No DARK
VALLEY

Books by
Jamie Langston Turner

Suncatchers

Some Wildflower in My Heart

By the Light of a Thousand Stars

A Garden to Keep

No Dark Valley

Winter Birds

No DARK
VALLEY

Published by Bethany House Publishers
11400 Hampshire Avenue South
Bloomington, Minnesota 55438

Bethany House Publishers is a division of
Baker Book House Company, Grand Rapids, Michigan.

Printed in the United States of America

ISBN 978-0-7642-0300-8

The Library of Congress has cataloged the original edition as follows:

Turner, Jamie L.
    No dark valley / by Jamie Langston Turner.
        p. cm.
    ISBN 0–7642–2730–0 (pbk.)
    1. Grandmothers—Death—Fiction. 2. Church membership—Fiction. 3. Southern States—Fiction. 4. Neighborhood—Fiction. 5. Young women—Fiction. I. Title.
    PS3570.U717N6 2004
    813'.54—dc22

                                                                        2004002032

IN MEMORY OF MY GRANDMOTHERS
LEONA HOLLAND THOMAS (1898–1988)
AND
KATE FLEMING LANGSTON (1900–1994)

The aged women likewise, that they be in behaviour
as becometh holiness . . . teachers of good things.
TITUS 2:3

Two of my best teachers about life were my grandmothers. Neither of them had an abundance of this world's goods, but they were both rich in things of eternal value. One was a preacher's wife in Mississippi, and the other was married to a barber and storekeeper in Georgia. One taught for a time in a one-room schoolhouse, one was ordained to perform wedding ceremonies, and both knew how to stretch a dollar. They both created beauty with their hands. One of them crocheted and tatted, while the other embroidered pillowcases and made patchwork quilts. Both of them lived through four wars and the Depression, and both knew the sorrow of burying a child. When I think of my grandmothers, I am struck with a deep sense of my "goodly heritage" and with a desire to match my steps to theirs, to radiate their godly contentment, their trust in their Savior, and their service to others. God laid it on my grandmothers' hearts in the 1940s to send their children, my parents, to Bob Jones College in Cleveland, Tennessee, and twenty-five years later my parents in turn felt a clear call to send me to BJU, where I sat under the teaching of intelligent, refined, Christlike men and women, heard sound Bible-based preaching, and was exposed to a vast array of cultural events in art, drama, and music. It has been my joy to give my life in service to the place that has given me so much.

JAMIE LANGSTON TURNER has been a teacher for thirty-seven years at both the elementary and college levels and has written extensively for a variety of periodicals, including *Faith for the Family*, *Moody*, and *Christian Reader*. Her first novel, *Suncatchers*, was published in 1995. Born in Mississippi, Jamie has lived in the South all her life and currently resides with her husband in South Carolina, where she teaches creative writing courses at Bob Jones University.

Part One

Seek Us When We Go Astray

Part Two
Hear, O Hear Us When We Pray

Part Three
Thou Hast Loved Us, Love Us Still

PART ONE:

SEEK US

WHEN

WE GO ASTRAY

1

The Birds Hush Their Singing

"We been hopin' you'd come," Aunt Beulah called, pushing the door open. She stepped out onto the porch, closing the door, then letting the screen slam behind her. "Come on inside before you freeze to death. Everybody's here eatin'." Her words came out in little white puffs. She was wearing a nubby black sweater over a navy blue dress and pink terry-cloth bedroom slippers on her feet.

Celia felt a sudden wave of panic. So that explained all the cars parked up and down the street. Aunt Beulah hadn't told her that everybody would be here at her house eating. If she had, Celia would never have agreed to come. She had expected only Aunt Beulah and Uncle Taylor to be here, not *everybody*. "Come on by the house first," Aunt Beulah had told her over the phone. "We can have us a little visit before we go to the funeral home."

"Now, tell me again which cow this is," Al said as they started up the sidewalk. On the drive here Celia had told him the names of her grandmother's five sisters—Clara, Bess, Beulah, Elsie, and Molly—to which Al had replied, "They sound like cows." He had then laughed, for what seemed to Celia a little too long, at his joke. He was right about their names, of course, though Celia had never thought of it before. And her grandmother's name had fit right in with the rest: Sadie.

"This one's Aunt Beulah," Celia said. "She's the only one of them who ever liked me."

"Watch out for that icy patch there!" Aunt Beulah called. "Molly nearly slipped on it earlier. I got Taylor to sprinkle some salt on it, but it might have refroze." She shaded her eyes as she watched Celia and Al make their way toward her. "I'm sure glad you could come, Celia. I told them you would." The implication, clearly, was *But nobody believed me.*

Aunt Beulah stepped back and opened the door again. Behind her Celia could see a roomful of people, all jammed together with plates of food balanced on their laps. She heard somebody cry out, "Mercy, you're lettin' the cold in, Beulah!"

Celia felt her knees go weak as she started up the steps, Al at her elbow. "I don't think I can do this," she said to him. "These people are perfectly capable of violence. There's no telling what they might do." She could picture herself lying in the middle of Aunt Beulah's living room, surrounded by all her Georgia kinfolk coming at her with their knives and forks.

"Don't worry. I'm here," Al said. "I won't let them do anything." He put his hand on her back. Celia knew he was looking forward to meeting her relatives, to see for himself if they were as weird as she had claimed.

"Come on, hon," Aunt Beulah said, beckoning. "Quick, get in here where it's warm!"

In that little space of time before she entered Aunt Beulah's house, Celia tried to imagine how all of this could be translated into the opening of a novel. She often did this with incidents in her life, although she didn't write fiction herself, in fact didn't even read much of it anymore. As a freelance editor, however, she had helped two or three novelists, certainly not very good ones, get their manuscripts ready to submit. It was exhausting, really. She had to wade through so much *bad* writing and then try to be halfway tactful when helping the writers, always a touchy lot, get things shaped up. During such projects she wondered why in the world she did it. Compared to her editing work, her other job at the Trio Gallery seemed like a summer vacation.

But today might not make such a good opening for a novel, she decided as she lifted her foot to step across the threshold. Far too many novels and movies started out with funerals, many of them in the dead of winter on a day like this one. If she *were* going to make it into fiction, however, she'd start with this speck of time right now, right before walking inside to face them all, with her heart thudding like a hammer inside her chest. She might start with a sentence like *Celia sucked in her breath and stepped across the threshold.*

The hum of talk stopped as they entered. Celia glanced around at the circle of faces and nodded. She didn't actually look at the faces, but at the wall slightly above their heads. She could sense that they were all looking her up and down, that she was being weighed in the balances of their narrow minds and found severely wanting.

"See here, I told you she would come," Aunt Beulah announced, closing the door. Celia could still feel the pocket of cold air they had brought in with them. Aunt Beulah touched her arm. "Y'all remember Celia, of course, and this here's her fiancé, Al."

Al nodded and smiled. "Glad to meet you all."

There were a few halfhearted replies. Mostly there was silence, though.

Fiancé? Celia thought. Where had Aunt Beulah gotten that? Certainly not from her. Celia was tempted to set her straight. "No, he's not my fiancé," she wanted to say. "We're not engaged." She wondered what they'd all do if she stood right there and told them the whole truth: "We don't have any intention of getting married. We've been keeping our own separate lives and just sleeping together whenever we feel like it." She wondered which one of them would lunge after her first. She remembered the tall oak tree in the middle of Aunt Beulah's backyard. That's probably the one they'd hang her from.

"Look, they didn't even wear coats," someone said from the far corner, and Celia saw it was Aunt Elsie. She hadn't changed a bit over the years. Same frizzy gray hair. Same squinty eyes. "Maybe they taught 'em not to wear coats up North," Aunt Elsie added. She gave a little scornful snort, then waved a chicken leg around. "Down here folks wear coats when it's freezing cold outside!" Aunt Elsie brought the chicken leg swiftly to her mouth and bit off a large chunk.

Celia wondered if she should remind them all that she lived in South Carolina, had done so for a good twelve years now. Evidently they were still holding it against her that she had left Georgia, the land of milk and honey, and gone to a college in Delaware all those years ago, where she had studied journalism.

Celia would never forget how horrified they all were when she announced that she was going to Blackrock College in Delaware. They had all had their say about it, coming over to her grandmother's house one by one to state their disapproval and offer gloomy forecasts of what happened to young people who went off to public universities, especially those in states other than their own. "It's in *Delaware,* not hell!" Celia had exploded one day after one of the aunts had left. And her grandmother had looked as if she'd been poked with a high-voltage wire. "Celie, we don't use that word in this house!" she had said.

"Well, come on out here to the table," Aunt Beulah said now. "We got more food than we can ever eat. Everybody's been so nice to help us out." As she followed Aunt Beulah across the living room and through the wide doorway into the dining room, Celia could feel every pair of eyes on her.

"Pretty little thing, ain't she?" she heard someone say.

"Pretty is as pretty does," Aunt Elsie declared.

Behind her, Celia heard another voice she recognized immediately as Aunt Clara's, apparently addressing the room at large. Aunt Clara's voice was deep and husky with an authoritarian tone. She had always been the bossy one among the sisters. "Sadie raised her all by herself, you know, after Celia's mama and daddy passed so sudden—and so *young*! Poor Sadie, workin' her fingers to the bone to raise that child, and never a crumb of thanks she got. Sulky and selfish and rebellious. Broke Sadie's heart over and over with her wild and willful ways."

Celia glanced up at Al with a look that said, "See, I told you they were all batty." He raised his eyebrows and emitted a low whistle.

Celia thought she heard someone in the living room make a shushing sound, but Aunt Clara either didn't hear it or ignored it. Aunt Clara had been hard of hearing years ago, so Celia could only imagine she was even more so now. Knowing Aunt Clara, it wouldn't have made any difference if she had heard it or not. If she had something to say, nothing could stop her. Celia could still hear her eighteen years ago, could still see her eyes flaming with indignation, her nose wrinkled up as if she smelled something spoiled: "Mark my words, you're going to send your poor grandmother to an early grave, young lady, if you go up there to that godless state university!" Celia had laughed right out loud. In her mind, her grandmother, sixty-nine at the time, was already ancient.

"See here, there's plenty!" Aunt Beulah raised her voice a little, perhaps to try to drown out Aunt Clara. "Y'all get you a plate and help yourself, and I'll go get the tea. I must've set it down out in the living room somewhere. Now take your fill—we got more'n enough for now and later, too. And we're not in any great big rush. We got us a whole hour before we got to be down to the mortuary."

From the other room Aunt Clara could still be heard. ". . . and *threw* away all her training, ever' last bit of it. Bowed Sadie down with grief to talk about it. Just *had* to go up North to some heathen college where they teach evolution and use drugs and let the boys and girls live in the same dormitories and fill up their minds with trash and . . ."

The dining room table bore a random assortment of food, all in Corning Ware dishes, Pyrex, tin plates, and plastic containers of every kind. Al caught her eye and winked. He looked as if life had suddenly gotten a lot more interesting. This was one of the things that most irritated Celia about Al—his enormous preoccupation with food. At times he could be so intelligent, so witty and sensitive to her moods, knowing exactly how much to say and when to quit prying, understanding her unspoken jokes, but then he'd turn around and act like some kind of *animal* when he got hungry.

Evidently no thought had been taken to arranging the food in any semblance of categories. It looked as if it had been set down in whatever order it had been delivered, then shoved over to make room for more. At one end sat a big platter of ham, surrounded by a basket of hush puppies, a dish of apple dumplings, and a plate of salmon croquettes. Corn-bread muffins, fruit cocktail, fried chicken, pinto beans, creamed corn, biscuits, custard pie, Jell-O salad—on and on it went.

Typical, thought Celia. It would never occur to these people, her Georgia relatives, to put all the meats together in one place, then the vegetables, salads, and desserts. Just throw them all together in a big hodgepodge and dig in. That was their way, always had been.

That was exactly how they approached life in general—mixed everything together in one big pot, stirred their religion in with whatever they did. Celia remembered how mortified she used to be when her grandmother was in Kmart or Piggly Wiggly, looking for cornstarch or floor wax one minute, then accosting a total stranger in the aisle the next, telling him bluntly that Jesus died to save sinful men or inviting him gruffly to a revival meeting at church. Celia would always walk away and hide out in another aisle.

Looking at the table, Celia couldn't help thinking how much Grandmother would have enjoyed this occasion, with all the people and all the food. She had loved family gatherings, would always arrive early and leave late, would sample some of every dish on the table, then go home grumbling about how she wished people wouldn't bring so much food. In her medicine chest Grandmother had a bottle, among all the others, on which she had printed "When you eat too much," and she would always shake a pill out of it after such a get-together and gulp it down. That was just like Christians, in Celia's opinion—always looking for easy answers to problems.

And Grandmother had always loved a funeral, too, had dragged Celia to dozens of them all over the county during the years they'd lived together on the other side of this pathetic little excuse of a town. It was too bad a person couldn't attend his own funeral, Celia thought. Maybe they should have rehearsals for them the way they did for weddings. That way the person could come and see how the service was going to go, then give suggestions for improvements, and after that go ahead and die.

Celia followed Al around the table, taking small helpings of a few dishes. Al's plate was heaped before he had made it halfway around, and he looked longingly at the other side of the table. There were two empty folding chairs in the dining room, angled into a corner beside the gas heater. The wallpaper—a design of large red roses twining in and out of a lattice—looked scorched above the heater and was curling apart at the seams. Celia was glad the living room was full. She would have hated to eat in there with all the aunts glaring at her, their small minds racing to think of all the wicked things she must have done since she left her grandmother's house eighteen years ago.

She thought Aunt Clara was through in the other room, but evidently she had just stopped a few moments to chew. "Sad how some folks'll wait till a funeral to come back and pay their respects," Celia heard her say. "Poor Sadie. What she wouldn't of *give* for that girl to come see her before she died. You'd sure think a body would have enough common decency to come visit their own grandmother when she was on her deathbed!"

But I didn't know she was on her deathbed! Celia felt like shouting. She kept quiet, though. She wasn't going to let these people get to her, not anymore. She didn't owe anybody any explanations for anything. She had nothing to apologize to them for. She had been done with that way of life for a long time.

Suddenly someone was standing in front of her. "Hey there, Celie." Celia looked up to find her second cousin Doreen grinning at her, holding a plate in one hand. She must have put on a good thirty pounds since Celia had last seen her, but it wasn't hard to recognize her with her round freckled face and curly red hair. Doreen wiped her other hand along the side of her dress, then cocked her index finger and thumb at Celia and made a shooting noise as if firing a gun. "Gotcha!" she said. "Remember how we used to all the time do that in the hall at school?" She laughed, showing broad yellow teeth. She had some fish sticks on her plate, Celia noticed, all cut up into small squares and slathered with ketchup.

"Hi, Doreen," Celia said. "How are you doing?"

"Ornery as always and up to no good," Doreen said. "How 'bout yourself?"

"I'm okay," said Celia. "Managing to keep busy."

Doreen laughed again. "Hey, remember that summer at Bible Memory Camp when I hid from you in that big old patch of poison ivy? And then jumped out and scared the livin' daylights out of you while you was walking by?"

Celia smiled and nodded. Doreen had always loved practical jokes, though they often backfired on her. The two of them had been good friends during the first two years she had lived with her grandmother but had drifted apart after that. Doreen could have been a lot of fun if she hadn't had such a religious streak.

"And then a little bit later I started itchin' and scratchin' like crazy," Doreen said. "I 'bout scratched myself raw before it was over. I remember that!"

Celia nodded again. She remembered a counselor threatening to tie Doreen's hands behind her back if she didn't quit scratching.

Doreen reached behind her and dragged a little red-haired boy out to stand in front of her. He looked down at the floor and twisted from side to side, three fingers jammed in his mouth. "This here's Ralph Junior," Doreen said. "Named after his daddy. You remember Ralph, don't you? He graduated same year you did. Played football."

Celia felt her stomach knot up as she glanced at the boy. Probably no more than four or five. She nodded at Doreen. She remembered Ralph all right. Big dumb Ralph Hubert, who reinforced every stereotype in the world about football players. She thought she remembered her grandmother writing her that he had gone into the army a year or so after graduating from high school, but she was already away at college by then and couldn't have cared less about any of the hicks she had gone to high school with. She looked back at Doreen's little boy and felt something like the cold point of a knife against soft skin.

"So you finally decided to get hitched yourself, huh?" Doreen said, nodding to Al. "Never too late. Better not wait around for ten years to have you a kid like I did, though. 'Course that wasn't the plan. I expected I'd just drop 'em out one after the other the way Billie Ruth did, but no sir, not me. Me and Ralph had to traipse all over to a hundred doctors 'fore we found out what was wrong, and then—"

"And how is Billie Ruth?" Celia asked.

"Oh, same as ever. Had her another baby couple of months ago—number eight. Imagine that, my sister's got eight, and I had to work like the dickens just to get me one. Mama told her she ought to get her tubes tied, but . . ."

Al spoke up, his mouth full. "And how old is Ralph Junior?" he asked. The boy scowled up at him briefly, then turned and buried his face in his mother's skirt.

"Five his next birthday," Doreen said proudly. "He goes to the four-year-old kindergarten school over at the Baptist church three days a week, don't you, Ralphie?" No response from Ralphie. "Here, show Cousin Celie and her friend how good you know your numbers, Ralphie." Doreen tried to pry him away from her legs, to no avail. "Come on, Ralphie, one . . . two . . . three . . . Count for us and show what a big boy you are." Ralphie wouldn't deliver.

"Oh well, maybe another time," Celia said.

"Yeah, maybe so," Doreen said. "Well, come on then, sport, let's go back out here to the kitchen and finish up your din-din." She grinned at Celia. "He loves fish fixed like this." She nodded toward the plate she was holding.

This came as no surprise to Celia. Breaded fish sticks that came frozen in a box would be exactly the kind of food her relatives would love. Give them a fresh fillet of flounder amandine or Chilean sea bass, and they wouldn't have a clue what it was.

Doreen waved. "Talk to you later, Celie." She jerked her head toward the kitchen. "We're eating out here with Candy. You remember Candy—she's married now and has her a baby. She's trying to nurse him, but she's afraid she doesn't have enough milk."

For a moment Celia didn't understand. Surely this wasn't the same Candy she remembered—Aunt Elsie's "change of life baby," as everybody had called her. The last time Celia had seen her, Candy was still dragging a blanket around and sucking her thumb. But that was over eighteen years ago, Celia realized, which would make her twenty or more now.

"And Ralph's coming to the funeral, so you can see him, too," Doreen was saying. "His boss is letting him off early today. He's one of the pall-bearers—I didn't know if you knew that. Your grandmother picked 'em all out herself before she passed."

Celia shook her head. "No, I didn't know." She waved back at Doreen as she steered Ralphie toward the kitchen. As they disappeared through the swinging door, the sound of a baby's wail broke forth, then suddenly stopped. A rushing sound filled Celia's head, like a semi passing by, and she took several deep breaths.

"Wow, there goes one classy woman," Al said, then laughed. "I can't understand how you escaped all this, Celia."

Celia watched him for a few moments. He had already picked two chicken wings clean and was busy now with a mound of spaghetti casserole. He was having trouble getting it to stay on his fork, however, so he finally took up his spoon and, with the aid of a corn-bread muffin as a pusher, began to make headway. Celia looked away. Bringing Al with her on this trip had seemed like such a good idea a couple of days ago.

She wondered if her grandmother had planned out the whole funeral. That would be just like something she would do. She probably had it all written down in one of her notebooks somewhere, right down to the songs that would be sung. This was something southerners were fond of doing. And knowing Grandmother, there would probably be dozens of songs.

Next to her Bible, her grandmother's favorite book had been the old brown hymnal they used at church. She even had her own personal copy of it that she carried back and forth to church. *Tabernacle Hymns Number Three* it said on the cover. And she sang those songs at home all hours of the day and night the whole three years Celia had lived with her. During that last awful year Celia would often turn her radio up full blast to block out the sound of her grandmother's singing.

Looking up at the roses on the wallpaper, Celia suddenly thought of the words of one of Grandmother's favorite songs: "I come to the garden alone, while the dew is still on the roses." She could remember her grandmother singing it over and over at home and calling out its number time and again at church on request night. In Celia's opinion it was a sappy maudlin song, one of those that sounded pretty but meant nothing. *Well,*

Grandmother, Celia thought, *it looks like the dew has all evaporated now and the roses have wilted and died on the trellis, just like you.*

And even though she tried hard to keep it from coming, she could clearly hear her grandmother's abrupt answer. "No, Celie, I haven't died. I only changed addresses is all. And the dew *is* still on the roses up here, and there's not a single thorn on 'em, either." As much as she disliked it, Celia couldn't stop a picture from forming, one of her grandmother strolling through a lush celestial garden with Jesus by her side. Or rather *stomping* through the garden. She had never known Grandmother to stroll anywhere.

Grandmother loved the second stanza of that song and would always close her eyes when she sang it at church: "He speaks, and the sound of his voice is so sweet the birds hush their singing." In Celia's opinion, if Grandmother was the one in that garden with Jesus, that explained the birds' falling silent. It had nothing to do with *his* voice—the poor birds were terrified of hers.

In the doorway from the living room appeared the bent figure of an old man with a white goatee. For a moment he stood absolutely still, peering into the dining room at Al and Celia. Then he shuffled forward toward the table and leaned down close. "Looking for some more of that cobbler," he said, staring hard at the chicken pot pie.

Aunt Beulah came back into the dining room carrying a brown plastic pitcher of tea. "No, Buford, that cobbler you're wantin' is down here," she said loudly and pointed him to the far end of the table.

"Uncle Buford," Celia whispered to Al. "I don't think I would have ever recognized him. He's shrunk." She watched as Aunt Beulah set the pitcher down and helped him fill his plate with cobbler. "He's Aunt Beulah's twin brother. The only boy in the family. He used to be a preacher—a very long-winded one."

"So there was a bull among the cows," Al said. "He looks like he could be Colonel Sanders' grandfather." He stabbed at his plate with his fork. "Hey, what are these little brown things, anyway? They're good."

"Crowder peas," Celia said. "He's married to Aunt Bernice, who used to dramatize the story of Elijah and Jezebel for all the neighbor kids. She made a very convincing Jezebel." Uncle Buford headed slowly back to the living room, stopping briefly to peer over at Celia and Al, then emitting a soft belch and moving on.

"Here, let me pour y'all some tea," Aunt Beulah said. "Sorry we got to use these little foam cups. They don't hardly hold enough to spit at." As she poured, Celia saw that her hands still shook the way they always had.

"Oh, now, see there, I've gone and dribbled some on your plate," Aunt Beulah said. Before moving away, she leaned in close to Celia and spoke confidingly, her rhinestone pendant dangling near Celia's chin. "Celia, hon, you don't have to rush, but I do want you and Al to come with me to the funeral parlor when you're done. I asked them to leave the casket open for a little bit before the funeral so you could see her if you got here in time. She looks so sweet. My, they did such a good job on her."

Aunt Beulah left with the pitcher of tea. "A 'good job'?" Al said. "Celia, these people are everything you said and more." He lifted a spoonful of stewed apples and examined them appreciatively. "But they can sure cook." He chewed for a moment, then said, "Hey, you don't have to go through with this, you know. We can leave. We can think up some excuse to tell them and go back home. Or don't tell them anything—just get in the car and leave. They can have the funeral without you. Nobody can make you stay."

Celia shook her head. "I've come this far, I might as well finish it." But it was more than that, though she knew Al would laugh if she told him about it. The truth was, she had made a promise to her grandmother years ago. Not that she wasn't above breaking a promise. She had done that often enough. But this one was different. It was the kind that would rise up to haunt you if you didn't keep it.

It was the last time she had seen her grandmother, actually. Fourteen years ago this spring. Grandmother had ridden a Trailways bus all the way up to Blackrock to attend Celia's college graduation. Celia had tried to discourage her, but she had her mind made up. "Everybody needs family at their graduation," she had said flatly. "I didn't pay for your education. Your daddy's money did that, along with your granddaddy Coleman's, but I still feel like I had a part in it." And then, as if Celia didn't already know what she meant, she went on to explain. "I prayed for you every single day, Celie."

It had been more than a little bother, she recalled, working out the details—having to borrow a friend's car to pick her grandmother up at the bus station, take her to a motel near the campus, get her to the graduation ceremony, take her somewhere to eat, take her back to the bus station, all that.

It amazed Celia at the time that the two of them were able to spend those two days together in Delaware pretending nothing had happened, as if they had parted four years earlier on the best of terms. Not that the two days had been without strain. Anybody watching them could probably have told that there was a volcanic history between them. But the eruptions were in the past, and they both took care to step over the landscape gingerly.

It was at the bus station at the end of the two days that the promise had been exacted, though Celia had never actually spoken the words *I promise.* Grandmother had handed her a small box and said, "Here, I wanted to give you something. You've done good in your studies, and I'm proud of you." Grandmother wasn't the sentimental type, so this was a surprising speech for her to make.

The box wasn't wrapped but had a piece of gold yarn around it, tied in a bow on top. "Go on, open it before I get on the bus," Grandmother had said. Inside, Celia had found a watch. Not a new watch, though. "It used to belong to your mother," Grandmother had said. "It was one of the few pretty things she ever owned. Your daddy gave it to her before they married, and she fussed at him for spending so much. She used it a long time, but then it needed a new crystal and she left off wearing it for a while. It was sitting at home on her dresser the day they went out to buy that clothes dryer. I put it back to save for you."

That was how Grandmother always referred to the day Celia's parents had died—"the day they went out to buy that clothes dryer." On their way back from the appliance store, they had been struck head on by a drunk driver in the middle of the day and killed instantly, both of them. This drunk couldn't wait till nighttime to get behind the wheel of his car. No, he'd had to take his joyride at four o'clock in the afternoon. Of course he staggered away from the accident unharmed while Celia's parents lay strapped in their seats, crushed to death. Celia was barely fifteen years old. She had been at home doing her geometry homework when it happened.

"I thought it'd make a nice graduation gift," her grandmother said that day at the bus station. "I got it out and took it to the jewelry store, and they cleaned it up and fixed it up like new."

Celia nodded, staring down at the watch. The face was tiny, not as big as her thumbnail, and the bracelet band folded over and snapped. "It does," she said. "It makes a very nice gift." If someone had asked her the day before to describe her mother's watch, she couldn't have, but now, touching her finger to its small face, it seemed altogether familiar, like something she had handled every day for many years.

"Well, good, I'm glad you like it," Grandmother said. "Here, you'd better close it back up and put it somewhere safe before somebody comes along and steals it. You might have to get the band adjusted. Your mother's wrist was about as big around as a stick." She grunted. " 'Course, you're not any bigger'n she was." She reached down and picked up her old red train case. "Well, I got to go get me a seat on the bus. I like one by the window." They stood facing each other for the briefest span of time, as if waiting for something, and then Grandmother said, "There's no telling when we'll see each other again, but I'm only asking you to promise me one thing, Celie. Nothing more, only this one thing."

Celia said nothing. She was old enough now to know the danger of promises.

"I want you to promise you'll come back home to see me buried when the time comes," Grandmother said.

Celia didn't know what to say, but Grandmother didn't wait for an answer. She moved away toward the bus, then stopped and turned around once more. "I tried, Celie. I did try. I didn't do very good, I know that, but I tried." And then she was gone. Celia watched her mount the steps into the bus, saw her move down the aisle and settle into a seat by the window. When the bus pulled out, she turned her head and looked out at Celia, but neither one of them waved.

2

On That Beautiful Shore

The funeral home didn't seem to Celia to be the most prosperous of enterprises. WALSH'S FUNERAL SERVICES the sign out front said. She remembered it from when she had lived here in Dunmore, since it was right off one of the main streets of town and you had to pass right by it to go practically anywhere. She had even attended several funerals here with her grandmother years ago, though it hadn't seemed to be in such a state of decline back then. But maybe it was always this way and she hadn't noticed. Lately, it seemed that everywhere she looked things were shabby and run-down.

She might be headed to her job at the art gallery, for instance, and glance out the window of her car at a red light and see the curb littered with cigarette butts, smashed pop cans, and burger bags. A heavy sadness would come over her to see how dirty it all looked. And sometimes the art gallery itself filled her with the same kind of sorrow. If she allowed herself to look away from the paintings and sculptures, her eyes would go straight to the long crack in the ceiling, the water stains on the wall around the front window, and the rusted vent, and she would feel an urge to weep.

Once recently, coming out of the grocery store, she had stopped beside the row of newspaper vending machines, sitting in a crooked row, and stared at the depressing sight. One was badly dented, as if someone had taken a baseball bat to it. On the pavement all around the machines were paper cups, straws, old chewing gum, candy wrappers, even a few half-eaten French fries.

Even her own apartment sometimes filled her with a melancholy aware-
ness of things going downhill. The harder she tried to keep it absolutely
spotless, the more she saw examples on every hand of breakdown, of the
accumulated years of wear and tear. One of the kitchen cupboards had
begun to sag away from the ceiling molding, and she had taken out a cereal
bowl recently to find a dead roach in it. Windowsills, baseboards, picture
frames—there was no way to keep dust from gathering. In housekeeping,
every principle of science worked against you—gravity, friction, all those
laws of thermodynamics.

Aunt Beulah's house had been sad, too. The peeling wallpaper, the
clutter everywhere, the scuffed hardwood floors and dusty bookshelves.
And now here it was again at the funeral home, more evidence of dilapi-
dation and neglect. The carpet, probably a pretty shade of rose at one
time, was faded and worn. Around the entrance it looked almost gray.
Tacky still-life prints hung on the walls—flowers and fruit, both of which
in real life started the inevitable process of decay almost as soon as they
were picked.

The man who came forward to meet them as they entered was everything you'd expect from a second-rate establishment. His black hair was
thickly oiled and combed straight back from his high pale forehead. He
wore a pained smile, perhaps in keeping with the atmosphere of mourn-
ing, and his dark suit had the sheen of cheap fabric. Moreover, it hung
loosely on him, obviously made for a more robust man than the one who
even now seemed to be wasting away inside it. In the breast pocket was
tucked a maroon handkerchief the same color as his necktie. His shoes
had a hard Formica shine.

He took Aunt Beulah's hand as if they were old friends. "Is this the
granddaughter you were telling me of?" he said softly, glancing toward
Celia. His voice was too lubricated, too womanly.

Aunt Beulah nodded. "Celia, this is Mr. Shelby, one of the directors
here. He's been such a help to us." She nodded again and addressed the
man. "This is Sadie's granddaughter, Celia, and her fiancé, Al. I wanted
them to see her before you closed the casket."

Mr. Shelby gave a little bow. "Just as we discussed," he said primly. "If
you'll come this way." The way he walked reminded Celia of someone on
a tightrope, the shiny pointed toes of his shoes touching first with each
small step. They passed silently across the carpeted lobby and into a hallway. "Here we are," he said, stopping at a doorway and motioning them

in. "Take your time. We're running well on schedule. We won't need to close the viewing for another half hour at least."

The *viewing*—the word made Celia cringe. The room was dimly lit, and eight or ten flower arrangements flanked the casket. "That one's yours." Aunt Beulah pointed to an arrangement of pink roses and miniature white carnations as they stepped forward. Celia noted that it was the largest arrangement there, which didn't surprise her, considering what little she knew of her grandmother's friends. Not exactly well-heeled, any of them. They'd be far more likely to give a donation to the missionary fund at church in memory of her grandmother than to order flowers, which most of them would see as throwing away good money.

The lid was open, and though Celia thought this whole concept of a viewing was barbaric, she knew she had to look. She had tried to brace herself for what she would see. Fourteen years was a long time. A lot of changes could take place in a person's appearance during that time, especially if there had been illness toward the end. As she stared down at her grandmother's face, however, she was amazed at how few the changes were. Her skin was as Celia remembered it, like cream parchment that had been crushed and then smoothed out again. Her features were the same—no evidence of drastic weight loss or great suffering. She might have simply lain down for a rest and drifted off.

The biggest difference was her hair. Someone had curled it, and it was longer than she used to wear it. She must have been really sick these past few months, Celia thought, or she never would have tolerated it that long. If there was one thing her grandmother was particular about concerning her appearance, it was her hair. It had to be kept short and away from her face. The longer style and the curls gave her a softer look, more grandmotherly. The way she used to wear it, short and brushed straight back, had always looked hard and manly in Celia's opinion. She had never looked like a grandmother who would bake cookies or hold you in her lap and read to you, although when Celia was younger she had done those very things whenever she came to visit.

They had dressed her in a cranberry suit with a large plastic-looking pearl brooch at the neck, and one gnarled, brown-mottled hand lay across the other. Celia's eyes rested on the hands. She realized she had rarely observed Grandmother's hands idle before.

"Doesn't she look precious?" Aunt Beulah whispered. It wasn't a word Celia had ever thought of using to describe her grandmother. Grim, industrious, practical, hard-nosed, judgmental—those all fit, but not *precious*.

She continued to stare at the hands—the hands that had opened a Bible every morning at breakfast and every night at supper and had traced the words as she read aloud to Celia. They were the hands that had persisted in knocking on Celia's bedroom door every Sunday morning during that last year they lived together and had touched her on the shoulder to let her know it was time to wake up and get ready for church. They were the hands that turned on the radio in her bedroom and time and time again moved the dial from Celia's favorite rock station to the Christian station that played gospel music and preaching twenty-four hours a day, then adjusted the volume so it practically burst her eardrums.

They were the hands that had always put together some sort of casserole for the potluck supper at church on the first Wednesday of every month and then helped to serve the plates of others as they went through the line. They were the hands that prepared a meal at home every other night of the month for the two of them, that set the table with her unmatched silverware and the dishes she had bought a place setting at a time through a special offer at the grocery store. Celia could see those dishes as clearly as if she were holding one in her hand right this minute. White, rather small for dinner plates actually, with a little gold scallop around the edge and in the center two little robins in a brown nest. A little old-fashioned, certainly not what you'd call fine china, already starting to discolor by the time Celia had left for college.

Celia had dropped one of the plates while washing dishes one day not long after coming to live with her grandmother. It had broken neatly into three large pieces in the sink, the two robins separated in the blink of an eye. Without a word her grandmother had reached over and let the soapy water out of the sink, then picked up the pieces and dumped them into the plastic pail she used as a trash can. Celia had begun crying, something she used to do regularly during those early days. Her grandmother had only six place settings of the dishes, and now only five plates were left. It was the thought of the incomplete set that filled Celia with dismay. And it couldn't be replaced. The grocery store had run the offer for only a few months years ago.

"It's only a plate, Celie," Grandmother had said. "Save your tears for things that matter." And she had turned to get the broom out of the pantry, then gone about sweeping the floor. She wasn't the kind of grandmother who kissed and hugged. At the time it had seemed harsh and unloving to Celia. It was one of the things she had used as justification for turning against her grandmother during her last year of high school.

Aunt Beulah put an arm around her now. "Y'all can stay here a few minutes, okay, honey? I need to go out and speak to Mr. Shelby about something. Is that all right?"

Celia nodded. "Sure, that's fine." She glanced at Al, who was bending over the flower arrangements, humming tunelessly and reading the names on the cards. She tried again to remember why she had thought it would be good to have him along. He looked at her and smiled. " 'Bethany Hills Virtuous Women Sunday School Class,' " he said, pointing to a card and winking. It was on a live plant in a basket—ivy, fern, and a small flowering vine of some kind. The whole thing would no doubt be dead within a few days.

She looked back at her grandmother in the casket. She had heard of people's faces looking strangely sweet and peaceful in death, but Grandmother's face looked . . . well, she couldn't really think of the right word for it. It wasn't really peaceful. Maybe *resigned* was the word. The face of someone who had known early on that life was a far cry from perfect and who had never seen her conviction overturned, yet someone who didn't question it, who knew that's just the way it was.

If she were a betting woman, Celia would be willing to lay down money that one of the songs they'd sing at the funeral would be "In the Sweet By and By." She knew she could sing the words to all three stanzas this very minute if she wanted to even though it had been years since she had last heard it. The chorus played through her mind now: "In the sweet by and by, we shall meet on that beautiful shore." They had sung it often at Bethany Hills Bible Tabernacle. No doubt it had been a favorite at all the churches here in Dunmore, Georgia.

She imagined most people would gasp with shock as they stepped through the pearly gates and gazed about at the splendor of heaven—if there even *was* such a place, which she doubted. But she couldn't for the life of her picture her grandmother doing such a thing. Her grandmother would take one look around, nod briskly, and say, "Nice—exactly what I expected it to be," then go on about her business.

There had been a time when Celia had thought she knew her grand-mother far too well and could hardly stand to be in the same room with her. But now, looking down at her lying in the casket, she felt that she hardly knew this woman with whom she had lived for three whole years.

She had expected to feel angry on this trip, and she had started out that way. Anger was the kind of emotion that could carry you through a funeral with perfect composure. She hadn't expected to look down at her grandmother and be flooded with this strange, mixed-up conglomeration of guilt, regret, curiosity, sadness. *This woman made my life miserable,* she tried to remind herself. *She didn't have a loving bone in her body. All she cared about was a bunch of rules in that big black Bible of hers.*

But even as the thoughts came, something deep inside spoke words she hadn't heard for years: "For now we see through a glass, darkly . . . but then shall I know even as also I am known." She shook her head to try to clear it. And once again her eyes traveled to her grandmother's hands. They were large hands, roughened by work like a man's.

She remembered the first day she had come to live at Grandmother's house after her parents' funeral. This time was different from all the other times she had visited. She was alone this time, and she was here to stay. Barely fifteen, she was just a few weeks into her sophomore year of high school. She hadn't been in on all the decisions, of course. It had all been arranged without her consent, presented to her as the way things were going to be from now on. As far as she knew, though, there had been no fight over who would get her. It certainly wasn't as if *everybody* had wanted her.

Her father's parents had never been much involved in her life and had both proceeded to die within two years of her parents' accident. They were even older than Grandmother, but as nonreligious as Grandmother was religious. Celia had called them Papa and Mums, not out of affection but because her mother had told her to. Papa had taught astronomy and physics at one time at a private college in Minnesota, their home state. Mums was an organic horticulturalist. The few times they had flown down to visit Celia's family at their home near Atlanta, they had observed everything with quiet disapproval. They appeared to be stymied as to how their youngest son had ended up in the South, married to a Georgia girl with whom he had fallen into the habit of attending church, in a lowly denomination like Baptist, no less.

They had picked at the meals Celia's mother had prepared and had gone to bed early. Mums told them one evening at supper about a study she had helped put together with a professional nutritionist to determine the correlation between a woman's fertility and a diet high in organic vegetables. It was clear to Celia, though she was only ten at the time, that Mums wasn't really talking in general terms but was pointedly telling her mother that her inferior diet was the cause of her inability to bear her son more than one child.

Whereas Grandmother's hugs were few and stiff, Mums was a violent hugger, at least of Celia and her father. She couldn't remember ever seeing Mums hug her mother. Celia remembered hating it after her parents died, the way Mums would suddenly fall upon her at all hours of the day and embrace her at length, shaking with silent tears. Papa and Mums had spent a week at their house, during which Celia started avoiding them, retreating to her bedroom and locking the door. She remembered the profound relief she felt when they finally left. She might grumble about having no say in her relocation, but she knew she never would have chosen to go live with *them*.

With so many people at their house for a whole week, going through closets and drawers and cupboards, dividing up everything, Celia had been in a daze. When she had asked to go back to school two days after the funeral, Papa and Mums had looked at her as if she had lost her mind. "You'll not be going to school there anymore," Mums had said, putting her hand over her heart and breathing deeply. "But I have to get my things from my locker," Celia had said, and Mums had once again rushed at her and thrown her arms around her. "Oh, you poor, poor little child," she had said. Celia remembered looking over Mums' shoulder that day to see Grandmother staring at them, unsmiling, from the doorway.

When Celia was told that Grandmother's house in Dunmore was to be her new home, she had the feeling of having known it all along. At the time she hadn't realized that a lot of parents plan ahead better than hers had, that many have it stipulated in their wills who is to take guardianship of their children if something happens to the two of them. It wasn't as if there were that many choices, though. Celia's mother had no living siblings, and her father's two brothers both lived in Minnesota and had large families of their own. Celia wasn't even sure she would recognize either of her uncles if she passed them on the street.

At some point during that week Celia had stopped outside the kitchen, where a conversation was in progress. She had known she was the subject of the discussion. She heard Mums' voice: " . . . and my heart isn't strong, you know. The angina's getting worse." There was silence, and then Papa

had added, "The doctor had to double her blood pressure medication."
As Celia tiptoed away, she heard Grandmother speak up. "Like I already
said, it won't be as big a change for her if she comes to my house."

Grandmother hadn't made a ceremony out of that first day. She had
handled it all with the same businesslike demeanor with which she paid
her bills each month. Aunt Beulah and Uncle Taylor had been the ones
to actually transport Celia from Atlanta to Dunmore. They had rented a
little Hertz trailer to pull behind their car so they could fit in the things
they were taking to Grandmother's. Most of it had been sold—furniture
and appliances and such—but Celia wanted to keep her bed and her
mother's cedar chest.

Celia's parents didn't have all that much, really. Her father had had
big plans to finish a graduate degree in finance and marketing, but a single
night course at a time made it slow going. The irony was that in spite of all
his interest in the stock market, his own investments never did very well.
At least that's the idea Celia had gotten as a child. He was always buying
and selling at the wrong times, it seemed. His job as co-owner of a shoe
store was an up-and-down kind of business, and one of Celia's clearest
recollections of him was the way he would sit at supper and bemoan the
plight of the small retailer in America.

Her mother would listen to him, a worried line between her eyebrows.
Celia would watch the two of them and take smaller and smaller bites, as
if by eating less she could ease the budget strain and make things better.
She could look back on her parents' marriage now and see that, though
without question they had loved each other, they hadn't balanced each
other out the way a married couple should. They were both worriers. She
never remembered her mother laughing off her father's woeful speeches,
whipping up a favorite dessert, for example, and saying something upbeat
like "Well, so what? We've got each other, and that's all that matters!"

It does something to a child's sense of security to be part of a family
like that. Celia knew that now. Her mother had always sewn all her own
clothes and Celia's, too, and had bought dented cans of food and ripped
boxes of cereal at the Savvy Shopper, a salvage grocery store. Birthdays and
Christmases were always celebrated, but cautiously. She loved her parents
deeply, but she had grown into a little worrier herself, always hoping her
father's accounts would balance, that he would have enough each month
to pay his two shoe clerks and the rent on his building, which was way too

high, that each sale he ran would generate a little more business than the last one, although they never got many customers compared to the hordes that flocked into the big discount places like Shoe Bonanza.

Of course, looking back on it, he must have done better than he had let on because after everything was liquidated and the money was put aside for Celia's college education, there was enough for the whole four years plus graduate school. As a child, however, Celia had never taken food and shelter for granted. As far as she knew, she might sit down for breakfast the next morning and be told there was nothing to eat.

She would watch her father reading the stock page of the newspaper and pray silently, *Please don't let him risk any money. Make him keep it all safe in the bank!* Oh, how earnestly she had prayed as a child, up until she was around seventeen actually. And even though she never had realized the incongruence between worrying and praying, not until her grandmother pointed it out to her after she came to live with her in Dunmore, she had been absolutely faithful in her prayers up until her defection from religion in twelfth grade. Somehow she had gotten it in her mind as a young child that if she prayed regularly, in a certain place at a certain time, covering things in a prescribed order, she could hold her world together. Safety came from following rules.

The day her parents had gone to get the clothes dryer, however, she had come home from school and been so eager to get to her geometry homework, which was her favorite class after a whole week of tenth grade, that she changed her schedule around and skipped praying. Her geometry teacher, Miss Augustine, was beautiful and used her hands gracefully as she explained things. She had a long elegant neck like Audrey Hepburn's, and she had worn the same pearl necklace around it every day so far, a necklace that Celia was sure Miss Augustine's boyfriend had given her. Celia sat right in front of her desk and studied her worshipfully.

So that day after school, thinking about how pleased Miss Augustine would be when she saw her neat, perfect homework paper, Celia took out her books and sat down at the desk in her room without taking time to read her daily chapter in Psalms and pray. She even postponed her clarinet practice that day, which usually came right after prayer time and right before taking her tennis racket outside to practice her backhand against the side of the garage. She intended to do it all later.

Her parents had brought her home from school that day and dropped her off, telling her they would be home in an hour, after they picked out a new clothes dryer. She remembered how happy her mother was. This was her first clothes dryer after being married for nineteen years and hanging clothes outdoors on a clothesline long past the time when women did that routinely.

The first thought that came to Celia's mind when she learned of the accident was "I skipped my prayers and look what happened." And she lived for the next two years with the assurance that her omission that day had caused her parents' death. She became fanatical about praying then, was dressed and waiting to accompany her grandmother to church every time the doors were open. She filled up notebooks with verses she copied from the Bible and concentrated hard on every word that Grandmother read during their devotions together at breakfast and supper.

When she finally woke up her senior year of high school and, with the help of three new friends, discovered how ridiculous a notion it was—that by doing her geometry homework before praying she was responsible for her parents' accident—she turned her back on everything else associated with her religion. Religion survived, Ansell had told her, only by making people feel guilty. It feeds off the gullible, Renee had said. It takes everything in life that's fun and puts it on the no-no list, Glenn had added. It didn't take Celia long at all to see the truth in what they said, and every day afterward she saw evidence all around of how manipulative a force religion was, how totally devoid it was at its very core of love and joy, those two Christian virtues they were always singing about at church.

Grandmother saw that year as a war and fought vigorously to keep Celia from being captured by the enemy. There were more battles than Celia could number. Every day Grandmother rose with fierce determination, ready to take up arms, and every day Celia, fortified by her new knowledge, her new way of thinking, and her new friends, resisted. Grandmother, however, never retreated, nor did she devise new tactics whereby she might circle around and surprise the foe. She wasn't very creative. She was a head-on fighter, very predictable. You could count on her to keep the front line steady, not giving an inch.

And the thing Celia couldn't get away from now, looking down at her grandmother in death, was the incredible expenditure of energy it must have taken. It tired her to think of it, and she was only thirty-six. Her grandmother had been almost seventy at the time. How could a woman that old keep it up day after weary day? How could she continue to open her Bible every morning and evening and start to read aloud, knowing full well what would follow?

Celia hadn't been all that creative herself, really. Sometimes she would begin shouting to cover the sound of her grandmother's voice, or she might put her hands over her ears and sing. Sometimes she would simply get up and storm out of the kitchen, slam her bedroom door, and turn her radio up full blast. She might even leave the house on foot and stay gone a couple of hours.

If she could find her grandmother's car keys, which she usually couldn't, she would take the car and speed off in the dark. Twice out of pure spite, not at all because she enjoyed it, Celia came home drunk. The first time, she stumbled and threw up all over the front porch. She didn't even remember how she got into bed that night. The next day when she left for school, two hours late, there was no sign on the front porch that anything had happened the night before.

As a believer in a literal heaven and hell, Grandmother must have gotten a glimpse of what hell was like during that year. And all the years after that, as she waited for Celia to come back, if not in body at least in spirit. *But I never did,* Celia thought now. *I got out for good.* The thought didn't give her the satisfied surge it had before, whenever she had let herself think about her escape from the stranglehold of religion. For some reason, all she could think of now was the withering and fading of an old woman's hope and peace, of her own part in a lasting disappointment.

Without even meaning to, Celia reached down and touched one of her grandmother's hands. It was cool and hard. She drew back quickly. She remembered that first day she had arrived at her grandmother's house with Aunt Beulah and Uncle Taylor. Grandmother had led her to the back bedroom, the one that had been added on with the bathroom, finally. Celia didn't remember it, of course, but the whole time her mother had lived in the house growing up, there had been only a path to a little rickety outhouse behind the garage.

Grandmother had walked into the bedroom, which was small and would barely be big enough to accommodate Celia's bed once it was set up, and had laid one of her hands on top of the old pine bureau that had been Celia's mother's as a girl. "You can put your things in here," she had said. Then she had opened the tiny closet and pointed. "Here's where you can hang things." She had turned and left the room then, saying, "You go ahead and get settled. I'm going to get our supper finished up."

Uncle Taylor and Aunt Beulah had carried the bed in and set it up, and then they had stayed for an early supper of pork chops and turnip greens. The pork chops were fried tough, not like her mother's tender slow-baked ones. "We'll go to the school tomorrow," Grandmother had said after Uncle Taylor and Aunt Beulah left. "You can go run you a bath if you want one. Try not to use much hot water. The tank doesn't hold much."

"Hey, Celia, you okay?" Al leaned close and studied her face. "She's gone now, Celia. You don't have to worry. She's not going to rise up and start preaching at you again." He squeezed her hand. "Never again, babe. You're free as a bird."

Celia suddenly laughed.

"What's the matter?" he said. "What's so funny?"

"Nothing," Celia said, shaking her head. "Nothing at all." The truth was, a picture had sprung into her mind. For some strange reason she had just remembered the time Grandmother had backed her Mercury Comet over a motorcycle in the parking lot of the Crystal Burger out on the old highway near their house in Dunmore.

She had gone inside to find the owner, who turned out to be a big hulking guy with a ponytail and a nose ring. Grandmother had told him about his motorcycle and walked with him outside to see the damage. Celia, sixteen at the time, had been there, hanging back in fear of what might happen. The guy had sworn colorfully and at great length, had looked like he wanted to punch Grandmother's lights out. A policeman had to come and write up a report, and right before they left, Grandmother had reached into her purse and pulled out a gospel tract. She stepped right up to the man whose motorcycle was so banged up it would have to be carried away, who was still so mad he could hardly see straight, and handed that tract to him. "Here, read this," she said in her blunt way. "If you're so bent on riding motorcycles, you better be sure you're going to heaven."

3

Where the Still Waters Flow

Aunt Beulah was suddenly standing beside her again. "If you've had enough time, Celia honey, we can go on out to the other room now before people start getting here for the funeral. I think they're about ready to close up the casket." *If I've had enough time?* Celia thought. She had had more than enough time. She took a deep breath and stepped back from the casket.

Aunt Beulah took her arm and led her out into the hallway. "We're supposed to meet back here in this other room," she said, "and then we'll all walk in together and sit in the family seats."

Celia wondered if Mr. Shelby had any idea how many seats he needed to reserve for the family. With all the aunts and uncles and assorted cousins, they'd probably take up at least a dozen pews. The thought came to her again how much her grandmother would have enjoyed all this. An idea popped into her head: What if it were true that people in heaven could look down and, with some sort of magical long-distance vision, see things on earth? What if Grandmother had been allowed to pull up a chair right at the brink of heaven so she could have a good view of the funeral?

She didn't realize she was smiling until Al gave her a long look. "Hey, what's going on?" he said. "You look like you know a secret."

"Maybe I do," she said, but she stopped smiling. Inside the family waiting room she chose a straight-back chair by the window. They were the first three in the room. She knew it would be full before long. She could hear their voices already, strident and contentious, with no sense of discretion.

She could imagine Aunt Elsie pointing her out to someone on their procession into the chapel: "Up there, that's Celia. Look at her worldly haircut and that little bit of a dress, and not even wearing a coat!" And then Aunt Clara would add her commentary: "Still as stubborn and contrary as she was before! Not one ounce of concern for the things of the Lord! Made poor Sadie's life one endless tribulation!" Even Doreen might chime in: "She used to be real sweet till she got mixed up with the wrong crowd in high school."

There was a little table by the window where she sat, and Celia looked hard at the artificial flower arrangement sitting on it. It was in a white wicker basket, an unseasonable mixture of fake irises, roses, and daffodils in colors much too bright for a January day. As could be expected, the petals and leaves were coated with a fine film of dust. The basket was too large for the arrangement in it, and it sat a little lopsided on the table.

Looking at the basket, Celia was taken back to a summer afternoon when she was sixteen, before she had gotten mixed up with the so-called wrong crowd, when she and Grandmother had gone blackberry picking along the railroad track that ran beside their house. They had spent hours filling their baskets and pails with berries. Grandmother could pick them twice as fast as Celia, deftly avoiding the thorns, and when her basket was full she came alongside Celia and helped her fill hers.

They didn't talk much, just picked. And broiled like hot dogs on a grill. Celia remembered how unbearable it was, how long the day had seemed. She wondered now why they hadn't risen early and done their picking in the morning when it was cooler. She hadn't complained, though, not even about the long sleeves Grandmother had insisted she wear. That was before she had wised up and found out about freedom. Those were still the days of conforming, of accompanying Grandmother to church and praying four times a day and doing as she was told.

They had finished with the baskets and set them side by side, then taken up two buckets they'd also brought along. The bushes were loaded with ripe berries, and even after both buckets were full, her grandmother put her hands on her hips and looked off down the tracks. "We could empty these and fill 'em all over again," she said, shaking her head. For a minute Celia was afraid she was going to insist they do just that, but she didn't. She took off her straw hat and bent over to wipe her forehead with the hem of her dress. "Let's go," she said, putting the hat back on. "Time to get us some supper."

After they ate that night, Grandmother took out some plastic grocery store bags and divided up all those berries, every last one. Then they walked up and down Old Campground Road delivering them to all the neighbors. Grandmother kept one bag for herself. One bag out of probably twelve or fourteen. The next day she made one blackberry pie and two jars of preserves. Not much to show for all that hot work under the July sun. Their fingers were stained for days afterward, and Celia had scratches all over her hands and wrists from the brambles.

Not that her grandmother made a proud show out of her generosity. Not at all. It had often seemed to Celia that Grandmother hardly knew how to go about being neighborly. It almost seemed as if she were embarrassed by her attempts. As Celia remembered it, she was terse, bordering on rude, in her presentation of the berries throughout the neighborhood that night. They certainly hadn't lingered over the task.

Her grandmother would thrust the bag at whoever came to the door and say, "Here, we got lots more'n we know what to do with. You take some." Then she'd wheel around and stalk back to Celia, who was waiting at the edge of the road. Since Grandmother's house was set off all by itself, they had walked quite a little distance in either direction, stopping at houses where lights were on. The whole process took more than an hour, and when they got home, her grandmother washed her hands for a long time in the kitchen sink, seemingly glad to be done with the whole business.

Celia sighed now and turned from the basket of flowers to look out the window. She saw a couple of cars pulling into the parking lot of the funeral home and felt herself wishing she could make time zoom ahead. If only she could suddenly be on the other side of the funeral, headed back home to normality. If only she could stay mad at Grandmother, if she could call up pictures of the hateful ways Grandmother had tried to control her life during that awful last year of high school, if she wouldn't keep seeing instead all these other images of earlier times when they lived together peaceably.

Al sat on the sofa by the window. Without looking directly at him, Celia could tell he was leaning forward, staring at her. "Celia, do you . . ." he started to say, then fell silent. Celia turned her head away from him. Again, she wished she had considered the effort it would take to have him along on this trip. The thought of riding all the way home with him after the funeral exhausted her.

Aunt Beulah had disappeared again, but Celia could hear her voice out in the hallway: "We're all meeting in here. Go on in. Celia's already in there waiting." Out of the corner of her eye, she saw several people enter the room, but she didn't look to see who they were. She heard one of them say, "I bet you the ground is hard as cement. Sure is a cold day for burying her." Someone else added, "Yep, I reckon it'll be a sparse turnout."

But when they all filed into the chapel fifteen minutes later, Celia saw that the place was packed. She couldn't help wondering who all these people were.

Grandmother's life had been so narrow. She had been born in a little town thirty miles away and had moved here to Dunmore after she married. Atlanta was about the farthest she had ever traveled. At one time Celia had thought it was pleasantly quaint to have a history like Grandmother's, confined to a tiny pinpoint on the map, but then she had changed her mind and seen it as a horrible way to live your life. "Don't you ever want to *go* places and *do* things?" she had asked her grandmother once, during the time she was starting to shake off her old way of thinking.

"I got plenty to do right here at home," Grandmother had replied evenly, and without so much as looking at Celia she had continued ripping an old sheet into rags.

Celia followed Aunt Beulah into the second row of the funeral chapel and sat down between her and Al. The organ was playing softly " 'Tis So Sweet to Trust in Jesus." Celia wondered if her grandmother had chosen even the prelude hymns. Probably so. Someone directly behind her blew his nose, a sudden loud honking sound, and Celia flinched. Al put a hand on her arm, but she pulled away.

She had always hated sudden loud noises. One of the hardest things to get used to when she had visited her grandmother as a little girl, and then later when she had lived with her, was the sudden blast of the train whistle as it rushed by the house. Actually, it wasn't anything like a whistle. It was more like a horn or *many* horns—a great sustained blast of a thousand tubas. She had finally learned to watch the clock and brace herself for it, but sometimes she would forget and be caught by surprise. Often she could feel the train coming before she actually heard it, but even then she was never fully prepared for the whistle.

She had never thought to ask her grandmother during all those years whatever possessed her to buy a house less than thirty yards from a rail-road track that was still in use. She remembered how the windows would rattle as the train rumbled by, how the floor would vibrate. No doubt her grandparents had gotten a low price for such a piece of real estate. They had probably thought they were getting a real bargain. Celia could imagine the former owners making sure they didn't schedule appoint-ments with potential buyers during one of the two times each day when the train came tearing by. She could picture them turning somersaults after her grandparents signed the papers, thanking their lucky stars for unloading the house, and then moving far away to a tranquil hillside out in the country.

Two men in dark suits walked into the chapel from a side door and sat in chairs on the small platform. Celia sensed a stirring in the rows behind her and saw that the casket was being borne in by eight men walking slowly down the center aisle. She wondered if any of her relatives knew that the custom at most funerals now was to place the casket on a rolling stand and let the pallbearers walk beside it instead of actually carrying it. Of course, maybe Walsh's Funeral Services didn't have such a rolling conveyance available. It didn't look like the kind of establishment that spent a lot of extra money on up-to-date amenities.

As the pallbearers made their way down the aisle, everyone turned sideways to watch the procession. Celia wondered if anyone else was think-ing about how much like a wedding this part was. The men were surefooted and kept the casket level. Mr. Shelby must have met with them and given them instructions beforehand. Maybe they had actually practiced it.

Celia picked out Doreen's husband at once. Ralph Hubert still had the build of a football player, carrying his part of the burden easily. He actually looked a lot better than Celia would have predicted. No potbelly or scruffy beard. If she didn't know who he was, she'd almost be tempted to call him handsome. She knew if he opened his mouth, though, every syllable he uttered would give him away as a very blue-collar small-town former high school football player who had graduated only because of the mercy of several teachers.

As they passed her row, Celia stared intently at the casket. *And this is how it all ends, Grandmother,* she thought. *You're put in a box, then carried in, then carried back out, then dumped in a hole. The end.* Of course Grandmother wouldn't agree. If she heard Celia sum it up that way, she'd turn at once in her Bible to the book of John and start reading aloud those verses about mansions, and then she'd flip back to Revelation and read about the twelve gates and the crystal river and the light that shines eternally and all the rest of it. If there was one thing Grandmother had had plenty of, it was faith.

Celia felt a thick suffocating sadness. How pathetic, she told herself, to live eighty-seven years in the same area and never see the world, to rise day after day and do the same things, to have such a long list of rules to live by, to miss out on so much. But even before she finished the thought, her grandmother's face, which she had seen less than a half hour ago in the open casket, rose before her—the set of her lips, the strong brow, the parchment skin—and she knew beyond a doubt that Grandmother would take issue with her on this point, also. "Don't go feeling sorry for me," she would say. "I did exactly what I was supposed to do. It suited me just fine."

At least I got away from here and didn't end up like her, Celia thought. *At least I've seen what the world outside the state of Georgia looks like. At least I know something about real life and art and culture.* Still, a disturbing thought nibbled at the edge of her mind. As far as *happiness* went, she knew that was probably one area in which she hadn't really surpassed her grandmother. Money, yes. Education, yes. Experience, at least of a certain kind, without a doubt. Even a moderate measure of success. But happiness? Not by a country mile, as her relatives were fond of saying.

Not that Grandmother had *seemed* all that happy on the outside. "Doesn't she ever smile?" Celia's friend Ansell had often said when he came to pick her up in his car. Or, "There she is, the old woman with the contagious laugh." But something spoke very clearly to Celia right this very minute as she watched the men gently place her grandmother's casket on a stand in front of the pulpit: *She was contented with her lot in life.* She couldn't have liked much of what had come her way, but she accepted it and went on living.

Grandmother had lived in the same little white frame house next to the railroad track for sixty-some years, had raised three children of her own in it, had planted a garden every spring and kept chickens in the backyard. Celia had seen her snatch up many a chicken with her bare hands and wring its neck for supper that night. Then she'd chop off its head with a little hatchet she kept in the shed. She'd fling the head out into the tall weeds behind the garage for the stray cats to fight over.

For all those years she had washed clothes and hung them on the line outside, sewed and mended and ironed, mowed the grass, scrubbed the floors, cooked meals. Not fancy meals and usually not even very good ones. She fixed the same things over and over, as Celia remembered it, and she didn't hold much to the principle of seasoning, believing that Americans used far too much salt. She also thought Americans ate their meat too rare, so she went to the other extreme. Though Celia had never taken the trouble to actually keep a tally, she knew that at least two out of every three meats her grandmother put on the table were seriously overcooked, usually downright burned.

A funny thing about human adaptability, though, was that you could get used to almost anything. Celia recalled the way her grandmother would fix fried potatoes—dice them up, then fry them in hot oil until they were dark brown. Very dark brown. Later, living in her first apartment, sharing her bed with a grad student named Benjie, Celia had made fried potatoes one night to go with the hamburgers Benjie had grilled on her hibachi. When she put them on the table, Benjie had laughed and said, "Whoa, what have we got here—potato pellets?" He took only a couple of bites, and Celia ate all the rest. He couldn't believe she actually *liked* them fixed that way, that she had been watching them carefully the whole time they cooked, deliberately waiting until they were almost black to transfer them from the skillet onto a paper towel.

One of the men stood behind the pulpit now and introduced himself as the pastor of "our dear sister, Mrs. Burnes." As far as looks went, he fit the bill for a backwater southern preacher. Tall and thin, with an apologetic stoop to his posture, everything about him bland and nondescript. He told about visiting Mrs. Burnes daily during her last week when "she knew she was soon to depart to Glory." And he read from what he claimed was her favorite passage of Scripture: Joshua 1:5–9.

The words were familiar to Celia. She could have recited them from memory. When the pastor came to the words "observe to do according to all the law" and "turn not from it to the right hand or to the left," Celia felt the old bitterness rise up within her. There was that same old rigid code of behavior being held up as the only way to live. Follow the rules! Stay inside the lines! Walk the straight and narrow!

When he came to the final words, the pastor slowed down and let each one hang in the air a little longer: " 'For the Lord thy God is with thee whithersoever thou goest.' " He closed the Bible and leaned forward.

"And that promise is as true for our departed friend today as it was for Joshua. Mrs. Burnes has gone to a new place, but the Lord God is still with her. In fact, he's with her now in an even better way, for she's resting in his bosom as a lamb with its shepherd." Celia suspected that this was intended as a transition so they could all stand and sing something like "Savior, Like a Shepherd Lead Us."

She continued to study the pastor as he returned to his seat. He wasn't the same pastor as the one she remembered from eighteen years ago. Pastor Thacker had been the name of that one, but he had probably retired or died by now. He'd been an old man even back then, but he'd had a strong voice, with which he had loudly denounced "the rampant worldliness creeping into our homes and churches." That was one thing Pastor Thacker had loved to harp on—how much like the world Christians were becoming. " 'Come out from among them, and be ye separate'!" he would shout at some point during almost every sermon he preached. She remembered the looks of silent reproach he gave her that last year the few times she went to church. She remembered the day he visited their house, no doubt at Grandmother's request, and tried to talk her out of going to a liberal state college.

Celia's prediction proved wrong. The congregation wasn't asked to sing "Savior, Like a Shepherd Lead Us" after all. But she hadn't been all that far off. The other man came to the pulpit now and began singing all by himself a song Celia remembered from the old book of *Tabernacle Hymns*: "The Lord Is My Shepherd." At least she had been right about the shepherd part. Next to her she saw Aunt Beulah wipe her eyes with an embroidered handkerchief.

Celia knew all the words to this hymn, also. "The Lord is my shepherd, no want shall I know." When the man got to the part that said "He leadeth my soul where the still waters flow," the pastor leaned forward in his chair and nodded earnestly.

She studied the pastor again. He was sitting with his hands on his knees, both feet flat on the floor, looking steadily at the man who was singing. He was probably in his late forties, Celia guessed, and not at all handsome, with thin hair he was clearly in the process of losing. He looked exactly like the kind of man who would be Grandmother's pastor. Not one glimmer of prosperity about him. He had probably "felt the call" early in life and devoted himself to studying the Bible as a youngster, never experiencing anything remotely close to an adventure.

But *adventure* wasn't a word people like Grandmother understood. The *sameness* of her life was remarkable to Celia. And totally unthinkable—she couldn't imagine such dullness. Not only had her grandmother lived in the same house for all those years, but she had also attended the same little clapboard church only three blocks from her house as long as she had lived there, and most of that time she had walked to services, even in winter.

She had owned only one car in her whole life—a tan Mercury Comet that her husband, Celia's grandfather, had bought used in 1970 only two years before he died. Actually, he had bought it wrecked at an auction and had gotten it home and fixed it up like new out in the barn. Before that they had gone everywhere in an old Chevy pickup. Grandmother was over fifty when she learned to drive the Comet, and she drove it mainly to the grocery store. Come to think of it, that was probably the great adventure of her life—learning to drive a car. The children were gone by then. There had been two boys, uncles Celia never really knew, and one girl, Celia's mother.

Everyone talked about how strange and sad it was that her grandmother had outlived not only her husband, whom Celia barely remembered, but also all three of her children. One son had died at the age of twenty-three in Vietnam, the same year Celia was born, and the other had died of cancer when Celia was in junior high. He had been only forty-seven. And in between the two boys, of course, Celia's mother had gone out with her husband one day to buy a clothes dryer.

There was a sudden metallic clanking in the rear of the chapel, and Al turned around to look. "They're setting up folding chairs in back," he whispered to Celia. "People are still standing."

Celia marveled again at the crowd that had come out on a cold January afternoon in the middle of the week. Church friends and neighbors—those had been her grandmother's main contacts. Now that she thought about it, though, Celia supposed that there would be enough of them to account for most of the people here at the funeral. After all, it wasn't a terribly big chapel, not as large as the auditorium of Bethany Hills Bible Tabernacle, for example.

Grandmother had never been what you'd call "a people person," though, so it was curious to Celia that so many would come to her funeral. She wasn't the kind of woman to talk on the telephone a lot or pay visits just to pass the time of day. For her, the time of day was not to be frittered away but spent profitably, which always meant some kind of work.

Her grandmother wasn't a leader at church, though she attended faithfully and served wherever she was needed. It had become one of Celia's frequent criticisms during that last year of high school, however, that her grandmother's service was so rigidly and sternly rendered, almost by rote. "You're just following a bunch of stupid rules somebody made up centuries ago!" Celia had said more than once. "They don't even have anything to do with *now*. I'd hate to live my life like you! You've never even known what it's like to have a good time!"

"Doesn't she ever smile?"—the first time Ansell had asked that question was when he had come to pick Celia up for a party at Renee's house. She had told Grandmother they were going to the library to work on some research for a debate they were having the next week in economics class. Ansell thought it was the funniest thing he'd ever heard. "And she *believed* you?" he asked. Celia said yes, though she wasn't at all sure about that. Grandmother had a way of looking through what a person said and knowing things intuitively.

It was early in Celia's friendship with Ansell and the others, and he pulled up in their gravel driveway in his red souped-up Camaro and honked the horn one long toot. Grandmother had been trimming some bushes at the other side of the house and, at the sound of the horn, came charging around to the driveway frowning and holding the long clippers in front of her with both hands as if ready to whack off somebody's head. She walked up to the car, according to Ansell's report, and said, "The only thing I can figure out, young mister, is that your hand must've slipped and landed on the horn by accident."

Celia flew out of the house about then and headed for the car. Ansell was looking at Grandmother with his mouth hanging open, as if she had posed a riddle he couldn't figure out. He had caught her meaning, of course, which was "Surely you wouldn't drive up to my house and sit in your car and *honk* for my granddaughter to come out instead of going up to the door like a gentleman." But Grandmother would have no way of knowing that one of Ansell's favorite ways to show his disdain for adults was to stare straight at them and act as if he was too slow to understand what they meant.

When Celia got into the car that day, Grandmother raised her voice and said, "Be home in time to . . ." but Ansell was already backing out by then, spraying gravel everywhere. He mimicked her grandmother all evening, giving his performance over and over for everybody at Renee's party. It kept getting more and more outrageous as the evening wore on, and everyone laughed and begged him to do it again whenever somebody new arrived.

He had Grandmother's gruff manner down pretty well, but the vocabulary was all wrong: "Hey there, young stud, my granddaughter is not some piece of trash you can pull in here and honk for! You need to get your sorry self out of that car and walk up to the door and behave like a gentleman, which I can see is a completely foreign idea to a slimeball like you!" Celia hadn't heard Grandmother's actual words, but she knew she would never have said *stud* or *slimeball*.

By the last time Ansell reenacted the scene that night, he was using even worse words, words that shocked Celia, though she tried not to let it show. She laughed along with everybody else. Part of the hilarity was that they were all out of their minds by the end of the night, except for Celia. She wouldn't have anything to do with drugs, and it took her a good while to get up the nerve even to take her first sip of beer. Even months later, after she had loosened up a little, she was always very cautious, rarely letting herself get as far gone as the others.

To be honest, it scared her. You don't grow up hearing about the evils of alcohol and then suddenly overnight start drinking. She had hated the sensation of drunkenness the couple of times it happened, especially the aftermath, and frankly, she also hated the taste of beer. Deep down, drinking seemed like such a low-class, pointless thing to do for fun, though she never told her new friends this. Anyway, she decided she could put up with the drinking, considering the fact that they were rescuing her from her old way of life.

When she came home that first night, Grandmother was up waiting for her, sitting in her old green recliner with her Bible open in her lap. Lifting her nose to sniff the air, she gave Celia a long level look, then read aloud part of a verse from James: " 'Know ye not that the friendship of the world is enmity with God?' "

Celia walked right past her without speaking, went back to the bathroom, and stared at herself in the mirror over the sink. *It's time to quit feeling guilty,* she told herself, *and start having fun.* When she turned to start her bath water, she was surprised to see a tall bottle of Avon bubble bath on the side of the tub. She knew it was for her. Grandmother had ordered it a couple of weeks earlier when a woman had come by the house with a catalog. She had called Celia from her bedroom that evening and asked her to choose the fragrance she wanted.

Celia knew it had pained her to spend money like that on something so unnecessary, but here it was. The Avon lady must have delivered it today. She unscrewed the lid and smelled it. "Spring Rain" was printed on the label. She wanted to pour a capful into the water and watch it turn into a mass of bubbles, but she wouldn't let herself. Instead, she put the lid back on tightly, then set the bottle on the floor and pushed it behind the trash can.

4

And the Morning Breaks Eternal

Finally it was all over, but not until after the mourners had sung three verses of "When the Roll Is Called Up Yonder" beside the grave. Surely the preacher could have condensed Grandmother's funeral instructions, Celia was thinking, out of consideration for the comfort of those attending. Why did they have to sing *three* stanzas? Wouldn't one be enough to give the effect? Grandmother would never know the difference anyway.

It was misting by now, and combined with the bitter cold, it was a miserable day to be standing around outdoors. Celia was glad she had put her long wool coat in the car before leaving home that morning. She had seen Aunt Elsie squinting at her as she and Al had walked toward the gray tent at the cemetery. Celia knew exactly what she must be thinking: *About time that girl put on something warm.*

Celia wondered why funerals had to drag out so long, especially this last tacked-on part at the graveside, and especially on such a cold day. She was sure she wouldn't be able to remember all the parts later on as she thought back over the day, but then she hoped she wouldn't be doing much thinking back over this day. Forget the earlier idea of making today into the beginning of a novel. The only thing she wanted now was to get it all over with and blot it from her memory.

Today would make a lousy novel anyway. Besides the funeral gimmick that opened so many bad novels, there were also way too many orphans in fiction. Orphans who had suffered through bleak childhoods, then carried their pitiful shipwrecked emotions into an adulthood doomed from the start. In many books, however, these orphans would eventually rise above their troubled past with great heartrending courage and accomplish admirable things, all of which turned out to be terribly contrived on the printed page.

Recently one of her longtime clients, a man named Frank Bledsoe, had brought her the opening chapters of a new novel he planned to publish himself, since his previous attempts to find a publishing house interested in his stories had proved fruitless. Celia had been telling Frank for years that his manuscripts lacked the important ingredient of believability, to which he always replied indignantly, "But it's all based on something that *really happened*. These are people I *really know*." Frank had never learned what she had learned years ago in college, that real life didn't always convert into good fiction. He also took himself way too seriously.

She had read only a few pages of Frank's newest manuscript before she recognized it for what it was: the dreaded autobiographical novel. Actually, she was a little surprised it had taken him this long to get around to writing it. On the first page it was established that the main character—a boy named Dean, which happened to be Frank's middle name—was an orphan, as was Frank. Celia had never told him that she, too, was an orphan. She had never told him much of anything else about herself, either, mainly because Frank always did most of the talking, and the topic he was most fond of discussing was himself.

He had never once blamed her for his many rejection letters but kept coming back, bringing yet another stack of pages for her to read, critique, and edit, sure that this one would be a bestseller. He paid her well, but with this most recent manuscript she was beginning to think no amount of money was worth having to slog through stuff like this. She thought of the manuscript now, on her desk at home, waiting for her attention. It was in one of those thick brown expandable folders, titled importantly "From Ashes to Fame."

Celia pulled the collar of her wool coat up tighter around her neck. Most of the people at the graveside service were standing, since Walsh's Funeral Services had set up only a dozen or so folding chairs, in which Grandmother's sisters and some of the other older relatives were sitting. The tent was too small for everyone to stand under, so a lot of people were huddled under umbrellas around the perimeter.

Celia leaned closer to Al. She couldn't remember being this cold in a long time. She wouldn't be surprised to hear later that they had set some kind of temperature record here in Georgia today.

After the last chorus of "When the Roll Is Called Up Yonder" came a benediction offered by Grandmother's pastor, who seemed to be trying to depict the concept of eternality by the length of his prayer. During the prayer Celia's mind whirled with snatches of the things she had seen and heard today. Like Frank Bledsoe's novels, it all lacked the quality of believ-ability, yet, as Frank was so fond of saying, it had all "really happened."

Sometime before this closing prayer, Uncle Buford had limped forward to recite the passage of Scripture about man's days being as the grass of the field, and at some other point the song leader had sung another solo, a hymn called "No Night There," which Celia remembered as another of Grandmother's favorites. Naturally, it was talking about heaven, calling it the "land of fadeless day" and the "city foursquare" and tritely listing the "gates of pearl" and the "crystal river" among its many mythical charms.

Somewhere in there Uncle Buford had also read the verse "For what is a man profited, if he shall gain the whole world, and lose his own soul?" For an old man hard of hearing and half blind standing outside in the freezing cold, his voice sounded wondrously strong. He stood unsupported at the head of the grave, throwing himself into his role of Scripture reader with great fervor, giving no evidence of wishing he were at home on such a dismal day taking an afternoon nap after all his second helpings at Aunt Beulah's house earlier.

But at long last it was over. The preacher finally wound up his prayer, and after the amen, the pallbearers came forward once more and lowered the casket into the ground. At this, Celia suddenly turned and left. It was as if a tight wire inside her had snapped. Didn't these people have any sense of when enough was enough? She supposed they were going to stand around now and watch the clods of dirt fall against the casket, or maybe even help out by taking turns with the shovel. They wouldn't know that this part was also out-of-date.

She had been standing behind all her aunts and uncles, off to the side a little for a quick getaway. Al caught up to her now and took her arm. He held his umbrella over her, and they walked toward his car in silence for a few moments. Then Al chuckled. "So, when the roll is called up yonder, I wonder where *we'll* be, huh?" Celia didn't answer. The trouble with all these old church songs was the way they clung like barnacles to your memory. Without wanting to, in fact trying hard *not* to, she heard the words of this one now: "When the trumpet of the Lord shall sound, and time shall be no more, and the morning breaks, eternal, bright and fair . . ."

She heard Aunt Beulah's voice floating above the others in the chorus, confidently asserting that when the roll was called up yonder, indeed *she* would be there. "I'll b'there" is how Aunt Beulah sang it. At the thought of her aunt, she stopped and turned around. They were all starting to move away slowly now, out from under the gray tent, back toward their cars. She didn't care about the rest of them, but she hated to leave without saying good-bye to Aunt Beulah.

"You ready to get in?" Al said, pressing her arm. "Here's the car right here. You don't need to hang around for any reason, do you? I mean, hey, there's not going to be a big *reading of the will* or anything, is there?" Celia could tell he was eager to get back on the road. He was probably already thinking about where they'd stop for supper. He had to be cold, too, not having brought an overcoat along as she had. At least he had on a turtleneck under his sport coat.

"No," Celia said, not sure of which question she was answering. It was funny that she hadn't even thought about the possibility of a will. She wondered if Grandmother had even had one. There sure wasn't anything of value in that little house of hers. It wasn't exactly full of antiques. There wasn't a single thing of Grandmother's Celia could ever remember wishing she could have—no table or chair or piece of jewelry or set of books. Not even a knickknack. Eighteen years ago she had been only too glad to wipe the dust of that cramped little house off her feet and get out of the crummy little town of Dunmore.

She didn't even want the bed she'd brought with her when she moved in with her grandmother. It hadn't been worth much, really—just a cheap one her parents had bought through the want ads. There was a bad gouge along the top of the headboard now where she had thrown her hand mirror one day after Grandmother had once again come into her room and turned the radio dial to the Christian station in Roswell.

The only thing from her childhood that she still had was her mother's cedar chest, which she had taken to college and kept ever since. She had it in the living room of her apartment now and used it for storing blankets and sweaters. She thought of the furniture in Grandmother's house, all of it unmatched secondhand stuff. She'd hate to fall heir to any of it. And she'd also hate to be the one stuck with the house itself, to have to put it up for sale. Maybe a deaf person would consider buying it. Or maybe somebody who worked for the railroad. Maybe they could get the train to slow down as it passed the house so they could hop on and off and thereby have a free ride to and from work every day.

She knew Al was wishing she would go ahead and get into the car so they could be first leaving the cemetery. With all these cars, there was sure to be a bit of a bottleneck getting out. Walsh's Funeral Services had furnished only two black limousines, which hadn't begun to accommodate the family. So most of them had driven out in their own cars and parked along the little single-lane road that wound through the cemetery.

But she really wanted to tell Aunt Beulah good-bye before she left. It surprised her that she wanted it so badly. Then, amazingly, in a development as luckily timed as those in all of Frank Bledsoe's bad stories, Celia saw her aunt Beulah break from the graveside crowd and head straight toward her, hanging on to Uncle Taylor's arm, pulling him along and waving a hand. "Celia, honey! Wait! I need to see you before you leave!"

Celia left the shelter of Al's umbrella and walked back to meet her aunt. She heard Al heave a sigh behind her.

"I have something for you," Aunt Beulah said. "Sadie told me to give it to you after the funeral was over. She was real particular about that part. She said it had to be *after* it was all over." Aunt Beulah's eyes were red, and she patted at them with her handkerchief, then smiled. "Your grandmother always did have things planned out a certain way, you know, and you couldn't do step two before step one, or she'd get real upset."

Celia nodded and fell into step beside Aunt Beulah. Nobody had to tell her about Grandmother's insistence on doing things a certain way. Uncle Taylor tried to extend the umbrella to include her, but the mist seemed to be swirling up from the ground. Celia could feel that her bangs had gone limp, could see them drooping into her eyes. She looked down at her feet and scolded herself again for wearing her new shoes that had cost far too much. The suede trim was going to be ruined, of course. She should have thought about the possibility of tromping through a muddy cemetery.

Al had already gotten into the car and started the engine. No doubt he had the heater turned on full blast. She could see him rubbing his hands in front of the vent, trying to thaw out. As they approached his car, Aunt Beulah stopped and opened her large pocketbook, which was made of a woven strawlike fabric more suitable for July than January. From it she took a book-size package, neatly wrapped in a brown Piggly Wiggly grocery sack and tied with string. She handed it to Celia.

On the top Celia recognized Grandmother's bold script: "To My Granddaughter Celia. Read This." Celia knew exactly what it was. She had seen the tattered book in Grandmother's lap hundreds of times. How like Grandmother to wrap it and tie it all up as if it were something precious and breakable.

Aunt Beulah stepped forward and hugged Celia. "I'm so glad you could come, Celie. I know how happy Sadie would be. I wish you'd come back and see us sometime. With Martha Sue and Jerry both in Mexico, I get so lonesome I could just sit down and cry." Celia had almost forgotten about Aunt Beulah's two children, both of whom must be in their fifties by now. Both of them had served for years as missionaries in different parts of Mexico. Martha Sue and her husband, David, had gone first, right out of Bible college, and then several years later when Martha Sue's brother, Jerry, went to visit them, he met a Mexican girl who attended their small church near Torreón and ended up marrying her, then staying in Mexico and starting another church farther north, near Delicias.

As Aunt Beulah hugged her, it struck Celia that her aunt, whom she had always thought of as a tall woman, wasn't much bigger than she was herself. No bigger than a minute, she thought. That's what her aunt Bess had always said about small thin people, in fact about Celia herself. "That girl's no bigger than a minute. We need to fatten her up, put some meat on her bones!" As a teenager, Celia had gotten tired of hearing it but had gradually learned to ignore it, finally figuring out that Aunt Bess, being portly herself, wanted everybody else to be fat, also.

Before releasing her, Aunt Beulah pressed her cheek against Celia's. Celia felt its cool slackness and couldn't help thinking how the funerals among Grandmother's siblings would start piling up now. Grandmother's was the first, but the others would come fast.

"Thanks, Aunt Beulah," she said. "It was good to see you." She opened the car door, and Al raced the engine ever so slightly. "Well, we've got to get back on the road now. Tomorrow's a work day and all."

Aunt Beulah nodded sadly. "Everything's so busy nowadays."

Celia got into the car and set the package in her lap. "I'm glad I got to see you before we left. I wanted to." She closed the door and waved at her aunt and uncle.

Aunt Beulah said something through the glass, and Celia rolled down the window a crack. "So he'll probably be sending you something in the mail," Aunt Beulah said.

"Who's that?" Celia said.

"Buford. He's the one who's settling up all your grandmother's affairs."

"Oh, okay." Celia waved again, closed the window, and they pulled away. She wondered for a moment what it was Uncle Buford would be sending her. She sincerely hoped Grandmother hadn't left unpaid bills behind. She wondered about the funeral expenses. Surely they wouldn't ask her to help with those.

"Hey, maybe your grandma had money stuffed in her mattress," Al said. He was driving down the winding little road a lot faster than he needed to be, considering the rain and the fact that it was in a cemetery. "Maybe she left it all to you."

"Grandmother didn't have money," Celia said shortly. She could hear the edge in her voice. "Granddaddy left her in debt when he died. She had to close their store and sell everything just to break clear. She lived off her social security check."

"Store? What kind of store did they have?"

Celia gave a short dry laugh. "Not much of one. It was one of those little neighborhood grocery stores. About the size of a storage shed."

Which was exactly what it had turned into when they closed it up. Celia could barely remember the store as it had been before that. She had been only four or five at the time her grandfather died. She did recall the cold bottles of pop in the big cooler with the sliding top, the little packages of peanuts clipped to a red wire rack, and the freezer where the Popsicles and ice cream sandwiches were kept. She also remembered the old coal heater and the tin can that sat beside it on the floor, into which her grandfather, with deadeye aim, had spit tobacco juice while he whittled little objects out of sticks.

"What's that you got there?" Al asked, nodding toward the package in her lap. "A book?"

Celia tossed it into the backseat. "Yep, that's my inheritance." She sighed and looked at her watch. Four o'clock already, which meant they wouldn't get home until almost eight, probably closer to nine if Al stopped to eat, which no doubt he would. She knew this would be a good time to thank him for taking the day off work to drive her here, but she couldn't force the words out of her mouth. More than anything she wished she were already home right now, that she didn't have to endure several hours of riding in a car. She hoped Al didn't plan to keep talking.

To give him a hint, she closed her eyes and adjusted the back of her seat until she was reclining. Al turned on the radio and finally found a station playing jazz. This was another thing that irritated Celia about Al. He thought he was a terrific jazz saxophonist, which he wasn't. He was a decent enough saxophonist, but he didn't have the keenness and security and creativity of a jazz player. As with any art, you had to know the rules before you could break them, and Al didn't know the rules. Besides that, anybody could play the saxophone. Everybody knew it was the easiest wind instrument to play.

She listened to him hum along with a trumpet rendition of "Tuxedo Junction," followed by a jazz arrangement of Bach's "Musette," of all the unlikely things. It was actually quite cleverly conceived, however, with some trading off between passages of vocalization and clarinet improvisation. She wondered if she could have ever gotten that good on her clarinet if she'd kept at it. Maybe she should get it back out and start practicing again. Maybe the community orchestra in Greenville or Anderson needed a clarinet. At least she could start getting in shape for the summer band that gave park concerts in Spartanburg.

Right before she fell asleep, she was in the process of remembering the concerto she had played as a high school junior, the one she had memorized for the state competition, the winner of which was invited to perform with the Georgia All-State Orchestra in the spring. It was a difficult piece, but she had played it flawlessly that day in Atlanta when her music teacher had driven her down for the final runoffs. Carl von Weber's Concerto no. 1 in F Minor for Clarinet and Orchestra—it was the pinnacle of her clarinet studies.

She had placed first and had played with the All-State Orchestra that year. She was something of a local celebrity for a while, since students from Dunmore didn't usually win statewide competitions. Her clarinet teacher had cried as she sat on the front row of the auditorium listening to her performance at the final concert in Atlanta. Later, during her senior year, her clarinet teacher had cried again when Celia stopped practicing and dropped out of band. Oh, the disappointed, droopy-faced looks she had suffered from adults that year! She hadn't quit the tennis team, though.

For some reason she had hung on to that, maybe because she liked the feeling of pounding something as hard as she could.

Celia had ridden down two days before the All-State concert in a school van, along with two twelfth-grade violinists and a tenth-grade cellist from nearby Rome, whose auditions had earned them chairs in the All-State Orchestra. Grandmother had put on her best dress, a dark brown print, and had driven her Mercury Comet all the way to Atlanta for the final concert. It had been on a Sunday afternoon, which smote her grandmother's conscience because it meant missing the evening service at Bethany Hills Bible Tabernacle, but she told Celia they would have their own church service at home that night when they returned. And they did.

As she was slipping toward sleep with the sounds of a jazz ensemble ripping through "American Patrol" on the radio, Celia remembered the ride back to Dunmore with her grandmother that Sunday almost twenty years ago now. "You played pretty," Grandmother said at last, her eyes on the road and her hands firmly clutching the steering wheel. She had greeted Celia after the concert with her customary businesslike nod, had helped her get her things into the car, said a word to her clarinet teacher, then consulted a road map before starting the car. She hadn't spoken of the concert until they were out on the interstate.

"You sure did," Grandmother said again. She even reached over and gave Celia's hand a single pat, something she rarely did. Then after a brief silence, "But I like the songs you play at church a lot better than that one." It wasn't that her grandmother disliked classical music. She just liked hymns better.

The last thing Celia saw before she fell asleep was the look on Grandmother's face as she would watch her play her clarinet at church, sometimes during the offering and sometimes right before the preacher's sermon. It wasn't a look of pride or great rapturous joy, but was closer to something like assurance or confirmation, as if she were thinking, "There, that's a good song. I sure hope people are thinking about the words to it."

It must have been close to an hour later when Celia bolted awake. "No! Wait!" she cried. "I want to go that way!" She sat up, pointing straight ahead. Al jerked the steering wheel a little, then exhaled slowly.

"Don't do that!" he said. "Don't ever do that. You almost made me . . ." He glanced over at Celia, and his voice softened. "Sorry. Another one of your dreams, huh?"

Celia pressed her fingertips against her eyelids and nodded. This one had been so real. She forced herself to breathe slowly. *It was only a dream,* she kept telling herself. *Only another dream.* But she could still see the images vividly stamped in her mind.

She had been crawling in a clump of poison ivy, peeking out to watch Grandmother pick her way along a narrow pebbled path toward a gleaming golden gate. Grandmother had kept looking back and motioning Celia to follow, but Celia kept ducking into the ivy. As Grandmother approached the gate, a huge red doorknob rotated slowly and the gate opened. An angel, glowing from the inside, stood at the portal holding a scroll. Hosts of other angels wearing white came forward like a welcoming committee to escort her grandmother through the gate.

Still, Grandmother cast one more anxious glance behind her. An angel placed on Grandmother's head a crown of glittering rubies, while a man on a motorcycle nearby held a gospel tract above his head, waving it around like a little banner. A group of people next to him also smiled and waved at her, their mouths all darkly stained with purple. They were all holding large baskets piled high with blackberries. A woman enveloped in frothy mounds of bubbles and carrying an Avon catalog ran up and hugged her.

The shiny gate slowly began to close, and Celia stepped out of the poison ivy. Someone behind her, whom she couldn't see, tugged her sleeve and said, "No, come this way." She felt herself being pulled backward. She heard the blare of a car horn, and the voice said, "Don't follow her—she never smiles." She yielded to the pull yet strained to see Grandmother. The gate was swinging shut inch by inch. She saw her cousin Doreen appear at the gate holding a silver toy gun, which she pointed at the person tugging on Celia. "Gotcha!" she said. There was a popping sound like a cork coming loose. "Now break loose and run!" Doreen yelled to Celia.

She saw Aunt Beulah, wearing pink slippers, come up behind Doreen and gesture to the glowing angel. She heard her aunt plead, "Don't call the roll yet!" And she saw her lean earnestly toward Celia, motioning her forward. "Hurry, Celie! Get in quick! Watch out for that icy patch!"

Behind Aunt Beulah the faces of Celia's mother and father materialized, but instead of having the bodies of people, they were two little robins sitting together in a brown nest. With one of her wings her mother held up a watch, the same one that had been Celia's graduation present from her grandmother, and shook it. "Time's running out, Celie!" she called softly. Red-haired Ralphie peered out from behind the gate and started counting: "One, two, three, four . . ."

But the arm kept pulling her backward, and the voice, which sounded young and old at the same time, kept repeating, "No, Celia, no fun there. Come this way. Come with me. Come on now." In the background she heard someone playing "No Night There" on the clarinet. She felt the ground shake, as if a train were thundering by, and then the cries of many babies filled the air.

"No! Wait! I want to go that way!" she called out at last, wrenching free and pointing ahead . . . toward a dark highway somewhere between Dunmore, Georgia, and Filbert, South Carolina.

Celia rubbed her eyes again, then opened them and looked out the window. She had to learn to tame her imagination one of these days. She had to find a way to stop dreaming so heavily, with such jumbled-up scenes, everything mixed together like Aunt Beulah's dinner table. She could trace every detail of the dream to some event or thought of the day, which settled her down somewhat, yet when she thought of the gate slowly swinging shut, she felt as if someone had his hands around her neck.

The funeral is over, Celia reminded herself. *Grandmother is gone for good, along with all her finger-pointing. Guilt is only a trick churches use.* She kept repeating these words to herself, trying to fall into slow, steady breathing.

Al reached over and took her hand. "It's really a pity, you know?" he said. "All those relatives of yours—they live their whole lives going to church and then they die. Then what? What do they have to show for living?" He laughed and shook his head. "Boy, those were some *crazy* people back there. They'd make a great comedy act." And although Celia agreed with him, had always said the same things herself, Al's words grated on her. Somehow her Bible-toting nutcase relatives didn't seem nearly as funny now as they did when she described them to him from a distance of eighteen years and a couple of hundred miles.

Al sighed and continued. "But really, it is sad, isn't it? Their little houses get sold to pay their debts and buy a coffin, and what's left? Nothing. And you inherit the grand sum of a book wrapped up in a brown paper sack."

Celia was quiet for several moments. It came to her in that instant with perfect conviction that Al's voice was not one she wanted to hear every day for the rest of her life. Not even every other day or once a week. She could well imagine today being the pivotal point in their relationship. months to come she might remember it and say to someone, "It was going fine until the day he drove me to my grandmother's funeral." And it was nothing she could begin to explain. She agreed with everything he said, yet hearing him say it made her want to open the door and fling herself onto the shoulder of the freeway, anything to keep from having to be confined with him for another minute.

She removed her hand from his, almost shook it off actually, and reached into the backseat for the package Aunt Beulah had given her. She raised the back of her seat and began untying the string.

"Hey, are you all right?" Al said. "You're not mad about anything, are you?" She thought she could detect a tone of wounded annoyance, could almost hear him thinking, *Hey, I took off work today to drive you here. I deserve to be treated better than this.*

"Don't worry about it," Celia said tersely. She had the string off now and was unwrapping the Piggly Wiggly sack from around the Bible. She wondered when her grandmother had done this. It was wrapped up very securely and neatly, not at all as if someone had done it in a hurry, and certainly not as if a dying person had done it. But she couldn't imagine her grandmother wrapping up her Bible well in advance of her death, either, not having it at her fingertips to leaf through, to write in, to trace the words she already knew so well by heart.

Celia sighed and looked out the window at the dying light of the January sky. Here was just another small mystery to add to all the other things she would never understand about her grandmother.

5

Marching Through Immanuel's Ground

Another reason her life would make a bad novel, Celia had decided, was that the characters would seem so stereotyped. Nobody would believe that one person could have so many rigidly religious relatives, all stuck in the rut of such predictable, countrified ways of viewing life, all trekking to church several times a week, all so unaware that the twentieth century had come and gone. You could get by with one or two characters like that in a book, for quirky splashes of color, but not dozens and dozens of them. The whole thing would turn into a farce.

She could remember her second year at college when she had taken a course in creative writing. She had tried to write a short story about an intelligent boy with relatives like her own, a boy who started feeling cramped in the small-town box he was born in and finally made the decision to run away from home to get away from a hyper-religious grandfather. The focal scene of the story had taken place at a family reunion, and she had been very proud of the way she had captured the comical hubbub of the occasion. She had, of course, drawn freely from her memory.

It hadn't worked, though. The story, like the whole course, was a disappointment. Part of the story's failure was probably due to trying to write from a boy's perspective, but another part, a big one, was that everybody who read the story said the characters seemed fake. They had passed their stories around in class that semester for what the teacher called "peer feedback," and this comment kept showing up on her evaluation forms. Everybody thought the characters were funny in an overdone sort of way but not at all believable. One person had written, "Is this supposed to be a satire?"

The professor of the class, who had grown up in Canada, told her in their private conference that the characters were all too "broadly drawn," that she needed "a majority of rational benchmark characters" instead of "so many abnormals" in order to tie the story more securely to the school of realism, which seemed to be the tradition of fiction in which she was attempting to write. He had stressed the word *attempting*. She remembered that clearly. He had offered a bit of praise at the end, though in a rather condescending tone. "You obviously have a great imagination," he had said, "and an eye for humorous detail." He might as well have patted her on the head and said, "Aren't you adorable?" At least she had had the sense to keep her mouth shut and not shoot back with "But they're all people I *really know*!" No one would have believed her anyway.

And the tone—that was another problem the teacher pointed out. He said he felt there was too much anger fueling the story, as if "you're writing about something you're too close to." Something she needed to have more time to sort through, he said, so that she could reveal some kind of cohesive pattern to the whole situation.

The creative writing class had been good for one thing, though. It had shown her how much effort an artist has to put into something to make it appear effortless. She had never tried to write fiction again after that semester, though she often thought she probably could now. Not that she had ever really been able to sort through her life yet, certainly not that she had found any cohesive pattern. She could spot a good story when she saw one, though. She could also spot a bad one, which is what she most often saw in the editing she did on the side. Poor Frank Bledsoe—she thought of the reams of awful stuff he kept churning out and bringing to her.

Most of her classmates in college considered her a novelty, a cute little immigrant from Dixie. A boy in one of her journalism classes, Danny Ingles, had always begged her to talk. "Say *anything*," he would plead. "Go ahead, just talk and keep on talking. Recite the Declaration of Independence or a nursery rhyme or read from the textbook . . . anything at all, I don't care. Just let me close my eyes and listen." Sometimes she'd comply, and he'd close his eyes and lift his face as if basking in the sun, then afterward sigh and say something like "Oh, Celia, love, you're the real thing."

She and Danny had even dated some, mostly for meals late at night at his favorite Italian and Chinese restaurants, had in fact even gone further than dating for a short while. He had gotten an apartment in town their junior year and asked her offhandedly one night after polishing off a double pepperoni pizza what she'd think about the idea of moving in with him and sharing expenses. "Not a whole lot" was her reply. Celia knew she'd get sick of living with the smell of garlic. If a food didn't reek of garlic, Danny wasn't much interested in it.

Everyone at college had been fascinated that she was from Georgia, had teased her about living on a plantation like Tara. They had no idea what a curious state Georgia was, made up of every possible socioeconomic stratum of society, from old-money aristocrats to poor white trash. But that probably wasn't so curious after all. Every state was most likely that way. She knew firsthand of at least one other, having lived in South Carolina for twelve years now.

She remembered clearly the first time she had seen a copy of the magazine called *Georgia: The Easy Life,* which featured full-color spreads of mansions all around the state and told all about the cultured people who lived in them. These people collected Jackson Pollock and de Kooning paintings. They attended the theater and hired chamber groups for their private dinners, where they served dishes such as Scalloped Artichoke Hearts, Stevens Tavern Turtle Gumbo, and Herb Roasted Lamb with Grape Sauce.

It was like looking at a travel brochure for a foreign country. For sure Celia had never rubbed shoulders with the likes of these people during her years in Dunmore, where the locals preferred Clint Eastwood movies and Hank Williams songs. Their idea of good art was sticking a calendar picture or an old greeting card inside a frame from Kmart.

But while her relatives and their homes and menus certainly never appeared in *Georgia: The Easy Life,* neither were they at the other extreme— the kind of down-and-outers you saw shuffling down to the welfare office with five or six ragged, runny-nosed children trailing along behind them, redneck mountain illiterates who lived in gullies and hollows, dipped snuff, and had old couches and rusted washing machines sitting on their front porches, people straight out of the movie *Deliverance,* with a mean streak as wide as the Chattahoochee.

Instead, her relatives were part of another group Celia called the Rabid Blue-Collar Fundamentalist Fringe. She pictured all the other people of Georgia as a multicolored tablecloth, and this group as a very tacky tasseled border all around the edges.

It was incredible to her, looking back on it, how much *alike* all her Georgia relatives were, every single man, woman, and child among them, and how truly funny they were if you could just step back and observe them from afar instead of having to live in the middle of them. She doubted there was a more homogeneous family in the entire country than the Georgia clan on her mother's side. For certain a more churchgoing gang you'd never find anywhere. Though her grandmother had attended Bethany Hills Bible Tabernacle, the rest of them went to churches on the other side of Dunmore, near the old GE plant, where many of them had worked all their lives.

Oh, the churches in Dunmore, Georgia! Everything else existed in moderation: one elementary school, one junior high, and one high school, two decent-sized grocery stores, one Laundromat, one drugstore, one theater, one beauty shop, and five restaurants—Haynie's Dinette, Shady Lane Bar-B-Q, Popinjay's Burgers, Dairy Queen, and Little Bud's Pizza Parlor. But when it came to churches, they had sprouted up all over town like toadstools after a hard rain. Everything from Roman Catholic to holy rollers.

On a Thursday night, two weeks after returning from her grandmother's funeral in Dunmore, Celia found herself sitting at Al's dining room table in Derby, South Carolina. He didn't know it yet, but in the trunk of her red Mustang, which was parked in his driveway that very minute, were all the possessions he'd left at her apartment over the past months—the clothes, the toiletries, his portable CD player, several books, coffee mugs. She had put them all into a couple of large garbage bags before she left home, with plans to return them to him tonight after she told him she didn't want to continue their relationship.

As she had expected, the trip to Georgia for her grandmother's funeral had indeed proved to be the breaking point for her. By the time they had arrived home that night, she had loathed the sound of Al's voice. She had avoided him now for two weeks, but when he had called and invited her over for tonight, she knew she shouldn't put it off any longer.

She was only mildly concerned about *how* she would tell him. She was familiar enough with the process by now to know that you didn't have to plan out every detail. The words always came somehow, sometimes more easily and gently than other times, but once a relationship had progressed to this fork in the road, she usually had very little concern for sparing the man's feelings. She wanted only one thing: out. And by now she was good at making it very clear and doing so quickly.

But first dinner had to be gotten out of the way. Besides fancying himself a proficient jazz saxophonist, Al also claimed to be a gourmet cook, and occasionally on weekends he liked to "do dinner," as he called it. "Come over tonight," he'd say to Celia on the phone, "and I'll do dinner." He never wanted her help, though in Celia's opinion the final results almost always showed that he could have used it. She had to give him credit for trying, though, and sometimes he actually pulled off a good meal.

Tonight the main dish was something he called Steak Charlotta, a recipe he'd seen in *Chef's Pride*. Evidently he had tried to get by with a cheaper cut of meat, however, hoping to disguise it by slow cooking it to the point of fork tenderness. He had run short of time, though, and he had called Celia at five to tell her to come at seven instead of six, and then when she did arrive, he delayed the dinner further by serving an appetizer he had obviously thrown together in haste. He was a little out of sorts, Celia could tell, though he tried to cover it up with a loud cheerful stream of random chatter.

It was almost eight o'clock when they finally sat down to the table, having finished the Pickle Fan appetizer, which was a mixture of cream cheese and horseradish spread over pieces of melba toast and garnished with a sweet gherkin cut lengthwise and fanned across the top. Celia had nibbled around the edges of one while Al had devoured four of them in four bites, a single swift bite per Pickle Fan. Celia had finally managed to wrap the remains of hers in her paper napkin and deposit it in the trash while Al went into the kitchen to check on the main course.

They were just sitting down to eat their Steak Charlotta, along with Corn Sesame Stir-Fry and Almond Supreme Green Bean Casserole, when the doorbell rang. "That reminds me, I forgot the rolls in the oven," he said, not even glancing at the door. The doorbell rang again, twice. He brought back the rolls—nice ones but clearly store-bought. He wasn't much for baking his own bread, though he had tried it upon occasion with less than satisfactory results.

From where she was sitting, Celia couldn't see who was at the door, though she knew whoever it was could no doubt see the lights on inside, could maybe even step to the side a little and see the two of them through the window, sitting at the table at one end of Al's living room. It was dark outside by now, but the porch light, which had been turned on when she arrived, was still on, which was probably the reason the person out there continued to ring the doorbell, taking the light as an invitation.

Al was taking great pains with his roll, using about three times more butter than he really needed. The doorbell rang again, and a voice called out, "Anybody home in there?" The screen door opened, and they heard several loud knocks on the door, followed by two more rings of the doorbell. Al calmly set down his knife, broke off half of his roll, and began to eat it.

"Yoo-hoo!" the voice said. It was a deep phlegmy voice but clearly a woman's. The doorbell rang again.

"Whoever it is, I don't think she's going away," Celia said.

He shrugged and picked up his fork. "I don't care if she stands out there all night. I don't answer the phone or the doorbell during meals." He took an enormous bite of green beans.

She already knew this, of course. Al allowed nothing to interfere with his eating. She had been sitting right here at this same table only a month ago when an ambulance had pulled into the driveway next door, siren wailing and lights flashing. They had been eating BLTs and cream of broccoli soup that Al had made, but he hadn't budged from his chair.

When Celia had gone to the door and thrown it open, he hadn't even looked up from his bowl. She had gone outside to see the next-door neighbor borne out the front door on a stretcher and had learned from his wife that he had fallen off a ladder trying to hang a mirror above the fireplace. By the time Celia had returned to the table, Al had already refilled his soup bowl. Between bites he had nodded toward the house next door and said slurpily, "So what's going on?"

Finally the doorbell quit ringing, and they heard the slow heavy sound of someone retreating down the front steps. Celia couldn't help wondering who it was. Probably somebody selling something for a booster club or soliciting donations for cancer research. She picked up her knife to cut a piece of her meat. She had to work at it, and as she did, Al glanced at her and sighed. He was not at all happy about the Steak Charlotta. He started cutting his own meat with exaggerated sawing motions, his lips pressed together tightly.

"How about steak knives?" Celia suggested. "After all, it *is* steak."

"The recipe said it would fall apart," he said testily. "I hate a recipe that raises your hopes like that."

"It would probably be fine if you could cook it another couple of hours."

"But we're eating *now*," Al said. "I want it ready *right now*, not in another couple of hours. I followed every step of the stupid recipe." It struck Celia with great force that marrying a man like Al would come down to conversations like this one. Their lives would revolve around meals; their moods would be determined by them. She looked at Al and suddenly thought of Mr. Ed, the horse on television reruns, content in his warm stable with plenty of oats and hay. She watched Al stab a bite of his steak and put it into his mouth almost angrily. She had never before noticed the rather horsey way he chewed his food, working his jaws sideways and showing a little too much gum, and without meaning to she laughed right out loud.

Al kept chewing, of course, but frowned at her. "What's so funny?"

"Oh, nothing really. I just remembered this joke I heard."

"Oh yeah?" He took a bite of his corn, followed by another one of green beans, then glared distrustfully at Celia. "What joke?"

"This horse goes into a bar and sits down," Celia said. "The bartender comes over and says, 'Hey, why the long face?' " She paused, then laughed again and shrugged. "Oh well, it seemed funny at the time."

Al grunted and continued to chew. A buzzer went off in the kitchen. "That's the dessert," he said. He took the rest of his roll with him and left the table again.

From the small dining area where she sat, Celia turned her eyes to Al's living room, took in the bachelor look of it all—the stacks of magazines and books by the lumpy recliner, the remote control resting on its padded arm, the blue-and-brown plaid sofa, the pale sheers drooping at the large front window, a cheap metal floor lamp with a crooked shade, the bare walls. She shuddered to think of the redecorating a woman would have to do here. Or the decorating—you could hardly call it redecorating when it looked like this.

Of course, in Al's defense, he hadn't lived here very long. He had bought the house and moved in only two months ago, after he had decided to keep his job at the bank and stay in the area awhile. Remembering the apartment he had moved from, however, Celia was fairly sure his house was going to look exactly this same way years from now. Al's domestic interests stopped at cooking.

For a moment she tried to imagine what it would be like to move in here as Mrs. Al Halston, and the thought was so horrible that she actually stuck out her tongue and made a face. She wished more than anything they were done with the meal so she could make her speech to Al, dump his stuff out of her trunk, and get home to her own apartment, full of good furniture and art.

Al came out of the kitchen whistling, which Celia translated as a sign that the dessert had turned out well.

"Save some room for Berry Berry Buckle," he said, seating himself again and taking up his fork. And though she hadn't asked, he began explaining the dessert to her. "It's kind of a cross between a cobbler and a cake," he said, "and you use three kinds of berries—raspberries, blackberries, and blueberries. I found the recipe in this old book that . . ."

As he talked on, it occurred to Celia that this had become something of a pattern, these pre-breakup dinners. She wondered how many she had sat through by now, picking at her food until enough time had passed and she could spring the news. It always seemed to work out that way, not that she planned it or anything, not as if she thought, *Well, I'll get one more good meal out of him and then split.*

She remembered the last guy, Ward, who used to work at the Derby *Daily News* before he moved over to Greenville to work for a bigger paper. She had first met him when she had gone to the Derby newspaper office to talk to the editor about a freelance article she had agreed to do. Ward had introduced himself as the new sports writer, although she discovered later that most of his work in the office consisted of other things besides covering sports. He took care of the billings, for one, and did obituaries for another, also worked with ads and even cleaned the bathroom in back. Sports writing was his first love, though, and his speech was peppered with sports analogies. In fact, this was the thing about Ward that, like Al's obsession with food, Celia had grown to detest.

If he was late because he got tied up with a project at work, for example, Ward couldn't give the real reason. Instead, he'd have to say something like "Wow, it took forever to chip my way out of that bunker" or "Sorry, the game went into overtime." If he was optimistic about something, he might say, "Hey, first and goal, on the two" or "Green flag and no pit stops." A tense situation might elicit "Whoa, sudden death shootout." When Celia had canceled a date one time, he had said, "No problem, we'll just roll out the tarp and take a rain delay."

Their last night together had been at a small restaurant trying hard to be trendy in downtown Greenville, a place called Ziggy's that used to be a shoe repair shop. When she had told him afterward that she didn't want to see him anymore, he had said, "Ejecting me from the game, huh? Sending me to the old locker room?" She had felt an immense wash of relief at that moment, knowing she wouldn't have to put up with him anymore. She had taken a deep breath, looked at him without flinching, and said, "Yes, you've struck out, double faulted, air balled, gotten sacked, and whatever else you want to call it."

Usually she would lose all interest in the man long before the final dinner, but at last she would be seized with the knowledge that she couldn't stand him another day, and she would accept an invitation to go out, knowing it would be the last time. Something always seemed to rip apart and come crashing down at some point in a relationship, like a tree struck by lightning in a sudden storm.

Before Ward there had been what she called her "C Sickness," a string of guys whose names had started with C. Chris, Clint, Casey, and Colin. All but one had been short relationships, but she had actually begun to think that Casey might be a marriage prospect until she went swimming with him one day. It was sometimes the silliest, smallest things that could trigger the end of a relationship. As she sat beside Casey on the edge of the pool that day, she noticed how white and nearly hairless his thighs were and how fat they looked pressed against the concrete. She had broken up with him a week later after a meal at a steakhouse over in Spartanburg.

Before the "C Sickness" period there was an older guy named Roy she had liked a lot. She had met him at a party, and they had spent three hours by themselves on a balcony talking about books, art, and theater. By the end of the evening she had imagined herself in love, her heart nearly bursting with the sudden influx, but then right before she left the party, she had learned that Roy's last name was Kluck, and her heart had suddenly sprung a leak and emptied itself.

The trouble with most men, she had decided long ago, was that they were too crass, too driven, too loud, and too full of themselves. They tried too hard to impress her, to make her smile, to prove themselves funny and smart and ambitious. She hated the quick, assessing way they looked at women walking by, top to bottom and back up again.

And they always, always imagined themselves to be great irresistible Casanovas, acting as if they had taken an advanced course in romancing a woman—no, more like they had written the book for the course. Sometimes she would feel like laughing right out loud, and sometimes she actually did, which they always misinterpreted as evidence that she was overcome with delight. The truth was, though she had met a few men she knew she could put up with, she had never met one she knew she couldn't do without. She was pretty much convinced by now that such a man didn't exist.

She had counted up to only the last seven or eight men by the time her dish of Berry Berry Buckle was set before her. One thing Celia liked about eating with Al was that she didn't have to search for things to talk about because he gave his full attention to his food, either eating it or delivering a monologue about it. This particular meal seemed to be going on forever, though, and Celia was starting to get restless.

The dessert was okay, though nothing to rave about—not as good as a regular cobbler made with only one kind of berry, in Celia's opinion, except that it was still warm. It did have that going for it. Al had added a scoop of vanilla ice cream to the top, and it was melting fast.

Al was finished with his serving before Celia was half done with hers. He dropped his spoon into his bowl, swiped at his mouth with his paper napkin, and emitted a satisfied sigh. At that exact moment the doorbell rang again.

Though Al didn't curse nearly as much as a lot of men did, he did so now. "That better not be the same idiot as a while ago," he said. Celia didn't reply, but she wondered what difference it made, or how he would find out if it was, or what he would do about it. He pushed back his chair and stalked to the door as if ready to throw the person off the porch bodily.

He jerked the door open and was almost run over as a large woman lumbered across the threshold. "Well, good! Somebody's home after all! I just *knew* in my heart somebody was in here, what with the lights on and the cars in the drive and all. It could be your doorbell doesn't work right. Sometimes ours won't if you don't punch the little button right square in the middle. Willard, he's my son-in-law, he says he's going to buy us a new one and wire it up hisself so we can have one we can count on. Folks don't know they got to push it just right, so there's no telling how many visits we've missed on account of them wires not meetin' up. I keep meaning to write us up a little tag and tape it by the doorbell, one that says Push Hard, but it keeps slipping my mind. But anyway, that's one reason I like to follow up with a knock or two when I go to somebody's door and maybe holler out a word of greeting on top of it all. I figure surely they'll hear at least one of 'em in case they got a faulty mechanism like ours, though I guess *you* must not of when I came around a little bit ago. Maybe you had your TV up too loud." She nodded toward Al's big screen. "They can sure make a racket." Then laughing, she said, "We don't have one at our house. We make enough racket by ourselves!"

During this stunning explosion of words, the old woman stood on the brown mat at the door and wiped her feet the whole time, slowly yet thoroughly. She wore black rubber boots, a voluminous gray wool cape, and a dark green scarf cinched about her head. She had to be at least six feet tall, with the heft of a tree trunk. In one hand she carried a plastic grocery bag that bulged with the rounded shapes of whatever was inside.

Celia had a bite of Berry Berry Buckle poised on her spoon but could make no progress toward eating it, so great was her astonishment at the arrival of the visitor. Had she put this woman into a story in her creative writing class, her college professor would have cried, "Hold on! Tone her down!" Compared to a character like her, Celia's Georgia relatives were only pale shadows. And Al likewise was rendered both motionless and speechless. If someone had broken into the house with an assault rifle and begun spraying them with bullets, they couldn't have been more incapacitated.

". . . over there kitty-cornered in that house with the front door that's painted red," the woman was saying now, pointing across the street. "That was the one thing I begged Willard for when we moved here a little over a year ago. 'Willard,' I said, 'I got just one request in all this revampin' you're doing, and that is a red door.' I always did want a house with a red front door, and I never in my whole life had one till now. It's such a handy way to tell folks where you live, to be able to say, 'Ours is the house with the red door!' " She paused and looked down at the bottom of her boots before stepping off the mat.

Al was staring at her as if she were a UFO and little Martians were coming out of her mouth.

"Here, mind if I set down just a minute?" the woman said, making for the sofa. "I been out too long, and my old joints is telling me it's high time to get back home and quit gallivantin' around the neighborhood in the nippy night air. But I was so hoping you'd be here when I stopped by for one last try—and you *are!*" She sat down heavily on the sofa, then looked over at Al and repeated, "You must not of heard me when I came by earlier."

Al closed the door slowly but remained standing near it. The woman set the plastic bag on the sofa beside her and turned to look at Celia, stretching her face into a spectacularly homely grin. "You must be this nice man's little lady friend," she said. "What's your name, honey?"

Al answered for her. "Celia Coleman."

The woman turned back to Al. "And what's—"

"Al," he said. "Al Halston."

The old woman nodded approvingly. "Celia and Al—them's nice names." She pointed back over her shoulder. "I'm Eldeen Rafferty. I live over there on the other side of the street. I been watching you come and go for weeks on end, out the window of our house—that one I was telling you about with the red door—but I couldn't never seem to get it timed right so's I could come pay you a visit when the both of you was here. I help baby-sit my little granddaughter, you see. But I do love to visit when I get a minute here and there."

She picked up the plastic bag beside her. "Well, anyway, here's the cause for me bustin' in on you young folks tonight. I brought you these. My daughter Jewel baked us up a double batch of muffins tonight to go with our supper, and I told her, 'Jewel,' I said, 'I'm aimin' to put some of these in a bag and carry 'em to our neighbor over there in that little white house.' I was so happy when I saw your car here," she said to Celia, " 'cause I been wantin' to meet you, too, and see if you was as pretty up close as you was from the window." She clenched her teeth into another frightful smile. "And you *are*!" she said. "Here, you can take these." She extended the bag toward Al, and he stepped over from the door.

"Thanks," he said. He opened the bag and looked inside.

"I apologize for not comin' over sooner," she continued, "but like I said, I baby-sit my little grandbaby during the day—Rosemary Jean's her name—and she's been teething bad, and then she had her a doozy of a ear infection for a spell and has been all fretful and out of sorts from it. So I been sticking close to home 'cause I sure didn't want to get her out during that awful cold snap we had."

One quick breath and she plowed ahead. "We moved here to this neighborhood a little over a year ago, and I been working on learning everybody's name up and down our street. I'm just about done, too, except I never can get that man down there in number 58—you know that house with the fence and the sign that says Beware of Dog—to come to the door." She lowered her voice and leaned forward. "He's got him a bad leg, from

what I can tell—it might even be one of them wooden legs—and I think
he needs him a hearing aid to boot."

She leaned forward a little more. "And I don't think he's got him a
dog at all 'cause I sure never seen one or even heard one. I think the sign's
there to discourage burglars and hooligans." She leaned back. " 'Course,
maybe he *did* have a dog and something happened to it. *We* had us a dog
named Hormel that got hisself hit by a car."

Dispenser of Too Much Information—that's what Celia called people like
this old woman, though she couldn't remember meeting anyone who fit
the label to quite the extent of this woman, who was still talking. " . . . and
I sure miss that little pooch, though I don't miss all his mischief. Why, he
could scoot under the fence and take off faster 'n a jackrabbit, he could!
Just had these short little stubs of legs, but, oh, he was a *quick* little feller.
One of them wiener dogs, you know."

She looked back and forth between Celia and Al, smiling. "So now I got
two more names to add to my list. Celia and Al." She paused and looked
down at her black rubber boots. "Most people don't realize how much
they count on their *feet,* you know. I'm sure thankful for mine. Woodmont
Street's my mission field, you see." She waved an arm back and forth and
around her head as if to encompass the whole neighborhood. "Some missionaries get to go to Africa and Japan and Brazil and what have you, but
no, God called *me* to go up and down Woodmont Street." She bared her
teeth in another smile. "And all ground's holy ground, I say. I'm marching
through Immanuel's ground—right here in Derby!"

So she was religious—Celia could have guessed as much. She knew
beyond a doubt that if she were to ask this woman to sing "Marching to
Zion," she would know every word by heart. An odd sensation overwhelmed
her at that instant. She looked intently at the old woman and was struck,
first of all, by how much she reminded her of her grandmother in a way
that had nothing at all to do with looks or the simple fact that neither
of them had a television. She could imagine the two of them striking up
a friendship, reciting Bible verses by the hour, listening to sermons on
the radio, and singing duets from the hymnal, though an octave apart—
Grandmother taking the soprano line while this woman sang the bass.

But they were an octave apart in more than a literal sense. The difference between them reached far beyond vocal pitch. It was the resonant
tone of what Eldeen Rafferty said, the whole eager attitude behind it, the
fullness of spirit, the peculiar light of her countenance. How different

this neighborly delivery of muffins than Grandmother's presentation of blackberries in Dunmore, Georgia, so many years ago. How funny, thought Celia, to meet someone so much like Grandmother, who was dead and buried in Georgia, yet someone at the same time so very, very different from her, so charged up with words, so happy, and so very much *alive*.

6

Where Bright Angel Feet Have Trod

The following afternoon Celia was working in the back room of the Trio Gallery. It had been another slow day, but she didn't mind that at all. In fact, she preferred it. If it weren't for the fact that the traffic in and out of the gallery had a pretty direct correlation to the amount of revenue generated, she wouldn't care if anybody ever came in.

But she especially didn't want to talk to people today, not after last night. After the old woman, Earlene or whatever her name was, had finally left Al's house, Celia had unburdened herself of her news, that she felt it was time for the two of them to go their separate ways. Al hadn't taken it very well, had been quite loud and accusatory. She had finally opened the front door and walked out while he was still talking. He hadn't followed her but had stood at the door and watched her take his bags of stuff out of her car and set them on the front lawn.

She had then backed out of his driveway, glancing behind her at the house with the red door. She wasn't sure, but she thought she saw a curtain move, as if a hand had pulled it aside for a peek. She didn't doubt for a minute that the old woman knew everybody's comings and goings along the whole street. Still, it was strange that she hadn't grated on Celia's nerves the way she should have, given her little missionary speech. No doubt she thought the Ten Commandments should be posted on every street corner. But underneath her religion—or maybe on top of it, Celia couldn't be sure—she had seemed like such a *nice* old lady. Odd as a three-dollar bill, but somebody you could love without even having to try.

Last night's breakup had affected Celia more than usual. It had come to her in a flash of certainty early this morning while she was splashing her face with water that she was getting too old for this sort of thing. Someone thirty-six years old should either go ahead and find somebody decent to marry, she told herself, or else give up and quit looking. Just resign herself to being single.

Anyway, marriage was far too risky. The thought of a commitment that huge made her go cold and hot at the same time. How could you ever *know* the person was right, that he would wear well with time, that you wouldn't get bored out of your mind before a month was over? The whole idea of what they called a "happy marriage" seemed like something out of a book of fairy tales. Well, no, actually fairy tales hardly ever dealt with marriage unless it was an unhappy one with wicked stepmothers and such. Fairy tales usually stopped with the falling-in-love part, glossing over all the years that followed with a "happily ever after" summary. The writers of those stories sure knew how to get out while they were ahead. These were the thoughts circling through her mind as she worked in the back room of the gallery.

When she had interviewed for this job ten years earlier, Celia had made it clear to the owners, two men and a woman who were all artists themselves, that she didn't have the gift of salesmanship. If that was what they wanted from her, they'd be better off hiring someone else. Her concept of a good art gallery director, she had said, was someone who allowed the visitors plenty of time and space to browse, someone who realized that good art spoke for itself, that it didn't need a cheerleader, but rather someone who would be waiting in the folds for quiet consultations if asked.

She had said it all with a perfectly straight face, though afterward she wondered how she had managed it, seeing that up until the actual job interview she had never given a passing thought to her concept of a good art gallery director. She had, in fact, interviewed for the job on a whim after hearing through the grapevine that the gallery was looking for a director.

Today she was packing up a set of prints to return to a dealer in Charleston. Ollie, one of the gallery owners, was going to drive the van down and deliver them in a couple of days. The show had been a successful one, and, thankfully, they were returning fewer than half of the prints they had exhibited. All the others had sold for prices anywhere from six hundred to three thousand dollars. The most expensive one, a large black and white of homes along the Charleston Battery, priced at five thousand, hadn't sold but had been greatly admired by everyone. She held it up now and studied it.

The dealer had told her that this particular artist had finished the woodcut from which this print was made only two weeks before he had died suddenly at the age of fifty. It was an incredible piece of work, so fine and detailed you could hardly believe the plate was carved from wood. She had seen steel plate prints that weren't nearly as delicate as this one.

Celia had already decided that anybody who could capture the Charleston waterfront this way with such grace in such a restricted medium, depicting it as neither too sweetly nostalgic nor too rigidly formal, must have been a fascinating person. To think that he had done it all using a block of wood, a carving tool, black ink, and white paper—well, she wished she could have met the artist. She was in the process of wondering what kind of husband such a man would make when she heard the electronic chime that signaled the entrance of a visitor to the gallery.

She set the print down with a sigh and left the workroom, hoping whoever it was wouldn't stay long. Maybe someone just needed directions to another shop along this stretch of road. People often stopped in to ask if they did framing here or sold cross-stitch thread, and Celia always directed them to the Framed for Keeps shop at the far end of the strip mall or the Yarn Barn a mile down the road next to the Exxon station.

Every now and then people came in "looking for a gift," they said, but they almost always left quickly, trying not to look shocked at the prices. Celia would never forget the woman who, immediately upon entering the gallery, had shown such enthusiasm for a small stone sculpture of a seahorse. She had misread the price on the card as fifteen dollars instead of fifteen *hundred* dollars and had actually started coughing in a choking sort of way when Celia corrected her misconception. Of course, other people, the serious collectors, came in to buy. And came back to buy again.

Exiting the workroom, Celia immediately recognized the woman who had just come in. She was a frequent visitor here at the Trio Gallery. She was standing inside the center viewing gallery now, where the new exhibit was on display. She had positioned herself in front of a large abstract oil painting swirled with hot, bold colors. Integrated into the painting were a number of other textures—a straggly forked twig, for instance, and a swatch of burlap, torn bits of paper, some crushed leaves.

The piece fit right in with the show's title: "From the Pit, Rising." A tornado had obviously gotten loose in that pit and flung out all sorts of things. It was wild and seething, unsettling yet oddly beautiful. The price was listed at forty-eight hundred dollars, and Celia had no doubt at all that it would sell. She had developed a pretty accurate feel by now for what would go home with somebody and what would be left.

More than once she had thought of herself in terms of an orphanage director, though the parallels were imperfect, of course. But this painting would be adopted, she felt quite sure. Though bigger children, for the most part, weren't as appealing to prospective parents as the little ones, there always seemed to be buyers for these grandly courageous paintings. And it did take courage to produce works of this size. If they didn't sell, the artist had to be prepared to store them somewhere.

Titled simply *Tumult,* the piece had been at the gallery for only two weeks, along with twenty other works by the same artist, Tara Larson, who was also one of the gallery's three owners, a thin slip of a woman in her forties. Over the years her art had become not only larger but also more and more . . . *tumultuous* was the only word Celia could think of to describe Tara's most recent pieces, especially the ones she had produced for this show. Yet if you saw Tara on the street, you might describe her as mousy.

Elizabeth Landis was the name of the woman who had just arrived at the art gallery, the one now staring intently at *Tumult,* stepping in closer and leaning forward slightly as if trying to decipher words spoken by someone with a heavy accent. Celia was glad at least that she wasn't a chatty woman. Usually Elizabeth Landis came in for short, quietly intense periods of time, and she liked to be left alone to wander from piece to piece. Rarely did she ask a question or offer a comment.

A year or so ago, however, she had bought a painting of wild jasmine vines, and as she was writing out the check for it, she had suddenly looked up at Celia and said, "I was so afraid on the way over here that someone else might have already gotten it. I didn't see how I could wake up tomorrow knowing I might not ever see it again." When she had stopped talking, her voice had quavered a little as if she were on the verge of crying. Celia had watched her carry the painting out of the gallery that day. When she had gotten to her car, Elizabeth Landis had held the painting out in front of her and looked at it a long time. Right before stooping to put it into the back, she had lifted her face and closed her eyes reverently.

Celia observed her now for a few moments and then spoke. "Oh, hello, Mrs. Landis." She said it in a breezy, off-handed way as she passed through the center gallery toward the reception desk out front, as if she were very busy and had just noticed Elizabeth on her way to take care of something else. She didn't stop to initiate a conversation of small talk with her, knowing that it would suit them both better if she didn't. If she had been forced to choose a customer for this afternoon, if there had to be one, she couldn't have done better than Elizabeth Landis.

Celia kept walking when Elizabeth answered. "I just stopped by to see the new show."

"Take your time," Celia called. "I'll be out here at the desk if you need anything." Secretly, of course, she was hoping Elizabeth Landis *wouldn't* take her time too much. She wanted to get the rest of those prints packed up, then take down some pieces that had been hanging in the side galleries for too long. She kept careful track of the rotation since that was something Ollie, Tara, and Craig had become quick to complain about.

Of course Celia knew for a fact that there had been no system of circulation before she had come along, that paintings had languished in the back storage bins forever while the same old things hung on display. After the first week of working here, she had asked Ollie one day about the high vertical storage shelves along the walls in the back room. She couldn't tell whether those were actual paintings standing up there all stacked together or maybe just old frames.

Nobody ever had the time to get a system organized, Ollie had told her, but that day he had suddenly been seized with the need for *her* to do so and had asked her to get started on it as soon as possible. "Tara doesn't care about organization," he had confided to Celia, shaking his head, "and Craig . . . well, he's even worse." Ollie had lifted both index fingers and twirled them around his head in little circles. "Craig's mind runs here, there, and everywhere."

Reaching the reception desk now, Celia sat down in her rolling chair and swung around to a smaller table on which she had stacked a group of photos of some watercolor paintings by a retired artist, Angela Worth-eimer, who lived in Hendersonville, North Carolina. Ollie had seen some of the paintings at a show in Asheville the year before and asked Celia to contact the artist about doing a show for the Trio Gallery. Though she had studied the photos many times by now and had even seen many of the originals after driving up to Asheville to pay the artist a visit, Celia looked through the stack again, hoping that an idea would come to her for the refreshment table on opening night.

Planning the receptions for the openings of shows was another part of her job she hadn't known about when she was hired. Actually, she had to admit that it was something else she had brought on herself. Before she had come along, Ollie, Tara, and Craig had taken turns planning the openings, most of which had been thrown together at the last minute without any thought as to a theme or an actual opening night program with artist's talk and refreshments. Two weeks after being hired, Celia had offered to plan a reception for an upcoming pottery show, and she had been doing them ever since.

Each of the three owners had spoken to her privately in those early days about the failings of the other two to open the gallery on time when it was their day to work and to plan ahead in booking the exhibits. It hadn't taken long for Celia to figure out that, though they secretly blamed one another, not one of them had a head for running a business. But she had sympathized with them. "You can't be an artist and a businessman at the same time," she had said to all three of them separately, though she didn't really believe it.

She discovered that they had been ready to close the gallery when they decided as a last effort to try to hire a director. Celia had heard through a friend at the newspaper, who knew a friend of one of the owners, that they were looking for somebody, and in one of the most uncharacteristically daring moves of her life, she had put on her gray wool dress and silver hoop earrings and had gone to the gallery to express her interest in the job.

"I am not an artist," she had told them forthrightly at the interview, "but you don't need another artist around here. You need someone who can keep things straight, and I can do that. I can learn whatever it is you need me to do. And though I'm not an artist, I do have a good eye for line and color and am moderately creative." She didn't tell them about winning the school art contest in ninth grade for her sketch of a woman's stockinged feet surrounded by dozens of pairs of shoes she was trying on. She doubted that they would be much impressed by that, although her father had been so proud he had hung the picture behind the cash register in his shoe store.

"I have computer skills," she continued, "and I've also worked as a journalist and freelance editor, so I can write, which I would think could help in a job like this." She was the third person they had interviewed, and they hired her on the spot. After she left the room that day, she heard one of them say—she thought it was Ollie—"I like her moxie. And I think she's teachable."

They wanted her to open the gallery every afternoon from one until five, including Saturdays, and as long as she devoted those hours to the business of the gallery, she was free to come in at any other times and use the desk and computer for whatever else she might want to do, which would come in handy, she decided, for her writing and editing on the side.

Elizabeth Landis continued making her way around the center gallery, stopping in front of each work, sometimes moving farther back, sometimes moving in closer. She glanced at her watch once, which raised Celia's hopes. It was already close to four o'clock, so maybe she had to get home and plan supper. Celia wondered if she was married, if she had kids at home. They had never talked with each other about things like that. She was an attractive woman in Celia's opinion, in an understated sort of way, tall and slim like a runner or maybe a former basketball player. Celia didn't have much to base it on, but she was sure Elizabeth was intelligent. She appeared to be in her late forties, though Celia didn't consider herself a good judge of ages.

Celia had separated the Wortheimer photos into three stacks according to subject, and she started through them all again. Because they were strictly representational, it had been quite easy to figure out categories for them: land, sky, and water. In the land group there were the meadows and fields, the houses and barns, flower gardens, and so forth. The sky group focused on sunsets and sunrises above the tips of evergreens or mountains, and the water pictures were lakes with lily pads and covered bridges over rushing brooks, also a couple of waterfalls, and Celia's personal favorite—a sidewalk scene depicting the aftermath of a rainstorm, with puddles and shiny wet leaves.

The show was coming up in a month, so she needed to get the details for opening night lined up. Thankfully, Angela Wortheimer had agreed to drive down to give a talk. Celia liked to somehow coordinate the reception with the paintings themselves whenever she could, but she had been struggling with an idea for the refreshment table for this one. Ollie's wife, Connie, who worked for a florist, sometimes helped her with the table, but she was coming up blank for this one, too. They really couldn't do anything seasonal since March was one of those in-between months, not really winter still but not yet spring, either.

Celia was thinking of putting together a large centerpiece using slender bare branches hung with silver wire balls and those miniature lights on a string. Maybe some moss underneath it all and tea candles in shallow clay pots artistically arranged under the branches. It wasn't all that exciting, really, and she didn't see a clear connection to the watercolor paintings, but it might work.

"You don't know anybody who plays tennis, do you?" The question startled Celia. She swung her chair around immediately and saw that Elizabeth Landis was now standing midway between the reception desk and the front door. It was clear that she was preparing to leave. She had picked up one of the leaflets listing the titles of the pieces in Tara's show and was rolling it into a little scroll.

Celia gave a small laugh. "Well, I played in high school and college, but I haven't kept up with it much since then." She had a sudden memory of the last time she had played tennis. It was with Ward, the sportswriter she had dated before Al. After Celia had won one easy set and was almost ready to close out the second, Ward pretended to have a pulled muscle in his thigh. He grimaced as he kneaded it, then took a few limping steps around the court and said, "Sorry, Celia, but the old horse has pulled up lame. I'm gonna have to take him outta the race."

An hour later, after they had gotten barbecue sandwiches at the drive-through over at C. C.'s in Filbert and eaten them in Ward's car, they stopped for hot fudge sundaes at the Dairy Queen. As they walked up to the order window together, Celia noticed that Ward's pulled thigh muscle had evidently healed itself.

Elizabeth moved a step closer to the reception desk. She had a hopeful light in her eyes. "Well, we really need another singles player," she said. "I'm the only one right now. I joined this team last fall, and we're getting ready to start practicing for our spring season in a couple of weeks, but we're . . . I mean, I don't know how good you are. You may be way above the rest of us. Or you may not even have Monday mornings free. That's when we play our matches." She shrugged. "Or you might not be interested at all. Most of us are older than you."

"Well, goodness, I haven't played in so long, I don't think I'd—"

"I didn't have any idea you played yourself," Elizabeth said. "I was just asking if you knew anybody who did. We're getting desperate to find somebody."

"Well, you'd have to be pretty desperate to want me," Celia said, laughing, although she knew this wasn't really true. She had played the number two singles position at Blackrock College and had lost only four matches during her entire four years on the team, one loss per year. She didn't have either the power or the wingspan of the number one player, Elena, who was five-ten, and she wasn't nearly as aggressive as Elena at the net. She found, however, that her small size tended to make her opponents overconfident, and this worked to her advantage, as consistency was her strong point. Surprisingly, she had ended up with a better overall record than Elena by the time they graduated.

Elizabeth was shaking her head. "Oh no, no, I didn't mean it that way. You could probably run circles around the rest of us. I just meant the season is going to be starting soon and if we don't find another singles player, then our doubles players are going to have to take turns filling in, and they all hate to play singles, and . . ." Her words trailed off, and she shrugged again. "I sure didn't know you played. I was just . . ." Something came to her, and her face fell a little. "We're a 4.0 team, and you'd have to get verified."

Celia sensed that Elizabeth was wishing now that she had never said anything. Though she wasn't letting on, she was probably starting to get worried that Celia wouldn't be good enough to get a 4.0 rating. She was probably thinking Celia had played a few intramural matches at some community college years ago.

There was a brief awkward moment before Celia made a quick decision. She had been thinking for some time that she needed to start doing something to keep in shape. She used to exercise to an aerobics tape, but more and more she was finding excuses not to. "You know, this interests me," she said. "I just might like to do it." She could hardly believe what she was saying. She rarely made up her mind so fast.

"They divide you into levels," Elizabeth said hesitantly. It was clear that Celia's interest was making her nervous. "These people called verifiers watch you play, and then they give you a rating. Our team . . . well, most of us have been playing a pretty long time, but the team itself is fairly new. Several of our players used to be on 3.5 teams but got bumped up, and we have one girl who used to be a 4.5 but got bumped down, and then there's another one who switched to our team from another 4.0 team, so it's kind of a funny mixture."

"But you're the only singles player?"

Elizabeth nodded. "We used to have two others, but one of them moved and the other one had foot surgery and is laying out. The competition's going to be really tough this season, but we think we have a pretty good chance of holding our own—if we find another singles player, that is."

"When does this happen—this getting verified?" Celia asked. "Is there time to do it before the season starts?"

Elizabeth laughed. "My team won't believe this. We've been looking for a singles player for months, and then I breeze in here and ask you out of the blue if you know anybody, and . . . well, they're not going to believe it when I tell them." She took another step closer. "And you really *are* interested in joining our team?" She laughed again. "You're not just teasing me, are you?"

Celia reached into the little tray on top of the desk and took a business card off the stack. "Here's my card. Let me know where to go and when. I'll get my racket out and dust it off."

"You have to join USTA, too," Elizabeth said.

"I can do that. I used to belong years ago."

Elizabeth took the card. "I'll give it to our captain, and she'll be in touch. I think there's a verification next weekend." She shook her head again. "I can't believe this."

After Elizabeth left, Celia headed back to the workroom, wondering what had come over her that she would leap into something big like joining a tennis team when she had plenty to do as it was. She would be glad when the effect of her grandmother's funeral had worn off. It had been over two weeks now, and she was still as restless as the day she had come back, still doing the oddest things for no good reason.

Passing a black faux marble pedestal, she stopped as she often did to look at the white limestone sculpture of an angel displayed on it. Or, more accurately, the bottom part of an angel. It had been fashioned to resemble an ancient sculpture that had been broken in half, with only the part from the waist down to the feet surviving. The jagged break at the top looked quite authentic, like something that had been damaged in an earthquake or a war, then left to crumble over the ages. Celia wondered exactly how the artist had done it. Maybe he had made a whole angel, then intentionally broken it. Maybe the top part was displayed in another gallery somewhere.

Anyway, the bottom part was beautiful. The folds of the angel's robe were gracefully fanned out, showing a bend of knee beneath, and the bare feet were planted on a small slab of granite, one foot turned slightly outward and the other poised on tiptoe, as if the angel were ready to ascend into the heavens.

When she had first started working here at the Trio Gallery ten years ago, Celia would never have looked twice at this piece. It would have mystified her that anybody would intentionally *break* something and call it art. She certainly wouldn't have considered buying it. Today, however, she knew that if she could spare the nine hundred dollars that it cost, she would lay it down in a minute for this sculpture. She had even thought of the exact place to put it in her apartment—on the small black table beside the front door. She had already overextended her budget, though, with a large silkscreen of red zinnias she had bought a few months ago.

It came to Celia right now that the only imperfect part of the angel, which was the work of a sculptor who lived like a hermit near Walhalla and did only two or three pieces each year, was its title. *Angel Feet* was what the artist had named it.

Celia had looked at this sculpture a hundred times before, and never until now had she thought it was poorly named. If she hadn't been to her grandmother's funeral, she doubted that the thought would have occurred to her. Ever since returning from Dunmore, Georgia, however, she had been plagued by words from her grandmother's hymns. They invaded her mind at the strangest times, such as right now. This was another cause of her restlessness—all these unbidden and altogether unwanted hymns haunting her at all hours of the day and night.

Angel Feet was a good enough start for a title, but it stopped short. The right title came to her now—*Where Bright Angel Feet Have Trod*. Probably no one else would recognize it as coming from "Shall We Gather at the River," another of her grandmother's favorites in *Tabernacle Hymns*. Such a title would have a little more flair, and as a playfully obscure allusion that most people wouldn't catch, it would be a lot more fun.

Well, this wasn't productive thinking. There sure wasn't anything *fun* about her grandmother's hymns, and she wasn't about to start suggesting to artists what they should name their pieces. She shook her head and continued on her way to the back room, passing a painting of a nude woman bent over a basin pouring water over her hair. *Saturday* was its simple title. Celia remembered as a little girl washing her hair on Saturday nights, with her mother's assistance, in preparation for looking her best at church on Sunday. Of course, she was always fully clothed when she washed her hair, and they did it at the kitchen sink, not over a basin.

An amusing thought crossed her mind as she entered the workroom and set about packing up the last few prints. She tried to imagine all of Grandmother's sisters and her brother, Buford, showing up en masse here at the Trio Gallery, maybe attending the opening of a new show. She could see them all studying the works of art, clucking their tongues at the nude hair washer ("Wicked, sinful nakedness!"), staring in bewilderment at the broken angel ("Why, somebody's done broke that thing in two!"), gaping at Tara Larson's *Tumult* ("And what in the name of common sense is *that* thing supposed to be?").

7

Some Melodious Sonnet

Within ten days two new things had happened in Celia's life. First, she had become an official member of the Holiday Winners tennis team, the same one Elizabeth Landis was on. The verification had been easy. She had requested a 4.0 rating, and after they watched her play, they gave it to her. The team captain, Bonnie Maggio, was at the courts that day. "Just stay loose and play in the middle of your game" was her advice beforehand. "If you impress them too much, they could deny you the 4.0 and give you a 4.5. You could still play on a team if that happened, but not ours." She grinned as she patted Celia's shoulder. "And you definitely want to be on ours. We have the most fun."

The second new thing happened on the same Monday she returned from her first practice with the Holiday Winners at the Holiday Inn courts in Greenville. One of the women on the team knew the manager of the motel and had talked him into letting them use their four courts as home base. Celia had met all the other team members that day, then had run home to shower and eat lunch before opening the art gallery at one.

The mail had just arrived as she was leaving her apartment, so she grabbed it out of the mailbox and tried to sort through it at stoplights on her way to work. Most of it was throwaway stuff, but one letter bore the name of a law firm in Dunmore, Georgia: Cassidy and Percy, Attorneys. Celia conjured up a picture at once of a shabby little room in an upstairs corner of a ramshackle building in downtown Dunmore with two aging lawyers, one of them blind and the other deaf, both of them wearing clacking dentures.

The letter took her completely by surprise. She was having such fun with the picture of two bumbling old hick lawyers, sporting suspenders and moth-eaten plaid vests and dozing off right in the middle of meetings with clients, that the first sentence didn't even sink in at first, and she had to reread it: *You are sole inheritor of the property at 604 Old Campground Road, Dunmore, Georgia.*

A car honked behind her, and she didn't have time to read further. Her mind was spinning, wondering what the rest of the letter said, but she had to wait nearly ten whole minutes to find out, until she pulled into the row of shops out on Highway 29, where the Trio was located. She had tried to sneak a few words at every stoplight, but wasn't that the way it went? Every time you wanted a light to turn red so you could take care of business—put on makeup or fill out a bank deposit slip or, in this case, read a letter—the green light shone cheerfully, interminably. But as soon as you were running the least bit late and were desperate for green lights, they were not to be had. Or else some moron at the head of the line would get distracted and sit through half the green light, or his car would die and he couldn't get it started again.

So finally, when Celia pulled around to the back of the Trio Gallery and parked in her usual spot, she read the rest of the letter. She had already recognized the address on Old Campground Road, of course, and could only figure out one way to interpret that first sentence, which indeed turned out to be the case. Her grandmother *had* made out a will before her death after all and, to Celia's dismay, had named her only granddaughter as the inheritor.

If this wasn't also par for the course, Celia thought. The things you wanted were so often out of reach, but then you'd turn around and get stuck with a piece of rundown no-account property to try to dispose of. The letter referred to "all edifices and equipage," and this struck her as very funny.

Let's see, she thought, besides the house, that would include the outbuildings—what used to be the little neighborhood store, the small dilapidated barn her grandfather had used as both a workshop and a garage, the former outhouse that had never been torn down, and an old chicken coop—maybe a few tools and old pieces of rusted equipment, and then the vast wealth of treasures inside the house: the ancient appliances, the odds and ends of cheap furniture, the chipped dishes, thin towels, discolored linens. Oh, she was one lucky granddaughter, she was. It struck her as so funny that she laughed out loud in her car. She opened the door and carried the letter inside with her. She wanted to reread it throughout the afternoon and be amused all over again.

"Sole inheritor!" she said to herself as she made her way around the gallery, switching off the security alarm, adjusting the thermostat, unlocking the front door. "I'm sole inheritor of a little matchbox of a house next to a railroad track!" She flipped the sign on the front door to Open, then twirled around and headed to the front desk to put her purse away and turn on the computer. "Sole inheritor!" she said merrily. "Maybe I should keep the house and tell people I have a vacation cottage in Georgia." A few minutes later when Ollie dropped by the gallery to take a look at some photos of a new artist's works they were considering for a show later in the year, Celia laughed and said, "I bet you didn't know you had a *sole inheritor* working for you, did you?"

"Yeah, no kidding?" Ollie said absently. He sat down in the chair in front of the desk, crossed his long legs, and picked up the photos. He looked hard at the one on top, a collection of overlapping iridescent ovals called *Under Glass,* then looked up at Celia as if something had finally registered. "Sole inheritor, huh?" he said. "Of what? Money? Stuff? Or both?" This was actually quite a speedy response for Ollie, who often answered questions minutes later or, even more often, not at all.

"Stuff," Celia said. "Definitely stuff." She was in the middle of checking her e-mail. As usual, there were a dozen or more messages she could delete without opening.

Ollie grunted and held the photo of the ovals out at arm's length in front of him. He studied it for a long time, then set it down flat on the desk and stood up to look at it from above. The first time she had looked at the photos, Celia had wondered if *Under Glass* was some sort of loose interpretation of what the artist remembered seeing under a microscope, but she knew better than to suggest such a thing to Ollie, Craig, or Tara. She had come to this job knowing you didn't try to find a *picture of something* in every piece of art. She remembered at least that much from her course in art appreciation at Blackrock College.

Ollie studied another couple of photos, even turned them around in circles to see them from every direction. Tara's method of looking through artists' photos or slides was cursory compared to Ollie's. "I see fast," she was fond of saying. "I can tell at a glance if it's right." And Craig fell somewhere in between Ollie and Tara. He would look through them once very quickly, then go back through a second time a little more slowly, and then zip through one last time.

The three owners had agreed years ago that they had to be unanimous in their decision to invite an artist for a show, and so far they had stuck with it, though not without some sparks of conflict. Whenever one of them disagreed with the other two, Celia always heard about it for days. The dissident might come to her privately and complain, "I don't know what they're thinking. It's all so *imitative*." And one of the other two might sigh and say something like "Well, when the guy becomes famous, we'll remember we had our chance to give him a show."

Ollie propped a photo up against the ivy plant on the desk and stepped back to look at it. "Sometimes stuff can translate into money, though, you know," he said to Celia.

"Not this stuff," she said.

"You never know," Ollie said. "Friend of mine in Ohio told me his cousin found an early Jasper Johns wrapped up in a beach towel in his aunt's attic when they were cleaning out her house. A *Jasper Johns*! Totally bizarre, he said, because the aunt was supposedly this conservative tee-totaler fanatic, some kind of foot-washing Plymouth Brethren sect or something, so what was she doing with a Jasper Johns?"

"Evidently hiding it," Celia said. She opened an e-mail from a collector in Raleigh who was looking to buy an Edmund Yaghjian painting, preferably an oil, and had heard Trio might have one. She began a reply, telling the woman they had had a Yaghjian show the year before but had returned all the unsold works to the family. Trio had an address where the collector could write, and Celia stopped for a minute to look it up.

Ollie picked up the photo from beside the ivy and brought it up close to his face, then returned it to the stack. " 'Severely tacky tastes,' my friend said. The aunt was an art collector but didn't have an eye. The whole house was pure kitsch top to bottom, but then she had this phenomenal piece of real art sitting up in her attic all wrapped up in a towel." Ollie picked up another photo and held it above his head, then looked up at it, turning it around and around as he did so. "So you never know, Cecilia. You never know what might turn up in your so-called *stuff*."

Ollie was the only person Celia knew who ever called her by her full name. He had told her once that as a boy he had dreamed of marrying

somebody named Cecilia because he had so admired St. Cecilia, the mar-
tyred patroness of music. In high school he had even painted a picture of
St. Cecilia in her legendary pose of playing the organ. He had entered it
in the Virginia Young Artists Expo and won first place. But then Connie
had come along shortly after high school, and he had given up on his
dream of marrying a Cecilia, though he still loved the name. Celia was
quite sure that her name had gained her favor in Ollie's eyes when she
was first interviewed for her job at Trio.

"Well, I knew my grandmother," Celia said now, "and I can safely say
there's no Jasper Johns in her attic." She laughed. "No attic even."

After he had looked at all the photos, Ollie told Celia that he voted
yes for booking the artist for a show. He already knew that Craig agreed,
because Craig was the one who had first seen the artist's work in Winston-
Salem and suggested they contact him. Celia had predicted when she first
saw the photos herself that all three owners would vote yes. She almost
always guessed right, and more than once Craig had suggested in his terse
way that they just let Celia make the final decision since she knew their
minds so well by now. He really disliked anything extra that took up his
time, especially looking through slides or photos of other artists' work.

"If Tara bucks us on this one, she needs to have her head examined,"
Ollie told Celia on his way out. Tara had been the lone holdout against
another artist recently, a woman from Savannah whose specialty was moon-
scape collagraphs in browns, grays, and blacks. Though Celia never said
so, she was glad Tara had voted no on that one. The thought of looking
at all those dark colors and pocked surfaces for six solid weeks hadn't
appealed to her in the least.

She was finishing her e-mail business a few minutes later when the
phone rang.

"Craig here," the voice said brusquely. She would have recognized
his voice anyway. "Need you to do something," he continued. Craig never
wasted time chitchatting. "I'm coming by today to pick up my Madonna.
Is it still out?"

"Uh, I don't . . . no, I don't think so," Celia said. She pretended to
be having trouble remembering, though she knew very well it was in a
storage bin, not out on display.

"Well, find it if you can. It'll save me some time. I'm in a hurry." As if
that were anything new, Celia thought. Craig sometimes stopped by the
gallery for a minute, literally, and then was gone. But before she could

say anything, she realized Craig had already hung up. Nothing new about that, either. Phone etiquette wasn't one of Craig's strong points, nor any other kind of etiquette for that matter.

With a sense of dread, she went back to the workroom and climbed up on a ladder over by the topmost bin. She might as well get it over with now. Underneath the dread, though, was another feeling—happy anticipation that the painting was going to leave the gallery. She would find it and set it by the back door, and that way she probably wouldn't even have to speak to Craig, which would suit them both. While Ollie sometimes dropped by the gallery just to talk, Craig never did. Craig was one of those men who seem to be engaged in a lifelong contest to see if they can use fewer words today than they did yesterday. Before long he would be down to grunts and hand gestures. It was remarkable to Celia that he was a teacher. She knew he couldn't be a very good one, since teaching required communicating. Of course, maybe he took on a different personality in the classroom, though she seriously doubted it.

Celia did try to rotate these things on the top shelf regularly, although because of their larger size, the inconvenience of getting to them, and the extra trouble and space required to hang them, it was very tempting to skip over them. She dutifully kept track, though, and kept careful records in a file named "Circulation." Only a few times had she deliberately skipped a turn for a certain painting. Celia felt a pang of guilt now as she scanned the frames in the top bin, for the Madonna was one of the pieces she knew she hadn't been fair with. It had been hidden away up here for a long time.

When Craig had first completed it four years ago and brought it to the gallery, she had instantly hated it, though she generally liked Craig's work more than either Tara's or Ollie's. She had hung the Madonna but had left it on display a shorter time than she usually did with single new works by the gallery's small stable of artists. She generally gave the three owners an even longer exhibit time if a work didn't sell, but she had made an exception with this one. She remembered the great relief of taking it down and storing it away on the highest shelf in the back.

She couldn't have gotten away with it had it been one of Tara's or Ollie's own works, but she had taken advantage of the fact that Craig so rarely came by the gallery and appeared to be in another world when he did come. He seemed so detached from everybody and everything, even his own art. As soon as he finished a painting, he either gave it away or dropped it off at the gallery, thereby divorcing himself from that one so he could immediately take up with a new piece.

He had told Celia once, in one of the few real conversations they had ever had, that he lived to paint and that what happened to the painting after he finished it wasn't of much consequence to him. It was the immediate pleasure of the creative process that "keeps the blood coursing through my veins." Those were the exact words he had said to Celia before standing up and walking out the door to get in his old green wood-paneled Chevy station wagon.

He lived with his mother and never mentioned a girlfriend. Not once had he seemed to notice that Celia was unmarried and available, for which she was glad, since she wasn't at all interested in dating him. He had a wispy mustache and an annoying habit of sucking on his teeth as if food were trapped between them. She had often wondered how he related to students and if they made fun of him behind his back. He taught at Harwood, a private college over near Spartanburg.

For a teacher he was quite prolific in his output, but Celia doubted that he had any idea how many unsold pieces he had in storage or loaned out to friends. For him to ask specifically about one of his paintings, therefore, was very unusual.

Some of these bigger pieces were heavy, but she knew the Madonna wasn't. It was actually quite light for its size. She spotted it now among the others, its slender gold frame looking out of place, even though it was just right for the piece. As she lifted it down, she felt her pulse quickening. It might have been out of her sight for a long time, but she had never gotten it out of her mind. She would see it most often at night in her dreams. She had put it up in the top bin partly for its size, of course, but also to get it as far away from her as possible.

She thought of a plan for right now. She wouldn't look at the painting directly. She would lightly brush it off with the feather duster, but she would not actually look at the picture itself, only at the frame and the very edges of the canvas. This was also how she had coped with it when it had been on display four years ago. She couldn't always avoid passing by it, but she could avert her eyes.

She turned the piece around backward and set it on the floor against a cupboard, then climbed back up the ladder. While she was at it, she might as well look through the other paintings up here. There was a large gouache and pastel of a mountain stream she remembered—one of Ollie's works, in fact, done during his early years before he had entered what he called his architectural phase. *Little Tweed Creek*, it was named. She would get that one down and put it back out.

Several minutes later she had moved things around in one of the small side galleries to accommodate two of the large works she had selected from the top bin. It would be a little crowded, but that was okay. She would be taking some other things down soon anyway, and she had a buyer for the carousel painting, so that one would be leaving in a few days.

Besides the Madonna and the mountain stream, she had also taken from the top bin a large enamel on canvas that reminded her of several magnified black Rorschach blots on a very pretty patterned field of blues, greens, and yellows. She had never understood why no one had bought the piece, cryptically titled *The Deep Twenty*. It was one of the few she had expected to be adopted quickly but had instead been stranded at the orphanage.

Tara had flatly declared *The Deep Twenty* too symmetrical, and Ollie was sure the artist had inadvertently hung it upside down. It would be a much stronger piece, he had argued, if the large blue background square were at the bottom instead of the top. When it was first displayed, he would stand in front of it, then lean over and contort himself sideways so he could study it upside down. "Yep, that's better," he would say. He even mentioned it to the artist one time, a cadaverous, scary-looking woman whose blond hair was about an inch long all over, but she made it very clear that she had *not* mistaken the top of the painting for the bottom.

Celia hung *Little Tweed Creek* above a collection of ceramic pots on a low shelf, and *The Deep Twenty* right above it, between the carousel painting and a crazily stitched fabric piece in three panels titled *sun moon stars,* a work which Tara scorned as "crafty," meaning it wasn't her idea of true art. This particular room was what Celia called her eclectic room—no unifying theme or common medium, just some miscellaneous things she liked most.

As she headed back to the workroom to get the Madonna ready for Craig to pick up, she kept concentrating on breathing deeply and steadily. She imagined her fingertips glowing red where she had touched the frame while getting it down. She gave herself a speech consisting of several short points, which she numbered as they came to her: (1) It's just a picture in a frame. (2) Treat it like merchandise. (3) Think about other things. And her final point was emphatic: (4) Don't look at it!

The Madonna piece—titled simply *Mother and Child*—was a batik, a laborious procedure of printing fabric using wax and dyes, adding one color at a time. The colors on this one were gorgeous muted maroons, purples, golds, jeweled greens, and blues. It had a mottled, somewhat fractured look, like stained glass. In fact, the Madonna herself appeared to be sitting in front of a stained-glass window of sorts, large blocks of dark, rich colors through which a mellow light diffused. The whole scene looked soft around the edges, slightly out of focus.

The Madonna, a more modern-looking version than the ones in Baroque and Renaissance paintings, was looking down so that her face was shadowed. Her long hair fell loose about her face and shoulders, and the neckline of her blue dress draped down in soft modest folds. She looked far more natural and unfettered than most Madonnas Celia had seen in other paintings, whose strained expressions often suggested they might be wearing uncomfortable undergarments. One hand of this Madonna was poised an inch above her baby's face, and her lips were slightly parted, as if she had just breathed, "Oh!" It was remarkable to Celia how a face could emanate pure joy without even the hint of a smile. Unlike other stiff, primly posed Madonnas in all the other paintings down through the ages, this one was not at all aware of herself. She was past smiling.

And the baby—the utter sweetness of the baby! He was wrapped in something dark crimson, and his small face was illuminated. His lips were open also in a tiny O of wonder as he gazed up at his mother. It didn't seem like a smart thing for the artist to do, drawing both mouths in puckered little circles that way, but it worked. You looked at those two mouths and couldn't imagine either one being otherwise.

Not that Celia actually saw any of this now. She was seeing it all in her memory. With the feather duster, she dusted off the frame first, then kept her eyes fixed on the top left corner as she lightly dusted the picture itself. When she picked it up by the wire to move it over by the door, she realized she was gritting her teeth. Relax, she told herself, it's just a picture.

She had meant to set it with its face against the wall next to the door, but at the last minute she turned it around. And then, as when passing a car accident, the perverse impulse to look where she knew she shouldn't forced itself upon her, and she stepped back and saw the whole thing. She didn't mean to and certainly didn't want to, but she did. For a moment she stopped breathing. There it was, exactly as she had remembered it, except even more beautiful. She wondered if anyone else had ever looked at a single piece of artwork and both loved and loathed it the way she did this one.

This is my punishment, she thought, but then quickly revised it. This is *part* of my punishment. Her punishment was far greater than this one Madonna picture. She was certain, though, that this piece would never sell, that though it might be leaving the gallery for now, it was destined to return, then remain there to haunt her forever. It was God's way of penalizing her for her sin. Whether it was stored away on the top shelf or hanging in plain view or even temporarily away from the premises, it would always be there, whispering to her. *Remember, remember, remember.* As if she needed a piece of art to help her remember.

So, okay, take a good hard look at it, she told herself now. Maybe if you look at it long enough, the effect will wear off. But she suddenly thought of all the warnings she had heard about not looking at the sun during an eclipse. It might seem harmless, but it could burn a hole in your retina. Nevertheless she stepped closer to the Madonna, knelt down, and looked right at it. She could see all the separate dots of color that made up the different parts. She had never noticed that the light around the baby's head was actually a collection of small, irregular flame shapes. She wondered if Craig knew about the flaming tongues in the Bible, signifying the coming of the Holy Spirit.

"Teach me some melodious sonnet, sung by flaming tongues above"— the words and tune leapt into her mind for no good reason but were quickly obliterated by the distant sound of a baby, one she had heard only days ago, in another woman's cart at the grocery store. Only one baby this time, not dozens of them, thankfully, and not crying, as they so often were in her dreams, but a single baby making waking-up noises—sleepy murmurs and small sucking sounds.

She stood up, turned the painting around, and slowly moved to the table to sit down. Sometimes she sat here in this same chair to eat when she came to the gallery early or stayed through supper, but food was the last thing on her mind right now. She saw the letter she had left there earlier, the one from the lawyers, and she stared at the envelope as she tried to breathe. She thought of the phrase "sole inheritor" and how it had made her laugh only an hour or so ago. And wasn't that also the way life went? One minute you felt like laughing, and the next thing you knew you were crying.

They had told her all those years ago that she was doing the wise thing, that bringing an unwanted baby into the world was wrong, that someday when the timing was right, everything would be fine. They hadn't told her about the dreams, about the sounds she would hear and the feeling of hands tightening around her neck and fists being punched into the pit of her stomach.

And then she heard the chime of someone entering the front door of the gallery. She could have predicted that if she'd been quick enough. As usual, just when you most needed to be alone, someone showed up.

8

Each Earthly Joy

"You here, Celia? It's just me." Celia recognized the voice, and her heart sank. She felt like hiding under the table. Boo Newman ran the gift shop two doors down from the Trio Gallery, and she never seemed to have enough to do since she had hired a girl to work afternoons. Now she visited up and down the strip mall, taking up everybody else's time. Jack Upton down at the State Farm Insurance office had told Celia that Boo had spent an entire hour at his place one day the week before telling him all about her pets—a menagerie of assorted cats and dogs and even a myna bird named Agrippa—and their many talents and physical maladies. She had finished the first hour of her visit and started on her second when a client had come into the State Farm office. Jack had told Celia he wanted to jump up and kiss the ground the man walked on.

Boo was really a harmless woman and good-hearted, but she could wear you out with her words and her simpleminded way of looking at everything. Her real name was Iona, but her father had nicknamed her Boo when she was a baby because she was born on Halloween. She told this to everyone she met, usually more than once.

Celia quickly went to the sink and splashed some water on her eyes, then dabbed them dry with a paper towel and went out into the gallery. Boo was standing in front of Tara Larson's *Tumult* piece, which had sold two days earlier, as Celia had known it would. The buyer lived up on Glassy Mountain in a new house with twelve-foot ceilings, and he had told Celia he needed something "huge and wild and earthy to fill a wall in the den."

He hadn't batted an eye at the price, had even jokingly offered her more if she'd let him take it home with him right then instead of having to wait till the show came down.

Boo Newman was standing with her hands on her very large hips as she looked at *Tumult*, and when she saw Celia come into the room, she shook her head and said, "I know exactly what you're going to tell me, but I'm going to speak my mind anyway. That is the *strangest* thing I've ever laid eyes on! I think Tara's art is getting downright evil-looking." She lifted one pudgy hand and waved it around. "So there, I guess I've proven all over again how out of step with the times I am, but I can't help it. I simply can't feature living with something like *that* hanging on your wall. I don't know why she can't paint real pictures of things people can recognize!" She pointed to the red dot on the wall beside the painting. "But somebody evidently doesn't agree with me. I see you sold it. Just think of what you could do with that much money!"

Celia didn't have the energy to carry on the same conversation with Boo that they'd had so many times before, so she just smiled and shrugged. "Everybody's got his own tastes." There was no reasoning with Boo; her idea of great art was the newest Precious Moments figurine.

Boo sighed and walked to the chair by the desk, the typical sign that she was settling in for a visit. She sat down gingerly, tilting herself a little sideways so she could wedge herself between the slender chrome arms of the chair. Once ensconced, her thighs spilled over and pooched out under the arms of the chair like two well-stuffed pillows. More than once Celia had imagined Boo trying to stand up too fast, the chair clamping onto her broad backside and coming with her.

Boo slipped her shoes off, then looked down at her puffy ankles. "I don't think those pills are doing me a bit of good," she said. "The doctor told me I'd see some difference right away, but I still feel as bloated as I ever did." Bloating was a frequent complaint of Boo's, and Celia had often been tempted to ask if the doctor had ever suggested she start exercising and go on a diet.

Celia didn't move toward the desk. She knew there was no way she could sit here and listen to this woman right now, and she felt bad for letting her get seated, for not having spoken up sooner. "I'm kind of busy in the back," she said. "I'm trying to reorganize some things and get ready for the new show next month. Sorry."

She knew she wouldn't be pressured for specifics, and she could be glad for that. Another good thing about Boo was that she didn't get her feelings hurt easily. Although Celia knew she would have had the most sympathetic of ears had she chosen to confide in Boo Newman, who unlike a lot of talkers was also a good listener, she didn't dare tell her the truth: *I need to go sit still for a while and try to erase the picture of the Madonna from my mind.* Boo loved talk shows where people told all their secrets and cried about them in public. She often shared the stories with Celia in great detail.

Boo was already putting her shoes back on, scrambling as much as a woman of her size could be said to scramble, trying to disengage herself from the armchair so she could be on her way. "Well, I needed to stop in down at the frame shop anyway to see if Ursula ever got that man's prisoner of war certificate framed. It was the *real* thing, not a duplicate. The man took it right from the German POW camp office when they were liberated. Went right in and ransacked the drawers and found it, then brought it all the way back home to Plum Branch, South Carolina, and had it in a scrapbook all these years." She stopped at the door and gave Celia a cheery wave. "It has his fingerprint on it, and you should see the size of that man's thumb!"

Boo opened the door, then stopped again. "Oh, wait, did I tell you Desi is pregnant? That's what I was meaning to tell you the other day when I stopped by and you were on the phone." Desi, short for Desiree, was the girl who worked for Boo in the afternoons. She had a tangle of jet-black curls piled messily on top of her head and wore blue, green, and bronze fingernail polish to match whichever color of eye shadow she was wearing that day.

Celia felt something twist inside her. "Is that so?" She pretended to straighten a painting on the wall next to where she was standing.

"Yes, but she says she wants to keep working if I'll have her." Boo shook her head. "There used to be a time when women didn't parade around in public when they were pregnant, but it's a different world now. Girls these days, they work right up till the day the baby's born." She opened the door. "Of course girls used to be married to the fathers of their babies, too." In earlier visits at the Trio, Boo had already covered at length the subject of Desi's cohabitation with a car mechanic who dropped her off at work every afternoon in a black Corvette with orange and yellow flames painted along the sides, its pulsating rock music jiggling the little suncatchers on the gift shop window.

"She hasn't told *him* yet," Boo said. "She's afraid he's not going to want her to have it." Right before she closed the door all the way, she added, "Desi wants the baby, though. She told me she's been cheating on her birth control pills for the past three months."

Finally she was gone. Celia fled to the back room and sat down again. It would always be this way, and she knew it. There would be no escape, ever. At any moment somebody could say something or she might see or do something that would bring it all back. The reminders would always be there, coming loose and crashing down on top of each other like a giant rockslide. She stared at her hands and remembered how they had trembled that day fourteen years ago when she had gone to the clinic, paid her money, and signed the papers. Well, no, they hadn't actually started trembling until after she had signed the papers, when they led her from the waiting room to another room in the back.

She remembered how cold the room was and how she couldn't quit shivering for days afterward. She had never asked anybody if that was normal—if everybody had that same deep-down frozen feeling in their bones. No one had warned her about the cold. She had been a graduate student at the time with a part-time job at a newspaper in Dover. A friend had driven her to and from the clinic, and she had stayed home from classes and work for three days, wrapped in blankets but unable to get warm. Right in the middle of summer, too.

And no one had warned her about this part of it, either—the smother-ing feeling she got every time she saw a mother with a baby, even a *picture* of a mother with a baby, or heard about someone getting pregnant or saw a pregnant woman or a new mother in a store. No one had told her about the dreams she would have almost every night for the rest of her life, all those babies she would see swirling around in her head, dead babies that should be silent but were instead emitting horrible wails.

No one had warned her that she would need to lay in a supply of pills to drug her into a dreamless sleep when the nights got especially long. Nobody at the clinic had bothered to tell her that she would look at children differently from that day on, that she would keep up with how old hers would have been, that she would feel an ice pick in her ribs whenever she saw a child that age.

She often found herself studying other women at the mall or in gro-cery stores, even clients who came into the art gallery, and she would wonder which of them had a secret like her own hidden away inside. At times she imagined she could spot the women who did have such a secret by a particular look in their eyes, but she had no way of knowing if she was right. If she happened to make eye contact with one of these grave, wistful-looking women in an aisle or a parking lot somewhere, she would fight the urge to touch her hand and say, "How long ago was yours?" or "Were the dreams especially bad last night?" She might pull up beside someone at a stoplight, take one look at her face, and think, "I know, oh, believe me, I *know.*"

It was hard for her to separate the guilt from the anger, she felt them both so much of the time. Part of her blamed her grandmother's God for not letting her forget, for making her feel so keenly the weight of her guilt, for not having used all that power he was supposed to have to keep her from having an abortion in the first place. It was only further evidence to her that the God worshiped at Bethany Hills Bible Tabernacle kept strict, unrelenting account of everything a person did and then proceeded to get even for all the years to come. Celia had decided long ago that she didn't want to have anything to do with that God, and she didn't know about any other. So what if it was true about heaven and hell? She would take her chances. Anyway, she couldn't imagine that heaven would be anything special with a God like that running things.

All of which meant that she blamed her grandmother, also, sometimes without even realizing she was doing it. Living with a woman like that had planted notions in Celia's head of constantly being watched and judged by the great almighty Record Keeper. It had activated her imagination to the point that it interfered with her enjoyment of life, even after she made her break with religion as a high school senior.

Renee and Ansell and her other friends used to laugh about Celia's conscience, calling it "the vermin within" and urging Celia to "exterminate" it by immersing herself in all the new things they were trying to teach her. "You know, *baptize* yourself with fun!" Ansell liked to say. Her own timidity and caution made her mad. If she didn't live with her grandmother, she had reasoned, she could have grown up with normal attitudes about enjoying life.

But another part of her blamed herself for slipping up that one time. She had always been so careful before then. And certainly since then. One of Celia's college roommates had teased her mercilessly about what she called Celia's "religious" approach to birth control. "Must be that heavy-duty Sunday school background of yours," the girl had said. Celia had told her all about her grandmother and Bethany Hills Bible Tabernacle.

That particular roommate was a history major named Amber, who regularly brought her boyfriend to their dorm room to spend the night. Celia had asked her once what she would do if she got pregnant, and Amber had laughed and waved it off. "It won't happen. But if it does, it's not like the end of the world. There *are* ways to take care of such problems, you know." Amber hadn't come back to school the next fall, and Celia never knew why.

She looked around her now, at the storage cupboards in the workroom, the sink and countertop, the small refrigerator, which held a leftover Caesar salad she planned to eat after she closed the gallery that evening and stayed late to work on the computer. At least that had been the plan when the day started. Now she wasn't so sure. This day seemed oddly distorted, as if it had lasted for a whole week already. She thought of that Bible story from her childhood, the one where somebody—was it Joshua?—had lifted his rod and made the sun stand still. Perhaps someone had done the same thing today. Surely it hadn't been only this morning that she had played tennis at the Holiday Inn.

Her eyes landed on the letter again—the one from the lawyers telling her she was the sole inheritor of her grandmother's house. She felt a sudden and surprising pang of envy toward her grandmother—Sadie Madeline Ellsworth Burnes, though most people had known her as just Sadie Burnes. How unencumbered her life had been. She had simply gotten out of bed every morning and set about doing her duty. She read her Bible, did some housework, cooked a little, listened to a radio preacher, sent a card to a missionary or a shut-in, swept the front porch, hung out a few clothes—on and on with things like that until the day was filled up and it was time for bed. She could lay her head on her pillow every night without dreading the dark hours ahead and the dreams that came with them, and when the sun came up the next day, she would get up and start all over again. She could look at a school bus full of children passing her house and feel no burden of guilt.

As she did so often, Celia felt an intense wish gripping her heart, the wish that somehow there could be a way to go back and redo the past. One little mistake and you were never a free woman again. One especially handsome sweet-talker—a well-built PE major of all things, oh, the shame of it!—and you lost your head one night and got careless, thinking just this one time wouldn't matter. But it did matter, and it kept on and on mattering because you had to remember it every single day and night for the rest of your life.

And to think she had actually paid four hundred dollars to torment herself for the rest of her life. But how could she have possibly known how far-reaching the effects of that visit to the clinic would be? She had been twenty-two, not exactly a kid, certainly old enough to think for herself, so why hadn't she taken more time to consider it all? Why, when she was usually on the indecisive side about every little thing, had she so swiftly made up her mind to do that one huge thing?

And even when she had felt the first stirrings of doubt as they led her to the back room of the clinic, when her hands started trembling and the cold started seeping into her, why hadn't she had the courage to say, "Wait a minute, I need to think this through some more"? She often wondered if other clinics had people who sat down and talked to the girls before they took their money and told them to undress, who warned them about this thing they were about to do and about what it would mean for all the years to follow.

The sweet-talking PE major had lost his appeal as soon as Celia had discovered she was pregnant. She wouldn't have thought of seeking his opinion concerning what she was about to do nor of asking him to help pay for it. She dropped him like a hot potato and never offered a word of explanation. Nor did he press her to. He immediately took up with a tall blond interior design major, and the two of them walked around campus looking like models for a college fashion magazine. Every time Celia saw him, she felt physically sick to think she had been so stupid.

"But life goes on," she said now, quite loudly, in the back room of the art gallery. This was the refrain she forced herself to say after each episode of guilt knocked her down. Sometimes she said it a dozen times a day; other times she could almost make it through a whole day without saying it once. The gallery was a good job for her, much better than the newspaper job she'd had before, where she'd had to be around too many people all the time and cover stories that far too often seemed to involve children.

Some would probably say it didn't make sense, that the newspaper job should have kept her thoughts so occupied that she wouldn't have time to dwell on her own problems, but it hadn't worked that way for her.

Coming to work at the Trio had been a great relief. Some days it was as if she had been granted a reprieve—not a pardon, never *that,* but at least a brief stay. At times she could get her mind on something here at the gallery and concentrate so hard she could actually forget for a while that a child would be alive today if it hadn't been for her carelessness.

And her selfishness. At some point during the last fourteen years, she had admitted to herself without even meaning to that this had been a big part of why she had gone to the clinic that day. She'd had things she wanted to do with her life, and a baby sure wasn't part of them, not right then. A simple choice—and a totally self-centered one. It had been a black day when she had realized this. How depressing that a person's own mind could turn against her that way. Nevertheless she had recognized it as the absolute truth.

She had long since given up arguing with herself that it wasn't really a *baby*—and all those other attempts at justifying the act. It was nothing more than a little mindless clump of cells, not really a person, she had tried to tell herself for years. And any child brought into the world deserved to be loved and *wanted,* which this one wouldn't be. And, of course, it could have easily been damaged in some way even at that early stage; maybe it would have been born deformed and never . . . blah, blah, blah. Oh, she knew them all, the same old tired thoughts.

She got up from the table and splashed water on her face again. She needed to go through the day's stack of mail, make a couple of phone calls, and then start working on the mailing for the next show, which ought to go out in a week or two.

She was sitting at the front desk a few minutes later when she saw a mustard-colored Volkswagen van pull up in front of the gallery. She recognized it at once as belonging to Macon Mahoney, one of the gallery's newer artists. She sighed—far too many people were showing up this afternoon.

She had always thought that Macon Mahoney could be a character in a book. He could have been somebody Tom Sawyer and Huck Finn ran across while drifting down the Mississippi River on a raft, some good-hearted fellow who joined up with them to try to get Jim to freedom. Or put him in a frock coat and top hat instead of his customary jeans and T-shirt, and he could be in a Dickens novel—maybe a kindly neighbor of the Cratchit family or another clerk, a nicer one, in the office where Uriah Heep worked. Half of what Macon Mahoney said didn't make sense to Celia, but the other half was very funny and witty and showed a child-like love of life she didn't often see in grown people. He was polite, too, and never acted as if he thought he was anything special, though in her opinion he was an artistic genius.

She watched him get out of his van now and walk around to open the side door. He got back inside the van, but she could see him crawling around in the back of it. She wondered what he was bringing in now, for surely this was the reason for his visit. He usually stopped by every other week or so, bringing something he had recently finished or, more often, something old he wanted to swap for another piece of his in the gallery. Celia rarely had to worry about rotating Macon's pieces because he kept them rotated himself. He was always changing things around at home or entering something in a contest or lending pieces out, sometimes even giving them away.

He was immensely talented, although Celia thought that he explored so many different forms and media that he still hadn't found his home ground. She liked almost everything he did, however, so she didn't know what advice she would give to an artist like him—if an artist like him would ever ask her opinion, that is. Would you tell a Macon Mahoney to keep experimenting and producing these highly unique pieces in every style, or would you tell him to spin a wheel and then zero in on whatever he happened to land on, forgetting everything else? A specialty was some-thing Macon didn't yet have, but was that a bad thing when you could do so much so well?

Celia remembered a lidded clay pot he had brought in with him the first day he had come to the gallery with color slides of his work. The pot looked like primitive southwestern art, a dusky mottled clay with crude figures of animals etched into it, like something you'd see on the wall of a cave, and she had fallen in love with it at first glance. In fact, she had bought it for herself before he left that day.

A "walk-in" is what they called artists like that who just showed up at a gallery to say, "Here I am and here are pictures of my stuff and wouldn't you love to represent me?" Dealers and gallery owners joked about them. The ratio of walk-ins that actually had something worth seeing to those who needed to find some other way to support themselves was probably about one to five thousand, but, amazingly, Macon Mahoney had been that one.

She would never forget it. It had been the first day of April last year when he had sauntered in and bowled her over with his art. She had almost asked him if it wasn't some kind of April Fool's joke, especially given the fact that he said such off-the-wall things. She thought surely he must be some famous rising artist from New York already represented by some big name like Castelli or Janis, but then it didn't make sense that somebody would go to the trouble to pull a prank like this.

It turned out that he was one of those rare undiscovered talents who had quietly matured in relative obscurity while he held down a part-time job at a health food store. Celia could tell from looking at his slides that he could only be expected to keep getting better. His studio was above a mattress store in Derby, one big room where he had both lived and worked until he married a music teacher in Berea the year before and moved into her house with her. Celia had known beyond a doubt that Craig, Ollie, and Tara would all vote to do a show of his work and then invite him to join the gallery, and she had been right.

Celia had gone to his studio a few days after his first visit, along with Tara, to see some of the works firsthand, and she had been astounded to think he had been living within twenty miles of the Trio for close to ten years and had never shown any of his work at a gallery. His new wife had been the one to first encourage him to visit some of the regional galleries and talk to some dealers about his work. He had never thought he was ready for that, had given most of his work away as gifts. And, in one of those odd connections you sometimes discover between two people you know, Celia had later learned that Elizabeth Landis had actually been the one to specifically suggest the Trio Gallery to him. It just happened that Elizabeth lived across the street from the woman Macon married.

He was out of the van now and walking toward the door with a rather large painting. Celia met him and opened the door for him.

"Hi, Macon. Got something new for us?"

" 'Ever reaping something new,' " he said, stepping sideways through the door. He turned the painting around and set it on the floor against the plate-glass window. "That was Tennyson," he said. "Could be *Lady of Shalott*, but I'm thinking not. Maybe *Locksley Hall* or *In Memoriam.* That's memori*am*, you know, not memori*al*. Some people get those words mixed up." He stepped back a few paces and scowled at the painting. " 'Perhaps a frail memorial, but sincere.' " He glanced up at Celia. "That's William C-o-w-p-e-r. Rhymes with blooper. Cowper—lots of people pronounce his name wrong. Great poet. Wrote a lot of hymn texts. Old guy—died over two hundred years ago."

After her first few confusing conversations with Macon Mahoney, Celia had finally asked him one day if there was a trick to interpreting what he was saying. Thereafter he had started identifying the sources of his quotations for her. Sometimes she still didn't see how it all tied together, but it did help some. She had wondered more than once how his wife ever carried on a conversation with him. She would love to ask him someday how he had proposed to her.

Right now the thought flitted through Celia's mind that she had seen William Cowper's name somewhere, but she didn't take time to try to place it. She was too busy looking at Macon's new painting. He generally favored representational art over abstract, but he liked to manipulate his subjects in unusual ways. She knew that to understand this painting fully, if such a thing were possible, she would have to study it a long time.

The entire background was dark gray, but the painting as a whole was anything but dark. The focal image was low and off-center: a large royal blue sphere representing the planet Earth with bright green land masses, not cartographically exact but easily recognizable as the continents in spite of their angular contours. All around the planet were silver-white splotches, streaks, and swirls, and several glowing orange and yellow spheres of various sizes—obviously other celestial bodies.

Above the planet, at the top of the painting, were the very large tips of a man's thumb and forefinger pinched together grasping a long, slender silvery thread attached to the planet. The thread wasn't exactly vertical, however, which gave the effect that the planet was being swung back and forth like a pendulum by the giant hand. There was a little bright red bow right above the planet, affixed to the thread, as if the whole thing were a Christmas ornament about to be hung.

But most curious of all were the tiny objects floating in space around the planet. They were recognizable shapes, some of them, such as a car, a house, a kite, a shoe, a bottle, but they weren't colored in. They were just empty outlines against the background, some of them laid right over the silver swirls and other heavenly bodies. The outline of a miniature skyscraper, upside down, appeared against one of the orange balls.

"Well," Celia said at last. Clearly Macon Mahoney believed some greater power was holding the world in space. That much she could see for herself.

" 'Tis not so deep as a well,' " Macon said. "Shakespeare—you probably already know that. *Romeo and Juliet*."

"Okay, tell me about these little things floating around," she said.

" 'Great princes have great playthings' " came the reply. "That's Cowper again. I've been reading him a lot."

"So they represent all our toys?"

" 'Men misuse their toys first, then cast them away.' I might have missed a word or two of that one, but it's close. More Cowper."

"Does it have a title—the painting?" Celia was always intrigued by the titles Macon gave his pieces.

"*Fade, Fade, Each Earthly Joy,*" he said.

Celia felt a chill go over her. How had Macon come to choose a hymn title for his painting? Or did he have any idea that it *was* a hymn title? Nothing he had said before today had given her the idea that he had any interest in anything religious.

She turned and looked at him. "You've got to be kidding, right?"

" 'The leopard shall lie down with the kid,' " he said solemnly. "That's from the Bible. Book called Isaiah."

9

Silent in the Grave

Celia was very glad to see five o'clock roll around. After she had closed everything up, she left through the back door, noticing as she went that the Madonna picture had disappeared. Evidently Craig had popped in sometime during the past hour and taken it. Thank goodness he hadn't bothered to say hello.

She knew she should stay and work on the article for the Derby *Daily News,* but it wasn't due until Friday, and she already had a good start on it. It could wait another day or two. It wasn't the most cheerful of assignments—a reprise of an unsolved murder in Derby that had been committed twenty years ago next week—and today she didn't feel like thinking about somebody killing a local woman in broad daylight as she was running the vacuum cleaner right in her own house while her husband was at work and her four children were at school.

Celia had also planned to stop by the grocery store on her way home, but that could wait, too. She headed home, trying to direct her thoughts to safe objective subjects. She tuned the radio to a station that played old rock and turned it up loud. Unfortunately, she couldn't sing along because all the songs were before her time, but she listened hard to the words, which, unlike the rock music she had become familiar with during the eighties, could actually be understood. "If you want to know if he loves you so," someone was singing now, "it's in his kiss, that's where it is, oh yeah, it's in his kiss." Well, she wasn't so sure that was a reliable proof of love.

As that one faded and the Beatles took over with "I Want to Hold

Your Hand," Celia remembered the time her grandmother had sat down at the supper table and proceeded to deliver a speech about the evils of kissing and holding hands. "It leads to bad trouble," she had said flatly, searching Celia's face for some response, which she didn't get since Celia had picked up Ansell's trick of the blank stare by now. If she *had* chosen to respond, it would have been with a laugh—to think that Grandmother actually thought she might heed her warning! Of course, she had to admit now that if she had listened to her advice, maybe . . . But it was too late for that kind of thinking. She reached over and switched the radio off.

At last she pulled into the driveway of her landlord's house and swung around to the back. Finally, after she had lived here all these years, the Stewarts had repaved their driveway and added an extension pad in back so she would have her own place to park instead of up on the street. The Stewarts were nice enough people, but when it came to making improvements in the apartment, they had a bad habit of putting things off, though they were always getting things replaced and remodeled on the main floor where *they* lived. Back in January Celia had had to endure several days of banging and drilling overhead while Patsy Stewart had new kitchen countertops and cupboards installed.

Fitting her key into the lock, Celia felt a great sense of relief to be home again. She surely couldn't complain too much about her basement apartment. As a walkout, it had its own access. No need to climb steps and always be running into her landlord. It was nicer than many apartments she had seen and thirty dollars a month less than the average one-bedroom in the area. And it had personality, not like all those boxy cookie-cutter units in apartment buildings. She had it tastefully decorated and filled with nice things she liked, and the Stewarts not only gave her the use of their washer and dryer but also allowed her generous storage space in the unfinished part of the basement, two benefits not always available to apartment renters. Even if she did have to put up with some noise from upstairs, it was much better now that their children were grown and gone.

She swung the door open and stepped inside, tossing her purse and keys on a chair. She took off her shoes and padded over to turn up the heat. Then she walked through each room, which didn't take long. It wasn't for the purpose of checking for intruders but rather to admire her art. She did this every morning as she was brushing her teeth and again every evening upon arriving home.

Currently her very favorite piece was a large canvas depicting a chair with odd angles. She had hung it next to the window in her living room. No normally fashioned person could sit comfortably in such a chair as the one pictured, but that was beside the point. Celia loved the painting for its wit and its wacky proportions. The artist, a sixty-year-old black man from Columbia named C. J. Tibbetts, had titled it *Perch*.

The color wasn't one Celia was usually drawn to, but as soon as she had seen the painting, which she had owned for almost a year now, she had known she had to have it. It was thirty-six by twenty-four inches, and the chair took up most of the surface area of the canvas. The background, which was a wavy wash of greens, blues, browns, and grays, gave you the impression that you were looking at a lake of shifting colors. The chair itself was a unique color: a peachy sort of tan with a shimmery cast and small speckles of dark red dribbled all over it. It tickled her to think of how much the colors reminded her of a fish, especially set against the waterlike background, and the title *Perch* was the clincher that C. J. Tibbetts had a sense of humor.

She continued through her apartment, ending up back in the living room in front of her most recent acquisition—a piece of Macon Mahoney's she had bought only a couple of months earlier. It was eight by twenty-six inches, short but wide. Called *Through the Blinds,* it depicted a stand of very black trees, but only the tops of the trees, with a slate-blue sky behind them. The whole scene was striped over with slender cream-colored horizontal lines every inch or so, which represented the blinds in the title. "That's what I used to see out my back window," Macon had told Celia. He had set up an easel right by that very window and painted the picture there.

It was one of his earlier pieces, he had told her, painted before he was married, when he lived in the apartment above the mattress store. The tree trunks were painted with automobile lacquer, which he discovered later could be dangerous to your health. "So it's a one and only," he had said that day when he brought it by the gallery along with a dozen or so of his older works, which he was getting ready to donate to a new dentist over in Spartanburg after checking with Celia to make sure she didn't want any of them for the gallery. The dentist, a friend of Macon's, was just starting his practice and didn't have anything on his walls yet except for two framed diplomas.

Celia had climbed into the back of Macon's van to look at what he had. They weren't bad, any of them, and several were quite good, although it was clear that his style had still been in its formative stages when these were done. She had kept two pieces to display at the gallery, feeling sure she could advertise them as Early Mahoney and sell them easily, and she bought *Through the Blinds* for herself. Macon let her have it for a song, and she didn't argue with him. Just paid him on the spot and happily took it home.

Unlike the dentist, she didn't have roomfuls of bare walls. In fact, she was running out of wall space and might soon have to start rotating her art the way she did at the gallery. She had found a place for *Through the Blinds,* however—she had hung it above a shelf on which she had displayed some smaller pieces of pottery and a sculpture of a very round washerwoman on her hands and knees.

Macon had said he didn't like the way the blinds ended up working against the effect he was trying to achieve, an effect he never did explain to Celia, who didn't want to hear it anyway since she *loved* the blinds and considered them a daring move that succeeded. It had to take courage to paint a picture and then draw lines across it. It was odd how a person was attracted instantly to certain pictures. Any art dealer would tell you that logic flies right out the window when people shop for art. At any rate, Celia liked *Through the Blinds* more every time she looked at it, could in fact imagine it surpassing the chair picture someday to become her favorite.

As she stood there looking at it, her mind turned again to Macon's visit to the gallery that afternoon and his new painting titled *Fade, Fade, Each Earthly Joy.* She thought of what he had told her before he left, and the revelation came rushing at her now with the same surprise and dismay she had felt at the time.

It turned out that he and his wife had recently been visiting a small church in Derby called The Church of the Open Door, which in itself was surprise enough, but furthermore, they had first attended at the invitation of Elizabeth Landis, their neighbor across the street, who attended the church regularly—Elizabeth Landis, the woman who had come into the Trio Gallery for years now, who had recruited Celia for her tennis team, and who, from all outward appearances, looked like a rational, normal human being. To think of her harboring *religion* inside her like a small but deadly explosive made Celia's mind reel.

During one of the services Macon and his wife had attended, he had run across the title "Fade, Fade, Each Earthly Joy" in the hymnbook. When he told Celia this, that's when it clicked in her mind where she had seen the name William Cowper before, the poet Macon had quoted. That was it—she had seen his name in the old brown *Tabernacle Hymns* they used every Sunday at Bethany Hills in Dunmore, Georgia, back when she used to pay attention not only to the words and music but also to the names of the people who *wrote* the words and music.

Such colorful names, some of them: Philip Bliss, John Grape, Charles Gabriel, Frances Havergal, Edwin Excell, Ira Sankey, Maltbie Babcock, and Augustus Toplady, to name a few. And William Cowper—she was pretty sure he was the one who had written the hymn that started out with the disturbingly vivid picture of a fountain filled with blood "drawn from Immanuel's veins."

How absolutely infuriating that everywhere she turned she kept being reminded of these stupid outdated hymns. As if to mock her now, she heard a voice inside her head, her grandmother's voice no less: "When this poor lisping, stammering tongue lies silent in the grave." *So why can't you lie silent in the grave like you're supposed to?* Celia thought. *Why do you have to keep bugging me?*

It further turned out that Macon Mahoney had begun to read the Bible lately and had already made it from Genesis all the way to Jeremiah. "Just checking things out," he had said to Celia. "Exploring the options." Celia had felt her heart go heavy. That's all she needed—an artist as refreshing and vibrant as Macon Mahoney getting religious and quoting the Bible every time he came around. What would make him do such a thing? she wondered.

On the one hand, she felt like shouting at him to ditch the church thing, to start reading ancient Chinese poetry, medical journals, real estate manuals, *anything* besides the Bible, but on the other hand, she knew if she spoke her mind like that, it would arouse Macon's curiosity, and he'd want to find out why she felt that way. For all his weirdness and apparent absentmindedness, Macon Mahoney had a deep interest in other people. He wasn't wrapped up in himself the way some artists seemed to be.

So Celia didn't dare ask for more information. She merely nodded, hoping he wouldn't start elaborating on these so-called options he was exploring. She didn't want to think about Elizabeth Landis inviting him to church. She didn't want to imagine him flipping through the hymnal and then going home to read his Bible.

"Well, I'm closing up in a few minutes," she said, then walked over to the desk and turned off the computer. "I need to get home. I'll find a good spot to hang your painting tomorrow if you're planning on leaving it here. Or were you just bringing it by to show me?" She pretended to be straightening some things on the desk.

Macon was quiet for a moment, and when she looked up again, he had cocked his head and was studying her. "Well, both actually. I brought it by to show you, yes, but I'm also leaving it." He raised his voice to an oratorical pitch. "My wife, the fair Theresa, hath banished it from our castle! 'Remove it from hence and take it thence,' says she, 'for our walls do groan with a surfeit of art.' And when I remonstrate, 'No, my sweet shrew, I cannot so soon relinquish my offspring,' she points to the door and says, 'Get thee to the gallery.' "

He paused again, and Celia walked over to turn the heat down. "And tomorrow is fine," Macon said behind her, now adopting a deep southern drawl. "Like Miss Scarlett said, 'After all, tomorrow is another day.' " He left after that without another word, but as he started up his van, he activated the sound system, and from the little trumpetlike amplifier sticking up on top came the sounds of a brawl in a western saloon, accompanied by the theme from the old *Bonanza* TV program.

Celia flipped the Open sign around to read Closed and stood for a moment watching Macon back up, then pull out of the parking lot. What a strange, strange man. She wondered if his wife had begun to regret marrying him. Or maybe she thought she was the luckiest woman alive.

Celia sighed now, turned from *Through the Blinds,* and walked into her kitchen. She wasn't really hungry yet, but she needed to keep busy. Macaroni and cheese, that's what she would make. She went to the stove and got out a pan, then turned on the water at the sink. As she watched it swirl down the drain, she thought of how fast a simple action could turn into irreversible consequences. Just as there was no way you could get that water back once it was sucked down the drain, neither could you undo things you had done. And just as you had to pay for every single drip of water you used, you also had to pay in some way for every careless action you committed. She set the pan down hard inside the sink.

She squeezed her eyes shut. This was going to be one of those long nights, she could tell. Too many things were spinning around in her head. No doubt she would need some help falling asleep later on. But for now, this was the plan—clatter around in the kitchen, make some noise and a little bit of a mess to clean up, also put something on in the background. As she walked into the living room to turn the television on, her eyes suddenly lighted on the shelf where she kept her videotapes. Without stopping to consider, she grabbed *Pride and Prejudice* and inserted it into her VCR. There, that would fill up space for a good long time.

She was glad her apartment was laid out in such a way that she could see the television from her kitchen. Most evenings she watched the news while she fixed and ate her supper, and more and more she was watching *Wheel of Fortune* after that, though she wouldn't have told anyone for the world. She often found herself comparing Pat Sajak with Alex Trebek on *Jeopardy*, another old-people's program she would never admit to watching.

After she put the pan of water on the stove to boil, she took a block of cheese out of the refrigerator, then got out the cutting board and grater. This was going to be real macaroni and cheese, not one of those box deals. It would take time to do it right, and it would leave her with two pans and the colander to clean up. She'd bake it in a Corning Ware dish and afterward would transfer what she didn't eat to a smaller freezer container, which would leave the Corning Ware dish to scrape out and scour. She would bake it a little longer than the recipe stipulated because she liked it with a crunch around the edges, which would make the dish harder to get clean, also.

So this could stretch out to a couple of hours if she took it nice and slow. She would warm up two leftover corn-bread muffins to go with the macaroni and cheese and butter them with real butter, then take her time eating it all. Actually, these were two things her grandmother had done pretty well in the area of cooking—macaroni and cheese and corn bread. They might have been the *only* things she had done well in the kitchen. How ironic that Celia was using them to try to occupy her mind, to keep her from thinking, among other things, about her grandmother.

Pride and Prejudice was one of those movies Celia could watch continuously and never get tired of. She had probably seen it at least ten or twelve times by now, all six hours of it. The last three of those times had been on a single Sunday, the previous Christmas Eve, when she had started it at seven in the morning after being awakened by the Stewarts' grandchildren upstairs. It sounded like they were jumping up and down all over the house on pogo sticks. The youngest, an infant, was crying at the top of his lungs. Celia had actually thought at first she was having another of her bad dreams, but finally it sank in that this was a real baby, alive, and in close proximity. Also not very happy.

She had lain in bed for a few minutes hoping the crying would stop, but when it didn't, she had hit on the idea of watching *Pride and Prejudice* and turning the volume up extra loud. Thankfully the baby seemed to be in one of the back bedrooms upstairs instead of in the den or kitchen, both of which were directly over her apartment. Other sounds were coming from the den and kitchen, however. Evidently someone was already up and thunking around in the kitchen getting breakfast. Something substantial, like a rolling pin or can of shortening, was dropped on the floor, followed by what sounded like the slamming of a door. She could hear people talking, then the sounds of laughter and small feet running through the hall.

Then the thudding of larger feet. She often wished she had the nerve to ask Milton Stewart why he had to plant his heels so heavily whenever he walked through the house. He wasn't that big a man, yet he sounded like Paul Bunyan with Babe the Blue Ox, the way he stomped around. And somehow this gene had been passed on to his sons, skinny boys both of them. She had moved into the apartment when the boys were in high school and had even gotten to where she could tell which of the three Stewart men was walking across the floor at any given time. When they were all three home and moving around, it sounded like a herd of stampeding buffalo up there. She had bought earplugs during those years, which helped some.

She lay in bed that Christmas Eve morning and wondered how long the Stewarts' sons would be staying. At the time she thought only one of them was home for Christmas, but it turned out that both of them were up there, along with their wives and four children of assorted sizes. So there, without warning, went her plans for a quiet Christmas Eve. That had been back when she was still seeing Al, who was supposed to come over the next day to spend Christmas Day with her. He was bringing the turkey, dressing, and a pumpkin pie, and she was supposed to make everything else.

But the ruckus overhead, rather than inspiring her to action, enervated her. She had meant to clean her apartment and get a start on her part of Christmas dinner that day, but instead she spent the entire day watching *Pride and Prejudice* three times back to back, ending at one o'clock Christmas morning. She had fixed herself a sandwich around noon and heated up some leftover pizza that night, but she never once paused the movie except to rewind it.

Upstairs the hubbub continued all day, but she heard it only as faint background noise. Having spent all those hours with the Bennet family in eighteenth-century England, she had more than a little trouble extracting herself from them, and when Al called at some point that evening to talk about their schedule for Christmas Day, she treated him somewhat shabbily on the phone, trying to hurry him up so she could get back into the movie.

Celia wasn't positive, but she thought that day may have actually been the very beginning of her disenchantment with Al. She wondered now if maybe she had subconsciously identified him with the insufferable Mr. Collins since his phone call had come right smack in the middle of Mr. Collins' proposal to Elizabeth. It had occurred to her that Al was about the same size as Mr. Collins, both of them tending toward paunchy, though Al was a little taller and therefore hid his better. She knew that over the years, however, he would have to start buying larger clothes.

Mr. Collins was one of her favorite characters in the movie, with all of his comical affectations, and as she stood in the kitchen grating cheese now, she found herself already looking forward to his first appearance on the screen. The opening credits were done by now, and Elizabeth Bennet had already viewed Bingley and Darcy from a distance as they surveyed nearby Netherfield on horseback.

The Bennet family was now leaving church, and Mrs. Bennet had just heard from someone that Netherfield was to be taken by a man of fortune, a man of "five thousand a year." She was all aflutter with the possibilities this could open up for her five daughters. Mrs. Bennet was another favorite character of Celia. Her fussy, melodramatic mannerisms, combined with her intense seriousness over all things trivial, were such fun to watch. Poor Mr. Bennet, having to put up with *that* his whole married life.

It was funny how she had come to love all the movies based on Jane Austen's books when she had detested the novels themselves in college. Once in a class called Critical Analysis of Literature—a class she had been forced to take because it was the only English elective she could fit into her schedule one semester—she had finally stated aloud her opinion of *Emma*, a novel they were required to read. Mercifully, she didn't remember her exact words, but the gist of her speech was that these people had *no life*, all they ever did was make polite social calls and play silly card games and every now and then get really wild and have a hokey little dance, besides which Austen's writing style was incredibly slow, and Celia didn't see why the class had to spend so much time on her.

She still remembered the amused smirks of some of her classmates, who no doubt agreed with her but were too timid to say so, and for sure she still remembered the teacher's comments to her after class that day when she asked Celia to stay behind for a moment. Her name was Dr. Quinn, and she had a small but conspicuous scar above one eyebrow that Celia wondered about. If she herself had such a scar, she knew she would wear long bangs to conceal it, but Dr. Quinn wore her hair pulled straight back. She stayed behind her desk and stared at Celia for a long time before she spoke, not unkindly really, but with something close to a puzzled expression. When she finally spoke, however, she sounded very certain, not puzzled at all.

"Miss Coleman," she said, "I recall one of my professors keeping me after class one day, it must have been thirty-five years ago now, when I was a student at Delaware State, to tell me that my slip was showing and she knew I would want to go to the restroom to fix it before proceeding to my next class. I wanted to see you for a moment after class today to tell you that something of yours is also showing—your immaturity and ignorance. Unfortunately it can't be fixed by ducking into a restroom for a few minutes, but it is my sincere hope that before you graduate you will understand the value of looking at literature in its own context, that you will not try to judge every book by how closely it matches your own extremely small and narrow experience of life."

Dr. Quinn had worn a brooch at the neck of her dress that day, and Celia could still picture it—a large oval onyx with a flower etched in the center, in a gold setting. Before Celia had left the classroom, Dr. Quinn had leaned over her lectern and said, almost gently, "You're a smart girl, Miss Coleman. Don't let yourself get blown around by every little current of contemporary thought that comes along. Don't think that your own generation has all the answers. Open up your mind."

Which had struck Celia as preposterous at the time. *Her* mind was wide open! It was all those people in Austen's books who were the stuffy ones, all prim and constricted, riding around in carriages and worrying about all the social conventions of the time! And, she suspected, Dr. Quinn herself wasn't so all-fired open-minded, either, or she wouldn't dress the way she did and offer her opinion in class that a fuddy-duddy writer like Jane Austen "was the brightest flower in the garden of British novelists." And that comment about Celia's "own generation"—why, people Dr. Quinn's age thought that *their* generation had all the answers!

Well, at some point Celia had grown up, thankfully, and now she could hardly believe she had had those thoughts about Austen's books, much less had the nerve to say them aloud in class. It was sad how much education was wasted on kids. How often she had wished she could go back and sit in some of those classes again.

Celia hadn't intended to grate the whole block of cheese, but she realized all of a sudden that she had. She certainly didn't need that much for a small recipe of macaroni and cheese, and now she wouldn't have cheese for a sandwich if she wanted it. Oh well, too late to undo it now—like the water down the drain, like the stupid comments in Dr. Quinn's class. She got out a zipped baggie and put the extra cheese into it, then stuck it in the freezer.

She was happy to realize as she proceeded through the recipe that she had hit on a good idea to fill up the hours. She was calmer now, and the thought of the finished macaroni and cheese and the anticipation of watching the rest of the movie made her feel proud of herself for coming up with a workable strategy. The article for the Derby *News* nagged at her a little, but she told herself she'd get back to it tomorrow for sure. She didn't usually like to procrastinate, but it couldn't be helped tonight.

She had discovered over the years that macaroni and cheese was even more flavorful if she sprinkled grated Parmesan cheese, along with the cheddar, between the layers. She also liked a little extra fresh-ground pepper. The white sauce was perfect this time, not too thick or too thin, and as she poured it slowly over the top of the casserole, from the VCR she heard Caroline Bingley tell Darcy that all the locals considered Elizabeth Bennet a great beauty. And just as Darcy curtly disagreed, right as he was delivering one of the funniest lines of the whole video—"I should as soon call her mother a wit"—Celia's telephone rang.

10

Of Every Good Possessed

"Celia, I have a favor to ask." It was Patsy Stewart from upstairs. She was most likely using the telephone back in her bedroom because Celia wasn't getting the stereo effect she always did when Patsy phoned her from the kitchen directly overhead.

Patsy had a low, husky voice, though as far as Celia knew, she had never been a smoker. If most of what she said weren't so mundane and totally devoid of double meaning, Patsy's voice could possibly be described with adjectives such as *sexy* or *sultry*. If every now and then she would say something ambiguous or suggestive, something with the faintest innuendo of naughtiness or flippancy, it might be an interesting Bette Davis kind of voice. If she were the least bit witty, it would make a great comedian's voice. But, like Mrs. Bennet, no one would ever accuse Patsy Stewart of being a wit.

Or another idea: Celia could imagine somebody with a voice like Patsy's sprinkling in endearments like darlin', honey, sweetheart. With a southern accent, *that* would be a voice you'd take notice of and remember, one with a distinctive sort of charm. Patsy wasn't one for endearments, though, and she barely even had an accent, though she had been born right here in South Carolina, in a small town called Greer over on the other side of Greenville. So as it was, her voice wasn't any of these things—not sexy or sultry or interesting or memorable in any way. It was merely husky and a little on the loud side.

So she had a favor to ask. Celia already smelled something thick and musty, like a mixture of obligation and dread, seeping down through the floor of Patsy's house and into her own apartment. In the brief second before she replied, Celia recalled that the last time Patsy had asked a favor had been when her husband, Milton, was in the hospital for a hernia operation a couple of weeks after Christmas. She had spent over an hour upstairs that time helping Patsy clear out her entire pantry, which was crawling with little black bugs. Some time back, Patsy had come across a sale on cornmeal and had bought three bags of it, which she had stored on a shelf of her pantry.

"I sure never expected it to go bad on me," she told Celia. "I thought I'd use it all up before something like this happened." It was hard to believe that a woman deep into her fifties with a long history of cooking behind her could think she could store that much cornmeal in a pantry without inviting trouble. That's when Celia told her about her grandmother's practice of always putting flour and cornmeal in the freezer so the bugs wouldn't get to it. Patsy said she'd have to try that next time.

The two of them stood at the door of the pantry closet for a long silent moment surveying the scene. Celia couldn't imagine how that many bugs could have taken over without Patsy noticing anything earlier. Evidently as far as their reproduction rate went, rabbits couldn't hold a candle to these little guys.

"I haven't cooked much since Christmas," Patsy told Celia, evidently guessing her thoughts. "After the boys left, we ate mostly leftovers, and then we had our new cupboards installed right after that, so I didn't cook for another week or so. And then with Milton's surgery, well . . . if I hadn't been hankering for a cup of hot cocoa when I got home from the hospital tonight, there's no telling when I would have discovered all this." She dragged a small stool inside the pantry, then started handing things from the top shelf down to Celia, who was holding a big plastic trash bag. Patsy wasn't taking any chances trying to salvage anything that was questionable.

The bugs were crawling all over almost everything, as if looking for a way in. Celia studied three or four of them, tiny dark ovals, wandering around on the outside of a box of raspberry Jell-O. She smashed one of them with her thumbnail, feeling the slightest crunch. She immediately wished she hadn't done that. She knew she'd have the feeling all night that her hands weren't clean.

It looked like the bugs had originated in the cornmeal and then had migrated throughout the pantry. Next to the cornmeal was a partially used bag of flour, which, although folded over securely and clipped at the top, was also crawling. Patsy started wondering aloud if the bugs had maybe started there instead and then somehow gained access to the cornmeal. She went on and on about this. Celia didn't say anything but felt like telling Patsy it didn't *matter* where they started, the point was they were everywhere now. An open box of cream of wheat, another of oatmeal, and two of dry cereal on the top shelf were also infested.

Celia stayed that night until the worst of it was cleaned up, then left Patsy vacuuming out the pantry while she cinched the bulging bag tightly and took it outside to the garbage can. As she dropped it in, she imagined all the bugs inside it, still teeming with life, probably still multiplying, all of them closed up inside that plastic bag with all that food. What a night they would have! She clamped the lid of the garbage can down tightly. She thought of the vacuum cleaner bag also—would the force of the suction kill them all, or would they crawl out and start all over again? Maybe they would crawl down the basement stairs to her apartment.

After she went back to her apartment, she kept seeing visions of her own cupboards overrun with bugs. She checked them all carefully to make sure Patsy's bugs hadn't already found their way downstairs to her kitchen. And later during the night she kept waking up with a prickly feeling, as if things were crawling all over her skin. She remembered the crunch of the bug against her thumbnail. Finally she got up and washed her hands a long time, then took something to make her fall asleep.

"They said they wouldn't stay long," Patsy was saying on the telephone now.

Celia had no idea what she was talking about. In remembering the bug incident, a thought popped into her mind: She had a partly used bag of cornmeal in her cupboard right now that she needed to check on. She scolded herself for not sticking it in the freezer after she opened it. She should probably go ahead and throw it out just to be on the safe side.

"So they'll be here in about thirty minutes if that's all right with you," Patsy said.

"I'm sorry. I missed part of that," Celia said. "The TV is up kind of loud. Who did you say was coming?"

Patsy raised her voice a little. "The people who are buying Lloyd's house next door. They made an offer on it yesterday, and I guess it's all settled now. Lloyd called this morning from Atlanta to tell us. He's sure glad to have it sold. They want to move in sometime next month."

Celia didn't see what any of this had to do with her. "Well, that's good. And so . . . they're coming over in thirty minutes, you said?"

"Right."

"Well, okay, but why do I need to know? Do you need me to do something?"

"Well, I thought you'd want to know. I didn't want to just show up at your door with two total strangers."

"At my door? You mean they're coming *here* to my apartment? What for?"

There was a pause, but when Patsy spoke again she gave no sign of impatience. She was like that, steady and dull. If somebody told her to, she'd repeat something twenty times in her loud, husky monotone and never once sigh or ask why. "They want to see the layout of your apartment," she said now, a little slower and even louder, no doubt thinking that would help Celia catch it this time around. "They're planning to finish out Lloyd's basement and make an apartment down there like we did, and they want to see how we did ours. The woman's brother is a handyman, and he's going to do most all the work for them. They want to get started on it soon as they can. I told them Milton could probably help some, since his hernia's all healed up now."

As if they were interested in Milton's hernia, Celia thought. More than anything she wanted to get back to *Pride and Prejudice,* then eat her macaroni and cheese in peace and try to get this long day behind her, this day that had twisted itself all out of proportion. If her whole life were a novel, as she often mused, this one day alone would take up at least four chapters. She wanted to finish the last few paragraphs, not drag it out longer. She sure didn't want two strangers coming to look around in her apartment.

But it was such a little thing, she didn't see how she could say no. "I really wasn't planning on company tonight," she said, then paused. "They said they wouldn't stay long?"

"I can ask them to wait for an hour or so if you'd rather," Patsy said. "They were wanting to drop in right away but said they could come around eight or so if that would suit you better. Or they could come tomorrow sometime. And you sure don't need to go to any trouble straightening things up. They're just—"

"No, no, it's not that," Celia said. The fact was, she kept things so neat she didn't need to do any straightening up. She was a little offended that Patsy would even suggest such a thing. "Oh, okay. Thirty minutes did you say? Tell them to come on, I guess."

"Well, I really don't need to tell them anything," Patsy said. "I said I'd call back if they needed to wait, but if it was okay with you, then I wouldn't call and they'd know they could come on."

"Fine, fine," Celia said. Honestly, Patsy Stewart had to be the most tedious person on the face of the earth. It was a wonder Milton hadn't died of boredom over the years. Of course, he wasn't much more exciting than she was. For fun, Milton Stewart shelled pecans. He had a friend across town who had pecan trees in his yard, and Milton brought them home by the sackful. Then every night after supper he sat in his recliner in front of the television and shelled them. That's what Patsy had told her. Every single night. He went over and got them during November and December and stored them in huge washtubs in the basement, then spent the rest of the year shelling them, a small bowlful every night.

Oh yes, the Stewarts led a reckless, zany life upstairs. Real party animals. Celia had no complaints, though. Milton was not only meticulous about his method of shelling pecans, using a toothbrush to clean out between all the little grooves, but he was also generous. He regularly gave Celia sandwich bags full of them, which she sometimes used in cookies but more often ate right out of the bag.

Evidently the people who were buying the house next door couldn't wait the entire thirty minutes, for they were there in twenty. The macaroni and cheese was in the oven baking when Celia heard the doorbell ring upstairs. She stopped *Pride and Prejudice* right as Elizabeth Bennet was tromping through muddy fields on her way to Netherfield to visit her sister Jane, who had taken ill while visiting the Bingleys. It had always puzzled Celia that the detail of Elizabeth's muddy shoes was never dealt with once she arrived at Netherfield.

She knew that when she restarted the movie, Elizabeth would be sitting beside Jane in one of the bedrooms, but whether Elizabeth had taken off her shoes at the door and was going around in her stocking feet or whether she had gotten a rag and brush and already cleaned them up, or perhaps had borrowed an extra pair from Bingley's sister or was wearing Jane's shoes or . . . Well, none of these possibilities was offered. The omission of this detail was one of the few imperfections in the movie in

Celia's opinion, and it surprised her how much it bothered her every time she watched it. No doubt the director of the movie was a man. A woman would have made sure the matter of the muddy shoes was settled.

A minute later she heard voices outside her front door, which actually faced the Stewarts' backyard, and then two short rings of the doorbell. She was glad Patsy had brought them around that way instead of coming downstairs through the basement and knocking on the hall door next to her bathroom, as she sometimes did when she had a question about something. The front door gave a better presentation of her apartment, Celia thought.

Celia opened the door and immediately wished she could slam it in their faces. Patsy had failed to mention that they would be bringing a baby with them, but there they stood, the happy little all-American family, smiling at her, all except the baby, who was staring about wide-eyed. Words were already spilling out of the woman's mouth about how much they appreciated this and they wouldn't stay but just a few minutes and they surely didn't want to inconvenience her and so forth and so on. Patsy stood behind them like a humorless chaperon. Celia clenched her teeth and stood aside so they could all enter.

"Here's your paper," Patsy said, handing it to Celia. "I picked it up for you." Celia thanked her and tossed it onto the couch. She had been in such a hurry to get to tennis practice this morning that she hadn't brought it in and then hadn't even noticed it when she came home later. She was ready to cancel the subscription anyway. Even though she still did a little writing for it from time to time, the Derby *Daily News* bored her.

The couple looked to be close to Celia's own age, the woman a little on the plump side but with shiny dark hair, perfectly straight white teeth, and enormous glamour-girl eyes. Patsy was introducing the couple in her slow, ponderous way, but Celia's mind was in such a state that all she caught was the woman's first name—Kimberly. The woman glanced up at the man and then cocked her head and smiled down at the baby, shifting into the silly kind of talk adults use with babies. "And this is baby Madison. Can Madison give the nice lady a smile?" Celia barely noticed the man except that he was tall. She tried not to look at the baby, but she couldn't help it. Madison—girl or boy, Celia couldn't tell at first—suddenly let out a string of gibberish, most of it unintelligible except for the last two words, which were very clearly "my ball." The baby appeared to be well over a year old, probably walking by now, which Celia hoped her parents wouldn't let her do inside her apartment.

Celia nodded and introduced herself by first name only. She didn't offer to shake hands, and neither did Kimberly, who was busy pulling the baby's hood back and smoothing its dark hair, which had a tiny white bow clipped in it. So evidently it was a girl. Celia looked away. This was all she needed today. It came to her suddenly that this was the first time a baby had ever been inside her apartment, at least a real baby. Her dreams didn't count.

"Go ahead and look around," she said. "I'm watching something in the kitchen." And she turned and left them.

She stood for a moment against the kitchen counter with her eyes closed, then filled the sink with sudsy water and slowly set about washing up the things she had used to make the macaroni and cheese. Breathe in and out nice and slow, she told herself, and they'll be gone before you know it. *And don't look at her anymore!*

As they proceeded through the apartment, she heard most of Patsy Stewart's commentary: "So Milton added this closet here to get rid of the wasted space" and "These are all new windows." And a few seconds later, "We found this carpet at a close-out sale, and Milton laid it by himself. It's made in these big squares so you can replace just one if you stain it." Then, "Lots of apartments only have showers, but Milton wanted a tub down here. He did all the plumbing himself."

Patsy was clearly enjoying herself, reciting all the wonderful things she and Milton had done to make the apartment nice, plus the added bonus of getting to look around and see how Celia was keeping things up. Celia had wondered before if Patsy ever took sneak peeks at the apartment during the day while she was at work. She had to admit that she herself would be tempted to do that if she owned a house and had a renter.

The woman, Kimberly, responded enthusiastically to everything Patsy said. "Oh, how handy!" "Yes, that's very nice." "What a great idea!" "We ought to think about doing this, Bruce." "You don't even feel like you're in a basement down here!" While they were still back in the bedroom, she heard Kimberly say sharply, "No no, don't touch!" and the baby started crying. "Oh, happy day," Kimberly said. "I hope she didn't break it."

Celia thought of all the things in her bedroom that could be broken. She hadn't heard anything fall over, though, and no sounds of glass breaking. On top of her bureau she had a clay figurine of an old Chinese man fishing. Maybe the baby had somehow grabbed the fishing pole, a tiny thing as slender as a toothpick, and snapped it in half. A baby certainly could break that. Or maybe she had knocked the whole figurine onto the floor. On the bedside table next to Celia's most expensive lamp, the one with the porcelain base and hand-stitched shade, was a beautiful sculpture of a nude couple embracing. Surely the baby hadn't broken either of those. Those would have made a loud sound.

Curious and a little worried, Celia quickly dried her hands and started toward the bedroom, only to find the others coming out into the living room again. She saw that the man was now carrying the baby, and Kimberly was holding a silver necklace in both hands, examining the clasp. "She still loves to play with my jewelry," she was saying to Patsy. "She broke my best gold chain last week."

"Maybe you ought to quit wearing it until she outgrows it." This was offered by the man. Typical of a man, Celia thought. Practical as the day is long. Always ready with a suggestion to fix any trouble.

Celia pretended to be checking the thermostat, relieved that it wasn't anything of hers that had gotten broken. While they went into the kitchen to look around, she went into the bedroom to stay out of their way. "Milton found this countertop in a Dumpster over at a construction site," Patsy said. "It was brand-new, but it must have been what was left over. It fit perfectly in here. And all the cabinets came from one of our neighbors. She was remodeling, so she gave us these, and Milton just repainted them."

Kimberly laughed. "Sounds like Milton ought to have one of those home repair shows on TV. Maybe he can help us out, huh, Bruce?"

With hardly a breath, Patsy forged ahead. "And we got a good sale on the refrigerator. It had a dent on the side that's against the wall, so they marked it down two hundred dollars. It has an ice maker, too." It occurred to Celia that Patsy was talking louder than she usually did, probably to make sure that Celia heard it all and would be filled anew with gratitude and admiration for all the talents her paragon of a landlord possessed.

Finally, after Patsy pointed out the second door into the bathroom, the one off the tiny hallway next to the kitchen, they were done. They came out of the kitchen into the living room, and Celia came out from the bedroom. The man, still holding the baby, stopped in front of the first oil painting Celia had ever bought and stared hard at it—a small still life including a vase of delphiniums, a pincushion, a wine jug, a string of beads, and several pine cones, all artfully arranged on a brilliant blue cloth. Celia wished he would step back a little. She could imagine the baby swinging out a fist and knocking the painting off the wall. Or spitting up all over it, though the baby looked a little too old to still be doing that.

Kimberly smiled at Celia and extended her hand. "You don't know how much we appreciate this," she said. "I sure hope we didn't mess up your schedule." Celia assured her they hadn't. "We're anxious to get started on this basement project," Kimberly continued. "My husband has to travel a lot, so we like the idea of somebody living in the basement."

Celia felt a prick of irritation. She hated it when women referred to "my husband" right in the presence of the man himself. Why didn't she just call him by his name. Bruce, wasn't it? "My husband" sounded so proprietorial, as if the woman wanted to remind any single women present that this man was already claimed, rubbing it in: "I have a man, but you don't."

She glanced up at the man, noticing for the first time that though he also had a nice smile and a head full of thick dark hair like his wife, the skin on one side of his neck and jaw was red and shriveled. She saw also that one of his hands bore the same scars. Celia wondered if he'd been in a fire and whether it had happened before or after he and Kimberly had met.

"Nice art you've got," he said, waving a hand around at the walls. "Lots of good stuff." Celia nodded and thanked him. At least he appreciated good art. And really, aside from the scars, he was a nice-looking guy. She looked at Kimberly. Except for the fact that she was considerably heavier than her husband, the two of them actually looked enough alike to be brother and sister. Funny how that so often was the case with married couples.

"You know," the man went on, looking back at the painting and pointing to the blue cloth, "that's the same blue you get when you react a copper ion with ammonia solution. Copper ammonia complex ion—that's the name for it."

Kimberly laughed. "Can you tell Bruce was a science major?"

There, at least she used his name.

Bruce smiled again. "Well, not exactly, but I did take a lot of science and math." Then he looked right at Celia and said, "You can get some beautiful colors in the lab. The barium salts usually make green, and strontium is a crimson red. Sometimes the copper goes to a pale blue instead of the royal blue like in that painting." With his free hand he pointed to the wall and started gesturing. "If you can picture the periodic chart, see, all the elements in the middle will make colors. The ones stacked on the sides will be clear. It's really—"

Kimberly broke in. "Hey, Bruce, we need to go and get out of this poor woman's hair. I'm sure she has more important things to do than stand around listening to you talk about the periodic chart." She held her hands out to the baby. "Here, Madison sweetie, come to Mama. Let's go home and get you to bed."

"My husband travels a lot, too," Patsy said. Such a remark, so ill-timed as to be irrelevant, was typical for Patsy.

But Kimberly touched her shoulder sympathetically and said, "Well, after we move in, we can sit around together and feel sorry for each other." Just then the baby reached up and touched Kimberly's earring. "Oh no, you don't, you little rascal, you," Kimberly said, catching her hand. They thanked Celia again and headed out the door.

"I've got to make up a test tonight," she heard Bruce say to Kimberly right before she shut the door behind them. Celia wondered briefly what kind of job he had that would involve both traveling a lot and making up tests. Maybe he did training sessions for some corporation or chemical tests for a research lab or something.

"Oh, happy day," Kimberly said. "Another late night."

Oh, happy day. Evidently it was a pet phrase of Kimberly's. One of Celia's aunts used to say the same thing. She was pretty sure it was Aunt Molly, though it could have been Aunt Bess. Or maybe it was both of them. Anyway, she knew for a fact that it used to make her grandmother mad to hear it. Her lips would get that same disapproving pucker as when Celia let loose with a bad word. It had always been Grandmother's opinion—and that's all it was, an opinion—that any phrase borrowed from the Bible and used carelessly was equivalent to taking the Lord's name in vain. And she had extended this "conviction," as she called it, to include words from hymns. As if the words to all those silly hymns were inscribed on the stone tablets Moses brought down from Mount Sinai!

"O Happy Day" was somewhere close to the back of *Tabernacle Hymns.* Celia remembered that much, along with the fact that it was on the left side of the page, at the bottom, under "Just As I Am," the hymn they used to sing at the end of every service at Bethany Hills Bible Tabernacle while the pastor begged, cajoled, and wheedled for one more soul to come forward and repent, sometimes stopping between stanzas to tell awful stories of people refusing to come, then stepping outside to get mowed down and killed instantly.

"O Happy Day" was a short hymn the way it was printed on the page, but it had a couple of repeats in it. A phrase from one of the stanzas came to her now as she stood there leaning against the front door: something about "this blissful center, rest." Rest sounded like a good thing to Celia, but something she knew would never be hers in any permanent sense.

As she turned and walked slowly back toward the kitchen, she tried to think of another song to drown out this one. What was that one she had heard so many times on the golden-oldies radio station on her way to and from work? "I can't see me lovin' nobody but you for all my life . . ." But she couldn't think of what came next, and once again a line from "O Happy Day" took over: "Nor ever from my Lord depart, with Him of every good possessed."

Of every good possessed—that was a joke. She often felt possessed all right, but not of anything good. Her grandmother used to talk about people who were demon possessed, had even used those words in connection with Celia's friend Ansell one time. Celia had laughed at her then, but later she found out a demon really could get inside a person's head. It was a demon called guilt. It could make you see and hear awful things, especially at nighttime. And it could take up residence inside you and torment you for years and years.

The hymn rolled on relentlessly, now the chorus: "Happy day, happy day, when Jesus washed my sins away." Celia stopped in the middle of the kitchen and stood very still. She closed her eyes and pictured her mind as a big computer screen. She imagined herself clicking on *Tabernacle Hymns*, then dragging it to the trash can and hitting Empty Trash. In school she had always been grateful for such a good memory. It helped with all the mindless memorizing that had to be done for tests. But it sure had its downside, too. How could it be that she hadn't thought of a certain stupid hymn for almost twenty years, yet here it was, playing through her mind note by note, word by word?

She opened the oven to check on the macaroni and cheese. It was starting to bubble up around the sides, but the timer still had several minutes to go. She went back to the living room, turned the television on again, and restarted the movie. She sat down on the sofa and watched as Elizabeth comforted her sister Jane in her bed at Netherfield. Somehow, though, the movie had lost its appeal for right now. She knew what would come next, and what would come after that, and somehow she wasn't all that interested anymore. After all, this wasn't even a real story about real people.

She picked up the newspaper she had thrown onto the sofa earlier and opened it. Here, these were real stories about real people. She scanned an article on the front page about vandalism at the Field Pea Restaurant over in Filbert, then another one about the low math scores on achievement tests in South Carolina. And here was one about road repairs out on Highway 11. She gave a little laugh. This stuff was about as interesting as what came out of Patsy Stewart's mouth.

As she flipped open the paper to find the editorial page, a circular slipped out and fell into her lap. *COME TO THRIFTY-MART! WE'VE GOT HEARTS!* it announced boldly. Pink and red hearts were splashed all over the front, along with pictures of frosted heart-shaped cakes, heart-shaped boxes of candy, teddy bears, red roses, and such.

Of course. She had almost forgotten that tomorrow was Valentine's Day. It wasn't a day you cared much about when you didn't have anybody to celebrate it with. Now that she thought about it, this was probably the first Valentine's Day in years and years that she would spend alone. Maybe the first one ever. Last year she had gone out to dinner at a nice restaurant in Greenville. Her date owned the floral shop where Connie, Ollie's wife, worked, and Connie had set it all up. She had just *known* Celia would fall madly in love with this guy, and she had talked him up so much to Celia for days before that no one could have possibly measured up.

And speaking of measuring up, it evidently hadn't occurred to Connie to mention not only that the man was about the same height as Celia, who had always been the shortest girl in her class, but also that he was five years younger. He had brought her flowers, which didn't much impress Celia, because she knew he had no doubt taken them from his shop at no cost. They were probably all the leftovers lying around after his helpers had assembled the bouquets that other taller men had bought for their real sweethearts.

He *was* funny, though, Celia had to admit that. She liked his sense of humor a lot, but that wasn't enough to make up for all the other things. At some point during the evening, she had found out he had a cat, and that, along with the fact that when he got his credit card receipt from the waiter he wrote in a chintzy tip, barely even ten percent, so the bill would come out to an even fifty dollars, was enough to make her turn him down when he asked her out again.

Edward, his name had been. Not Ed or Eddie, he had been swift to point out, but Edward. Al had come along shortly after Edward, and though he had lasted longer than Edward, she had ended up dumping him like all the others. It was becoming increasingly clear to Celia that for every single man close to her age, there was also a very good reason for his still being unclaimed.

The timer went off in the kitchen just after Mrs. Bennet arrived at Netherfield with her younger daughters in tow to see how Jane was doing and to pronounce her still too ill to be moved. The camera focused on Mr. Darcy's face as Mrs. Bennet made a pointed comment about "gentlemanly behavior," an area in which she obviously felt Darcy to be lacking.

Darcy's intelligent eyes and dark hair suddenly made Celia think of Bruce, whatever his last name was. Husband of Kimberly and father of Madison, she reminded herself. She wondered briefly what he would give Kimberly for Valentine's Day. She imagined him going to a jewelry store to buy a new gold chain to replace the one Madison had broken. She glanced back at the television and saw that the camera had shifted to Darcy taking a bath. The servant was pouring a large pitcher of water over him. Even soaking wet, Darcy had to be one of the handsomest men Celia had ever seen.

She wondered if one side of Bruce's entire body had been burned, or just his neck and hands. She imagined gently rubbing salve onto his scars.

O happy day, Celia thought as she slowly rose from the sofa to go to the kitchen. I've sunk to fantasizing about fictional characters and married men. And as she prepared to eat her supper, the same bleak thought settled upon her that kept coming to mind more and more these days. She envisioned herself growing old, and doing so alone, without husband or children to love her.

11

A Green Hill Far Away

March was finally almost over. On the last Monday of the month, Celia won her fifth straight tennis match for her new team, and as she came off the court, Bonnie Maggio, her team captain, met her at the gate, slung an arm around her, and proceeded to tell her how well she had played.

It had been a hard match, a three-setter that went to a tiebreak in the third. There had been talk beforehand that her opponent, a muscular thirty-year-old named Donna Cobb, used to play at the 4.5 level but had been out for a couple of years and decided to rate herself down for this season "until she got her game back." In Celia's opinion, the woman's game was back, if she had ever lost it in the first place.

Other teams in the area were complaining loudly about Donna Cobb, saying it wasn't fair that she was playing on a 4.0 team. One team captain had written a letter of protest to the state league coordinator. Bonnie Maggio hadn't said much. She had advised the whole team to keep quiet because they all knew by now that Celia was also probably closer to a 4.5 than a 4.0. If Donna Cobb's team went on to the state championship in May, she had a good chance of being disqualified when the ever-watchful state verifiers came around during one of her matches and saw how good she was. Of course, this was exactly what Bonnie Maggio was worried about concerning Celia, also.

"We pamper our singles players," Bonnie told her now, guiding her toward a chair over in the shade, where several other team members were seated. "Here she is. She did it again," Bonnie called to the other women.

"Hail the conquering hero and all that. Here, y'all take care of our little girl while I go get her something to drink." Bonnie liked to tease Celia about being the youngest player on the team. Except for Anastasia Elsey, who had recently turned thirty-eight, the other team members were all in their forties and fifties.

As Celia's team members congratulated her, Celia noticed that Donna Cobb was standing over by the food, which was spread out on a large wrought-iron table, above which a large multistriped umbrella was mounted. She was talking to a cluster of her own teammates, shaking her head and gesturing angrily. Celia had played a lot of bad losers in her life, but this woman topped them all, questioning line calls, refusing to call out the score when she fell behind, cursing audibly whenever Celia put one away at the net. When it was time to shake hands at the end of the match, she had barely touched Celia's hand before pulling away quickly, as if afraid of contracting hoof-and-mouth disease. She had zipped her racket into its case furiously, then jammed it into her tennis bag and stomped off the court without speaking.

"That is one ticked-off gal," Tammy Elias said. "Losing is probably something she never does."

Celia could see why. She still didn't know how she had managed to pull it off. Donna Cobb could make two of Celia. She walked like a man, and her biceps were huge. Her serve and overhead volleys could take your breath away.

"So glad we could give her this new experience," said Elizabeth Landis. She was sitting in the chair next to Celia. Bonnie Maggio had treated Elizabeth like a queen all season, too, thanking her over and over for "finding Celia for us." The team had all had a good laugh over Elizabeth's story about just happening to mention their need of another singles player to Celia one day at the Trio Gallery.

They still had one match in progress on the second court—the number two doubles—so they all turned their attention back to that. Jane Kimbrell and Gloria McGregor were a strong partnership, but lately they'd been having trouble with consistency and had lost their last two matches. They were now in the third set at five games apiece, having split the first two sets 7–6, 6–7. The team needed this last match for the win.

Bonnie returned with a cup of ice and a can of Coke for Celia and flopped down on the grass beside her to watch Jane and Gloria. Celia was so tired she wasn't sure she could even pop the tab on her Coke. She sat there looking down at it for a minute, wishing she didn't have to go to work this afternoon. She'd love to just go home, shower, and go straight to bed. When she had agreed to play tennis this season, she had never dreamed she would have matches like the one today—not exactly what you would call "recreational tennis."

She lifted her eyes and looked off toward Paris Mountain. This was a beautiful country club nestled among wooded hills and small lakes. Most of the women on the other team lived in the nearby subdivision, an exclusive private community called Gateway Greens on the outskirts of Greenville. They all belonged to the country club and took weekly lessons from a pro, whereas Celia's team, the Holiday Winners, played on borrowed courts at a motel and set up a rickety folding table for the food when they hosted a home match.

Celia's teammates, a mixed lot including everything from an interior decorator to a day-care worker, lived in houses scattered all over Derby, Filbert, and Berea. One of them, a part-time grocery store clerk named Cindy Petrarch, even lived in a trailer. But every time they had had a match so far this season, Celia had come away with the conviction that the women on the Holiday Winners got along better and had more fun than those on the other teams. She liked being part of a ragtag group that nobody took very seriously until after they finished playing them.

Elizabeth Landis must have noticed that Celia's attention wasn't on the doubles match because she leaned over to her and said quietly, "This is a pretty place, isn't it? Everything's so green—the name sure fits." Celia nodded and looked back to the court. The four players were changing sides, which must mean it was now 6–5. She wondered who had won that last game.

"Come on, girls," Bonnie called to them. "You can do it."

"Okay now, if Gloria can just hold her serve," Judy Howell said. Only a week earlier, it had been Gloria who had double-faulted and then blown an easy overhead to lose the last two points of the match.

The first point was short as Jane poached at the net and hit a sharply angled shot that was impossible to return.

"Hang in there, girls," Bonnie said under her breath.

But they lost the next point when they both rushed the net and one of the opponents landed a lob behind them.

Ellen Myers covered her eyes with one hand. "I can't watch this," she said. It was a long point that finally ended when one of the opponents netted an easy return.

"That's like me," Betsy Harris said. "Luck up on the hard ones and miss the easy ones."

"Yeah, you ought to be more consistent like me," Judy said. "I miss both kinds."

Gloria won the next point when she passed the net opponent with a line drive down the alley, so now it was 40–15.

"This would sure be a nice time for an ace," Bonnie said. And no sooner had she gotten the words out of her mouth than that's exactly what happened. The serve went in low and hard right down the middle, and the woman receiving it, obviously expecting one of Gloria's signature spinouts near the sideline, couldn't adjust fast enough. She swung late and awkwardly, totally missing the ball.

Bonnie and several of the others were on their feet at once, calling out congratulations and heading for the gate to welcome Jane and Gloria off the court. Betsy Harris announced her intention of checking out the food and walked off in that direction. "Come on, y'all go with me," she called back to Celia and Elizabeth. But Celia couldn't force herself to get up.

"We'll be there in a minute," Elizabeth said, laughing and waving her on. "Save us some."

Celia had been a little wary of Elizabeth Landis ever since Macon Mahoney had talked about going to her church. She sure wasn't interested in being close friends with anybody who went around inviting people to church. She took another sip of her Coke and hoped Elizabeth would get up and leave.

But she didn't. Instead, she took in a deep breath and said, "I love being out here away from town. No factories, no McDonald's, no traffic." She pointed off to the left. "I keep looking out there between those two green hills expecting a shepherd to come out holding a little white lamb. Or maybe a few horses galloping out or a little girl herding geese or something picturesque like that." She held up a hand and smiled. "I know, I know. You don't have to tell me I'm strange. My sister told me that last night on the phone. Came right out and called me strange." She laughed. "Of course, maybe it had something to do with the fact that I was quoting poetry to her, which she despises."

The reference to poetry surprised Celia. She wondered what Elizabeth would say if she knew that her pointing out the green hills of the golf course had caused a line of poetry to spring to her own mind: "There is a green hill far away, outside a city wall." She guessed you could call it poetry. It wasn't a hymn they had sung very often at Bethany Hills Bible Tabernacle, and she couldn't believe she even remembered it and that it had popped into her head out of nowhere. She wondered if they still sang a song like that at churches today, if maybe Elizabeth would know it and be able to hum a few bars.

"Come to think of it, I think the actual word she used was *weird,* not *strange,*" Elizabeth said, still smiling. "I get absolutely no respect from my little sister."

Celia was also surprised that Elizabeth Landis was talking so much. She had always gotten the idea that she was reserved, for she often sat apart from the others, not in an unfriendly sort of way but just keeping to herself, watching. You could tell a lot was going on in her mind, but she didn't let much of it out. At least not usually. But for some reason Elizabeth seemed to have suddenly turned talkative today. Maybe the others were rubbing off on her.

As a group, the team was usually very chatty, with several of the women talking at the same time. And laughing—there was always plenty of that with this bunch. They seemed to know everything about each other and often joked about personal details. "So did you ever wear that black nightgown for George?" one of them might ask, or "Did Carlyle's mother fix Spam again when y'all went over for supper the other night?" or "What did the doctor say about that rash?" They all knew one another's history.

Celia really hadn't thought much about the social part of being on a tennis team. She hadn't realized they would stand around and talk so much before the practices and matches and then eat and talk some more afterward. Of course, she could leave as soon as she finished a match every time, but somehow she found herself hanging around, sometimes almost against her will, it seemed. She'd tell herself to get in the car and *go,* but then she'd delay for a few minutes, and before she knew it, she'd be sitting right in the middle of them, or off to one side more often, like Elizabeth, holding a plate in one hand and a can of pop in the other and listening to the whirl of talk around her. She couldn't get over these women—they all seemed so openhearted and unpretentious, as if they had arrived at the place in life where you didn't have to try to impress anybody.

She hadn't been part of a group for a long time, had in fact taken care to avoid such a risk. You never knew, for instance, when someone would make a high-voltage comment, such as two weeks earlier, when Ellen Myers had been complaining about her youngest daughter, a fourteen-year-old, and her all-night phone marathons with her friends. And Jenny Steel had piped up and said, "Hey, why don't you send her over to stay with Celia for a couple of weeks?" She had looked right at Celia and grinned. "Wouldn't you like a little excitement at your place?"

Celia had felt her spine stiffen and her face force itself into a smile as the others had laughed. Naturally Ellen and Jenny had no way of knowing that Celia would have a teenager of her own if she hadn't done what she did. None of them could possibly know that the month of March always seemed twice as long to Celia than any other month, that if Celia hadn't done what she did, another child would be having a birthday this month. This year she would have turned fourteen. Or he. Usually in her worst dreams during the longest nights, the child was a boy.

And right before today's match, Carol Sawyer had passed around a picture of her brand-new grandson. Carol had just gotten back from helping out a week at her daughter's house and couldn't quit talking about how sweet the baby was. They had named him Sawyer, too, which pleased her to no end. Celia had pretended to look at the picture when it came to her, but she had really looked down at the sidewalk where they were standing, then passed the picture along quickly.

She hadn't expected so many women to be on the team in the first place, which naturally intensified the socializing part. When Elizabeth had first invited her to join, she had imagined a team of around six or eight players, not fifteen. That was before she knew that for every match five courts were going at the same time—three doubles and two singles— so you had to have plenty of extra players available. She had learned all fourteen of her teammates' names by now, but she was still sorting out all the relatives. Since she was the only one who wasn't married, everybody else had other names connected with theirs—husbands, children, sons-in-law, daughters-in-law, even grandchildren.

Anastasia Elsey, who wore a perky ponytail and form-fitting tops that showed off her well-endowed figure, was the only other one who didn't have children besides Celia, but Anastasia was married. She and her husband were "waiting," she had told them all, several times. They wanted to have their house paid off before they had children, which would happen in two years, when she was forty. She cited case after case of women she knew who had babies in their forties.

People who had their lives overplanned like that annoyed Celia, but at least it made for one less person talking about her kids all the time. Not that Anastasia had any trouble finding other things to talk about. Though they all tolerated her good-naturedly, even teased with her, Celia had seen looks pass between some of the others when Anastasia got going.

None of them seemed to mind that Celia was quiet, and they didn't ask a lot of probing questions, so she was glad for that. They were probably relieved that she didn't require a lot of attention. They were all friendly, except for Nan Meachum, who was frequently in a bad mood—"the team melancholic," Bonnie Maggio called her. Nan had a sharp wit, though, and could be incredibly funny when she wasn't mad at something or somebody.

Elizabeth wasn't talking anymore now but seemed to be studying her teammates, who were gathered around Jane and Gloria. Betsy Harris walked back from the food table holding a plastic plate filled with chips, dip, celery, a sandwich, some grapes, and a brownie. "They don't do food as good as we do," she said, biting into a celery stick. "But I decided to be a martyr and try to choke it down anyway." She grinned and walked on to meet the others. "Time to eat!" she called out to them. "I volunteered to be the taste tester in case of food poisoning."

Elizabeth smiled, then turned to face Celia and took a deep breath. "Okay, I can't put it off any longer. I have something to ask you." She licked her lips nervously. "Two things, really."

Celia felt her heart sink. She was pretty sure she knew what was coming, and she started trying to formulate an answer. *No, I usually work on Sundays. No, I'm out of town a lot on the weekends.* This last one wasn't really true, but she had been known to get in her car sometimes and take a long drive on a Sunday afternoon. But, thankfully, she was wrong about Elizabeth's question.

"Do you ever let people buy things in installments?" Elizabeth said. The words poured out as if they had been pent up a long time.

Because her mind had been on another track, it took a moment for Celia to understand. "Oh . . . you mean at the gallery? Well, yes, we've done that before," she said. "It's not something we broadcast, but if people ask, we can almost always work something out."

"I was afraid you'd . . . well, I didn't really think the artists would go for that," Elizabeth said. "It's not the same when you get your money a little bit at a time instead of all at once." She went on to tell Celia about the piece she had her eye on. It was Ollie's painting of *Little Tweed Creek,* which Celia had put back out on display several weeks ago. Elizabeth had seen it when she came to the opening of Angela Wortheimer's watercolors, and it seemed she hadn't been able to get it out of her mind since. "I even dreamed about it last night," she told Celia. She could pay a hundred dollars a month for the next year, she said, if the gallery could agree to that. She'd understand, too, if there had to be some kind of carrying fee added on.

"Well, stop by sometime, and we'll see what we can do," Celia said. She'd have to talk with Ollie, of course, but she was sure he would agree. No one else had shown much interest in the piece.

"Does that mean . . . well, can you hold it for me?" Elizabeth said. "Say if you go in to work this afternoon and somebody comes in and wants to buy it and can pay the whole amount right now, would you tell them it was already spoken for?" She was sitting forward a little in her chair now, looking at Celia hungrily as if her answer would be the climax in a long suspenseful plot.

"Well, I have to talk to Ollie about it first, but I don't think you have anything to worry about."

"Could I come in this afternoon? I mean, I hate to seem pushy, but do you think you could check on it today?" Elizabeth suddenly seemed embarrassed by her eagerness. She shook her head and sat back in her chair. "Sorry. I need to calm down, don't I? It's just that I'm subbing at Derby High the rest of this week, so today's my only free day, and I really, *really* want this painting. I'd hate to think I'd finally gotten up the nerve to ask you about it and then somehow missed my opportunity."

The rest of the team had drifted off to the food table by now. Celia wasn't all that hungry, but she thought she might like a little bit of the fruit and maybe a brownie. Forcing herself up from her chair, she told Elizabeth to come in sometime around four, and she'd try to have an answer for her. "Or you could call if you'd rather," she said. "That might save you a trip."

Elizabeth's face clouded. "If a hundred a month isn't enough, tell him I could maybe pay two hundred some months."

"No, no, I meant in case I can't get in touch with him today," Celia said. "Don't worry. I'll hold the painting for you." She was a little amused by Elizabeth's almost childlike desperation, but she sympathized, also. She herself had wanted certain pieces of art so much that she had lost sleep over them and had been willing to spend a lot more than she should to buy them. She had bought things through the gallery by paying in installments, also, had put horrible strains on her budget so she could get yet another painting or sculpture. Sometimes she would lie awake at night and mentally rearrange all the things on her walls to fit in another piece she especially wanted. Her walls were full of nail holes from all the times she had moved paintings around.

She wondered if it was similar to what Connie, Ollie's wife, had told her about working at a dress shop one time. Connie had filled all her closets to the point of bursting because she brought home so many new clothes. She finally decided to quit her job and go to work for a florist. "I'd get so frustrated every morning getting dressed," Connie had said. "There was simply too much to choose from." At her new job she wore mostly pants and a T-shirt under a blue smock. She had given a lot of her clothes away and claimed to be much happier and more balanced now. She wasn't as tempted to bring home floral sprays as she had been new outfits.

But it wasn't the same thing at all. Art was totally different from clothing. In Celia's opinion you could never have too much art. Art wasn't something you bought to adorn yourself for public show. It was something you took home to expand and elevate your soul.

If the national economy took a dip, it was Celia's thinking that that was the perfect time to buy something beautiful to look at instead of hoarding your money and watching the stock market reports. She had gently expressed this opinion to more than one potential buyer at the gallery who was hesitating because his investments had recently lost money.

And she got different responses from different people. One woman, she recalled, had turned to her, her face blooming with joy, and breathed, "Yes, you're absolutely right. I'll take it home with me right now." And she had quickly written out a check for over three thousand dollars. Another collector, however, an elderly man who wore an eye patch, had wheeled on her and snapped, "It's attitudes like that that lead to bankruptcy!"

Elizabeth rose from her chair now and walked with Celia over to the food table. "Oh, and the other thing I wanted to ask you about," she said, stopping, and again Celia felt a heavy sense of dread as she prepared for an invitation to church. But, again, she was wrong.

"I'm supposed to speak to a poetry club in May," Elizabeth said, "and I wondered if you'd be interested in coming." She rolled her eyes and made a face. "Not to hear me, but . . . well, I have an ulterior motive." Celia didn't say anything. She knew all about religious people and their ulterior motives.

"My part of the meeting is supposed to be about poetry and art," Elizabeth continued. "I'm supposed to show some pictures of famous works of art and discuss the poems that have been inspired by them. It's not supposed to last very long, only about fifteen or twenty minutes—that's what I was told." Celia still didn't say anything. She really didn't know much about poetry and didn't have any particular interest in learning. She also didn't see where this was leading.

She must have been frowning because Elizabeth added, "I know, it does seem impossible, doesn't it? I mean, how can you even talk about *one* painting and poem in that amount of time? But I'm planning to do a few shorter poems, certainly not that long one about Seurat's *Sunday* painting and probably not even Ferlinghetti's poem about *The Kiss,* even though that one is really intriguing the way it turns around at the end. I'm thinking I'll probably do Williams' poem about Demuth's *Number Five* painting and Anne Sexton's *Starry Night* poem for sure and maybe one other one. Maybe Auden's poem about Brueghel's *Fall of Icarus.*" She shook her head. "I'll just barely have time to mention a couple of things about each one, but I think I'd rather do it that way than spend the whole time on one, you know?"

Celia nodded but still didn't say anything. She knew about the paintings—anybody who knew anything about art history would recognize those—but the poems were a mystery. She hadn't heard of any of them. She had no idea that anybody sat around writing poems about famous paintings.

One thing this tennis team was showing her more and more was that these women had a lot of experiences she didn't know anything about. In a way she envied them for the fullness of their lives, for their maturity, for letting their hair turn gray without apology as they went right ahead enjoying life. There was a lot to be said for being in your forties and fifties, she had decided. She wished like everything that as she got older she could have that same depth, that placid acceptance of life's ups and downs, that sense of security and the ability to throw her head back and laugh.

" . . . and suggested we do some sort of assignment just for fun," Elizabeth went on. "I told her I could maybe bring in a painting of my own and talk about it a little and then let the women try writing poems about it. They'll work on them at home and bring them back to the next meeting to read."

Celia nodded again. She was trying really hard to follow all this.

"But then I had another idea, a much better one . . . if you think you'd have time to do it." Elizabeth was talking a little faster now. "And if you don't, I promise I'll understand, but it shouldn't take long, really. I don't want you to feel—"

Elizabeth stopped and took another deep breath. "Okay, I'll get to the point. I was wondering if they'd let you bring something from the gallery, some painting you particularly like maybe and would feel comfortable talking about, and then after my part of the meeting, you could show the work and speak for a few minutes about it, point out some things about the technique and style and maybe even tell something about the artist. They might have some questions, too, and you could answer those." She stopped talking abruptly, her eyes full of hope.

So that was it. A speaking engagement. Celia had never heard of a poetry club around here. She wondered if it was held over in Greenville. The small outlying towns of Filbert, Derby, and Berea didn't exactly strike her as centers of literary pursuits.

"Hey, you two, y'all better quit talking and come get some food before it's gone!" Cindy Petrarch called to Celia and Elizabeth from the food table.

"Yeah, Betsy's filling up her second plate," Darla Smith said. Neither Cindy nor Darla had played that morning but had come to watch. Looking at them both, dressed nicely in slacks, pretty sweaters, and jewelry, with their hair neatly combed, Celia suddenly remembered how sweaty and disheveled she felt and how she needed to get home to shower and clean up before she went to work.

"Let me think about it," she said to Elizabeth. "I can probably come up with something. The meeting's next month, did you say?"

"No, not till May," Elizabeth said. "So you've got plenty of time. It's always the third Monday night of the month. You wouldn't have to speak long . . . and we always have refreshments afterward." As if that would be the clinching point, thought Celia.

Elizabeth laughed. "Not that you strike me as the kind of person who would be swayed by the enticement of refreshments."

Celia laughed, too. She couldn't help it. She had to admit something to herself. Church attendance notwithstanding, she liked Elizabeth Landis.

She liked her a lot. In a lot of ways the two of them seemed to think alike. "Well, I was beginning to wonder if I looked like a will-work-for-food kind of person," she said.

They locked eyes for the briefest of moments, then turned and headed toward the food table together.

12

With Every Morning Sacrifice

It was about two weeks later, on a Saturday afternoon, that Celia unlocked the front door of her grandmother's house in Dunmore, Georgia, and stepped into the living room. The house had a sweetish medicinal smell, like a mixture of rotting fruit and Vicks VapoRub, with a touch of something else slightly rancid, like old bacon grease.

She knew that the phone lines between her aunts' houses had been buzzing with spiteful, gossipy complaints about how long it was taking her to get around to coming to Dunmore to see about her grandmother's property. Even Aunt Beulah had finally called her sometime in mid-March to find out when she was coming, speaking gently but insistently. "We're afraid somebody's going to break in and do mischief to Sadie's things" was how she put it.

Celia had been tempted to snap back with "Hey, I didn't ask to be named sole inheritor." But she couldn't bring herself to be rude to Aunt Beulah. As for anyone breaking into her grandmother's house, well, that was laughable in Celia's opinion. If you were intent on robbery, you sure wouldn't target a pitiful little tin box of a house beside a railroad track, not if you had any sense.

She had known she couldn't put off the job indefinitely, however, and besides, the property was paid for, so there was at least a small chance of selling it and making a little money, though Celia still couldn't imagine who would want to buy it. But at last she had made arrangements with Ollie to be away from the gallery both Saturday and Monday so she could drive to Georgia and check things out. "So Cecilia's gonna go gloat over all her loot, huh?" he had said, and Celia had rolled her eyes and said, "Yeah, right, all my loot."

So here she was surveying her domain. Walking through the house took all of two minutes, and when she returned to the living room, she felt so tired and weighed down from all the dark, dank memories lurking in every corner that she locked the door again, got into her car, and drove to Dunmore's only motel, a family-owned enterprise at the edge of town called the Sunny Side Up. She checked in, then bought a small pizza at Little Bud's Pizza Parlor across the road and took it back to her motel room. While she sat on the bed and ate her pizza, she used the remote control to switch among the four stations that came in clearly on the television.

A little later she called Aunt Beulah from the motel and asked if she thought she could come over to her grandmother's house tomorrow and help her go through some things. The thought of being cooped up in that little house by herself gave her the creeps. At least it was warm and springlike outside, so she could open up the doors and windows to let in some fresh air.

Aunt Beulah agreed to come over the next day, but not till after church, of course. She hesitated before asking Celia timidly if she'd like to come to church with her, to the Believers of Christ Church on the other side of Dunmore. "Or maybe you were planning to go to Bethany Hills, since that's right down the street," she said. Celia let her know quickly that she hadn't planned any such thing and would just meet her at Grandmother's house the next afternoon whenever Aunt Beulah could get there.

"Oh, but we want you to eat dinner with us," Aunt Beulah said. "I couldn't stand it if I thought you had driven all the way here from South Carolina and then didn't eat at least one meal with us. Can't you come over first and let me feed you some pot roast? We usually eat sometime around one. I always put our dinner in the oven on Sunday morning, so it doesn't take too long to get it on the table once church lets out." She paused, then added, "It would just be your uncle Taylor and me and you." She was smart, Aunt Beulah was, no doubt realizing that Celia wouldn't want to take a chance on having to eat at the same table with any of the other aunts.

Celia put her off, though, claiming the need to use every minute on Sunday to go through stuff before she had to leave Monday afternoon and promising Aunt Beulah she'd come over for a meal when she came back to Dunmore this summer to tie up all the loose ends.

"But what will you eat?" Aunt Beulah asked. Regular meals had always been a major concern among Grandmother and her sisters. Celia put her off again, assuring her she'd be fine, that she'd probably grab something at Popinjay's Burgers on her way over to her grandmother's house.

Finally she got off the phone with Aunt Beulah and resumed flipping channels on the television. Sometime after midnight she sat through a mindless sci-fi movie called *Alligator*, in which a man-eating alligator lived in a sewer and terrorized Chicago. On another weekend night it might have been funny, something to laugh about later with Ollie or Connie at the gallery or maybe Elizabeth Landis or Bonnie Maggio after a tennis match, but tonight she simply sat on the bed and thought about what a sad thing it was that people spent time and money making such movies and, even sadder, that other people actually watched them from beginning to end.

Every time a commercial came on, though, she quickly changed to another channel. Commercials made her jittery now, ever since that one she had seen for the first time a month or so ago. She'd had no idea they made commercials like that. It had come out of nowhere, starting deceptively with a little soft piano music and two hands scooping out two holes in some dirt. Then each hand dropped a seed into one of the holes and smoothed the dirt over it.

A second later the hand on the left had dug back into the earth and removed the seed, leaving an empty hole, but on the right a little sprout had appeared, then green leaves. And still the innocent tinkly piano music had continued, and Celia hadn't caught on, although she should have seen what was coming and rebuked herself afterward for being so slow. The rest of it happened so fast she couldn't even reach for the remote to turn it off.

On the side of the screen where the little plant was growing came a swift succession of superimposed images—first, a closeup of a baby laughing, then one crying, then one a little older reaching up to slap at the keys of a piano, then one chewing contentedly on a cob of corn, then a toddler taking his first unsteady steps, then a preschooler smashing his face against a windowpane, then an older child running through a sprinkler, and finally a little girl stooping to bury her face inside the golden cup of a daffodil. And as the piano music faded away, the words *Choose Life*, along with an 800 number, came across the screen, and a voice said soothingly, "Facing an unexpected pregnancy? Call for help." By the time it was over, Celia knew what it must feel like to fall from a great height and land on a hard, immovable surface. The commercial probably hadn't lasted more than a minute, but it had been a long paralyzing minute.

Before that, she had always been able to see the dangerous commercials coming. There would be some giveaway image at the very beginning, a baby sitting inside a tire, for example, or a little kid eating breakfast cereal maybe, something that would warn her: *Turn it off!* Pretty soon she responded almost instinctively, before the picture even showed up on the screen. She had even grown a little smug about the way she was able to protect herself by sensing what was coming. And then along came that stupid Choose Life commercial to catch her off guard.

And movie theaters—she had grown wary of those, too, ever since Ward had taken her to *The Cider House Rules,* that awful movie about the orphanage that was also an abortion clinic. She had been ambushed by that one, had felt like she was being slowly asphyxiated as she sat trapped in the middle of a row at the theater.

She didn't get much sleep that night, nor had she expected to, not within the city limits of Dunmore, Georgia. She got up early Sunday morning and headed to her grandmother's house after eating a package of small cake doughnuts from the vending machine in the motel lobby. She knew better than to try to get anything to eat at Haynie's Dinette because Haynie Peeler had always prided herself on not opening her doors on Sunday. She knew something like that would never have changed over the years here in Dunmore.

By eight o'clock Celia was at her grandmother's house sorting through things, and she kept at it by herself for a good six hours. Her aunt showed up around two, and they worked hard for another four hours. Celia was glad that at least the refrigerator had already been emptied and cleaned. The aunts had done that when Grandmother had gone into the hospital two weeks before she died.

At six o'clock Aunt Beulah apologized profusely for having to leave but explained to Celia that it was her week to staff the library table at church before and after the evening service and then work in the nursery during the service, and she just hated to ask someone to substitute for her because it would mean that person wouldn't get to hear the sermon.

"They do try to pipe in the preaching to the nursery," she said, "but you only get to hear bits and pieces of it in all the hubbub." She chuckled and added, "Some of those babies can really set up a ruckus. Why, the last time I was on nursery duty, this one baby—"

But Celia cut her off quickly, thanking her for her help and telling her she understood completely. She went to the front door ahead of her aunt and held the screen door open for her, repeating her thanks and saying whatever nonsense came to mind just to fill up space until Aunt Beulah was out of the house and safely on her way. Celia left a couple of hours later, since the electricity was turned off and daylight was fading.

On Monday morning when she unlocked the house, she felt the smallest whisper of hope as she realized she'd be leaving Dunmore this afternoon. Only a few more hours, thank goodness, and this trip would be history. Around ten o'clock she folded over the flaps of the last box of old books and magazines and glanced at her watch.

The Holiday Winners would have already started their weekly match back in Derby by now. She wondered how it was going. Nan Meachum was having to play singles today since Celia wasn't there, but Celia knew she would do fine. Besides having a strong all-around game, Nan was so cranky she often unnerved her opponents, closing out matches before anybody else had even started a second set. It struck Celia that exactly two weeks ago right now, she had been playing the first set of her exhausting tennis match against Donna Cobb. She shook her head. *That* had been an entertaining little lark compared to what she had been doing here at her grandmother's house for the past couple of days.

She walked to the window facing the railroad track, lifted the cheap vinyl window shade, and gazed out toward the woods beyond. It wasn't much of a woods, really. The whole scene looked bleak and beaten down. The pine trees were scraggly and stunted along the track, and a small mis-shapen dogwood tree, looking like some kind of mutant species, leaned sideways at a crazy angle and bore only a smattering of pink blossoms along a couple of scrawny branches. Along the banks of dry red dirt grew a snarl of blackberry bushes. No doubt they would produce their usual abundance of fruit later in the summer, but right now they looked totally unmotivated.

Celia thought about the small deep pond farther back in the woods. She could imagine its waters having stagnated over the years, now emitting a greenish vapor that floated through the woods like a phantom. A little boy had drowned in that pond years before Celia had come to live here, and her grandmother had warned her about it constantly. Once during her senior year of high school, out of spite, Celia had run off into the woods one night, knowing Grandmother would follow her with a flashlight, which she had.

Celia had simply circled back to the house and was soaking in the bathtub by the time her grandmother came back. She remembered feeling so proud of herself as she heard footsteps come down the hallway toward the bathroom, then stop outside the door. "Celie, you in there?" her grandmother had called sharply, rattling the doorknob, which was of course locked.

Celia remembered scolding herself at the time for laughing out loud, for as soon as her grandmother had started back down the hall, she realized she should have kept absolutely quiet. *That* would have been the perfect answer to the question. Ansell was always telling her that silence was the best way to show contempt—not answering back, not even laughing. Ansell had always told her she was too quick to offer an apology or explanation. "You don't owe anybody anything," he was always saying. "Never let people figure you out. Always keep 'em guessing."

Before she left for home this afternoon, Celia thought now, maybe she would walk into the woods and see if the pond was still there. But she immediately dismissed the idea. There would be no pleasure in seeing it again. The thought of worrying her grandmother sick didn't hold any of its former appeal, and all Celia could picture now as she remembered the pond in the woods was the beam of a flashlight bobbing up and down along its edges in the black of night.

The storage building that used to be her grandparents' little neighborhood grocery store was off to the right, next to the narrow dirt road that led out to the abandoned Boy Scout camp. The store had always been a sad sight, in Celia's opinion, and it was even more so now, with its peeling paint, sagging screen door, and grimy windowpanes. Sitting a little lopsided on cement blocks, it appeared that the ground had shifted, or maybe the building itself had. Maybe the cement blocks had gradually sunk deeper into the earth over on the side of the store where her grandfather used to keep the heavy cooler of soft drinks and the freezer of ice cream and Popsicles. Anyway, the perspective seemed slightly off, as if a child had drawn it without the aid of a ruler.

My inheritance, Celia thought. *All mine.* But all the humor had gone out of it now that she was actually here. She shifted over a little and looked out the other direction, toward the back of the house where the garage stood. Her grandmother had always called it "the barn" because it was big enough for a car, a truck, a dilapidated tractor, all her grandfather's old tools, and a couple of animal stalls, where her grandmother had at one time kept a few goats. It had two broad doors that hung crookedly and were secured by a padlock, if *secured* could be used of such a flimsy arrangement.

It surely wouldn't take much effort to break down one of those doors, both of which appeared ready to fall off the hinges. Celia wondered briefly where the key to the padlock was. Maybe it was one of the extra ones she had gotten from the lawyer—on the cheap key ring with the little glow-in-the-dark plastic disk on it stamped with the words *Jesus saves.*

She wasn't at all eager to find the key, though. The thought of opening the barn and having to look at and dispose of whatever ancient, rusted, mildewed junk was out there gave her a sick, oppressive feeling. She had had her fill yesterday and this morning of going through somebody else's useless, worn-out things. And to think, she had just gotten started. She would have her work cut out for her when she came back later this summer to finalize everything.

Celia moved away from the window and walked to the kitchen. She stood in the doorway and looked at the things she had laid out on the old porcelain table the day before, things she had set aside to think about keeping. If someone had asked her months ago what she would want from her grandmother's house, she would have instantly replied, "Not one single thing."

But the tabletop was quite full. It had surprised her to realize how unobservant she must have been when she lived here every day—or rather, how her memory had shut down once she left. All the things on the table were things she remembered her grandmother using regularly, but it was only in seeing them again after all these years that her memory was stirred. She doubted that she would ever have thought of them again if she hadn't come here and started going through Grandmother's cupboards and drawers.

She walked over to the table now and picked up the set of hand-held beaters, with the little crank wheel on the side and the label *Mister Mixer* imprinted on its metal handle. She could picture her grandmother standing right here at this very table holding the top handle of the Mister Mixer tightly with her left hand and turning the little crank with her right hand so that the beaters whirred around in whatever batter she happened to be mixing up, most often corn bread or sweet muffins. Sometimes she used the beaters to whip up evaporated milk, which she would mix in with Jell-O and call dessert. That was about as fancy as dessert had ever gotten at Grandmother's house.

Since her grandmother had had no countertop to amount to anything, the porcelain table served an all-purpose function in the tiny kitchen. Positioned as it was, directly in the center, it took up most of the space, leaving about two feet on all four sides. Depending on which side of the table you were sitting at, you could easily reach over to the stove, refrigerator, sink, or dish cupboard. Grandmother's kitchen made Celia's apartment kitchen back home seem spacious.

She put the Mister Mixer down and picked up one of the plates. She ran a finger around the scalloped edge, then set it back down with the others. She couldn't believe it yesterday when she had seen that the robin's-nest plates were still in the cupboard, all five of them, along with four other plain white plates she had never seen. She didn't care anything about those, but she had set the robin's-nest ones on the table to take home with her. She certainly didn't need any more plates, but somehow she couldn't stand to think of selling them at the yard sale Aunt Beulah was going to help her with when she came back in June, nor of donating them to the Salvation Army if nobody bought them at the yard sale.

Celia sat down wearily at the table and closed her eyes. She hadn't slept well last night, again. She had dreamed a whole string of short troubling dreams, not about babies this time, but about old women. Or rather about one old woman—an old woman chasing chickens through the yard, chopping weeds with a hoe, hanging threadbare clothes on a line, driving an old Mercury Comet, bending over a big black Bible. She had kept waking up all night wishing dawn would come.

Sitting here at Grandmother's kitchen table, Celia could almost imagine that it was twenty years ago and if she opened her eyes, she might see her grandmother, with her blue bibbed apron tied around her waist, which for some strange reason had always appeared to be higher up than a normal person's waist, somewhere around the middle of her ribcage. Under the apron, she'd be wearing a shapeless old dress the color of catfish or gravel.

Biscuits, that's what she'd be pulling out of the oven. She'd scoot them off the baking sheet with a spatula, dumping them into a basket lined with a clean dish towel, then set them on the table along with the old glass syrup dispenser. First you opened up your biscuit and put a pat of butter in the middle and closed it back up. After the butter melted, you laid it open and drizzled the syrup over both halves, then ate it with a fork for breakfast.

But first you prayed, or you sat and tried not to listen as Grandmother prayed, on and on and on. In the background the Christian radio station would be blaring out some gospel song or some rabid preacher's hellfire sermon. But over the top of that, droning on and on, would be Grandmother's voice, flat and businesslike, going through a whole litany of entreaties for divine assistance—everything from weather concerns to Aunt Clara's migraine headaches to the missionary family in Cameroon whose house had burned down.

A sudden knock at the front door startled Celia. It must be Aunt Beulah. She had said she'd drop by today before Celia left. "Come on in!" Celia called, then remembered she hadn't left the front door unlocked this morning. She walked quickly to the living room, and as she swung the door open, she said, "Sorry, I meant to—"

She stopped and stared at the two people standing on the other side of the screen door, neither of which was Aunt Beulah. The man, tall but slight of frame, spoke first. "Good morning. We thought we saw somebody here over the weekend." He was wearing a navy polyester knit sport shirt, the pocket of which was stuffed messily with note paper, two pens, and a pair of glasses. He had a receding hairline, and the hair he did have was as wispy as duck down. Celia had the vague feeling that she knew him.

The woman, almost as short as Celia herself, could have been the man's twin sister except for the extreme difference in height. Here it was again, another married couple who looked alike. At least Celia assumed they were married. The woman's hair, a washed-out brown going to gray, was thin and nondescript, and both of them looked as if a good stout wind could carry them off. She wore a plain white blouse and a denim skirt and carried a small straw purse that gaped open at the top and exposed everything inside, which, like the contents of her husband's pocket, seemed to be stuffed in haphazardly.

The woman did have one arresting feature of her own, though—a pair of amazingly blue eyes, a darker blue than your average blue eyes, with a slight tinge of something close to violet, the color Celia imagined the South Pacific to be, although she had never seen it. Or maybe the summer sky right before twilight in Wyoming, though she'd never seen that, either. "We just wanted to stop by and say hi," she said to Celia. "We knew Sadie real well." She was talking louder than a woman her size normally talked and certainly louder than she needed to. It was a Sunday school teacher's voice.

Celia pushed the screen door open. "Well, sure, come on in. I'm kind of in the middle of—"

"Oh, we're not staying," the woman said, shaking her head and backing up a little, but still talking as loud. "I know how busy you must be. We're not even coming in. We just wanted to let you know we'd be glad to help out in any way if you need us." Then she stopped and shook her head. "Sorry, we forgot to tell you our names."

At that, both the man and woman laughed and started speaking over top of each other, then stopped and laughed again and started all over. It was clear that they were trying to introduce themselves, and out of it all, Celia finally managed to catch the name Davidson, which she guessed to be their last name, and she soon pieced it together that the man was the preacher of Bethany Hills Bible Tabernacle and the woman was indeed his wife. Then it hit her why the man had seemed familiar. He had been the preacher in charge of Grandmother's funeral back in January.

"We just live a few houses down the road," the woman said, waving a hand back over her shoulder. "We'd be happy to help if you need anything. I know all about cleaning out and getting ready to move, believe me. We've done plenty of it ourselves."

Celia stepped out onto the porch and closed the screen behind her. "Well, thanks," she said. "I think I'm fine, though. I'm almost done for now."

The man fumbled in his pocket for a scrap of paper and a pen. "We figure you must be Sadie's granddaughter. She used to talk about you a lot." He peered down at her and smiled, his pen now poised like a newspaper reporter ready to write something down.

Oh, I'm sure she did, Celia was tempted to say. *And I can just imagine some of the things she said.*

"Sorry, I can't remember your name, though," he said. "I sure should because we heard it over and over, but . . ."

His wife swatted him gently on the arm. "Why, it's Celia. Don't you remember?" She looked at Celia and made a face, as if to say, *Men—what would they do without us?*

Her husband smiled and nodded. "Oh yes, of course, that's it. I remember now." He wrote something down, then said slowly, "But since she was your mother's mother, I don't guess your last name would be Burnes, would it?"

"No, it's Coleman," Celia said as she saw her aunt Beulah's green Pontiac pull up in the driveway. Good, she thought, now maybe these people would take a hint and leave so she could get back to work.

But that didn't happen till another full hour had passed, after Aunt Beulah had made the mistake of mentioning an old treadle sewing machine stacked up with all of Sadie's old quilts next to the washing machine, and after the preacher's wife—Denise, her name turned out to be—had expressed great interest in it, thus eliciting an invitation from Aunt Beulah to walk through the house to the back porch to see it. They had ended up removing the whole stack of quilts so that Denise could get a better look at the old sewing machine, and then they had brought them all back out into the living room and unfolded each quilt to examine it front and back.

"You'll want to keep some of these," Aunt Beulah said to Celia, and Denise quickly added, "Oh, absolutely!" Even the preacher seemed to be interested in the quilts, patchwork all of them, which in Celia's opinion were certainly not samples of fine workmanship, though they did possess a simple homespun charm in the style of folk art. It would be fun, she decided, to have one or two at home, among all her good art, to look at every now and then, to remind herself of how ordinary country people used to live. Maybe she should even display one on a wall somehow if she could find a place for it, or maybe get one of those quilt racks. After all, there would be nothing shameful about having a few crafts mixed in with all her art, especially if they were authentic crafts instead of the fake commercial stuff.

"Sadie used to make these when her children were little," Aunt Beulah said, running a finger over a square of pink cotton printed with little white rabbits. Well now, that made even more of a difference, Celia thought. She hadn't realized that her grandmother had made the quilts herself. She didn't remember seeing any of them while she was living here. One more thing she had failed to notice all those years ago. Surely the quilts hadn't been on the back porch right in plain sight back then. "She'd get up early, real early in the morning before anybody else was up," Aunt Beulah said, "and work on them before she fixed breakfast."

The preacher, wearing his glasses now, sat down on a small footstool and examined one of the quilts. "Look at all these stitches," he said, shaking his head. "Think of the time this took."

"She made the squares out of old clothes," Aunt Beulah continued. "I used to give her some of ours. In fact, I'm almost sure this red plaid came from a pair of Jerry's pajamas." Which Celia figured must be why they looked so faded. Most likely the clothes were already ragged with wear by the time Grandmother turned them into quilt squares. Aunt Beulah lifted the quilt to her nose. Celia could imagine thousands of mildew spores pouring into her aunt's lungs. There was no telling how long those quilts had been on the back porch, unprotected from the humid Georgia air. Whatever she decided to keep would have to be dry-cleaned.

"I think this is the best one," Aunt Beulah said. "You ought to put it in the kitchen with your other things, Celie. Here, I'll help you fold it back up." And together they folded it.

"Maybe I'll take a couple of them," Celia said as she headed to the kitchen with the folded quilt. She had her eye on another one that had a white cotton square right in the middle of all the other multicolored ones, stamped with blue letters: *Dean's Pork Sausage.* That one had personality.

The tabletop in the kitchen was almost full, but she moved some things over and placed the quilt next to Grandmother's old brown copy of *Tabernacle Hymns Number Three,* which she had run across quite early in her sorting, back in Grandmother's bedroom on a little table. Everything inside her had told her to throw it in the trash bag or put it in the pile of things to donate to the Salvation Army, but instead she had taken it to the kitchen table. It was, in fact, one of the first things she had set aside to keep.

As she stood at the kitchen table now, staring at the hymnal, she heard the preacher back in the living room, his voice still full of wonder. "Just think of it," he said. "Think of how much sleep she must have sacrificed every morning to make all these."

With every morning sacrifice. Celia touched her finger to the raised design of a small torch on the cover of the hymnal. She knew she could open the book right this minute and find the hymn the phrase came from. Again the thought came to her that she ought to get as far away from this book as she could. She ought to take it out in the woods, throw it into the pond, and let it sink to the bottom. *Take it home and you'll be doomed for the rest of your life,* she told herself. *You'll hear her voice every time you turn around.*

But a few hours later, when she had finally gotten rid of the preacher and his wife, said good-bye to Aunt Beulah, and locked up her grandmother's house, the hymnbook was inside one of the three cardboard boxes she had loaded into the trunk of her car. She started her car, then backed out of the driveway to head out of town, and though she should have peeled off as fast as she could go, for some reason she couldn't begin to explain, she paused once more to look at the house. She imagined her grandmother's hand pulling aside the cheap organdy curtains at the front window, her lips pinched together as she watched Celia drive off.

13

Ten Thousand Charms

By the time she had pulled into the Stewarts' driveway back in Derby and unlocked her door, Celia felt as if she were returning from an assault on Mount Everest. It was odd how physically tiring it could be simply to sort through things in closets and drawers. The lack of sleep no doubt accounted for some of her exhaustion, as well as the emotional strain of being back in Dunmore and handling her grandmother's things.

And guilt—that could wear a person down, too. The whole weekend she had felt bound up and suffocated with guilt in spite of her vigorous attempts to reason it away. *You're free from it all,* she had kept telling herself. *She's not here anymore to point her finger and spout off a long list of no-no's. Sure, you've messed up, everybody has, but it's over and done. Get on with life!* Nothing worked, though. In Grandmother's house she felt something large and dismal looming over her at every turn, glaring at her, rustling around reproachfully behind her back. Her little pep talks were useless.

It took several trips to get everything from the trunk of her car into her apartment. As she set each of the three boxes on the floor of her living room, she wondered again if it wasn't a huge mistake to bring all this stuff home. There was no way to explain why she had kept some of it—the old radio, for instance. Every part of her had screamed out to trash it, yet she had watched her own hand reach down and unplug it, then lift it from Grandmother's nightstand and carry it to the kitchen table. Later, even as a voice inside her was yelling, *You'll regret this!* she had placed it inside one of the cardboard boxes.

Maybe she should leave everything packed up. She could store the boxes in the Stewarts' basement and never have to look inside them. She could take them over right now and put them in the storage area with her other things. She wondered if it would be possible to forget all about them, or if she would wake up through the night and hear faint scrabbling sounds coming from the other side of her basement door. Or maybe eerie strains of old hymns or the soft whir of beaters or the strident tones of a radio preacher's voice. She knew very well what her imagination was capable of.

She suddenly remembered something Ansell used to say to her in his low, lazy voice: "All those years of moral rectitude have warped your psyche, Celia. In the parade of life, you could carry the banner for the Society of Religion-Induced Stress Syndrome." He had loved to taunt her about what he called her "plethora of hang-ups." More than once, though, Celia had suspected it was her religious background that so intrigued him, that without it she wouldn't have been nearly so welcome in his small select circle of friends, that he fancied in their unlikely friendship something of a conquest.

Ansell had always imagined himself a great intellectual, had talked about studying philosophy in college and writing essays and poetry that, once decoded by the critics, would turn the world on its head. Only he wouldn't care, of course. The world could do whatever it wanted. He didn't need its praise, would actually shun it if he got it. He was above all that.

And as for criticism, well, he was like the peak of an ancient pyramid, he used to say, and when it stormed, whether a measly few drops of fault-finding or a gully washer of condemnation, it just ran right down to the base and soaked into the sand. Nothing could touch him up at the top. He would live somewhere in solitude after college, he said, away from the abysmally ignorant masses, and spend his days thinking, reading, and writing. How he planned to finance his hermitic existence was never a topic of discussion, though maybe he should have thought about that part, since his family wasn't wealthy. His father taught math at their local high school, and his mother worked at the Dunmore post office.

Celia checked the car once more, then locked her front door and went into the kitchen to make some popcorn. That would be her supper tonight—a bag of popcorn and a Coke. Her grandmother and Aunt Beulah would be horrified.

She had stopped for a late lunch at a Burger King drive-through sometime around three, about an hour outside of Dunmore, but was so out of it that she had forgotten to tell them to hold the onions and ketchup. As soon as she had realized her mistake, she had stopped along the road and pulled off the onions, then tried to wipe off all the ketchup with a napkin, but it was no good. She could still taste the onion, had even bit down on a little piece she had missed, and the bun was soggy with the ketchup that had already soaked in.

She had eaten a few bites, then thrown the rest away. As she drove on, she wished she had never stopped. She kept seeing the white paper napkins smeared with ketchup, which metamorphosed into splotches of blood on a white sheet, another image that often showed up in her bad dreams. Even after she stopped at a gas station to wash her hands, she couldn't get the bloodstains out of her mind.

That was another thing Ansell had teased her about—her squeamish-ness over blood, which in his opinion was also somehow tangled up with her fundamentalist background and all those songs and sermons about blood. And in his habit of reducing everything to the same level of seri-ousness, he always went on to say that this religious perversion was also undoubtedly the source of her dislike of ketchup and tomato products in general.

Which in turn always led to another of his favorite subjects—what he called her finicky eating habits. "Just give her a chicken wing and some corn bread," he'd drawl to a waiter whenever they drove over to Carters-ville or Rome to eat. He would often order lunch for her when they ate at Haynie's Dinette, adopting a bored tone to underscore his point about the lack of variety in her diet: "One grilled cheese sandwich, fries, and a large Coke." He was always telling her that she was missing out on all the good stuff in the way of food. "Shrimp, onion rings, mushrooms, pasta, tacos . . ." He had memorized a whole list, and if he was in cheerful spirits, he'd really lay it on thick, throwing up his hands in mock dismay. "Why, you don't even like Chinese—no chop suey, no chow mein, no moo goo gai pan!"

But again, Celia had sensed that this was something else he found interesting about her, that if she were to suddenly begin eating anything and everything, part of her novelty would wear off. Glenn and Renee, the other two in what Ansell called their "core four," always took their cues from Ansell, joining in on the teasing or falling silent, depending on his moods. Once Glenn had misread him and poked fun at Celia about something—maybe something she was wearing, she couldn't remember now—and Ansell had almost wrenched his arm out of its socket. She could still see Glenn, kneading his arm and trying to act casual. "Hey, it was a *joke*," he had said, to which Ansell had replied, "So get a new one. That one wasn't funny."

As the popcorn popped, Celia filled a glass with ice, then opened a can of Coke and slowly poured it in. How had she gotten off on Ansell? she wondered. Thinking about him was certainly not the thing to lift her out of her weekend depression. She had been so cautious over the last couple of days in Dunmore, making sure she never drove past his parents' house, and now here she was, letting him mill around inside her head and talk to her, smiling his slow, cynical smile.

Ansell had been the whole reason she had gone to Blackrock College in Delaware. He had an uncle—actually only a half-brother of his mother's—who was on the music faculty there, one of the few adults for whom Ansell seemed to have some measure of admiration, though he had met him only once when he was twelve. From what Ansell had told Celia, this uncle was something of an eccentric, a pianist and composer who had never married and who lived in a house he had designed himself, surrounded by a wrought-iron fence and guarded by two Dobermans. Celia had the idea that Ansell was hoping to insinuate himself somehow into the uncle's good graces, to be invited inside the wrought-iron fence, to win his confidence, perhaps at some point even to live there while he finished up his college courses.

The microwave beeped, and she removed the bag of popcorn, then carefully opened it and watched the steam rise. *Oh, the dreams of youth,* she thought. *They drift up just like that and vanish.* She emptied the popcorn into a bowl and sat down at the kitchen table.

Ansell's uncle had turned out to be an alcoholic, an old tenured professor just putting in his time whenever he could drag himself to campus. Celia would never forget the look on a girl's face, a music student, when she and Ansell went to the music building in search of the uncle's studio a week or so after arriving on campus. They had found the studio, but a girl was in it, sitting on the piano bench practicing a bassoon. "I'm looking for my uncle," Ansell said. "Is he here?"

The girl looked down, apparently from embarrassment, and then reached down to her case as if searching for something. "You mean Professor Gambrell? He's your uncle?" She wasn't looking at them. "Well, uh, no, he hasn't been in today, I don't think—or yesterday, either. He lets us use his studio to practice, but he . . . well, I don't think he's in very often." She straightened, then shrugged. That's when she finally looked right at them, and Celia recognized it at once as a look of pity. Ansell, on the other hand, didn't choose to interpret it that way. He slammed the door shut and pronounced the girl an idiot.

He finally made contact with his uncle a few weeks later, catching him in his studio during what must have been one of his rare appearances. He was with a student, presumably teaching a piano lesson, but was actually slumped in an armchair with his eyes closed while the student played something bombastic, and badly, according to Ansell. They eventually noticed him standing in the doorway, but the uncle couldn't seem to process the information Ansell tried to give him. "I am no one's uncle," he kept saying. "I have no brothers or sisters," and then, incoherently, "I will refer you to my attorney, young man." Ansell tried to act indifferent about it all when he told Celia, but she could sense the flimsiness of the facade. She could hear the anger behind his words, as if he felt betrayed.

Evidently Ansell wasn't cut out for college life, for he lasted only two months. Perhaps inspired by his uncle's example, he began drinking himself into a blind stupor every night and missed most of his classes during the day. He turned on Celia and called her unspeakable names when she tried to talk to him. Something in their relationship suddenly disintegrated, like an airplane exploding in midair, the pieces flying everywhere.

Then one day he simply disappeared from campus. Most of his things were still in his dorm room, but his roommate said he hadn't talked to him in days. Celia remembered the feeling of liberty and happy independence after Ansell left campus, though she wouldn't have admitted it to anybody for the world. She hadn't realized how much he had controlled her life until he was gone, how she was always looking to him to tell her what to do, how she would never make plans on her own until she checked with him. In an upside-down sort of way, she supposed that Ansell had simply replaced her grandmother. She talked to his mother on the telephone a few times and tried to sound sorrowful and comforting, though deep inside she felt ashamed for her insincerity.

He was finally discovered hitchhiking somewhere in West Virginia, and his parents drove up from Georgia to pick him up and take him home. His mother called Celia to tell her he had been found and to let her know they were coming to the college to pack up his things before heading home.

Celia didn't even see him to say good-bye. She made sure she was holed up in a distant corner of the library the morning they came. How curious a thing their friendship was. With a great sense of wonder, she kept remembering how only months earlier he had almost torn someone's arm off for what he took to be an insult to her. And now that he was leaving college, the only feeling she could muster was relief.

Shortly after Christmas that year, a holiday Celia had spent mostly alone on a deserted campus, her grandmother sent her a newspaper clipping telling of Ansell's death. He had taken his father's car to Florida and driven it off a bridge somewhere. "Alcohol and drugs were thought to have played a part in the accident," the clipping reported at the end.

It had always puzzled Celia somewhat that she hadn't felt more guilt and responsibility over Ansell's death, but after a brief shocking jolt, she had put it behind her. He had made his own choices—that was a fact. It saddened her but also educated her. When it came to friendship, nothing was certain. You could think you were close to somebody, but then it could all fall apart in the snap of a finger.

After Ansell was gone, she changed her major from literature, which had been totally his idea, to journalism. Not that she was unhappy with her major—she actually liked it quite a lot—and not that she was all that interested in journalism, which seemed pretty dry in comparison, but the simple act of changing her major gave her a feeling of independence she hadn't felt in a long time.

Celia looked down at the bowl of popcorn and was surprised to find it nearly half gone. She glanced out the kitchen window and noticed that the sky, which had been as bright as day when she had arrived home less than an hour earlier, had grown suddenly darker. Upstairs she heard water running and heavy footsteps going down the hall. Must be time for Milton's bath. Patsy had told her once that Milton liked to take bubble baths, and Celia had always thought less of him for that. Men should take showers and leave the bubbles to kids and women. She would never marry a man who—

She stood up from the table suddenly and dumped the rest of the popcorn in the trash. She wondered if she would ever stop setting these ridiculous standards for prospective husbands. Why should she care what kind of baths Milton Stewart took? Let him sit in mounds of scented bubbles for all she cared. Let him make a holy ritual of it if he wanted.

Let him light aromatic candles, use perfumed soaps, and listen to Enya as he soaked all night.

She took the empty bowl to the sink and ran water into it, then walked back into the living room and looked at the three boxes on the floor. She wouldn't think of those now. She would unpack her suitcase first and worry about the boxes later. Maybe she would take a hot bubble bath herself before bed. She pushed the boxes against the wall, then carried her suitcase into the bedroom and set it on the bed.

Her digital alarm clock was flashing, which meant the power must have gone off while she was away. She checked her watch so she could reset the clock and was surprised to see that it was only a minute shy of seven. It seemed more like midnight. She sat down slowly on the edge of the bed and picked up the clock. She was surprised at how heavy it felt. Having to punch the reset button enough times to get to seven o'clock suddenly struck her as a monumental effort. As she sat staring at the flashing display, she heard two things, one right after the other.

First, her doorbell sounded, followed almost immediately by a deep rumble of thunder, neither of which was a welcome sound. She didn't want to talk to anybody right now, and she hated nighttime storms. As the years had gone by and many of the other reasons for wanting to get married had evaporated, this one remained: A husband could gather you in his arms at night and hold you until a storm had passed. So far, however, she had never found a man she wanted to put up with during all the other times of the day and night for that occasional comfort.

The doorbell sounded again right away. Whoever was at her door was impatient. Celia was tempted to ignore it. Who could it be, anyway? People hardly ever came to her door, since it was at the back of the Stewarts' house. Patsy Stewart surely wouldn't be coming around to her outside door. She would come down through the basement if she needed to see her, or else she would call on the telephone.

Celia's doorbell was generally put to use only when she was dating someone, which she certainly wasn't doing now, thank goodness. As it rang a third time, long and insistent, she got up from the bed and walked into the living room, wishing she hadn't left so many lights on. She could hardly pretend to be away from home or asleep when every room was lit up like a ball park. At least the blinds were closed.

The last time she had heard someone ring the doorbell this relentlessly was when that funny old woman had come to Al's door the night she broke up with him. For an instant the woman's scary-looking smile flashed into Celia's mind, and she wondered if the Muffin Lady was still making her rounds in Al's neighborhood. She wondered if the old woman, from her post by her front window, had noticed that Celia no longer went over to Al's house. Maybe she had taken him an extra batch of muffins as a gesture of consolation.

Milton Stewart had recently installed a motion sensor light at the back of the house, so Celia's doorstep was illuminated when she looked through the peephole to see who it was. She didn't recognize the man at first. Big smile, tall, good-looking—or at least she thought he probably was. It was a little hard to tell with his face stretched out so wide from the optical distortion of the peephole. A silly thought ran through Celia's mind. What would this man do, she wondered, if she threw open the door, flung herself into his arms, and cried, "You're just in time, Prince Charming! Please hold me till the storm passes."

It took a moment for her to register surprise that the man was actually standing there waving at her, or rather at the peephole. Somehow he must have sensed that she was peeking out at him. He took a small step back so that his face turned into a size that fit the rest of his body, but he continued to wave. He cocked his head, and Celia could see then that the smile was of the wistful, apologetic sort, with maybe a touch of despair mixed in.

That was when the thick dark hair triggered a memory—yes, she had it now. It was the man who had visited her apartment a while back, the one who was moving in next door, who looked like Mr. Darcy in *Pride and Prejudice,* except for his scars. Celia knew they had been doing a lot of work next door during the past weeks. She had seen cars in the driveway on the other side of the house and boxes of trash left out by the curb. Bruce, that was the man's name. Kimberly's husband and baby Madison's father.

All foolish notions of Prince Charming having now vanished, Celia opened the door. Besides the fact that he was a married man, it was clear as soon as he spoke that his mission was anything but romantic. "Do you have a plunger?" he asked. Another sudden clap of thunder made them both jump, and almost simultaneously Celia heard a loud crack, as if lightning had split a tree. Bruce evidently heard it, too, for he leapt forward toward Celia's threshold, then immediately looked embarrassed. It was already raining, Celia noticed, the raindrops pattering against the leaves of the backyard trees with a sound like a roomful of distant typewriters.

"Here, step inside," Celia said at exactly the same time that Bruce said, "Sorry, I hate lightning. It scares me to death." So much for this guy comforting anybody during a nighttime storm, Celia thought. She imagined him curling up beside Kimberly at the first rumble of thunder, whimpering and shaking like a puppy until it blew over.

The screen blew shut as Bruce stepped inside. Behind him Celia could see the trees tossing and swaying. The tall pines always made her nervous during storms. Several years ago one blew down in a neighbor's yard during a high wind and fell on the Stewarts' house and crashed right through the bay window in their living room.

"Uh, about that plunger," Bruce said. "We've got a plugged toilet, and, well, I can't seem to find—"

"Yes, of course I have one," Celia said, whirling around. "Hang on. I'll get it." Bruce was wearing a half-untucked wine-colored golf shirt, she noticed, with an unusual satiny sheen and a little zipper affair at the neck. If she had seen it on a mannequin in a store, she would have immediately pronounced it tacky. She wondered why he didn't wear turtlenecks to hide the burn scars on his neck.

Another violent boom of thunder sounded as she headed back to the bathroom closet. When she returned with the plunger, Bruce was standing even farther from the door, over by Macon Mahoney's painting, *Through the Blinds.* He was stooped down a little, studying it, or at least pretending to.

"Here you go," Celia said, handing him the plunger as an amusing thought came to her. It had once been a preoccupation of hers to imagine bizarre ways of meeting eligible men, to wonder if anybody ever met the man she was going to marry like *this,* or like *this.* And the thought that came to Celia now was *I wonder if anyone ever met her future husband when he showed up at her door and asked to borrow a toilet plunger.*

She supposed she'd never get over this habit of imagining weird ways of couples meeting each other, even though she had given up on it for herself. She thought now of Boo Newman, who ran the gift shop near the gallery, and how she and her husband had met when Boo had mistakenly gone inside the men's restroom at a gas station.

And a couple of years ago an acquaintance of hers, another stringer at the Derby newspaper named Joan Spalding, had met the man she ended up marrying by running into him, literally, by a pickle display at the grocery store. For several weeks after Joan told her about it, Celia had been highly alert every time she had gone to the grocery store, but she hadn't seen any available-looking men, much less run into any.

Oh yes, she had heard some pretty wild stories from people about how they met their spouses, had done one of her first newspaper assignments about that very subject—a Valentine's Day feature for the Dover paper one year fresh out of grad school. And she still found such stories interesting. Of course, there were plenty of dull, ordinary ways that people met their spouses, too. Patsy and Milton Stewart, for instance, had worked together at a Waffle House one summer, and Ollie and Connie had sat by each other in history class in college.

Celia had finally concluded, however, though only in the last year or so, that, first of all, you never found something you were actively seeking and, second, all the eligible men her age were significantly flawed. And, to be fair, in her heart she knew she wouldn't exactly be any man's dream girl, either. She might be okay to look at, but what man would want to marry someone who had blithely gone to a clinic to get rid of something *living*? It always, always came back to that.

Celia must have been frowning because Bruce looked at her quizzically and said, "Anything wrong?" She shook her head, and he laughed, holding up the plunger. "I guess we don't really know each other well enough to make jokes about this." He headed for the door, pausing briefly to scan the sky. The storm was in full force now. "Don't worry, I'll bring it back," he said, then opened the screen and ran toward his house, holding the plunger over his head like a tiny inverted rubber umbrella.

She should have offered him a real umbrella, but it was too late now. Celia watched him as he dashed across the Stewarts' backyard and headed toward the driveway. He'd be soaked by the time he got inside his house. At least the trees sheltered him from some of the rain.

Celia wondered why he hadn't offered to stay home and deal with the overflow in the bathroom while Kimberly went next door to borrow a plunger. That would seem like the gentlemanly, husbandly thing to do. Of course, then *she* would have gotten drenched by the rain instead of him, but even that would be better than having to sop up a toilet disaster. Celia's idea of the perfect man would be one who would stick around when things got messy, who would wade in and get dirty instead of running next door. She sighed as she realized she was making lists of qualifications again.

Celia stood at the door and watched the trees thrash around. It wasn't as frightening, she decided, to watch a storm in progress as it was to lie in bed in the dark and listen to one. She couldn't remember ever giving her full attention like this to a storm, facing it head on. There was something majestic about the unleashing of such power. The sky was still just light enough that she could see the seething charcoal storm clouds against the twilight sky and the lacy effect of the swaying treetops with their new growth of spring leaves. If you could separate yourself from any disturbing memories of earlier storms, it actually made a beautiful picture.

She observed the storm for several minutes. She even stepped out to stand on her little concrete square of a porch beneath the awning over her door. She closed her eyes for a few moments. Combined with the coppery smell of rain and the cool sweeping drafts of air, this could almost be interpreted as a restful experience. The wind blew rain into her face, and she could feel her hair lifting and swishing about. She opened her eyes again and stayed there watching until the lightning began fading to sporadic glints and the thunder to a low grumble.

She was opening the door to return inside when she heard a voice. It was Bruce again, loping across the Stewarts' driveway toward her, brandishing the toilet plunger. His wet shirt was completely untucked now, and his hair was untidily plastered against his forehead from the rain. "Hey, it worked!" he said. "Very efficient piece of household equipment."

He handed it to her. "Thanks. Hope we won't be needing to borrow it again. I know Kimberly's got one somewhere, but who knows where. Her system for storing things doesn't always make much sense." He paused, then added, "Knowing her, it's probably in the china cabinet or maybe in Madison's toy box." Celia shouldn't have cared, but it rubbed her the wrong way that he would criticize his wife behind her back. Even if he was teasing, the little dig was totally unnecessary.

He gave her a goofy grin. "Well, uh, thanks again," he said. "Oh, and don't worry—I washed it off good with hot soapy water, so it's not . . . well, you know . . ."

"Okay, okay, that's fine," Celia said, turning to go back inside. Honestly, Kimberly should consider putting a piece of masking tape over her husband's mouth before letting him out in public.

"Well, see you 'round," Bruce said through the screen door. Celia nodded to him, then closed and latched the door. She hated to seem rude, but she had nothing more to say to this man.

As she returned the plunger to the bathroom closet, for some odd reason she had a sudden memory of her grandmother also closing the door in someone's face. It was the summer before Celia had left for college—she remembered that clearly—and it was suppertime. She and Grandmother were eating together silently in the kitchen when the knock came at the front door.

The two boys—they didn't look much older than Celia herself—were dressed in black pants, white shirts, and neckties. Jehovah's Witnesses or Mormons or something like that, she couldn't recall exactly now. They began talking, politely but insistently, as soon as Grandmother opened the door. The one who stood in front and did most of the talking was tall and handsome, with the rugged looks of a cowboy.

Grandmother didn't invite them in but stood and conversed with them through the screen, trying to refute everything they were saying by quoting Bible verses, which they would immediately counter with other verses. Celia made a note to ask her grandmother sometime why it was that everybody at Bethany Hills was so sure *theirs* was the only right religion. Why did they have to argue with other people who also claimed to believe the Bible?

After she had gotten the drift of the conversation, Celia remembered thinking how strange it was that a guy who looked like the Marlboro Man would be going door to door talking so fervently about religion. She went back to eating, trying to finish before Grandmother came back. She had things she wanted to do, and the sooner she got done with supper, the sooner she could leave.

She wished now that she could remember what they were eating that night, not that it mattered one bit. For some reason she found herself thinking a lot lately about her grandmother's cooking. How funny that she should want to remember something that was so forgettable.

Anyway, the conversation went on until, evidently, her grandmother realized she wasn't making any headway with these two young zealots. Not that she ever once got tongue-tied. Oh no. Her store of Scripture flowed forth abundantly, but there came a point when Celia could tell that her determination to get through to them was waning.

And Celia would never forget what her grandmother said at that point. She raised her voice, actually interrupted the handsome one, who was in the process of saying something about a figurative versus a literal hell, and switched from quoting Scripture to quoting a hymn. And in such a commanding, authoritative voice! Celia didn't get up to look, but she would have bet money that her grandmother was pointing directly at the two boys as she recited: " 'Come ye sinners, poor and needy! Weak and wounded, sick and sore! Jesus ready stands to save you! Full of pity, love and power!' " And with the last word, Celia heard her shut the door firmly and turn the bolt.

She remembered her grandmother's return to the table that night, how she had sat down wearily and bowed her head for the longest time. Celia had heard her breathing heavily, had seen her lips moving, had known she was praying for the souls of those two boys just as she prayed for Celia's soul day after day.

Oh, Grandmother's solution for everything was so simple. Just arise and go to Jesus. Let him embrace you in his arms and lead you back to the safety of the flock. And somehow Grandmother believed, she really and truly believed, that in the dry, dusty fold of religion, with its high fences and securely latched gate, there were ten thousand charms, if not more.

14

Just Beyond the Shining River

"You better give it to someone else," Celia said. "I'm afraid I won't be able to fit it in this week." It was the first day of May, a Sunday afternoon, and Celia was sitting cross-legged in the middle of her bed, talking on the phone with Mike Owen, who liked to introduce himself as "the editor-in-chief of the Derby *Daily News,*" which was true but nothing to brag about in Celia's opinion.

The book she had been reading was lying facedown on the bedspread. Ollie had lent the book to her, and she had found it fascinating so far: *Making the Mummies Dance* by Thomas Hoving, a former director of the Metropolitan Museum of Art. It told all sorts of inside scoop about the Met—the incredibly high prices of certain acquisitions, quarrels among the board members, dealings with major donors, auctions, scouting trips abroad, scandals in the art world, and such. She was eager to get back to reading, especially now that she knew what this phone conversation was about.

She couldn't remember the last time she had flatly turned down a newspaper assignment from Mike. Not that she hadn't tried before, but somehow he always managed to talk her into it. This time he wouldn't, though. He might as well save his breath.

"Debra can't do it," Mike said. "She's swamped with the library renovation feature, plus all the Greek Festival stuff. And I wouldn't give something like this to Lorenzo. It's not a guy thing." He paused. "I really need you, kid. You're the best. You know that."

She knew he'd try flattery eventually, but usually it wasn't so soon. "Sorry, Mike. Can't do it. How about Joan? She's good—and twice as fast as the rest of us."

"She can't. She's already doing two concert reviews and the Clinton bluegrass thing for me this week, plus her usual poetry fillers," he said. "And she's got a full-time job, you know." Whenever things got tight, Mike liked to drop little reminders that Celia's afternoon hours at the art gallery gave her more free time than his other stringers, as if he thought she sat at home every morning lounging around in her pajamas.

Ever since Wanda had left the paper in March, Mike had become a real nuisance, phoning every week about assignments he didn't have a writer for. "Well, if you'd quit spinning your wheels and hire another full-time reporter," she told him now, "you wouldn't keep running into this problem. You can't expect me to keep dropping everything to bail you out of a jam."

"Hey, I don't own the paper, Celia. You know that. It's not my decision. I've told Mr. Fields the situation, and he's still—"

"Well, I can't do it. This is a bad week for me. Tennis playoffs start tomorrow, and we have a new show opening at the gallery on Thursday night. I've still got a lot to do for that." There, not just one reasonable-sounding excuse, but two. Actually, only one of the excuses was valid, though.

She heard Mike sigh. Though he had tried hard to hide it, he hadn't been at all happy when she had told him back in February that she'd joined a tennis team that had matches and occasional practices in the mornings. Usually it was only one morning a week, but this week was different, and she couldn't do anything about the schedule even if she wanted to do the article for Mike, which she definitely didn't. The three playoff matches were scheduled for Monday, Tuesday, and Thursday mornings, and the team needed her at every match. Whichever team won this week would go to the state championship in Charleston in early June.

The second part of her excuse might be stretching the truth, however, since things were pretty well under control for the new art show. She and Ollie were hanging the pieces tomorrow, three whole days early, and she had the refreshment table and decorations all set for Thursday. She was using a lot of scarves, old hats, and costume jewelry for the table, and the refreshments were going to be cheese straws, pastel mints, meringue cookies, and cinnamon peach tea, all of which Connie was bringing in on Thursday.

Celia was looking forward to this new show—oils and acrylics in vibrant colors, mostly interior scenes with a wry twist. The artist, Lenny Bullard, was a native of Yemassee, South Carolina, but you'd never guess his rural background from this new show. And you probably wouldn't guess his gender, either.

Celia's favorite piece in the whole show, the one she had chosen to depict on the postcard mailing, was a large painting of a women's upscale lingerie shop. The mannequins, the customers, the merchandise, the shop owner, the decor—it all said "snobbery," but with such good-natured satire that you had to smile. She also liked the painting of a lady's bureau, showing an open jewelry box with necklaces draped over the side, an arrangement of peacock feathers in an Oriental vase, a small crystal clock, a poppy red scarf, and several scattered earrings and hatpins. Obviously that woman had been in a hurry.

Angela Wortheimer's watercolor show had gone well, but Celia was glad it was down now. All those placid scenes in pastel colors had grown tiresome after a few days. Nothing to stir the imagination in all that tranquillity. Even the one Celia had liked best—the wet sidewalk scene—hadn't kept her interest. During the six weeks of looking at the paintings every day, she had grown to believe that Angela had a good eye but not a whole lot of fire in her soul. Quite a few pieces had sold, though, so a lot of people evidently didn't care whether an artist had fire in her soul.

Regarding Lenny Bullard's work, however, some people might turn it around and say he had plenty of fire in his soul but not a very good eye. Another of his paintings flashed into Celia's mind: a small beauty shop with five swivel chairs, slightly tilted in different directions, in a rainbow of sherbet colors. The name of the shop could be read backward through the plate glass window in the background—Lovelier Than Thou. The letters were leaning crookedly, hardly a sign maker's dream.

She realized Mike was talking again and wondered if she had missed much. Probably not. He seemed to have shifted into a lecturing mode.

" . . . and you know those are invariably the things I learn the most from," he was saying. "So, really, we both know a person can always make time for important things, right? And believe me, kid, this is important. And *fun*—hey, it'll be a whole lot more fun than most of the stuff I give you." He paused to chuckle. "You know, like murders and such. Oh, and by the way, people are still writing in and calling about that one. I probably already told you that, though. Everybody and his brother thinks he has a clue that's gonna solve that case. And who knows? One of them actually might. But anyway, the point is, that was some good writing you did. As usual. You really know how to snag the reader."

More flattery. He really must be desperate. "And then the Teacher Appreciation feature," he added, "and the big thing about book clubs in the area, and that hot-air-balloon event a couple weeks ago—well, you've really helped us out, Celia, and I was really, really counting on you for this one." He paused as if hoping her sense of obligation would kick in. *After all, you did leave us in a lurch ten years ago,* she could feel him thinking over the phone. *You did promise to keep freelancing for us as needed when you up and quit the newspaper to work at an art gallery, of all places.*

She could hear him tapping on something in the background. She tried to say something but suddenly found that she couldn't put a sentence together. Maybe it was Mike's mention of her recent articles, but for some reason at this very minute it struck her all at once, with swift and sure conviction, that she was tired of writing for the newspaper. Tired in a very permanent way. Absolutely fed up. She wouldn't care if she never had another call from Mike, if she never again saw her by-line in the Derby *Daily News.*

And the freelance editing jobs she kept doing for people—she suddenly knew without a doubt that she couldn't face another one. She thought of poor misguided, eternally optimistic Frank Bledsoe, who had called again a few days ago to ask about her progress on editing his latest manuscript, a collection of inspirational short cameos titled *Folks Who Failed*—well, there was no way in the world Celia could in good conscience keep accepting the man's money.

Some weeks ago she had finally given back to Frank the opening chapters of his dreadful autobiographical novel *From Ashes to Fame* and had broken it to him gently that this one would require more effort than she was able to give in order to make it publishable, at which time he had briskly pulled out another manuscript, the *Folks Who Failed* one, and asked her to "take a look at this when you have a minute." Such resilience that man had!

She couldn't believe now that she had actually let him put yet another manuscript into her hands, that she hadn't looked him square in the eye and said, "It's over, Frank. Kaput, adios, the end. Sorry, I can't help you anymore. Your writing is hopeless. Go home and take up herb gardening. Raise carrier pigeons. Start a coin collection. Restore vintage cars." She wondered how she had managed all these years to keep trying to fix up other people's writing when she hated doing it so much.

And writing articles for Mike—why, that was like doing homework. None of it was anything she *wanted* to write. She was tired of being told what to write and then seeing it printed on the kind of paper people threw away, shredded up for packing material, or wrapped fish bones in.

So at the exact same moment Celia was experiencing a revelation—that she had totally lost interest in what she had two degrees in from Blackrock College and had for the past ten years considered to be her second job— she was also wondering if there was any way she could swing it financially with only her job at the gallery. All this while trying to maintain some semblance of paying attention to Mike on the other end of the phone.

"I mean, we've *got* to have something for Mother's Day," he was saying now, his voice having taken on a wheedling note. "We'd never hear the end of it from our readers if we didn't. You'd be so perfect for this, Celia. And think of how much you'd learn. Think of how many pitfalls you could avoid after listening to all these other women talk. And as far as the time factor goes, why, you could probably do all the interviews in the normal course of your day. Just talk to women wherever you go. Right there at the art gallery, in the grocery store, in your neighborhood—why, you could—"

"I said I can't do it," Celia said. "And I mean it, Mike. It doesn't matter how little time you think it'll take. Anything is too much. I can't do it. Not this week." Her mind was still whirling over her revelation, but she didn't think this was the right time to break the news to him. She needed to think about it some more, to look at her budget and figure some things out first. You didn't cut off a supply of income on the spur of the moment.

"And you could think of it as a gift for your own mother." Mike was good at the pretend-you-didn't-hear game, another ploy he sometimes used to get his way. "Wouldn't she be proud to read something you wrote specially for Mother's Day? Can't you see her carrying it around and showing it to—"

"My mother died twenty years ago," Celia said. She felt sure she had told Mike about her parents at some point during all the time she had known him, but if she had, he had obviously forgotten. "Anyway," she added as he cleared his throat and made apologetic noises on the other end, "I don't think an article about the mistakes mothers make would have thrilled her all that much."

That was the concept of the article, as Mike had explained it to her at the beginning of their phone talk—to ask a dozen or so older mothers what they'd do differently if they had their child-rearing years to do all over again. "Another Shot at Motherhood" was the title Mike had suggested. The whole thing struck Celia as being a little depressing, not to mention insulting. Asking mothers to criticize themselves, then compiling it all into an article so that thousands of other people could read about their private blunders in dealing with their kids. Who wanted to open up the paper on Mother's Day and see a chronicle of mistakes committed by the segment of the population that was supposed to be setting the moral tone for the next generation? It didn't seem like much of a way to honor mothers. Granted, it might make a pretty interesting article for some other day, but not for Mother's Day.

Mike seemed to catch what she was implying, for he said, "Hey, wait a minute. You know what? You've got a point there. Guess I hadn't thought about it like that." But instead of dropping the whole idea, he suddenly hatched an even worse one. "So let's see . . . say, how about this? How about doing something personal, some memory of your own mother before she died? That would work. Some nice little vignette. Warm and fuzzy."

She should have cut him off, but she wasn't quick enough. She was distracted by a thought that flitted across her mind: Why didn't people take her seriously when she said no? Maybe it was her size, maybe her voice, maybe the simple fact that she was a woman. "You could sort of reminisce about your childhood," Mike continued. "Maybe you've got some nugget about your mom—you know, one of those meaningful moments from childhood you could build the piece around. This could be great, Celia! We're on the right track now!" He was doing his best imitation of The Editor As Motivator-Cheerleader-Nurturer.

She couldn't believe she had let him get this far. Motherhood was not a subject she was going to write an article about—not now, not ever. Not from any perspective. She didn't even want to *think* about the subject, much less write about it. Anyway, she had just decided that her writing days were over. Maybe she should go ahead and tell him now. Or maybe she should try an appeal to his sympathy first. Maybe that would get him off her back for now.

"Mother's Day brings back a lot of painful memories I'd rather not dredge up," she said quietly. That much was certainly true.

"Well, I can appreciate that," Mike said quickly, "but, you know, Celia, maybe this could be therapeutic in a way. I mean, maybe you could—"

"No, I can't do it." She let out a little gasp, which was part acting. "I really am busy this week, Mike, but even if I had the time, I couldn't do a Mother's Day piece. I just couldn't. End of discussion."

Though Mike rarely swore, he did so now, but softly, not in anger. "Okay, kid," he said after a long pause. "I give up. I'm gonna hang up now so I can start beating the bushes to find somebody else to do it. Got any other suggestions for me? That's the least you could do."

Celia thought a moment. "How about that English teacher over in Filbert who covered the dog show a while back?"

Mike let out a snort of laughter. "You mean the one who had the love affair with adjectives? The one who called the winner of the show a . . . what was it? 'A sprightly, self-assertive schnauzer with a stately stance and a squared-off schnoz'—something like that?"

"I think it was a soldierly stance."

"Whatever. Can you imagine what somebody like that would do with an article about mothers?" Mike groaned. "Give me a buzz, kid, if you have any more bright ideas, okay?" Celia felt a flood of relief when she heard him hang up.

Motherhood—it would always be there, nibbling at her conscience. As long as she lived, there would be daily reminders that she wasn't a mother herself and because of what she had done she didn't deserve to ever be one. On Mother's Day she was always smitten with the thought that she didn't have a mother of her own and, furthermore, that her mother would have been heartbroken to know what she had done.

She closed her eyes for a minute before settling back against her pillows and picking up her book again. She had been right in the middle of an interesting story about the Met's acquisition of a huge, remarkably beautiful vase unearthed on the island of Crete and all the political difficulties associated with purchasing it and getting it out of its country of origin. She tried getting back into it but found her concentration gone.

As she closed the book and laid it on the table beside her bed, she let her eyes rest a moment on the sculpture of the nude couple embracing. It was a funny thing how she so often took only quick glances at this piece of art that she had paid more for than any other in her apartment. She had wondered before if it was another hangover from her upbringing, the whole Bible-belt phobia about nudity. Or maybe it wasn't that complicated. Maybe it just hit a nerve, seeing two people in love. She reached over and picked up the sculpture. It was heavy, though only seven or eight inches high. She made herself look directly at it.

The stylized figures were dull bronze and very smooth. The woman was sitting, her knees drawn up, and the man was kneeling beside her, facing her, his head resting on hers. Looking at it up close, Celia felt both happy and sad. Happy because it was so beautiful, but sad because it reminded her that she had no one to kneel beside her and embrace her and that, except for short-term flings, she probably never would. No one to help her ride out the storms through the long nights.

Celia clearly remembered stooping in front of the piece many times a day during the sculptor's exhibit at the Trio nine or ten years earlier. It had caught her eye the first time she had studied the artist's slides, and when he brought all the pieces down from Raleigh, North Carolina, in the back of his van for the opening of his show some months later and set this one on the floor in a corner with several others, she had felt something scrunch up in the pit of her stomach. Those were the days before she had given up hope, when she still considered it entirely within the realm of possibility that she would eventually meet someone she couldn't live without.

Before opening night she had placed a red dot beside the number of the sculpture, which was displayed on a small pedestal, to indicate that it had already been sold. And though she had inherited much of her father's cautious regard for money, she had gone to the bank and taken out of her savings account five thousand dollars in order to bring the piece home and call it hers. She had set it reverently on the table beside her bed, and though her churchgoing days were long gone, she felt that someone ought to say a benediction over something so beautiful.

She recalled a woman coming to the Trio before the show came down, firmly clutching the hand of her young son as she walked through the door. Celia hated to see people bring their children to the gallery, for more reasons than one. She could still hear the little boy's voice as they moved from piece to piece: "What is that?" "That looks like a robot." "Is that a horse?" And when they came to *Embrace,* he had laughed, a high chirping laugh that his mother tried to shush. "Those people don't have any arms!" he had said. And it was true in the strictest sense. Yet every curve of the smooth bodies left no doubt in the viewer's mind that they were indeed embracing, and very intimately. Arms were totally unnecessary. Celia liked to think of it as a perfect example of the artist's power to suggest something from nothing and of the ability of the human eye to see beyond the literal.

Celia sat up straighter and leaned slightly forward, drawing her knees up much like the woman's posture, then set the sculpture on top of them so that her eyes were only inches away from it. She turned it around in a slow circle to study it from every angle. She wondered what it would be like to be able to do this for a living, to actually create the pieces instead of just showing and selling them as she did. She ran her hand down the smooth arc of the man's back, then the woman's. Then she traced a finger from the top of each head, across the smooth face, down to the neck, chest, around the inside curve of the stomach, and then to the knees. The woman's breasts were full and her stomach slightly rounded, but Celia could easily circle her waist with her thumb and index finger.

Celia studied the sculpture a minute longer, then finally set it back on her nightstand, turned off the lamp, and once more lay back against her pillows. She had intended to read for an hour or so and then take a Sunday afternoon nap, a habit she had developed as a child. When she closed her eyes, though, all she could see was the sculpture of the nude couple, except that now they were moving slightly. Then for some reason, perhaps because of Mike's mentioning her mother on the phone, the two people suddenly turned into her parents. She opened her eyes and shook her head. This certainly wasn't something she wanted to imagine. She would hate to see her parents every time she glanced at the bronze sculpture.

Though she had never asked anyone, Celia guessed that most orphans spent long hours thinking about their parents. If they never knew them, they probably tried to imagine what they looked like, how they laughed, what things in life gave them special pleasure. If they could remember them, they probably relived favorite incidents, trying to bring into focus a closeup picture of their faces, recalling exact words and small telling actions.

Which was exactly what Celia had tried *not* to do for almost twenty years. The first couple of years after they died, she had thought about her parents constantly. She had even talked to them at night after she said her prayers in her dark bedroom at Grandmother's house. She would tell them about school, about the changing of seasons, about the people of Dunmore. She would describe the daily details of life with Grandmother—her chickens, a sack of tomatoes that showed up on their doormat, the zinnias by the front steps, the potluck supper at church. She would always end her talks by asking their forgiveness for neglecting her prayers the day they died, and more often than not she would end up crying. She had learned to keep a box of tissues by her bed during those two years.

But it all changed her senior year of high school after she met Ansell and the others. After that, whenever she found herself thinking about one of her parents or seeing their faces in her mind, she immediately tried to erase the picture and move on to something else. She quit talking to them at night. It was her newly formed opinion that nothing good could come of dwelling on how things used to be. The biggest reason, though, was that she wanted to avoid their eyes. She didn't want to imagine their disappointment in her. She could bear her grandmother's wrath—her stern reproofs, her grunts of disapproval, her banging around in the kitchen—but not her parents' silent grief.

And later, in college, it was the same. She knew beyond a doubt that her parents wouldn't be proud of the person she had turned out to be, so she continued to block them from her memory. After her grandmother had come to her graduation, Celia had worn her mother's watch only a few weeks before taking it off, putting it in a box, and shoving it to the back of a drawer. She couldn't stand its tiny face staring up at her all day long.

After her visit to the clinic, it was even worse. She couldn't begin to imagine what words her mother would have spoken to her if she had known, nor what deep lines would have creased her father's already worried brow. Old Testament phrases would echo through her mind whenever their faces crossed her mind: "ashamed and confounded," "sackcloth and ashes," "weeping and wailing," "the day of desolation." Her parents often spiraled through her dreams, their heads bowed with sorrow, tears streaming from their eyes, and she would wake up trembling. She imagined she could hear her mother's old watch ticking faintly in the back of her drawer, like a baby's heartbeat.

She remembered something a former boyfriend had told her. It must have been eight years ago now, because her car was eight years old. His name was Todd Robard, and he had majored in psychology in college, though he owned a small car dealership over in Greenville, which is where she had met him while shopping for her Ford Mustang, the same one she still drove. It was Todd who had talked her into getting a red one.

"Face your fear." That's what Todd had said that came back to her now. He had tried repeatedly to probe into her past, wanting her to "open up her shell," as he called it, but she had always managed to elude his questions. Of all the men she had ever dated, Todd Robard was probably the most insightful, and therefore the one who scared her most. Whereas other men let her do most of the talking, Todd liked to discuss and analyze things, freely expressing not only his opinions but also his feelings.

During the couple of months they dated, Todd had been in the process of remodeling his house and had asked her one night, which turned out to be the last night they were together, to come over and help him install insulation and new wiring. Celia laughed, then accepted. And it was fun at first. Todd ordered a pizza, and they sat on his kitchen floor, which was covered with brown paper to protect it. The work wasn't hard. He did most of it, asking her only to help measure, hand him the staple gun, and tap on the kitchen ceiling to help him locate the old wires in the attic.

It was later, after they had cleaned up and were eating shortbread cookies straight out of the bag, that Todd leaned forward, put a hand on each of her shoulders, and said, "Whatever it is that's haunting those pretty eyes of yours, Celia, needs to be dealt with. Quit running from it. Turn around and face your fear. Cut off the dragon's head." He said it kindly, but it was clear that he wasn't the type to let a matter drop. She could tell from the precise way he had cut the bats of insulation, folded the winged edges out so neatly, and stapled them at exact intervals that he liked to tackle a problem systematically and see it through to completion. And though, looking back on it now, he might have been exactly what she needed, she never saw him again after that night.

"Face your fear"—it sounded so easy. But how did you go about doing that? And what exactly did she fear? *Okay, make a list,* she told herself. She sat up and opened the drawer of her nightstand to get a pen and note pad. She wondered what Todd would say if he knew that his long-ago advice had lodged in her memory and was finally bearing fruit.

She first wrote the word *Fears* at the top, then numbered from one through five, as if she were about to take a spelling test, although she had no idea why she chose to stop at five. She went back to number one, thought a moment, then wrote, *Living with what I did fourteen years ago.* She went down to number two, paused again, then wrote, *Being alone.* The rest followed quickly: Number three was *Nighttime,* number four, *Children,* and number five, *Grandmother.* This fifth one surprised her a little, but as she studied the list, she soon saw the connection among all five. Numbers two through five were actually only subpoints of number one, and *Grandmother* wasn't really her grandmother as a person, but rather what she believed— her whole system of religion, of paying for your sins, or more specifically, of burning in hell for eternity because of your sins.

She could feel herself breathing harder. Here she was, almost thirty-seven years old, and she could probably expect to live at least another thirty-seven years. Yet, as her eyes ran up and down her list of five, she saw no relief in the years to come. She thought of her tennis teammates, their hearts and minds continuing to expand gracefully as they grew older, surrounded by their families and a lifetime of happy memories. Then she saw herself, shut inside her apartment, choking for breathing space as she filled her walls with more and more art, driving back and forth between home and work, watching television, running the vacuum, hearing snatches of old hymns, waking up during the night, alone.

Life would be so much easier if you could talk yourself into believing, as Grandmother had, that sins could be washed away like magic, that prayers were answered, that someday you'd die and go to heaven, where it was always daytime, where there was "no dark valley"—there was a song about that in Grandmother's hymnal.

It was a hymn her grandmother had sung a lot at the kitchen sink, the light chink of dishes bumping each other under the sudsy water as she sang, "There'll be no dark valley when Jesus comes to gather his loved ones home." And "no more sorrow" and "no more weeping"—she'd go through all the stanzas. Grandmother's creed said you simply did your Christian duty day in and day out, even in the dark valleys of life on this earth, of which there were plenty, until the angels rang those golden bells for you and transported you to that sweet land "just beyond the shining river."

Of course, the catch in Grandmother's religion was that everything was so black and white, that there was no fun in that creed of hers. So many pleasures were labeled "sin," and sin was punished by a God who didn't spare the rod, who applied that rod with a might heavy hand and kept the fires of hell stoked with a steady supply of unrepentant sinners.

Celia ripped the list of fears out of the note pad and crumpled it slowly in one fist. The trash can, a white wicker one, was neatly positioned in the corner over beside her dresser. She swung her legs over the side of the bed, took aim, and let go—a high loopy lob. The paper ball fell considerably short. On the tennis court, it would have made an easy putaway for the opponent at the net.

15

Yonder Sacred Throng

Two days later, on Tuesday morning, during the second playoff match against a Greenville team, Celia was receiving a serve from a woman named Sissy when all at once she thought of her clarinet. She tried to put it out of her mind because she really did want to close out this match. The temperature was already in the high eighties and climbing at the tennis club in Greenville, where the playoffs were being held. The clarinet wouldn't go away, though. It must have originated from the sound of a crow that had perched itself on the corner of the fence. Not that she would ever, during her clarinet-playing days, have compared the sound of her instrument to the strident caw of a crow.

Perhaps the thought was further encouraged by the heat. As she pushed her visor up and wiped her brow with the back of her hand, she suddenly remembered for some strange reason how hot she used to get wearing her band uniform during the halftime shows in tenth and eleventh grades—the dark blue pants, the long-sleeved jacket, and the snug taxi-style cap. The uniforms, which were purchased with November in mind, were beastly hot under the stadium lights at those September football games in Georgia.

Another stimulus could have been the jazzy big-band sound of Benny Goodman blasting from a Porsche convertible that had pulled into the parking lot beside the court she was playing on. It stopped as soon as the driver cut the engine, but she had heard it clearly. At any rate, it all must have combined—the crow, the heat, the music—to make her think of her clarinet.

Her opponent, Sissy, had to be the world's longest ball bouncer before a serve. At some point during the match, Celia had started counting the number of bounces. The record so far was eighteen, though it was usually only ten or twelve. She wondered if in the history of tennis anyone had ever lodged a complaint against an opponent for excessive pre-serve ball bouncing. It could be considered a delay-of-game tactic. Sissy was down 15–40 in this game and 2–4 in the second set, so maybe she was trying to revise her strategy during all that ball bouncing.

But now, when Celia needed to bear down and concentrate on breaking Sissy's serve to bring the match within one game of being finished, she was instead trying to remember when she had last played her clarinet and exactly what piece she had played. She had thought about getting it back out this summer and seeing if she could play in a couple of the park concerts in Spartanburg, but so far she hadn't even taken the case out of her closet and dusted it off. She had been meaning to ask Elizabeth Landis if her husband, the band director at Harwood College, had any suggestions for a former clarinetist on how to go about easing back into it after an almost twenty-year hiatus. Maybe she should find a teacher and start lessons again.

Fortunately for Celia, Sissy must have lost her concentration, too, for she hit Celia's service return a good three feet long, putting Celia ahead in the set 5–2. But when they changed sides, Sissy dusted her palms with rosin, took a quick swig of Gatorade, then strode back onto the court without even sitting down, apparently eager to get started on her comeback. Celia took another drink from her thermos and wiped off her racket grip before getting up from the bench and walking to her side of the court. People who tried to rush between changes always annoyed her. "See, I'm in better shape than you," they seemed to be saying. "I don't need to stop and catch my breath."

If Celia could win this game, the match would be over. Sissy wasn't really much competition, but these were the matches that sometimes turned on you. You'd get overconfident, let your mind wander, blow a few easy shots, and then before you knew it, the other person would catch up. A few points later, and you'd be behind. She was far from behind now, however, so there was plenty of time to get her attention back on the game.

As she walked to the service line, she reminded herself that these were the local playoffs, not just a regular match, and that the winning team would advance to the state championship. She remembered Bonnie Maggio's words to the team this morning when they had met for what Bonnie always referred to as their "prematch rah-rah": "Okay, girls, go out there and dominate your court. Play like it all depends on *you* whether the team wins or loses this match. Fight for every point." Bonnie had gone on to remind them about the playoffs the year before, when two teams ended up tied and they had to count individual games to determine the winner.

Celia wished she knew how the other singles and the three doubles matches were going, but she and Sissy had been assigned to the end court next to the parking lot, while all the others were up closer to the clubhouse. The Holiday Winners had won four out of the five courts the day before, against a team from Oconee, but the Greenville team they were playing today was a stronger team overall.

Celia took her place behind the service line and began her own ball bouncing. Okay, focus on what you're doing, she told herself. Keep your mind on the court and make every shot count. Win this game and the match is yours. Pretend that we've already won two courts and lost two, and yours is the deciding one.

Just as she tossed the ball up to serve, however, the person driving the Porsche started it up again, and Benny Goodman picked right up where he had left off. Her serve went into the net, then started rolling back into the court. She took her time retrieving it so the Porsche could leave before she served again. She went down the T with her second serve, forcing Sissy to hit a backhand return, a soft midcourt shot that Celia returned deep and down the line for a winner.

Three points later, however, the score was tied at 30–all. A second crow had now stationed itself on the adjacent court, on top of the fence, and had joined the other one in what seemed to be a cawing contest. Three of Celia's teammates who weren't playing today had also walked over to see how things were going. They were standing quietly outside the fence, but she was still very much aware of their presence. Watch the ball, she told herself. Forget the crows, forget the spectators.

As she tossed the ball up to serve, she caught sight of another crow flying over the far corner of the court. Was this a third one, she wondered, or one of the others moving to a better spot? Her toss was off, so she caught the ball and tried again. Evidently there were a lot more than two or three crows, because suddenly a great raucous chorus went up, ragged and argumentative. It sounded like it was coming from somewhere behind her. The first guy must be the head honcho, summoning them all for a meeting.

Celia's serve landed long, and she saw Sissy relax and move in. Though this could be seen as the time for caution, she decided to go for her second serve instead of letting up. She bounced the ball several times, then served hard to the corner of the service box. And it worked. The ball skipped off the line with such speed that it caught Sissy by surprise, and though she got her racket on it, it blooped off sideways and landed in the next court.

Celia heard one of her teammates say, "Way to go, Celia." Sissy stepped up to where the serve had landed and scowled down at the court, as if looking for a ball mark, then moved over to the ad court. She danced lightly on the tips of her toes as Celia prepared to serve, as if to say, "Okay, try that again. I'm ready now."

But a few seconds later they were shaking hands at the net, Celia having won the final point when Sissy's service return hit the tape and dropped back onto her own side of the court. As they walked to the benches, Celia saw that the crows appeared to be settled in the trees on the other side of the parking lot, where it sounded like a heated family conference was going on. Celia nodded toward them and said to Sissy, "Interesting sound effects today, huh?"

Sissy sighed. "Yeah, they should do something about that. You shouldn't have to put up with stuff like that during playoffs. I'm going to complain to Melanie." Melanie, one of the league coordinators, was the one monitoring today's match. Celia glanced quickly at Sissy to see if she was teasing, but evidently she wasn't. Grim-faced, she was shoving her things back into her tennis bag.

Celia tried to imagine exactly what Sissy would say to Melanie: "The crows distracted me" maybe. And while they were at it, Celia could chime in with her own complaints. "Yeah, and Sissy bounced the ball too many times, and a Porsche was playing loud music."

Sissy zipped up her bag and left the court, shoving past Celia's teammates at the gate. Celia wondered if Sissy would go home and tell everybody she could have won today if it hadn't been for those crows that made so much noise at a critical point in the match. Celia wondered if anyone would point out to her that her opponent must have heard the same crows.

An hour later the whole team was sitting inside Wendy's eating lunch.

Ollie was going to open the gallery today, so Celia didn't have to be there till two. The Holiday Winners were in good spirits. They had taken today's match against the Greenville team, winning three of the five courts. Elizabeth Landis had lost her singles match in a disappointing three-set match, and Ellen Myers and Carol Sawyer had also lost in two close sets.

But with Celia's win and the other two doubles, they had taken their second playoff match. Now they would have a day off to rest before their last one on Thursday, and if they could win that one, they were going to Charleston. It would be a tough match on Thursday. They were playing a team from their own division, one they had played during the regular season—the Gateway Greens team, the one Donna Cobb played on.

There were about five different conversations going on at the long row of tables they had moved together. Elizabeth, who was sitting next to Celia at one end, was still trying to replay her match to figure out how she had let it slip away from her. Celia had seen most of the last set but couldn't give her much help. From what she could tell, Elizabeth had been playing smart, not making many unforced errors, and keeping her opponent on the run. But the other woman, who looked to be in her twenties, was a gazelle. She could get to anything and could usually place it well.

"I *hate* to lose," Elizabeth said to Celia now.

"Probably because you haven't had much practice doing it," Celia said, smiling. This was only Elizabeth's second loss of the ten matches they had played this season, and the other one had been in early March after she had been in bed for a week with the flu.

Tammy Elias must have been listening in because she leaned over the table and said to Celia, "Well, look who's talking. And how many matches have *you* lost this season?"

"Oh, I've been lucky," Celia said with a wave of her hand.

"I wish I had that kind of luck," Tammy said.

"Yeah, how about sharing?" Elizabeth said, laughing. One thing Celia had discovered about Elizabeth was that she often changed subjects abruptly, which she did now. "You're still planning on coming to our poetry club, aren't you?"

"Oh no, I had completely forgotten," Celia said, clapping her hand over her mouth. She was teasing, of course. This was only about the ninth or tenth time Elizabeth had mentioned it since she had first asked her in March.

Elizabeth made a face. "Okay, okay. What I really meant was, has Ollie decided yet about letting you bring something from the gallery?" Celia had told her a couple of weeks ago that Ollie didn't think their insurance would permit a piece to be taken out of the gallery for something like that. If anything happened to it, he wasn't sure they would cover it.

Their insurers had gotten picky lately. A few weeks ago they had told the gallery they couldn't display any paintings in the front window, as they had done for years—or rather, if they continued doing so, the company wouldn't cover any damage to those pieces. There had been a lot of talk about a gallery in Columbia that had recently been the target of vandalism in the form of drive-by shootings through the plate-glass window. Several expensive pieces had been ruined.

Celia shook her head. "He still hasn't found out for sure. But he said he'd let me have something of his own from his studio at home if they say no. Ollie's got some great stuff, especially his older work. I'm thinking of one in particular that would be the perfect thing. Lots of possibilities for writing material."

Elizabeth held up a hand. "Hey, you don't have to convince me about Ollie's work. I know it's good. Remember, I'm the proud owner of *Little Tweed Creek*. I look at it every day on my wall and can't believe it's really mine." For a moment she looked as if she had fallen into a trance. Some of Frank Bledsoe's bad fiction came to Celia's mind. He had always liked to describe characters as having "a certain faraway look" or "slipping into a moment of serene reverie."

Elizabeth carefully examined a French fry, then slowly brought it to her mouth, bit it in half, and chewed contemplatively. "Well, anyway," she said brightly, the moment of serene reverie apparently ended, "I know whatever you bring will be great. I'll quit bugging you about it."

Just then there was a loud burst of laughter from the other end of the table. Several other people at nearby tables looked over curiously. "Hey, y'all gotta listen to this," Betsy Harris called out. "Listen to what Gloria's mother-in-law did this time. Go on, tell 'em, Gloria."

It was a good seven hours later, after she had gotten home from work that evening, that Celia opened her hall closet and got up on a chair to reach to the back of the top shelf and pull out her clarinet case. She took it into the kitchen and wiped it off with a damp paper towel, then slowly opened it. She wouldn't have been surprised if dozens of moths had fluttered out, or maybe a bat, or if some kind of wood-boring insect had had a feast over the years, but from all appearances the clarinet was perfectly fine.

The packet of reeds had to be useless, though. She took one out and stuck it in her mouth, sucking on it while she slowly put her clarinet together. Then she inserted the reed into the mouthpiece and tried playing a C scale. To her great surprise, she got a strong, completely identifiable clarinet sound. She played another scale or two, then stopped. What she really needed was some music to play. She used to have an old leather satchel with several books and pieces of sheet music in it, but she couldn't remember where it was, or even *if* it still was. Maybe she had discarded it somewhere along the line, though she couldn't imagine doing so.

She checked the closet again, but it wasn't there, and she surely didn't feel like going through all her trunks and boxes stored in the Stewarts' basement. Suddenly she remembered something and almost immediately wished she hadn't. Grandmother's hymnal—it was in one of the three boxes she had brought back from Georgia. In fact, she knew exactly which box it was in. If she was desperate for music and wasn't picky about what kind, it could be easily had.

She walked over to the door leading from her hall into the laundry area and flipped the lock. Generally, the only time she used this door was when she did her laundry on Thursday mornings in Patsy Stewart's washing machine. Her storage area was just outside the door, against the other side of her bedroom wall, and she had set the three boxes of Grandmother's things right in front. She opened the smallest of the three. There was the brown hymnal, *Tabernacle Hymns Number Three,* right on top, as she had known it would be.

She took it out, then closed the box and returned to her kitchen. She sat down at the table again, and as she reached forward to open the book, she heard something drop hard on the Stewarts' kitchen floor upstairs, accompanied by the shattering of glass. The thought crossed her mind that maybe it was a warning that she shouldn't tamper with the hymnal. *Go put it back in the box,* something told her. *Then move the box over to the Stewarts' side of the basement and mix it in with their things so you can never find it.* An image popped into her mind of rows and rows of identical boxes stacked up in a huge warehouse, like the ones at the very end of *Raiders of the Lost Ark.* It was one of the few movies she owned. You knew at the end of that movie that the box containing the lost ark would never again see the light of day.

Overhead she heard Milton's voice raised in alarm as heavy footsteps pounded through the hall. Then she heard Patsy's voice, followed by a moment of total silence, then laughter, then more talking. Whatever it was, it hadn't been much of a catastrophe.

Celia once again reached forward to open the hymnal. She remembered the sudden atmospheric upheaval earlier in *Raiders of the Lost Ark* when the Ark of the Covenant was finally uncovered and displayed in full view. As it was about to be touched, all hell broke loose—or rather, heaven. Swords of lightning, huge splintery cracks of thunder, howling winds, graveyard shrieks and wails. "The wrath of God"—that's what Indiana Jones had called it. He had told Marian not to look at it, and that's how they had survived while all the Nazis melted in the great heat.

No such pyrotechnics occurred now when Celia touched the hymnal, however, and she gave a little laugh as she opened it. It was just an old, old hymnbook, nothing more. But she was cautious, turning to the back instead of flipping it open to the middle. She found herself looking down at the very last hymn in the book. Number 352, "All Hail the Power." Okay, here were staff lines and notes, key signatures, meter, the whole works. This is what she wanted—any kind of music to play on her clarinet.

She played the hymn four times, twice through each of the two tunes printed on the page. Though she tried hard to look at only the notes, the words jumped out at her. And even if they hadn't been printed right in front of her, she knew she would have heard them anyway. "All Hail the Power" had been a heavyweight Sunday morning song at Bethany Hills, not a Sunday night or Wednesday night song like "Glory to His Name" or "Sound the Battle Cry."

"O that with yonder sacred throng we at his feet may fall," she heard during her fourth time through the melody, and for some silly reason she suddenly saw a very clear picture take shape in her mind, a picture of an enormous crowd of people looking toward a bright light. And she knew for a certainty that her grandmother was in that crowd—her parents, also. She stopped playing and immediately looked over at her kitchen counter, staring hard at her canisters with their bright yellow lids.

She tried picking up the tune again without looking back at the music and finished it with only one minor slip. That's what she should have done anyway—tried playing by ear. She had always been pretty good at that.

Across the page from "All Hail the Power" was a page titled *Responsive Readings*. Celia remembered the procedure well. The preacher or song leader or sometimes a deacon would read the first verse, and the whole congregation would join in whenever the text shifted to boldface type. This would usually come after the second hymn, right before the offertory. One thing Bethany Hills knew how to do was stick to a routine. She remembered one deacon in particular, Brother Dooley, who was a poor reader and always butchered his half of the responsive readings, doing things like mixing up *immorality* and *immortality*, and once when reading John 3 had had Nicodemus address Jesus as *Rabbit* instead of *Rabbi*. Another time he had pronounced *naked* as one syllable, rhyming it with *baked*. "Naked came I out of my mother's womb, and naked shall I return," he had read.

Celia had tried to make a joke of it once, and only once, a few months after coming to live with her grandmother, when they were having their Bible reading after supper one night. She was still timidly trying to figure Grandmother out, to see if there were any sunlit corners in her dark personality. It was Celia's turn to read, and she had purposely mispronounced naked as Brother Dooley had the Sunday before, even stressing it a little: ". . . but all things are *naked* and opened unto the eyes of him with whom we have to do." Her grandmother had immediately lifted her eyes from her Bible and fixed them on Celia's face reprovingly. "Don't make fun of the less fortunate" was all she had said, or needed to.

Celia saw now that the first responsive reading was titled "The Holy Scriptures," and before she could close the book, she caught sight of the second verse, the one in bold print for the congregation to read: "But continue thou in the things which thou hast learned and hast been assured of, knowing of whom thou hast learned them." Her eyes leapt ahead to the next verse, "And that from a child thou hast known the holy scriptures," but she closed the book firmly and pushed it away from her, as if it were emitting noxious fumes. It was a passage she had heard often, though. She knew it went on to talk about being "wise unto salvation."

She twisted her clarinet apart and put it back into the case. What a stupid idea it had been to use Grandmother's hymnal for clarinet practice. She should have listened to the voice that had warned her not to. Now she had all those pesky words spinning around in her head: "The things which thou hast learned" and "from a child thou hast known" and "O that with yonder sacred throng." Something else to keep her awake tonight.

As she snapped the case shut, she noticed the nametag hanging from the handle. Turning it over, she saw her name printed neatly on the little card inserted behind the plastic shield: CECILIA ANNETTE COLEMAN. The ink had faded over the years, but she recognized it at once as her mother's printing.

And suddenly a whole day from the past came back to her. It would have been twenty-two years ago, almost twenty-three now, on the second day of August, the day she had turned fourteen. That had been the day her mother had printed her name on a little white card and inserted it into the luggage tag, taken off an old suitcase, then affixed it to her clarinet case, which, being secondhand, didn't have one of its own.

"Some nugget about your mom"—wasn't that what Mike had said on the phone recently? "One of those meaningful moments from childhood." If she ever did write anything about her mother, this might be the nugget, the meaningful moment—her fourteenth birthday. It had been a mild, pleasant, fairly low-key birthday up until the big surprise that evening.

Celia always knew that part of the reason her father was so concerned about finances was that, unlike many of her friends at school, hers was a one-income family. Though her mother had taught first grade before Celia was born, she had quit her job and stayed home after discovering, jubilantly, that she was finally pregnant after nine long years of waiting and hoping. Or *trying*, as Celia had heard people describe it today. Thereafter, when filling out forms with a blank for occupation, her mother had proudly written in "homemaker, wife, and mother." And her father approved wholeheartedly. He wanted her mother to stay home. He liked being the sole breadwinner, even if it did worry him sick at times.

Her mother was a skilled seamstress, though, and gradually, as Celia got older, she took on sewing projects to make a little extra money. After several years, her father cleared out the spare bedroom and made it into a sewing room with a big worktable in the middle and a three-sided mirror mounted in the corner. Her mother used an old Singer sewing machine that had hardly any attachments, but nobody seemed to care about her equipment when she could turn out such perfect draperies and neatly tailored dresses.

Every month her parents made a ritual of sitting at the kitchen table and paying all the bills together, during which time Celia would sit quietly in the living room right around the corner, pretending to read or do homework, listening for signs of trouble. She remembered the feeling of relief when it was over, when the last stamp was licked and stuck on the last envelope, when her mother would sigh and say something like "Okay, that leaves fifteen dollars to put in the fund."

"The fund" was for a new sewing machine her mother had her eye on, one "with all the bells and whistles," as she called it. The fund had been a fourth presence in their home for as long as Celia could remember. It was raided regularly, however, to pay for emergencies, such as a brake job or a dental bill, and once her mother had taken fifty dollars out of it to send Celia to a summer camp sponsored by the Baptist church they attended in Lawrenceville, Georgia. And when Celia started clarinet lessons in sixth grade, her mother paid for them out of her sewing money, which meant less left over for the fund.

Keenly aware of the extra expense, Celia threw herself into her lessons and practiced fiercely. If she was going to strain the budget, she was going to make sure her parents saw results. And they did. Her teacher, Mrs. Campbell, had nothing but praise for her efforts in spite of the cast-off instrument Celia was using, which had been the one her father had played in high school.

He had told her that if she did well on the clarinet, he would take her out and show her how to use the tennis racket in his closet, which he had also used in high school. The summer before eighth grade he had kept his promise, and she had picked up on tennis as quickly and as well as she had on clarinet.

Several times, as Celia continued to improve, Mrs. Campbell had suggested to her mother that they look for a better clarinet, and her mother had always acted embarrassed and said, "I'll tell my husband, and we'll think about it." Which made Celia wonder if she should back off and stop improving so her teacher would quit talking about her parents spending more money. By then, however, she loved playing so much she couldn't make herself ease up.

And it made her parents happy, too. Her junior high had a band, and in seventh grade Celia sat first chair among the ten clarinets. She liked seeing her parents in the audience when the band gave a concert. She liked the way the worry lines in her father's face smoothed out when he listened to her practice at home. "You're already better than I was when I graduated from high school," he told her one day when she was thirteen.

Her fourteenth birthday had started out pretty much as expected. It was early August, hot as all get-out in Lawrenceville, Georgia, and when she woke up that morning, she lay in bed and rehearsed the joys ahead.

She knew her mother was trying to finish up a bridesmaid's dress today and was meeting with another woman who was moving into a brand-new house and wanted all new window treatments, which was the new term for what everybody used to call draperies or curtains. But at three o'clock, her mother had promised, they would ride the bus downtown to JCPenney to look at school clothes.

It had never seemed odd to Celia at all that her birthday presents were always necessities, never luxuries. School clothes, shoes, backpacks, notebooks, pens and pencils—these were the standard gifts. But this year was different. This year she got to help pick her own clothes, so even though some of the surprise would be missing, it made her feel grown-up to participate in the selection.

Celia got her own breakfast that morning, a bowl of Cream of Wheat and a piece of cinnamon toast, and ate it while she watched a rerun of *Perry Mason,* then practiced her clarinet for a while, read her Bible for the standard fifteen minutes, tidied her room, took some clothes off the clothesline for her mother and folded them, and read two chapters in a book her Sunday school teacher had given her, *A Girl of the Limberlost.*

She heard her mother talk to the bridesmaid on the phone and, later, to the rich lady who was getting all new window treatments. The bridesmaid came over for her final fitting around noon, and the rich lady arrived early, so the two of them overlapped a little. Celia herself went to the door to let the rich lady in, a tall, skinny, magazine-model type wearing a bright turquoise pantsuit and aggressively made up with heavy mascara and deep purplish lipstick. As she escorted her to her mother's sewing room, Celia could feel the lady's eyes behind her, taking in every detail of their modest home. It worried her a little, the way she looked down from her great height so condescendingly. What if she decided not to use her mother, to give her business to someone with more social class?

She shouldn't have worried, though. As her mother explained to her later when they were on their way downtown to JCPenney, people like that really preferred their hired help to be of humble means. Her mother didn't laugh all that often, but when she did, it was a beautiful sound, almost like singing. Celia remembered that she had laughed that day on the bus as she told Celia how rich people sometimes liked to boast to each other about such discoveries as "this amazing tailor I found in this little dump of a shop on the west end of town" or "the most exquisite *artist* of a carpenter whose shop is the filthiest little hole in the wall you ever saw." If the workman himself were freakish in some way—say, a midget or a paraplegic—all the better for their story.

When Celia wondered aloud what the rich lady would tell her friends about *them,* her mother laughed again and, in a rare show of playacting, said in a breathy, gushy voice, accompanied by much hand fluttering, "You wouldn't believe this little plain sparrow of a seamstress I ran across over in those shacks behind the bus depot! Does the most astounding things with this absolute *relic* of a sewing machine!" Then, evidently afraid she had gone too far and not wanting to set a bad example, her mother grew serious again. "I'm just teasing, you understand," she said, patting Celia's hand. "We all have our little oddities."

They rode the rest of the way in silence, Celia reviewing the way things stacked up in unequal portions in life, some people having so much money and others not nearly enough. It troubled her to hear her mother describe herself as a plain sparrow. She was a small woman and didn't go in much for fancy things, but in Celia's opinion she was much, much prettier than the rich lady in her turquoise pantsuit. And the part about the shacks— that bothered her, too. Theirs wasn't a grand house by any means, but it was clean and neat and plenty big for the three of them.

After a supper of grilled hamburgers that night, which was Celia's birthday choice, she opened her presents—the things she had already picked out and tried on earlier that day, which her mother had brought home and wrapped. Celia remembered searching her father's face as she opened each one, hoping he wouldn't think they had spent too much money. But if he did, he didn't show it. Grandmother had sent her a copy of *Little Women,* and Papa and Mums had sent a card and a ten-dollar bill.

After the gifts they had cake—yellow cake with white icing, decorated with brightly colored candy sprinkles—and then Celia started back to her bedroom to put her new things away. That's when her father called her back. "Oh, say, Celie, there's one more present we almost forgot about."

Another present? Celia was astonished. Had she heard right? She had opened all the things she had picked out downtown. And it was plenty! They shouldn't have spent more money on something else. Maybe her father was teasing, though it wasn't like him to tease.

She turned back, clutching her new school clothes to her chest, and looked at her parents quizzically. Her mother laughed her beautiful sing-ing laugh and said, "You should see your face!" And her father pulled out from under the table another present, a rectangular shape wrapped in shiny lime green paper with a big bow of curly white crinkle ribbon.

Astonishment heaped on top of astonishment as Celia put her clothes down on a chair and set about opening the surprise gift. She could hardly get her breath while she was unwrapping it, and afterward—well, she didn't remember if she had even been able to get a word out. She did remember staring at it for a long, long time and at some point crying over the gift itself, the money it must have cost, her parents' happy faces, and of course her own immense delight.

It was a new clarinet, at least new to her. As she lifted it gently out of its case, her mother told her the story. Her father had seen it in a pawn shop downtown one day and had called Mrs. Campbell to come down and take a look at it. Mrs. Campbell had tried not to let on in front of the shop owner as she looked it over, had even scowled and made some deprecating remarks about the finger pads and such, but she told Celia's father as soon as they went back out on the sidewalk that it was a wonderful instrument worth about ten times what they were asking for it. She said the quality was such that Celia could play it all the way through college.

"Play it for us right now!" her father said, and Celia went to get a reed from her old case. She still couldn't believe it—a new clarinet! How in the world had her parents paid for it? Just the week before, she had heard her father talking about needing to find a plumber to replace some pipes under the house.

When she came back to the kitchen, her mother had found a marker and was neatly printing Celia's name on a little card. "Look, I got the nametag off that old brown suitcase in the attic," she said. "We'll put it on your case so nobody gets it mixed up with theirs."

And as Celia picked up her new clarinet, the truth struck her. Her mother's sewing machine fund had once again been robbed, in a very big way. She glanced over at her mother, who was smiling as her small fingers slipped the name card behind the little plastic cover of the tag, and Celia knew that those same hands would be using the old Singer relic for many, many months to come. No bells and whistles anytime soon.

Celia ran her thumb over the nametag now. The years might have faded the letters, but every detail of her fourteenth birthday was as clear as type rolled freshly inked off the press. She wasn't surprised to find herself crying. This was a memory that warranted great bucketfuls of tears . . . her dear, sweet, good parents, both of them so full of joy at the gift they had given her.

If she had been reading one of Frank Bledsoe's deplorable stories and come across the phrase "her dear, sweet, good parents," she would have slashed through it with her red pen and written in the margin, "Too gooey—cut the mush!" But those were the three best adjectives to describe her parents. They were other things, also—strict, frugal, serious, nervous. But first they were dear, sweet, and good. If she wrote the phrase herself, about her parents, and some editor told her to tone down the sentimentality, she would have to refuse, clinging to the higher standard of honesty.

As she walked back to the hall closet to put her clarinet away, Celia knew she was crying not only for the loss of her parents and their goodness, for the huge gap their death had left in her life, but also for what she knew would be their vast disappointment if they could see her today and know the things she had done. She was crying over the happy memory of her long-ago fourteenth birthday. And she was crying, also, because she was once again stabbed in the heart by the realization that right this very minute another fourteen-year-old could be alive if she hadn't done the things she had done.

16

Not a Shadow, Not a Sigh

Celia arrived promptly at seven o'clock. Cars were parked in front of Elizabeth Landis's house on both sides of the street, but Elizabeth had told Celia to pull into the driveway, since she would need to unload the painting she was bringing to the poetry club meeting. Celia was looking forward to having this evening behind her. She was afraid Elizabeth was expecting too much of her, and she suspected that this whole poetry club business was a little corny. She couldn't figure out, though, how someone seemingly as classy as Elizabeth would be part of something corny.

The Women Well Versed—that was what they called themselves. The name was actually what had raised the first question mark in Celia's mind about the seriousness of the group. They met once a month at a member's home, and this month Elizabeth had volunteered her house. It was a brick ranch style, nothing pretentious but comfortable looking, with two big pots of red geraniums on the front steps and an American flag hanging by the front door, which was standing open.

From the driveway Celia could see through the bay window into the living room, which was softly lit but apparently unoccupied. The women must be meeting in another room. Maybe they were all in the kitchen sampling the refreshments.

Celia got out of her car and looked around. It was a peaceful-looking neighborhood, different in two important ways from many of the new subdivisions she had seen. First, it had a lot of trees, all kinds of full-grown ones—pine, oak, poplar, sweet gum. There was a beautiful Japanese maple by the mailbox in Elizabeth's front yard. And second, the houses weren't replicas of each other. Each one had its own personality. Too bad so few developers today understood how to plan new neighborhoods.

Celia knew Macon Mahoney lived across the street from Elizabeth, and she turned to study his house for a moment. She didn't know what she was expecting, but, except for his mustard-colored Volkswagen van in the driveway, she was struck by how normal it all looked. You'd never know, if you were strolling up the sidewalk admiring the hydrangea bushes planted in front of the porch, that when you mounted the steps and rang the doorbell, a kooky guy like Macon would come to the door and say something totally incomprehensible. When Celia had suggested to Elizabeth that she ask Macon to come to the poetry meeting instead of her and talk about one of his own paintings, Elizabeth had laughed and shaken her head. "You know Macon," she had said. "Nobody can follow a word he says."

As Celia turned back to look at Elizabeth's house, a man came out the front door. "You must be the guest speaker," he said to her as he came down the steps. Celia didn't like the sound of that. A guest speaker was someone who gave a full-fledged, well-outlined speech, someone who did it often and well, not somebody who was about to chat extemporaneously for ten or fifteen minutes about a painting.

She recognized the man as Elizabeth's husband, Ken Landis. She had seen him in person once, conducting a July Fourth outdoor concert over at Harwood, and his picture had been in the paper a couple of times for other community events. He had also won some kind of award for musical composition not too long ago, and the Derby paper had printed an announcement, along with another picture of him in a tuxedo, holding a baton.

They shook hands and introduced themselves. He wasn't what you'd call a breathtakingly handsome man, Celia thought, but he had the kind of decidedly masculine looks—the dark straight hair, the deep-set eyes, the angular jawline—that could probably grow on you to the point that someday, when describing him, you might use the word *handsome* without even meaning to.

"Liz sent me out to help you with the painting," he said, glancing at Celia's Mustang. He seemed a little uneasy to Celia, not nearly as warm and outgoing as he had come across in the July Fourth concert, when he had turned to address the audience between numbers. It must be one of those cases where the public persona was totally different from the private one.

The painting, covered by a thin blue blanket, was standing upright in Celia's car, leaning against the backseat. It was tight getting it out because her Mustang was a two-door, but Ken was careful and took his time. She closed the car door, then followed him up to the front door, where Elizabeth was now waiting. She greeted Celia and held the screen open for them. "I was hoping you wouldn't forget," she said to Celia, winking.

"All I can say is I hope you don't nag your husband as much as you did me about this meeting tonight," Celia said, to which Ken replied, "Oh, she does, she does, believe me." He set the painting down inside the front door.

"We're meeting in the den," Elizabeth said.

"Oh, that's right," Ken said, picking the painting up again.

"Men," sighed Elizabeth. "You have to tell them everything."

"And that's something women are so good at—telling *everything*," Ken said.

They smiled at each other but sideways, almost shyly, and only for the briefest second before each of them looked quickly away. It was almost as if they were new at teasing, trying it out to see how it worked.

As the three of them walked back to the den, Celia found herself wondering what kind of long-term relationship it was that produced smiles like the ones she had just observed. Was it that Elizabeth and her husband were closer than most couples? Or perhaps not as close? She assumed they had been married for at least twenty-five years. She had heard Elizabeth talk about a grown daughter and a son in college.

Was it possible that two people could be married that long and still maintain a sort of old-fashioned reserve around each other? Or maybe this was only a phase for Elizabeth and Ken. Maybe their marriage had long periods of intense closeness, followed by wintry spells, then gradually warming again. Maybe they were in transition right now, moving into early spring. Or maybe—and this was probably more likely—she had completely misread their smiles. She knew that, as a single woman, she tended to spend too much time scrutinizing married people, concocting theories that were probably nowhere close to the truth.

Suddenly she found herself at the doorway of the den, a large room with lots of windows, bookshelves, and art. All the women, already seated in a big circle around the room, grew quiet. Elizabeth put her arm around

Celia's shoulder and pulled her forward to stand beside her, then began introducing her. Most of the women were married, Celia noticed. She had often wondered if her own quickness in spotting wedding and engagement rings was superior to that of other single women. Maybe it was working in the field of art for so many years that had given her such a sharp eye for details.

Someone had once told her that the spotting-a-wedding-ring talent was in direct proportion to how badly you wanted to be married yourself, but Celia wasn't so sure about that. She certainly didn't consider herself overly anxious to get married, not anymore. She could list dozens of advantages of being single. She could point to any number of marriages she wouldn't want to be any part of. Still, it was uncanny, and maybe a little amusing, how fast her eyes could sweep across a group of people and separate them into married and single. It wasn't hard, really. The ring finger on their left hand wasn't something most people tried to hide.

Sometimes married men didn't wear a ring, though. She knew that. If they worked with heavy machinery, for example. Or sometimes a ring got too small or caused a rash, and they left off wearing it. Often Celia's eagle eyes could detect a slight paleness, the faintest indentation on a man's third finger that spoke of a ring having been worn for a long time, then taken off.

Sometimes men wore their rings on unconventional fingers, too. Ollie wore his on his middle finger, for example. He had weighed 250 pounds when he married Connie but had gone on a diet and dropped about eighty pounds several years ago, so instead of getting his wedding ring resized, he had started wearing it on his middle finger. Celia had noticed that Bruce, her new next-door neighbor, wore his on his right hand, probably because of the scars on his left hand. Mike Owen down at the newspaper office wore his on a chain around his neck.

She shifted her eyes from the circle of women to the art on the walls as Elizabeth went on a little too long in her introduction. Celia knew Elizabeth loved art, but she was surprised at how much of it she had collected. Every spare section of wall that wasn't windows or bookshelves was covered with groupings of pictures, all sizes and subjects, in a variety of media—etchings, oils, prints, collagraphs, linocuts, photographs, watercolors, even some needlework. "And she's on my tennis team, too," Elizabeth was saying now. "She's our number one singles player, which means she has to play the really tough opponents while I get the easier ones."

Which wasn't exactly the way it always worked out. Celia could have broken in and set her straight, could have reminded her of their last playoff match two weeks earlier when the other team had reversed their number one and two singles players so that Elizabeth, instead of Celia, had been paired with Donna Cobb. Team captains sandbagged like this all the time—switched the order around for tactical advantage, sacrificing one court in hopes of having a better chance on another.

But it hadn't worked out for the other team. Elizabeth, still chagrined over her loss two days earlier, had come to the match full of resolve. When it was announced that her opponent was Donna Cobb, she had set her jaw and headed to the court to get started. And according to the ones who had seen the entire match, she had played "out of her mind," making shots she had never made before and keeping Donna off balance by changing the pace of the game at crucial points. It made Donna's second defeat of the season, and if she had been mad at her loss to Celia back in March, she was livid at this one.

Afterward, Nan Meachum had overheard Donna in the restroom with one of her own teammates, crying and yelling about how she was "ten times better than a puffball player like that." Nan had wanted to call out from her stall and remind Donna about Elizabeth's two service aces and some of the overhead slams and cross-court winners she couldn't even get her racket on. She had wanted to ask Donna exactly what her definition of a puffball was.

Elizabeth's victory had been even sweeter because it was the one that gave them the third win they needed to take the match, and therefore come in first in the playoff series. Two of the doubles lost, but the other doubles and both singles won. Celia had ended up with the number two player on a court behind Elizabeth's, and her match had stretched out much longer than it should have. She hadn't played her best tennis that day by any means, but in spite of missing far too many shots, she had managed to pull it out and win 6–4, 7–6. The team was now making plans to leave for Charleston in three weeks for the state playoffs.

Elizabeth finally wound up her introduction and asked Celia to sit in the chair closest to the door, where Ken had placed the painting on a makeshift easel against the wall, making sure the blanket still covered the front of it before he quickly disappeared. "We'll wait just another minute or two before starting," Elizabeth said to everyone in general. "I think we're all here but Michelle, and she wasn't sure she was coming. One of the kids was running a fever."

Just then there was the sound of deep bleating laughter from out in the kitchen, as if from a very large sheep, followed by the tread of heavy footsteps coming toward the den. "I'm a-comin'! Don't give up on me!" a voice called—a thick sticky bass voice you might hear on cartoons.

"Oh, here comes Eldeen," Elizabeth said. "I'd forgotten she was in the bathroom." Something about the name Eldeen and the peculiar sound of her voice sparked Celia's memory. It was one of those times when she felt that she was about to experience something she had already done before—something, strangely, that she both wanted to repeat and wished she could avoid.

It was hard to decide what would be the first adjective you'd use to describe the woman who came through the doorway of the den and made her way to her seat at the end of the sofa. *Big* might be a place to start. Or *old*. Those would be the obvious ones. There were others, of course— *talkative,* for from her mouth issued a mighty flow of words, and *outlandish,* for her clothing appeared to have been chosen in the dark. She wore a bright red cotton print dress with a splashy pattern of large white daisies, enormous brown sandals with white socks, and a bright teal blazer made of a nubby synthetic fabric.

Although the other women seemed to regard Eldeen's entrance quite casually, Celia couldn't take her eyes off the spectacle. How could you ever get *used* to someone who looked like that? Apparently addressing Elizabeth, Eldeen was explaining her delay in returning, laying it all to Elizabeth's account for having magazines in the bathroom: " . . . the most *interesting* article in one of them old *National Geography* magazines you got in that wicker basket by the commode," she was saying. "Whenever there's read-ing material in the lavatory, I got to watch myself or I'll lose track of the time. I reckon that's one of my besetting sins—though I can't see where it's a sin to want to broaden your mind, can you? There's just so much to learn in the world, I can't soak it all up fast enough!"

She lowered herself heavily onto the sofa, expressing hope that she could get back up once she got settled into the cushions. Then she leaned forward and continued talking to Elizabeth, who was sitting in a ladder-back chair three seats away. "Many's the time Jewel's come a-tappin' at the bathroom door, sayin', 'Mama? Mama? It sure is quiet in there. You all right?' Not meanin' to be nosy, she's not, but just wantin' to make sure what happened to that woman over in Powdersville doesn't happen to me. You know, that one that slipped on the tile floor and banged her head against the bathtub and fell down unconscious and stayed that way for the longest time before her husband got in from plantin' corn, expectin' his supper to be on the table, and the kitchen just as dark and still as a sepulcher, and he had to go all around the house callin' her name till he found her just comin' out of her spell, a-settin' on the bathroom floor rubbin' her head, all bewildered and full of perplexity!"

The woman sitting next to Eldeen on the sofa, a tranquil, pretty, normal-sized woman who didn't look like she could possibly be related to her, placed her hand on Eldeen's arm in a daughterly sort of way, a gesture which, if intended to stanch the tide of the older woman's words, failed altogether. "I always start out tellin' myself I'm just going to look at the pictures, nothing more," Eldeen said, "and then before I know it, I start reading the captions under the pictures, and then my appetite's so whetted I read a little tidge of the beginning, and then I just give in and start reading the whole kit and caboodle. This article I got started looking at a minute ago was about these men in Africa that hunts pythons, them big old snakes that can squeeze the breath out of a human person."

By now most of the other women had stopped their various conversations and were listening to Eldeen. "They carry little torches, you see, and they wiggle theirself down these long dark burrows, where the python's a-layin' all snugged up asleep in his den, and they *snatch* 'em real quick right behind their head"—to illustrate, she reached a man-sized hand behind her own head and grabbed her neck—"and then they drag 'em out and slit open their throats and . . ."

This time the other woman must have exerted a little more pressure on Eldeen's arm, for Eldeen lost her rhythm and looked over at her. The younger woman whispered something, at which Eldeen burst out with a great honk of laughter, followed by another series of deep, sheeplike baas, then clamped her hand over her mouth briefly. "Oh yes, I know it. I know it!" she said. "I'll stop now, I promise. We didn't come here to listen to me talk about snake huntin'. We got us a meeting to get started! You go right ahead, Elizabeth honey, and I'll be quiet as a little church mouse." She laughed again and added, "A *mouse*—now that reminds me. The article said that's one thing them pythons like to eat!"

Elizabeth smiled and looked down, smoothing her skirt, a pale apricot knit. Celia always liked the colors Elizabeth put together. From the first time she had come into the gallery years ago, Celia could tell she had a flair for color, and not your traditional combinations, either. That day she had been wearing cranberry-colored slacks and a bulky sweater the blue of a robin's egg. Tonight with her apricot skirt, she had on a sleek tunic-style top the color of a clay pot, with the sleeves pushed up. Her only jewelry was a large silver pin shaped like a conch shell.

"Well, all right," she said, nodding toward the attractive woman seated to her right. "I guess we'll go ahead and get started now, Margaret. I thought maybe we could go around first, starting with you, and give our names for Celia." The other woman, whom Celia took to be the leader of the group, nodded and gave her name. "Margaret Tuttle," she said, smiling at Celia.

When it got around to Eldeen's turn, she said, "Eldeen Rafferty, and just one more little thing about them pythons . . . they don't spit out poison like some snakes, but they got these long teeth in the back that curves backwards and can tear up flesh like saw blades!" She grinned, a grisly-looking grimace of a smile, then said, "There, I'm done. Oh, and I guess I was out of the room when this little lady got introduced." She nodded toward Celia.

Celia had already identified Eldeen by now, of course, as the nighttime visitor, the bringer of muffins, the persistent Woodmont Street welcoming-committee-of-one who had come to Al Halston's house the night she broke up with him back in February. The woman who claimed to be marching through Immanuel's land, whose finger was on the pulse of the whole neighborhood, who kept watch at her front window on the comings and goings of everyone along the street.

Yet Celia also remembered the curious feeling she had had as Eldeen left Al's house that night—the simultaneous rush of relief at getting rid of her, mixed with the inexplicable desire to follow her out and give her a hug. She remembered wondering what it would have been like to have a grandmother like her instead of the solemn, poker-faced one she had been saddled with. Even though the woman had made no secret of her religion, she seemed to have a broad imagination and a generous spirit. You could tolerate a little religion in a grandmother like that.

Though Eldeen had crossed Celia's mind a number of times since February, never had she suspected they would someday be thrown together again. Now as Elizabeth repeated Celia's name and an abridged version of her introduction for Eldeen's benefit, the older woman cocked her head and stared at her intently. But evidently she didn't make the connection with Al, for afterward she broke into another alarming smile and stated her pleasure in making Celia's acquaintance. Then, surprisingly, she fell silent and allowed the meeting to continue.

The painting Celia had chosen to bring to the meeting was one of what Ollie referred to as his "experientials," which fell between his earlier objective landscapes and the moody mythological abstracts he had dabbled in before his most recent exploration of architectural themes, or "playing around with the line," as he liked to describe his current style. Personally, Celia thought Ollie's earlier work was superior to his later stuff, but she knew artists had to be free to roam, so she never spoke up and agreed when his wife, Connie, openly expressed her opinion about the direction he was going, which she did quite often without mincing words.

"Get back to humanity," Connie was fond of saying. "These things you're doing now aren't what people want hanging on their walls at home. They're sure not what *I* want hanging on *our* walls. That last thing looked like a blueprint you'd roll up and put a rubber band around." Not that the recent pieces didn't have the mark of an acknowledged master of color, line, and form. They were good art, no doubt about it, but not terribly appealing to the average collector who came into the Trio Gallery with the dual ambition of investing and decorating. "People have to feel art tugging at them," Connie would say. "The stuff you're doing now is for the connoisseur, not for the nice person who's looking for something to hang above his mantel or go over a new sofa."

Ollie would argue good-naturedly, accusing Connie of lapses in her logic. "You and your false dichotomies," he might say, laughing. "As if a connoisseur can't also be a nice person."

"Well, anyway, you need to get back to humanity," she would always repeat at some point in their debate. "Something people feel drawn to, not all this gothic, sterile stuff."

Connie often seemed to fling words around indiscriminately, yet somehow they always managed to communicate quite precisely. Like *gothic* and *sterile,* two words that had seemed to fall off her tongue at random. Ollie's style during his mythological phase had indeed been somewhat gothic, full of dark brooding stylized figures arranged in highly allegorical contexts, while the spare lines of his more recent architectural pieces did give each piece the cold, sterile feel of an office or waiting room. "You've gone from way too much to way too little," Connie also liked to say. "Keep on and pretty soon you'll be down to blank canvases with a little dot in the middle."

But Celia herself would never say such things to Ollie's face. Instead, she used words like *mystical* and *evocative* or *uncluttered* and *innovative*. And then there was *interesting*. That was always a highly useful word, too.

The painting she had chosen for tonight, though, was one of Connie's favorites. She was out of town for a few days, visiting her mother in Irmo, or Ollie might have had trouble getting her permission to take it off the wall. "This way she'll never know," he said when Celia had stopped by to get it.

He had offered her anything in his studio, but none of those pieces seemed suited to tonight's purposes. To be polite, she had nevertheless looked at them all. She knew she'd see many of them again when Ollie did his next show of new works at the gallery. When she had hesitated, then asked if he'd let her take the painting in the entryway by the front door, the one titled *Beyond,* he had agreed at once, as long as it was back on the wall by the time Connie came home.

After a few words from Margaret Tuttle by way of introducing the goal of this evening's format, which was the composition of original poems by the women themselves, Elizabeth spoke briefly about three well-known paintings and read the three poems inspired by them. She had distributed handouts containing small prints of each painting, along with the text of each poem. In addition, she had larger color prints of the three paintings, which showed more detail than the handouts.

Elizabeth had evidently changed her mind about which paintings and poems to use, for they were different from the ones she had mentioned to Celia earlier. There were a few comments and questions after Elizabeth's part. Concerning Cathy Song's poem about Kitagawa Utamaro's *Girl Powdering Her Neck,* Eldeen observed, "How'd she know them was maple leaves on that lady's kimono? Looks to me more like little birds a-flittin' through the air." Another woman asked what a "meerschaum" was in Delmore Schwartz's poem about the painting by Seurat, and someone else noted how the verb tense shifted in the third poem by Molly Peacock.

Then Elizabeth turned the floor over to Celia to "share with us a fine work by a contemporary artist living right here in our own corner of the world." Celia enjoyed the sensation of unveiling Ollie's painting, of lifting off the blue blanket and hearing the admiring murmurs of the women. It was a large painting, around thirty-six by fifty-two inches. She loved standing right next to it and basking in its beauty and power. And when she started talking, she had no trouble finding words for *Beyond.* There was so much to be said, in fact, that it was hard to find a place to stop. She defined terms such as *impasto, Mars pigments, ochre,* and *copal* as she went along. The women listened closely, as if preparing for a test over the material. Most of them were taking notes.

The painting, richly suggestive of a thousand things, combined golds, oranges, grays, and browns with so many subtle gradations you'd think you were looking at something in real life, except for the fact that you couldn't identify an actual scene or object. It could be any number of things if you were bent on trying to find a picture of something in it—the sky above a canyon, the intimate parts of a giant flower, the Florida Keys at dusk, a woman lying in a pool of sunlight, an oil spill, the interior of a topaz mine—which made it the perfect piece for the poetry club to write about.

After Celia's talk, the idea was for the women to come up to the easel a few at a time and examine the painting at close range, ask questions, and then go back to their seats and start writing their poems. They wouldn't be able to finish them that night, most likely, but they were to jot down ideas, certain phrases that came to mind, decide on a unifying theme, maybe get a few lines put together. Elizabeth, Margaret, and Celia were all available for consultation during this half hour of initial rough drafting, and then at the next monthly meeting they were to bring back their finished poems, revised and polished, to share with one another.

When Eldeen came up to view the painting, Celia noticed that she had evidently already decided on a theme for her poem, for in her spiral notebook she had printed on the top line in large, childish letters, *WHEN WE GET TO HEAVEN.* She stooped and craned her neck forward so her nose was about ten or twelve inches from the bottom of the painting, and she scanned her eyes back and forth across the canvas, turning her head from side to side, as spectators did while watching a tennis match, gradually straightening as she went higher, until she was again standing to her full height.

Being so close to her, Celia could easily imagine Eldeen being featured at a carnival, alongside the Sword Eater, the Two-Headed Man, and the Bearded Lady. They could bill her as the Huge Funny Old Woman. It might not sound all that strange, but people would sure get their money's worth if they gave her a chance.

After Eldeen's close-up perusal, she stepped back and took another good long look at the painting, then whispered to Celia loudly, so as not to disturb the others, "That there's a picture of the shinin' pathway to heaven, clear as clear can be!" She pointed to the bottom corner of the canvas. "Right now we're standin' outside, don't you see, way off here in the valley of shadows a-lookin' at it from afar."

Then she pointed to the broad, curved band of gold running through the center. "There's the road leadin' to the celestial city. See how it keeps a-gettin' brighter as it goes along? And right there—see? See that splotch of yellow, like the sky's busted a hole in itself? Why, that's the light of eternity spillin' out the gate! And all this up here"—she waved her hand at the bleeding layers of reds, oranges, and golds at the top—"all this here's the reflected glory and majesty and splendor of the Almighty God and his precious son, Jesus, whose blood ran down the old rugged cross of Calvary to give old Eldeen Rafferty a ticket to show at the gate!" She leaned even closer to Celia then and added, still talking in a stage whisper, "And I don't know if you know it or not, honey, but he'll give *you* a ticket, too, if he already hasn't!"

Not a word of which surprised Celia one bit. Why hadn't she thought of heaven as a potential topic for the poems springing from a painting titled *Beyond*? Knowing that Elizabeth was a churchgoer, she should have known there would be others in the group. It would be the most natural thing in the world for someone wired together like Eldeen to interpret the painting this way. Celia glanced back at Eldeen, who was smiling at her hopefully, and revised the sign on Eldeen's carnival exhibit: Huge Funny Old Religious Woman.

She thought again, as she had that other time at Al's house, of how much her grandmother and Eldeen could have found to talk about—two women totally different in temperament but standing on the same unshakable bedrock. Celia let herself imagine for a moment what it would have been like if Eldeen had been one of their neighbors in Dunmore, Georgia, if she and Grandmother had visited back and forth and traded recipes with each other. Maybe she would have rubbed off on Grandmother a little, could have eased the lines around her grim mouth and made her laugh once in a while.

"See, here's how my poem starts out," Eldeen said, showing Celia her spiral notebook. "There's a song we sing at church with almost the same words, except it says, 'When we *all* get to heaven,' but I left out the *all* because, sad to say, we're not *all* going to get there." She patted Celia's hand, quite hard. "But I hope *you* are, honey, I sure do. I can talk to you during refreshments and tell you how to get there if you want me to, that is, if you don't already know." She squeezed her hand, again quite hard. "You sure are a pretty little angel of a thing. You look like you *belong* in heaven, like you're just down here amongst us on loan!" She let go of Celia's hand. "You know, I keep thinking I've met you *somewhere* before, but I just can't put my finger on it." Celia let it pass. She didn't want to bring up Al Halston's name. Eldeen turned around and moved back to her seat on the sofa.

Celia looked back at the painting and immediately thought of something. She recalled that she had played "When We All Get to Heaven" on her clarinet at Bethany Hills Bible Tabernacle one Sunday for an offertory. It had been her grandmother's special request. That would have been twenty years ago now.

She knew she would never be able to look at Ollie's painting the same again. Now it would always be a depiction of heaven. Even as she looked at it now, she was assailed by phrases from the song: "In the mansions bright and blessed," "Soon the pearly gates will open," "Not a shadow, not a sigh."

From the sofa came the sound of Eldeen's laughter. She was bent over saying something to her daughter—or trying to. She had changed from a sheepy sort of laugh now to a gooselike one, a goose whose honking mechanism seemed to be stuck. Celia knew she would hear Eldeen's laughter for the rest of her life. One more thing to weave into her nighttime dreams. And her voice, too: "All this here's the reflected glory and majesty and splendor of the Almighty God!"

17

Frail Children of Dust

On the last day of May, a Tuesday, Celia was preparing to close up the gallery at five o'clock when Elizabeth Landis walked in. With her was the woman named Margaret, the leader of the poetry club, whom Celia had met at Elizabeth's house two weeks earlier. Margaret was one of the few middle-aged women who, in Celia's opinion, could truthfully be spoken of as beautiful in a physical sense without having to pad the word by including character, wisdom, experience, and all that, although, by all appearances, Margaret Tuttle seemed to possess those attributes, as well. You wouldn't have to qualify the adjective with any kind of concession for her age: "beautiful for a woman of fifty," for example. One glance at Margaret and the word *beautiful* sprang to mind with nothing tacked on. At least that's what Celia thought, and she had always considered herself a good judge of looks.

"I know it's closing time," Elizabeth said, "but we were driving by, and I wanted to show Margaret that one painting—you know, the gardenia one." Celia knew you didn't just happen to drive by the Trio Gallery. They must be headed to or from Greenville.

"Help yourself," Celia said. "I'm just trying to clear off the desk a little." The state playoffs started at the end of this week, and she wanted to leave things in good order for Tara and Ollie, who would take turns filling in for her at the gallery. She held up a handful of notes, all sizes, scribbled on scraps of paper. "Ollie's always leaving me reminders about things he wants me to check on, then I forget to throw them away afterward." She had often wondered what it said about her that she was so fastidious at home yet could tolerate an amazing amount of clutter on her desk at work.

The painting Elizabeth was talking about, the "gardenia one," as she called it, which was actually titled *Writing Table,* had sold on opening night. Celia had never before seen the woman who bought it, which was unusual. Most often she knew the buyers by name, had dealt with them before. Sometimes a friend of the artist, someone from out of town, might buy a work, but Lenny Bullard hadn't known this woman, either. She carried herself with the air of someone long accustomed to buying expensive things, however, and Celia had no doubt that she would make good on her commitment. She had left her card with Celia before driving off in a white Mercedes. The card identified her as "Justine Cunningham, Designer" at a place called Mercado Custom Interiors in Greenville.

"We won't be but a minute," Elizabeth said now. She and Margaret went into the central gallery, and though they were hidden from Celia's view, she could hear them. "That's it," she heard Elizabeth say, after which there was a pause before Margaret replied, "Yes, I see what you mean." Another pause, then Margaret again: "What arresting colors." A longer pause, then, "What a marvel that an artist can achieve such an elevated tone with such whimsy and buoyancy of style. I can see why you are struggling to keep the tenth commandment, Elizabeth." They both laughed.

Margaret hadn't talked much at the poetry club meeting, but Celia remembered wondering that night if she had written out her comments ahead of time and memorized them. She had never heard anyone speak extemporaneously with such formal grace. Most of the people she talked to on a regular basis didn't use words like *arresting, whimsy,* and *buoyancy* in a normal conversation.

"Yep, too bad that's somebody else's red dot," Elizabeth said with a sigh, referring to the fact that it was marked as sold. "But there's no way I could have bought it," she went on. "I've already overspent on art. The way I figure it, though, if I visit it enough times before the show comes down, it can be mine in a certain sense. I have this special gallery in my mind."

So Elizabeth had another hankering. Celia could have guessed it, though they had never really talked about it. Elizabeth had come to the opening of Lenny Bullard's show several weeks ago and had hung around longer than usual after Lenny's brief artist's talk, walking around slowly from painting to painting. Celia had seen her standing at length in front of the one titled *Writing Table* with something like anticipation written all over her face, looking like a ship coming into harbor, drawing nearer and nearer to a wondrous landmark on shore.

Celia had seen the look many times before on the faces of true art lovers. It was completely different from the that-would-match-my-new-wingback-chair look. This emigrant-gazing-at-the-Statue-of-Liberty look was the soul-hungry look of someone who didn't care one whit about using the painting for decoration, whose mind and heart were fixed on beauty as an emblem of goodness and hope.

Writing Table wasn't Celia's favorite piece in the show, but she could see how it would appeal to the likes of Elizabeth and Margaret, both of whom loved poetry. The perspective was interesting—the writing table was seen through a bedroom window, yet quite close up, as if the observer were a voyeur hoping to get a peek of something on a very different order. In front of the window there was a gardenia bush in bloom, so the writing table was actually forced into the background, though it was the title of the painting.

Lenny Bullard had outdone himself with the gardenias. They were gorgeous—sensuous full-blown blossoms with white petals smooth as buttermilk, others starting to open, some still spiraled up tightly in long creamy buds, all nestled within clusters of glossy dark green leaves. The brushwork on the open petals was exquisite, three or four strokes per petal, in colors ranging from the whitest white to the palest tinge of buttery yellow. You could spend a long time just reveling in the gardenias, practically smelling them, before you moved past them to the window and then inside to the writing table.

It was strange how the coolness of the gardenias in the foreground could temporarily block your attention from the bonfire of colors behind them. On the writing table, obviously a woman's, were scattered the accouterments of what looked to be a leisure poet. These included several sheets of bright yellow paper fanned out, a chunky uncapped fountain pen striped in all the colors of the rainbow, a pair of eyeglasses with wild chartreuse and pink polka-dotted frames, a peacock blue teacup with only a sip of raspberry-colored tea left in the bottom, two orange crackers lying in the matching saucer, a small banker's lamp with a green shade, a slim volume of poetry with a white cover, titled *Night Poems,* and a lady's wristwatch with a bracelet band of red scarabs like miniature stoplights strung together. The table itself was a shocking shade of lavender, with a chair of dark purple. Concerning the use of color, Margaret's word *arresting* was quite mild. If using color were a crime, this artist would be locked up for life.

Incongruously, however, a black-and-white picture with torn edges appeared in the midst of all this color, propped up against the base of the banker's lamp. And this was where the painting got really interesting, for it seemed that the poet, departed from the scene temporarily, perhaps to go brew another pot of tea, was in the process of composing a poem about this photograph. She had already completed two stanzas and started a third, all written in a tiny, delicate cursive, which could be read by twisting your neck and looking at the yellow paper sideways. The title was simply "Yellow":

> The hottest yellow I know
> Ignites the October page
> Of a calendar: a black
> And white photo of birch trees.
> Against the bass monotone—
> Trunks stretching off the page, wide
> Mouth of dark behind, then gray
> Hills—those leaves play piccolo.
> That white should turn to yellow
> Doesn't follow logic, yet . . .

These were the words she heard Elizabeth reading aloud to Margaret now. She read them slowly, seeming to taste every word. Since Celia herself didn't really know what to think of the poem as poetry, she listened carefully for Margaret's response. Maybe it would be something she could use if anybody asked her about it.

Margaret laughed softly. "Well, the artist is clearly having fun with his audience, is he not?"

"And with his subject, don't you think?" said Elizabeth.

"Oh, to be sure. In the midst of a profusion of color, he seems to be praising the absence of color. Yet the title of his poem is 'Yellow.' "

"Written on yellow paper no less. And the title of the book on the table is *Night Poems,* but it has a white cover, which goes along with the black-and-white photo, I guess."

Celia turned off the computer, rose from her desk, and walked into the exhibit room. The painting was on the far wall, and the two women were standing side by side, their backs to her.

Elizabeth bent forward and pointed. "I can't get over that little picture of the birch trees. Look at how lifelike it is. I mean, this guy takes all kinds of liberties with realism—all these distorted angles and funky colors—and then he sticks in this little cameo, all tidy and precise. It almost looks like it's in a different medium, doesn't it? Like a pencil etching or something." She moved back again and shook her head. "Interesting. So, so interesting. You're practically beat senseless by all this color, but in the end your eyes land on that one little spot of black and white."

"Seven syllables per line," Margaret said.

"Yes, I saw that. It's not bad, really, though he probably shouldn't give up painting to write poetry."

Again they both laughed. "Perhaps someone else wrote the poem," Margaret said.

"Maybe so," Elizabeth said. "Maybe his wife did."

"Is he married?" Margaret asked. She sounded surprised, as Celia herself had been surprised upon learning that Lenny was a family man. He even had grandchildren. That wasn't something you expected out of a man who consistently chose such feminine subjects to paint.

"Not anymore," Elizabeth said. "He talked a little about his wife on opening night. Said she died ten years ago of cancer. That's when he started painting her things—her dresser, her desk, her jewelry box, her closet—"

"And the places she used to go," Celia added. "The beauty shop and all." She was standing slightly behind Elizabeth now.

Elizabeth turned and smiled at her. "I really enjoyed his talk that night," she said. "He seemed like such a nice man."

Celia nodded. "He really is." She had noticed the first time she met Lenny Bullard, at his home a year or so ago, that he wasn't wearing a wedding ring, which didn't prove anything, especially in the art world. Still, it piqued her interest. He was a compact man but muscular, built like a wrestler, and it was easy to imagine him not breaking a sweat as he carried a bride over the threshold, even toted her around the whole house.

He was probably in his late forties or early fifties, but a nice-looking man. She had barely had time to wonder about his marital status, however, before he pointed to a crayon picture of a farm on his refrigerator and spoke proudly of his grandson, who had drawn it and who wanted to be an artist like his grandpa someday. And a little later he talked openly about his wife. Anyone could tell he was still deeply in love with her, that remarrying was clearly not something he was likely to do anytime soon.

The discovery of Lenny Bullard made a great story. Tara had run across one of his paintings hanging behind the cash register in a small mom-and-pop restaurant over near Mount Chesney, and she made some inquiries about the artist, who turned out to be a brother of the mom or pop. She got his name and address, and a few weeks later, after a phone call, Ollie and Celia had driven to Yemassee to visit him, which was the start of it all. Lenny had been shocked and overwhelmed that a real gallery wanted to do a whole show of his work. He had shown his stuff mainly at regional arts and crafts festivals and local flea markets. He had no idea he was as good as he was, nor, evidently, did anyone else down around Yemassee. Of course, it didn't usually happen that way at all. Artists weren't usually plucked out of obscurity. It made almost as good a story as Macon Mahoney walking in out of nowhere.

"So you think it's a pretty good poem?" Celia asked Elizabeth.

"Not bad," Elizabeth said. "Not bad at all. He's got a ways to go, you understand. It's not finished. But he's got a kind of interesting thing going."

Celia nodded. "Seven syllables in a line," she said, then deciding to be honest, added, "I really hadn't noticed until I heard Margaret say it."

"Well, I promised we wouldn't stay long," Elizabeth said, looking at her watch. "It's past five now." She glanced at Margaret, then back at Celia. "Okay, now for the second reason we stopped by." Celia felt her neck go tense. It had surprised her somewhat that Elizabeth had been so quiet about her religion since they had been on the tennis team together. She sensed now that the silence was about to be broken. "I really did want to show Margaret the painting," Elizabeth continued, "but we were also wondering if we could talk you into joining us for supper." She explained to Celia that they were on their way to Greenville to eat at a place called Aunt Cassie's Kitchen. Judy Howell on the tennis team had told Elizabeth about it. "Good country cooking and cheap—that's how Judy described it," she said. She went on to say that their husbands were both busy tonight, so they were having a ladies' night out.

The idea instantly made Celia nervous—eating out with two married women, trapped in an unfamiliar place, not knowing where the conversation might go. She knew Elizabeth, of course, but not Margaret, and to tell the truth, Margaret intimidated her a little. Her eyes had the wise, penetrating look of someone who could extract secrets you never intended to yield. Her beautiful face, her scholarly speech, her quiet dignity—they could hypnotize a person. She had a way of studying you that went beyond just friendly interest. It seemed that she *knew*.

"You would honor us with your company," Margaret said to Celia.

And right then, as if to demonstrate Margaret's hypnotic effect, though Celia's mind was waving a thousand red flags, though sirens were screaming in her ears, she heard herself say, "Well, okay, I guess so. I was just going to fix a sandwich at home."

They waited out on the sidewalk while she adjusted the air conditioning, activated the alarm, and turned off the lights. As she was flipping the sign to read Closed, the phone rang. She had no intention of answering it, but she waited nonetheless to see if someone would leave a message. Within seconds she heard Craig's voice, clearly exasperated. He didn't have to identify himself. No one else talked that rudely on the phone. "So you're gone already," he said. "I needed something," and then he hung up. Celia wasn't about to call him back. It was ten minutes past closing time. It irritated her that he made it sound like she had skipped out early.

She stepped outside and locked the door. Boo Newman, several doors down at the gift shop, was locking up, also. She hadn't stopped by the gallery in over a week, which pleased Celia just fine. But she cried out merrily now, "Hello, Celia! I'm coming down to see you tomorrow. Have I got a story for you!"

It was decided that they would all go in Elizabeth's car and leave Celia's Mustang at the gallery to pick up on the way home. Celia would have preferred to follow them in her car, but Elizabeth wouldn't hear of it. Thankfully, the conversation as they rode to Greenville was harmless, most of it relating to the gallery. Both Elizabeth and Margaret seemed consumed with curiosity about the everyday workings of an art gallery and plied her with question after question.

Celia didn't really mind all the questions, since they filled up time, and she liked the arrangement, with her sitting in the backseat giving her answers to the backs of their heads. She didn't rush her answers, even cast about for extra details to include. With every passing mile, what worried her more and more, though, was where the conversation would lead after Elizabeth and Margaret grew tired of the art gallery.

She knew how it went when women got together. She had been with the tennis team enough times to know that. But, ironically, the larger group was probably less risky. The smaller the number of women, the more personal and specific the talk would most likely get. So why in the world had she done this? What did she care about Aunt Cassie's Kitchen and its cheap good country cooking? What she was wishing for more than anything as the minutes passed was the safety of her own apartment, her own kitchen table, her own sandwich.

Elizabeth remarked about how interesting the layout of a new show always was and asked who decided how and where each piece was to be hung. She was obviously expecting Celia to describe some kind of complicated mathematical method of formatting, complete with graph paper and slide rules. Both Elizabeth and Margaret therefore thought it was very funny when she told them that though she usually came up with the groupings and general locations, Ollie most often did the actual hanging, using a procedure he had perfected called "the shoulder and nose method."

They were nearing the city limits of Greenville now, so she tried hard to concentrate on giving a relentlessly thorough explanation of the procedure, which might last until they got to the restaurant. For the shoulder part of Ollie's method, she told them, he needed a long piece of yarn, a hammer, and couple of nails. He stood against the end of a wall so that his shoulder touched it, and then he drove in a nail at that point and wrapped the yarn around the nail. Then he walked the yarn down to the other end of the wall, stood against the wall again, and drove another nail, then tied the yarn to that. This gave him a reference line.

Next he eyeballed all the pieces Celia had laid out to be hung on that wall, then, starting in the middle, he stepped up to the carpeted wall until his nose touched it and with his finger marked the place. He then fished a nail out of his pocket with the other hand and placed it a couple or three inches to the left of the spot, then took the hammer, which was tucked into his waistband, and pounded the nail in. Then he hammered in another nail to the right of the spot so that each painting hung by two nails instead of one. That gave greater stability.

Ollie had hung so many shows by now that the art of centering and spacing had almost become intuitive. And Celia had watched and helped so many times that she could do it herself if necessary, which she had had to do the time Ollie had been rushed to the hospital for an emergency appendectomy. She could have asked Craig or Tara to come in and help that time, but she decided it wasn't worth the trouble. So she did it herself, copying Ollie's basic technique but modifying the "shoulder and nose method" to the "chin and top of the head method" to compensate for the difference in their heights. And though it had taken her longer than Ollie, the results were basically the same.

Margaret asked if there was ever much damage to worry about—pieces getting broken or smudged with fingerprints—and if people were held liable for breakage as in any other store. No major catastrophes, Celia told them, only minor stuff—a couple of broken frames that were easily replaced, and once she herself had snapped off the very tip of a tail feather on a polychromed wood sculpture of a rooster when she was moving things around in one of the rooms.

When she had shown it to Ollie the next day, he had laughed as if at a piddling concern, then had taken a magic marker out of the desk drawer and colored over the broken end, after which he spit on his finger and rubbed it in. "Piece of cake, Cecilia. Eric will never know, believe me. Anyway, he trusts my judgment. He would thank me for fixing it." He had held the rooster out at arm's length. "I actually think it's even a little better now." Celia had marveled at Ollie's nerve, tampering with somebody else's art, and wondered if the artist, Eric Lynch, would ever trust Ollie again if he had seen him using a magic marker and rubbing saliva on his sculpture.

True to Elizabeth's description, Aunt Cassie's Kitchen was nothing fancy. A simple storefront building with plate-glass windows, it was located between a Goodwill store and a beauty supply outlet on the west end of Greenville, out near Interstate 85. Though it was owned and operated by a black family, the clientele appeared to be a mix of all races and tongues. It wasn't much past five-thirty, yet the place was almost full.

A noisy table of black teenagers occupied a back corner, while several Mexicans wearing red Dink's Car Wash shirts sat near the door. They must have just gotten off work, for their shirts were wet, making Celia think the workers might have gone through the car wash themselves. A black-haired woman in a sari sat with two small wide-eyed children at a table by the window. Celia looked past them quickly, shifting her attention to a grizzled old man hunkered over a plate of barbecued ribs at another table, with unkempt hair down around his shoulders and his beard collected into a ponytail, cinched with a rubber band.

"Judy said we'd see a cross section of Greenville if we came here," Elizabeth said after they were seated in one of only two low-backed booths, both of them situated close to the kitchen. Celia wished they had sat at a table instead of a booth. At a table you had more space, and your view was broader. In a booth you felt backed up against a wall, especially if you were sitting on one side by yourself, as Celia was, with two pairs of eyes facing you directly across the table.

Single sheets of paper propped up behind the ketchup bottle served as the menus, listing in hand-printed capital letters six different "plates," all the same price and each consisting of a meat and two vegetables, plus drink, corn bread, and cobbler. Celia decided quickly on the fried chicken breast with rice and gravy and green beans. While Elizabeth and Margaret were still looking at the menu, she studied the restaurant, noticing that the floor was surprisingly clean for the number of people that evidently walked across it every day. The Formica tabletop also looked spotless.

A black woman in a flowered apron was wiping off an empty table by the window, taking her time about it. That was the secret to clean restaurant tables, Celia decided—let grown women do it instead of teenagers. The woman even picked up the salt and pepper shakers and wiped them off, then the napkin dispenser. Celia wondered if that might be Aunt Cassie herself, but she saw three or four other women moving in and out of the kitchen who also might qualify. It looked like a whole family of sisters ran the place, with maybe a couple of brothers and nephews thrown in. Maybe Aunt Cassie was the mother of the clan, having earned the right to sit in comfort at home while her children took care of the business.

An older couple sat at a nearby table, and Celia noticed how thin and feeble they both looked. They were eating silently and with great concentration, as if they needed every ounce of their energy to cut their meat loaf and butter their corn bread. She watched them for a moment and then moved on to another table, where two yuppie-looking men in shirts and ties sat reading the *Wall Street Journal.* How like men, she thought, to go out to eat together and then not say a word to each other. Of course, that would suit her fine right now, she realized. She would love to eat quickly and quietly and get back home.

Suddenly she was aware that Elizabeth and Margaret had stopped reading the menu and were both looking at her. She wondered if one of them had asked her a question, but before she could say anything, a waitress, maybe one of Aunt Cassie's daughters, showed up at their table and took an order pad out of her apron pocket.

"Hey there," she said. "Y'all know what you want?" She reached back and pulled a pencil out of her knot of coiled braids. She was plump and had one of the widest smiles Celia had ever seen, adorned by a spectacular gold tooth. A jolly sort, she expressed approval at all their selections: "Yes'm, that's real good." "We just cooked up a fresh batch of chicken." "Mmm, you sure gonna like them butter beans." She promised to be right back with their tea.

After she left, neither Elizabeth nor Margaret seemed to be in any hurry to start a conversation. Elizabeth was looking for something in her purse, while Margaret, after replacing the menus behind the ketchup bottle, was straightening up the other items next to the napkin dispenser. Celia watched her remove a napkin, wipe it across the table, and examine it.

Elizabeth noticed it, too. "Margaret's extra particular," she said, glancing up. Then she went back to digging in her purse. Evidently she still hadn't found whatever she was looking for. "This is a real adventure for her—eating out. She'll probably figure out a way to inspect the kitchen before we eat."

A different waitress, a young girl no more than fifteen, pretty and quick, brought their glasses of tea. She was gone in a flash.

"Elizabeth is of the opinion that I need to get out more," Margaret said, smiling. "She has undertaken a campaign to acquaint me with a variety of restaurants. Sometimes we bring our husbands along." She smiled and held up the paper napkin she had used to wipe the table. "Thus far Aunt Cassie is to be commended for cleanliness." She folded the napkin neatly and placed it on top of the dispenser.

"It's a little like the vaccination principle," Elizabeth said. "I'm introducing her to public germs a few at a time, building up her immunity so that one of these days she'll actually go to a restaurant without bringing her own silverware along."

They all laughed. Apparently she was teasing, for Margaret took Aunt Cassie's utensils from the napkin they were wrapped in and laid them out, arranging each one on the proper side as carefully as she would set the table for company.

"There it is," Elizabeth said, pulling a wrinkled scrap of paper out of her purse. "I knew it was in here somewhere." She smoothed the paper out, then cleared her throat. "Okay, this is part of a poem I ran across the other day. See what you think. Don't worry, it's short."

So while they waited for their meat loaf, fried chicken, and pork chop plates at Aunt Cassie's Kitchen, Elizabeth read aloud a poem titled "Early Shift at Duke's Donuts." Celia wondered if anyone else had ever read poetry at one of Aunt Cassie's tables. Elizabeth had found the poem in an old issue of a writing magazine, she said, in an article called "Sharpening Your Poems to a Point." It was a descriptive poem, bursting at the seams with the sights, sounds, and smells of a doughnut shop in Alabama. Celia was glad it wasn't one of those enigmatic poems by somebody like Wallace Stevens or T. S. Eliot or some other poet whose intellect was up in the stratosphere somewhere. The point of this poem seemed to be, simply put, that the world was gloriously full of all manner of people, although she couldn't help wondering if there was something else she might be missing.

Evidently not, though, for after she finished reading it, Elizabeth looked up, her eyes shining, and said, "Isn't that great? Doesn't he capture the whole seething mass of humanity right there in that doughnut shop?" Then she nodded toward the other tables in the restaurant and said, "Just like right here. Look at all these people. Isn't it fascinating?"

For several long moments the three of them sat in silence, looking around at the seething mass of humanity in Aunt Cassie's Kitchen in Greenville, South Carolina. And an idea suddenly hit Celia: *We're all alike*, she thought. She couldn't remember ever being hit so hard with an idea so elementary. She looked at another table, where three elderly women were finishing up, spoonfuls of cobbler moving slowly from their little green plastic bowls to their mouths. That could be the three of us a few years down the road, she thought.

She glanced back at the old man with the rubber band around his long gray ponytail of a beard. On the most fundamental level, she thought, there's not an ounce of difference between us. I might work at an art gallery, but I'm no different really, certainly no better, than someone who spends his days working on telephone poles or digging ditches. At another table she saw a man tip over his glass of tea. The woman he was with jumped up with a squeak of dismay and started soaking it up with napkins, her lips tightly clamped, obviously holding back a dam-burst of angry words.

We're born, we live, and we die, Celia thought. We have dreams, we mess up, we muddle by. We all have our own little glimmers of light, but in the end we fade away. We're blown off the face of the earth like dust. She imagined a hand holding a giant leaf blower, knocking a hole through the ceiling and aiming it at everybody inside Aunt Cassie's Kitchen. She imagined all of them swirling out the door like little bits of debris.

She caught herself before she spoke aloud, before she said the phrase that jumped out of Grandmother's brown hymnal like a jack-in-the-box. "Frail children of dust"—that's what we all are, she thought. Those old guys who wrote the words to the hymns might have gone overboard a lot of the time, but they did get a few things right. "Frail children of dust" summed it up perfectly.

Finally Margaret spoke. "And to think that each person in here has a unique view of the room. My view includes you, for example," she said to Celia, "but yours does not. Yours includes me, but mine does not." Thankfully, their food came then so that Celia was spared the effort of thinking up a suitable reply to *that*.

Elizabeth said, "I hope you don't mind if we say grace, Celia." And for the first time since leaving her grandmother's house, Celia bowed her head and listened to someone pray over a meal.

18

The Burning of the Noonday Heat

A week later, on the screened porch of a rented condo in Charleston, another very simple truth hit Celia. This one came about as a result of something Betsy Harris said as the tennis team was discussing the lineup for the next day's match at the state playoffs. It would be their third match, and it would mean the difference between advancing to the semifinals and being eliminated.

It had always seemed to Celia that big things sank into her mind slowly, things other people appeared to grasp instinctively. She knew it wasn't an intelligence problem, but it had something to do with the big-picture way of thinking as opposed to her more microscopic view of life—or "the forest versus the trees," as Elizabeth Landis had called it the day they had eaten supper together at Aunt Cassie's Kitchen. Sometimes you were too close to a situation to see the truth, Elizabeth had said that day.

It was almost ten o'clock at night, and the Holiday Winners had just returned from eating a late supper at a little restaurant called the Mustard Seed. They had played their second match that afternoon and had won, giving them two wins and no losses—tied with the Hilton Head team they were scheduled to play the next day. Bonnie Maggio had agonized over the lineup for the decisive third match, and she was clearly nervous as she opened the floor for discussion.

The meeting had a séance-like atmosphere, for Carol Sawyer had found some tea candles in a cupboard and had come up with the idea of placing them inside coffee mugs and setting them all around the screened porch. She had suggested to Bonnie that they meet out here instead of in the living room, and Bonnie had been all for the idea, no doubt thinking it would be easier to have a potentially touchy discussion in the dark than in bright light.

Celia didn't envy Bonnie her job as team captain. With fifteen women on the team and only eight playing in a given match, that meant seven had to sit out each time. It didn't much affect Celia and Elizabeth because no one else really wanted to play singles, but there were times when feelings were hurt because certain people didn't get to play as much as they wanted to.

"Before we left home, I know we talked about everybody getting to play at least one match in Charleston," Bonnie said by way of opening the meeting, "so I want to know if everybody still agrees with that."

Nan Meachum wasn't the type to give much thought to hurt feelings. "Well, we came to win, didn't we?" she said. "I think it's dumb to get this far and then not go out with our strongest lineup in the critical match." As one of the best doubles players, she knew such a lineup would include herself.

Judy Howell, who was Nan's regular doubles partner, spoke up. "I agree. If our goal is to win, we can't hold back. I guarantee Hilton Head's going to be playing their first string."

Bonnie looked around the circle in the flickering light. "Someone else?" When no one spoke, she said, "How about somebody who hasn't played yet?" Everyone was well aware that this included only Ellen Myers, Gloria McGregor, and Betsy Harris.

"Well, we did talk about this back at home," Gloria said, "and we did say anybody who spends the money to come should get to play at least one match." She paused to blow her nose, but everybody knew it was only her allergies. Gloria was unfailingly even-tempered and good-humored. "But in my opinion," she continued, "being a team means we rely on each other in a pinch, and we're in a pinch now. I'm more than willing to give up my right to play so that we'll have a better chance to win tomorrow." She blew her nose again. "Besides, I'm planning to take a double dose of my medicine tonight. I might still be asleep during the match tomorrow."

During the comments that followed, only one timid objection was raised by Cindy Petrarch, who suggested that the ones who hadn't played yet might be fresher than the ones who had played both matches so far, and therefore might perform better in tomorrow's match. On the other hand, Darla Smith said, the ones who had already played might feel warmed up and in a groove, and therefore more confident going into such a big match.

Anastasia Elsey started repeating everything Nan and Judy had said earlier until Betsy Harris finally interrupted her and offered these words: "Hey, we're all grown-ups here. Everybody knows who our best players are, and everybody knows I'm not one of them." She laughed, and so did several others. "Like my mama used to say, what's good isn't always what's fun. What's good right now is for us to win. It might not be fun for some of us to sit out, but hey, we got something bigger going on here." Betsy reached over and socked Bonnie in the arm. "Just because Bonnie doesn't let me play much doesn't mean she doesn't love me. She might be mean, but she's looking out for the team."

Celia didn't hear much of what went on after that because Betsy's words had called to mind "the forest versus the trees" way of seeing things that Elizabeth had talked about just a week ago. Right there on a screened porch in Charleston, this thought exploded into a truth that she had steadfastly refused to consider before now, a possibility that she had always slammed the door on when the slightest suggestion of it came tapping at her heart. Now, in an instant, the fact dropped down upon her like a sure blessing, like a garment that was tailor-made for her and all she had to do was lift her arms and let it slip down over her.

Actually it was a confirmation of something that Margaret Tuttle had already said the week before at Aunt Cassie's Kitchen, which had followed Elizabeth's comment about looking at the forest instead of the trees. Somehow they had moved—or rather leapt, sprung, catapulted—from the poem Elizabeth had read at the table, the one titled "Early Shift at Duke's Donuts," to the subject of the good things that can come out of suffering. Celia had no idea how the transition had taken place, but suddenly there they were, talking about the heartaches they had been through.

Not her, of course—she was only listening, that is, at first. Elizabeth and Margaret were astonishingly forthright in their divulging of personal trials. Sometime after Elizabeth said grace, Celia remembered cutting into her corn-bread muffin and placing a pat of butter between the two halves, then closing it up again and staring at it intently as Elizabeth said, "I'm such a chicken when it comes to telling people what God has done for me, so I asked Margaret to come with me for moral support." That's when it dawned on Celia that the whole thing had been premeditated, that Elizabeth had singled her out for special attention and had carefully timed her stop by the art gallery that day. It hadn't been a spur-of-the-moment idea as she was driving by the Trio.

Elizabeth had asked Margaret to talk first because, she said, the story really started with her. And somehow, between bites of her pork chop and mashed potatoes, Margaret told Celia a remarkable account of how as a girl she had lost her mother, had been preyed upon by her grandfather, and had lost her four-year-old son. She didn't dwell on the details, but there was no mistaking the depth of her suffering. For a short while they ate in silence before she took up her story again. After many years, she said, a friend had come along to rescue her, to teach her again what love meant, and to lead her back to God.

"Her name was Birdie," Margaret said, "and I loved her with all my heart."

Someone came to refill their glasses of tea, and Margaret stopped again for a moment, during which time Celia felt the tug of wanting to hear the rest of the story, yet wishing she could stop up her ears against it at the same time. After the waitress left, Margaret told about Birdie's sudden death and about her own vow to take up Birdie's work on earth. She spoke briefly about her husband, Thomas, who "had waited patiently for me through the long drought." At last, she said, when she had lifted her eyes to heaven and the "gentle showers of faith, hope, and love had begun their work" in her heart, she and Thomas discovered a joy they had never known.

Ten minutes—that's all it took to sum up almost forty years of human pain and divine redemption. The orange Sunkist clock on the wall behind Aunt Cassie's cash register had shown six o'clock when Margaret began talking and ten minutes past when she finished up with "I do not speak of these things to bring attention to myself but to testify of God's power to heal a broken heart."

At which point Elizabeth picked up the story and, as she was finishing up her meat loaf and butter beans, told how Margaret had indeed taken up Birdie's mantle of ministering to others by coming alongside her during her own time of trouble. Elizabeth was wearing a short-sleeved olive green sweater and a necklace with a large coppery pendant, and Celia noticed how exactly her eyes matched the color of her sweater. If someone had asked Celia what color Elizabeth Landis's eyes were, she wouldn't have known, but evidently they were that sort of vague, accommodating gray-blue-green that takes on whatever color it's near.

Elizabeth gave few details but made it clear that her trouble somehow included her husband, Ken. "God used Margaret," she said, "to teach me about grace. She told me first about God's grace to me, and then showed me how I could be a giver of grace myself. God used her to help Ken and me repair our home." She laid her hand on Margaret's arm and added, "She's still teaching me how to give myself to other people."

There was an awkward moment when Elizabeth stopped. Celia felt something rising in her throat, something like a choking sob or a cry for help, but she managed to swallow hard, then took a long drink of tea followed by a deep breath to calm herself. Common sense suggested that it was her turn to talk, but she didn't trust herself right now. Who knew what would come out of her mouth if she tried to speak. She might start screaming and never stop.

Thankfully, just then a minor disturbance distracted everybody's attention for a little while. One of the three elderly women sitting at a nearby table somehow stumbled as she was getting up to leave and went down on her knees. Her pocketbook went flying and slid right under the feet of the old man with his beard in a ponytail. Maybe he looked a lot older than he really was, though, because he jumped up as lithe as a panther and dashed to her assistance. The two yuppie-looking men absorbed in their newspaper glanced over with only the mildest interest, then went back to reading.

The woman wasn't hurt, but the bearded man gallantly insisted on walking her out to the car. Before she could stop herself, Celia's imagination got cranked up. Maybe neither one of them was married, and this time next year the woman might be telling someone, "We met at Aunt Cassie's Kitchen one day when I slipped on the floor and he helped me up." By then she might have talked him into cutting off his beard and sprucing himself up a little.

The incident passed, and Celia started eating her apple cobbler, taking quick bites one right after the other. She was ready to leave this place and get back to the quiet of her apartment. She didn't want to hear anybody else talk about hardships and recoveries. Her head suddenly felt swollen with the stories she had just heard. Her ears felt as if they were filling up with water, the same way they sometimes felt after a long tennis match.

Elizabeth spoke again, her voice soft, almost pleading. "We didn't ask you here to pump you, Celia," she said. "We're both sort of closed-up types ourselves, and we don't want you thinking we go around telling our sob stories to everybody and then try to trap people into revealing all their deep dark secrets. I had to practically twist Margaret's arm to get her to do this with me."

Margaret nodded. "These are not things we wish to make public."

So why pick on me? Celia thought. *I didn't ask to hear any of it!*

"Like I said, I'm a chicken," Elizabeth said. "I've been praying for you, but I was so afraid to say anything. I would start to, then back out. I hate being nosy, but God kept on telling me to talk to you."

"Elizabeth has been telling me about you for months," Margaret said. "I felt that I already knew you when you came to our poetry meeting a few weeks ago. I, too, have been praying for you."

"But *why?*" Celia said, looking straight at Elizabeth. "Why me? Do I look like some horrible sinner or something?"

Elizabeth shook her head slowly. She set her spoon down and wiped her mouth, then folded her arms and leaned forward. "You're a beautiful girl, Celia," she said, "but your eyes are sad. I've had this feeling that you were carrying around something heavy, and I've wanted so badly to help." She paused. "If there's any way I could, that is. But then, I might be wrong. Maybe you're not sad at all. Maybe I'm imagining things. I've been known to do that."

There it was again . . . that thing about her sad eyes. Celia was tired of hearing it. How did a person get rid of a malady like that? There were all manner of medications for everything else, not to mention all the little cosmetic tricks to disguise a pointed chin or to make your face look thinner, but what could you do about something like sad eyes? That went too deep for pills or makeup to change. That was a soul sickness.

At last Celia trusted herself to open her mouth, but she spoke lightly, casually, and she avoided looking at either Elizabeth or Margaret directly, fearful that her eyes might get more specific, might give away more than her general sadness. "Well, both of my parents died when I was fifteen," Celia said. There, that should satisfy them. Anybody without either a mother or father would have cause to look sad.

Margaret made a sympathetic sound, and Elizabeth said softly, "I'm sorry. That must have been awful for you."

And though neither one of them pressed her for more information, for some reason Celia heard herself add, "My grandmother took me in."

Her voice seemed to come from somewhere outside her body, reverberating all around her, as if she were at one end of a tunnel and the words were being spoken from the other end. And even as she noted this distortion of sound, she marveled not only that she had felt compelled to mention her grandmother but that she had chosen that particular way of saying it: "My grandmother took me in." Was that really what she had said? Why hadn't she stated it the way it really was? "I had no choice but to go live with my grandmother, and I hated every minute of it."

"Your grandmother must have loved you," Margaret said, and though Celia couldn't be sure, she thought she heard herself laugh at that. But then again, maybe she hadn't laughed. Maybe she had only stared in confused silence.

It was a short time after that, before they left Aunt Cassie's, that Elizabeth mentioned the forest and the trees in regard to different ways of thinking. "I've always been better at seeing the parts than the whole big picture," she said. Celia didn't remember how that had fit into their conversation, but it had made an impression. It had suggested a question, which she had shoved to the back of her mind to think about later: Could it be that she herself had looked so closely at all the negatives of living with her grandmother that she had missed something larger?

And now, sitting in the flickering light of a screened porch two hundred miles away and a week later, the question came back to her, and she saw the truth in what Margaret and Elizabeth had said. And also in what Betsy Harris had just said about love. Somebody could do things you didn't like but still love you. Somebody could be perceived as mean but still want the best for you.

Grandmother loved me. It was as simple and undeniable a truth as the ones listed in the Declaration of Independence, those self-evident ones about all men being created equal, about being endowed with the inalienable rights of life, liberty, and the pursuit of happiness. *Grandmother loved me.* Maybe she had stifled Celia's liberty, had discouraged the pursuit of what Celia considered happiness, but she had certainly, most assuredly, loved her.

Somehow she left the porch of the condo and found herself alone in the small bedroom she was sharing with Tammy Elias. Celia was sitting on the edge of the bed staring up at the wallpaper border of sailboats and leaping dolphins when Elizabeth peeked in. "Bonnie sent me to check on you," she said. "You're okay, aren't you? She was wondering if today's match did you in. She got worried when you left the meeting so suddenly."

Celia nodded. "I'm fine," she said. "Just thinking—you know, forest and trees and all that. There's a big picture I'm trying to see."

Elizabeth cocked her head and studied her. She looked as if she had a hundred questions she wanted to ask, but when she spoke, the only one that came out was "So I can tell her you're on for tomorrow?"

"Oh sure. I'm going to try to get to bed pretty soon and rest up."

Elizabeth hesitated at the door and said, "Is there anything . . . ?"

But Celia stood up briskly and threw back the bedspread. "Tell her I'm feeling great. I'll be ready to hit the courts in the morning." She took her pajamas out of her suitcase and walked toward the bathroom. "Night, Elizabeth," she said and closed the door.

It was shortly after noon the next day, and Celia was sitting on the ground with her back against a tree at the country club in Charleston where the state tournament was being held. She had just finished her match, and her long winning streak for the season was over. She had not gone down without a fight, though. She and her opponent, a twenty-something woman named Kristin, had slugged it out for over two hours in the scorching heat, splitting sets 7–6, 5–7.

Instead of playing a third set, the state tournament rules required what was called a third-set tiebreak, what amounted to a single long game to determine the winner. The first one to reach ten points and be ahead by two took the match. Tied at 10–all in the tiebreak, Celia had dumped a service return into the net and then in the next point had sent a lob only inches long.

So in the end the difference between winning and losing had come down to a couple of inches. You could come that close and your performance would still be recorded as a loss, just as surely as if the score had been 6–0, 6–0. Nobody cared whether *it was as close as it could have possibly been.* The fact was that you lost, period. In fact, in a tennis match you could actually win more points, even more games, and still come out the loser. Celia had often wondered if there was something wrong with a scoring system like that. It reminded her of the way the electoral college worked in national elections.

She couldn't remember ever being so hot. She had played lots of other matches in the heat of the day, but she couldn't remember anything quite like today. The weather report that morning had predicted a heat index of 115 degrees with humidity up around ninety percent. She was almost becoming used to the way stray lines from her grandmother's hymns had started finding their way into everything she did, waiting for her around every bend, sidling up alongside her at the most unexpected times. "The burning of the noonday heat" was the phrase that slipped into her mind now from "Beneath the Cross of Jesus," a hymn the organist had always played during Communion at Bethany Hills.

She leaned her head back against the tree trunk and closed her eyes. Even though her match had lasted two hours, the other four matches were still going on. That was because she had gotten on the court almost a full hour before anyone else. The number-one singles player always went on first in a tournament, and the others were assigned courts as they came available. Things had gotten backed up today because of the heat. People were taking longer breaks between games and sets, and the officials and timekeepers weren't saying a thing about it. Nobody wanted a player conking out here at the country club in the middle of the state championship.

Anastasia Elsey was the only one who had been waiting for her after the match, and she had patted Celia's arm comfortingly, then dashed off to spread the news of the loss to the other team members, all of whom were over watching Nan and Judy, who were engaged in a doubles match that was "nip and tuck," as Anastasia put it. She didn't know who was ahead on the other courts, but she thought Elizabeth might have won the first set of her match.

Celia dreaded facing her team. They had grown to count on her winning. Glad that none of the rest of them were around right then, she had walked to the rear of the clubhouse, away from the courts, where she had dropped her bag and collapsed under a tree. Every inch of her was dripping wet. She had her towel slung around her neck, but it was as wet as the rest of her.

So here was another fact of life: All good things came to an end. You couldn't go on winning forever. There would always be someone who could beat you. Even your best talents, considerable though they might be, could always be topped by somebody somewhere.

The team still had a chance, of course, depending on how the other matches were going. If they could take three of the other four courts, they would play in the semifinals tomorrow morning, and if they won that, they'd go on to the finals tomorrow afternoon. She was so tired and hot right now, though, that she couldn't let herself think of having to play two matches tomorrow.

She heard a celebratory shout go up on one of the courts down where the men's matches were being played. You could tell it was men by the way their voices carried, by the sustained roaring effect and guttural grunts. Evidently somebody had just won and made his team very happy. But that meant somebody had lost, too, maybe even in a squeaker like the one she had just played. She knew exactly how that man must feel right now. All that effort for nothing, only to be reduced on the master score sheet to a big fat zero.

All of which reminded her that seven of her teammates were still out on the courts battling it out under the hot sun while she sat here in the shade. She pulled herself to her feet and headed over to the courts to see how things were going.

Bonnie Maggio, who wasn't playing this match, saw her coming and hurried to meet her. "There you are, girl. I've been looking everywhere for you. Tough match." She squeezed Celia's shoulder. "I watched most of your first set and part of the second. That girl was a machine." She took Celia's bag from her and hoisted it to her shoulder. "Don't beat yourself up. You played hard." She grinned, her eyes crinkling into slits. "Hey, look at it this way. Maybe they won't bump you up to 4.5 now that you've finally lost a match."

As they walked over to where the rest of the team was sitting, Bonnie told her that Elizabeth had indeed won the first set of her match and was tied at five-all in the second. Nan and Judy had lost the first set 5–7 but were up one game in the second, and Jenny and Carol had lost the first set and were trailing in the second. They weren't sure about Cindy and Jane's match, because they weren't using the scorekeeping numbers on their court and nobody could hear them call out a score before a game. "We've got a chance, though," Bonnie said. "Nobody's giving up. We might win this thing yet."

Bonnie made Celia sit in her canvas chair while she sat on the grass beside her. It was hard enough to follow the score of one match, much less three or four, so Celia decided to focus on Elizabeth's court, which was right next to the one Nan and Judy were playing on. Focusing on anything was a little difficult at the moment, though, since Anastasia Elsey, seated on the other side of her, was talking nonstop, delivering a running commentary on every shot, on every player on the courts, and on every person who walked by. She changed subjects so often that it was impossible to keep up with her, and when she said, "Good grief, she sure thinks she's hot stuff, doesn't she?" Celia had no idea who it was she was talking about.

Horror vacui—the Latin term for "the horror of empty space"—was what came to her mind all at once, something she had read about in an art magazine a long time ago. It was originally a concept in art tracing its roots to India, she thought, or maybe to the Middle East, where an artist's skill seemed to be determined by how much he could cram into a single painting, as if the tiniest blank space meant that his imagination had run dry. The concept also carried over to many other areas. In interior decorating, for example—the compulsion to fill up all the available space. Celia had often suspected, in fact, that she herself was approaching that point in the way she kept packing more art onto the walls of her apartment.

And, of course, in social settings, there were always those people, such as Anastasia, who seemed to have a horror of the empty space of silence. Celia decided it would be an interesting contest to have Anastasia Elsey and Eldeen Rafferty in the same room together.

As Celia watched a particularly long point during which Elizabeth's opponent ran her from one side of the court to the other, then up and back several times, something caught her eye outside the fence where they were playing. A little girl stood watching the match, her face pressed up against the fence, her fingers clutching the chain links. She was as skinny as one of the fence posts and had long blond braids. After Elizabeth won the point by drilling a shot down the line, the little girl called out, "That's okay, Mom! You can do it! Come on!"

Celia looked more closely at Elizabeth's opponent—a tall gangling woman who didn't exactly look like a spring chicken but, like Elizabeth, was evidently the kind of player who sank her teeth in and wouldn't let go of a point. Celia had learned not to underestimate singles players like her, who looked like they were past their prime but somehow had a battery that never wore down. What they lacked in power and technique, they often more than made up for in consistency and sheer determination.

"You must feel awful about losing your match," Anastasia said beside her. "That girl you played sure strutted off the court, didn't she? Did you see that tattoo on her arm? I never could get close enough to see what the picture was. Did you?"

Too tired to talk, Celia merely shook her head and kept her eyes on Elizabeth's match. She always avoided looking at children close up, but she sometimes studied them from afar, and for some reason right now she kept coming back to the little girl by the fence. It took only seconds for her to realize why. At this distance, some forty feet away, the child looked exactly like Celia herself at that age, skinny with long braided pigtails.

Her parents, being frugal as they were, hadn't filled up dozens of photo albums the way some parents of only children did, but they had taken a moderate number of pictures, and Celia's mother had neatly labeled them all with occasion and date and filed them in order in a shoebox. Owning a shoe store as he did, Celia's father had ready access to shoeboxes, which they used for everything at home. Her mother's recipe box, covered with yellow wrapping paper, had once held a pair of child-size bedroom slippers. It had sat on the kitchen counter next to the canisters the whole time Celia was growing up.

"But don't worry," Anastasia said. "I have a gut feeling that Elizabeth's going to pull this one out for us."

"Good shot, Mom!" the little girl shouted now and clapped her hands. Her mother had just scored on a drop shot.

"I wish that kid would be quiet," Anastasia said. "Somebody ought to make her get away from the fence."

Though Celia was pulling for Elizabeth, something in her wanted the mother of this little girl, whose voice rang out so clearly and so hopefully, who twirled around in a joyful little circle as she clapped her hands, to do well, also. She felt a wrenching deep inside when she thought of what it must be like for that woman to hear her own daughter cheering her on after every point. She let herself wonder for a moment what it would have been like in her own match against Kristin if she had heard a voice like this urging her on from the sidelines. That would have to add an extra charge to anybody's battery.

And then again the cloud descended. She would never ever hear a child's voice saying to her, "Good shot, Mom!" She had been too stupid, selfish, and shortsighted one day almost fifteen years ago to ever earn the right to hear something like that. She shut her eyes tight and lowered her head, which suddenly felt too heavy to hold up.

Anastasia leaned over to her. "Hey, I know exactly what you must be thinking right now," she said in Celia's ear.

Celia didn't even lift her head as she answered, her eyes still closed, "Oh no, I don't think you do."

19

On the Page White and Fair

Celia had always known that someday she would find herself in this place again, especially since she had all but promised to come a couple of months ago. But now that she was here, it didn't seem quite real. She felt as though she were in some kind of time warp. She glanced to either side, halfway expecting to see her grandmother seated beside her, but the only people on the pew with her were ones she had never seen before.

A sixtyish couple sat across the aisle from her, the man with only a few sprigs of pale hair sprouting around his ears and the woman crowned with a hairdo that reminded Celia of the huge paper wasp nest she had found in Grandmother's barn the day before. The couple smiled at her as she sat down, and the man said, "Glad you could come out to worship with us this morning."

The first thing Celia noticed as she sat down—in fact, the thing she was most curious about, the thing that probably, even more than her tacit acceptance of the invitation back in April, had made her come this morning—was that the hymnbook in the rack in front of her bore on its cover the title *Tabernacle Hymns* and below it, in smaller letters, *Number Four*. This edition had a green cover but was about the same size as the old brown one of her grandmother's and had the same torch emblem embossed beneath the title.

So Bethany Hills had simply reordered the same hymnal when the old ones wore out. She could have expected as much. She remembered thinking, when she used to visit Grandmother's church as a little girl, that the hymnal was made especially for this church, since they both had *Tabernacle* in their names, but her mother had explained that it was just something called a coincidence. She took the green hymnal out of the rack now and examined it. If all of them were as worn as this one, the deacons here at Bethany Hills needed to approve funds to order the Number Five edition sometime soon.

Celia flipped through the pages. All the same old hymns were there. As much as she wanted to feel scornful about this tangible evidence that a whole group of people had remained entrenched in mindless tradition, for some strange reason she felt the smallest prickle of satisfaction that they hadn't changed hymnals.

Up on the platform sat the preacher, not old Brother Thacker from eighteen years ago, but the other one who had come to Grandmother's house when Celia was there back in April, the one whose wife, Denise, had said to Celia right before she walked out the door that day, "Well, we'll be looking for you at one of our services when you come back in June, all right?" And like a spineless ninny, Celia had nodded dumbly, realizing as she did so that people like these would interpret that as a commitment. She should have said what she felt: "No, I won't be coming to church. I escaped from that cage a long time ago and don't intend to get caught up again."

And, of course, Denise had just *had* to drive by Grandmother's house yesterday as Celia and Aunt Beulah were having the yard sale. Naturally she had stopped her car and greeted them, even bought three of Grandmother's aprons and a flour sifter before leaving. And, as Celia had known she would, she had repeated the invitation to come to church the next day, giving the exact times of the services in a tone that implied her certainty that Celia would be at one of them.

And so, here she was. This was exactly the kind of thing that Ansell and the others used to laugh at her for in high school—her heightened sense of obligation. "One of life's finest thrills is letting people down," Ansell would often say. But she had never found that to be the case. Even after she had started letting people down and had gotten quite proficient at it, she had never considered it a thrill. There was always that little beesting of guilt she never could reason away completely.

The organist was the same one from years ago—Mrs. Abbott, who swayed and dipped and sang along with the congregation as she played. Her hair had gone gray, and she looked a little rounder, but her face still had that same alert scorekeeper's gleam as she scanned the faces of the congregation, checking out who was here this morning, all the while playing "Blessed Be the Name." Mrs. Abbott hardly ever used printed music, rarely looked down at the keyboard, and could play anything in any key you wanted. She used to accompany Celia for all her clarinet solos.

The pianist was someone she didn't recognize—a young woman with exceedingly straight posture who sat on the bench, hands in her lap, staring intently at the open hymnal in front of her, as if reviewing for a hard test she was worried about. At eleven o'clock a door opened behind the platform, and the choir started filing in. Celia recognized one of the men at once as Rodney Ruskin, who used to be the church treasurer and give the financial reports at the monthly business meetings. It was amazing how little he had changed in almost twenty years. It wasn't really fair the way men seemed to age more slowly than women. She recognized a couple of the women in the choir, also—Mrs. Vanzetti, who used to teach the junior high Sunday school class, and Mrs. Gerard, who used to sing solos that were always just slightly too high for her range.

It turned out that Celia was to be treated to the full menu of church business this morning, for in addition to the table laid out with the silver Communion trays, the preacher announced that today's service would conclude with the baptism of "two new converts" and a "baby dedication." Too bad they couldn't add a missionary slide show and a church discipline session to make it complete, Celia thought. Well, she would slip out before these add-ons at the end of the service. She wasn't about to sit through a baby dedication.

As the preacher moved from the announcements to greeting the visitors, a plain little rabbit-faced woman walked down the aisle looking for a place to sit. She was wearing a tan shirtwaist dress with a straw belt, not a good choice for someone whose complexion was already totally lacking color. Except for her eyes—those Pacific blue, western-sky eyes that looked completely out of place in such a nondescript face.

It was Denise Davidson, the preacher's wife. Unfortunately, she spotted Celia right away and stopped at the end of her pew to greet her, then craned her neck to see past her, checking if there was room to squeeze in one more, which there was. Everybody shifted down some, and with a sinking heart Celia moved over to let her sit on the end, realizing that her chance of a quick and early exit had just died a sudden death.

"I see that the late Mrs. Davidson has arrived," the preacher said, and everybody laughed and looked back at his wife, who waved her hand and smiled. The ushers came forward to distribute visitors' cards, and Denise Davidson waved her hand again to secure one for Celia. If it had been left up to Celia, she would never have identified herself as a visitor. She would have looked the other way until the usher passed her pew. But now, with the preacher's wife sitting right at her elbow, she felt obligated to fill it out.

A task, however, which though simple enough proved to be a challenge because of all the activity that followed—standing up for a hymn, sitting back down, finding the responsive reading in the hymnal, standing up again, shaking hands during a segment called "greeting the brethren," sitting back down, watching two teenaged girls carry their violins to the platform during a deacon's long pre-offering prayer, listening to them play a vigorous rendition of "Since Jesus Came Into My Heart" while the offering plates were passed and thinking that, in spite of a pitch problem here and there, they were really much better than she had expected, then singing another hymn, and then watching as the song leader turned around to direct the choir special.

No one had known Celia was going to be there this morning, so it couldn't have been planned. And even if someone had known she would be in the service today, no one could have possibly remembered that the choir had sung this exact song, the very same arrangement, almost twenty-two years ago on the Sunday morning she had been baptized by Brother Thacker in this church. It had been only a couple of months after she had come to live with her grandmother.

She had talked with her parents earlier that summer about being baptized, and they had been very happy. She had told them that she wanted to talk to the pastor of their church in Lawrenceville about it sometime that fall after she turned fifteen. The trip to buy the clothes dryer had changed all that, though, and in addition to her guilt over skipping her prayer and Bible reading the afternoon they died, Celia had worried that her delay in getting baptized had had something to do with their accident. If she hadn't put it off so long after she had walked the aisle for salvation at the age of eight, then maybe God wouldn't have had to punish her that way.

After coming to Dunmore, she had wasted no time speaking to her grandmother about her desire to be baptized, for what other horrible penalties might she have to suffer if she didn't get that requirement taken care of? She remembered wishing Brother Thacker would hurry up and get her under the water that Sunday morning as she had stood with him in the baptistry. He had talked far too long about the meaning of baptism, had quoted Scripture, had asked Celia to give a word of testimony about her salvation, had spoken sadly about the loss of her parents and how glad they would have been to witness this happy occasion, and then finally, finally had placed the white handkerchief over her mouth and nose and lowered her into the water.

She hadn't held back the way some of the younger children did, the way the little Childers boy had, who had gripped the edge of the baptistry a couple of weeks earlier and wouldn't let go, had even started crying and had to be pried loose by his father, who came up finally to assist Brother Thacker. But not Celia. No, she had let herself go, giving herself to the water, pushing into it and almost causing Brother Thacker to lose his hold of her, interrupting his rhythm a little as he had recited his blessing: "In the name of the Father, and of the Son, and of the Holy Ghost. Buried in the likeness of his death and raised in the likeness of his resurrection."

She had been baptized at the very beginning of the service. That's the way Brother Thacker always did it, not at the end the way this new preacher did. So by the time the choir sang their special number right before the sermon that morning, she was already dried off and dressed, sitting back in the congregation, her hair pulled back into a slick ponytail. And when the choir had sung "Is My Name Written There?" her heart had leapt with the answer: "Yes! Yes, it is! My name *is* written there on the page white and fair." It was all signed, sealed, and delivered now. All the boxes in the checklist filled in. No loose ends. Nothing that an angry God might see as unfinished business.

The choir didn't sound much different today than it had all those years ago, not much better certainly, but not much worse, either. There seemed to be a few more men in the back row than there used to be, and the basses sang out boldly on their repeated phrase at the end of the chorus: "Yes, my name's written there!" What a bizarre coincidence that this would be the song they were singing on the only day she would be sitting in a service. She wondered how many times they had sung it in the past twenty-two years, what kind of rotation schedule the Bethany Hills Bible Tabernacle Choir had, if they even had a schedule. One thing was clear to her by now: The changes that had taken place in this church over the past twenty-plus years could be listed in full on a Post-it note. The very smallest size they made.

By the time a man and woman came forward to sing a duet before the sermon, Celia had filled in only her name on the visitor's card. How did they expect people to fill these out when there were so many things going on in such swift succession? And what were they going to do with this information after she filled it out? Were they going to use her address to start sending her all kinds of letters and pamphlets, trying to shoehorn their narrow brand of religion back into her life?

She was staring down at her name on the card when the man and woman sang the first words of their duet. They were singing without accompaniment, which made the surprise all the greater, since there was no introduction to prepare her. When she saw Denise Davidson glance over at her quickly, she wondered if she had involuntarily done something to give away her shock—maybe jerked suddenly or uttered a sharp yip of pain. She tried to make her face absolutely blank as she focused her eyes on the wall behind the singers, trying hard to block out what they were singing.

It was a rock wall, flanking the baptistry, and it called to mind another source of guilt Celia had struggled with as a girl. The rocks were irregularly shaped, all sizes and different shades of gray and brown, and when her mind used to wander from Brother Thacker's sermons, she would sit in the congregation and try to find pictures on the wall. One grouping of rocks on the left side looked like a stout hiker with a large pack on his back, and on the right there was a little man kicking a box. Right above the baptistry a three-legged dog was standing on its head. She found them all now with no trouble. The rock wall was another thing that hadn't changed a bit.

She remembered how she used to pray for forgiveness every time she let herself start playing the little find-the-picture game in church. She knew it was sinful to let your mind wander when Brother Thacker was preaching, but that rock wall was in such a bad place, right behind his head, and often she would catch herself falling into the temptation before she was even aware of it. She would look back down at her notebook, where she kept sermon notes, and see that she had broken off right in the middle of a sentence: *Our biggest concern in life should be . . .* it might read, or *God only asks that we . . .* She often went home from church feeling totally unworthy, wondering what the ends of those sentences had been and fearing what God was going to have to do next to teach her a lesson.

The man singing the song now was a tenor and the woman an alto, so he sang the melody while she harmonized. The song wasn't in the Tabernacle hymnal, but it was one Celia used to hear regularly at Bethany Hills. And at home, too. She had even played it once as an offertory on her clarinet at her grandmother's request. She wasn't sure, but she thought she remembered that some jazz musician had written it, either the words or the music, maybe both—some big-band guy. The two people singing it now weren't jazzing it up, though. They were singing it straight. No scooped notes, no breathiness, no embellishments of any kind: "Precious Lord, take my hand, lead me on, help me stand."

It went on to beg for guidance through the storms of life, when a person's strength was at its end, when he was about to fall. "Precious Lord, take my hand," it kept repeating. The man and woman started out in unison on the last verse, and Celia shifted her eyes from the rock wall to look right at them. Something about the woman's face, a hollow sagging look around the eyes even though she was obviously trying to smile with her mouth, sent a chill up Celia's backbone. She reminded Celia of pictures she had seen of victims of the Holocaust marching in long lines, women whose children had been yanked from their arms, whose eyes said, "We know our days are numbered, and we wish the number would hurry up and expire."

The last verse of the song wasn't one Celia remembered. "Though the night be long," the two people sang, "in my heart there's a song." Long nights—Celia had known plenty of those, but she sure hadn't heard any songs during them. Whoever wrote those words must have lived in a fantasy world. As they came to the last "Take my hand, precious Lord, lead me home," Celia wondered all of a sudden why Grandmother had omitted this song from her funeral plans. It was one she used to sing and hum around the house all the time, probably more than any other. It could very well have been her favorite song. And it would have fit right in with the theme of heaven at her funeral.

Maybe she had chosen her funeral songs strictly from the *Tabernacle Hymns,* though. Celia could imagine her sitting up in bed one night, thumbing through the pages, making a list of all the possibilities to be sung over her dead body. She might have stayed up late that night to wash down the shelves of her dish cupboard, then stir up a bowl of Jell-O, then

mend a tablecloth, then run a measly two inches of water in the tub for
her bath, after which she might have climbed into bed and picked out
hymns for her own funeral. To a woman like Grandmother, who saw birth
and death as just two more days in a person's life, it would have seemed
like the most natural thing in the world to do: clean house, cook, bathe,
plan your funeral.

For some reason a vision of Grandmother's large hands rose again
before Celia. Perhaps it was the suggestion in the song of Jesus taking
her grandmother's hand and leading her home, or maybe it was because
Celia had spent the last few days touching her things, the things her
grandmother herself had handled, and laying them out on tables for
the yard sale. Though there wasn't an elegant item among them, almost
everything had sold. Aunt Beulah had boxed up the few remaining items
and taken them to the Salvation Army.

A neighbor a half mile down on Old Campground Road had bought
all five of the old quilts. A wiry little woman with three barefoot children
trailing along behind her, she had the looks of someone who planned
to put the quilts to good everyday use come winter. Aunt Clara, who had
stopped by to nose around the tables, had asked Celia if she was *sure* she
wanted to part with those quilts, and Aunt Beulah had sprung to her
defense, telling Aunt Clara that Celia had already selected the two best
ones for keepsakes.

Celia thought now of the one she had out on display at home. After
having it dry cleaned, she had draped it over her mother's old cedar chest
in her living room. It was the one with the *Dean's Pork Sausage* square right
in the middle among all the printed, striped, and polka-dot ones. She had
arranged the quilt so that that square was on top. At the other end of the
cedar chest, she had placed a few other things she had brought home
from Grandmother's: a chipped enamel dipper, an old candle snuffer, an
ancient checkerboard, a cookie jar shaped like a big red apple.

In the midst of all her good paintings and sculptures, all her tasteful
furnishings, she knew that some people might think this little exhibit
was totally out of character. Celia didn't care, though. She didn't like the
overplanned effect so many interior designers went in for these days. Mix
it up—that was the way she liked things.

All of a sudden something funny hit her. She remembered the dinner table at Aunt Beulah's house the day of Grandmother's funeral, how
everything was all crowded together with no attempt made to categorize

the dishes. She also remembered how contemptuous she had felt when she saw how disorganized it all was. And now here she was five months later declaring "mix it up" to be her preferred decorating style. It made her wonder what other glaring inconsistencies she had overlooked in her personal life.

The preacher was well into his sermon before Celia started actually listening. He was preaching from the book of Joshua, about the sin of Achan. Nothing much had changed here, either. Brother Thacker had also been partial to the subject of God's punishment of sin. This new preacher was getting to the part where Achan finally admitted his guilt of hiding the Babylonian garment in his tent, along with the silver and gold. No doubt he would soon come to the stoning, the sure and severe penalty that always followed a digression from the law.

Celia tuned out and let her mind retreat again, trying to imagine how long it would take for a person to die of stoning. Maybe, as a grotesque form of mercy, they tried to aim for the head first to knock the person unconscious right away so that he couldn't feel himself being battered to death. Probably not, though. They didn't give much thought back in Bible days to the criminal's comfort during his punishment. Stoning, beheading, crucifixion—it was all brutal.

Next to her she heard Denise say right out loud, "That's right," and Celia snapped back to listening. The next thing she heard the preacher say made her wonder if he had suddenly lost his place in his notes. "God loved Achan," he said. "He loved his sons and daughters, too." Celia glanced around to see if anybody else gave any sign of thinking that God had a mighty unusual way of showing his love. No one else was reacting, though, except for a nod of agreement here and there.

"God could have wiped out all the children of Israel that day for the sin of Achan," the preacher continued. *Except that he would have thwarted his own plan of sending a messiah through the line of David,* Celia thought. But she didn't have much time to feel superior, for no sooner had she formed the thought than the preacher added in his Georgia drawl, "But Jesus had to be born of Mary, of the house and lineage of David, so God mercifully preserved the race, though once again Israel had grievously disregarded his commandments."

He went on to catalog all the times God could have destroyed Israel down through the ages for their sins against him. The flood, the tower of Babel, the golden calf, the grumbling in the wilderness, the intermarrying

with the Canaanites, on and on through the long list of individual short-
comings and deceptions of the people all the way from Adam and Eve
straight through to Peter's denial of Christ in the New Testament and, of
course, the ultimate failure of the race as a whole: the refusal to accept
Jesus as the Messiah.

" 'It is of the Lord's mercies that we are not consumed,' " the preacher
said, " 'because his compassions fail not. They are new every morning: great
is thy faithfulness.' " It was God's hand, he went on to say, that held sinners
"from being dropped into the pit of hell right this very minute." He even
waxed eloquent for a minute or two, alluding to Jonathan Edwards' famous
sermon, painting a graphic picture of God holding the world over the
raging flames of hell like someone dangling a spider over a campfire.

Celia couldn't help being reminded of Macon Mahoney's painting
Fade, Fade, Each Earthly Joy. She saw the hand at the top of the canvas,
clasping the slender thread with two fingers, swinging the ball of the Earth
back and forth like a toy on a string, and she wondered if Macon had been
thinking of Jonathan Edwards' sermon when he painted the picture.

" 'There are the black clouds of God's wrath now hanging directly
over your heads, full of the dreadful storm, and big with thunder,' " the
preacher was saying, " 'and were it not for the restraining hand of God, it
would immediately burst forth upon you.' " Celia was pretty sure he was
quoting directly from Jonathan Edwards now, and when he added, " 'The
sovereign pleasure of God, for the present, stays his rough wind,' " she
was positive. But when he said, "Every one of us in this room should get
down on their knees and thank God for his patience with us," she knew
he was back to his own words again.

It was an interesting effect, she decided, to hear the powerful drama
of an eighteenth-century New England preacher's sermon coming out
of the mouth of a man whose every syllable gave him away as a native
southerner, who, when he shifted back into his own words, had a little
trouble with pronoun case and antecedent agreement.

He was wrapping up his sermon when he said something that took
Celia back. Furthermore, she had a feeling that it would keep coming
back to her in the days that followed. "But for every instance of God's
judgment in Scripture," he said, "I'll show you two of his great mercy." And
right before the Communion service, he wound things up with "God's
love is the theme that runs from Genesis through Revelation. He delights
in blessing anyone who gives their life to him. And now we move into a

celebration of his greatest blessing—the gift of his Son, who gave himself for us on the cross."

This was evidently the cue for the deacons to rise from their pews and come forward to pass the plates of Communion bread and the cups of grape juice. Mrs. Abbott at the organ began playing "When I Survey the Wondrous Cross," and people bowed their heads as if weighed down with shame. Celia passed the plates without taking anything. She didn't even want to be here, so there was no way she was going to compound her hypocrisy by actually participating in the service. She had sung along with the hymns, but that was somehow different.

The two baptisms after that were uneventful, although the second one, a fortyish man, did raise his hands when he was lifted up out of the water and say, "Thank you, Lord Jesus," right out loud.

When a young couple came forward with a baby wearing a long white dress, Celia closed her eyes. *Just hang on through this and you'll be done,* she told herself. *Think about something else.* She tried shifting her thoughts to all sorts of other things outside the four walls of Bethany Hills Bible Tabernacle, but all she could hear was the preacher's voice saying, "For every instance of God's judgment, I'll show you two of his mercy." She found herself arguing with him now. Every guilt-ridden day of her life, she felt God's judgment, but the double measure of mercy—well, she sure hadn't experienced that.

When the baby started crying, a lone thin wail, as she had known it surely would, she thought of a question for the preacher: "So where's that mercy you were talking about a while ago?"

The thought came to her that the eye-for-an-eye justice of the Old Testament could actually be seen as a form of mercy, if you didn't believe in the idea of eternal life, that is. With swift tit-for-tat retribution your punishment would be over and done. You kill someone and you die. You wouldn't have to live with the effects of your sin every day of your life. You wouldn't have to suffer through the dreadful storms of long sleepless nights and the thunder of infant voices.

20

Till the Last Beam Fadeth

At first Celia had thought of it as a total miracle that somebody wanted to buy Grandmother's house, but then she had learned that the train no longer kept its daily schedule along that stretch of track. With that drawback out of the way, she could see how somebody might want a small clean house like her grandmother's, even though it would need a new roof in the next few years and the kitchen was no bigger than a walk-in closet. Maybe a widow or a retired couple, somebody who didn't do a lot of cooking, would find it just right.

But it turned out to be a newly married couple. And one of the biggest surprises was that they were paying cash, so there was no loan approval to wait for. Evidently the girl's father, an orthodontist, was giving them the house as a wedding present. They wanted to move in soon, in July, so they'd be all settled by the time school started. They were both teachers in Dunmore, one at the high school and the other at an elementary school. They had come by twice already to take some measurements while Celia had been here this time, and it was clear that they were champing at the bit to start hanging curtains and unpacking dishes.

This couple was a great mystery to Celia, and she marveled that they hailed from right here in Dunmore. They looked like they belonged in some big city like Atlanta or Savannah. They were both good-looking in a wholesome, all-American way—shiny brown hair, clear fresh complexions, straight white teeth. Their names were Luke and Ashley Franco, and they both had one whole year of teaching under their belts.

The first time they came by the house, Celia had two more names for her list of married couples who looked like each other. Here they were, the Franco twins, with their shiny-faced star quarterback and head cheerleader kind of good looks. She added them at once to the preacher and his wife, the look-alike Davidsons, and her next-door neighbors back home, Bruce and Kimberly, whose last name she didn't even know, who, not counting his scars and her extra weight, could also be siblings.

Now that she thought about it, though, it wasn't just the couples she had met recently. Milton and Patsy Stewart looked alike, too. They were almost exactly the same height and body build, wore the same bland smiles, and from a distance appeared to have something perched on top of their heads, Patsy's hairdo looking like a helmet with earflaps and Morton's like an upside-down mixing bowl. Even Ollie and Connie favored each other, with their Scandinavian kind of good looks, both tall and big-boned with blue eyes and blond hair going gray. And Boo Newman's husband was as plump as she was, though Celia had seen him only a couple of times through the art gallery window and couldn't judge how much they looked alike in the face. She thought also of her Coleman grandparents, Papa and Mums, who had looked a lot like the farm couple in the famous *American Gothic* painting—stiff, responsible, and deadpan, though her grandfather had been a scientist not a farmer.

She thought also of her own parents. When she was growing up, she didn't think anything about it, but now she could see that they, too, had looked like they came from the same gene pool. People had called her mother "cute"—she remembered that clearly—and her father, in spite of the fact that he was a chronic worrier, had a boyish grin and a smattering of leftover freckles across his nose—Sally Field and Ron Howard kind of faces. Gidget and Opie.

Of course, she knew she could make a list of an equal number of couples who didn't even remotely resemble each other, but once she got past Aunt Beulah and Uncle Taylor and Elizabeth and Ken Landis, she lost interest. It was more fun to think about couples who looked alike and to hypothesize about why it so often happened that way. Did they gravitate toward each other in the first place because they recognized something familiar in the other person's face, or was it that true intimacy, physical and emotional, somehow worked its way out of the soul and into their features? In other words, was the resemblance a cause or a result of the relationship, or maybe a little of both?

Oh, these were the kinds of things Celia could spend hours contemplating, and with no good results. What did it matter, really? Maybe the whole subject of couples looking alike was just something she had dreamed up. Maybe nobody else saw it at all. Sometimes she had to laugh at herself for getting so carried away. She had once read somewhere that marriage was never more interesting than to someone who was single.

The closing for the house was scheduled for Tuesday, two days after Celia had attended Bethany Hills Bible Tabernacle. When it was over, she would be around thirty-four thousand dollars richer, not counting what they'd brought in from the yard sale. She would give Aunt Beulah something for all her help with sorting things and organizing the sale. And Uncle Taylor, too. There was no way she could have cleared out the storage building and barn without his help. He had filled up the bed of his pickup truck countless times and carried loads to the dump, to the Salvation Army, to his own workshop. Luke Franco had been interested in the old tractor and several other things in the barn, so some of it was staying.

Late Tuesday morning before the one o'clock closing at the lawyer's office, Celia went out to the barn one last time to make sure the paper wasps were all gone, that there wasn't a contingent hanging around the rafters somewhere trying to build another nest. She also wanted to check the inside of the old store again to see if she had overlooked anything there. Ashley Franco had asked to keep the coal stove that had been shoved into a corner, had said she wanted Luke to clean it up and paint it with black enamel to use as an end table in the living room.

Celia swung open the barn door and stepped inside. It looked like a totally different place than it had five days ago. It was big enough and clean enough now to hold a moderate-sized square dance in. She smiled at the thought of sending invitations to Grandmother's sisters and her brother, Buford, and the legions of cousins. One of those preprinted ones that read, "You are cordially invited to" and then had a blank after it, in which she would write "A Square Dance!" in big bold letters. In the blank after "Where," she would write "The Late Sadie Burnes's Barn on Old Campground Road." What pleasure she could derive from such a parting shot as she took her leave of Dunmore, Georgia.

She could imagine all the aunts on the telephone, gasping at the thought of holding a *dance* on Sadie's property. They would never catch that it was a joke. They would assume the invitation was for real. She'd be willing to bet that every one of them would sneak by in their cars at the appointed time, hoping to catch a horrified glimpse of swirling petticoats and stomping feet in the barn. It would almost be worth the time and trouble to hang around and watch their disappointment when they found it was a hoax.

Celia walked around inside the barn, squinting up at all the rafters. No sign of more wasp nests. She was circling back toward the door when she saw a small box behind the tractor. She hadn't noticed it before, and obviously Uncle Taylor hadn't, either. When she opened the top, she saw that it was more than half full of broken walnut shells. No telling how long they'd been here. Years ago there had been an old walnut tree out near the railroad track, but some men from a county work crew had cut it down the summer after Celia had come to live with her grandmother. They said the branches were too close to the track.

Grandmother hadn't been happy about losing the tree even though the railroad line had paid her a little something for it. She kept talking about how she would miss it. She had gathered the walnuts every fall and, like Milton Stewart back home, had spent hours in the evenings cracking the hard shells and picking out the nutmeats. The Thanksgiving after Celia came to live with her, Grandmother had cooked a turkey outdoors in the open pit her long-dead husband had dug for that purpose. She had placed walnut shells on top of the coals, telling Celia it would give the bird a better flavor. And it *had* tasted good, even though, as usual, Grandmother had overcooked it. The skin had been charred black, and the meat was dry.

Grandmother grumbled about the loss of the walnut tree for weeks and weeks. Celia, however, had gotten in on enough of the gathering and shelling of walnuts during that one fall to make her want to hug the men who had cut it down, but she stayed quiet and never let on. She tried to look sympathetic when Grandmother talked about not having walnuts for pies and cookies and not having the shells to use for roasting in the pit. To be honest, Celia knew by now that Grandmother's pies and cookies would never win any blue ribbons at the Georgia State Fair, and she still remembered how hard it had been to chew that turkey.

She couldn't help wondering now how long this box of walnut shells had been sitting out here. It would have been over twenty summers since the tree was cut down. No doubt Grandmother had forgotten all about them, for she never would have willingly let something go to waste. She would have built an outdoor fire and cooked over it every night if she had to until the shells were used up. So what could have happened to make her grandmother forget about them?

As Celia looked down into the box of broken shells, an idea suddenly took shape that until this minute had never entered her mind. She had thought plenty over the years about how her own life had been turned upside down by coming to live with her grandmother, but right this minute she stood very still and thought about the ways in which her coming here had changed her grandmother's life, had interrupted her days and maybe made her forget things like a box of walnut shells stored in the barn.

Well into her sixties at the time, Grandmother would have already lived alone as a widow for over ten years, having closed down the little store after her husband's death and having sold his pickup truck and a few personal effects in order to pay off his debts. For over ten years she would have been living off her monthly social security check, recording in a ledger how every penny was spent. Celia had run across those ledgers while cleaning out her grandmother's drawers.

She didn't know all the details of the financial arrangements, but she knew her grandmother had received some kind of government money for taking her in. Not that anyone had ever sat Celia down and explained it all to her. Ansell had been the one to tell her, when she was seventeen, that the government gave money to guardians of orphans. "What? You think the old bat's doing it out of the goodness of her heart?" he had said to Celia. "Get real, Celia."

During her last year of high school, Celia had said some pretty ugly things about the money when she had been angry at her grandmother. She had accused her more than once of hoarding *her* money to use for herself later. She had to use the accusation of hoarding because it was clear her grandmother wasn't spending it on extravagances. The only things she ever bought were the weekly groceries, gas, and school clothes for Celia.

She remembered now how surprised she had been when she turned eighteen and learned how much money was available to her for her college education. She had gotten five thousand from Papa and Mums Coleman, the bulk of their estate going to an endowment fund at the college where Papa had taught. But there was much, much more than five thousand in what Grandmother called her "college fund." This was when Celia had formed the assumption that her father's investments must have done a lot better than he let on. And who could tell? Maybe that was the case.

Right now, though, standing in the barn staring down at the walnut shells, she allowed a thought to circle around and round in her mind. Maybe Grandmother *had been* hoarding money all those years, but maybe she had been hoarding it for Celia's education, to add to whatever was already there from the sale of her parents' assets.

Then suddenly she came to her senses. *Wait a minute,* she told herself. *She was a stingy old woman. Don't start making her out to be a kindhearted philanthropist.* She made herself think of the leather jacket she had wanted so badly her senior year. It wasn't the most expensive one by any means, but at least it was real leather even if it was in the Sears catalog. She had shown it to her grandmother that fall, when the days had started turning cooler, and had strongly hinted that it would be a great Christmas present. Several times after that she had seen her grandmother slowly turning the pages of the catalog as she sat in her rocking chair by the gas heater.

One large box with Celia's name on it had appeared under the small artificial tree that Christmas, and even though they had had a rocky time at home for the preceding few months, Celia had actually let herself believe that she was getting the leather jacket for Christmas.

When she had opened the present on Christmas morning, it wasn't the jacket, of course, but a bright blue wool parka with a hood and little oblong wooden buttons that slipped through loops. She hadn't disguised her disappointment, hadn't even tried to, and when Grandmother said, "This one's more practical, Celie," Celia had replied, "Yeah, and it's also a lot cheaper and uglier," then had left the parka in the box on the floor and shut herself up in her bedroom.

She wondered now why she hadn't refused to wear it altogether or why she hadn't marched down to Sears and gotten a refund, then bought something else she wanted with the money. She didn't recall that such an idea had even occurred to her. Instead, she had eventually worn the stupid parka, had worn it a lot, in fact. For being such a rebel, she surely hadn't had much backbone. It had kept her warm through six Delaware winters at Blackrock College until she got her master's degree and her first full-time job at a newspaper in Dover. She had even put it on and worn it in bed in the middle of the summer fourteen years ago, in the days following her trip to the clinic when she couldn't get warm.

And the really funny thing was that when she had gone to a department store in Delaware after starting her first job, to finally buy a leather jacket, she had felt lightheaded and short of breath when she looked at the price tags. She had tried on a dozen or more and had gone away without buying one.

She had returned another day and tried again, then found herself wandering over to the other coats and jackets, finally settling on a tan wool pea coat that would be more practical. For days after, she had been so mad at herself that she finally went back and bought a leather jacket just to prove—well, she wasn't sure what she was proving, really, maybe just that she could do whatever she wanted to. But the fact was that for the next several winters she wore the tan pea coat ten times as much as the leather jacket.

Celia gave herself a little shake and looked at her watch. She couldn't be wasting time like this standing out here in the barn reliving the past. She picked up the box of walnut shells and headed around to the back of the barn toward the old creek bed. It had dried up many years ago and was now full of weeds, dead branches, and pinecones. She would dump the shells in there and throw the box away.

Surely, she thought later, she would have remembered the cat incident at some point, even if she hadn't gone down by the creek bed behind the barn. Something like that would *have* to come back to you sometime. You couldn't repress such a memory permanently. How odd, though, to consider the seemingly random chain of events that led up to the moment of remembering—discovering the paper-wasp nests in the first place, using the free time before the closing at the lawyer's office to return to the barn for another check, finding the box of walnut shells, deciding to dispose of them, walking purposefully to the creek bed, and then, on the way back to the house, the sudden violent erupting of the memory from years gone by. For weeks after, it made her nervous, wondering how many other closed compartments were to burst open on her unawares.

As soon as it happened, she knew this was another of those moments that would come back to her at all hours, especially in the nighttime. Even as she sat in the lawyer's office two hours later, she had trouble following the proceedings. She kept replaying what had just happened, saw herself tromping through the tall grass behind the barn, then reaching the creek bed and turning the box over, watching the shells fall out and disappear beneath the thick growth of weeds, then mindlessly heading back toward the barn, carrying the box by one of the top flaps.

And then . . . seeing it. There, about two feet from the back side of the barn, was a small crude-looking cross of sorts, tilted a little to one side. She had never actually seen it here in this place before, but she remembered with absolute clarity the day her grandmother had nailed it together out on the front porch. Celia had watched her from the living room window as she went into the old store and emerged a minute later with two short pieces of one-by-two. She watched her lay one piece on top of the other to form a cross, then lift her hammer there on the front porch and furiously drive two nails through the center, after which she stomped back toward the barn, holding the cross in one hand and the bucket in the other. In the bucket was a dead cat.

It was a nasty, spiteful gray cat, with an unpredictable streak running through him. He would lunge at the silliest things without warning, like a leaf skittering across the driveway, or a shadow moving across a windowpane, or a dish towel flapping on the clothesline. On the other hand, he was very predictable about other things. Every single time the train whizzed by, for example, Smoky could be found hiding behind the big tin washtub on the back porch.

Celia hated him from the moment she laid eyes on him, and the feeling was evidently mutual. The cat always watched her resentfully, as if she were trespassing on his turf, and at times she thought he had a greedy hungry look in his eye, as he might if she were a very large rodent he'd like to rip into.

He was a stray that had shown up on her grandmother's back doorstep only weeks after Celia herself had moved in. He was half-starved and flea-bitten, and though her grandmother usually didn't have a sympathetic bone in her body, for some reason she started feeding this mangy creature. She even used some of her grocery money to buy flea shampoo and dipped the cat within an inch of his life, over and over, suffering scratches all over her arms and face in the process. One day she gave him a name: Smoky, because his fur was smoky gray. She let the cat stay on the back porch and cut a little hole in the bottom of the screen door so he could get in and out. But he wasn't an indoor cat. As much as she loved him, Grandmother never would have stood for an animal in the house.

And amazingly, the cat seemed to love the old woman, too. He would purr softly and rub himself against her when she took a bowl of milk and a plate of scraps out to the back porch. Whenever Grandmother swept the back steps, Smoky would meow so pitifully at her that she'd always

put down her broom, sit down on the steps, and take him into her lap
for a brief minute.

Celia couldn't count the times she had seen them on the back steps,
her grandmother gently stroking Smoky's gray fur and talking to him,
never in a babyish crooning voice the way a lot of pet owners did, but always
very sensibly in her ordinary voice, usually reciting her day's agenda for
him. "I got to finish up the sweeping," she might say, "and then trim the
bushes in the front yard. And I got to put in a load of wash, then hang it
out, then call up Molly and ask her when she's aimin' to bring over those
cucumbers so we can put up some pickles."

Celia had never had much contact with cats, or dogs, either. Neither
one of her parents liked animals, especially not in the house, and they
had always made it clear that a pet would cost money they should be using
on other more important things. As a child, Celia had had only one pet
briefly, a blue parakeet named Chipper, but he was a messy, loud bird who
hated his cage and bolted for freedom whenever Celia opened the little
door. He would fly to the top of her mother's nicest draperies and dirty
them with droppings. One day he flew right out the front door as her
father came in from work, and though she was sad for a day or two, she
soon realized that life at home was a lot less complicated without Chipper.
She had never asked for another pet after that.

Maybe Smoky sensed in her an aversion to animals. Or maybe he liked
only old women, not teenaged girls. Whatever it was, he clearly avoided
her. The few times she took his food out to the back porch, he made no
move to welcome her but stared at her with his evil green eyes from his
favorite spot under the old wringer washing machine. She tried a few
times in the beginning to stoop down and pet him, but he hissed at her
and retreated behind some paint cans. "Well, I don't like you either, dumb
cat," she finally said, but not loud enough for Grandmother to hear, and
after that she quit trying to make friends with him.

Whenever Grandmother was working in the yard, Smoky would station
himself near her, curled up under a bush somewhere or up against the
house. On summer evenings after supper Grandmother would often sit
on the front porch in the swing, snapping beans or mending something
or cutting pictures out of magazines to glue onto the homemade cards she
sent to missionaries. Smoky would always be lying right next to her, usually asleep. She didn't generally talk to him in the evenings on the porch

swing, only on the back steps, but as she worked, she would frequently look down at him with something very close to a smile on her lips.

To Celia's way of thinking, there was nothing in the least bit endearing or winsome about Smoky. He was snooty and temperamental. When he caught birds or chipmunks in the backyard, he proudly paraded around with them in his mouth, their little heads hanging out one side and their tails out the other. If he happened to see Celia, he would stop in his tracks and glare at her distrustfully. *As if I want that disgusting thing,* she would think. If he saw Grandmother, however, he would walk straight to her and lovingly lay his prize at her feet.

Part of Celia's dislike of Smoky, she suspected now, was that deep down she was jealous of him, for he had appropriated Grandmother's affection in a way she didn't seem to be able to do. He and Grandmother seemed to have such an easy, natural relationship, each one giving and receiving gentleness as a matter of course. Theirs was a staunch silent friendship, and she felt at times like an intruder. During her senior year of high school, she had often used Smoky to excuse her wild behavior and her disrespect to her grandmother. Though she wouldn't have stooped to say such things aloud, she had often thought, *If you acted like you cared for me half as much as you do that cat, maybe things would be different.*

In the lawyer's office Celia realized that she was now being asked to sign papers. She saw Ashley Franco studying her from across the table and wondered if she had done anything to give away the fact that she hadn't heard a word that had been said in the last few minutes. For all she knew, they could have lowered the cost of the house and gypped her out of ten thousand dollars. She ought to check the papers carefully before signing.

But even as the lawyer's assistant slid the papers over to her, the printed words began swimming before her eyes, and once again the image of the wooden cross in the ground behind the barn rose before her. The human mind was a curious thing. How could she have possibly blotted from her memory such a horrible day? The answer suggested itself at once. Maybe it was because she had had so many other horrible days since that one.

She could still see the hoe her grandmother was using to break up the ground on either side of the front steps that March day, jabbing furiously at the hard ground in preparation for planting dahlias. Less than six feet away from her, Celia herself was sitting in the porch swing, something she rarely did during those last few months at Grandmother's house. The two of them weren't talking right then, but there were hot bitter words still hanging in the air.

The subject had been the high school prom. Celia had demanded money for a dress, to which her grandmother had replied that a Christian girl didn't have any business going to an event where the devil was going to be having his way all night long, to which Celia had replied that maybe a Christian girl didn't, but *she* was going to, and if Grandmother didn't fork over the money out of the hoard that was rightfully Celia's anyway, she'd find some other way to get the dress. Over and over she kept repeating to herself Ansell's advice: "Stick up for yourself, Celia. Don't let the old witch run your life."

Celia rarely looked directly at her grandmother during these blowups because she knew she'd lose her nerve if she did. Right now she sat on the swing with one leg tucked up under her and looked instead at her grandmother's hoe. It was a big hoe, much too big for the job at hand in Celia's opinion, but Grandmother wielded it with the ease of someone who had many years of experience with farm implements. She wasn't a tall woman, but she was strong. With her large hands she gripped the handle of the hoe firmly and chopped at the dirt like a madwoman. Any worms hiding in that flower bed would be mincemeat before she was done.

Smoky was on the porch, too, lying beside the front door, his wicked tail swishing ever so slightly as he watched Grandmother hack away with the hoe. Celia was waiting for Grandmother to speak, waiting for some kind of commitment about the money for the dress. As the seconds ticked by, she grew worried, for she had learned by now that total silence wasn't a good sign. If Grandmother continued to grumble and mutter objections, it meant she was beginning to concede defeat. If she said nothing, then her mind was already made up.

Though it was late March and still cool, Celia was barefoot, another thing her grandmother frowned upon, along with almost everything else she did, and as she continued to watch the rise and fall of the hoe, she must have started wiggling the foot that wasn't tucked under her, the one hanging down from the swing. Maybe it was twitching in rhythm with the hoe. She wasn't aware of doing it, or she surely would have stopped, for she knew Smoky's neurotic behavior well enough by now. It wasn't until later, after Smoky pounced, that she realized what she must have been doing.

All she remembered was a sudden projectile of snarling gray fur and the shocking pain of claws and teeth sinking into her bare foot. She screamed, she remembered that, too. But the cat latched on, going for a kill, and wouldn't let go. When she tried to shake him off, she felt a ripping of flesh and the warmth of blood. It was almost as if Smoky had waited long enough and now was finally taking his revenge on her for the past two and a half years.

Somehow she had managed to get off the swing and began hopping around the porch, blood dripping from her foot, but still Smoky hung on. Snarls, shouts, screams, it was hard to tell where they were all coming from—the porch was pure bedlam. For a brief moment Celia pictured a terrifying scene of the cat launching himself from her foot to her face, scratching out her eyes, ripping her scalp open. She heard her screams escalate and felt herself going weak, as she imagined a person must feel right before fainting, and then all at once she heard a mighty whack against the floor of the porch and saw Grandmother's hoe come down inches from her foot.

Smoky immediately went limp and released his hold. Both Grandmother and Celia stood motionless for several long seconds, staring down at the cat, whose hindquarters were almost severed from the rest of his body. Later Celia would generate a fresh wave of anger at her grandmother for coming so close to chopping her foot off with the stupid hoe, but for now she was stunned by the amount of blood pooling under Smoky, mingling with her own blood, and she suddenly saw the floor of the porch start to spin and felt herself falling down into a gaping black hole. When she came to, she was lying on the porch close to the door and Grandmother was bent over her foot, sponging it gently with warm soapy water in a tin bucket.

"This'll hurt," she told Celia bluntly, then applied something that felt like liquid fire and started wrapping the foot with a long strip of gauze. Over this she put a length of stretchy bandage, clamping the end with a little silver clip. Celia didn't dare turn her head to the left to see if all the blood was still there, or the mutilated cat. She didn't say a word, just kept her eyes fastened on Grandmother's face, unyielding and intent as she bent over her work.

Though it didn't make a bit of sense, Celia's dazed mind kept pulling up pictures from Bible stories—the Good Samaritan, Jesus washing the disciples' feet, Mary wiping the feet of Jesus with her hair, and, most inexplicably, the Crucifixion. When it was done, Celia made herself look only at the screen door while Grandmother helped her stand up and hobble into the house to lie down on the couch in the living room.

Always squeamish about blood, Celia couldn't quit thinking about all that blood on the front porch. How would they ever clean it all off? The front door had been left ajar, and through the screen she could hear her grandmother thumping around out there, grunting softly as she . . . did what? Celia couldn't resist limping over to the window to look out. She covered her mouth as she watched Grandmother running the hose right over the planks of the porch, the water washing the blood over the edge, down into the flowerbed where the dahlias were to be planted. She didn't see the cat anywhere.

She continued watching as her grandmother got down on her hands and knees and scrubbed for all she was worth with a large stiff-bristled brush, then rinsed the floor again and again. She did it all with such grim purpose, the same way she did everything. If Celia had been asked to pick a hymn that personified her grandmother best, she would have chosen "Work, for the Night Is Coming." If asked on any given morning what she was going to do to fill up the day, Grandmother would have lifted her chin and said, "I'm going to *work*, that's what. I'm going to work through the morning hours, right on through the sunny noon and the sunset skies. I'm going to work *till the last beam fadeth*. That's what I'm going to do today."

When she finished with the floor, Celia saw her grandmother get up and head out toward the store, then return shortly with the two pieces of wood, a hammer, and nails. She watched her fashion the cross, then saw her pick up the tin bucket from the top step and gaze down into it silently, her mouth set in a taut line. That's when Celia knew where the cat was. How like Grandmother. She had emptied the soapy water she had used to cleanse Celia's foot and put Smoky's dead body in the very same bucket. Same receptacle for victim and culprit alike.

"Uh, here you go, one more time, Ms. Coleman," the lawyer said, clearing his throat, which made Celia think he had probably already said it before. And as she wrote her name another time on a line at the bottom of yet another page, Celia once again saw her grandmother tuck the hammer into her apron pocket, then pick up the cross with one hand and the bucket with the other. She saw her walk around the side of the house and disappear behind the barn to bury her cat.

21

Those Wide, Extended Plains

The next day when Celia was on her way back to South Carolina, her mind returned again and again to the cat incident. Never had she paused to think about Grandmother's loss all those years ago. Her main concerns that day had been whether she could play tennis in an upcoming match against a rival school in nearby Burma and whether she could wear a pair of slinky sandals with her prom dress next month.

She had never bothered to wonder about trivial things such as how Grandmother felt about losing the only pet she had ever had or whether she stayed awake that night, and for nights after, thinking about the fact that she had killed that pet with her own hands. And neither had Celia stopped to reflect for even a minute on what it said about her grandmother's feelings for her that she would bring her hoe down so swiftly on the soft gray fur of Smoky's back.

Superficial wounds, that's what Grandmother had labeled Celia's injured foot when they argued later that day about making a doctor's appointment. Though Celia brought up the possibility of rabies, Grandmother hadn't given it a passing thought. "I kept up with his shots," she said gruffly. And she had. Though she always took Smoky to a mobile clinic that didn't charge much, she was faithful about it and kept a careful record of the dates in the same ledger where she accounted for every penny of the budget.

Oh yes, she had spent money on Smoky's rabies shots all right, but when it came to taking her own granddaughter to a doctor, Celia had pointed out, that was a different matter. Celia knew it was the money more than anything that made Grandmother reluctant about seeing a doctor, and she came right out and said so, accused her of caring more about money than about whether Celia was maimed for life.

Her grandmother had shot her an inscrutable look but had relented and called the same elderly doctor who had tended to Granddaddy during his last illness. Celia was disappointed when Dr. York confirmed her grandmother's diagnosis. Surely anything that had hurt so much and produced so much dark blood all over the porch couldn't be merely superficial. There was some swelling, which he said would subside within the next few days.

The foot, Dr. York had told her, was a pretty tough appendage, capable of withstanding all kinds of abuse. "Not a whole lot of meat on these bones," he had said with a smile. The cat had raked at her skin but hadn't torn away big chunks of flesh. "My guess is that he was just playing with you," he added. "If he had wanted to hurt you, he sure could have, big old cat like that."

Celia could have explained that Smoky wasn't a playful cat, that he hated her as much as she hated him, and that he most certainly *had* wanted to hurt her, but she decided it wasn't worth the effort, especially not with Grandmother sitting right there ready to dispute her word. Though Dr. York complimented Grandmother on her dressing of the wound, he had taken Celia through another painful cleansing, followed by more antiseptic that felt like he was pouring hot tar over her foot, and a tight rebandaging.

In the car on the way home, Celia had called into question both Dr. York's eyesight and his soundness of mind, to which Grandmother hadn't bothered to reply. For three days Celia had to bathe with her foot sticking out of the bathtub, and then for another few days she wore only a light bandage, and finally no bandage "so the air can get to it and make it scab up dry," as her grandmother put it.

Two weeks later she rebandaged it and played in the tennis match against Burma, winning in two sets, and four weeks later she wore a pair of silver sandals and a light blue gauzy dress with a sequined bodice to the Dunmore High School prom. When Ansell came by to pick her up that night, she had flown out of the house before Grandmother could intercept her and add a coda to the dirge she had been singing ever since she gave Celia thirty whole dollars to buy a dress. As if thirty dollars were enough to buy anything fit to wear—that had been her first thought. But, remarkably, it turned out that it was. Her friend Renee knew about a consignment shop over in Cartersville, where she and Celia found the blue dress for only eighteen dollars.

"I never thought I'd see the day when my own flesh and blood would want to consort with evil"—that was the main tune of Grandmother's sad song. She also interjected dire warnings about "not letting anybody force you into doing things," which, being interpreted, meant no drinking, no smoking, no drugs, and, above all, no sex. She had to know by now that Celia had dabbled in both drinking and smoking, but she would have no way of knowing that neither one really appealed to her, and Celia wasn't about to tell her. She knew Grandmother was probably worried to a frazzle about whether she had tried drugs and sex, but she had no intention of enlightening her about those, either. If she was going to act the way she did, Celia reasoned, then it served her right to be eaten up with worry.

Actually, prom night wasn't something Celia wanted to think about, and as she drove south on Highway 41 toward Calhoun, she tried to put it out of her mind and concentrate on other things. She had called Ollie at the gallery two days ago, and he had told her about Macon Mahoney's wanting another show in the fall. She did have a six-week slot starting in mid-November that was still unfilled, so that would save her the trouble of having to come up with something.

Ollie had also told her about selling two more of Lenny Bullard's pieces to a collector from Flat Rock, North Carolina, and about Craig running into an old classmate of his from college and how this man had a French friend, a brilliant artist, who was in the States, living in Greenville for a couple of years with his wife, who had some kind of short-term contract with Michelin. The gallery might be able to work a deal with him, Craig thought, to show his stuff. According to Ollie, Craig had seen some of it and was uncharacteristically enthusiastic about it.

So Celia tried to turn her thoughts homeward, thinking about what she could do for opening night if Macon Mahoney really did have enough new pieces for another show. He was hoping for a mystical theme was how Ollie put it—or, as Macon himself had described it, "supernaturalism, the afterlife, antimaterialism, and such," which sounded a bit worrisome to Celia. They sure couldn't allow any of their artists to use the gallery as a platform for promoting a particular religious or political ideology.

She thought about what she could do with the refreshment table for a

show with a mystical slant. Maybe she could work the theme of the decorations around outer space—hang colored balls from the ceiling to suggest
planets, sprinkle glitter on a black velvet tablecloth, and such.

She tried thinking about her car, too. It had been burning oil lately,
and she knew enough to recognize that as a bad sign. Uncle Taylor had
looked it over while she had been in Dunmore and told her she might be
facing what he called a "ring job," not a cheap repair. Maybe it was time to
start thinking about a trade-in on a new car, or at least a newer one.

This was the second Mustang she had owned, so maybe she should
try something else, or at least switch to a four-door. There were getting to
be too many times when a two-door was inconvenient. And tone down the
color, too—a dark blue would be nice. Maybe she should go back over to
the car dealership in Greenville and see if Todd Robard still owned it and
was still giving free psychological counseling. No doubt he was married
and had a couple of kids by now. But the whole complicated prospect of
buying a new car gave her no pleasure. It would be less expensive to get
the ring job and keep driving this one for now.

She thought about the money she had just received from the sale of
Grandmother's house. How funny that she had netted twice as much as
she had expected. If anyone had asked her six months ago to estimate
what her grandmother's estate would total, she would have laughed, first
of all, at the use of such a high-sounding word as *estate* for the property
on Old Campground Road, and second, she would have guessed no more
than fifteen thousand. For all she knew back then, the house might not
even be paid off yet.

To be sure it was a meager inheritance, but an inheritance nonetheless. She could use it to buy a car if she decided to go to the trouble one
of these days. Or maybe she should put all the money into mutual funds
or a money market account, then buy a car with interest-free monthly
payments over five years. The deals they were offering on new cars now
made it silly to pay cash up front. But again she dismissed the idea of a
new car. She didn't really need one if she got her Mustang repaired. It
had only sixty-five thousand miles on it.

She had toyed with the idea over the past several years, too, of going
out on a limb and buying a house. She could certainly do that now, using
Grandmother's money as a down payment for something nice, maybe in
a moderately classy neighborhood on the outskirts of Greenville so she'd
be a little closer to the gallery. And she could afford house payments now

that the three owners of the Trio Gallery had expanded her hours to full time. Ollie had been glad to hand over the bookkeeping to her, something he had always hated and never been very good at.

But she thought about the idea of packing up to move, then redecorating a whole house, buying new furniture to fill it up, spreading out her art over more wall space. None of it really excited her. All the work, all the money it would take, all the time before she got it the way she really wanted it, all the repairs and improvements that would be her responsibility as a homeowner—really, her apartment was all she needed and more. Before she had left home for this trip, in fact, Patsy Stewart had told her that while she was gone Milton planned to take up the linoleum from Celia's kitchen floor and replace it. They had even let Celia choose what she wanted. There was something very secure in having a good landlord to take care of your needs, even to anticipate a few of those needs before you thought about them.

Of course, there was the old argument about throwing your money away every month as a renter instead of building up equity. That used to worry her a lot more than it did now, though. Over the past few years she had begun to realize how much money Patsy and Milton spent on their house just to keep it up, and she knew it was a never-ending process. Some emergency was always lurking around the corner, waiting until the most inopportune time to need fixing or replacing, like the hot water tank that went out one weekend last spring. And the fact wasn't lost on her that Milton saved a bundle by doing many of the home jobs himself. If she owned a house, she would have to hire somebody to do it all—more money sucked out of her bank account.

But as hard as she tried not to let it, prom night kept slipping back into her thoughts. She had imagined herself so free when she had skipped down the steps to meet Ansell that night, not even waiting to see if he would behave with a little more decorum than usual by coming to the door for her. All those old customs were out of date anyway. She hadn't been given a curfew, and she surely didn't want to hang around and risk being given one. She wanted to feel like everybody else for a change. Tonight was prom night, the climax of every girl's high school years, a time to forget about rules and restraints and bothersome grandmothers who thought "Thou shalt not dance" should be the eleventh commandment.

Suddenly a car coming toward her, going north on Highway 41, honked and blinked its lights. For a moment Celia bristled. What in the world was that guy doing? Then she realized how fast she was driving. Maybe the other car was trying to warn her about something. She eased up on the gas pedal, and no sooner had the speedometer fallen below sixty than she saw it up ahead—a police car pulled over in a thicket of trees by a roadside park. She wished she could thank that other driver now. She had never gotten a speeding ticket in her life, though one of the men she used to date—she thought maybe it was Chris—got them routinely, usually not bothering to go to court but simply mailing in his two or three hundred dollars each time.

She would hate spending two hundred dollars on something like that. What a waste. At the thought she couldn't help smiling a little. At least she recognized the irony of it all. The more money a person had, the more he tended to clutch it to himself. And another thing that struck her just now was how much she had grown to be like her father in regard to money.

Not that she invested in stocks and kept up with the Dow average every day as he had. Utilities, mutual funds, and money markets were as daring as she ever got. But she often found herself fretting over her finances, shifting money around, hyperventilating over whether to write a check or charge a certain item, counting the cash in her billfold over and over and stashing little wads of it in the different zippered compartments of her purse. She wondered if it could be partly due to the fact that she was single and had no husband to take care of paying the bills. She wondered if it would get worse as she got older until she got to be as bad a penny pincher as her grandmother had been. That would be awful.

She remembered Ansell taking a roll of bills out of his pocket after she got into the car on prom night. He had grinned at her and said, "Hot time tonight, baby." It had surprised her—not the money, but his calling her "baby." He never did that. He hadn't rented a tux for the prom the way some of the guys did. Ansell wouldn't have thought of doing something so "rich-boy sissy," as he called it. He was wearing one of his father's old sport coats, a deep burnt orange, with a white silk handkerchief peeking out of the pocket, and a pair of loose-fitting white linen pants he had found at the same consignment shop in Cartersville where Celia had gotten her dress. Ansell liked to imagine that he looked like Robert Redford in the movie *Out of Africa,* which they had driven to Rome to see the year before.

He had already told Celia not to expect anything traditional and normal tonight, so she wasn't looking for flowers or candy of any kind. Instead, he handed her a brown paper bag as they backed out of the driveway, inside which she found a large coconut. "In lieu of the standard," he told her, winking. The wink was something else he never did. Ansell had painted a goofy face on the coconut and given it the name Derwood. He had also written a long poem about it, typed and folded up inside the paper bag, a bawdy saga about Derwood's attempts to seduce a girl coconut named Gladys. This he insisted Celia read aloud after they had picked up Glenn and Renee.

The plan was, he told them all, to bust Derwood open later on in the evening and drink the milk together around a fire. He had brought goblets along, also a book of poems by W. H. Auden, and they were going to have a little *carpe diem* ceremony up at the old quarry. He had an audiocassette of music from the forties he was planning to play in the background.

Just south of Adairsville on Highway 41, Celia decided to go ahead and get on I-75. Though the scenery wouldn't be as interesting, she could make better time. Maybe all the interstate traffic would keep her mind off things she didn't want to think about. From the interstate outside Rome, she could see what looked like a new subdivision. Children were playing on a swing set in one backyard, and a woman in a big straw hat was watering flowers in another. Garbage cans were lined up beside driveways, and Celia wrinkled her nose at the thought of all the disgusting things oozing inside them. She imagined for a moment the inside of the garbage truck, where all those cans would be dumped, where the impact would puncture the bags, where all that nasty stuff would comingle and send up putrid vapors.

All of a sudden she remembered going with Grandmother a few times to the landfill. Most people paid the city of Dunmore a fee for garbage pickup, but on Old Campground Road, which was outside the city limits, they had a choice, and Grandmother had chosen not to pay. Every couple of weeks she put their collection of garbage into the trunk of her Mercury Comet and drove it out to the landfill herself, then hurled each bag into the pit reserved for Fresh Garbage. There was actually a printed sign with those words on it. At the time Celia hadn't thought anything of it, but now it seemed like the ultimate oxymoron.

Instead of buying regular garbage bags with twist ties, Grandmother had always used plastic grocery bags and knotted the handles together tightly. Because the grocery bags were smaller, that meant she had more of them to throw, and Celia could still see her now, giving each bag a brisk little half swing above her head before letting go, like David wielding his slingshot. And right now, even as Celia remembered the raw, rank smell of the place, the crows that picked among the heaps of trash, and the clouds of black flies, she couldn't help thinking a little sheepishly of all the plastic grocery bags stored in her kitchen cupboard back home, especially to be used for trash so she wouldn't have to spend the money for real garbage bags.

Oh yes, Grandmother had rubbed off on her in ways she never intended. She also thought guiltily of the drawerful of used aluminum foil in her kitchen right this very minute. How many times she had started to throw away all those neatly folded squares, but somehow she just couldn't. They were still perfectly usable. What an embarrassment if anyone were to find them.

Her mind returned to the landfill. She remembered the toothless old man who sat out there year-round to make sure all the rules in the fine art of garbage disposal were followed. Uncle Shep was what everybody called him. Celia had always been sure his clothes were salvaged from other people's trash, and she used to imagine him scrabbling about in the pit every evening for his supper.

She passed another row of backyards in another subdivision along the interstate. She saw a community swimming pool full of little bodies bobbing up and down, and nearby were two tennis courts, where a man appeared to be giving lessons to several children, all of whom no doubt wished they were over at the pool instead. Balls were scattered all over the courts, and two little boys were swinging their rackets at each other's head.

Tennis—Celia reminded herself that that was something she needed to be thinking about again. She had talked with Bonnie Maggio before leaving on this trip and told her she'd try to be at every practice after she got home from Georgia. In four weeks the team would be leaving for Louisville, Kentucky, for the Southeastern Regional Championships. It was still hard for them all to believe they had squeaked by with the victory in Charleston two weeks ago. Their chances had looked so bleak at first, then suddenly it had gotten incredibly close, and then somehow they had pulled it out.

"The competition's going to be even tougher in Louisville," Bonnie had told them at their first practice after returning from Charleston. "We've got to be in top shape or we won't have a prayer." The higher you went in the playoffs, she reminded them, the better the teams got. And younger, too. "They're going to take one look at us walking onto the courts and think they've got the match in the bag," she said, smiling.

Judy Howell had piped up and said, "And aren't they going to be surprised when us old bags get out there and whip up on them."

Celia tried hard to keep her mind on tennis, but prom night kept nagging at her. How irritating the way her thoughts always seemed to insist on finishing a story. She might succeed for a short time in weaning her attention from a certain subject, but always, always, her mind would circle around and move in again from a different angle. Maybe that came from all those journalism courses in college, that drive to get all the facts laid out. Still, it seemed that a person ought to be able to stop thinking about something if she wanted to, to pull it right out by the roots like a pesky weed. After all, it was *her* mind. If she couldn't control it, then who could?

Ansell had decided they wouldn't go to the prom right away but would drive around for a little while listening to the radio, maybe even go out to the old quarry and make sure things were in good order for their ceremony around the fire later. Nobody in the car disagreed with him, although Celia's preference would have been to go to the prom first and save the driving around for afterward. As for the old quarry, that could wait indefinitely for all she cared. Why did they have to go all the way up there to read poetry and drink coconut milk? That place gave her the creeps.

She wanted to see everybody from school, what they were wearing, who was together, even the decorations and the band. The juniors had decorated the gymnasium, and though it was supposed to be a secret, everybody knew the theme was Paris and there was a miniature Eiffel Tower set up in the middle of the dance floor. Ansell had pronounced the whole thing hokey, though, so Celia didn't dare act too eager to get there.

In the backseat Renee and Glenn were following Ansell's lead. Sure, they said, by all means let's drive around. Nah, we're in no hurry to get there. Why, we wouldn't care if we skipped the whole stupid thing! Who wants to be all jammed up together in the gym anyway, bumping into a fake Eiffel Tower, with chaperons standing along the walls smiling and nodding, talking among themselves about what fun the young folks were having?

Then Ansell turned the radio up so loud that nobody tried to talk over it, and before long they were on the dirt road that led out to the quarry. He turned the radio down a little to comment on what a boring bunch of kids they went to school with, one of his pet subjects. Not more than a handful in the whole student body of Dunmore High who had enough imagination and gumption to try anything adventurous, even something as childishly predictable as spiking the punch. Glenn, Renee, and Celia all agreed, laughing condescendingly at the thought of their classmates, all scrubbed and gussied up, flocking mindlessly right this minute to the gymnasium for a night of High School Fun. "The pathetic conforming masses," Ansell called them. "Dwarf minds," said Glenn. "Future Sunday school teachers of America," Renee added.

Yeah, Glenn and Renee said, this is a lot more fun. Yeah, Celia agreed as she pictured the No Trespassing signs they had seen posted all over the place last time they had driven out here. She surely didn't care about getting out of the car and walking around up on the hillside above the lake. There had been a lot of rain recently, and she imagined getting her silver sandals and the hem of her blue dress all muddy. Which also reminded her that Ansell hadn't even shown the courtesy yet of complimenting her on how she looked.

In Celia's opinion the old quarry was a depressing place, a close second to the landfill. She never could figure out what attracted Ansell to it so much. She had been here only two times before, and both times she had felt a great sense of relief when she left. Last Halloween, when she had been a newcomer to the group, the four of them plus three other girls had come out to build a bonfire and roast hot dogs. They had all piled into Ansell's car together. Ansell got drunk that night, and two of the girls went off for a walk with him while the rest of them sat around the fire and talked and laughed. That was the first time Celia had a drink of beer, and the taste of it made her sick to her stomach.

Later in the evening Renee got mad at one of the other girls and started walking home. After a while Glenn took Ansell's keys and drove off to find her, leaving the rest of them sitting around for over an hour, trying to act like they were still having a good time. It was such a pointless night that Celia couldn't figure out why she ever agreed to go out with Ansell and the others the next time they asked, but she did—and the next time, and the next time after that. Part of it, she knew now, was simply the heady feeling of being part of a select group.

Talk about embarrassment. Embarrassment wasn't reusing plastic bags and tin foil. Embarrassment was letting a jerk like Ansell control your whole life for over a year. The shame of that year rushed over her right now, and she saw herself returning home after three in the morning on prom night, the left shoulder of her blue dress ripped, her makeup smeared, and her hair pulled out of the pretty rhinestone clip. Glenn had brought her home after Ansell had driven his car into a ditch.

Oh, to be able to go back and revise your life as if it had been a rough draft. Only one thing about that whole night made Celia the least bit glad now, and that was the fact that when Ansell started fiddling with the zipper of her dress, the word *no* had erupted from some deep buried place within her. Even after she pushed him away, he pretended not to hear or believe her until she raised her voice and shouted the word again, louder this time.

Surprisingly, it was the first time he had ever tried anything with her, and she saw now that he had no doubt planned it as the grand finale of their carpe diem ritual. He had kept her in the trophy case long enough, and now it was time to take her out and handle her. But somehow everything flew apart at that moment. Suddenly everything seemed dirty—the filmy coating of the coconut milk inside her mouth, the cheap wine on Ansell's breath, the dying ashes of the fire, the spongy earth and damp pine needles, the scratchy blanket beneath them. The night air felt heavy, and the black sky was starless. Even her silver sandals looked shoddy and sleazy, lying on their sides at the edge of the blanket.

She remembered leaping up from the blanket, stepping right on top of Ansell's book of poetry, fumbling to get her sandals back on, and walking to the car. The windows were down, and she could hear Renee laughing hysterically in the backseat. Her laughter died, however, as soon as Celia yanked open the door and got in the front seat. There was a great deal of scrambling around in back, and Glenn said, "Hey, what's the deal?"

It was after that, on the way back down from the quarry, that Ansell, in a silent fury, drove his car off the side of the road. The ditch wasn't very deep, but there was no getting out of it. The tires spun hopelessly in the soft earth. Celia didn't even remember what happened next, except that Glenn had ended up delivering her home in his father's pickup truck sometime after three in the morning. He had walked her to the front door, and through the crack where the window shade didn't quite cover the pane, she saw that her grandmother was asleep in her recliner in the living room, her chin resting on her breastbone, her Bible spread open in her lap.

Strangely, Celia couldn't remember how things had ever returned to normal with Ansell after that. If she had had an ounce of sense in her head, their relationship should have been over at that point. But it wasn't. The disappointment of prom night, the blowup at the end, the wrecked car—somehow the whole failed evening had evaporated like fog, and within days they were back together as if nothing had happened. It was impossible to believe she had been so easy to manipulate.

The only reference ever made to prom night was sometime the following summer when Ansell had dropped her off in the driveway one night and said casually, "Wait until I get you away from this place." He had glanced toward the house, where Grandmother, hands planted on her hips, had appeared at the front door, scowling out into the night toward the car. "That old woman won't be around much longer to play games with your mind." Celia had opened the door to get out. "I'll show you things up at Blackrock," Ansell had added in his slow drawl, "that'll make you wonder why you pushed me away that night."

Interstate traffic was heavier than she expected for a Wednesday, but finally she made it around Atlanta and got on I-85 toward Greenville. She passed the exit to Lawrenceville, where she used to live as a child. How long ago it seemed now.

From the interstate, she kept looking out over the Georgia countryside. The sun was high in the sky, and all looked green and peaceful. "All o'er those wide extended plains shines one eternal day." She had sung those words at Bethany Hills just three days ago when she had returned for the evening service on Sunday night, something she never would have done if Denise Davidson hadn't coerced her into it. She thought of the preacher's wife now, sitting beside her in the pew, smiling over at her as she joyfully sang, "Oh, who will come and go with me? I am bound for the promised land," her vivid blue eyes almost making you forget how extraordinarily homely she was.

22

No Other Fount

As she pulled into the Stewarts' driveway and parked at the back of the house, Celia felt a great flood of relief that she was finally back home. Realizing how exhausted she was, she allowed herself a sudden silly wish that someone would bring out a stretcher and carry her inside her apartment. The output of energy required to get from her car to her apartment, not to mention transferring her suitcase and all the other stuff, was more than she wanted to think about right now. Maybe she should roll down the windows a little bit, tilt her bucket seat back, and take a nap before tackling it.

She actually did close her eyes for several long moments, during which a swift succession of images flashed through her mind of things she had seen and done over the past few days. If by some weird contortion of time she had to go back and repeat those days the way that guy kept having to do in the movie *Groundhog Day,* she knew she'd rather die. She tried to pep herself up by saying these words aloud right there in her car before she opened the door: "You will never ever have to return to Dunmore, Georgia, again as long as you live. It's all over." Spoken aloud, they didn't sound quite as satisfying as she expected them to, so she said them again a little more forcefully.

Aunt Beulah was the only one she would miss seeing, but she could call her whenever she wanted. As for all those others, she was more than glad to be rid of them. She would never again have to walk inside that little box of a house that held all the echoes of all the arguments she and her grandmother had ever had and all the collected smells of all the bad cooking, or hear the clucking tongues of all her other aunts, or drive past her old high school and remember the droopy faces of her disappointed band director and other teachers, or glance out the front door of Grandmother's house and see the little steeple of Bethany Hills Bible Tabernacle down the road. She wouldn't have to plan her errands around town so as to avoid the road leading out to the old rock quarry, or the street where Ansell's parents still lived, or the cemetery where Grandmother was buried.

And she would never have to look into those disconcertingly blue eyes of Denise Davidson again and hear her ask nosy questions such as the one she had asked last Sunday night after the evening service, which Celia still couldn't figure out why she had attended when she had been so glad to escape that morning. Celia had been in even more of a hurry to leave that night, to get back to her motel room and wind down, maybe get a bite to eat and watch something on television to help her relax and drive today's sermons out of her head. If she was lucky, she might be able to get some sleep later on, and if it was too long in coming she had her pills with her. She had two busy days ahead of her, and she was most eager to finish it all up so she could get out of this sorry little town once and for all.

When she had tried to slip past Denise that night, however, she felt a hand on her arm. "Wait, Celia, let me walk you out to your car," Denise said, and though Celia thought of a dozen ways to decline, none of them came out of her mouth. "Newt and I are going up to see his mother for a few days tomorrow, so I probably won't see you again," Denise said behind her as they threaded their way past the people crowding the aisles and heading toward the door, and Celia had to bite her tongue to keep from saying, "Well, I certainly hope not." Someone called to Denise, asking her if she'd heard how somebody's surgery had gone, but she answered, "I can't stop right now, but I'll be back in a jiffy to talk to you!"

Out in the parking lot Denise kept up a steady trickle of talk as they walked toward Celia's Mustang, mostly predictable platitudes about how happy and fulfilled she always felt on Sunday night after the blessings of the Lord's Day and how thankful she always was when people visited their church and how *especially* glad she was that Celia had come to *both* services today. But she dropped the trivia and got down to business when they finally arrived at Celia's car. It was not quite seven o'clock yet, so it was still light outside. And besides the light, Denise and she were almost exactly the same height, meaning that Celia got the full effect of Denise's eyes when they turned on her, a straight-line view right into the heart of those two hot, steady blue torches.

"I can't let you leave without asking you something, Celia." Denise clutched her Bible against her as if afraid someone was going to try to steal it. "I owe it to your grandmother to do this. She was so worried about you before she died. She couldn't talk about anything else those last couple of days." She looked down at her feet quickly, then looked back up and took a deep breath. Celia was tempted to open her own mouth and recite the words along with her, so sure she was of what was coming. But she would have been wrong, for Denise put it a different way from the old standard "Are you saved?" Instead, she said, "Have you ever truly trusted in the blood of Jesus to wash away your sins?"

Perhaps it was the way she always approached people when casting her net for lost souls, or maybe she used a different line every time. Maybe this particular cliché was inspired by one of the hymns they had sung in church tonight: "What can wash away my sin? Nothing but the blood of Jesus." The song leader had gotten creative, directing the women on the first stanza to sing the question and the men to respond with the rousing answer, then reversing it on the second stanza, urging the women to "really raise the roof" on the repeated phrase: "Nothing but the blood of Jesus!"

It had struck Celia that the sound of women's voices alone had a sadly empty, shallow sound—nothing that came anywhere close to raising the roof. She remembered the way her high school band conductor used to complain when the low brass played too timidly: "I don't hear any *bottom!*" he would bellow. But the song leader at Bethany Hills hadn't seemed to notice. He had even given the children a special stanza all their own, which sounded even more bottomless and tooty, like a little choir of flutes and piccolos.

But now, to answer the question. Denise's blue eyes were boring into hers, glowing with concern, waiting for a reply. It was a sticky night, thick with humidity, and Celia suddenly felt so closed in that she wasn't sure she could even frame a complete sentence. Some children were playing chase nearby, and their squeals and laughter filled her with sorrow. How many of them would have heavy hearts by the time they were her age? How many of them would stumble and make horrible decisions they would regret for the rest of their lives? She felt like running over to them right now, shaking them one by one and saying, "Listen here, be good! Don't do anything stupid! Think a good long time before making important decisions!"

But the question—it was still hovering in the air, and Denise was still waiting. Celia's mind spun around and around. She glanced to the left of the parking lot, at the little white house that served as the parsonage. Put a steeple on that roof and it would be a miniature of the church itself. She looked back at Denise, holding her Bible in front of her like a shield against fiery darts. So many pictures and allegories in this religion. Pastor Davidson—wasn't he a picture of God shepherding his little bleating flock of stupid, compliant sheep? And here was Denise, stepping into the role of the Holy Spirit, trying to stir up Celia's conscience with her probing blue eyes like tongues of fire.

If Celia answered no, then an earnest invitation to let Denise take her Bible and show her the plan of salvation would follow. If she said yes, she'd be treated to a sermonette about backsliding, getting right with God, rededicating her life, manifesting the fruit of the Spirit, and all those sorts of things. And if she said, "I don't want to talk about it, and it's really none of your business"—well, she might think that, but it would be awfully hard to actually say it.

Denise reached out imploringly with one hand. It was such a little hand, no bigger than a girl's. "Jesus can make you white as snow, Celia."

"Oh, precious is the flow," said Celia.

Denise cocked her head and came a step closer. "What? What did you say?"

Celia shook her head. "Sorry, I was just thinking of that song."

Denise still looked puzzled. "Well, I'm not—"

"You know, 'Nothing But the Blood,' " Celia said. "The one we sang tonight."

Denise's face cleared. "Oh. Why, yes. That's a wonderful old song." She smiled. "And it's so *true*! 'No other fount I know, nothing but the blood of Jesus.' We can try all kinds of different ways of getting to heaven, Celia, but the fact is, there's only one way, and that's by believing in Jesus' shed blood on Calvary. I know you must have heard all this before, but I just feel like I have to say it anyway. Sometimes the things you've heard all your life are the hardest to believe."

Celia felt a little shudder go through her. "You know, there's an awful lot of blood in that hymnbook," she said. She wasn't trying to be a smart aleck. The words just popped out. "I wonder how many songs there are about blood."

Denise's forehead wrinkled. Her blue eyes were still fastened on Celia's face. "A lot," she said. "A whole lot, Celia. And there's a reason for that. It's the whole foundation of everything we believe. Jesus' death wasn't a pretty one. He didn't just close his eyes and die peacefully at home in his sleep one day. It wasn't quick and easy, either. He didn't have a heart attack where he was alive one minute and dead the next." She shook her head. "I'm not meaning to be disrespectful, but I just want you to see how God had it all planned out. You see, there *had* to be blood spilled, like all those animals sacrificed in the Old Testament. The Crucifixion shows us just how much Jesus loved us—that he was willing to go through the most horrible, gruesome kind of death for us. The wounds of his hands and feet testify to that great love."

Celia should have interrupted her, but at the same time she was thinking of what she could say to stop her, she was also thinking about how clearly and convincingly Denise Davidson spoke. No doubt she taught a Sunday school class, probably a ladies' Bible study, also. Maybe she had even been a schoolteacher at some point.

"I bet you homeschooled your kids, didn't you?" Celia said, immediately wishing she hadn't. Usually she measured every word so carefully before speaking, but here she stood, saying anything that sprang to mind.

Denise's eyes flickered away from Celia's for a moment, but she looked back quickly. "No," she said. "I would have loved that, but, well . . . Newt and I never had any children." Though she was trying for a light tone, there was no mistaking what was underneath. Celia was angry at herself. She never *ever* brought up the subject of children with other people, always fearful that the questions might be turned back on her, so why had she done it with this woman she hardly knew? She felt reckless and, now, altogether unkind and lowdown.

Neither one of them seemed to know what to say next. So part of that deep ocean blue in Denise's eyes was sadness, Celia thought. For the first time, it came to her that maybe she had something in common with this woman besides being short. They were both childless, sure, but it wasn't just that. She didn't know the circumstances behind Denise's childlessness, and she certainly had no plans to open it up for discussion, but as the seconds passed, the thought grew stronger that maybe the sadness she felt over what she had done all those years ago was in some small way similar to what Denise felt about having borne no children.

You would never dare say such a thing, though. She could well imagine this soft-spoken, low-key woman flying into a rage at such a suggestion, slapping her right across the cheek. How could a woman who had gotten *rid* of a child she had considered an inconvenience ever in a million years understand the sorrow of a woman who wanted children and couldn't have them? No, Denise Davidson would never be able to sympathize with somebody like Celia. If she knew what Celia had done, she wouldn't be standing here asking her if she was washed in Jesus' blood. She wouldn't want anybody like Celia having a chance to go to heaven, as if there were a chance of that anyway.

"Well, anyway, all this talk about being washed in blood doesn't make sense to me," Celia said. The thought had come to her that maybe she could find her way out of this by walking straight into it head on. Maybe she could distract Denise with an argument Ansell used to have fun with. "I mean, all these songs that talk about being *clean* after being dunked in a fountain of blood," she said, "well, think about it. Does that make sense to you? Would you feel *clean* if you had a bucket of blood poured over your head?" A look came into Denise's eyes that was hard to describe—some combination of puzzlement and horror, with a touch of wonder.

All of a sudden Celia heard a tapping on glass and realized how stuffy the inside of her car was getting. Bruce, the man who lived next door, was standing outside her window knocking with the knuckle of an index finger while holding up the other hand, from which was streaming . . . blood.

How eerie. She had just been thinking about all those hymns about blood and Denise Davidson's words about the Crucifixion, and now here was her next-door neighbor showing her his bleeding hand. She felt her stomach lurch, and she looked away quickly. What would he do, she wondered, if she got sick to her stomach right here in front of him? The thought of him trying to touch her with that bloody hand to help her impelled her to open the door at once and get out. She made sure she kept her eyes away from his hand, though.

"I'm glad I saw you pull in," Bruce said. "What great timing. You got a Band-Aid? I've torn the house apart trying to find where Kimberly keeps them."

Men and their ineptitude—their total dependence on their wives for the simplest things! He ought to be humiliated to admit that he didn't know where his wife kept the Band-Aids, but, in fact, he looked quite amused by it. "I was ripping out some old chair rail in the dining room," he said by way of explanation, "and I completely forgot it had nails in it when I picked it up to carry it out. Dumb, huh?"

It *had* to be a nail wound, of course, and right in the palm, just to make it match up all the more. Celia turned and headed for her front door, fingering through her keys to find the right one. "Were they rusty?" she asked, then scolded herself. She didn't want to prolong this any more than she had to. Get him a Band-Aid and send him on his way—that was her goal right now.

"Yeah, I thought about that," Bruce said, "but I washed it out with soap and peroxide. Plus, I had a tetanus shot a year ago when my foot ended up inside a dog's mouth. An old stray my sister dragged home." He laughed. "Lousy little mutt. I was just playing with him, but he couldn't take a joke. They put him down after that out of respect for my pain. Ever had an animal attack your bare foot? It hurts, let me tell you."

Celia unlocked the front door and stepped inside. Bruce followed her. Another weird coincidence—they had both suffered foot injuries from other people's pets. But she wasn't about to tell him the story of Smoky, the devil cat. She just wanted to get rid of this man so she could get on about her business. "Stay here," she said, then worried that she sounded a little too curt and distrustful, she added, "I'll get it and be right back."

As she headed to the bathroom, it came to her that Bruce must have changed jobs recently. She distinctly remembered Kimberly saying he traveled a lot, but it seemed to Celia that he had been home most of the summer so far. And at all hours of the day, too. Maybe he had started some kind of business he ran out of their house. She wondered if he was going to keep coming to her door with strange needs. Why couldn't he go to another neighbor for help?

Frankly, he made her feel uncomfortable. He seemed a little too friendly for a married man. She thought back to the day when he had tried to intercept her between her car and apartment to engage her in a conversation about the Norman Rockwell exhibit coming to Atlanta. She had cut him off, hoping to send a clear message, and he hadn't bothered her again until the toilet plunger incident.

But here he was again. She wondered where Kimberly was right now. Maybe she had gotten tired of Bruce and his bumbling ways and had taken baby Madison and gone home to her mother's. That would be easy to understand.

When Celia came back, Bruce was stooped down over by the cedar chest. He had his hurt palm against his mouth, as if he was sucking on his wound, and with the other hand he was touching her grandmother's patchwork quilt. She imagined little droplets of blood on the patches—something a man wouldn't even be aware of. She wanted to call out, "Don't touch that!" but couldn't think of a nicer way to say it. "Here," she said, "I brought you a couple of extras." She handed him three Band-Aids.

"Hey, good deal," he said. "Thanks. Now I can go hurt myself in two other places." He tucked two of the Band-Aids into his shirt pocket, then started to unwrap the other one. "Rats," he said, holding his hand out toward her. "There it goes again." A bright new bubble of blood was swelling up. He clamped it back against his mouth.

Celia swallowed hard and looked down. She had never once touched her tongue to blood. If the sight of it sickened her, she could only imagine what the taste of it would do.

"Would you mind?" Bruce said, his words muffled as he handed her the Band-Aid. And though every part of her resisted the thought of touching a bleeding person, even if it was just the palm of a hand, she took the Band-Aid and peeled off the backing. Bruce removed his hand from his mouth and flattened his palm against his jeans to dry it off, then held it out. The tiniest little veins of red were already appearing as Celia quickly applied the white pad to the wound and then pressed the sticky ends down firmly. She wanted to shoo him out the door and say, "There now, go on out and play." She also wanted very badly to go wash her hands.

"Good job, nurse," Bruce said, examining his palm carefully. "How about we put on another one to be extra sure—you know, cross them like an X." As if she couldn't figure that out. He fished another Band-Aid out of his pocket and held it out to her. Not seeing any other choice, she took it, ripped off the wrapping, and, not quite as gently this time, put it over the other one.

With his other hand Bruce patted all around the circumference of his palm, making sure the Band-Aids were secure. "Guess I'm going to have to keep it stretched out like this for a while, huh?" he said cheerfully, holding his hand out flat. " 'Cause if I cup it, the Band-Aids buckle up, see?"

Oh, he was a quick one, he was. Kimberly ought to keep this man leashed and muzzled, Celia thought. Standing as close as she was to him, Celia could see the burn scars on the back of his hand. At least, she assumed they were burn scars. It could be seen as a scary-looking hand, actually—with the skin all tight and shriveled. It wasn't a uniform color, either, but a mottled pinkish red. She wondered all of a sudden how the skin would feel if she touched it.

And then she had a horrible thought of Kimberly walking up to the door and looking in on the two of them, seeing them face to face, watching Celia reach out to touch Bruce's scars. She stepped back quickly and bent to gather up the little bits of wrapping from the Band-Aids. She dropped them into the trash can, then walked to the door, hoping Bruce would take the hint and leave. He did follow her out, all right, but unfortunately, his plan was to repay her great kindness in giving him a Band-Aid by helping her carry all her things from her car.

"Where've you been?" he asked as he hoisted her suitcase from the trunk.

"Georgia."

"Yeah? What part?"

"Dunmore." What a damp, heavy sound it had, like a soggy lump of uncooked dough. For some reason Celia suddenly remembered one of the ridiculous lines of their high school pep song: "Hear us cheer, and hear us roar. We're the best 'cause we've *Done More!*" They were supposed to yell those last words so no one would miss the clever pun.

" . . . earlier today, and she was telling me about growing up in some little spot in the road in Georgia," Bruce was saying, "but it wasn't Dunmore. It was . . . oh, I remember now. Burma. That's it. Burma, Georgia. I thought it was funny because there used to be this two-laner we'd take to get to my aunt's house in Alabama, and it had these Burma Shave signs along the side of the road."

Funny he should mention Burma, Georgia. That's where Elizabeth Landis had grown up. Celia and she had discovered that when they rode to Charleston in the same car for state playoffs. Burma was only about forty miles from Dunmore, so the two high schools had played each other in sports, but, of course, Elizabeth had been done with high school during the three years Celia lived with her grandmother.

"Said she was just driving by and thought she'd stop," Bruce said. "Funny how you don't expect to see people out of their regular zone, you know." He gave a short laugh. "I didn't recognize her at first."

Well, Celia had no earthly idea who Bruce was talking about, and since it didn't matter anyway, she said nothing.

Finally the car was empty. She had brought back a lot more than she had intended on this trip, most of it stuff she knew she'd never use, so once again she'd have to add to her stack of boxes in the Stewarts' basement. The last thing Bruce brought inside and set on the floor was a brown paper bag of twelve embroidered placemats Aunt Beulah had given her. "This is a whole set I made for a real sweet girl who was getting married at church," she had told Celia, "but the boy got killed in a car wreck two weeks before the wedding, so I've had them in a drawer all these years, just hating to let go of them. I never could find anybody else I wanted to give them to." Then she had thrust the paper bag at Celia, adding, "But I'm too old to be clinging to things, and I've finally found somebody I want to have them. They're all yours, Celie honey, if you'll have them."

They weren't at all the kind of thing Celia would choose for herself—reversible blue-and-white gingham with a pink flower pattern embroidered in each corner—but she wouldn't have hurt Aunt Beulah's feelings for the world. So she admired them at great length, told Aunt Beulah how nice they would look with her blue dishes, waxed grateful that there were so many of them, and by the time she finished had actually formed a mental picture of them on her own kitchen table, which was set for company, with white cloth napkins folded in the shape of little sailboats and a bouquet of pink roses in the center. It was funny how fast you could get used to things if you just gave in a little, how you could hate the whole country style of decorating on one hand yet make room for dashes of it here and there without compromising your standards to any great extent.

As she watched Bruce jog back toward his house a minute later, Celia was once again glad the neighbors' driveway was on the other side of their house. She would hate to always be running into Bruce and Kimberly, having to smile and think of polite things to say, always feeling that they were watching her go and come. It was bad enough as it was. She remembered when Lloyd and his wife had lived next door—that was a much better arrangement. Never once had either of them come to Celia's door to ask for something. They used to visit back and forth with Patsy and Milton, but they left Celia alone. And then when the house sat vacant all that time—that was better yet.

She closed and locked her door, then turned around to face the mess of sacks and boxes on her floor. More stuff. She hated the thought of adding more baggage to her life than she already had. That was another reason she didn't want a house. All those extra rooms would only give you an excuse to collect more *things,* and it had always been her experience that things generally translated into more work—arranging, dusting, repairing, rearranging, dusting again, on and on it went. Not to mention earning the money it took to buy the things in the first place.

She lifted her eyes and looked around at the walls of her living room. That was the good thing about art. With a minimum of upkeep you had something truly beautiful and valuable that would last a lifetime. And it didn't take up a bit of floor space. It was funny, she supposed, how she could be so stingy and practical about some things, but then turn around and talk herself into buying a painting that cost a thousand dollars or more.

She looked back at the boxes and bags on the floor. Dump them all out and the whole pile wouldn't be worth anywhere close to a thousand dollars. Well, if she went ahead and stacked them with all her other stuff in the basement right now, she wouldn't have to feel depressed every time she walked through the living room. Might as well get it out of the way. She picked up two brown paper sacks and walked toward the door at the end of her hallway. Passing the kitchen, she saw the new linoleum—she had almost forgotten about it. She flipped on the light and studied it for a minute. It was nice. Simple, understated, neutral tones, new, shiny, clean—all the things she liked. If she weren't so tired, maybe she could feel more excited about it.

As she proceeded into the storage area, she remembered something the preacher had said in one of his sermons on Sunday. Not that she wanted to remember it. In fact, she had tried hard over the past few days to expunge that whole day from her memory. "Once you get a glimpse of Jesus," he had said, "nothing down here on earth holds much attraction." Beside her, Denise Davidson had nodded and murmured, "That's right." Out of the corner of her eye, Celia could even see her write it down on a piece of paper in her Bible.

The preacher was on a roll and, no doubt trying to be poetic, rattled off a whole string of these little Christian banalities. "Once you fall in love with the Savior," he said, "the things of this life seem pretty trivial," and "Once you cast your lot with the Almighty, you forget about all the little trinkets that clutter up your life." And nobody around her seemed to catch on that he was repeating himself over and over. They all acted like every statement was something brand-new. There were *amen*s all over the place, and Denise scribbled away furiously on her piece of paper. "Once you experience the mercies of God," said the preacher, "it sort of spoils the pleasures this old world offers."

The mercies of God—it wasn't a concept old Brother Thacker used to talk much about, his sermons always leaning as they did toward the judgments of God. Then later, out in the parking lot before she escaped, Celia heard it again from Denise. She had paused a long time after Celia's complaint about the illogical connection between blood and cleansing, then had evidently decided to ignore it for the time being. "God wants you to be his child, Celia," she said at length. "He reaches out to you in love and mercy. Nobody is beyond his saving power. Nobody."

"Not even the chiefest of sinners, huh?" Celia said. It was a phrase she remembered from years ago. She wasn't trying to be sarcastic, though, and Denise seemed to know it.

"That's right," she said kindly. "Not even the chiefest of sinners." She smiled, and her eyes scrunched up into little blue stars. "And that could describe most of us, you know."

Celia opened her door at that point and got inside her car. But she rolled down the window after she started the engine and looked up at Denise for a long moment. "Thank you for your interest in me," she told her, "but I need to leave now." And as she backed out, she waved to Denise and said, "See you later," as if they were parting for just a few hours instead of forever.

23

Pilgrim Through This Barren Land

Five weeks later on the first of August, after Celia and the Holiday Winners had come back from the USTA Southeastern Regional Tournament in Louisville, Kentucky, Celia was returning her suitcase to her storage area in the basement when she noticed how asymmetrical and messy it all looked. She stepped back and studied the stacks. If she took the time to move all the plastic sacks and paper bags to the same side, it would help some.

So she set her suitcase down and picked up two brown grocery sacks with the tops folded over. This wouldn't take long, since most of them didn't weigh much. She had forgotten what all was in them, and now certainly wasn't the time to do an inventory. She had to finish tidying her apartment and then get supper going for her company tonight. Just move them, she told herself, and don't start digging through them.

Now that this last tennis trip was over, it was time to settle down again and give her full attention to the art gallery. After all, it was already August, and summer would soon be over. Ollie and Tara had been good to fill in for her at the Trio, but everybody was ready for things to get back to normal.

A new show had gone up the week before, while Celia was in Louisville, and Connie had been in charge of the reception table. The artist, Yvette Song, did mostly delicate pen-and-ink drawings of Oriental subjects, and Celia had suggested they go the predictable route with the refreshments and table decorations, serving tea, rice cakes, goldfish crackers, and homemade fortune cookies. They rigged up a pretty little trickling fountain as a centerpiece, along with a rock garden and a couple of bonsai.

Before she left for her tennis trip, Celia had found some miniature paper lanterns to string above the table and had typed out over a hundred little sayings about art for Connie to insert into the fortune cookies she was making, things like "Where the spirit does not work with the hand, there is no art," and "The excellency of every art is its intensity." She wasn't even sure she agreed with them all, but if somebody famous said it, like Leonardo da Vinci or John Keats, she knew the art crowd would love them.

It was the first time in ten years that Celia had not been there on the opening night of a show, and she hoped it was the last. She had been sitting with her teammates in a steakhouse in Louisville that Thursday night of the opening, and she was sure the others must have noticed how fidgety she had been the whole time, although they couldn't have known it was because her mind was back at the Trio, wondering how things were going—if there was a good turnout, if Craig had remembered to meet Yvette at the airport that afternoon, if Ollie had gotten all the pieces hung in plenty of time, if Connie had run into any snags with the fortune cookies, what kind of speaker Yvette had turned out to be, and so forth.

Her teammates probably thought she was just nervous because of the match against the Arkansas team the next morning. They all knew they had to really be on top of things to pull off a win at this level, where the competition was cutthroat. It was rumored that one of the Arkansas singles players hadn't lost a single set since the beginning of the season back in February.

As it had turned out, the Holiday Winners did perform well enough to beat the Arkansas team the next day but not the Tennessee team after that. And something inside Celia was secretly glad. She had had enough traveling for a while, and she had no desire to pack up again in a few months and fly to Tucson for the nationals. Maybe another year, but not this one.

A few seconds later, as Celia lifted a sack that was considerably heavier than the others, she momentarily forgot her resolve not to look inside. When she opened it, she saw that it contained nothing but steno pads. A fusty smell came wafting up from inside the sack. Oh yes, Grandmother's makeshift diaries. There must be more than two dozen of them, the exact kind of steno pads Celia herself had used as a sophomore in high school when they still offered courses like typing and shorthand, both of which her grandmother had insisted she take that year. "A girl can always use secretary skills," she had told both Celia and the school counselor when they had gone to Dunmore High that first day to get Celia enrolled.

And Grandmother had been so interested in those two courses for some reason! Celia had heard her on the telephone with various aunts that whole year, proudly announcing that Celia was "earning high marks in her secretary classes." From time to time Celia would find her poring over her Gregg typing and shorthand manuals.

One of the few times Celia could remember her grandmother laughing, as a matter of fact, was when Celia found her reading aloud the practice exercises for the letters *x, y,* and *z* in Celia's typing manual. "Rex and Alex mixed the extra beeswax exactly," Grandmother had said. "Yes, young Sally played with a cymbal and a yellow yo-yo." Standing in the doorway behind her, Celia saw her grandmother's shoulders shaking. "Zesty zebras zigzagged crazily in the Zanesville Zoo," Grandmother concluded, and then she leaned back and actually laughed right out loud. Celia was so surprised that she had tiptoed back to her bedroom without a word.

Several years later when she was away at college, her grandmother had written that the high school had a brand-new computer laboratory, according to the newspaper, and was selling all their typewriters for twenty-five dollars each. "Seems like a pure waste to me to get rid of perfectly good equipment," she had written. Instead of typing and shorthand, she reported, they were offering Computer Skills. It was funny how Celia could tell just from Grandmother's handwriting, darker and more angular in that paragraph, that she thought the whole thing was a pack of foolishness, one more sign that the world was going to pot.

Of course, it wouldn't have mattered if someone had pointed out that Dunmore High actually lagged way behind the times, that other schools all over the nation had switched from typewriters to computers a couple of years earlier. In Grandmother's opinion they should have held out and refused to give in. So what if everybody else changed? If everybody else jumped off a cliff, did that make it right? What was wrong with the old ways? They should have stuck with their typewriters and steno pads.

But evidently Grandmother had taken advantage of the new ways when she ran across a bargain on steno pads around that same time. Celia set the sack down and counted them now. Thirty-one of them, all identical, all filled up from front to back with Grandmother's handwriting. About half of them had a red sticker on the back marked Clearance, with the price of twenty-five cents stamped below. So Grandmother might have frowned upon Dunmore High's surrendering so easily in the war of technology, but she sure had been quick enough to pick up a few spoils from that particular battle.

Celia had flipped through several of them while clearing out the house back in Dunmore, and why she hadn't tossed them in a trash bag right then she couldn't say. Another thing she couldn't say was why she had never before realized her grandmother had such a compulsion to write things down, even the most insignificant of details. She guessed she should have known from the number of letters her grandmother wrote and the kinds of letters, too—always crammed with the trivia and tedium of everyday life on Old Campground Road.

And Grandmother's Bible—that should have been another clue. Every page was heavily underlined, and the margins were crowded with hand-written notes of all kinds—cross-references, sermon outlines, definitions of words, even little corny pithy sayings like "An excuse is a lie with a thin skin of reason around it," or "Never doubt in the dark what God told you in the light." So why should Celia have been surprised to find steno pad after steno pad filled to the brim and overflowing with words, words, and more words?

As far as women went, Grandmother hadn't been that much of a talker, not to the extent of someone like Aunt Clara or Boo Newman or Anastasia Elsey. And certainly not like that old woman named Eldeen that Celia still thought about from time to time. Once not long ago, in fact, she had rounded the corner in the Winn-Dixie and had seen in front of her a very large woman hunched over a shopping cart, shuffling through a handful of coupons. Celia had stopped dead still at the end of the aisle, wondering whether to go speak to her or run the other direction. She had decided to skip that aisle but had seen the old woman again later by the dairy case and found that it wasn't Eldeen after all.

She had been a little surprised to feel a twinge of disappointment. It was funny how a person you hardly even knew, didn't really *want* to know, could stick with you like that. Sometimes during the night when she was trying to get to sleep, Celia would think about Eldeen and try to imagine what it would be like to live next door to her. She would hear her deep sticky voice at odd times during the day: "I can tell you how to get yourself a ticket if you want me to," or "Yes, sir, I'm marching through Immanuel's ground right here in Derby!"

Her grandmother might not have done much talking in person, but she had evidently done her share of it on paper, far more than Celia had known at the time. The diaries were just one more of the many, many things she hadn't noticed as a girl. She tried now to picture Grandmother sitting in the living room bent over a steno pad, filling the lines with words. Surely she could remember something like that. But it was no good—the picture wouldn't focus. Maybe Grandmother had done her diary writing in her bedroom with the door closed.

Thinking back over it, Celia was fairly certain now that her grandmother had approved of her majoring in journalism in college, though she never actually said so. Maybe some of her approval had to do with the fact that it involved writing, something Grandmother thought was important. She had always wanted Celia to be a teacher, but spending her days in a classroom wasn't Celia's idea of a fulfilling life. Nor was the life of a secretary, another acceptable career in Grandmother's opinion. Celia knew that answering the phone and typing letters would get boring in a hurry.

Which was exactly what journalism had turned out to be. Covering dinky little community events, sitting in on dull school board meetings, interviewing local politicians, and all that—it had given her a steady job, sure, but not one she really cared about. She had often wished she could make up tantalizing tidbits and stick them in. So what if they weren't true? At least they'd be interesting! *City Councilman Brant Hummel spoke out boldly against the increased funding for the new arts center, an unsightly piece of dark green lettuce wedged between his front teeth,* or *Gail Penninger, the youngest member of the school board, was out of town for Tuesday's meeting, having gone to Columbia for a breast implant.*

Back when she had changed her major to journalism, after Ansell's departure from Blackrock, it sounded like something you could make a career out of, more than literature. She had liked the possibility of traveling and interviewing famous people. Besides, she had been ready to assert herself, to do things nobody else suggested. Journalism hadn't been a hard major, nor a particularly enjoyable one—certainly nothing she was passionate about. But she had done well enough to get an internship with a small newspaper in Blackrock, which eventually worked into a job with a larger newspaper in nearby Dover during grad school and later another job with a paper here in South Carolina.

It was amazing that she had stayed in the field so long after discovering how little she liked it. She remembered the feeling of exhilaration after landing the job at the Trio Gallery. The thing she couldn't get over in those early days was driving to work with a sense of eagerness, stepping outside her dark little world for a while and actually looking forward to what the day would hold. Not that she could ever totally escape, but sometimes for hours at a time the weight of who she really was would be lifted and she might even notice that the sun was shining outside.

Twenty minutes later, after Celia had moved all the bags and rearranged a few boxes, she turned to leave the storage area. She even got all the way to the door leading to her apartment. But then she stopped. Her hand was on the doorknob as she paused to look back at her storage area. It looked much better now, as if someone had actually drawn up a design. She knew exactly which sack it was that held the steno pads. She stared at it for several long seconds, then quickly returned to it, opened the top, and took out four of the pads.

If anyone had asked her how she had made her selection of four, she might have said, "Oh, I just picked them at random." But if forced to tell the truth, she would have to admit that she had first checked the front cover of each, where the year was boldly printed in Grandmother's no-nonsense handwriting, and she had intentionally chosen the diaries of the four calendar years she herself was in residence at the little house by the railroad track on Old Campground Road. She wouldn't read them right away, but they might come in handy during one of her long nights. All that minutiae would be just the thing to put a person to sleep.

Several hours later, Elizabeth Landis was sitting at Celia's kitchen table. Somehow on the way back from Louisville the week before, headed south on I-75, the subject of macaroni and cheese had come up, and right there in the backseat of Jenny Steel's Ford Blazer, Celia had told Elizabeth that although she wasn't much of a cook, that was one dish she knew how to do well.

Elizabeth had turned to Celia with the expression of someone beholding the amber waves of grain, the purple mountain majesties, and the fruited plains all at the same time. "That's one of my absolute favorites," she had said. "Do you make good corn bread, too?" Not bad, Celia had told her. She made it in a cast-iron skillet the way her grandmother used to, except she usually managed to take it out of the oven before it was charred.

So before it was all over, Celia had surprised herself by inviting Elizabeth to her apartment for supper on Monday night. It had been a long time since she had cooked for anyone. Before she had broken it off with Al, she used to make supper for him every now and then, but he had been no fun to cook for. Regardless of what she had served, he always spent a good part of the meal telling her about better recipes he had for the same dishes.

"Where in the world did you get these plates?" Elizabeth said now. Her tone was one of great wonder. For some reason Celia had pulled out two of Grandmother's old robin's-nest plates when she was setting the table, along with two of Aunt Beulah's gingham placemats. Nothing else seemed to go as well with the meal she had fixed.

"They were my grandmother's," Celia said. "Real classy grocery store bargains from way back."

Elizabeth picked one up and turned it over.

Celia laughed. "I've checked, too, dozens of times," she said. "Not a thing there. I guess the company that made them didn't want to claim responsibility."

Elizabeth shook her head. "Bad decision." She turned the plate back over and held it out at arm's length, admiring it. "Don't you wonder how many other people bought plates like this through that grocery store deal?" she said. "And how many people still use them?" The funny thing was that Celia had indeed wondered that very thing when she had set the table less than an hour ago.

Elizabeth set the plate back down in front of her and patted the edge. "I can't tell you how much I like them. I've got a soft spot for old things—authentic old things, I mean, not this stuff they make nowadays that's supposed to look like it came out of grandma's kitchen when it's really brand-new. I noticed the quilt in your living room. Was that your grandmother's, too?"

Celia nodded. "Made from old clothes and rags." She poured two glasses of tea, then took the macaroni and cheese out of the oven and set it on a hot pad in the middle of the table. It was bubbling up around the edges. Then she took up the field peas and zucchini squash and put serving spoons in each of the bowls. Last, she took the covered dish of ham out of the oven and set it on the table. "The corn bread's almost done," she said. "I'll get it after we've served everything else." She sat down across from Elizabeth. "I like to butter my corn bread right out of the oven."

Elizabeth nodded. "This all looks and smells wonderful, Celia. Maybe I'll get inspired after tonight. Ken's so easy to please I'm afraid I take a lot of shortcuts these days." She sighed, smiling down at her plate. "Every once in a while I'll get motivated and surprise him with a real spread, but it gets harder after the nest is empty."

"I guess I should have told you to bring him along," Celia said. She had actually thought about it but had decided one person for supper was more than enough when you hadn't done it in so long. Anyway, she couldn't imagine having somebody like Elizabeth's husband, a genuine professional musician, sitting in her apartment. She never had gotten around to inquiring about playing in the outdoor summer band concerts he conducted. Besides, he probably had clarinets running out his ears. If she played oboe or bassoon, that would be different.

Elizabeth shook her head. "Oh no. He was fixed up for tonight. He had it all planned out. He picked up a hamburger, then headed straight back to his study. He's composing a new piece for his wind ensemble to play this fall. Not that he wouldn't enjoy a meal like this some other night."

"Well, don't think I cook like this all the time," Celia said. "I'm big on salads and sandwiches. Sometimes it's not even that much." She remembered the apple, redskin peanuts, and cheese slices she had eaten for supper the night before.

Celia had already prepared herself for the likelihood of Elizabeth's saying grace over the food. People who did it in public most often did it in private, too. There was a moment of awkward silence, though, with both of them busily unfolding their napkins, straightening their silverware, adjusting their chairs before Celia finally said, "Well, it's okay with me if you want to say a blessing."

And Elizabeth did. No fancy rhetoric, just a simple prayer of thanks for the food and the friendship, and when it was over, Elizabeth looked up and said, "Now, feed me till I want no more." She looked suddenly ashamed and added, "Sorry, I shouldn't have said that. It's something we sing at church. I didn't mean to make fun."

"Oh, no problem," Celia said. She knew exactly which song it came from, and the tune to "Guide Me, O Thou Great Jehovah" started ponderously through her mind as they served their plates. She had just gotten to the line "Pilgrim through this barren land" when the timer went off. She rose quickly and took the skillet out of the oven. After running a knife around the outside, she cut the corn bread into wedges. She was pleased to see that the crust was exactly the right color and crispness.

She lifted the wedges out of the skillet one by one onto a plate, reconstructing the circle of corn bread. She wondered what Elizabeth would say if she started singing, "Bread of heaven, bread of heaven, feed me till I want no more" right now. She didn't do it, but she wouldn't have had a chance anyway, for Elizabeth immediately went into raptures over the prospect of what she called "*real* honest-to-goodness southern corn bread."

Celia turned to put the skillet in the sink, then ran some water into it. For some reason she had always been fascinated by the immediate, almost fanatical response of a hot skillet to water, both the quick angry hiss and the clouds of rising steam. But it scared her a little, too, and she always made sure to stand well away from the sink. She remembered watching her grandmother do this same thing in her kitchen, only Grandmother always stood right up next to the sink. Hot skillets and hissing steam didn't scare Grandmother one bit.

"You know, this meal doesn't really match you," Elizabeth said as Celia brought the corn bread over and sat down across from her again. Elizabeth took a wedge of corn bread, cut it open, and placed a pat of real butter inside. "I mean, from what I know about you—how you dress and where you work and all—I would expect something really uptown, you know, *haute cuisine* and hors d'oeuvres and dishes I wouldn't even recognize." She smiled and leaned forward. "But you'll never know how glad I am that you cook like *this* instead of like that."

"Well, I guess that's a compliment," Celia said, smiling.

"Oh, it is," said Elizabeth. "It most definitely is."

Celia had already thought of several topics of conversation for tonight, things that would be safe and could expand into a variety of other topics. She was about to open her mouth and introduce one of them—something she had recently read in a tennis magazine about Venus and Serena Williams—when Elizabeth said, "Isn't it funny that so much of the time things turn out to be so different from what you think they are at first?"

"Right," said Celia. She handed Elizabeth the dish of ham. "Here, help yourself."

"Take this zucchini, for instance," Elizabeth said, setting her fork down. "While you were over at the sink, I snitched a little bite to see if I could be polite and take at least a small serving." She wrinkled her nose. "Usually I don't do squash. But you know what? I actually liked it. So by the time you came back to the table, here I sat with a decent-sized help- ing of squash on my plate. Ken won't believe it when I tell him. He likes squash, but I never fix it. You'll have to tell me how you do this." She slid a piece of ham onto her plate.

"Oh, it's simple," Celia said. She was relieved that Elizabeth's state- ment about things being different from what you first thought was about nothing more than squash.

"And, of course, the same goes for people, too," said Elizabeth. "You remember my friend Margaret, who went to Aunt Cassie's with us that night? A lot of people think she's aloof and hard to get to know. But she's not really. She's as soft as butter on the inside."

Celia remembered Margaret's face across from hers at the restaurant table. Fifty if she was a day, yet that word immediately sprang to her mind again—*beautiful.* Dark curly hair threaded with silver, deep violet-blue eyes. Not as startling a blue as those of Denise Davidson, yet eyes that, like Denise's, gazed at you intently and spoke clearly of a heart ready to open up and take you in. Celia could see, though, how people could take one look at somebody like Margaret, so tall and attractive, could listen to her formal way of speaking, and write her off as unapproachable.

"And you," said Elizabeth. "You're a lot different from what I first thought, too."

Celia didn't like where this seemed to be headed. "Well, I could say the same about you," she told Elizabeth. "I used to think you were so quiet, but now I can hardly get a word in edgewise when I'm around you." There. Return the shot with a clean cross-court volley. Okay, now, what were those other topics she was going to use for conversation? "I think that woman in your poetry club must be rubbing off on you," she hurried on. "You know, Eldeen whatever-her-name-was, the one who talked so much. Which reminds me, I've been meaning to ask you how all those poems turned out—you know, the ones they wrote about Ollie's painting."

Elizabeth had bitten off the end of her wedge of corn bread and was chewing slowly, her eyes closed and a blissful smile on her face. "That is really, really good," she said. "I'm so glad you don't make your corn bread sweet. So many people do, and it ruins it in my opinion. I was afraid to ask you ahead of time if you used sugar in your recipe, and I had already told myself to act nice and eat it anyway if you did, but I can't tell you what a pleasant turn of events this is." She opened her eyes.

"Sugar hides the cornmeal flavor," Celia said. "If you're going to eat corn bread, you've got to taste the cornmeal." As soon as she had said it, she realized it was something her grandmother used to say after every family get-together. Both Aunt Molly and Aunt Elsie used to make sweet corn bread and bring it whenever they had a potluck supper, and Grandmother would always fuss about it afterward.

"Exactly," said Elizabeth. "If you want a sweet bread, eat blueberry muffins or something."

"Right," said Celia.

They both laughed.

"Well, now that we've got that settled, where were we?" Elizabeth said. "Oh yes, I was saying that you're not at all what I first thought you were like."

Celia shook her head. "No, we were done with that. I asked you about the poems, remember."

"Poems—oh yes." Elizabeth removed the slice of lemon on the rim of her glass, squeezed it into her tea, then dropped it into her glass and wiped her fingertips on her napkin. "I read one yesterday that I can't get off my mind. It was by a Greek poet, Ritsos I think was his last name. I'd never read anything by him before. He compared lemon slices to yellow wheels on a miniature carriage." She paused. "In fact, that was the title of the poem—'Miniature.' " She took a drink of tea, then stared down at the lemon slice in her glass. "I don't think I'll ever be able to look at a lemon slice again without thinking of yellow carriage wheels, just like I can't ever look at a dogwood tree without thinking of that description about the petals being burned with the tip of a cigarette."

Celia had no idea what description she was talking about. Why hadn't she sliced the lemon the way she usually did, in pudgy practical little triangles? Why had she gone and evoked images of wheel rims and spokes by trying to copy the way they did it in restaurants?

"Or a dead possum on the road without thinking of candy corn," Elizabeth added.

"Candy corn?" Celia said. She couldn't keep up with all this. She felt like she was suddenly having a conversation with Macon Mahoney.

Elizabeth laughed. "It was something Travis said one time."

"Travis?"

"My son, Travis. When he was a little kid, I mean really little, like three or four, he pointed to a picture of a possum in one of his nature books and said, 'Candy corn.' I told him no, it was a possum, and then he put his finger on its nose and said emphatically, 'Candy corn.' And you know what? That possum's nose did look exactly like a little piece of candy corn stuck on the end of its snout. So now every time I see a dead possum on the road, I think of candy corn."

One thing Celia had always appreciated about Elizabeth was that she wasn't forever talking about her children the way a lot of the women on the tennis team did. It never ceased to amaze Celia how mothers naturally assumed that you wanted to know all about their kids' accomplishments, their interests, their personalities, their illnesses, every little fact of their short histories. Whenever someone started talking about something one of her children or grandchildren said or did, Celia tried to ease away from the group. And if she was stuck and couldn't escape, say at a table or in a car, she would drift away to some other place in her thoughts.

Which is what she almost started doing now until she realized that Elizabeth had already quit talking about Travis and had returned to the subject of food. Celia was surprised. That had to be a record for the shortest amount of time spent by a mother recounting the charms of her child.

". . . one of my very favorites," Elizabeth was saying now as she studied the forkful of field peas she was preparing to put into her mouth. "I like all the brown vegetables," she continued. "Crowders, blackeyes, colored limas, pinto beans—the whole bunch of them. Of course, it makes a difference when you grow up on them. My mother fixed them a lot."

Celia nodded. "We ate them a lot, too."

They ate in silence for several long seconds, during which Celia heard Patsy Stewart clomping down the basement stairs, followed by a thump as she dropped her laundry basket on the floor, followed shortly by a metallic clank as she shut the lid of the washer. These were sounds as familiar to Celia as her own heartbeat. Always on a regular schedule, too—Monday, Wednesday, and Friday nights without fail, around six-thirty, after Patsy and Milton had eaten supper. Then right after *Wheel of Fortune* Patsy would plod back down to transfer the washed clothes to the dryer, and sometime after *Jeopardy* she would come back down to fold them, using the big table next to the dryer. This part would take only a few minutes so that by eight-fifteen or so she was climbing back up the steps with her basket of clean folded laundry.

Celia had often wondered if Patsy ever considered varying her routine just for fun. Naturally, she couldn't say too much, being a creature of habit herself. For all she knew, Patsy could listen to her doing her own laundry every Thursday night or see her driving off to do her weekly grocery shopping every Friday morning and think, *Well, there goes Celia again, regular as clockwork.*

Elizabeth took another bite of her corn bread and chewed contentedly. Just as she appeared ready to say something, Celia decided to try again. "So what about those poems—the ones the poetry club wrote? Were there any good ones?"

Elizabeth started nodding. "Well, there were some very—"

But just then a most startling sound interrupted whatever it was she was going to say. Although Elizabeth merely stopped and stared curiously toward the kitchen window, from where the sound seemed to come, Celia herself actually gasped out loud. She felt a quick fluttering of her heart. There it was again, a series of high-pitched sirenlike mewlings that sounded exactly like . . . well, exactly like a baby.

And then a vision appeared at the kitchen window. A flash of jet black fur and suddenly there was a cat perched right on the windowsill. He must have leapt straight up from the ground in that odd springy way cats had of getting somewhere quickly. Celia had never seen this cat around here, so at first she was more surprised than annoyed. And the cat itself seemed scared, smashed up against the window screen like that, swiveling its head as if looking for a way of escape. Celia might have remained merely surprised in a detached sort of way if the cat hadn't kept emitting those horrible demanding infantlike cries.

Just as she felt her anger rising, she saw a hand reach up to retrieve the cat, and when Celia saw the scars, she knew exactly whose hand it was. What a low-class thing to do—creep up to somebody's kitchen window right at suppertime. She wondered if this was his idea of a joke, to chase a cat, the very animal she most detested, up to her window and then leave it there to screech its fool head off. She felt like calling Kimberly on the phone and saying, "Please come get your husband. He's prowling around my apartment again."

24

Fathomless Billows of Love

It was long past midnight. Celia didn't know exactly how long, but she was wondering how she was ever going to be able to get out of bed in a few hours and go to work at the gallery. It had been an awful night so far, and it showed no promise of improvement. Contrary to what she had originally told herself, even though she hadn't really believed it at the time, Grandmother's diaries were not the thing to read before bedtime, not if you were hoping to get some sleep.

She was tempted to reach over and switch on the light but decided against it. For now she preferred lying in the dark. She didn't want to look at the clock, which she always turned around backward before bedtime. If she woke up in the middle of the night, she never wanted to know how little time she had left before the alarm went off.

She wouldn't let herself take a pill. No, this was a night she had to get through by herself. She couldn't take the easy way out. For what must have been at least two hours now, she had tried projecting pictures onto the screen of her mind, a technique by which she sometimes tricked herself into sleep. She had started out by calling up happy times in her childhood—a surprise picnic outing to the Etowah River on her tenth birthday, a blue dragon she had made out of modeling clay and won a prize for, the first time she had waded in the waters of the Atlantic Ocean, a train ride to Mobile, Alabama. But even the happy times had sad parts attached to them. She had slipped on a rock in the Etowah River and twisted her foot, for example, and she had eaten a hot dog on the train ride that made her sick to her stomach.

When the childhood scenes gave out, she had remained very still with her eyes closed, picturing herself standing in a large field, digging for more pleasant memories with a little silver pickax. Over and over she lifted the pickax and brought it down. Surely there were multitudes of other good memories underneath all the bad ones. She even imagined that she heard the soft plunging sound of the pickax as it sank into the loose soil, little glints of mica and quartz chips flying up with every stroke.

And, happily, she at last began to see the pickax uncover what she took to be more good memories. These took the form of glowing gems, which she reached down and plucked out with her hands. But all of them were coated with dirt and long slimy tentacles, and when she tried to brush them off or pinch off the tentacles, one by one the gems broke open and oozed yellow like the yolks of eggs. Then before she could stop the film in her mind, the solid ground under her feet began to turn into a slushy bog, and she saw herself slowly sinking, sputtering and glub-glubbing in a cartoonish way as she went under, holding her silver pickax above her head.

And as she sank, she heard her grandmother's diaries intoning aloud in a low bass voice, much slower than normal, like an old LP record played on the wrong speed: "Spent two hours on my knees after Celie left for school, beseeching the Lord to rescue her soul from the devil." "Celia still out as I write this at midnight. Oh, Lord, preserve my Celie from destruction!" "Tried to get Celie up for Sunday school. Said she was sick but was gone when I got back from church." "That boy's got Satan in his eyes. Came for Celia after supper. Honked the horn and she left. Oh, Father God, bring her back."

For some reason, Celia had decided to start with the diary of her last year in Dunmore instead of at the beginning. Perhaps she had wanted to get the worst one out of the way first. Maybe it was better to see the end already full-blown than to watch it taking shape. How awful it would be to read straight through from her innocent grieving fifteen-year-old self to what she had turned into that last year.

And then there was the entry that was probably the real reason she had started with the last diary, the entry she had been especially curious about, the one she had sought out first, before turning back to January 1 to read straight through the year. It was on March 22: "Had a bad thing happen today. Smoky went after Celie's foot on the porch. Killed him with the hoe. Buried him out back. Cleaned up the scratches and bandaged her foot. Later this P.M. took her to Dr. York. Said she ought to be fine. Please heal her foot like new, precious Lord. Help me know what to do. I'm so weak in body and spirit. Put your hand on Celie, dear Jesus. Planted dahlias today. Scrubbed the blood off the porch. I will never leave thee nor forsake thee, that's what you promised, and I believe it. Sweep over my spirit forever, I pray, in fathomless billows of love."

Someone examining Grandmother's diaries for style would have to laugh. All the staccato sentences without subjects, the shifts from narrating to imploring to quoting, mixing in Scripture with hymn texts, inserting a homely detail like the planting of dahlias right in the middle of reporting a crisis. But Celia didn't laugh. It wasn't the style she was looking at anyway, but the content.

She didn't know what she had expected. The entry shouldn't have surprised her, but it did. The fact that Grandmother had dispensed with her beloved pet in two economical, passionless sentences—well, it should have just added more proof to what Celia had maintained for all these years: Grandmother was cold and unfeeling. But it didn't, mainly because of all those other sentences, the ones about Celia and her soul. And the admission of weakness—that was another surprise.

Sometimes in the past, taking inventories and reciting lists had helped Celia get to sleep, so to get her mind off Grandmother she now turned to reciting the U. S. presidents, something she used to be able to rattle off with ease. She got stalled, however, after Rutherford B. Hayes. She wrestled with it a while, backing up for another running start, but again and again coming to an empty space after Hayes. She tried moving ahead to Chester Arthur, Grover Cleveland, Benjamin Harrison, William McKinley, and Theodore Roosevelt, hoping the omitted name would come to her if she pretended not to care. But it was no good. She was stumped. And because she knew the reciting trick worked only if you could fall into a trancelike repetition, she gave it up.

A mental tour of the art gallery sometimes helped, so she imagined herself stepping inside the Trio now, looking at the new wire sculpture of a cobra in a basket that stood by the door on a tall wooden pedestal. Macon Mahoney had brought the piece in a couple of weeks earlier, having fashioned it out of a single long piece of fine copper wire, one end of which was the cobra's tongue. She had marveled over it ever since, that art could result from something so utilitarian as a length of wire.

She turned from the sculpture and proceeded through the entry area into the central gallery, slowly passing each of Yvette Song's pen-and-ink sketches—*Old Father Eating, Ling Su With Duck, Rice Moon, Boy on Bamboo Stilts, River Bath*—but all at once she stopped. There on the floor, propped against the doorjamb leading into one of the side rooms, was the Madonna painting. It was facing her head on, exactly where she had found it this morning upon her arrival at work. Evidently Craig had returned it to the gallery. She had always known it would come back, but she hadn't been prepared for it.

The mental tour of the art gallery stopped abruptly, and Celia's head filled with a sudden shrill buzz, like the sustained whine of a mosquito. She threw off the covers, then sat up in bed and turned on the lamp. Reaching over to her nightstand, she picked up the digital clock. It read 3:03.

She got up and went into the bathroom. Only the night-light was on, but she could clearly see Grandmother's steno-pad diary on the floor beside the bathtub where she had dropped it hours ago. It was still open to the last page, the entry for December 31 of that last horrible year.

By then Celia had been at Blackrock College for four full months, far away from Dunmore, Georgia. But not far away from Grandmother's prayers. "Wrote Celie a letter today," that final entry said. "Please, Father God, let me get one from her soon. Hope she got my Christmas package. Please, Jesus Shepherd, wrap your arms of love around her and deliver her from the evil one."

That letter from Grandmother must have been the one with the news of Ansell's death in it. Celia had always wanted to throw her grandmother's letters in the trash can without reading them, but she never could make herself do it. Something in her wouldn't allow this last flimsy thread between them to be broken. So she had always ripped them open with a vengeance, read them hastily, then tossed them away. This particular one, with the newspaper clipping about Ansell, had fallen from her hands, however, onto the cheap green carpet of her dorm room, where it had stayed for two days until she had picked it up and slowly crushed it into a small tight ball.

She had taken a long walk sometime later, the paper ball stuffed inside the pocket of her parka, and had thrown it away in a Dumpster she saw in back of a burger place. Never again would she have to worry about Ansell showing up to resume control of her life. He was dead, buried, gone forever. She felt like laughing but was afraid it would turn into crying.

Never had she felt more alone than those two weeks during Christmas break when she was one of only a handful of students who hadn't gone home, but it wasn't a totally unpleasant feeling. She had discovered a love of solitude. Not once did she consider calling her grandmother, though her grandmother had called her two weeks earlier, a long-distance call that Celia knew was against her principles. "You coming home for Christmas?" That was the first thing she had said when Celia answered the phone. Celia had said no, she was staying on campus to work, though she had no intention of doing so nor did she have any prospect of a job.

The phone call hadn't lasted long. The only other thing Celia remembered her grandmother saying was "Have you gotten my letters?" Celia had said yes, nothing more. No word of appreciation, no apologies for not having answered them, no promises to write when things slowed down after exams.

And she hadn't written, not a single letter, even though the Christmas package from Grandmother had included a box of orange stationery with a decorative border of turkeys and pumpkins around each sheet, a bright green 50% OFF sticker still affixed to the lid. Trust Grandmother to buy something no one else had wanted, something left over from another season, then to leave the evidence of her penny-pinching ways right in plain sight.

Besides the stationery, the Christmas package had included a sheet of postage stamps, a crocheted bookmark in the shape of a cross, a pair of thick black knee socks, a plastic shower cap, and a paperback devotional book titled *Every Day With Jesus.* Funny how she could still remember every item in that box, a cast-off shoebox with $9.99 stamped over the original price of $19.99, wrapped with brown butcher paper and masking tape.

It would have been the simplest thing in the world to write Grandmother a letter on that orange stationery, to lick one of the stamps and put it on the envelope, then stick it in the mailbox that was only a few steps from the front door of her dorm at Blackrock. She had had plenty of free time during Christmas break that year. It wouldn't have had to be a long letter, just something short and general with a polite thank-you for the package. Just a gesture of common courtesy. She could picture Grandmother reaching into her mailbox on Old Campground Road, pulling out the orange envelope, and hurrying inside to open it. She would have called all the aunts one by one to tell them she'd heard from Celia; she would have carried the letter to church with her, then kept it tucked in her apron pocket for weeks afterward.

But no, Celia had been too proud and angry to write a letter. Too proud of herself for escaping her grandmother's house and too angry that she couldn't forget her. How cruel children could be. For that's all she had been back then, a selfish, stubborn child. And now, of course, she got to carry this around with her for the rest of her life, this weighty realization of the day-by-day, year-by-year disappointment her grandmother must have endured every time she opened her mailbox. It would be hard to pick out five things to do differently if she could do them over—there were so many more than five—but Celia knew for a fact that writing Grandmother a letter would be one of them.

With her foot Celia flipped the back cover of Grandmother's diary over to close it, then turned on the overhead bathroom light and stepped to the sink. She leaned forward and looked at herself in the mirror. *You are a miserable specimen of humanity,* she said to her reflection. She got up even closer and studied her eyes, the sad eyes everybody kept talking about. She really couldn't see what was so sad about them. They looked like normal eyes to her, except for the puffy eyelids right now. A man she used to date had called her eyes "bleen," since he claimed they looked blue part of the time and green the others.

She stepped back away from the sink, still looking at herself, turning her head from side to side. She needed a good trim, something short and perky to make her look like a young professional. This cut had grown out too long, was dragging her face down. The same man who had called her eyes bleen had described her hair as "dusky blond," which he said sounded much nicer than "dirty blond." He had always called her Beautiful, never Celia.

Derrick Templeton—that had been the guy's name. He had been nice enough until she discovered some of his odd obsessions, one of which was the comic strip character Garfield. He had entire scrapbooks of Garfield comic strips from newspapers, all kinds of Garfield trinkets, like mugs and key chains and T-shirts, even a stuffed Garfield he kept on his bed. And then it hit her—Garfield, that was the missing president she had been trying to think of. James Garfield.

Well, at least that was one tiny success in a whole night of failures.

She gathered up her hair and scrunched it up close to her head. Yes, she definitely needed a haircut. She knew that the cost was the main cause of her putting it off so long. Twenty minutes in a swivel chair and you had to fork over thirty bucks to somebody who had taken a one-year cosmetology course.

She thought of the last hairdresser who had given her a cut, a twenty-something over in Greenville at one of the malls. She had told Celia she was lucky that her hair color was the best for not showing gray. Celia had felt like slapping her at the time.

That same girl had also asked if she was married, then when Celia said no, she had set her lips in a way that seemed to say, "Well, let me hurry up and finish this old maid's haircut so I can get on to somebody more interesting." And Celia still couldn't believe what else she herself had said without even thinking! As a follow-up to her "no," she had added, "At least not yet," after which she had spent the next fifteen minutes rebuking herself. Why should she care what this little twit of a girl at a beauty shop thought about her marital status? And who was she trying to fool? Any woman like herself, within sneezing distance of her thirty-seventh birthday, shouldn't be holding out any hopes of marriage. Besides, she *could* get married if she wanted to. Finding a man was not the problem—it was finding one she couldn't live without.

Which suddenly reminded her of something. If it was past midnight, that meant it was now the second of August—her birthday. She wondered how many other people forgot their own birthdays. If someone were to offer to buy her whatever she wanted most for a birthday gift right now, she'd have to tell them to put their money away unless they knew where a clear conscience was for sale.

She turned on the water at the sink, dampened a washcloth, and pressed it against her eyelids. She thought about the little white bottle inside the medicine chest. She could so easily take it out, unscrew the lid, shake out a pill, gulp it down, and return to bed for at least a few hours of sound sleep. Or she could tough it out. She could take a good hard look at herself for the rest of the night and decide what she was going to do.

She wet the washcloth again and reapplied it to her eyelids. After several long moments she opened her eyes again and saw that nothing had changed. She still had the hollow-eyed look of a person who had either been awake too late or crying too hard, or maybe both. No one would look at this face right now and think "cute" or "young." If she told someone right now that she was thirty-seven years old, they would say, "Only thirty-seven? Is that all?"

She knew she had always cared too much about her looks. She sometimes wondered how different her life might have been had she not been pretty. Maybe things would have been a lot better. She found herself suddenly thinking about the preacher's wife in Dunmore. Plain little Denise Davidson, with her very clear, very direct, very blue eyes, which were no doubt closed in peaceful sleep right now. She thought of Denise and Newt, their heads side by side on their pillows in the small white parsonage next to the church on Old Campground Road.

She wondered if Denise ever had nights when she couldn't sleep. Probably not. People with clean consciences usually slept well. But maybe Denise was a worrier. Maybe she stayed awake fretting over their finances or a recalcitrant church member or an upcoming doctor's appointment. She remembered what Denise had said to her that evening in the parking lot outside the church: "God reaches out to you in love and mercy. Nobody is beyond his saving power." And just what did a naïve little goody-goody like Denise Davidson know about the great distances a person could travel away from God, about all the bridges he could burn as he fled further and further?

Celia went back into her bedroom and sat on the edge of the bed. She remembered a time long ago when she used to fall asleep praying in bed. When she first went to live with Grandmother, she was always afraid she hadn't prayed enough that day. She would force herself to lie awake, working her way through a long list of petitions until somewhere along the way she slipped into a dream and was out for the night. She also remembered the last year, when she would see Grandmother's light still on late at night, shining through the crack under her bedroom door. Sometimes as Celia tiptoed past her door, she would hear her voice, never in a loud showy display of piety but low and earnest, the words indistinguishable.

"Didn't sleep good last night"—that was a recurring phrase she had run across in Grandmother's diary. Often the reason followed: "Came a hard rain and kept it up till near dawn," or "Heartburn from Molly's chili," or, more often, something like "Celia not home till past 2 A.M." Never anything like "Bad dreams," though. Grandmother would probably have considered it a sin to have bad dreams. She wouldn't have approved of anything that showed too active an imagination or hinted at hidden guilt.

Well, one good thing about staying awake all night was that it kept the bad dreams at bay. No crying babies tonight, no disappointed looks on the faces of her parents, no snarling cats or old women in caskets. But besides not being able to function tomorrow, staying awake had other drawbacks tonight. It left too much time to think about what had happened at the kitchen window earlier that evening. She was still mortified over it.

She had behaved horribly, had known it even as she spoke the words, and had been so ashamed afterward that she had actually broken down and cried in front of Elizabeth. They had finished the meal, cleaned up the kitchen together, and even sat in the living room talking for a good hour after that, but Celia had wished the whole time that she could go hide in a closet. Not that Elizabeth hadn't done her best to smooth things over, to salve Celia's embarrassment first with cheerful talk, then with confidences of some of her own past blunders.

But nothing could wipe away the feeling of meanness Celia felt, the echo she still heard of her small-minded accusations, her tone of hysteria. Oh, how unspeakably arrogant she must have sounded to Bruce! How petty and childish she had felt as soon as the words were out of her mouth. Perhaps it had been her loss of control, however, that had opened her up to what happened after Elizabeth left. Maybe she would have put off reading her grandmother's diaries indefinitely if she hadn't already erred so badly that night. Maybe after recognizing your blatant fallibility in one area, you were more willing to consider it in others.

Whatever the cause, she had opened one of the diaries around ten o'clock, while soaking in the bathtub, and had closed it an hour and a half later after the water was cool. She hadn't shed a tear during the whole reading of it, but at the end she had been overcome with remorse and pity, with the pain of her many failures, had bowed her head and let the tears come. She had watched them fall from her face into the bath water, had thought, *I am washing myself with my own tears,* and had wished they could possess some healing for her guilt, some retroactive power to comfort her grandmother's broken heart.

So what was to be done? How could she ever know those fathomless billows of peace the hymn talked about? Her eyes lighted on the telephone beside her bed. What would Denise Davidson say if Celia called her right now? It would be easy to find out her phone number from directory assistance. But her husband would no doubt answer the phone. And what would Celia say to the Reverend Davidson? "Hi, Newt, do you know that song that goes 'Peace, peace, wonderful peace'? Well, I keep hearing it in my mind, and I know it's past three in the morning, but I can't sleep, see, and I need your wife to explain something we talked about in the parking lot six weeks ago, about how the balancing act works between sin and mercy."

Oh, the silly things that went through your mind when you were sleep deprived. Celia heaved a sigh and got up from the bed. She walked out into the living room. Maybe she could fall asleep on the couch. Maybe she should turn on the television and see what kinds of things came on at this time of morning. But she felt too restless to lie down again.

She went to her front door and unlocked it. She opened the screen and stepped out onto the concrete stoop in her bare feet. She looked up at the treetops, then past them to the black sky. One especially bright star stood out from the rest—a sign maybe? But then she saw it was only an airplane, and soon it was out of sight. It was a still night yet mild for early August. *I must do something.* The thought was bearing down on her. *I can't go on this way.* And then without meaning to, she fixed her eyes on the night sky and said aloud, "Show me how to start."

She turned and looked across the driveway to Kimberly and Bruce's house. She saw again the look of shock, then anger, in his eyes through the kitchen window earlier that night. Holding the struggling cat against his chest, he might have presented a comical image, but when he had spoken he was deadly serious. She had been too flustered at the end to make amends, and she couldn't imagine bringing herself to apologize now. No, she would just ignore him and hope that he would, like any typical male, forget the specifics of the incident over time.

She stepped back inside and locked the door. As she turned to go back to her bedroom, her eyes landed on the small table beside the door, the one where she always laid her mail and keys. She usually discarded junk mail right away, but because she had been busy preparing for Elizabeth's supper visit, she hadn't done so that afternoon. And there, right on top, was a piece of junk mail with these words printed in bright red letters on the envelope: *Do you need help? Write for free information.* The return address was Marchant & Buchanan, Public Auctions—certainly not an enterprise to lend the kind of help Celia needed, but she looked again at the message.

"Write for free information"—maybe this was a place to start. And instantly a person came to mind, the same one she had thought of only minutes earlier. How curious that a totally silly thought could transform itself into something that seemed not only feasible but absolutely right. She would write a letter to Denise Davidson. An old-fashioned letter, the kind she never wrote her grandmother. In fact, she couldn't remember the last time she had written a real letter to anyone. She knew she had some stationery in a drawer in her bedroom. She would get it out now, sit right down, and write a letter for help.

And suddenly she couldn't wait to do it. The idea was like a little shiny key to a door that had long been bolted shut. She went straight to the right bureau drawer, removed the stationery, and headed for the kitchen table. She wouldn't worry about what Denise Davidson would think of her. She had already shown her shabby side to Bruce and Elizabeth earlier tonight, so she might as well push it a step further. She would set things down on paper tonight that would take Denise's breath away. Then she would see what the preacher's wife had to say about the subject of mercy after this.

Celia could see why the Roman Catholic idea of confession had its appeal. There had to be some feeling of cleansing after verbalizing your worst sins out loud to another person, some sense of transferring a small part of a heavy burden. She knew, of course, that Denise couldn't expiate her sins, but it would be interesting to see what a sheltered soul like her would say when she knew the truth about Celia.

As Celia arranged a sheet of plain white stationery on the table in front of her and took the cap off her pen, Denise's blue eyes once again rose before her. She also thought of Elizabeth, with her kind, searching gray-green eyes that seemed to want to say more than she allowed her lips to speak. She thought of her grandmother's tired old eyes peering out from all the frown lines around them, the irises a weak watery blue, the whites like discolored porcelain. She thought of her own sad, sleepy eyes reflected in the bathroom mirror.

And right before setting her pen to paper, she glanced up at the kitchen window and remembered Bruce's angry dark eyes. How instructive it might be, she thought suddenly, to be able to see yourself through someone else's eyes, to view a movie of yourself at the end of every day.

She could imagine her own protests if such a movie were shown of this very day: *But that's not the real me!* she would say. Which would be absolutely true. No, such a movie couldn't begin to show the *real* Cecilia Annette Coleman, with all the deep ugly cracks of sin beneath the surface faults of today.

PART TWO:

HEAR, O HEAR US WHEN WE PRAY

25

One Holy Passion

On a Sunday afternoon in late October, Bruce Healey was sitting at the patio table in the backyard trying to carve a jack-o'-lantern to surprise Madison when he saw Celia pull into the driveway next door and park her red Mustang. It still surprised him that a woman like her, so efficient, sensible, and reclusive, drove a red Mustang instead of, say, a dark brown Volvo 280.

He had already gotten all the stringy goop and seeds out of the pumpkin and was working on the second eye—a simple triangular design, which was turning out to be larger than the first eye and a little lower on the face, down toward the middle of its cheek actually. So it would be a freak, but who cared? Nobody expected perfection when it came to jack-o'-lanterns.

He paused for a moment to watch Celia get out of her car and walk to her front door. He opened his mouth to call to her but for some reason decided against it. He realized he even had a legitimate question already framed and ready to ask: "How many trick-or-treaters usually come around this neighborhood on Halloween?" In fact, he knew in his heart that he was sitting here in the backyard with the express hope of seeing her. But something about the brisk, beeline way she was moving toward the door kept him from speaking. Not that it was much different from the way she normally walked to the door—as if she had just remembered she'd left a cake in the oven. After watching her disappear inside her apartment, shutting the door firmly behind her, he turned his attention back to the jack-o'-lantern's enormous misaligned eye.

Bruce Healey had met a lot of women in his life. All shapes and sizes, young and old, all kinds of dull and fascinating personalities, faces that made you look twice, others that made you wish you hadn't. When he was in college, he used to say he could never get married because he'd always be wondering about all those other women he hadn't had a chance to meet.

Sometimes in grad school in Montgomery, Alabama, he had sat in coffeehouses just thinking about all the women he had been with, his mind always wandering eventually to the more eccentric ones. The red-headed vegetarian from Hattiesburg who had had her first name legally changed from Audrey to Unity; the blond six-footer from Mobile who could bench-press one-eighty; Tamara something from Kosciusko who sang backup for an Elvis impersonator on weekends; those twin sisters—Tanya and Sonja—from Memphis who competed in demolition derbies; and dozens and dozens of others. His friends liked to joke that he was particularly attracted to the weird types.

Although he didn't really like the idea of lumping girls into categories, he had often said to other guys in his bragging days, "Name a type, I've met her." And he probably had. He had passed through a lot of towns in the South, the region of the country he considered the only reasonable place to settle down permanently, and a good number in the Midwest and Northeast, too, meeting girls everywhere he went. His friends envied him, mostly good-naturedly, because not only did Bruce really like girls, but for some reason none of the guys could figure out, girls really liked him back.

And it was a sad, pitiful thing, Bruce used to tell them, that they couldn't see why girls liked him so much. It was as fundamental a principle as the ones in science books—geotropism, photosynthesis, entropy, friction, cytokinesis, evaporation, thermodynamics, on and on. Simple cause and effect. It all boiled down, as he tried to explain from time to time, to the fact that he had a very high regard for the whole female population. And women could tell it.

Women were smarter in different ways from men. They were more loyal, they could be incredibly tough, they sensed things without being told, they kept the world running with their attention to detail, they had more compassion, could keep track of so many different things at the same time, and, obviously, there was the whole physical part of it. All that soft roundness—with a few exceptions, such as the blond six-footer. That woman had biceps as hard as baseballs and a torso like a steel cage.

But really, there was nothing difficult about it all. If you treated people right, they would like you. That's what his mother had told him on his first day of kindergarten as she had stooped down in front of him at the door and planted a wet, sloppy kiss on his forehead, which he had instinctively known he shouldn't wipe off because it might hurt her feelings.

When he thought of his mother now, as a grown man, *this* was the picture that most often came to mind instead of all the other more recent and less pleasant ones he could have conjured up: That day, about thirty-five years ago when she had kissed him at the front door and said, "Remember, be nice to everybody, Brucie, and they'll be nice back to you." And it had worked except in a very few cases, none of which could really be laid to the fault of the principle itself.

It had worked especially well with girls. Even in elementary school, girls had liked him because he had been nice to them. Not in a sissy, simpering way, but forthrightly and courteously. He had often wondered why it was that he understood this basic fact about women so much better than most of the other men he knew. Or at least he thought he did most of the time. There were always those other times after an encounter with a woman when he came away feeling that he'd had all his neat little theories shoved inside a paper bag, shaken up, and then released in a high stiff wind.

But even those times contributed to the fun. Those were the times that had always pointed him back to the ultimate pleasure of life: The Mystery of Womankind. Those were the times that helped fuel what he used to call his "one holy passion," a phrase he had heard somewhere and thought was a good way to describe his avid pursuit of that ultimate pleasure. He didn't call it that anymore. For one thing, he had pretty much given up the pursuit, and for another, he had heard those exact three words sung in a hymn at church not long ago in reference to loving God, something that legitimately deserved the adjective *holy*.

But anyway, the point still stood. It was good to be surprised, to have your predictions overturned when it came to dealing with women. If you could ever definitively interpret and label them, could ever really, finally corral and corner them, pin them down and identify their secrets, you'd ruin the grandest adventure in life.

Of course that adventure was mostly a thing of the past now. He tried to keep from thinking about all the casual liaisons he had made in years gone by, and whenever he saw an especially attractive woman walk by now, he tried to avert his eyes, at least most of the time. It was hard, though— a lot harder than most women realized. Any man trying to clean up his heart and mind these days had a really hard row to hoe with all the visual stimulation coming at him from all directions.

Bruce set to work on the jack-o'-lantern's mouth now, first marking the outline with a smaller knife, curving the grin up higher on the side where the eye was in its normal position. He would make it a big goofy snaggletoothed grin. Madison would like that.

Of all the girls and women he had ever met, though, he had never met one quite like the little ice cube next door. Celia was her name, a name that matched her perfectly, that sounded cold and zipped up like a plastic freezer bag. The first night Bruce had laid eyes on her, back in February sometime, Kimberly had said to him after they left her apartment, "Not exactly Miss Hospitality, was she?" And he had said, "Miss Hostility is more like it."

When he was honest with himself, he had to admit that his great gift for understanding and attracting women hadn't really paid such great dividends in the end. He could have used all that time in his youth a lot more profitably. And during those same honest moments, there was always that bad business of three years ago to remind him over and over that solving the mystery of womankind was something no mortal man should ever try to do. Things that seemed like such fun at first so often turned into tragedy.

The first night he had met Celia, when he and Kimberly had dropped by to see her apartment, he got the feeling she didn't want to be anywhere near them, yet, on the other hand, it seemed as though she wanted to follow them around with the vacuum cleaner and dustcloth to make sure they didn't mess anything up. Besides understanding women better, Bruce was also pretty sure that he paid more attention to details than the average man, and one thing he had noticed that first night was that the mail on the table by Celia's door was spread out in a tidy little fan. It made him want to knock it on the floor just to see what she would do.

But the looks she had given him weren't anything compared to the ones she had given Kimberly and Madison. She looked at them as if they were gigantic cockroaches she wanted to douse with Raid. She was no doubt worried that Madison was going to spit up huge geysers of curdled milk onto one of her paintings, which would also have been fun to see. That was something else that intrigued him about the woman—she lived in a basement apartment that, once you got inside, looked like some kind of art gallery. And it turned out that she worked at an art gallery, which explained why all the stuff covering her walls made it hard to see what color they were painted, though he had noticed they were a butter-scotch gold. She had nice stuff, though. Very, very nice. If a person was into collecting *things*, that is, which was another way he had changed his thinking of late.

He and Kimberly hadn't lingered that night, although Patsy Stewart had kept insisting that they see just this one more feature that her brilliant handyman of a husband had thought of adding to the apartment. When Bruce met older women, he often tried to imagine what they had been like when they were younger. He knew exactly what kind of girl Patsy Stewart must have been—stodgy and serious, tediously dull and industrious, explaining everything in great yawn-inducing detail, always concerned that everybody follow the rules. She had probably had that same hairdo since high school, too, lacquered hard like a football helmet. In his girl-chasing days, he never ever would have gone after a Patsy Stewart type.

When he thought about what it would be like to be married for years and years and years to somebody like her, he knew it would take a special kind of man, someone who wasn't all that concerned about earthly plea-sures. At church Pastor Monroe was always talking about storing up trea-sures in heaven. Well, maybe there were going to be endurance rewards up there for people like Patsy Stewart's husband.

But he knew if he were ever to say anything like that out loud, at least in the hearing of women, he'd probably be whapped on the side of the head with somebody's pocketbook. "You think men are the only ones who have to put up with duds for spouses?" somebody would scream, and he'd feel the blows of other pocketbooks on other parts of his body. And he could try to explain himself till he turned blue in the face—"Hey, wait a minute, I was talking about people in general, *anybody* stuck in a boring marriage, not just men"—but the attack wouldn't stop until he was lying senseless on the ground. Women had developed such an edge these days, a lot of them anyway. They used to be able to take a joke better.

Anyway, if a man happened to be interested, if he had any energy left after a couple of decades of hedonism, if he hadn't witnessed the tragic side of love or the whole tragedy called life really, if he hadn't decided to clean up his act once and for all, this woman next door could be looked upon as a challenge. When he and Kimberly had gotten into the car that night, Kimberly had laughed again about the extremely high chill factor in Celia's apartment. "The ultimate touch-me-not," she had called the woman.

But Bruce had shaken his head. No, that was much too mild, he had said. She was way beyond touch-me-not. She was look-at-me-not, speak-to-me-not, be-in-the-same-room-with-me-not, breathe-the-same-air-as-me-not. And Kimberly had laughed and bounced Madison on her knee and said she sure wouldn't be running over to borrow eggs and sugar from *her*. "I don't think she'll be giving you any come-hither looks," she had told Bruce, to which he had replied, "Nope, only the go-thither kind."

The jack-o'-lantern's mouth was almost done now. Maybe he would skip the nose since there wasn't much room left with the eyes and mouth spread out the way they were. No, Madison might notice the absence of a nose. She knew all the body parts, said their names as she pointed to them. He wouldn't want to confuse her by omitting something as important as the nose. Maybe a little round hole would serve the purpose. He certainly couldn't make it too big or the whole face might collapse in on itself. Maybe he should get out his drill and make two little nostrils.

He heard Celia's front door slam and looked back over to see her get in her car again and back out of the driveway. She was carrying her tennis bag this time and wearing a short white skirt. She was good at backing out of the driveway, going quite fast and using only the rearview mirror the whole way until she got up to the top, ready to enter the street. Then she would turn her head to look for cars both ways.

Bruce checked his watch. Almost four o'clock. She wouldn't be home till almost dark probably, and by then he would have left for church. What would she say, he wondered, if she knew how many times he had watched her come and go, flying down the driveway and stopping on a dime in the exact center of her parking pad, then later rocketing backward as if the world depended on her getting somewhere on time?

One Saturday shortly after they had moved in next door to her, he had seen Celia pull into her driveway while he was in the backyard mixing paint. He was converting part of the basement into an apartment by then, following some of Milton Stewart's suggestions, even accepting Milton's offer to help with the plumbing and electrical.

Together the two of them had knocked through the basement wall and installed an exterior door to make it a walk-out apartment like the Stewarts'.

To Kimberly, who fortunately was one of the few women who could still take a joke, Bruce had quipped that he was letting poor Milton help as a favor, to give him an excuse to get out of the house. "He's got to be in the terminal stages of boredom living with the likes of Patsy," he had said. "I'm just giving him a little shot of morphine." And Kimberly had laughed before popping him with Madison's diaper bag.

It was actually Milton who had told him, after Bruce had asked a few questions, that Celia used to work for a newspaper but now worked at an art gallery. That in itself was interesting. To go from a daily immersion in the dry facts of journalism to the imaginative world of art revealed some strange conflicts at work in the woman. There wasn't any wondering about which job she liked best, though. Her apartment was packed with art, not newspapers.

But even if you hadn't seen her apartment and had never heard the clipped, sparse way she talked when forced to give an answer and couldn't read her body language, something about her eyes would tell anybody with half a brain that she had the brooding, melancholy temperament of an artist. Or at least an art lover. Either that or she was mad at the world about something—or maybe just deeply sad. At his age Bruce had been around the block enough times to know that mad and sad were often flip sides of the same coin.

The two different jobs were particularly intriguing to Bruce, because he himself had those same bipolar tugs in his own background—the solid world of facts and the fluid world of art. In his case it was science and math on the one hand and drama and film on the other. So when Bruce had happened to see Celia pull into her driveway late that Saturday afternoon in March while Milton was still inside wiring the kitchenette in the basement apartment, he had called out, "Hey, could I ask you something?"

She was already out of her car and walking toward her front door by then, carrying a couple of plastic Wal-Mart bags. She turned her head but kept walking, slowing down only slightly and frowning, as if to say, *A person can always ask, but there's no guarantee that he'll get an answer.* He had the feeling he'd better talk fast or she might vanish inside while he was in midsentence. He broke into a trot and actually stepped through the low hedge into the Stewarts' backyard as he talked so by the time he had finished his question, he was standing up on the driveway extension right beside her Mustang.

His question was something he had been mulling over in the past hour or so. It didn't come out quite as he had it planned. He stumbled around a bit and ended badly. "I saw in the paper where there was this Norman Rockwell exhibit coming to Atlanta next week." No response from the snow queen, so he forged ahead. "Well, see, I was wondering if real artists would ever go to something like that. I mean, you know, would they think his stuff was too commercial to be real art?"

Still no sign of an inclination to answer. He rushed on. "Or too sentimental maybe? You know, sort of like how a real poet would think of somebody who writes Hallmark cards." He laughed a fake-sounding laugh. "Or like the difference between a symphony and a kazoo," he added, realizing even as he spoke that he was sinking to new depths of lame humor.

He was looking into the sun, which made it hard to see her face clearly. He heard her answer, though, as she inserted her key into the lock on her front door.

"You'd be an idiot not to acknowledge Norman Rockwell as a real artist," she said.

He held up his hands and pretended to be insulted. "Hey, let's not get personal."

She didn't joke back, though. The door was open by now, and she stepped inside. As she closed it, she added, "You couldn't begin to touch an original Rockwell if it came up for auction."

He tried again, laughing once more. "So I'm not only an idiot but an impoverished one, huh?" he said. He could have told her about his grandmother's money, but he knew that would come across as bragging. Anyway, the door was already closed. He remembered waiting for a few seconds on the off chance that she might open the door and add something lighthearted and conciliatory. But when she didn't, he made his way back through the hedge to his own backyard, feeling exactly like the idiot she had implied he was.

Then there was another time, that night maybe a couple of weeks or so after that, when Kimberly and Madison were out, and water started dripping through the basement ceiling. It turned out that Kimberly had flushed one of the upstairs toilets right before she had run out to get in her van, not realizing that sometime earlier Madison had dropped a little pint-sized stuffed monkey into that very toilet, never dreaming as she drove merrily off to buy groceries, which was something most normal people did during the daytime instead of at night, that the water in the toilet was slowly rising higher and higher, then spilling over the edge and splashing onto the ceramic tile floor, and that by the time she arrived at Winn-Dixie and got Madison happily settled in the front of the grocery buggy, it was running toward the corner of the bathroom where the floor sloped downward, already beginning its seepage through baseboard, past subflooring, through insulation, around joists, and past ceiling tiles to drip onto the new Formica countertop in the basement kitchenette.

Luckily, Bruce had been laying carpet in the basement that evening, so he caught the problem early. He was reciting Oberon's final speech in *A Midsummer Night's Dream* at the exact moment he registered the sound of the sixth or seventh drip against the Formica, which made him look up from the hallway floor and into the kitchenette. His first thought coming out of the sixteenth century back to the twenty-first was that the leak must somehow be connected with the rainstorm that had finally gotten started after a good half hour of earnest preliminary thunder.

He even had time to feel a flush of anger over it, especially since the man who had sold them the house had claimed that the roof was only five years old, before it hit him that a leak in the roof couldn't possibly reach the basement this fast. At that point he ran upstairs, saw the situation, and threw down armfuls of towels, then started yanking open closet doors searching for a plunger, which he never found because, for some reason that was further evidence of the Mystery of Womankind, Kimberly had decided to store the plunger next to the washing machine in the laundry room off the kitchen, a place he would never have thought to look because it would hardly be convenient for the kinds of disasters that necessitated its use.

The storm now revving itself up to full gear, he ran out the side door and across the backyard to Celia's door. He knew she was home because her car was there and lights were on. He rang the doorbell, rang it several times, in fact, before she opened the door the tiniest crack and looked at him with those sad eyes of hers, a frown creasing her forehead.

It was another frigid reception, which was no surprise. What did surprise him, though, was how tongue-tied he felt again. What was it about this woman? And he didn't exactly come across as John Wayne or Arnold Schwarzenegger when he flinched visibly at a huge crack of lightning. He tried a few light, off-handed comments, but she didn't yield an inch.

She let him borrow a plunger, though, and when he returned it a little later, he stammered out a few other dumb things in an attempt to act witty and manly before she almost caught his heel in the door in her haste to get rid of him. He could only hope he had come across less klutzy than he felt. It made him a little mad, actually, since he used to be so good at bluffing his way through awkward moments. How could such a small person, a little frozen minnow of a woman, make him feel like a twelve-year-old? It was enough to make him wish he had gone to Patsy Stewart's front door instead of Celia's even if Patsy would have been a lot slower and not nearly so nice to look at. She would probably have delivered a lengthy admonition about how to avoid such mishaps in the future and would have called Milton to come and give some pointers on how to repair the damage.

Then in June Bruce had done the stupidest of all stupid things. Celia had been gone for several days. Milton had told him she was in Georgia closing out her grandmother's affairs. Kimberly had been bugging Bruce to rip out the dining room chair rail, which some former obviously color-blind owner had painted lime green. She wanted to wallpaper the whole room and didn't want to mess with the chair rail, which, besides being an ugly color, also had two conspicuous gouges in it that looked like somebody had hacked at it with an ax.

So one day when Kimberly packed up Madison and took her to the kiddie pool at the YMCA, Bruce tackled the chair rail. It didn't take him long. He leaned the pieces against the front steps, then went back in to get his hammer so he could remove all the nails before stacking the boards out by the street for pickup. Just as he stepped out the front door again, hammer in hand, he saw Celia's red Mustang flash down the Stewarts' driveway toward her parking pad. So she was back already from her grandmother's. Like a doofus, he reached down without thinking or looking and grabbed one of the lengths of chair rail only to feel an immediate stab of pain as a nail dug into his palm.

At the bathroom sink inside, he washed the wound with soap and water, then let the water run over it while he looked for a Band-Aid in the medicine cabinet, all the drawers, even the small closet next to the sink. Where in the world did Kimberly keep the Band-Aids? Every time he removed his hand from the flow of water, it started bleeding again. He grabbed a wad of tissue and pressed it against his palm, then hurried to the other bathroom to look. No luck.

How irritating. What if Madison hurt herself and needed a Band-Aid? What would Kimberly do then? What was so hard about keeping some basic first-aid supplies on hand and storing them in a convenient and likely place? He remembered the toilet plunger. Maybe the Band-Aids were in some similarly illogical place. Maybe he should look in the refrigerator or the file cabinet.

But then, maybe he could put the situation to good use, he thought as he made his way out the front door and down the Stewarts' driveway toward Celia's apartment. Although part of his mind was saying, "Don't be a fool, leave her alone, give it up," another part was saying, "Just ask for a Band-Aid, make it short, play it cool." But he needed to act like his injury was cause for some concern, not just a minor scrape, or he would look ridiculous once again.

This time would be different. He would act mature and serious, yet brave and low-key. He would hold back a little, not seem so eager to please. He wouldn't talk himself into a corner this time. He would call on all his old skills with women, which he didn't use that much anymore, though he knew he surely must still have them. He would try just this one more time to correct her opinion of him and then let it go and never bother her again. By now he knew that she must think he was one of those learning-disabled adults who couldn't function independently, who was given small menial jobs around the house.

He was surprised to see that she was still sitting in her car, almost as if she were waiting for him to show up, though he knew for sure that wasn't the case. Arriving at the car, he saw that her eyes were closed. He knew she couldn't be asleep because women didn't fall asleep that fast, especially ones torqued up as tight as this one. He tapped lightly on the window of her Mustang with a knuckle, and from the way she jumped, you would have thought he had fired a gun at her point-blank.

Naturally all his intentions of acting intelligent and winsome fell flat. He couldn't seem to open his mouth without uttering something inane. But once again she gave him what he asked for, though with the same disapproving set of her mouth as before. As if she were thinking, *How many more times is this man going to show up at my door on the pretext of needing something? Can't he do anything for himself?* After the Band-Aids were in place, he helped her carry her things in, but it was clear that she wished he hadn't offered. After he left, he imagined her going around with a sponge and disinfectant, wiping all the surfaces he had touched.

Then the hot volley of words through her kitchen window that day back in August. As if he had purposely waited until she had company for supper, then somehow beamed Kimberly's new cat over to set up a howl on her window ledge. How was he to know the demented cat would be lurking in the basement, waiting to bolt out the door as soon as he opened it? And how was he to know it would streak across the backyard toward the Stewarts' house and fling itself up against Celia's kitchen window? Bruce had seen the light on in the kitchen, but how was he to know Celia was just sitting down with a supper guest?

The least she could do was show a little gratitude to him for chasing the cat down and taking it away. But no, not Her Royal Rudeness. She opened the window and let loose, telling him she didn't appreciate a joke like that, if it was supposed to be a joke, that she despised cats, and that if that was his cat, she'd better not ever see it around her apartment again or she would . . . blah blah blah.

Something suddenly snapped inside him, and he got angry, returning to the window to fire back a few insults of his own, which may have been the best thing he could have done because it pushed her to say something that finally cleared up a major misconception in her thinking. And just what would *Kimberly* think about him hanging around under her window, she had asked, to which he had replied that he didn't know that Kimberly would think much about it one way or the other.

"Oh, I think she would," Celia said, at which point Bruce saw the curious face of another woman, who turned out to be Celia's dinner guest, peering at him from behind Celia. And at the exact same moment that he was realizing that he knew this other woman, he heard Celia say, "I think any wife would have something to say about her husband spending a little too much time next door, especially if the person next door happened to be a single woman."

And then it was as if the sky suddenly burst open and a thousand pieces of a wacky puzzle suddenly rained down and fell right side up into a huge, full-color picture. Evidently Celia had somehow gotten it into her misguided head that Kimberly was his *wife* instead of his sister. And it wasn't at all easy to convince her otherwise. She held out for a while, insisting through the window that no, he *was so* married, that he was just trying to pull another prank. "*Another* prank?" he wanted to say. "And when did I ever pull the first one?"

Fortunately, the other woman standing behind her, the one who often subbed at the school where he taught, had even subbed for him a couple of times, whose name he suddenly remembered—Elizabeth Landis—stepped forward and stood up for him, telling Celia that she knew him, that he was trustworthy, reasonably sane, gainfully employed as a teacher, and, as far as she knew, unmarried.

But ever since then, almost three whole months now, the two of them hadn't spoken much. He couldn't believe she would actually think he'd be so low and unscrupulous as to flirt with her less than fifty yards away from his wife and child, all of which was proof that she must think pretty highly of her charms.

The jack-o'-lantern was done now. Bruce centered it on the table, put its little stem cap back on, then stepped away to study the finished product. Well, no one would ever mistake him for an artist, that was for sure. His middle schoolers could do better than that. Madison could do better than that. As he tried to form his mouth into a close approximation of the jack-o'-lantern's grin, he heard a rap-rap and looked up to see Kimberly standing at the nursery window upstairs, holding Madison. He saw Kimberly's mouth moving as she pointed at him, and he could imagine what she was saying to Madison. "There, see Uncle Brucie? See him standing there grinning? Isn't he a silly man?"

26

Fast Falls the Eventide

That night after church, Bruce's friend Virgil Dunlop asked if he and his wife could stop by to see his apartment sometime. Virgil had helped Bruce move in back in March, but he had never seen the basement apartment after it was finished and everything was in place.

"Well, there's not really much to see," Bruce said, "but sure, come on by. How about right now? I could probably use some decorating tips." As they headed toward the door of the church, Bruce realized this would be the first time he would have real company in his new apartment. Thus far Kimberly, Madison, and Milton Stewart had been his only visitors.

He really didn't want any decorating tips, though. He had just said that. He was perfectly satisfied with his present decor, which, if asked, he would describe as Monochromatic Minimalist. He liked the spare, uncluttered, neutral look of his apartment and took care to keep it that way. Not that he was a fastidious housekeeper by any means. He could go for several weeks before breaking down and vacuuming the carpet, and he had been known to write notes to himself or record telephone numbers by means of his index finger on a dusty tabletop. One thing he wouldn't tolerate anymore, though, was a lot of unnecessary stuff lying around.

Before they separated in the parking lot outside the church, Joan, Virgil Dunlop's wife, said, "Say, why don't we bring a pizza with us when we come by? Or did you already eat before church?"

"I did, but that wouldn't keep me from eating again," Bruce said.

When he got home twenty minutes later, he unlocked his door and took his jacket immediately to the bedroom to hang in the closet. He laid his Bible on his desk, where he kept all his books and papers from school in neat stacks, transporting them back and forth in his black leather briefcase.

Back in the living room, he looked around. When you didn't have much to get messed up, it sure made things easier. He always went upstairs to play with Madison rather than bringing her downstairs. That way none of her toys found their way into his apartment. Except for the dishes in the kitchen sink and the books on his desk, someone could peek into his apartment and think it was uninhabited, that it was kept in reserve for the occasional guest.

His living quarters hadn't always been so sparsely furnished and free of junk, though. He used to have quite a reputation as a pack rat back in college. At the end of his four years at Jackson State University, he had boxes full of stuff he had saved. The last roommate he'd had, a muscular guy named Rush Stapleton, majoring in physical education and coaching, used to tell Bruce regularly that he reminded him a lot of his sister back home, who saved every shred of evidence against the day that someone might accuse her of not having been sought out by the opposite sex— every movie ticket, every withered corsage, heart cutouts from the box tops of Valentine candy, notes passed in the hallway, pictures, birthday cards, you name it.

Bruce was unfazed by Rush's mocking. He didn't consider it at all effeminate that he liked to save mementos of all the different girls he had been with. He laughed, told Rush it was a pity, not to mention a great irony, that big beefy PE types like him were so insecure about their manhood, and then went right on stuffing his boxes with everything from play programs and restaurant menus to small tokens either snitched or left behind—a hair clip, a flashy button, an earring, a pressed flower, a bottle of red nail polish labeled Fox on Fire.

"Someone runs across all this," Rush said once, "they're sure gonna wonder about your sexual orientation." To which Bruce had replied, "Let them wonder all they want. I have a list of girls as long as my arm who'll be glad to testify enthusiastically as to my sexual orientation."

During his early days of bachelorhood after college, while he was floundering around in different jobs, Bruce had spent a great deal of money on furnishing an apartment in Birmingham, Alabama, where he had lived and worked for over seven years. Back then he imagined that the goal of having your own place was to fill it up. He had bought way too much, a lot of stuff he didn't need and ended up not even really liking.

But he had carted it all with him when he had moved from Birmingham to Montgomery and had kept adding to it for another five years. It was in Montgomery that he had gone back to school for his teaching degree, an addendum to his education that was cheerfully financed by his grandmother, and when he started teaching science and math to middle schoolers a couple of years later, he resumed spending his paychecks on stereo cabinets and bookshelves, appliances, tables, lamps, computer accessories, furniture of all kinds, even sets of dishes and flatware.

The turning point had come four years ago when his mother had moved into an assisted living facility, which in Bruce's opinion was nothing more than a glorified nursing home, and Bruce, Kimberly, and their older sister, Suzanne, had spent two weeks that summer working like dogs to clear out her house back in Mississippi.

At some point during those two scorching weeks in Mississippi, Bruce had experienced a blinding moment of truth while sitting in his mother's attic: If he kept on buying the way he was right then, someday people would have to wade through all his stuff just as he and his sisters were doing at their mother's house. He imagined people holding up things of his and, before tossing them in the discard pile, making faces and saying, "What a piece of junk," or "Whatever possessed Bruce to pay money for this?"

Not that about other people's opinions mattered, but the thought of collecting stuff just for the sake of *having* it had suddenly seemed not only pointless to him but also repulsive. He had been holding a big tacky light fixture in his hands at the moment of the epiphany, something he actually remembered his mother purchasing and bringing home years ago to hang in the entryway by the front door. It looked like some kind of clunky wooden flying saucer with a big bubblelike globe of streaky pale green glass in the center. Six spokes radiated from the globe, and at the end of each spoke was suspended a smaller globe of the same pale green, so that the whole thing gave off a substantial amount of light, far more than was needed for their small foyer.

More than once Bruce remembered a visitor stepping inside their front door and looking up startled by the exceedingly bright light, like someone caught in a police sting. The first time he had attended church with his friend Virgil Dunlop, in fact, he had thought about this very light fixture when Pastor Monroe had read a verse from Isaiah: "The people that walked in darkness have seen a great light." Later, when he heard about Ezekiel's vision of a wheel in the middle of a wheel, he thought of it again, wondering if the designer of his mother's light fixture had had a similar vision.

But his father had dutifully hung the thing for his mother, replacing a small, far more tasteful fixture with the amazing whirligig from outer space, only to take it down and move it several months later when she decided it was too big for the entryway but would work fine in the kitchen where she needed more light anyway.

Bruce didn't know exactly when it had also been deemed unsuitable for the kitchen, but here it was, sitting in the attic, a dusty reject. The truth was, as he thought of the migration of his mother's light fixture, it reminded him of a prissy wooden floor lamp with a little circular table skirting the pole that he had picked up at a sale. He had shifted that lamp around all over his apartment until he had recently shoved it into a closet behind some old sport coats he never wore anymore. He sat very still and thought of his apartment back home, visualizing each jam-packed room, imagining on every object a bright red tag marked Acquisition.

Sitting in the attic that day, Bruce had made a vow to change. He was going to pare his life down to the essentials. He didn't know how long he sat there with the light fixture in his hands, but finally Suzanne had called up to him and told him there were sandwiches and drinks in the kitchen if he was hungry. And he had set the fixture aside and come down to find that it had grown dark outdoors, which he took to be an extension of his revelation: Night was coming on, and he must mend his ways.

And so he had changed. He had gone back home to Montgomery and had a gigantic sale one Saturday and Sunday, opening up his entire apartment to anyone who had read the ad in the paper: "Too much stuff. Bring a truck and make an offer." On one side of his bedroom he had put everything he wanted to keep, which wasn't much. His friends told him he was crazy, but he didn't care. Once the sale started, he felt himself growing lighter and lighter.

So when he heard Pastor Monroe preach a sermon on the rich young ruler, it struck Bruce funny that he himself, before he had ever learned of salvation, had unwittingly followed Christ's injunction not only to go and sell what he had, but also to give to the poor, for more than once he had yielded to sudden inexplicable impulses of generosity.

Like the time in a grocery store in Montgomery when he had been in the checkout line behind a woman with four small children, one of them a fretful baby with hungry-looking eyes. He had observed the few things in her grocery cart, had watched her slowly unfold a ten-dollar bill from her change purse and hand it to the cashier, as if wrenching herself away from an old friend, then carefully count the change before putting it away. He still remembered the look in her eyes, which was closer to fear than anything else he could think of, when he followed her outside and gave her all the cash in his billfold, which was ninety-two dollars.

The whole point of the story of the rich young ruler, though—if he understood it correctly—had to do with the *means* of salvation, which was never ever because of anything man did. So although things like weeding out your possessions and giving away money were good, they didn't amount to a hill of beans when it came to earning divine favor. But at least he had been able to get out of Montgomery faster when the time came since all his worldly goods had fit into the bed of his Ford 250 XLT.

And when he showed up at Suzanne's house in Columbia, South Carolina, she took one look at the pickup and said, "You can't be serious! This is it? This is all you have?" Even Kimberly, who was newly married at the time and also living in Columbia, said, "Oh, Bruce, what happened? You have *nothing*, absolutely nothing!" Typical of Kimberly, she cried openly about it, shed real tears for her poor brother's misfortune until he finally got her attention. "Hey, Kimbo, look at me," he said, getting right in her face. "Do I look sad?" To which Suzanne sniffed and said, "You don't have enough sense to be sad."

But his sisters soon forgot about the contents of his pickup truck when he told them why he had left Montgomery. He didn't try to gloss it over— he told them the whole story, introducing it with a modified quotation from the movie *Judgment at Nuremberg:* "It is not easy to tell the truth, but I must admit it whatever the pain and humiliation."

And his sisters immediately launched into a sympathetic flurry of plans for him to relocate there in Columbia, refusing to accept the fact that this was just a visit. Suzanne was never happier than when she had someone's life to repair. She wanted him to stay at her house and sleep on the daybed in the rec room. "You need to be here with us," she kept saying. "You're vulnerable; you need to be around family; you need to rest." As if it would be restful to live in a rec room in the same house with her and her three sullen teenagers.

It was Kimberly, whom Suzanne always described as ditzy, who came up with a workable plan. She and her husband, Matt, were moving from Columbia to Greenville in a month or so, only a hundred miles away, and for the first few years of his new job with BMW, Matt was going to have to travel a lot. They had already made arrangements to rent a house until they found one to buy, so why couldn't Bruce move with them to Greenville and live with them, at least for a while? That way Kimberly wouldn't be so nervous when Matt was out of town. Bruce could surely get a job teaching somewhere in the area, and because he didn't have much stuff, he could fit it all into their extra bedroom.

It all seemed so simple that Suzanne was sure there was some major hidden defect in the plan. She did her best to create one, recited whole lists of potential hitches, but in the end Bruce drove his pickup to Greenville and moved in with Kimberly and Matt.

Which had led to his meeting Virgil Dunlop, a history teacher at Berea Middle School, not far from Greenville, where Bruce ended up teaching. Which in turn had led to months and months of verbal warfare with Virgil, first about the existence of God and, later, after Bruce was beginning to consider that yes, okay, there might be a God, about the puzzling nature of a God who allowed such horror to go on in the world he had supposedly created and that he supposedly *loved* so much. Unspeakable horror such as war and murder and starvation and painful disfiguring diseases, all of it coupled with such unrelenting sorrow, like what had happened to Bruce's own father and mother, and of course to Bruce himself.

It had actually been quite easy to surrender on the point of God's existence, Bruce himself having supplied much of the evidence in his arguments with Virgil, citing flaws that had always troubled him in the theory of evolution. He remembered speaking up one time in a college physics class, long before he had even met Virgil Dunlop, and asking the teacher how scientists could explain the origin of all these interactions between matter and energy that kept the world in microfine balance, all the properties and phenomena of nature, down to every little intricate function of the human body—how had it all fallen together in an interdependent way that just happened to work? To believe in a God who created it all made a lot more sense to Bruce than that physics teacher's answer had.

The time came when he finally agreed to go with Virgil to one church service—one and *only one,* he kept reminding him—where he read along with the words as the congregation sang a hymn from the old red hymnals that the First Baptist Church had donated to Community Baptist when they ordered new, more modern ones. "Abide with me; fast falls the eventide," it started out. Oddly, though he had never heard the song before, Bruce felt that the words were somehow coming from somewhere inside him, as if they were an echo from an old storybook he knew well.

Though he had never prayed one time during his adult life, had never had any interest in doing such a thing, he glanced at those sitting around him and found himself wondering what it would be like to be the kind of good clean man with the simple faith it would take to make this song his life's prayer. A man like Virgil Dunlop, who, with his pink skin and thinning reddish hair, could never in anyone's wildest dreams be called handsome, yet whose eyes told you he could be trusted.

The hymn talked about the deepening darkness, about the failure of people and things to give lasting comfort. It spoke of man's helplessness, of the swiftness of "life's little day" and the dimming of earth's joys. And beside him, Virgil sang out confidently with the words that Bruce would hear again that night and for many nights thereafter as he tried to go to sleep: "O Thou who changest not, abide with me. . . . Through cloud and sunshine, Lord, abide with me. . . . In life, in death, O Lord, abide with me." What would it be like, he wondered, to have an abiding, unchangeable, omnipotent *presence* with you every single moment of your life?

Without seeming to, Bruce had watched Virgil Dunlop like a hawk during the first year or so of their acquaintance. Pretending not to be much interested, he had observed his every move. When Virgil had met a woman who wasn't "saved," as he put it, the very woman he had ended up marrying, in fact, the woman who was coming over to Bruce's apartment this very night, Bruce had watched him especially closely, for he knew there was no surer thing than a woman to make a man throw over all his so-called convictions.

Bruce remembered things he had given up for women in the past, though in each case only temporarily—things he would never have relinquished in his right mind. Things like red meat, caffeine, late-night talk shows, doughnuts, open windows, and such. He had refrained from carrying books and opening doors for one woman in grad school who called such things a "slap in the face of every able-bodied woman."

And for a girl named Bunny, he had agreed one year not to watch the Miss America Pageant on television, although it was something he had done every fall since his early teens. It didn't matter one bit that he made it clear to Bunny that the main reason he watched it was to laugh at the whole farce, especially the part where they asked the girls questions about current events or politics or social issues in an attempt to show that it wasn't just a beauty contest. He also loved watching all the hilarious efforts to display the qualification called "talent," which very few of the contestants actually possessed, although a recent marimba player and a singer who sounded like Barbra Streisand had both come close.

But Bunny, not exactly the brightest candle on the birthday cake, had turned steely on him and said she couldn't possibly have a relationship with any man who watched such a *sexist* program. Which was exactly what Bruce was trying to get her to see—that the amusement derived from the whole Miss America thing was that it was so blatantly sexist while pretending not to be. He even slipped and told her that he could never truly respect anybody who entered a beauty contest, which he secretly suspected that Bunny had done at some point in her past. With a name like Bunny—well, you just knew certain things.

Anyway, he and Bunny had gone to a movie the night of the Miss America Pageant, a movie that Bunny had selected, in which one beautiful blonde was chopped into pieces, another was tortured for hours by a psycho, and yet another was strangled and thrown off a bridge. He knew there was no way Bunny would catch on to the fact, even if he tried to explain it in the simplest terms, that this particular movie was far more sexist in its depiction of the value of women than the Miss America Pageant.

Concerning the woman Virgil Dunlop had met—after colliding with her in a grocery store aisle of all things—it was clear that he was very interested in her. His manner of approach was so different, however, from what Bruce had always found successful, so deliberate in pace, so measured and careful, that Bruce was certain nothing so seemingly passionless could qualify as real love. He had considered giving Virgil a few words of advice, but with the memory of the fiasco in Montgomery still so fresh in his mind, he had kept quiet and watched.

And he still felt the shock of it all, now more than a year later, that the woman, apparently a mature, intelligent, artistic person, had eventually come around to Virgil's religious views, had begun going to church with him, and had agreed within months to marry him, apparently responding quite warmly to his poky and cautious method of courtship. Here was just more proof of the great mystery—how could you ever figure women out?

Living with Kimberly and Matt had worked fine. At first he spent so much time at school that he did little more than sleep at their house. Later, however, Bruce had been the one to take Kimberly to the hospital when Madison was born three weeks early, and though some bachelors might want no part of a household where a new baby lived, Bruce found that he actually wanted to stay home more after that. As an uncle, he was so crazy about Madison that he couldn't imagine what kind of overpowering, incapacitating love a father must feel.

Though he already knew he was different from most men in a lot of ways, the fact was confirmed whenever his brother-in-law was home, for Bruce would marvel that Matt could hold his daughter so casually in one arm while gesturing with the other hand and talking about the stock market or a football game or a new BMW prototype, could at other times walk right by her crib without stopping to lean over and gasp in amazement that she *was,* could blithely wolf down his own dinner at the table without even noticing all the cunning ways she devised of getting food to her mouth. Not that Bruce doubted for a second that Matt loved Madison. He was just so nonchalant about it.

When Matt and Kimberly had found a bigger house, one with a basement that could be converted into an apartment, he had moved with them again, doing most of the move himself during his spring break with the help of a few friends, since Matt was out of town again. And he had done most of the work on the apartment, too, with some help from Milton Stewart.

Not that he planned to live with his sister and her family indefinitely, serving as a stand-in for Matt, but for now it was working. Matt and Kimberly would be in a bind right now without him, for though Kimberly had planned to take Madison and go with Matt while he was on a three-month job in Germany this fall, everything had changed when she had discovered she was pregnant again. "I wouldn't leave Kim if you weren't here to keep an eye on things," Matt had told Bruce before he left in September. And Bruce had wanted to say, "What about Madison? How can you leave *her* for three months?"

Bruce picked up the newspaper from the floor beside his couch now and stuffed it in the trash can. That was about all the tidying he needed to do in here. He let his eyes travel around his living room and tried to imagine what it would look like to a person seeing it for the first time. As for decorations, he had only a few items that he wouldn't consider giving up for any amount of money, though it wasn't at all likely that anyone would be stepping forward to make an offer, as they were rather odd things. One was a small butter churn that had been used by someone in his family generations ago. It was one of the few things he had taken when they cleared out his mother's house four years ago. He had filled it with dried stalks of flowers and twisted twigs he had picked up on some of his weekend hikes.

The butter churn stood on a small plain maple table he had bought with his first paycheck from his first teaching job seven years ago, when he knew for certain that, after several false starts at other jobs, he had finally found a vocation that was his for keeps. The extra years of schooling, which included a semester of student teaching with a teacher not a whole lot older than he was, hadn't deterred him once the idea of teaching science and math to kids had hatched in his mind. Looking back on it, the only thing that was hard for him to believe was that it had taken him so long to gravitate toward teaching.

Maybe if his mother hadn't gotten so distracted taking care of his father, she could have given him some suggestions to save all the wasted time—he had tried sitting at a desk, standing behind a sales counter, processing loan applications, tallying columns of figures, balancing books. Majoring in business had been a colossal mistake, but back in college he hadn't been overly concerned about long-range career goals. All his goals back then had been mostly short-term, and they always involved girls. He had been good at math, had been able to coast through his accounting classes with a minimum of effort, which left him with a lot of free time to spend on his many short-term goals.

Besides the butter churn, he had a lamp he really liked. It had a black metal base in the shape of a slender tree trunk with a fat black toad sitting beside it, and the shade, the really stunning feature of the lamp, was made of mica, giving off a warm amber glow that turned out to be more ornamental than functional. When it was turned on, the lamp provided one of the few spots of real color in his living room, which was mainly different shades of tan. Beside the lamp sat an old pair of World War I binoculars that one of his great-uncles had taken from a dead German soldier.

In one corner of the living room was propped a flagpole from which hung, curiously, a large flag of Qatar, which he had found neatly folded in a trunk among his father's collection of foreign coins and stamps, college pennants, and baseball caps. The flag had appealed to Bruce for two reasons: first, because of its simple design, a rectangle with a sawtooth dividing line, and second, because of its colors, white on one side of the jagged line and brown on the other. He thought it was probably the only brown flag in existence.

At first he hadn't known what country the flag represented, hadn't even known for sure that it *was* a flag until he was looking through an atlas one day while cleaning out his mother's house and saw the name *Qatar* printed under a flag exactly like the one he had found in his father's trunk. As far as he knew, his father had never set foot in Qatar. Bruce wondered if his father had even known where Qatar was.

The walls of his living room were mostly bare except for a mounted pair of cow horns that had been his father's as a child, an old shotgun, and, above his beige-and-brown tweed sofa, The Painting.

After he had found out that Celia next door worked at an art gallery, he had meant to ask her to take a look at The Painting sometime and give him her opinion of it. But then she kept acting so paranoid whenever he came anywhere near her that he had never followed up. It didn't matter anyway what she thought about it or what kind of actual monetary value any appraiser placed on it. It might not be what so-called experts would call great art, though Bruce thought there was a good chance that it could be, but what mattered most was that he liked it.

The Painting, which was untitled and unsigned, had suggested different things to him at different times, but if pressed to give it a name, he would call it *Bridge at Nighttime.* It was an oil painting, mostly black, gray, brown, cream, and white with a few brushstrokes of the darkest, deepest blue. The frame was a brushed silver less than an inch wide. Bruce had no idea who had painted it or where it had come from. His grandmother had been an artist in her youth, but she had done mainly portraits, which she always signed.

He had discovered it in his father's workshop, leaning against a wall behind a stack of boxes labeled Garage Sale that contained all sorts of useless trifles. Before she lost the love of her life and therefore her love of life, his mother had been fond of garage sales, not only of going to them but also of organizing her own. Whether she had intended to sell The Painting at an upcoming garage sale or had purchased it and never got around to hanging it in her own house, Bruce had no way of knowing. When he had tried to ask her about it four years ago, she had merely shaken her head and said, "Oh, Bruce, Bruce, it's all just a bunch of . . ."

and had trailed off before screaming a single curse word, a word she would never have let him say while growing up.

Thankfully, she or somebody else had wrapped butcher paper around the painting so that it had been spared an accumulation of dust and dirt over the years. Bruce hadn't even shown it to Kimberly or Suzanne, both of whom were busy amassing piles of stuff to take home, but had set it in his pickup truck with the few other things he was taking.

After she moved into the assisted living place, Bruce had quit asking his mother much of anything. He had learned that any question about what she had been served for supper or whether she had gone to bingo or exercise class the day before would be met with the same response: a dry flat laugh punctuated at the end by a single word of profanity. Yet she was perfectly capable of lucidity. Over the telephone one day she had said out of the blue, "Remember that pistachio green suit I bought you for your fourteenth birthday? It came from Packard's Menswear in Hattiesburg. I sold it for five dollars to a Negro boy after you left for college."

In the kitchenette Bruce pulled an extra chair up to his card table and set out three glasses and three bottles of cold IBC root beer, along with forks, plates, and napkins. Nothing fancy, but it would do. No sooner had he decided to seat Joan Dunlop facing the window and sink instead of one of the bare walls than he laughed out loud. Here he was again, finagling a way to please a woman.

He thought about Joan Dunlop, whose face, though not pretty in the classical sense, had its own kind of beauty. She had silky black hair, Oriental fine, and a smile that went up higher on one side of her mouth than the other. She wasn't a woman who laughed very much, and never mindlessly. Bruce had already decided that she must have gone through some rough spots in life to give her such dark incisive eyes. She seemed to size a person up in a glance. She didn't joke around much, but she had a kind of serious pleasantness that made you want to behave well in her presence, like a favorite respected teacher.

As a girl, she had likely been studious, but not stuffily so, and smart as a whip, with a wicked wit if she chose to use it, which she probably didn't often do. Not one of the popular girls, maybe even a little unsure of herself, though she shouldn't have been. Middle of the road as far as looks went, but not much concerned about it. Not very interested in school affairs, but appearing to have her eyes fixed instead on some large threatening object in the distance, some weight of responsibility other girls didn't have.

Back in the living room, the thought of running the dustcloth over a few surfaces crossed Bruce's mind, but he dismissed it in favor of selecting some CDs for background music. His collection of CDs was much smaller than his collection of videotapes, but the ones he owned he really liked. He chose one called "Mountain Songs," played by flute and guitar, and another of Sylvia McNair singing Jerome Kern songs.

And just as he heard the opening tune of "Barbara Allen," there were footsteps at his door, a sharp knock, and the voice of Virgil Dunlop. "Come on, Healey, open up! Food's here!"

27

Emblem of Suffering

November was Bruce's favorite month, partly because he still enjoyed celebrating his birthday but also because of the way the world turned gold in the fall. October was pretty, of course, and in these parts was considered the peak month for fall foliage, but November was even better, in Bruce's opinion, when the leaves floated down and spattered the ground with color. They couldn't be allowed to collect indefinitely, however, which led to days like today—leaf blower in hand under a pure blue sky.

It was Friday afternoon, and Bruce was glad for the weekend that stretched out before him. If he took care of the leaves now, he would have the day free tomorrow. There was no better time than fall to hike in the North Carolina mountains. He already had it planned. He would get up early, then wash his truck and take off for the day, pick up a sandwich somewhere, hike, take some pictures, maybe poke around over in Walhalla, Westminster, Clayton. Just walking down the main street of some of those little mountain towns did his soul good, transported him back to a time when things were innocent and uncomplicated.

He looked up at the sky before cranking up the leaf blower, trying to think again of just the right word for that particular color of blue, that solid layer-upon-layer of absolutely serious blue. It was different from the pale, hopeful blue of a spring sky or the lazy, meandering blue of the summer sky, and certainly from the exhausted, washed-out blue of a winter sky. This blue looked like it was baked on, enamel hard.

He heard a car door close and looked over to see his neighbor, Celia, firing backward out of her driveway. It was unusual for her to be home at this time of day. She usually didn't get in until five-thirty or six. Maybe she was playing in a tennis tournament.

He wondered if she had noticed him standing stock-still in his back-yard holding a leaf blower and staring up into the sky. There was a time when he might have cared, but since their argument through her window three months ago, he had reached the definite conclusion that any woman with that many hang-ups was a lot more trouble than she could possibly be worth, regardless of how nice she was to look at. He was done with women anyway, at least when it came to any kind of personal relationship. The Montgomery experience had changed him for good.

He had talked at length with Virgil Dunlop about how God could expect bachelors to keep the seventh commandment, and he had decided that the best way for him to do it was to simply stay away from women. That's why every time he had slipped and found himself at Celia's apartment door, he had hated himself for his weakness. He could only look at their big shouting match back in August as a blessing. He had watched her off and on since then, sure, but for the most part he had been delivered of the temptation to talk to her.

Kimberly and Suzanne had both been hinting for months now that it was time for him to start dating again. Kimberly had even tried the old trick of bringing somebody home for him to meet one day back in July. She'd used the pretext of needing his help in choosing fabric for reup-holstering a sofa. And there was nothing really wrong with the woman, nothing at all that he could see. She was a trim, tan, thirty-something elementary schoolteacher named Lindsay, who divided her time in the summer between lifeguarding at the YMCA, which was how Kimberly and Madison had met her, and interior decorating, which was something she did year-round on the side.

Kimberly had wanted Lindsay to see the colors in the living room where the sofa would go, she said, and also give her some advice about using a cornice board as part of the front window treatment. Then she had called downstairs and asked Bruce to come up and see the swatches of fabric she was considering, to help her decide on one—if there was ever a more transparent matchmaking ruse, Bruce couldn't imagine what it would be—and then later loudly asked Lindsay to repeat her full name and phone number before she left, both of which she wrote down on a piece of paper. "I'll keep this handy right here beside the telephone,"

Kimberly said, patting it conspicuously as if to say, "Right here, Bruce, here's where it will be in case you'd like to follow up."

As soon as the front door closed, Bruce said, "Nice try, Kimbo, but don't ever do that again, not ever. I'll do my own picking when the time is right, okay?"

Though Kimberly pretended at first not to know what in the world he was talking about, she finally shrugged her shoulders and said, "Oh well, no crime in trying." Later she said to Madison, as Bruce sat at the kitchen table with them one night, "Here, punkin, let's try some peas. Just 'cuz we had an itsy little problem with them once doesn't mean we can't try again, does it, sweetie? We mustn't make up our minds too soon about anything, huh? Give things a second chance. Isn't that right?"

To which Bruce replied, also addressing Madison, "Tell Mommy that Uncle Brucie catches her dark cryptic meaning and that he likes her clever analogy with the peas but that he's not ready yet to *try again,* okay, cupcake?"

Well, here he was still standing in the middle of the backyard looking up at the blue sky. He'd better get going on these leaves. No time to be thinking about women or groping for words to capture a certain color. He started the blower. Lately he had been doing things like this more and more—getting all ready to do something, then stopping before he even got started and staring off into space, often because he was trying to think of the most precise word to describe some sight or sound. It sounded like something an old person would do, or a boring introvert.

He had been so inspired by the beauty of fall this year that he had even sat down and tried writing out an entire paragraph of description one Sunday afternoon recently, just to see if he could. He sat outdoors to do it, right outside his apartment door at Kimberly's patio table. The paragraph wasn't bad, really. He read it over and over, both silently and aloud, revising it a little each time. He was really struggling with the sky part, though, searching for an adjective that never did come to him and still hadn't.

He even went upstairs while Kimberly and Madison were napping in the den and looked through the big shoebox where Kimberly kept crayons for Madison to scribble with. Sometimes those labels on crayons had just the right word: thistle pink, adobe orange, pine green, buttercream yellow. He sifted through them, past mulberry red and frosty gray, past plum purple and mahogany brown, until he spotted a tip of blue exactly the color he wanted. He dug it out, held it up, and read: sky blue. So much for any help there. He looked up to see Kimberly standing in the doorway of the nursery, sleepy-eyed and puzzled. "You want a coloring book, too, Brucie?" she asked.

As he moved up along the side of the backyard now, Bruce remembered how he had worked out regular arrangements with girls in high school and college to write his papers for him. So how did it happen, he wondered, that he was just now starting to discover something satisfying about putting words down on paper, manipulating the order and fitting them together? He wondered if he could have been a writer if he had started earlier. He was always wondering if he could have been this or that if he had chosen to try. That was the trouble with life—you didn't have time to try everything.

He loved his teaching job and had no intention of changing jobs, but he couldn't help wondering about other fields, such as medicine, for instance. He had always enjoyed the channel on television that showed real operations in progress, and he had often pictured himself as the surgeon, removing a tumor here, cauterizing a bleeding ulcer there, performing delicate heart surgery, transplanting a liver, reattaching a severed hand.

And whenever he flipped past the *Antiques Road Show* on television, he paused to wonder what it would be like to be able to tell people the history behind their treasures and trinkets, to assign an exact price to a vase or a figurine right on the spot. When he watched the dog shows on television, he imagined being the judge for Best in Show, examining the dogs' teeth, confidently placing his hands on their haunches, telling the trainers to take them around one more time, then pointing at the winner and saying with assurance, "That one—the Kerry blue terrier. He's the best."

He had mused over all kinds of jobs—photographer, chef, architect, automobile designer, sportscaster, auctioneer, veterinarian, pilot, criminal investigator, on and on. Cinema had always fascinated him, also. In high school and college, though, he had decided he'd rather star in a movie than be on the technical end directing or filming, and he had even taken a couple of acting classes as electives, in which he had done quite well. But a writer—now that seemed a cut above most of the others.

Since he had added the role of drama coach to his teaching load at Berea Middle School, he was always thinking of ideas for new plays, though as of yet he hadn't gotten around to developing any of them. Maybe he should consider trying to write an article sometime for one of the area newspapers, maybe a short piece about good places to hike or the benefits of drama in the middle school. He was sure he could write as well as some of the people who wrote for the Derby *Daily News* and the Filbert *Nutshell*. He had read an article with Celia's by-line on it back in the spring sometime, something about an unsolved local murder, and it was far more interesting and a lot better than most of the others. Maybe if he ever wrote something and got it printed, Celia would see it and strike up a conversation with him about it.

Something caught his eye, and he looked up to see Kimberly standing on the patio waving a bright red dish towel. He turned off the leaf blower. "I'm making stroganoff," she called to him. "You want to eat with us?" Though she was a good fifty feet away, he thought she looked a little tired. She had stopped waving the towel and was standing with one fist pressed into her ribs as if easing a pain. It only made sense, though. Carrying another person around inside you had to add some physical stress to your life. She had put on quite a bit of weight with this baby and still had almost three months to go.

Bruce pretended to consider. "But that would mean saving my sliced ham on rye for another day."

She nodded. "Another day, another sandwich. It'll keep." She glanced up at the nursery window. "Maddy should be awake any time. I'm surprised she's not already, with all that racket you're making. I thought we'd eat around six or so."

Bruce wondered if Kimberly was on to something new—trying to plan her day according to a schedule. That would be a real switch. But he wasn't going to criticize if she was offering him a home-cooked meal. He looked at his watch. It was a little past four-thirty. He'd be there right at six, he told her. If somebody had tried to tell him five years ago that one day before he turned forty his plans for a Friday evening would include nothing more than eating stroganoff with his sister and niece, he would have laughed.

He turned the leaf blower back on. Another hour and he could be finished with both the back and front yards. The front yard wasn't much bigger than his flag of Qatar, thanks to the large island of mulched azaleas and monkey grass Kimberly had planted in the middle. Of course, while the island cut down on his time when mowing the lawn, it actually complicated the leaf-blowing job unless he just blew the leaves up under the bushes, which was what he might do today.

As he continued his work, he thought about the play he had recently begun rehearsing with the drama club at school. It was quite an ambitious undertaking—an adaptation of *A Midsummer Night's Dream* that he had trimmed and customized for young actors. When he had announced to the kids after the fall play—a silly shallow drama called *Humpty Dumpty and the Pack Rats*—that they would be preparing something by Shakespeare for March, a great yowl of protest had gone up.

But he had pretended to be amazed and a little scornful at their response, telling them they were acting like the little mush minds everyone accused them of being and telling them that of all the plays he had ever been in, his high school role as Oberon in *A Midsummer Night's Dream* was his very favorite. He promised them they'd like it if they'd just give it a try, and already most of them were coming around. One of the loudest objectors, a boy named DeReese Pascoe, who had lobbied for a rap drama about rival gangs in Chicago, was trying hard not to show how delighted he was with his role as Puck.

Bruce thought about how proud his grandmother had been when she had come to see him as Oberon in the high school play. Neither of his parents had come because his father had taken sick by then and his mother wouldn't leave his side. Though he knew he had performed well for a high school kid, his grandmother had acted like he was Sir Laurence Olivier. When she had died two years ago, he had lost his most enthusiastic cheerleader.

But he didn't want to let himself think about his grandmother now because that always led to thinking about his mother. He had loved them both, but in such different ways. In his childhood, his mother had been the sun around which his little planet orbited and his grandmother a bright but distant moon. Over time their roles had reversed. And eventually they had both become falling stars, though in the end his grandmother's glow had been by far the steadier of the two. She had outlived her own daughter by a full year, sitting up with her day and night during that last week.

He disliked thinking about what time had done to them both, but that's the way it was. His mother had turned her back on life, changed from an angel to a harpy, and his grandmother, though she embraced life, couldn't do anything about getting old and weak and finally had to release her hold. At least his grandmother had had plenty of money to take care of both herself and her daughter in what was supposedly the nicest assisted living facility in the whole state of Mississippi. Even so, Bruce had nothing good to say about the Magnolia Lane Home. Not that he could have taken care of his mother and grandmother any better than the people there had. And not that he had even offered to try, which had given him plenty to feel guilty about. It was a sad thing that love and guilt were so often tied up together.

Bruce was at the very back of the lot now, corralling the new leaves and blowing them into the long row of old ones near the alley, where they would all eventually be sucked up by one of the decrepit trucks sent around by the county. After this, the front yard would probably take less than a half hour. Then time to clean up and go upstairs for beef stroganoff with Kimberly and Madison. He wondered if there was another uncle alive who looked forward to spending an evening with his niece as much as he did. He often found it hard not to talk about Maddy too much at church or school, realizing he might sound like one of those bachelors who had no life.

The thought of beef stroganoff was already making his mouth water, which was a little worrisome. It had begun to occur to him recently that food seemed to be on his mind way too much these days. Back during his tomcatting days, he had liked to eat, like any man, but back then he could take it or leave it. If something more important came along, like a woman, he could skip a meal without thinking twice about it.

He wouldn't think of skipping a meal these days. Even though Kimberly kept telling him he looked a lot better now that he wasn't such a string bean, he knew he needed to take up something aerobic again. Hiking on weekends wasn't enough to keep in shape.

As he turned the leaf blower off and started toward the front yard, he noticed that Celia's car was back on its parking pad already. So much for the tennis tournament idea.

Maybe he should take up tennis again. He had played a few times in high school and had even made it to the semifinals in a city tournament when he was sixteen. Of course, there were only five boys who signed up for that tournament, and in Kimberly's version of the story, the other four were on crutches. But the truth was, he used to have a pretty good backhand, actually more consistent than his forehand. Maybe he should inquire at the YMCA and see if they had any kind of local tennis league he could sign up for.

Then after he got good again, he could challenge Celia and take her down a notch or two. Or very likely he could beat her right now. After all, he was a man, and she was so small. Milton Stewart had told him she was on a team that had won the state championship, which probably meant she was pretty decent, but surely he could beat her just by virtue of his superior power. But here he was, letting his mind get away from him again. No, he would never challenge her, he reminded himself, because he was never planning to talk to her again.

Cutting between the house and the driveway next door, Bruce suddenly stopped. He turned toward the Stewarts' house and listened. The sound was coming from Celia's apartment, and it was something he recognized. A clarinet—he was fairly sure that's what it was. He wasn't a musician by any stretch, but his grandmother had always played classical music whenever he had visited her as a child, and he still remembered the recording of *Peter and the Wolf,* which was one of his favorites. Yes, he was sure what he was hearing now was a clarinet. He noticed that Celia's kitchen window was open a few inches, the same window they had argued through.

He suddenly remembered a girl he had taken to a homecoming football game in high school years ago, Deanna or Leanna he thought her name was, who had played clarinet in the band. She had had to go sit with the band during halftime while the homecoming court paraded onto the field to the strains of "The Shadow of Your Smile," and later he had gotten her to play her part for him in the backseat of his car out by the airstrip, where the smell of burning leaves from somebody's backyard floated over the empty field. It really didn't sound much like the song, though, since her part wasn't the melody.

He kept listening now. It was a clarinet, no question. Once or twice before, he had heard music coming from an open window of Celia's apartment, but that was always recorded music and usually something orchestral. This was simple and unadorned, an unaccompanied clarinet solo. Surely it wasn't the radio or a CD. So was it Celia? Did she play the clarinet? He could see that—former journalist, art lover, perfectionist, tennis player, clarinetist, world-class expert on antisocial behavior. Yes, it all fit.

And the song she was playing—there was no doubt about that, either. It was a song he had heard a jazz combo play in Vidalia, Louisiana, one summer when he went to visit Marlo Arturo, a girl he thought he had fallen in love with his junior year of college at Jackson State. Turned out he hadn't, but they'd had a good couple of days together anyway. "Precious Lord, Take My Hand"—that was the song.

He could still hear the saxophone wailing the melody in that dim little smoky bar on the Mississippi River as Marlo sang the words in her breathy voice and ran her long slim fingers over the scars on his hand. It was a Tommy Dorsey song, she had told him, and Tommy Dorsey and her grandfather had been poker buddies, though Bruce couldn't be sure about that last part, since he had learned by then that Marlo liked to make up things to impress people. She had also told him that she had gone to an exercise class led by Jane Fonda in person and that she had become close friends with Jimmy Carter's daughter at a summer camp in high school.

So anyway, here was that same song all these years later, wafting out of a window from his neighbor's apartment, evoking a whole host of images, from the spicy scent of burning leaves at an airstrip in Mississippi to the black heavy-lidded eyes of a girl named Marlo in Louisiana. The tune broke off all of a sudden. Afraid that Celia had seen him staring at her open window, Bruce quickly resumed his walk to the front yard. He couldn't help wondering, though, what had made her stop playing. He wished she hadn't.

He wished he could remember all the words to the song. The melody itself was an odd mixture of blues and religion. It had a brooding sultry nightclub sound, yet there was something almost a little desperate in it, something that made you think of someone who was afraid of the dark. He wondered if there was anything Celia was afraid of. Probably not, a self-sufficient little piece of work like her.

He restarted the leaf blower and tackled the front yard. Within twenty minutes he was finished. It would have been quicker to go around the other side of the house to put the blower away in the garage, but he found himself once more walking on the side by the Stewarts' driveway, hoping he might hear the clarinet again. When he did, he felt glad and also disgusted with himself for feeling glad.

Amazingly, it was another song he recognized, this one a gospel song they had sung from the hymnbook he shared with Virgil Dunlop the second time he had gone to church with him about a year ago, the time that wasn't supposed to happen after the first. It was a song the people at church obviously loved, for they had sung it a number of times since then. "On a hill far away stood an old rugged cross," it started out. By this time Virgil and he had gone around and around about Christianity, about what kind of God it was these people called their "loving and almighty heavenly father" on the one hand, yet who evidently used his love and power very selectively if one read the front page of the newspaper every day.

"The emblem of suffering and shame" was another phrase in the song. Bruce remembered looking down at his hands later that night during the preacher's simple sermon about the Crucifixion. It really hadn't been that much of a leap for him to believe in a love so strong it was willing to die for someone else. After all, he bore an emblem of suffering on his own scarred hands. Not that his suffering had been for any noble and glorious cause, not at all. It had actually been quite stupid—the wild irrational act of a little boy upon seeing the utility shed on fire and knowing his cat and her new kittens were inside it. He remembered his sister Suzanne standing beside his bed days after the incident, shaking her head in all her teenage superiority and saying, "You almost died for a *cat*, Brucie."

But still, that's what love meant. That you would let yourself get hurt before someone you loved. "For 'twas on that old cross Jesus suffered and died"—those were the words he heard now as the clarinet tune continued. Strangely enough, it was the thought of Madison, who had not been quite a year old at the time, that had finally hit him so hard that night during the preacher's sermon about God's giving his son to die on that old rugged cross.

Sure, he could imagine laying down his own life for Madison in an instant, but what if somebody asked him to sacrifice *Madison's* life in order for some grand purpose to be accomplished? No way in the world would he be able to suffer like that. *And you're not even her father,* he thought. *You're only her uncle.*

Yet God had been willing to do this. He had given up his only son to suffer a painful and extended and publicly shameful death for . . . and that's when it had really struck him. For a whole world of proud, selfish, short-sighted, willful, ignorant sinners like himself.

The song ended, and Bruce realized he was standing dead still again, staring into space. Quickly now he headed toward the garage on the other side of the backyard, stopping briefly to blow a few new leaves off the patio. That was the way it went this time of year. You got the yard cleared one minute only to see it start filling up again the next. As he turned from the patio, he heard a noise at the upstairs window and looked up to see Maddy's face, at least the top part of it, peering out at him. She had both her palms raised and was slapping at the window.

"Hey there, Maddy!" Bruce called. "Uncle Brucie is coming up for supper!" He lifted the leaf blower and waved it back and forth. He even turned it on so she could hear it. Madison loved loud mechanical noises, which was only one of the many ways she was unique. She clapped her hands whenever he raced the engine of his pickup or ran the lawn mower. Airplanes and big trucks seemed to fascinate her, and she went into fits of giggles when Bruce made machine gun noises. She even liked the sound of thunder. While Bruce himself would scramble to get inside, Madison would look up into the sky wide-eyed, hoping to *see* it.

But she didn't seem to be smiling now. He could only see her eyes, though, so he wasn't sure, but it almost looked as if she was crying. He turned the leaf blower off. Madison was batting at the window with her fists now, and Bruce could hear her wailing.

Bruce felt himself getting irritated the way he always did when Kimberly took too long to attend to Madison's needs. Surely she must hear her crying and banging on the window in the nursery. He knew he ought to cut his sister some slack. After all, she was probably in the kitchen putting his supper together. But good grief, couldn't she stop for at least a minute? Maddy was throwing a regular little fit up there.

"Hold on, Maddy!" Bruce called. "I'll be right there!" He set the leaf blower by the door and raced inside. It would be a lot quicker to go upstairs through his apartment than to go around to the side and through the kitchen.

28

Music in the Sinner's Ears

As he took the stairs three at a time, Bruce could still hear Madison crying in the nursery, as well as a new sound—a high-pitched whistle, which turned out to be the smoke alarm. There was no sign of Kimberly in the kitchen, and she was obviously not going to come anywhere close to meeting her announced suppertime of six o'clock. The only indication that the meal was underway was the smoke billowing from an open pan on the stove, where the ground beef had gone far past the browning stage.

Bruce grabbed the pan and set it in the sink, then turned the stove off and headed for the nursery. "Kimberly! Where are you?" he called as he raced down the hallway, noting the empty bathroom on the right and living room on the left. "It's okay, Maddy! Uncle Bruce is coming!"

His first impression upon entering the nursery and seeing Kimberly lying on the floor was that the cat was somehow to blame because he was crouched only inches from Kimberly's face, his tail swishing slowly as he studied her intently. Bruce had seen cats position themselves that way after wounding a chipmunk or bird, waiting for it to move so they could pounce again. Madison came toddling toward him from the window, her arms outstretched, crying, "My mommy! My mommy!" On the floor were scattered what had to be hundreds of marbles. The big tin can Kimberly stored them in was overturned, its lid having rolled halfway across the floor.

Bruce knelt over his sister. "Kimberly! Can you hear me?" He thought he saw her eyelids flutter, but she made no other move. She was lying on her side, a peaceful look on her face as though she had just lain down for a short nap in her oversized red sweats, which were about the only thing she could fit into these days. Madison threw herself against him, wailing, "Mommy! Mommy fall!" Bruce pulled her close with one arm and tried to comfort her while he brushed Kimberly's thick hair back off her forehead.

"Everything's all right, Maddy, Uncle Bruce is here," he said in one breath, then in the next, "Kimberly! Kimberly, can you open your eyes?" Still no response. He felt for a pulse. Faint but steady. The smoke alarm was still squealing out in the kitchen.

It must have been the marbles. They were everywhere. He imagined the scenario. While he was blithely blowing leaves and daydreaming outdoors, Maddy had obviously awakened from her nap and started playing. Kimberly was in the kitchen, no doubt having gotten sidetracked from her supper preparations and now scrambling to get the beef stroganoff started, when she must have heard the crash of the tin of marbles.

Somehow Maddy, agile little monkey that she was, must have pulled it off the top shelf of the bookcase, where it usually sat. It would have made quite a crash against the hardwood floor, a sound which probably filled Madison with glee. That, plus the cheerful bouncing of the marbles in every direction, had surely rendered her awestruck. Bruce could envision her watching the popcorn effect of the marbles, her hands clasped under her chin and her eyes shining like dark little marbles themselves. She may have even shrieked with the thrill of it all, which had probably alarmed Kimberly further.

And when Kimberly dashed in from the kitchen, it must have been like one of those funny movies, like when the bad guys get outfoxed by the kid's booby traps in *Home Alone,* except it wasn't at all funny, because this was real and Kimberly was his sister and she was six months pregnant. He turned quickly to Madison. "Let go a minute, sweetie," he said, peeling her off him. "Uncle Bruce has to get help."

He had never dialed 9-1-1 before but had imagined doing so and had come close one time while helping to judge a science fair over at Berea High when a kid named Hardy Biddle had faked a seizure. Then when Bruce realized it was only a joke, he had jerked him to his feet with such violence he thought the kid really might need an ambulance by the time he was through with him. That was one unforgettable boy. You met him once and immediately had a new understanding of the term "problem child."

Several times while watching TV programs in which emergencies were reenacted, Bruce had wondered what it would be like to be a 9–1–1 telephone dispatcher. He had always thought he'd be good at calming distraught callers and sending help on its way.

He grabbed the portable phone from the kitchen wall now and dialed the numbers as he ran back to the nursery. Madison was kneeling beside her mother, patting her head, actually smacking at it quite hard. "Mommy! Get up, Mommy!" she said tearfully.

"Let's don't touch Mommy right now," Bruce said as the dispatcher answered. But amazingly, right when he opened his mouth and started talking into the phone, Kimberly's eyes flew open. He heard Madison catch her breath and whisper, "Mommy!"

Kimberly didn't try to get up or move, though. Without raising her head, she cut her eyes all around the room, taking in Madison, Bruce, the nursery walls, the marbles on the floor all around her. Fear suddenly filled her face as she heard Bruce's words to the dispatcher. She put a quick hand to her stomach.

"Don't move, Kimbo," he said. "They're sending an ambulance." Bruce answered a few questions, and the dispatcher told him EMS was on the way. And indeed, only seconds after hanging up he heard a distant siren. Surely they couldn't be responding already, could they? But as he listened he heard the siren growing louder and louder. He had read something in the paper recently about a proposed salary raise for paramedics, and he thought now that whatever raise was being considered couldn't possibly be enough for these people who rushed so promptly to the aid of their fellowman at all hours of the day and night.

He was kneeling beside Kimberly again, his hand lightly rubbing her forehead. Madison was pressed against him on the other side, peering around at her mother's face. The cat had retreated and was perched on the windowsill, observing everything with characteristic feline passivity. "Hang in there, sis," he said. "It'll be okay. They'll be here in a minute. Hear the siren?"

He kept listening, barely allowing himself to breathe, as the siren got closer, until it sounded like it was turning onto their street. "Stay right here, Kim, don't move. I'm going out to let them in." He picked Madison up and carried her with him, stopping long enough to sweep aside the marbles around the doorway with his foot. He surely didn't want the ambulance workers to trip and fall. It was a wonder he hadn't gone sprawling himself, the way they covered the floor.

As he headed toward the front door, his thoughts were springing in every direction, just as the marbles must have done. What should he do next? Should he go to the hospital with Kimberly? They would probably let him ride in the ambulance. But what about Madison? He couldn't take her along. You didn't take a two-year-old on a trip like that. But he couldn't leave her at home by herself.

He thought of Matt across the ocean, totally oblivious that his pregnant wife had fallen. As Bruce had wondered for many weeks now, why wouldn't a husband do everything in his power to stick right by his wife's side while she was carrying his child? Why would he fly across the Atlantic Ocean when so much was at stake at home? But Matt was in Germany—that was an inalterable fact. So who could help out right now?

Amazingly, unlike his disorderly thoughts, the events that followed seemed to unfold exactly on cue, not at all as he would have expected at a time like this. As he opened the door, the ambulance pulled up to the curb, much like a well-timed film script, and two paramedics came trotting across the front yard, cutting right through Kimberly's island of azaleas. The one in front, a burly man, carried a large medical satchel. Bruce felt Madison clutch his neck tighter. She had never been this close to an ambulance before.

Bruce saw Patsy Stewart standing in her front yard, stalwartly taking it all in. He quickly stepped out onto the porch and swung the screen door open. "Straight through to the hall and then left," he said to the paramedics, and at that very minute an idea presented itself to him: Maybe he could leave Madison with Patsy Stewart. No doubt Patsy would still be out in the yard when the ambulance left. She had the look of a Buckingham Palace guard, spine ramrod straight, chin lifted, a look that said, "I will not leave my post."

In the nursery the paramedics were asking Kimberly questions, checking her vital signs, jotting things down. Bruce stood in the doorway holding Madison. The house still smelled of burned meat, but the smoke alarm had finally given up. The cat on the windowsill was leisurely licking a paw, indifferent to the crisis at hand, the very tip of his black tail flicking sporadically. Bruce thought of his father's shotgun downstairs on his apartment wall. He'd like to pick that smug cat right off his comfortable perch with a single bullet. Stupid cat. Kimberly hadn't even settled on a name for him yet, kept trying different ones out and discarding them as unsuitable. She didn't like his suggestion of Dumbo.

The woman paramedic, who had the sharp popeyed look of a small hairless dog and who certainly didn't look strong enough to hold up one end of a stretcher, had stood and was speaking into her phone, all crackly with static, condensing the situation into sentence fragments.

The male paramedic, who was kneeling beside Kimberly, glanced up at Bruce. "Something burning?"

Bruce shook his head. "Not anymore."

"Let's get the stretcher," the woman said as soon as she finished talking on her phone, and when she hurried past Bruce at the doorway, she flashed him a sympathetic smile. "Don't you worry, hon, we'll take real good care of her," she said, and suddenly Bruce changed his mind about her. He could understand perfectly how some man could love this woman with her nearly bald head and her little Chihuahua face. You could give up a lot in the area of looks for a woman with a warm heart. He hoped this one had a good husband and grateful children.

Soon the paramedics had returned, and within seconds they had moved Kimberly and were carrying her out on the stretcher, one end of which the woman held up with perfect ease. Dickson County Hospital— that's where they were taking her. Bruce had asked twice just to be sure, had promised to follow in his pickup as soon as he took Madison next door.

Patsy hadn't moved an inch. She was still standing in the Stewarts' front yard like a piece of lawn statuary. Bruce saw that Celia had also come outside but was standing off by herself closer to the driveway, her arms folded tightly in front of her. She had on a pair of faded blue jeans and a red flannel shirt. He couldn't remember ever seeing her so dressed down before. Somehow the outfit wasn't what he had envisioned when he had heard her playing the clarinet earlier, although he wasn't sure what proper clarinet-playing attire would be.

He suddenly remembered seeing a contestant in the Miss America Pageant on TV years ago playing a clarinet during the talent portion, wearing a long black dress, slightly flared at the bottom, with silver buttons all the way down the side, so as she played she looked something like a tall slim clarinet herself, which was probably the whole idea behind her choice of a costume. Funny the things you thought about at a time like this.

He was surprised to see Celia. Didn't she know that by coming outside she was appearing to care about what went on in someone else's life?

"What happened?" Patsy called to him. For the briefest instant Bruce wondered why Milton wasn't outside, too. Then he remembered that Milton had told him he was going to visit his nephew in Hendersonville for a few days, to help him rewire his house. His nephew was an amputee, Milton had said, and competed in wheelchair sports. Bruce took a deep breath and started down the front steps toward the Stewarts' yard, shaking his head to try to clear any other irrelevant thoughts from his mind. He couldn't let himself dawdle. He had to hurry. He had to streamline his thoughts. Kimberly might need him.

The steps, which he had blown clear of leaves just a half hour ago, were now littered with several new ones. That very leaf, that big hand-shaped one right there, Bruce thought, could have detached itself from the sycamore tree at the very moment Madison had tipped over the marbles, and by the time it had drifted its lazy way down to the front step, Kimberly could have been lying unconscious on the nursery floor. So much could happen in the time it took a leaf to fall.

Even as he started across the lawn toward the Stewarts', he had no idea that he was going to do what he did only seconds later. "My sister had an accident," he called out to Patsy as he reached the driveway. "She's expecting a baby, you know." Funny, too, how you instinctively tailored your speech to your audience even in a crisis. Somehow he knew Patsy Stewart would be of the mind that *pregnant* wasn't a word to be used in public, especially by an unmarried man. It might be the twenty-first century, but this was still the South.

She spoke again, maybe even asked another question, but he didn't hear her clearly. Something was suddenly shifting around inside his head. He started across the driveway, then stopped. Celia was standing down to his right on the other side of the driveway, Patsy in the front yard, up the slight grade to his left.

Madison raised her voice, twisted around in his arms to look directly at Celia, and said clearly, "My mommy fall down."

"Fall?" Patsy said. "Did she say fall?" When she didn't get an immediate answer, she said, "Did she hit her head?" Then, "How far along is she?" and "Are you going to the hospital?"

The questions were coming too fast. Bruce could think of only one thing to say, and he said it: "Yes." And even as he said it, he felt his feet make a slight change in direction so that he found himself walking straight toward Celia. It was a strange moment as he approached her, the look on her face almost as panicky as the one he had seen on Kim's face as they strapped her onto the stretcher. He wouldn't have been surprised if Celia had raised her hands and stepped back, shaking her head no, or if she had turned around and bolted for her apartment. But she didn't. She stood absolutely still and watched him get closer and closer, her eyebrows drawn down, her mouth slightly open, as if groping for words that wouldn't come.

And when he handed Madison to her, she took her with a small resigned sigh, almost as if she had known this time would come, as if she had been dreading it like an old nightmare. Madison stared fixedly at Celia, their noses not three inches apart. "My mommy fall," she whispered, and Celia nodded, still frowning.

"I'll come back and get her as soon as I can," Bruce said. "I don't know how long. I hope it won't . . . I mean . . . hey, I know, I'll leave my apartment door open so you can get inside and . . ." He made a face. "She might need a diaper. They're upstairs in the nursery. But watch out for the marbles." Celia looked puzzled. "You'll see them," he said. "Oh, and she hasn't had supper. Wait, maybe I should . . ."

"No, you go," Celia said. "You go take care of your sister." Bruce thought he might have imagined it, but it really did sound like she put a little extra stress on the word *sister*. He didn't have time now to wonder about it, but later it would be worth mulling over the very remote possibility that maybe she felt the least bit sorry about their argument through her kitchen window that day, about her misjudgment of him and her testy words, some empty threat about how she'd better never see that cat hanging around her apartment again. Or maybe her threat had been directed at Bruce himself. Thinking back, he couldn't remember exactly who had said what that day.

On his way to the hospital only minutes later, Bruce couldn't help worrying about Madison. Had he done right in leaving her with Celia? Would Patsy have been a better choice? If he ever had a child of his own, he knew he'd never be able to trust anybody as a baby-sitter, not even a nun or a Girl Scout leader or a grandmother with umpteen grandchildren. He thought of the scowl on Celia's face when he had handed Madison to her. He hoped she wouldn't forget to feed her. He should have told her how much Madison liked applesauce, grits, and dark brown toast. Those would be easy to fix.

It came to him that this rushing to the emergency room seemed familiar. Not necessarily something he had done himself, though. Maybe it was just that he had read about ER scenes a lot in the suspense novels he used to like. Or maybe he had watched too much television. People were always getting hauled to the ER on TV.

He wondered again, as he often did, if anybody else's mind worked the way his did, if other people ever imagined they were writing about their lives as if they were episodes in a book, and as soon as the first few words started forming themselves, he stopped and wondered if any other person in the whole world was using this same tactic right this very moment to distance himself from his trouble.

He doubted it, although there had been that girl he had met in Natchez years ago, a very intelligent Jewish brunette who used to make up impromptu limericks about the places they went, things they did, people they saw. She was very witty, that girl, and about five times smarter than any other girl he'd ever gone out with. Wasn't all hung up on the Ten Commandments, either, like you'd expect from a Jew; in fact, she regularly broke several of them.

Speeding to the emergency room, Bruce remembered a particularly clever Jewish girl from Natchez, who never once, during his acquaintance with her, had kept the Sabbath holy. The words fell together easily. That kind of story opening would tease the reader in both directions, past and future. He wouldn't ever use it, though, as it might sound a little irreverent. He wouldn't want to come across as making fun of the Bible.

Or how about trying a limerick of his own? *There once was a mommy named Kim, whose figure was not very trim; She heard a loud crash, she made a quick dash* . . . But he stalled on an ending. He tried several, but none of them would work. The mind a fascinating piece of equipment. So much of what it did seemed to be diversionary, to keep from overloading itself with reality. He eased up on the accelerator. It wouldn't do to get pulled over or, worse, to have an accident on his way to the hospital.

What he needed to do right now was to pray. He was ashamed that thus far his thoughts had been so scattered that he hadn't even stopped to form a genuine prayer, only a few frantic *help me*'s in between everything else. Strangely, though, with every *help me* he had seemed to hear an immediate response: "Don't be afraid; I'm here; it's all right."

He thought of his sister and the baby she was carrying. He knew he could play the male role and act strong on the outside for her sake and Madison's if something bad happened, but he could imagine himself crumbling inside, lying awake at night, walking around like a drugged man for days on end, losing his train of thought right in the middle of explaining genetic mutations to his students and wandering out of the classroom into the hallway.

He started praying as he drove, then broke off when he heard another siren and saw a fire truck zip by going the opposite direction. So many tragedies overlapping one another. He thought of the pan in Kimberly's kitchen. He *had* turned the stove off, hadn't he?

His mind returned to the earlier thought—would Madison be all right in Celia's care? What were they doing right now? Surely Celia wouldn't treat a child, a baby really, as rudely as she had treated him in the past. Maybe he should have left her with Patsy after all, even though he hated to think of a beautiful, perfect little girl like Madison having to spend even a few minutes with dull, unimaginative Patsy.

Maybe Celia would play something on her clarinet. Madison loved music. Or maybe she had drawing paper and paints in her apartment and would let Madison finger-paint. Probably not, though. That would be messy. He remembered how tidy Celia's apartment was, how fastidious she always looked. He remembered an old movie his mother had liked—*Father Goose* with Cary Grant—in which Leslie Caron called herself a "picture straightener" type. That was Celia. He could imagine her making regular rounds in her apartment to straighten all her paintings. But then maybe Celia had a hidden side. Maybe she secretly loved kids and noise and a little unpredictability.

He thought of a conversation he had had yesterday with Elizabeth Landis, who had accepted a permanent job at his school a few weeks ago when an eighth-grade English teacher had suddenly resigned due to "health problems." That was the official announcement at their weekly faculty meeting, though they all knew it had to do with the protracted divorce she was going through. "Severe depression" hardly began to describe the woman's mental state now, though the way she used to talk about her husband in the teachers' lounge would have made you think she'd welcome a divorce.

Elizabeth, who had already been called on to sub for this same teacher many times since school had started in September, had stepped right into the job, and because their classrooms were catty-cornered to each other's, Bruce and she had fallen into visiting for a few minutes after school each day. She had even volunteered to help with the recent auditions for *A Midsummer Night's Dream* and was sitting in on some of the rehearsals.

Bruce judged that Elizabeth was probably a good ten years older than he was, and he had already decided she must have been one of the smart, quiet girls back when she was in school. But not boring, definitely not that. She was a tall woman and pretty in a natural understated way. She had a fertile mind and a quick sense of humor when you got to know her. Married, of course—the good ones always were—but Bruce had thought more than once that if he had been born a decade earlier or she a decade later, he would have spotted her a mile off as somebody worth pursuing, though a smart woman like her probably wouldn't have given him the time of day, since his attention up until the last couple of years hadn't exactly been aimed at a woman's mind. He wondered if Elizabeth's husband knew what a very nice wife he had. He was a musician, she had told Bruce.

Elizabeth had come to his classroom yesterday to show him some poems her eighth graders had written. Bruce had been sitting at his desk absentmindedly twirling a ruler around on top of a pencil—the same ruler and pencil he had confiscated from a boy an hour earlier who had been doing the same thing with them. He was thinking about how poorly most of his seventh graders had done on the chapter test that day over the major plant groups, wondering if he was expecting too much to think that they would recall the difference between xylem and phloem, between ferns and club mosses, between gymnosperms and angiosperms, all of which he thought he had made crystal clear in class but evidently hadn't.

Elizabeth laughed at him from the door. "Reverting to your childhood, huh?" she said, then came in and sat on one of the student desks facing him. She handed him the poems.

He could feel her watching him read them. He tried to make a few comments that wouldn't give him away as a total nitwit when it came to poetry. She told him she had gotten the idea for the assignment from a meeting she had been to recently—a poetry club she sometimes attended. And oh, she said, he'd be interested to know that his next-door neighbor, Celia, had spoken to her poetry club one time back in May.

Though Bruce pretended disinterest at the mention of Celia, Elizabeth must have read something different on his face, for she paused. "You know, I really think the two of you could become friends," she said. "I've thought that ever since I found out you live right next door to each other."

Bruce could still picture the astonishment on Elizabeth's face as she had stood behind Celia that day in August listening to the two of them exchange insults through the window. "One of you would have to make the first move, though," she said, rising to pick up the poems from Bruce's desk. "One person always has to do that."

He didn't say a word, merely shrugged, picked up the ruler once more and gave it another vigorous twirl. First move? Is that what she had said? If she only knew. Elizabeth had heard the argument that day, but she didn't know about all his first and second and third attempts to be friendly before that. Not unless Celia had told her, and he felt sure she hadn't. The only thing Elizabeth knew about was that one conversation, white-hot and razor-edged—and whatever else Celia had chosen to tell her, which would be nothing that painted him in a favorable light.

Before she left his classroom, she paused at the door and said, "Celia is a lot different from your first impression of her. She really is. You need to be patient with her, give her a chance. I think she's got some things in her background that make her . . . well, let's say not the easiest person to get close to. I don't even know what they all are, but I'm working on it. She's really very nice, Bruce. Very nice. We're on the same tennis team, you know."

And how was he supposed to know that? Bruce thought. He had never figured Elizabeth for a tennis player, though he could see it now. She seemed a lot more languid and low-key than Celia, however, so he wondered how quick she was on the court. Maybe he should play her sometime. Surely he could beat a woman ten years older than himself. That would be pretty humiliating if he couldn't.

Not that he had a superinflated ego like some men. He remembered all the mean stuff men had said about the woman golfer who had sneaked into an "open" tournament in Asheville last year and who had placed twelfth out of sixty-two entrants. Vic Darnell, that was how she had signed her name on the registration form, but later it came to light that Vic was short for Victoria. Bruce had applauded her at the time, though he had paused to wonder whether he would feel differently if he had been one of the fifty men who ranked below her.

After Elizabeth had left his classroom yesterday, Bruce had roused himself to flip through a book he had picked up from the Derby Library, titled *Plays for Today's Young Teens,* and right before slamming the book shut, he had come across a play called *First Impressions.* Funny coincidence. Well, he had certainly not been guilty of forming a hasty first impression of Celia. No, he had remained generously fair-minded, he thought, until the fifth or sixth impression had confirmed the first one: Celia, with her nose in the air, rode a very high horse.

Bruce suddenly realized he needed to turn on his headlights. Driving along toward the hospital, both impatient to get there and dreading what he might learn, he could hear again the sound of hymns drifting out of Celia's apartment. He wondered how she knew a song like "The Old Rugged Cross." Could it be that she knew other hymns, maybe some of the same ones they sang at Community Baptist every Sunday? He wondered if phrases from those songs ever came to her at odd times during the day or night, as they did to him. Surely not.

He doubted that the two of them had a single thing in common. He couldn't imagine someone as confident as Celia fretting about past sins, for example, the way he had done late one night recently while eating a miserable supper of canned corned beef hash. He couldn't imagine her suddenly standing up as he had, pounding a fist on the table and declaring right out loud, "He breaks the power of canceled sin! He sets the prisoner free!"

Surely somebody as cool and efficient as Celia had never gone on a hike and felt overcome at the sight of a red sunset or a cloudless blue sky or a foggy mountaintop. Surely she had never declared, "O for a thousand tongues to sing!" as he had done the day before on his way to school upon seeing the autumn colors of Paris Mountain. Impossible that someone like her could hear the name of Jesus and think of it as "music in the sinner's ears." Though Bruce had no trouble thinking of himself as a sinner in great need of large daily doses of God's grace, he felt sure that Celia had no such low opinion of herself.

As he pulled into the parking lot by the emergency entrance of the hospital, he prayed, again. Surely the God who could open the ears of the deaf, touch the eyes of the blind, and cause the lame to leap for joy could take care of Kimberly.

29

Deathbeds Are Coming

When he got to the emergency room, they had him fill out some papers. They told him that emergency room traffic was especially heavy today, that another doctor had just been called to come in. Because Kimberly was considered high priority, a doctor would be examining her as soon as possible, but they had taken her to X ray "for some pictures" a moment ago. "Things are a zoo back there," the woman at the desk told Bruce, jerking her head toward the double doors, "but have a seat and somebody will be out to take you back pretty soon."

The waiting room was crowded. Bruce sat down next to a white-haired man who was opening the lid of a Styrofoam tray. In one section was a mound of spaghetti, in another a lackluster salad that consisted of the palest yellowish green lettuce and two wedges of a hard pinkish tomato, and in the other a piece of toast. The man studied it all silently for a few seconds, then grunted and closed the lid slowly. When Bruce glanced at his face, he saw that the old man was crying. He knew he ought to say something, to offer a word of comfort, but as he opened his mouth to speak, the man got up and shuffled out the door and down the hall, leaving his Styrofoam tray on his chair.

Bruce realized how hungry he was. He eyed the food tray and wondered if the old man would come back to claim it. Then he remembered some vending machines he had passed down the hall, and a minute later he had returned with a can of root beer and a granola bar. This time he settled into one of the brown vinyl chairs across from the television.

Two middle-aged women on the loveseat beside him were engaged in a conversation. One of them was wearing a purple raincoat and sneakers, and the other one was dressed in what looked like a square-dancing costume, with a red peasant-style blouse and a turquoise skirt with billows of red petticoats, which she was managing to keep in check only by clamping her hands on top of her chubby white knees. She had on little white ruffled anklets with her black patent Mary Janes and a big turquoise bow in her pouffy bleached hair. Bruce wondered if maybe her square-dancing partner had had a heart attack right in the middle of a do-si-do.

The two women were talking so loud he couldn't help hearing every word. They were discussing, of all things, the virtues of various brands of paper towels. The square dancer seemed to favor the pick-a-size kind with the rows of perforations close together so you could tear off just a little strip if that was all you needed, which the other one pronounced too expensive. "Yes, but at least they give you a clean tear," said the square dancer, "not like those off-brands that rip everywhere but where you want them to." She had a good point there, the other woman admitted. The cheap ones were bad to tear crooked, but still . . .

And then they got off on prints versus plain old white, the square dancer suggesting that some of the prints had pictures she didn't necessarily want in her kitchen. Why, her mother-in-law had given her some with green and orange kangaroos stamped all over them.

It was all so typically *female*. How many such conversations had Bruce overheard in break rooms and teachers' lounges over the years? Long discussions about a difficult pregnancy or somebody's new dinette set or the look on so-and-so's face when she said something. He used to like to play devil's advocate and join in, turning the whole conversation into an argument until the women caught on, which was usually very soon, that he was mocking them.

One woman had thrown a book at him once, literally—a heavy hardback geography book—and asked him why he didn't go talk with the men about something *really* intellectual, like cars or sports stats. "Then for a little excitement, you could all go watch that cop show on TV," she had said. "You know, the one with high-speed chases and shootouts on the freeway." She had even added a few sound effects, quite authentic-sounding ones, especially for a woman.

She had been very funny, that woman. Every time she saw him after that she would ask him if he'd seen any good brawls in basketball games lately or watched any footage of wars. "You men have such *important* things on your mind," she'd say. "It's a wonder you can even hold down a full-time job."

The conversation about paper towels stopped abruptly when the woman in the raincoat left. Three other women were sitting in chairs on the other side of Bruce. They were apparently related, since one of them had her feet propped companionably in the lap of one of the others. The two younger ones were probably sisters, he decided, both of them quite large with moon-shaped faces. The one with her feet propped up had her hair pulled back into a greasy ponytail. The other one was holding a folded-up section of the newspaper, from which she was reading aloud the daily horoscope, sign by sign. The women in this waiting room didn't seem overly concerned about whatever emergency had brought them here, Bruce thought.

"Here's Scorpio," the sister with the newspaper said. "That's your sign, ain't it, Mama? It says here, 'Changing your focus from yourself to others will bring you good luck in the coming days. Look for ways to do favors, and you will receive favors in return,' " to which the older woman replied dryly, "Well, that's a pure-D lie. I been givin' and givin' and givin' my whole life, and I ain't never got nothin' in return."

The one with the ponytail took the newspaper and started reading aloud the letters of the scrambled-up words in the daily Jumble Puzzle. " 'A-B-I-S-S,' " she read, and they all appeared stumped, though Bruce had the answer at once: *basis.* Just as he was ready to speak up and offer his help, the mother said, "They done forgot to mix up the letters on that one! It's abyss, A-B-I-S-S. You know, that pit where the devil's gonna be throwed."

The one holding the paper smacked it against the arm of the chair. "Betcha they thought they was gonna fool ever'body on that one," she said, and she carefully wrote the letters in the spaces. The mother grunted and said, "I hate a person that's always tryin' to bamboozle other folks."

The third time they called for "Mr. Wilson" in the waiting room, it dawned on Bruce that they might be looking for him. Maybe they had overlooked the fact that his last name wasn't the same as his married sister's, even though he had filled out the admitting papers with all the right information.

He jumped up from his chair and walked over to the woman at the desk, who was writing something on a form. She wasn't the same one he had talked to when he first arrived. This woman had a severe look about her, one that said life here at the emergency room desk had taught her not to expect anything good. She was wearing a pair of those skinny little reading glasses on the end of her nose, and her lips were pursed as if she were sucking on a sour ball. "Excuse me, did somebody just call for me?" he asked her.

"Are you Mr. Wilson?" she said without looking up.

"No."

She scowled up at him, over the top of the tiny frames. "Mr. Wilson is the only one we've been calling for, sir. Have a seat and we'll call you when a doctor finishes with your patient." She gave a little sigh, repursed her lips, and turned back to her writing. Bruce felt like a schoolchild who had gotten out of his seat during quiet time.

"My sister is Mrs. Wilson," he said. "Kimberly Wilson. I thought maybe you—"

The woman stood up immediately. "Well, why didn't you say so? The doctor's been out twice already asking for you. Let me go back and see what I can do." She headed for the door, adding, "These doctors are really busy, you know. They're handling *emergencies*. They can't wait around forever."

Bruce was taken aback by her terseness. A woman like that shouldn't be working in a hospital, especially not at the emergency room desk. They needed somebody with a soft voice, somebody patient and compassionate who didn't treat people like they were naughty kindergartners. He could imagine this battle-ax snapping her fingers and barking at some distraught relative, "Nope, sorry, she died on the operating table. Just like that. Here, sign this before the undertaker comes for the corpse."

Bruce thought of several things he could have said, but she disappeared through the double doors before he got anything out.

It turned out to be a woman doctor, and she wasn't much better than the receptionist. He could forgive her more easily, though, because the dark circles under her eyes told him she had probably been on duty for a long, long time. Dr. Vollnogle—that's how she introduced herself when she finally barreled through the double doors with a curt nod and a quick hard handshake. She was a hefty woman, not fat but broad-shouldered and muscular. Bruce wondered if she had ever competed in weight lifting or shot put. Her lips were tucked in at the corners as if she were holding back the words her laser-beam eyes were shooting at him: "And where were you when I came out looking for you earlier?"

Bruce decided to forgo an explanation, especially since she didn't give him a chance to offer one. The news was good, though she fired it at him like a round of ammunition. Kimberly was stable, all vital signs strong, talking coherently, no concussion, no bleeding, baby was apparently fine, hadn't dropped, good strong heartbeat, no complications, only injury was a sprained ankle.

"The mother's, I assume?" Bruce said, then immediately wished he hadn't.

Dr. Vollnogle gave him a long look, as if he were a puppy that had wet on her new carpet. "Yes, Mr. Wilson, the mother's."

Bruce grabbed her hand and shook it. "The name's Healey," he said. "Bruce Healey. But thank you, Doctor! Thank you very much. I know you're busy, and I appreciate your time. Thanks for the good news."

"We're going to keep her overnight, though," Dr. Vollnogle said, removing her hand from his, "to make sure we didn't miss anything. Sometimes a fall like hers can have delayed effects."

"Oh, I don't think hers will," he said. "She used to fall all the time as a kid. She'd trip and hit her head on something, then bounce right up and keep going. And she was always bad about passing out when she was really hungry. She'd just keel right over. There goes Kimbo again, we'd say. We used to tell her that's why she was slow at catching jokes, because of all the head injuries." He laughed.

Dr. Vollnogle didn't seem to think it was funny, any of it. Her eyes were scanning his face as if she knew she'd have to give a description to the police later. Bruce wondered if she had ever considered a career in education. He could see her as a teacher, the kind who got all the bad kids because the principal knew she could handle them.

"We'll be moving her to a room in a little while," the doctor said, taking a step back. She put her hand against one of the double doors. "You can come back and see her if you want to." She was still looking at him suspiciously; no doubt she thought he'd had his own share of head injuries in the past.

"And why wouldn't I want to?" Bruce said cheerfully. "After all, she's the only little sister I have." He saw something suddenly click in the doctor's eyes. "Oh yes, she's my *sister*," he said. "Maybe I didn't say that. I did tell the other person, but . . . well, so you were probably thinking she's my . . . no, no, she's not. She's my sister. That's why our names are different, see. Her husband's overseas, and I'm . . . well, living at their house and helping her out. And her daughter, too. My niece. Her name's Madison, and she's two, and . . . well, you're not the first one who's misunderstood the relationship, believe me."

But the doctor was already several steps ahead of him, turning a corner and waving him toward a cubicle. "She's right in here," she called out to him. Then she poked her head into the cubicle and said, "Your brother's here, Mrs. Wilson. You need to get well really fast so you can keep an eye on him. He doesn't need to be running around loose." Then she flashed Bruce a smile and was gone.

Well. So Dr. Vollnogle had a little reservoir of good humor she kept hidden underneath that crusty exterior.

Kimberly was glad to see him but sorry she had caused such trouble. Sticking out from under the covers, her left foot was elevated on a pillow, the ankle encased in ice packs.

No, no, it wasn't the marbles at all, she told him. She had put the ground beef on to brown—oh, and had Bruce found it and turned off the stove? Good, good. So anyway, she heard Madison playing in her room and went back to peek in on her. And then suddenly, just as she got to the nursery door and saw Madison standing on a chair reaching up to the bookshelf, she felt herself going weak all over—"that woozy kind of faint feeling" is how she described it.

But it was different from all the times before, she said. Not a sudden blackout, not a pitching forward with great gusto, but a gradual *fizzling* like the air being let out of an inner tube. And right in the middle of crumpling to the floor, she heard this enormous clatter, which must have been the marble tin falling from the shelf, and then felt her foot twisting under her as her full weight came down on it. And as everything faded to blackness, she heard Madison's voice crying, "Mommy!" So Bruce had actually guessed it all wrong. The marbles accompanied the fall rather than actually causing it.

Kimberly tried wiggling her foot a little, breathing in sharply. She winced. Well, no, she admitted to Bruce, she didn't really *remember* when she had last eaten because she had gotten busy working on Madison's scrapbook that day, which was a new hobby one of her friends at the pool had introduced her to last summer, and well, okay, okay, she guessed she *had* sort of lost track of time after Maddy went down for her nap.

But she was trying to be extra careful about eating, really she was because she knew how important it was, especially when you were pregnant, and yes, yes, she had given Madison a peanut butter sandwich and some Fruit Loops at noon—surely he didn't think she'd forget to feed Maddy!—but she had wanted to finish a glitter border in the scrapbook before she ate anything herself, and, well, time got away from her.

The glitter border had led to something else, and something else after that, and . . . no, she absolutely *never ever* would let it happen again, she promised. After all, it wasn't like this happened every day—just think of how long it had been since the last time. He didn't have to look at her that way, like she was one of his junior high students. And he needn't think he had to start monitoring her food intake and checking up on her all the time. She had only forgotten this *one* time. She wasn't a child, for heaven's sake. And by the way, where was Madison anyway?

Her mouth dropped open. Surely he was kidding. Bruce had actually left Maddy with that snob next door? Well, he needed to leave *right now* and go get her. What had he been thinking of?

Madison was fine, he told her. He had been hit with a really strong feeling that he could trust Celia, and Kimberly knew, didn't she, how unerring his instincts about women usually were?

You mean like that girl in Montgomery a few years ago? Kimberly asked, to which he replied without hesitation, yes, like that girl in Montgomery, the one who had raised huge red flags in his mind soon after he had met her, the one he had tried to ease away from repeatedly, who not only ignored his first early hints but later his outright declarations that no, he did not now nor would he ever love her, the one who had *lied* to him.

Bruce called Patsy Stewart to give her a report on Kimberly and to ask her to tell Celia. But he wouldn't leave the hospital until Kimberly was transferred to a regular room. When he finally said good-bye, Kimberly squeezed his hand and said, "I'm sorry, Bruce. That was mean of me to bring that up. I don't deserve you."

He leaned down and kissed her on the forehead. "You're right, kid," he said. "I think I'll tell them to keep you here a week or two and poke you with needles every couple of hours."

Twenty minutes later Bruce found himself doing something he had promised himself never to do again: He was standing at Celia's door, his hand raised to knock. Her porch light was on, which he took to mean she was expecting him, probably eagerly. Not to see him, of course, but to get rid of Madison.

He stood there for several long moments listening for sounds coming from inside but hearing nothing. So at least Maddy must be behaving herself. Hopefully she was already asleep, since it was well past her bedtime, or what should be her bedtime. Kimberly was bad about keeping her up too late, letting her watch cartoon tapes and feeding her snacks at all hours.

In Bruce's opinion a child should be in bed at least by eight o'clock, though he had developed this opinion only in the past couple of years. Before Maddy, he had never given a passing thought to kids and their bedtimes, except for when he was a kid himself, of course. Back then he had had a vast repertoire of tricks to delay his own bedtime and had even succeeded with a number of them because his mother had been such a soft touch.

He knocked, waited a few seconds, then knocked again a little louder. He didn't want to use the doorbell, as it might wake Madison. He heard a light bump from inside and soon the sound of someone fumbling with the deadbolt. He smiled and waved apologetically at the little viewer hole in case she was checking to see who it was. The door swung open, and Celia unlocked the screen, then pushed it open to let him in.

She was still wearing the jeans and flannel shirt. She put a finger to her lips and pointed to the couch where Madison lay sleeping, a patchwork quilt folded over her. The television was on but turned down so low he could barely hear it. The news was on, and the anchorman was earnestly delivering his scripted speech. The look on his face was quite pleasant, but you couldn't tell anything by that. These news people had a way of reporting the most horrendous events with the same serene expression as when they told about a community wiener roast or the annual Christmas parade.

Bruce had planned simply to pick Madison up and go home immediately, but somehow he found himself sitting next to the sofa in a large chair upholstered in a cream-and-rose print. And the next minute Celia was handing him a mug of something hot, which she announced as mulled cider, something he didn't usually even like. And there was a saucer of sugar cookies on the glass-topped table next to him. Were those for him? he wondered. Had she offered him one? Suddenly he thought of the beef stroganoff Kimberly had been planning to feed him for supper. Cider and cookies were a mighty poor substitute for a plate of real food, but not wanting to seem ungrateful, he took a small sip from his mug, at which time he felt like he had put a blowtorch to his tongue.

"It's hot," she said in a tone of voice that made Bruce think maybe she had already warned him.

"No kidding," he said. He lowered his head and blew into the cup until his eyes quit watering.

"Sorry."

He shook his head. "Oh, no problem." He shrugged. "I didn't need those taste buds anyway." He pointed to the tip of his tongue. "Those are the sweet ones, you know, so maybe now I won't be so tempted every time I pass Krispy Kreme." That was dumb, he thought. What happened to him every time he opened his mouth in front of this woman? He used to be so good at clever repartee.

"So she's okay?" she said.

"Who?"

"Your sister." There it was again, the faintest hint of extra emphasis on the word *sister*. But maybe this time it was her way of saying, "Who else would I be asking about, nincompoop?"

"Oh, Kimberly—yes, as a matter of fact, she is. Just a sprained ankle is all."

Madison stirred a little under the quilt and stuck two fingers in her mouth. Bruce saw Celia stiffen and glance nervously at her. He could imagine what kind of mother she would make—the fretful, overly solicitous type, the kind who would draw up a schedule and stick to it relentlessly. Kimberly wasn't perfect, but at least she gave Madison plenty of room to breathe.

Bruce noticed something he hadn't seen earlier. A basket with several plastic tubes of tennis balls in it was sitting beside the couch.

Celia must have seen him looking at it. "We tried playing a little game."

"A game?"

"She caught on pretty fast," she said. "It was sort of like bowling. I set up the empty cans and showed her how to roll the ball to try to knock them down."

Bruce could hardly believe it. So much for his unerring instincts about women. So Celia had actually let her hair down enough to play a game with Madison—an indoor game with balls, no less, balls that could hit things and break them and make a mess on the floor.

He couldn't think of anything to say, so he picked up a sugar cookie off the saucer and bit into it. It was the soft homemade kind, the kind his mother used to make at Christmastime, shaped like stars and Christmas trees and sprinkled with red and green sugar crystals. This one was round, though, with a hint of lemon and sprinkled with regular white sugar. Before he knew it, he had finished the whole thing. He took another one. "These are good," he said. He could have popped it in his mouth whole, but he forced himself to take several bites and chew slowly. His granola bar at the hospital had long since worn off.

He took another cautious sip of his hot cider. It had an exceedingly tangy, almost fermented taste. A picture of rotting apple peels on top of a steaming compost pile rose before him. The drink was a little cooler now at least, but his mouth still burned from the earlier taste. He pressed the tip of his tongue against his teeth and knew he would be reminded of tonight for days to come until the soreness faded.

"I had the weirdest sensation on the way to the hospital," he said suddenly, realizing he should try to think this out before launching into it. Too late now. "As if I'd done it all before, or like I had expected all along that I'd be doing it eventually. Like it was inevitable." Celia looked at him, her chin lifted, her eyes studying him closely. "But at the same time," he continued, "something was telling me it was going to be all right. Even when I started praying, it was like I heard an actual voice in my head, saying, 'It's okay. She's not going to lose the baby.' I can't explain it. It was like something I was reading in a book. Like it was real and unreal at the same time." He made a face. "I know it must sound dumb."

Celia shook her head. "No, not really," she answered slowly. "I think I know what you mean."

"You do?" Bruce said. "Do you ever . . . ? No, never mind."

"What?"

"Nothing." He took another sip of his cider, then another. This stuff was potent. He hoped he could walk straight after he stood up from the chair.

"I've had the same feeling," Celia said. "That feeling of almost *knowing* something's going to happen. You're surprised but not *really* surprised."

Neither of them spoke for a long moment. Madison made a little sucking noise on her fingers, then stopped. Looking into his mug, Bruce saw that half of his cider was gone. He set it down gently on top of an *American Art Review* magazine lying on the glass-topped table. "Well, I guess I need to . . ." he started, at the same instant Celia said, "The other night I . . ."

They both stopped. For a second Bruce couldn't think of a thing to say. He used to be so good at tossing off witticisms to cover up small embarrassments, but here he sat, his mind as blank as a concrete wall.

"You go first," he said. "The other night you what? Washed the windows? Made soup? Did your laundry? Baked these cookies?" Then realizing he must sound like some kind of male chauvinist who thought all women spent every waking hour at home doing domestic things, he added, "Watched a movie? Read a book? Played—" He caught himself before he said "the clarinet." What if she thought he hung around her apartment eavesdropping? He cleared his throat. "Played tennis?" he finished. Okay, so now she knew he must have seen her in her tennis skirt, carrying her bag to and from her car.

She was staring at his mouth with a slightly pained expression, maybe wondering what other absurd things were going to come out of it. She shook her head. "Well, no, none of that is what I was going to say. It wasn't important anyway." She glanced at a clock on the glass-topped table—a sturdy modern-looking model made of brushed pewter, with large black hands and numbers.

Bruce stood up, forgetting the napkin in his lap, which now fluttered to the floor. He picked it up and wadded it into a ball, then aimed it at the little wicker trash basket beside the television. Of course he missed— and the second before he let it go, he had *known* he would miss, just like Celia was saying a minute ago. Another skill he had lost around women. He used to be able to sink a paper wad in a trash can from the other side of a room. Maybe he should tell her about the time he had scored thirty points in a basketball game in high school, but he decided she would neither care nor believe him.

Celia was already bending down to retrieve the wadded napkin when the whole scene before him suddenly struck Bruce with a force he couldn't remember since the grand moment of illumination in his mother's attic four years ago. It must have been the combined effect of the cookies and the mulled cider and the pleasant decor of Celia's apartment, so different from his own stark quarters next door, and probably also the sight of Celia herself, so small and nice to look at, and even Madison sleeping peacefully on the couch. Add to all that the fact that he was tired, having been at the hospital a good part of the night.

A home and a family of my own—what a nice thing that would be. This was the thought that leapt into his mind at that instant, a host of others crowding in behind it. Time was running short. He was almost forty, past his prime. Half of his life was already behind him. What used to give him such a suffocating feeling—the idea of sticking with one woman for good—now made him think of the high, clear ting of a silver fork tapped against fine crystal. And children, little bright-eyed Healeys splashing in bathtubs and riding tricycles and playing in mud—how could he live the rest of his life without them? He wanted to drive around in a van with one of those bumper stickers that said *I'm the proud parent of a terrific kid.*

It was astonishing how often he was reminded these days of life's brevity. Every day at school he thought of it. You couldn't teach middle school science without a clear understanding of the vulnerability of living organisms. You couldn't look through a microscope without thinking, *Well, these little guys won't be around for very long.* He thought about all the depressing material in the upcoming chapter, the one they would start this very week—all about disruptions in the rhythms of ecosystems, decomposition, the food chain, overpopulation, air pollutants, hazardous wastes. Often he would look into the faces of his students and wonder which of them would die first, which diseases or accidents would claim their lives.

At church, too, the thought was repeatedly driven home. All those verses comparing life to a vapor, to the grass that withers, and so on. And all those hymns declaring that traveling days would soon be over, eternity was drawing near, shadows were falling. He thought of the one they had sung last Sunday—"Softly and Tenderly." He had heard the song years before he had started going to church, but only the first stanza of it. It was in a movie, one that he had bought for his video collection, *The Trip to Bountiful,* which he loved for its fine atmospheric detail and its simple linear plot that could be summed up in one short sentence: "An old woman goes home." But the movie hadn't included all the words of the hymn, like those in the third stanza. "Time is now fleeting," it said, "the moments are passing," and "deathbeds are coming."

He had felt like a cold hand had touched him when they sang that last one: "Deathbeds are coming." He remembered noticing the tempo and dynamic markings at the end of the chorus. He knew just enough about music to know what *rit.* and *pp* meant—slower and very soft. Like someone's dying breaths. He thought of his father, with his hearty laugh and good looks, wasting away to a skeleton before all the suffering was done. He thought of his mother, so pretty and full of life before his father's illness, but turning into a shrew and dying before she was seventy. And his grandmother—holding out till she was ninety, dying in her wheelchair right in the middle of a *Matlock* rerun.

Oh sure, heaven sounded like a great place, and he planned to take up residence there someday, but right now he happened to be living on earth, and wasn't it true that God, like the father that he was, wanted Bruce Healey to be happy? So what was with this idea of his that he had to deny himself the pleasures of earth in order to be fit for heaven? You couldn't punish yourself forever for past faults. Well, okay, you *could,* but you shouldn't.

God didn't operate that way. Hundreds of times he had visualized the concept of grace as a mighty river, sparkling clear, gushing through the open door of his heart and carrying away with it all the dirt and debris of his past transgressions. He had opened that door himself, by a ready act of his will, the second time he had gone to church with Virgil Dunlop. So why did the picture keep blurring? Why was he still trying to secure his salvation by withholding from himself good things he felt he didn't deserve?

Not that this particular woman—this strangely sad little person who lived next door to him—was anybody he should ever get mixed up with romantically, but maybe they could at least be friends someday. Maybe God wanted him to help her in some way. Maybe she could meet one of his friends and then she could introduce him to somebody she knew, and the four of them could do stuff together.

Maybe it was time to let that whole thing in Montgomery be swept away by that river of God's grace. *A home and a family*—maybe he should actually dare to set them as goals.

So all that was what was swirling through his mind during the time it took Celia to throw his paper napkin into the trash can, walk a few steps to the couch, and lift the quilt off Madison so Bruce could pick her up.

And then something happened and everything was upside-down again. As quick as the flip of a switch, Bruce found himself holding Madison on the porch stoop outside Celia's front door staring out at the black night and wondering if his mind was playing tricks or if he really had spent several companionable minutes sitting in Celia's living room eating cookies and drinking cider.

Maybe he shouldn't have tried to ease himself out the door with small talk. Maybe he should have left silently with a friendly wave of gratitude. But no, he had started talking again, had thanked her for keeping Madison, had thanked her for the cookies, had even felt compelled to thank her for the cider he hadn't finished. And then he ran out of things to thank her for, but he wasn't quite out the door yet, so he had added lamely, "Speaking of cider, by the way, did you ever see that movie *The Cider House Rules?*"

And suddenly everything had changed. He couldn't remember what her answer to his question had been, if she had even answered. All he knew was that he was now standing outside her door, which had been firmly closed as soon as his heel had cleared the threshold.

He looked down at Madison, still sound asleep on his shoulder, then stood for a moment looking up at the stars through the treetops. Then stepping out into the backyard, he headed for the break in the hedge. At least one thing was still certain, he thought: Women were indeed a mystery. There was no hope of ever figuring them out.

30

All His Jewels, Precious Jewels

It was a Thursday, exactly a week before Thanksgiving, and Bruce was driving Kimberly and Madison to the Purple Calliope, a restaurant in Derby that advertised itself as having a "family atmosphere." Besides C. C.'s, a barbecue place, and Juno's, which was where all the retirees ate, the only other decent sit-down restaurant in the area was the Field Pea over on Highway 11 in Filbert, unless you drove all the way into Greenville, which Bruce didn't want to do on a school night.

He had told Kimberly that Madison would like the Purple Calliope, which supposedly had an actual purple calliope on display, along with several other unusual musical instruments hanging on the wall. They also provided crayons and paper placemats with pictures on them for children to color. Virgil Dunlop had recommended the place to him, said it was good for kids.

"So how does it feel to reach the big four-o?" Kimberly said. They were in her van, and she reached forward to adjust the temperature. These days she was always complaining about being too hot.

"No different really than the big three-nine last year or the big three-eight the year before that," Bruce said, not altogether truthfully. The fact was, he had thought about being forty years old all day, had tried to walk with an even sprightlier step at school, and had worked hard at being especially good-natured with his students and the other teachers so as to prove to himself and everybody else that he still possessed all his youthful vigor. But it did seem to him that it had taken a little more effort to act spry and happy today than before.

Kim pulled out an old road map from the glove compartment and started fanning herself with it. "Just wait till you're carrying around thirty extra pounds."

Not to mention the extra twenty or thirty you were already carrying around, Bruce thought but wisely didn't say. Kimberly could be a knockout if she'd trim down to what she used to be before she got married. She had thick dark hair, which she wore long and loose, and a pair of "fine eyes," as Darcy described Elizabeth Bennet's eyes in *Pride and Prejudice,* a movie which Bruce actually had in his video collection in spite of the fact that he knew most men would consider it one of the dreaded so-called chick flicks. Their grandmother had always said Kimberly was the spitting image of Mary Ann Mobley, who had won the Miss America Pageant as Miss Mississippi in 1959. In her trimmer days, others had said she favored Vivien Leigh in *Gone With the Wind.*

"Hope this place we're going to has good steaks," Kimberly said. "What else did your friend say about it?"

" 'Of all the gin joints in the world, I have to pick this one,' " he said. He also had *Casablanca* in his video collection, had watched it so many times he could practically recite the whole thing from memory.

"You're not funny," Kimberly said. She was used to his quoting lines from his favorite movies. She flipped her visor mirror down and adjusted it so she could see Madison in her car seat behind her. "How's my pumpkin doing back there?" she said. Madison, usually so full of chatter at home, was always quiet in the car, her little eyes wide with wonder as she took in all the sights and sounds along the way.

"Speaking of pumpkins, you really ought to toss that jack-o'-lantern sometime soon, you know," Bruce said. In spite of its facial imperfections, it had been a big hit with Madison, so much so that it was still sitting in Kimberly's bay window, and every night Madison insisted on lighting the candle inside.

Kimberly laughed. "Maybe before Christmas." She was in a very good mood tonight, and it was clear that she wasn't having to pretend. Of course, being only thirty years old, it was easy for her to be so perky, Bruce thought.

Though he doubted that his parents had given much thought to the concept of family planning, his mother had had her three children almost exactly ten years apart. It was one of those odd patterns kids accept about their families without thinking. Kimberly's thirtieth birthday had been last month, and Suzanne's fiftieth was coming up in December. Which meant the three of them hadn't exactly been best buddies growing up. They had one photograph of Suzanne in her cap and gown at her college graduation holding Kimberly, who was two, with Bruce standing beside them, a gangly twelve-year-old.

A year later in another photo, one of Suzanne in her wedding dress— her first one, which had barely been dry cleaned and stored in a box before the marriage fell apart—Bruce was all spruced up as a junior groomsman, and Kimberly, the flower girl, was wearing a lacy pink dress and holding a basket of rose petals. Except for the fact that all of them had the same dark hair and eyes, "the same incredible good looks," as Bruce was fond of saying, no one would guess they were siblings. People did sometimes mistake Suzanne for Kimberly's mother, however, especially when they saw the way she bossed her around.

The birthday meal tonight had been Kimberly's idea, and she also had a present for Bruce afterward, she had told him. The biggest reason she was so cheerful, though, had nothing to do with his birthday or her age. Matt, her husband, was coming home from Germany in five days and would be here through Christmas and for two months after that before he had to go anywhere again. He would be at the table for Thanksgiving dinner, he would help decorate the Christmas tree, and best of all, he would be here when the baby was born in late January.

Though the Purple Calliope wasn't crowded, the hostess seated them right next to a table of five people who were finishing up their dessert. Bruce almost asked to be moved but didn't want to come across as old and crotchety on his fortieth birthday. Besides that, the five people presented a challenge. He sometimes liked to make up stories about the people he saw in restaurants, but this little group wasn't exactly a typical set. He had a feeling he had seen the man somewhere before, but the real challenge was in sorting out the relationships among the five people.

The old woman was easy. She had to be the mother of either the younger woman or the man. He was tempted to go with the man at first because this old woman, like the man, was on the large side, but something about the way the younger woman kept leaning over to her, touching her arm and speaking confidingly, made him change his mind. Daughters were more likely to act that way than daughters-in-law. So the old woman and the younger one must be mother and daughter, he decided, though they surely didn't look it. Adoption—that was the answer. The old woman, unable to bear children because of a rare genetic disease, had taken the girl in as a foster child and then later adopted her. And now she lived with the family in a split-level—had her own bedroom and bath.

And the baby, not quite as old as Madison—she must belong to the younger woman and the man, which would of course make the old woman her grandmother. But the ages weren't exactly right since the baby's mother, if that's who she was, looked to be in her late forties and also older than the man by several years. But Bruce could make this work—okay, the couple had married late and had a baby right off. Both had lost their first spouses in sudden, untimely deaths, then had met at a monthly meeting of PLATA, People Living Alone after Tragic Accidents. This matched with the attentive, courteous way they were treating each other—they couldn't have been married long.

So that left the boy, probably eighteen or nineteen, who, in spite of the fact that he should be slouched down in his chair, looking bored and sulky at having to waste an evening in a restaurant with his family, instead looked all scrubbed and respectful, sporting a collared shirt and a trim haircut no less. But Bruce could fit him in somehow—he was good at this.

" . . . anything you want," Kimberly was saying. "You only turn forty once, you know."

Bruce laughed. "Well, that's true of every age, isn't it?" he said. "I don't remember turning twenty-five but one time."

"Doggie," Madison said, pointing to the picture on her place mat.

The boy must be from the woman's earlier marriage, Bruce reasoned, and he was maybe a little socially backward, having grown up without a father during his adolescent years. An avid amateur magician, the kid spent hours mastering new tricks, his current one involving a green parrot, a yellow scarf, and three decks of playing cards. His new stepfather was trying to bond with him, but with the new baby and the mother-in-law, it was slow going.

Bruce turned his attention back to the man—not exactly fat, but definitely stout. The more he looked at him, the more certain he felt that he knew him somehow, had seen him more than once. He must work somewhere that Bruce frequented. It was often hard to place a person out of his normal context.

"I apologize for my brother," Kimberly said. "He's very shy in front of women he doesn't know. Just bring us both sweet tea. And a glass of milk for her." She motioned to Madison.

Bruce looked up to see a waitress leaving their table.

"Hey, what's wrong with you?" Kimberly said, waving her menu at him. "You look like you're in a trance. Are you sleepy already?"

Bruce shook his head. "No, not yet. My bedtime's not till nine." Though he followed up with a laugh, he knew he wasn't exaggerating all that much. It had actually started to worry him a little lately that he was going to bed so early, earlier in fact than Madison most nights. If that wasn't a sign of growing old, he didn't know what was. A few short years ago he was staying up regularly till past midnight, then bounding out of bed ready to go at six the next morning.

Madison pointed to her place mat again, where she had scribbled several blue circles next to the dog. "Mommy," she said.

"How pretty," Kimberly said. "That must be my ankle."

"If you'd kept it iced like the doctor said, the bruising would—"

"Yes, yes, I know all about it," Kimberly said. "And elevated, too. If I'd kept it iced and elevated like a good girl, my boo-boo would all be gone. Thank you, Dr. Healey."

There was a sudden resonant outburst from the nearby table, like the squawk of a very large woodwind instrument. It must have been the old woman, for she had both hands covering her mouth now, and she was shaking with laughter. It must have been something the baby had done, since the other three were all looking at the little girl and smiling. Kimberly turned around and looked behind her, and the old woman must have noticed.

"Oh, beg your pardon over there," she called out to Kimberly. "I've gone and disturbed your family. Sorry, honey, me and my big mouth. I just get so tickled at my little grandbaby, I can't help it. But I see you got you a little missy of your own there, so you probably know exactly what I mean. It's been so long since Joe Leonard here was a baby that I keep forgettin' how *comical* little folks can be without even tryin'!" She emitted another reedy honk of laughter.

Bruce noticed that the boy tucked his hands under him and sat forward, his head down. He might look different in a lot of ways from the average teenager nowadays, but he evidently felt the same as every other young person down through the ages when an older relative does something embarrassing in public. The younger woman was busy with the baby's mouth now, wetting a napkin in her glass of water and wiping off what looked like chocolate icing.

But the old woman wasn't stopping. "Aren't babies just the limit when it comes to gettin' their dinner all over theirself? Does yours do that like our Rosemary Jean does?" Without pausing for an answer, she went right on. "I keep tellin' Jewel—that's my daughter here settin' by me—that we oughta carry one of them big tin wash buckets around with us so's we can hose her down every time she puts something in her mouth, or *around* her mouth I should say, seein' as how most of it never makes it inside!"

Her daughter patted the old woman's hand and said something, at which time the others appeared to start getting ready to leave. The boy pushed his chair back, though he still sat on his hands. He was smiling, though, Bruce noticed, even though he was still looking down, so at least he must be able to see the humor in it all. The man helped his wife into her coat and then picked up the baby. Right before standing up, the boy reached for his napkin and wiped his mouth in a careful circle, no doubt worried that his grandmother might start a discourse on the state of his mouth, too. Then he pulled out his grandmother's chair and helped her arrange an enormous cape around her shoulders.

As the family filed by Bruce and Kimberly's table, Bruce took a good look at the baby, who, he was pleased to notice, couldn't hold a candle to Madison in the looks department. The old woman, who was bringing up the rear, stopped by their table and said jovially, "Well, I hope you folks enjoy your supper as much as we did. It's my son-in-law's birthday, you see, and we came here to celebrate, even though Jewel was originally plannin' to make him his favorite meal of pork chops and fried onion rings at home, but Willard said no, no, no, he didn't want her slavin' in the hot kitchen, so he brought us all here, and lo and behold, when they found out it was his birthday, why, they brought out the prettiest little chocolate cake you ever did see for all of us to share at the end, so if you ever have you a birthday, be sure and tell 'em, and you'll get you a good meal and some free birthday cake to boot!"

She glanced up toward the front door. "Oh, Jewel's wavin' me to come on, so I better go so's we can get my grandbaby in bed. Little folks shouldn't be up too late, you know." She cut her eyes over at Madison, who was staring up at her with the fascination she usually reserved for semitrucks and police cars. "You sure are a pretty little missy," she said.

"Why, you're pretty as a china doll!" And she smiled down at Madison, one quick beam of scary intensity, then turned and moved away slowly.

"Thank you," Bruce managed to say as she lumbered off. He wondered what kind of ratio that was, his two words to her . . . how many? A hundred? Two hundred? His mind, usually so nimble when it came to imagining what kind of girl an older woman had been in her youth, was absolutely paralyzed. He couldn't begin to come up with even an inkling of an idea. Before tonight he had been so sure he had met every kind of woman there was, but here was one in a league of her own.

The old woman's son-in-law was standing by the door waiting to receive her, a patient smile on his round face.

"She walks kind of like you do these days," Bruce said to Kimberly. "She's got the waddle down pat—just needs to work a little on the limp."

"Thank you very much," Kimberly said. "At least you didn't say she *talks* like me. Then I'd really be mad." Madison was still staring at the woman's back. It made Bruce think of the time they had gone to a circus in Greenville and Madison had seen a real elephant up close.

All of a sudden the waitress was there again, placing their drinks on the table. She was sixty if she was a day, with hair that was unnaturally black, lips too carefully outlined with red, and dark penciled eyebrows. Along with her black uniform and sheer white frilly apron, she had on a little cap like nurses wore and squeaky rubber-soled shoes. The clothes didn't match the face—she looked like somebody who had come to a costume party as a waitress. One look at her face and Bruce could see this woman had led a hard life.

He glanced back to the door and saw that the old woman was finally exiting. Right before the door swung shut behind her, she looked back into the restaurant and gave a gracious little nod, as if leaving a stage amid wild applause.

Bruce gave his head a single brisk shake. He briefly considered the possibility that the woman could have been putting on. Maybe she liked to act that way to see what kind of response she would get from people. The whole family could be in on it. Well, if that was the case, they had gotten about as much response from him and Kimberly as from a couple of tree stumps. Maybe they were all laughing about it right now in the car on their way home.

He heard Kimberly giving her order to the waitress and tried to turn his attention to the menu. But all he could think of was the old woman.

What had she been *wearing* under that cape? Was it something big and purple? Or was he getting her mixed up with the calliope over by the wall? She did have on big red earrings, he remembered that, so surely she hadn't been wearing a purple dress. And her shoes—they had squeaked, hadn't they? Or was he thinking of the waitress's shoes?

Suddenly he sensed a long pause and felt Kimberly nudge his foot under the table. "You'll have to excuse him," she said to the waitress. "He turned forty today. I think he's having trouble accepting it."

Well, he wasn't about to let any over-the-hill waitress think he was brooding over turning forty. "I'll take the sirloin," he said, looking up with a smile. "Medium rare," he added, and as he started to say, "baked potato with butter and sour cream," he remembered all of a sudden exactly where he had seen the old woman's son-in-law before.

It was at the library—the Derby Public Library. The man worked there. Maybe he was even the one in charge. Bruce did remember now that the man—Willard, the old lady had called him—had ordered a new collection of children's plays for him two years ago when he first started the after-school drama club at Berea Middle School.

The waitress cleared her throat. "Baked potato, fries, or rice, sir?"

"Yes," he said.

Kimberly laughed. "Sure, bring him all three. The birthday boy can have whatever he wants."

"Just kidding," Bruce said. "I want a baked potato with butter and sour cream." And then before the waitress could ask, he added, "And honey mustard dressing on my salad. On the side, please." She gathered up the menus, a little smirk of a smile on her face as she looked Bruce right in the eye, as if to say, "I know your type, sweetheart, all tensed up and preoccupied. I'd sure like to help loosen you up."

Well, Bruce knew her type, too—he could tell her more about herself than she could. And he knew exactly what she had been like as a girl, too—the kind with a reputation among all the football players. He wondered if she had told her name while he had been daydreaming. No doubt it ended with an *i*—Tawni or Nikki or Brandi. He closed his eyes briefly and scolded himself. He used to be so proud of the fact that he never stereotyped people, especially women.

The waitress left, and Kimberly unwrapped two crackers for Madison. "Hey, you're okay, aren't you, Bruce?" she said slowly. "You're not back into drugs again, are you?" She laughed. She sometimes poked fun at Bruce, but usually kindly, about his new standards of behavior since he'd "turned religious," as she called it. "You're sure not the wild big brother I used to have," she had said more than once. She stopped laughing now and grew serious. "No, I mean, really—you're not worried about anything, are you, Bruce?"

"Me? Worried?" He shook his head. "Naah, I'm just hungry is all. It is almost seven, you know."

"Yeah, I know." She started playing with the cellophane wrapper from the crackers. They both watched Madison for a little while, bent over her place mat and coloring furiously, changing crayons frequently and pausing every now and then to enlighten them as to what she was drawing right on top of all the other already-printed pictures: "Unca Buce," "titty tat," "bunny wabbit," and so forth. Bruce thought it must be a sign of intelligence and creativity that she preferred drawing her own pictures, such as they were, instead of wasting her time coloring somebody else's.

When she pointed to a red squiggle and said, "Dack," he glanced at Kimberly and they smiled. "Dack" was the jack-o'-lantern Bruce had made for her. It was sad, Bruce thought, that it wasn't until after the jack-o'-lantern that she thought to add "Daddy" to her place mat. He wondered how Matt would like it if he knew he came in after a pumpkin in order of importance in his daughter's life.

As the waitress came back with their salads and a dish of applesauce for Madison, Bruce realized again how they must look—the three of them sitting at the table together like the well-adjusted all-American family: daddy, mommy, baby, and another one on the way. He was suddenly filled with an unspeakable sadness that he was sitting here instead of Matt, that it was Kimberly instead of somebody else who was with him—not that he had any specific names, but just somebody else, somebody who was his wife, not his sister. And Madison, beautiful funny smart little Madison, would always be only his niece, never his own daughter.

He thought back to the family who had left a minute ago. How was it that a tub of a man like Willard whatever-his-name-was could get married and have a kid and look absolutely pleased with life, while he, Bruce Healey, who had always had his pick of girls, was still single and not getting any younger? How had it happened that he had been alive forty whole years already and was living in his sister's basement, eating pathetic meals every night and watching movies on his VCR to make up for the life he didn't have? He looked down at his tossed salad and wondered how he could get through the next couple of hours until bedtime.

"Happy birthday to you; happy birthday to you," Kimberly started singing before the waitress had even taken two steps away from their table. Madison lifted her head and looked back and forth between Kimberly and him, a yellow crayon poised in midair. "Happy birthday, dear Brucie; happy birthday to you!" Kimberly finished.

Madison dropped the crayon and clapped her hands. "Birfday!" she said.

Bruce looked at his sister's bright face. He saw Madison's dark eyes sparkling and thought of the hymn they had sung at church on Promotion Sunday back in September when all the children came forward and stood up front to be officially assigned to their new Sunday school classes. "When he cometh, when he cometh to make up his jewels," the song started. "All his jewels, precious jewels, his loved and his own." Jewel— wasn't that what the old woman had called her daughter? What a nice name for a woman.

They hadn't sung the song before, nor since, but it had stuck with Bruce. Little children—it would be hard to think of them as "precious jewels" if you only mingled with middle schoolers all day every day. But he had Madison to remind him of how they started out—sweet and innocent and trusting. So full of awe at anything new, which was almost everything. Soaking up your love like little sponges, then pouring it back to you so generously. Madison was smiling at him now, laughing actually, her little white teeth all lined up like beads on a bracelet.

Okay, you can do this, Bruce told himself. You can rise above yourself and act happy for their sake. He smiled and bobbed his head several times, as if to a whole roomful of well-wishers. "You're really wanting to make sure they bring us one of those free cakes, aren't you?" he said to Kimberly.

The waitress heard him, for she said, "I've already told 'em in the back we got another birthday." She jerked her head in the direction of the table where the old woman and her family had sat. "People over *there* had one, too." She gave a little sigh, as if the people over there had worn her out.

Though he wasn't sure why he asked it, Bruce said, "Do you know how old the guy was?"

The waitress narrowed her eyes and appeared to be thinking hard. "Nope," she said, shaking her head, "but I'd say several years older than you, for sure." She raised her dark eyebrows and winked at him before leaving again.

Bruce was mortified. Now without a doubt she was convinced that he was all stressed out over his age. Which he wasn't! He definitely wasn't.

Kimberly had already gotten a good start on her salad, Bruce noticed, and Madison had abandoned her place mat and crayons in favor of the applesauce. Whereas all her playing was done with great exuberance, she had grown into a curiously tidy little eater. He watched her fill her spoon with applesauce and carefully lift it to her mouth.

Bruce picked up his little cup of honey mustard dressing and drizzled it over his salad. "Forty years old—just think," he said. There, if he talked about it openly, Kimberly would see how unbothered he was by his age. "I think it's a great age. You've gotten over trying to impress people, so you can focus now on what's really important."

"Yeah, in the few short years left," Kimberly said. She daintily picked a slice of cucumber from her salad bowl and popped it into her mouth, then munched contentedly, careful not to make eye contact with Bruce. He had often wondered how he would view Kimberly if she were somebody else's sister instead of his. Would he have been attracted to her, say, if she had been another single teacher at Berea Middle School when he started teaching there a couple of years ago? Probably not right then, not after what he'd just been through with that other woman in Montgomery, but how about later?

Kimberly had a lot going for her. Maybe she was a little undisciplined in some ways, but she was very funny and very big-hearted and very good-looking in spite of her extra weight right now.

"Hey, I just thought of something," Kimberly said. "Wasn't Daddy around forty when he ran in the Memphis Marathon that year? Wasn't that the picture Mom always kept on her nightstand?"

It was true. Bruce had a fairly distinct memory of it, though he had been only five at the time. Kimberly hadn't been born yet, but somehow she knew her father's history better than any of them.

They had made a family vacation out of it, or tried to. Suzanne, who had been fifteen, had pouted all the way to Memphis and back because she was missing some party somebody was giving back home in Missis-sippi. She had complained about everything he did in the backseat, had even kicked him once when he was clicking two Popsicle sticks together, making harmless little noises.

He still remembered her bare foot, with its bright red toenails, swinging suddenly out of nowhere and landing a good one on his leg. And though he was only five and the kick was entirely unjustified in his thinking, he hadn't set up a wail about it, which must have stirred Suzanne to remorse, for she had immediately handed him a Milky Way candy bar and put a finger to her lips so he wouldn't tell. Even at five, he knew she was talking about the kick not the candy, and he had kept quiet about both. Already he was learning some important things about getting along with women.

"He was something, wasn't he?" Kimberly said.

Bruce nodded. "They both were." Poor Kimbo, she had been only eleven when their father had died. She had worshiped him, had cried for weeks after the funeral.

It was a subject Bruce never brought up—his parents—though Kimberly was always looking for opportunities to do so, always trying to analyze what went wrong and why. For Bruce it was a subject that opened up too many *if only*s and never led to anything productive.

What went wrong was very simple—his father had gotten cancer in his early fifties, had wasted away over the course of three horrible years, and had died an agonizing death at fifty-six, after which his mother had simply given up and willed herself to join him. At eleven, Kimberly had suffered more than any of them, for she had not only lost her father but her mother, also, whose emotional erosion began the day her husband died but dragged out over the next seventeen years.

The why of his father's death had been an awful question to wrestle with, the kind of question there's no answer for. Added to the enormous unfairness of it all, when his father had been such an all-round great guy—virile, handsome, strong, friendly, could pick up anything and do it well—was the ugly guilt that still reared its head during weak moments, even though Bruce knew in his heart that God's river of grace was broad and deep enough to carry away even that. *If only I had been there that last day to say good-bye*—that was the biggest *if only* concerning his father, the one that invariably started thrashing around inside his head at the very mention of his father's death.

And he could so easily have been there. That was the part that gnawed at his soul. His mother had called him that morning, had told him his father probably wouldn't last the day. She had said it before, had urged him home on numerous occasions, but she sounded different this time, more desperate and sure. He had started up Highway 49 from Jackson, meaning to go straight home. It was his senior year at Jackson State, with only three weeks of classes left before graduation. He had dinked around for four years, but, as he liked to tell it, he had perfected the art of dinking to the point that he could still pull a B average.

If he had just kept his eyes on the road driving through the town of Belzoni, maybe the impulse to wander wouldn't have struck. Maybe he would have made it all the way up to the junction of Highway 82, where he would have turned west at Indianola and headed home. But he didn't do that. Instead, he slowed down going through Belzoni, which was wise, considering the fact that he had already gotten two speeding tickets in towns along Highway 49. But approaching the Phillips 66 gas station, he had slowed down even more, had in fact turned in to get gas even though he still had half a tank.

And she was there, as he had figured she would be. The only woman he had ever known named Fiona. He had loved to say it when he first met her at Jackson State their freshman year—"Fiona from Belzoni." That's how he had introduced her to everybody when they went out, which was an off-and-on thing practically all year. She had had a jillion boyfriends herself, so it didn't bother her that Bruce came and went.

She was almost engaged to somebody back home, she had told them all, but she sure didn't act like it. She meant to have fun, she said, since this was her only year for college. Her daddy ran a Phillips 66 gas station in Belzoni, she said, and she was taking it over next year after she took a couple of classes in business management and computers and accounting. She had a raspy voice that always sounded like the onset of laryngitis and a faceful of freckles you could play dot-to-dot with. Not your typical southern belle.

She was behind the counter when he went in to pay for his gas that day, a ball cap on and a pencil behind her ear. She still wore no makeup, not even a tinge of lipstick. Her shirt had a streak of grease across the pocket, right under the little name patch with Fiona stitched in cursive. But somehow she struck Bruce at that moment as the most beautiful girl he had seen in a long time.

She had grinned at him right off, spoken his name in her same old friendly unpretentious way. "Hey there, Bruce Healey. I always knew some-day you'd come walking through that door." A few months later in a movie theater, he would recall those words when he heard Marian say almost the exact same thing to Indiana Jones in *Raiders of the Lost Ark*.

"So you're a fortune teller," Bruce had said, laughing. "Well, here I am. Got a coffee break coming up anytime soon?"

The coffee break had stretched into a lot more than just coffee back at her apartment. The engagement with the hometown guy hadn't worked out, she had told him, though there were signs everywhere in her apartment that a man spent a lot of time there. She had told Bruce to stop again on his way through sometime, and he had said he would.

Back on the road again, he was surprised when he looked at his watch and found he had spent almost two hours in Belzoni. Maybe on another trip he would have stopped again to see Fiona if he hadn't found, upon arriving at home that day, that his father had died an hour earlier and had been asking for him at the end.

So you make a selfish choice and for the rest of your life, you regret it. And every time you hear the word *father*, you feel like crud. You never bring up the subject yourself, and you try to evade it whenever someone else does, but you make sure it's never far from your mind by choosing, perversely, to wear your father's wedding ring, so that every time you look at your right hand, you'll see it and be reminded of the heavy price you have to pay and keep on paying for a thoughtless spree.

Not that the wedding ring had served to alter his behavior all that much—he had still spent way too much time on women after that—but at least it had made a difference when his grandmother had called three years ago from the Magnolia Lane Home and said his mother was failing and wasn't expected to live.

He had been teaching in Montgomery at the time and had gotten in his pickup truck in the middle of the day and driven straight through Alabama and Mississippi, zipping past towns all along the way where he knew all kinds of girls—Selma, Demopolis, Meridian, Jackson. He had gone by way of Vicksburg this time so as to avoid Belzoni, taking Highway 61 north instead of Highway 49, and he had arrived at his mother's bedside in time to feel the squeeze of her hand, which was quite strong for a woman who was dying, to see her eyes flutter open as she felt the gold wedding band on his finger, and to hear her utter one word: "Donald." Not *his* name, of course, but the name of his father, whose death had extinguished her in every important way. She had breathed for seventeen years after he died, but she had not really lived.

"You think you could run a marathon?" Kimberly asked him now. "We'd come cheer for Uncle Bruce, wouldn't we, Maddy?" He saw that his steak was now sitting before him, his salad pushed over to the side. He was holding a steak knife in his right hand, which he didn't remember picking up.

Madison was squeezing a puffy roll in one hand. She waved it around, then took a big bite and chortled something that neither of them could understand except that it ended with "Unca Buce!"

A marathon. Now there was an idea. Though jogging had never appealed to him, maybe he should pick it up. Maybe sometime this next year, before he turned forty-one, he could enter a big race as his father had done. That's what he needed: a goal. He thought of the verses he had read in his Bible the night before, where Paul had talked about enduring affliction, fighting the good fight, finishing his course.

He looked at Kimberly across the table and smiled. "A marathon!" he said, raising a finger as if suddenly seizing on a brilliant idea. " 'I shall run that I may obtain!' " Though Kimberly could pick up on most of his movie quotes, he knew she'd never recognize one from the Bible.

Kimberly smashed up part of her baked potato and placed it on a saucer in front of Madison. "Isn't Uncle Brucie a funny man?" she said. "A funny *old* man?"

"Well, that makes me feel better," he said. "On the way here you said I *wasn't* funny, and I've been worrying about it ever since."

As he placed a bite of steak in his mouth, he imagined himself and a hundred other runners gathered at the starting line, poised for the gunshot. He saw himself move quickly into the lead, round a curve, and leave everyone else far behind. He wondered what it would be like if somewhere along the course someone would snap a picture of him, then put it in a frame and keep it on her nightstand.

31

Mount Pisgah's Lofty Height

At first Bruce worked the sound into his dream. A steady *thwump thwump thwump* like a heavyweight sparring with a punching bag. The dream was nothing that would hold together as a story, as usual, but a crazy mélange of people, places, and things. Just once he would like to have a plot in one of his dreams, some single obstacle to overcome, followed by a logical sequence of events that led to a triumph. Instead, his dreams were mostly composed of many obstacles, one after the other, against which he struggled mightily but never prevailed.

Such as with the punching bag, which was actually nothing more than a gigantic roll of paper towels stamped with green cats. Though it didn't weigh much, it kept swinging back and knocking him down, so that only every other thwump represented him landing a punch. The alternating thwumps were him getting hit by the paper towels, which didn't seem to be fastened to anything, but bounced around and came at him from all directions. *Thwump, thwump, thwump, thwump* . . . the sounds stopped for a moment, and in his dream Bruce crawled across the floor, sweating profusely, toward a tiny doorway to escape.

Then again, *thwump, thwump, thwump!* He squeezed himself through the door and suddenly found himself in the middle of a steamy jungle, right in the path of a . . . he couldn't really tell what it was except that it was wearing a gray cape and had two huge legs like Doric columns coming straight for him. He was on the ground, unable to advance through the dense tangle of undergrowth, but whatever it was bearing down on him was plowing through the trees and vines as if they were mere grass clippings, calling out, "A good meal and free birthday cake to boot!"

He was scrambling around on all fours, trying to find a way out, when all of a sudden the sounds stopped again and he was sliding down a slippery mudbank into a murky jungle river. Little heads were poking up above the water all around him—shriveled jack-o'-lantern heads with little fiery orange tongues flicking in and out. He tried to climb up the bank, but it was too slick. So he took a deep breath, dove down into the dark waters . . .

Which led to a huge underground tunnel where marathon runners were lined up behind a rotund bass drummer with a tall red plume on his helmet. *Thwump, thwump, thwump* went the bass drum. "Ready, set, go!" called the bass drummer. The echo was tremendous, a hundred times worse than thunder, and Bruce clapped his hands over his ears. It was hot in the tunnel, and he found it hard to breathe.

The runners, who filled the entire width of the tunnel, were running straight at him. He was destined to be trampled if he didn't get up off the floor and do something fast. Suddenly it came to him. He would join the race!

Thwump, thwump, thwump—they were coming closer. He stood up to meet them but saw the lead runner's mouth fall open as a look of loathing filled his eyes. The whole group came to a dead standstill and stared at him, many of them turning their heads away in disgust. Catlike snarls and hisses rose from their ranks. Then Bruce understood—he wasn't wearing the right clothes! Slowly he let his eyes travel down to see what he was wearing. . . .

And saw that he was absolutely stark naked. And his body, which he actually used to be quite proud of, looked . . . well, downright paunchy. The thought came to him that he really *did* need to start training for a marathon, and very soon.

Mortified, he turned to flee but could get no traction on the floor, which was covered with marbles. He heard boos and jeers behind him, then *thwump, thwump, thwump.* He realized with horror that the runners were throwing food at him—rotten apples, cans of corn beef hash, styrofoam cartons of leftover spaghetti.

He opened his mouth to yell . . . and woke up. He lay absolutely still for several long seconds, absorbing the fact that he was in his own bed, that the covers were all bunched up around his feet somewhere, and that the sun looked very bright behind the closed blinds.

Though he generally couldn't remember anything specific about his dreams, only that he had wrestled all night and come out the big loser, today was one of those unusual days when everything came back to him in vivid detail. At least he didn't take his dreams too seriously, didn't try to dissect them for symbolism.

As he lay there thinking about the paper towels and the jack-o'-lanterns in the river and the bass drummer, he remembered something he had heard a professor say long ago in some course at Jackson State. This professor had said people who dreamed in color usually had high IQs. Funny that he couldn't even remember what course it was, but he distinctly remembered this off-the-cuff tidbit shared by a professor who wore a bad toupee.

Thwump, thwump, thwump. There it was again, but this time it wasn't in a dream. It was coming from somewhere outdoors. He got out of bed and walked over to the window beside his desk. When he opened the blinds, he saw that the sun was already quite high in the sky. He glanced down at the old windup alarm clock on the desk. Ten-fifteen—he could hardly believe he had slept so late. For him, sleeping in on Saturday usually meant eight o'clock at the latest.

Thwump. There was nothing in the backyard that he could see, but when he stood over to the side and looked toward the Stewarts' backyard, the mystery was solved. Patsy Stewart had a double clothesline on the far side of their lot, and though Bruce had never seen any clothes hanging on it, he saw that something quite large was now draped over it—something dark and heavy like a rug. And Celia was beating on it for all she was worth.

He closed his eyes tight, then opened them again. No doubt about it, she was definitely beating a rug with what looked like a broom. Isn't that what women used to do in lieu of carpet cleaning? He was pretty sure he had seen his grandmother do it when he was a boy. How in the world had a little person like Celia gotten that big rug out there by herself? How could she have spread all that bulk out on top of the clothesline? Maybe it wasn't a rug after all. Maybe it was a big bedspread or blanket or something.

He squinted but it didn't help. Everything looked a little blurry around the edges—Celia, the clothesline, the rug or whatever it was, even the trees. The other teachers at school had teased him last week about turning forty, telling him his body would start falling apart now. And he didn't doubt it one bit. He had already seen signs of deterioration. He was sure, for instance, that his eyesight wasn't what it used to be.

Without even thinking about what he was doing and how it would look if anyone saw him, he walked to the living room and picked up the old pair of World War I binoculars and brought them back to the bedroom window. He stood right up next to the blinds and adjusted the binoculars until Celia came into clear focus. Her hair was pulled back behind her ears with a headband, and her mouth was set in a straight line. She held the broom like a baseball bat as she swung it over and over. He couldn't help wondering if she had ever been on a softball team. If so, he pitied the poor pitcher, trying to hit such a small strike zone.

Yes, it did appear to be a rug, but not a big bulky one. This one looked like one of those woven cotton rugs, and with the binoculars he could even see the colors—maroon, tan, and olive. He tried to remember if it was from her living room, but he couldn't form a picture of what covered her floor, though he was sure he had looked right at it several times.

His bedroom had two windows, and he moved to the side one now for an even better view. This was the window closest to the Stewarts' driveway, the one through which he often saw Celia come and go. She was rearranging the rug now, pulling it over a little more, then lighting into it again with the broom. She stopped and walked around to the other side, then started in again on that side, whapping it over and over with the flat side of the broom. Bruce couldn't see any big clouds of dust flying out, so he wondered why she didn't just stop and call it a job well done.

But now it looked like she was trying to turn the rug over. She propped the broom against the clothesline pole, then set about very systematically folding the rug back from one end until it was doubled, sliding it over and folding it back a little more until she had it all spread out with the underside on top.

Bruce studied her face again as she picked up the broom to start a new round of beating. He saw her examine the ends of the broom straws first, plucking off . . . what? Stray bits of grass? Rug fibers? She reached up to her forehead and tucked a wisp of hair back under her headband, then positioned herself again like a batter at the plate and lit into the rug anew. What a serious, methodical little person she was. He wondered what she did for fun. He knew she played tennis, but did she consider it fun, or did she approach it like a job?

He watched her move back and forth, top to bottom, pounding each square inch on one side, then coming around to do the other side. Now her back was toward the window as she raised the broom once more. He wondered if she ever had dreams like the ones he had just had, if she ever woke up in a sweat. Did a person like her ever feel as unworthy as he did when he loosed his hold on the concept of God's grace and let his mind dwell too long on the things he had done in the past? No, she probably had no guilt, no regrets about past relationships with men.

He wondered if she had even had any past relationships with men. What kind of man would succeed at getting through that prickly hedge of . . . he thought for a moment and came up with the term *moody arrogance.* Surely men had tried before him. After all, she was very pretty—looked sort of like the actress Meg Ryan, only smaller and with sadder eyes. He was certain somebody with her looks would have been pursued by lots of men.

So what kinds of encounters with men did she have in her background that would make her still single? Had she ever given anybody half a chance, or had she told them all to buzz off at the first sign of interest? He doubted that she was forty yet. Milton Stewart had told him earlier this year that Patsy figured her for midthirties. Nope, she'd never been married as far as he knew, Milton had said. Yep, she used to keep company with a right smart number of men, but none of them must have panned out. Seemed like she mostly stuck to herself lately. You can say that again, Bruce had almost said. He couldn't imagine what it would take to scrabble up the side of *that* mountain. He sure had no intention himself of ever trying again.

He wondered, though, if she ever thought about being married, ever considered, as he had started doing recently, what a nice thing it might be to have a family of her own. He recalled a line from the video Kimberly had given him for his birthday two days ago—a movie, coincidentally, in which Meg Ryan starred. It was one he hadn't seen in the theater when it first came out. Videos were one of Kimberly's favorite things to give him for birthdays and Christmases, mainly because they made easy gifts and she knew how much he liked movies. The only problem was that she sometimes forgot what she had already given him and repeated herself. Another slight problem was that she usually gave him movies *she* really liked, which didn't always translate into movies he wanted in his collection, in which case he could simply slip them into her video cabinet after a couple of months, and she would think they were hers. If she accidentally gave him a duplicate copy of something, he could always take it back and exchange it for something he really wanted. That's how he had added *Empire of the Sun* to his collection last Christmas and *Room With a View* the year before. He didn't collect movies just for the pleasure of possession, just to see the number grow. When he selected a new video to buy, it was because he wanted to watch it over and over.

He still wasn't sure whether he'd keep Kimberly's most recent gift in his collection, but he had watched it twice in succession last night and had actually enjoyed it both times. Which didn't necessarily mean automatic acceptance, though. Sometimes a movie could sustain multiple satisfactory viewings but still wouldn't be something he wanted to own for the rest of his life.

"It's easier to get killed by a terrorist than to find a husband after the age of forty." That was the line from the movie that he thought about now as he watched Celia pounding away at the rug. He wondered if she had seen the movie, and if so, if she had laughed at the line. And if she had laughed, had it been because she thought it was truly funny and ridiculous or because she was covering up for the little nagging worry that it might be true? For that matter, was *he* trying to cover up a worry of his own when he laughed at it? Could it apply to finding a wife as well as a husband?

Of course, the reference to terrorists wasn't as funny in the post-9/11 years as it probably was when the movie first came out. *Sleepless in Seattle*— that was the name of it, and though the whole plot was highly improbable, there was a gem of a scene midway through that had made him laugh out loud, when a woman was summarizing the plot of an old Cary Grant-Deborah Kerr movie and she got so emotional she started crying about the heroine's crippled legs. The two men listening to her followed up with a merciless satire, pretending to weep and blow their noses as they talked about *The Dirty Dozen*.

Celia stopped beating the rug all of a sudden and whirled around to look behind her. It looked, in fact, as if she were staring directly at Bruce's bedroom window, the one where he now stood in his underwear and T-shirt aiming a pair of binoculars at her. He stepped back quickly. Thankfully, he hadn't raised the blinds. What would Celia say if she saw him spying on her? What in the world had he been thinking? True, it wasn't quite the same as a peeping-tom situation, with him inside and her outside, but she might not catch the difference.

He knew she couldn't see him from where she was, but it was still unnerving the way she was staring in his direction. When she raised her hand and waved, he was totally mystified until he heard voices and saw Kimberly and Madison come into view right in front of his window. Kimberly was holding Maddy's hand, and the two of them were walking slowly down the Stewarts' driveway toward their backyard. "She saw you from upstairs," Kimberly called to Celia, "and wanted to come say hello."

And wonder of wonders, Celia put her broom down and started walking toward them, saying something as she came. Bruce wished he could tell what it was. She was facing into the sun, and she put up a hand to shield her eyes. Madison was waving both hands at her now. "Cela!" he heard her cry. It was odd that Madison had taken so readily to somebody as standoffish as Celia, but she had.

The three of them met right beside Celia's Mustang, and Celia stooped down and took both of Maddy's little hands in her own, or, more accurately, let Maddy take hold of *hers*. She said something else, just to Madison this time, and even though it was clear that Maddy was the instigator in all this, Celia still smiled down at her and allowed herself to be pulled around in a circle. Watching the two of them, he wondered if Celia ever wished she had a beautiful little girl of her own.

He sometimes suspected there were single women who, if they had to pick, would far rather have a child than a husband. Even with all the hassle that accompanied children—all the diapers, the lost sleep, the crying fits, the terrible twos and later the torturous teens, not to mention the whole horrible childbirth thing before you even got them home—they were still "a ton less trouble than men," according to Suzanne. Even with two divorces under her belt, though, his big sister wasn't as jaded as she liked to put on. She still went out with men regularly and quite hopefully, too, always looking for one, as she had once told Bruce, "as nice as you and Daddy."

So that line in the movie about a woman over the age of forty finding a husband—the real pity it was most likely hinting at was being childless rather than husbandless. Even though a lot of women today wouldn't hesitate to have a baby without a husband, Bruce knew a husband was still a desirable accessory for most women with children. Like a medal you win and then stick in a drawer somewhere.

But Celia hadn't let down her guard too long, he noticed now. Already she was backing away from Madison and Kimberly, still smiling though, even waving politely and saying something else to Madison—maybe something like "Well, it's been nice, honey, but I've got a schedule to keep. I've got to get back to flailing the living daylights out of my rug."

Bruce turned from the window and took the binoculars back to the living room. The empty cover of the new video was sitting on the sofa. Even if *Sleepless in Seattle* ended up in Kimberly's collection like several others she had given him—such as *Enchanted April* and *Out of Africa,* to name a couple—he still wanted to go back and watch that one scene another time or two before taking it upstairs. He walked over to the VCR and ejected the video, then slipped it back into the cover and put it on the bottom shelf of the bookcase next to the television, where he usually put newcomers and rentals. All the others, the ones that had been officially accepted into his collection, were in alphabetical order on the upper shelves.

He stood there, scanning all the titles he owned. He wondered what kinds of movies Celia liked, if she had favorites that she watched over and over. He sincerely doubted that she had seen *The Untouchables* and *Hunt for Red October* as many times as he had, but there had to be some in his collection that she really liked, maybe something like *Casablanca* or *Rear Window.* Maybe *Pride and Prejudice*—he wondered if she had ever watched that one.

If he would ever ask her over for dinner and a movie, say—though it was a preposterous idea—which movie would he select for the cool and caustic Miss . . . Now wait a minute, this was funny. He wasn't even sure of her last name. He closed his eyes and tried to remember if Milton had told it to him at some point and he had merely forgotten. When he was younger, he used to be very bad about not bothering to learn girls' last names, though he noticed that girls always seemed to know a guy's last name.

He had known a girl once who told him she always said her first name aloud with the last name of any boy who asked her out, to see if they sounded right together. She would write them together several times, too, as if signing a check or a letter, and if they didn't fit together, she wouldn't waste her time. Bruce had laughed at her, told her she was mighty picky for somebody named Shannon Worm. That really was the girl's name; he remembered that one all right. Shannon *Worm*. But she had a perfectly logical explanation. She had put up with her last name for so long, she said, that she wasn't about to trade it in for another bummer.

He opened his eyes again and looked at his video collection. Maybe Celia didn't like movies—something that wasn't real. She had been a journalist, after all. Maybe she only watched documentaries. He remembered how suddenly angry she had become when he had mentioned the movie *The Cider House Rules* to her that night.

Maybe there was something in the movie that had touched a sore spot. He didn't own the movie, so he couldn't go back and watch it to try to figure it out. But maybe it wasn't the movie at all. Maybe she had simply reached her limit of social interaction for the day and wanted him out of her apartment.

Surely somebody like Celia wouldn't have that feeling he had discovered in some of his church friends, that moviegoing was bad. He remembered very clearly the discussion in Sunday school, almost a year ago now, when the topic had been something called Christian Liberty. Virgil Dunlop had been teaching the lesson that day. Bruce had heard of people who thought things like movies and dancing and smoking and swearing were wrong—people like the Amish and Quakers and ultraconservative Baptists—but he had never actually carried on conversations with any of them.

From what he could tell, the discussion in Sunday school hadn't really changed anybody's mind, but it seemed to make them all think more about why they did or didn't do certain things. A man named Lyman Maxwell had been the main spokesman against movies, a specific issue that came up toward the end of the lesson that day. His wife, a jolly white-haired woman everybody called Bugsy, interjected comments that didn't always make a whole lot of sense but did help to keep everybody in good spirits. Early in the discussion she stated that she had been to only one movie as a girl, and all she could remember about it was that a boy's britches fell down at school when he reached up to pull the map down.

Lyman forced a point on the basis of that comment by following up with "See? Out of a whole movie, she comes away with *that*. Movies put pictures in your mind you can't purge out, even after fifty years!"

Lyman's main argument, however, was that by attending movies, you were supporting Hollywood, which was a hotbed of corruption and the single biggest shaper of culture and attitudes in modern-day America.

"Things folks yawn at today when they see 'em on the screen woulda scorched their hair back in the fifties," Lyman said. "Them moviemakers are leading the whole country downhill a little bit at a time, and the Christians are tagging right along with 'em!"

"Well, that's what the ratings are for," another man said. "You can decide for yourself whether you want to go to an R-rated movie or to a PG. You get to pick—nobody forces you or tricks you into it. Just like you can choose whether to read a good book or a trashy one. Or go to a beer joint at night or to the Dairy Queen."

"But it's all Hollywood!" Lyman said. "You might pay your money to see something PG, but it all goes into the same pot! And besides that, even them PG movies got bad stuff slipped in here and there, real easy and underhanded so's you don't hardly notice it."

A soft-spoken woman Bruce had never heard say a word in any other Sunday school discussion raised her hand and leaned forward to say, "And people who see you in line to buy a ticket at the theater don't stop to find out whether you're going to a kiddie movie or something R-rated. They see you going to a movie, and it might be a stumbling block to a weaker brother."

Another woman spoke up. "Well, anything you do could be a stumbling block to *somebody*." She gave a huffy sigh. "I think there's people that go around *looking* for things to be offended at."

"Like those Boy Scouts that come around to the door selling candy bars and popcorn," Bugsy said. There was a silent pause as people weighed the analogy. Several laughed.

"Yeah, exactly like that, Bugsy!" somebody in the back said. This time everybody laughed.

Virgil Dunlop, standing at a podium in front, said, "I wonder, would it help anybody resolve the issue of movies if we asked ourselves each time, 'Will this make me more Christlike?' Or is that too rigid a standard for something that's supposed to be merely entertainment?"

"So we have different standards in our entertainment than our other activities?" This was from Virgil's wife, Joan.

"Well, I'm not saying we should," Virgil said, "but do we?" Nobody spoke for a moment. "I mean, okay, before you decide to drive to Atlanta for a Braves game," he continued, "does anybody say, 'How will this help me in my walk for Christ?' "

"I'm new to all this," Bruce said, "but that's a good question. *Does* anybody ask that?" He looked at Virgil. "Do *you?*"

"Way to pin me down in front of everybody, pal. Thanks a lot."

Bugsy's laughter rang out above everyone else's, louder and longer. "Cracker jack!" she said. Bruce thought maybe it was the mention of a ballgame that elicited that one.

"Or maybe we should approach it from the other angle," Virgil said. "Maybe we should ask, 'Will this make me *less* Christlike?' "

"If you want to see a movie bad enough," Lyman said, "you oughta wait till it comes on the TV. They clean 'em up for that."

"Or rent a video and watch it at home," the soft-spoken woman said. "That way you're doing it in private with only your conscience to answer to. You don't have to worry about anybody else seeing you and judging you one way or the other."

"But people see you go into a video store, too," Joan Dunlop said, "so I don't see the difference, really, if it's other people we're worried about. They might think you're sneaking in to rent an R-rated movie. I don't get the difference between watching it in private and watching it at a theater."

"I think it's sure a sad state of affairs when we have to plan our lives around how some other person is going to *judge* us." This was from a man in the front row.

"If your argument is against Hollywood as a whole," Bruce said, "I don't catch the thing about waiting till the movie is on TV or renting a video. Hollywood gets their cut of all that, too."

Virgil nodded. "Yes, you're still supporting Hollywood regardless of where you see the movie. Good point, Bruce."

Lyman Maxwell seemed to have no response to this.

"Missionaries could sure use more money," Bugsy said. "That little Schwartz couple in Argentina that lost their baby and had all them medical bills . . ."

Right then the bell rang indicating an end to the Sunday school period. But miraculously, Bugsy's last comment made perfect sense to Bruce, and before the closing prayer had ended, he had made a decision. Lest somebody judge him, though, it was going to be a private decision. He would have to see if he had what it took to stick by it. And for almost a whole year he had, though he had to admit it had been really tempting to cave in several times.

He had an envelope in his top desk drawer marked *Movie Money for Missionaries,* and every time he read a review or heard about a new movie he really wanted to see, one he knew he would have gone to see if he hadn't made his decision, he put the cost of a ticket into the envelope. Sometimes, if he didn't have the cash on hand, he wrote out an IOU for the amount and stuck it in the envelope instead. At Christmas he planned to total it all up and write out a check for the full amount, then put it in the offering at church and designate it for the mission fund.

He didn't know what he had proved exactly, except that he could make a decision and follow through. And for somebody who had gone to at least one movie a week for a good part of his life, it hadn't been easy. Of course, it wasn't like going cold turkey, because he still had his video collection, for which he had been very thankful as the months wore on.

It was funny, though, how different it was now, with his new way of looking at everything. He had found it harder and harder to watch certain movies and then be in the right frame of mind to read his Bible and pray before bedtime. After watching *The Godfather,* for example, there wasn't much of a chance he was going to transition smoothly into a sweet hour of prayer. He might try to pray on those nights, and try earnestly, but instead of being on Mount Pisgah's lofty height, he would feel like he was much farther south, in a hot, smoky, closed-up space from which his prayers couldn't find a way out.

And he wasn't sure whether he should be worried or not at the way all these hymns were taking over his thinking, springing up all over the place like dandelions, their little seeds blowing into all corners of his life the same way lines of movies used to do. And to think the only hymns he used to be familiar with were a few he had heard in movies. He would never forget his surprise when he looked through the alphabetical index of the old hymnbook out of curiosity the first time he visited Community Baptist with Virgil, checking for the hymn titles from the movie *Sergeant York*—the ones they sang in the little backwoods church in the early 1900s, where Alvin York's mother prayed for the soul of her wild son. And there they all were. "Beulah Land" and "When the Roll Is Called Up Yonder" and "The Sweet By and By."

In a way it grieved him to feel himself becoming critical of movies he had always loved so much, picking out little flaws here and there that had never bothered him before. Not *Sergeant York*—that was one he could imagine them showing at church maybe for July Fourth or Veteran's Day—but he was thinking of other titles in his collection. More than once he had come close to admitting that Lyman Maxwell and some of the others might have a point when they hinted at the powerful suggestions beneath the text of a movie, the insinuation into one's mind of certain attitudes, language, lifestyles, and so forth. He tried to make himself smile at their alarm over the "corrupting influence of Hollywood," but he couldn't always pull it off.

Not that he was about to give up something he enjoyed so much and something that was so good in so many ways. Not at all. He surely had no intention of becoming one of those extremists who avoided something altogether just because a certain part *had* been wrongly used. He couldn't help wondering, though, if over the years to come he might not pare down his collection even further, might become even more selective about admitting new titles.

He turned away from his bookcase now, from the collection of which he had always been so proud. At one time, and not too terribly long ago, he had considered changing over to a DVD player, which gave a much sharper picture, and he had actually checked to see which of his videos were available in DVD format, had made a list of them and stuck it somewhere, he couldn't remember where. Now it seemed like a big investment with very unreliable returns.

He walked down the hall back to his bedroom. He really ought to try to get something done before noon. He had some grades to record from the last couple of weeks, also a pile of laundry he really ought to tackle, as well as dirty dishes in the sink. But the thought of staying in his apartment on one of the few Saturdays in his favorite month was something he couldn't do. Giving up movies for a year, okay, he could handle that, but not spending a Saturday inside.

Pulling on a pair of jeans a minute later, he asked himself a question: So have I gained anything from a year of movie abstinence? Then another: Have I lost anything? These were questions to ponder, maybe in his truck on his way to the mountains a little later today. He did know one thing right now, though—that come Christmas, he would have somewhere close to four hundred dollars to put into the offering plate at church.

He glanced back out the window after he had put on his favorite sweatshirt—the one the drama kids had given him last year that said *TEACHERS ARE A CLASS ACT*—and saw Celia headed for her apartment, solemnly and slowly, carrying the neatly folded rug out in front of her.

Put a crown on it and she'd look like an attendant at a coronation. He watched her struggle a little to get the door open with her hands full, then lift an elbow to hold the screen while she eased inside backward. On her face was the look of someone who planned to spend the rest of the day indoors doing important things like reorganizing her spice rack or checking through all her clothes for loose buttons.

Again it struck Bruce that the two of them were as different as night and day. If he ever did find a woman, it could never be somebody as starched and trussed up as she was. A woman had to know how to let down and have a good laugh. "Maybe you could help her learn how to," he said out loud, then laughed. This was something he would never ever do again—try to help a woman become a different person. He had learned his lesson in Montgomery.

At the door of his bedroom, right before turning off the light, he thought about making his bed but talked himself out of it with an excuse the deceptive side of his brain often attempted on Saturdays: He would change the sheets later today. *Oh, sure you will,* his smarter schoolteacher side said.

32

Where No Tears Will Ever Fall

Nate Bianchi was only thirteen but almost as tall as Bruce and a good twenty pounds heavier, with jet-black hair parted smack down the middle and the hint of a mustache already shadowing his upper lip. With a different personality, the kid could be downright menacing, but as it was he was a marshmallow. Of all the Drama Club members, Nate was the least likely to stir things up, though Bruce could tell he secretly enjoyed seeing others do so, maybe even wished he had the courage to be a troublemaker himself.

"Hey, Nate, I want you to try something today," Bruce said to him after school two days later. Bruce was standing outside the music room, where they were still having their *A Midsummer Night's Dream* rehearsals. After Christmas they would be moving to the auditorium to practice on stage.

He had zipped out of his classroom right away today, counting on Nate being the first one to rehearsal, as he usually was. He knew that his speech, if it was going to have any success at all, would have a better chance if delivered to Nate in private rather than during rehearsal with the whole cast present. He moved away from the door to stand over by the band lockers, and so did Nate, the look on his face saying, "Please don't ask me to do something weird in front of everybody."

To a timid soul like Nate, the part of Bottom, the simpleminded weaver who imagines he is a donkey beloved by Titania, was already sorely trying. To make him utter lines such as "I must to the barber's, monsieur, for methinks I am marvellous hairy about the face" almost seemed cruel, though Bruce kept reminding himself of one important fact: The boy had not only joined the Drama Club voluntarily, as had all the others, but he had also auditioned specifically for the part of Bottom.

The name Bottom had been met with snorts of laughter and had quickly degenerated, as Bruce had known it would, into various vulgar synonyms, to which he had responded with a sigh and feigned weariness: "Middle school humor is so predictable. At least you could try something a little more sophisticated, like Posterior or Derriere. Or something scientific like Glutei." Thankfully, they had soon grown tired of the little game, probably because they had gotten no rise out of Nate.

Others had read Bottom's lines more expressively during tryouts, but after Bruce, with Elizabeth Landis's help, had shuffled the parts around so the strongest actors were given the biggest roles, the only reasonable match for Nate was Bottom. A big boy like him certainly wouldn't work out as Peaseblossom or one of the other woodland fairies.

And the very mention of fairies had also elicited plenty of wisecracks and giggles at first. Bruce had approached it all very matter-of-factly, however, suggesting that while some middle school students might be too immature to realize these were fairies in the folklore sense—miniature sprites like Tinker Bell and Tom Thumb who worked magic and pulled pranks—he was certain the seventh and eighth graders at Berea Middle School would be able to handle it. Surely they weren't so narrow-minded as to think that everything had always been the way it was today. So after Bruce had worked some magic of his own to soften them all up to the whole idea of Shakespeare, DeReese Pascoe—who had loudly declared early on, "I ain't bein' no *fairy*"—had soon embraced the coveted role of Puck. And Titus Oldenburg, who followed DeReese's lead in everything, was Oberon, king of the fairies.

Five years ago Bruce might have slung an arm around Nate's shoulder to talk to him, but he had stopped doing that after an ugly lawsuit four years earlier down in Montgomery, where a parent had accused a male teacher of touching her son inappropriately. It had been splashed all over the front page news for days and talked about in every teachers' lounge in the state of Alabama, not to mention in faculty meetings, where principals had been very pointed in their warnings about physical contact with students. Except for one small slipup, the time he had yanked that Hardy Biddle kid up off the floor over at the high school science fair— and thankfully nothing had come of that—Bruce had kept his hands to himself. He had learned more than one lesson about physical contact in Montgomery.

As was his custom now in delicate situations with students, Bruce put his hands in his pockets and looked down at the floor as he addressed Nate, facing him squarely but glancing up only for the briefest moments at well-timed pauses to assure the boy that he was indeed speaking directly to him but that he didn't want to make a big deal out of any of this. Bruce had very carefully planned what he was going to say to Nate, down to exact word choices.

"You've got one of my favorite roles in this whole play, you know," he started out. His first quick look at Nate's face told him the boy was listening closely. "Bottom is a magnificent character—not very bright, but so dignified in his own way and unshakable and good-hearted. Such a noble and likable character." Another glance. Nate was frowning a little, as if he wasn't sure he liked the idea of being not very bright but noble. Probably he was thinking of the way DeReese got to leap about the stage and say things like "Up and down, up and down, I will lead them up and down" and "What fools these mortals be," while he, Nate, had to lumber about and *be* one of the mortal fools, with lines like "O night, O night! alack, alack, alack" and "Thus die I, thus, thus, thus."

"Yet so *funny* in his own way," Bruce continued. "One of the best comic roles in all of Shakespeare. I can't imagine this play without the character of Bottom. It would lose so much of its . . . vim and vibrancy." Though he pretended to be speaking spontaneously, this was all carefully scripted. Bruce liked the sound of *vim and vibrancy*, and besides that, he was attempting a little flattery by suggesting that he was sure Nate had not only heard of those words but also actually knew what they meant. And he *was* sure—Nate was a smart boy. His lowest test grade so far in Life Science had been ninety-eight percent.

No response from Nate now, but none was called for. His lips were firmly pressed together, his black eyes unreadable as he waited to see where this was headed. Bruce even wondered if maybe the boy knew he was playacting, that every word was premeditated. Maybe he was standing there thinking, "Ooh, way to go, Mr. Healey, I'm exceedingly impressed with *vim* and *vibrancy.*"

Bruce forged ahead. "Bottom is a key figure in two of the three plots in the play, but no doubt you already know that." And it was true. Bruce knew Nate probably had a better overall view of the play than anybody else in the cast. For starters, he had clearly been paying attention the day Bruce had introduced the storyline and characters of the play, the same way he paid attention in class instead of goofing around the way so many boys did, laughing and making bathroom noises, boys for whom school was no more than a slightly advanced form of day care. Anything they happened to learn was purely by accident.

That very day in Nate's class alone, for example, Bruce had stopped one boy who was deeply engrossed in drawing the torso of a naked woman on the palm of his hand with a ballpoint pen, and not two minutes later he had confiscated a watch from another boy who was aiming its face in such a way as to make little circles of light dance all over the wall and ceiling. Yet another boy had taken bites from his homework paper and was chewing them into little soggy wads. Bruce had calmly walked back to his desk with the trash can and motioned for a deposit. All of this while Nate sat listening carefully to Bruce talk about the respiratory systems of amphibians and reptiles.

"So Bottom has to be played by someone really intelligent, see," he continued now, "which illustrates one of the many ironies of drama. Only a smart actor can convincingly pull off a simpleminded character like Bottom."

Nate cocked his head ever so slightly, as if measuring the logic of what Bruce was saying.

"So much of it is the timing of the lines, of course, and the . . . well, the sincerity of them. I remember when I was in this same play in high school, the guy who did Bottom never did get it quite right. He did try, I'll give him that, but you could always tell that underneath it all he was worried about looking stupid, especially since Bottom loses both Titania and Thisbe in the end. He was a big handsome guy like you but was all hung up on being cool and suave. I think he was afraid the role would ruin his image with the girls."

There was the faintest beginning of a smile in one corner of Nate's mouth. Very observant of others, Nate Bianchi no doubt knew exactly what kind of boy Bruce was describing, could identify several at Berea Middle School by name, a couple of whom were even in Drama Club.

"So I just want to suggest something for you to consider," Bruce said. "Maybe it'll help, maybe it won't." He shrugged as if it didn't much matter to him one way or the other. "You know your lines really well already"— actually, Bruce suspected that Nate knew everyone's lines by now—"and you've got a great sense of timing, but I want you to try . . . well, *pretending* a little more today that you really are a dimwit. Try having fun being somebody who's the total opposite of yourself."

Bruce took his hands out of his pockets and pointed an index finger at Nate. "*You've* got the biggest challenge that way, you know. I mean, DeReese really is kind of puckish already, right? And Jonathan, ladies' man that he is, doesn't have to strain too hard to play the love-struck Lysander. But you have the hardest role. You have to push yourself to the other end of the spectrum from where you naturally are, and then somehow make yourself not care that you're foolish—or maybe it would be better to say *not aware*."

He paused again and looked straight into Nate's eyes, holding his gaze for several long seconds. "Does any of this make sense?" he said. "Can you try to forget the rest of us are watching Nate Bianchi and just let yourself become poor old slow dumb Bottom?"

Nate started to speak, then cleared his throat and started again. "Well, I think so, yes. Yes, sir, I'll try."

Though it was a gradually diminishing courtesy among kids, even here in the South, to say, "Yes, sir" and "Yes, ma'am" to their teachers, and though Bruce knew it had to be further proof that he was getting old, it nevertheless always pleased him to hear it. He nodded and smiled. "Well, give it your best shot today, and let's see what happens." He looked down the hall. "Ah, here comes the lovely Titania now with Mustardseed and Hermia. Things are about to get cranked up." He moved toward the doorway. "Say, Nate, can you give me a hand in here? Let's move those two stacks of chairs over by the windows."

Ten minutes later almost everybody was there, all of them talking at the same time. It always amused Bruce the way middle schoolers could carry on conversations in which everyone was talking and no one was listening. Roomfuls of women had this talent also, but they could do it sitting still. With middle schoolers, the talking was always accompanied by the same teeming movement of certain pond specimens he had observed under the microscope. Bruce often praised his classes for learning so well those two important babyhood skills of walking and talking. Then he would follow up with a line for which he was now famous at Berea Middle School: "Okay now, all you overgrown tots, time to play the quiet game. Dip your hips and zip your lips."

Elizabeth Landis came in just as Bruce got everybody settled down to

start. With her was a girl Bruce assumed was the new seventh-grader who
had moved to Berea from Rhode Island. Elizabeth had told Bruce about
the girl. She was interested in being in the Drama Club and wondered if
there was anything she could do in *A Midsummer Night's Dream*. Sure, bring
her to rehearsal, we can always use another fairy, he had said. Provided
she's not too big, he had added. Oh no, not at all, perfect size for a fairy,
Elizabeth had said, and he saw now that she was right. In fact, this girl
would probably be the smallest fairy of them all.

For such a little girl, she didn't seem in the least intimidated to
be in a new situation. She was wearing a blue chambray shirt and a
pair of overalls, with one hand in a back pocket. As she and Elizabeth
came up front and sat down in two empty chairs, her eyes were busy
trying to take in everything—the other students, the high ceiling, the
green linoleum floor, the piano in one corner with the crepe paper
cornucopia and turkey sitting on top of it, the pictures of composers
on the bulletin board, an old record player on a rolling cart. After she
sat down, her feet barely touching the floor, she zeroed in on Bruce,
who was in the process of reviewing the new cuts they had made in act
5 and reminding Puck of his new cue to enter for his important closing lines. Hardly anyone was listening, however, because all eyes were
on the new arrival.

So he finally stopped midsentence. "Okay, okay, I give up. We have
somebody new," he said, then looked at Elizabeth. "You want to introduce
her?"

"This is Maggie," Elizabeth said. "She's from Rhode Island."

Maggie grinned and fluttered her fingers over her head in a little
wave that from anyone else might have looked silly and affected. She
wore small round glasses, had a sparkle in her eyes and short black hair
in a sort of rag-mop style. She looked a lot like Harry Potter, but without the lightning scar on her forehead. It was funny, Bruce thought,
how you could tell almost instantly if a kid was going to fit in, and if so,
where. Maggie had all the signs of winning a spot for herself right in
the middle of things.

"She was in a community play last summer up in Rhode Island," Elizabeth added. "Played Scout in *To Kill a Mockingbird*. She really likes drama
and thinks it's cool that we're doing Shakespeare."

Bruce couldn't help wondering how the folks up in Rhode Island
had handled *To Kill a Mockingbird*, a story set in the Deep South. He

wondered if they had attempted southern accents, a doomed endeavor for any northerner. He could see Maggie doing justice to the part of Scout but wondered who had played Atticus Finch and how many light-years away from Gregory Peck's performance the poor man had fallen. He had a sudden desire to see the movie again. Maybe he'd do that tonight. He had it in his collection.

Maggie's bright eyes were still on him, Bruce noticed, full of questions she wanted to ask, her chin lifted, her glasses perched on top of her . . . wasn't it called a "button nose" in books?

"Okay, Maggie," he said, "first of all, I like your name, so you can be relieved about that." He didn't tell her it was mainly because it was so close to Maddy or that he also liked everything else about her. "What's the rest of it?"

"Trump," she said. "Maggie Trump." No one seemed to think it was a funny last name. They were all staring at the back of her dark shiny hair, some of them openmouthed, as if a leprechaun had suddenly leapt into their midst. Several of the girls looked over at Priscilla Bernard, whose opinion carried a lot of weight concerning the social standing at Berea Middle, but right now Priscilla was chewing on the inside of her mouth, staring at Maggie along with everybody else and remaining noncommittal.

"Okay, good. Maggie Trump," Bruce said. "Second, since you're new, I'll tell you what I tell all my students at the beginning of every year, only you get the short version because we need to get on with our rehearsal." She was smiling up at him expectantly, swinging her feet now, which were crossed at the ankles.

Middle-school girls often annoyed Bruce, though in a mild way he could smile about. He thought it was a pity they had to camp out in such an unattractive stage for so long, that they couldn't shoot directly from the cuteness of elementary school to the beginnings of genuine femininity in high school. Even though some of them were already filling out their bodies to astounding proportions while others were as flat chested as Olympic gymnasts, they all behaved the same—shrieking hysterically at the most trivial things, whispering in conspiratorial clumps in the hallway, watching each other slyly.

But Maggie Trump seemed different. She had been in the room less than two minutes, but already she came across as refreshingly straightforward. He couldn't imagine her ever staying after class to ask him unnecessary questions in that awkwardly flirtatious way a lot of middle-school girls had. Or saying spiteful things about other girls behind their backs. But then, maybe she was a slow bloomer. Maybe she simply hadn't hit true middle-school gawkiness yet.

As he did in the fall with every new class of students, Bruce now turned his face sideways and pointed to the scars along his neck and jawline. "As you see, I have scars," he said to Maggie. He held up his left hand. "Here, too." He pushed up the sleeve of his sweater. "And here, all up and down my arm." Maggie's eyes took it all in, and she gave a little half nod, as if to say, "Yes, I was wondering about those."

"And here's why," he continued, pausing dramatically. "As a child, I rushed heroically into a raging fire . . . but sadly, the victim died."

Maggie's brow furrowed, and she pushed her lower lip out a little in a show of sympathy. The other kids, all familiar with the story, were rolling their eyes as they awaited the punch line. "I was only seven," Bruce continued, "so I got these scars a long, long time before any of you made your debut into this world kicking and screaming like the little brats you were until you got to Berea Middle and we started whipping you into shape. I hardly think about my scars anymore, but I know other people wonder. So because of my keen understanding of human curiosity in general, and especially my deep insight into the notorious nosiness of adolescents, I like to set everyone's mind at ease. So . . . I was in a fire, okay?"

This was always his cue to start faking some emotion, which he did now. When he spoke again, his voice was low and quavery. "But it was too late for . . . for *her*. I couldn't . . . save her . . . because she was . . . she was already *gone* by the time they pulled me out." He wiped at the corner of his eye. Maggie was studying him gravely, but her look of sympathy had changed into something closer to suspicion. It was clear this kid wasn't easy to hoodwink.

"I was only seven when I lost her," he said sadly. "I had to grow up the best I could without her." He decided to skip the loud nose-blowing part that usually went here, but he did drop his head and rub at his nose briefly before looking up again. "No more of her comforting presence, no more soft murmurs, no more loving caresses of her . . . paw." There were a few titters of laughter as he closed his eyes, then inhaled deeply and shakily and concluded with, "No, I never found another cat to replace Tabitha."

Everybody laughed. Maggie grinned and shook her head. Alex Bower piped up from the back and said, "Was there anything left of her after the fire? Like a skeleton or claws or anything?"

"That's sick," said one of the girls.

"Only a few tufts of silky fur and the faint echo of her meow," Bruce said, placing his hand over his heart.

DeReese laughed and said almost the exact same thing his sister Suzanne had said all those years ago: "He almost got hisself killed trying to save a *cat.*"

Bruce put on a face of sorrow. "There's always someone standing by to criticize any act of human kindness." Then he clapped his hands sharply. "Okay, more than enough of all that. Whose idea was it to waste all this time anyway? Let's get started." He nodded his head in Maggie's direction. "We're glad to have you with us, Maggie Trump. We'll find a place for you in the fairy troupe." Already Bruce was wondering if he should let her try the long speech at the opening of act 2, which none of the other fairies had been able to do justice to, though all of them had tried. The lines needed a light, lyrical quality, and he had a feeling that Maggie Trump might be able to do it.

It was almost five o'clock when Bruce walked with Elizabeth out to the parking lot. Rehearsal had gone especially well that afternoon, and though Bruce was wishing he could take full credit for Nate Bianchi's improved performance as Bottom, he suspected there were more factors at work than his little inspirational talk with the boy beforehand. For one thing, it was obvious that Nate was not following the admonition to forget about his audience but, rather, had been uncommonly aware of his audience that day, particularly of the newest little fairy, who, not being involved in act 5, had remained in her chair on the front row, absorbing every detail of the rehearsal.

She was a great audience member, responding openly and warmly to everything—nodding, smiling, laughing out loud several times, even clapping her hands after Puck's "Good night unto you all" at the end. For some reason the whole mood of the rehearsal that day had been more buoyant than usual. The air in the music room had seemed cleaner and crisper, conducting the sound waves at an invigorating clip. Everything fell into place smoothly, no lapses of memory.

And Nate—well, the transformation was remarkable. He seemed to turn a corner midway through his first speech, during which he addressed first the night and then the wall. It was as if he had suddenly found himself on a scary carnival ride and had finally decided to settle back and enjoy it. Maggie wasn't the only one who laughed when he delivered his lines to the Moon as the ill-fated Pyramus, and then discovered Thisbe's mantle on the ground: "How can it be? Oh, dainty duck! Oh, dear! Thy mantle good, What, stained with blood!" And he had it exactly right. Not just close, but exactly right, with precisely the perfect blend of solemnity and humor.

And Bruce wasn't sure *how* he knew Nate was performing for Maggie, but he knew it. Maybe it was the single sideways glance Nate had shot in her direction the first time she laughed, or maybe it was simply the vast extent of his improvement, which couldn't be laid to anything as mundane as a pep talk from an adult. But still it mystified Bruce—so the kid had had this capability in a deep well inside him all along, but suddenly it had bubbled up to the surface when a girl's face lit up with pleasure at the sound of his voice?

To see such early evidence of womankind's magical powers blew him away. He wanted to laugh and cry both. "Oh, Nate," he wanted to say, "you're in for a lifetime of it, buddy. Retreat, hunker down, regroup! Let yourself start caring what a woman thinks, and you'll never be your own man again."

But surely his talk with Nate had to be at least partly responsible for the change, he argued. He wasn't willing to give it all up to Maggie. Both he and Elizabeth had witnessed Nate hanging around after rehearsal, however—something he never did. They had seen him rummaging around in his backpack, pretending to look for something but obviously filling up time until Priscilla and the other fairies had finished talking to Maggie and left. They had seen him follow Maggie and Tamara out into the hallway and trail after them, then suddenly feel the need for a long drink at the water fountain when Maggie said good-bye to Tamara and stopped at her locker.

"Wouldn't you hate to go back to those days?" Elizabeth had said to Bruce after they watched Maggie catch sight of Nate and call out something to him, at which exact point his thirst was immediately slaked and he pretended to notice her for the first time, then hastened in her direction. The thought of Nate Bianchi and a *girl* made Bruce realize all over again how life continually turned all your expectations wacky. And though he groaned and nodded at Elizabeth's question, he actually remembered thoroughly enjoying the adventure of those days.

While they waited around for everyone to clear out of the hallway and head home, Bruce felt a strong desire flood over him, a wish so powerful it made him ache inside. Really two wishes. First, he wished he could go back to those days and start all over with girls and do it right this time. And second, he wanted to call after Nate and pull him aside for another talk, this time about real life instead of acting. He wanted to say things to this boy that he wished someone had said to him as a thirteen-year-old.

He wanted to exhort him to be careful, to watch his step with girls, to guard his mind and his hands and his mouth so that he didn't have to live with hundreds and hundreds of regrets later on. He wanted to tell him that a girl's body was something you didn't mess around with, that he must regard it as sacred and never treat it as a toy, that he should control his natural curiosity, all those male urges to explore and conquer, and save them for one woman way down the road of life, somebody he wanted to spend his whole future with, somebody who would be the mother of his children.

How his old friends would laugh at him now, he thought as he went back to his classroom to pick up his briefcase. He, Bruce Healey, who had made a career of exploring and conquering, now talking up abstinence and monogamy.

"Great rehearsal today," Elizabeth said a few minutes later as they were leaving the building together. "I wonder what got into Nate."

"Oh, I had a few words with him," Bruce said, then laughed and shook his head. "Life is full of mysteries I can't begin to explain."

He pictured Nate, struggling to fill up his expanding body with some semblance of manliness. He saw him walking down the hall beside Maggie, so small and weak in comparison, yet in some ways the less vulnerable of the two. He imagined Nate glancing down at Maggie, his heart thudding at the smile on her upturned face, suddenly wishing he could . . . what? Bruce knew only too well the kinds of things boys wished. Again, he wanted to snatch Nate away and lecture him, maybe bind and gag him for a few years.

He wanted to tell him how horrible it was to bear the weight of sins of the flesh, to try to squelch images of things he never should have seen and done, to feel beaten down at the thought that he didn't deserve a woman's love and trust when he had sailed so thoughtlessly through so many conquests. God might forgive a multitude of sins—and Bruce firmly believed in God's inexhaustible grace—but where would he ever find a woman who had that kind of enormous capacity to forgive? "Squander your youth," he wanted to say, "and you'll have a lifetime to make heavy payments."

He knew he could never initiate such a talk with Nate or any other boy, though, for once he started, he wouldn't be able to stop. He would end up grabbing the boy's shoulders and shaking him till his teeth rattled in his head. He would rant like a wild man: "I know what you're thinking about, but *stop it*! Don't do it! Don't you dare lay a finger on a girl! You'll be sorry for the rest of your life if you do this evil thing! Find a school just for boys and go there!" They would lock him away for sure, either in jail or the loony bin.

He remembered watching Maddy in the backyard with Kimberly recently, being struck with the awful thought of somebody trying to harm her. He had stood there wondering how Kimberly and Matt would ever be able to send her away from home when she reached school age, to a place where boys were lurking everywhere with their lustful eyes and itchy hands. He could well imagine himself following her to school, then later hiding in the backseats of cars when she went out on dates, carrying a very sharp knife with him at all times. He couldn't bear the thought of attending her wedding someday, having to stand by and see some pea-brained boy put a ring on her finger and promise to love and cherish her forever, then watching them get into a car and go off to live together. How did parents weather such sorrow?

He had been ashamed of himself later for the way he had let his imagination run wild that day, like a girl's, and had even dreamed another awful dream that night with no satisfying conclusion, only a series of blunders on his part as he fought to get to Maddy, who was somewhere out of his sight, crying, "Help, Unca Buce! Help!" He had awakened with a start and slowly raised a hand to feel his face, hoping it wasn't wet. Surely, surely he hadn't reached the point of *crying* in his sleep.

Often these days when he thought about all the things that could go wrong in life, he found himself wondering at length about heaven, trying to conceive of a place of eternal peace and light and joy, a place on the other side of this world where he would be welcomed and would stand redeemed, where he would know and be known. There was a time when he had laughed about the concept of heaven, saying he'd be bored to tears in such a place. That was before he understood that heaven was a place "where no tears will ever fall," as the hymn said, one of the ones written by the blind woman.

"So how does that sound?" Elizabeth said. "You hungry?" Suddenly Bruce realized they were standing next to Elizabeth's car. The parking lot was almost empty. Only one other car was still there besides his and Elizabeth's.

"Well, I was going to try jogging for a little while tonight," Bruce said, "but food sounds better." He had no idea what it was she had suggested.

"Okay, then, we'll meet you there. Is six okay?"

"Sure," he said. "And where did you say that was?"

She smiled and shook her head. "C. C.'s—you know, the barbecue place over in Filbert?"

"Oh sure, sure." He opened the door for her. "Sorry, I was just thinking about something."

"Oh, I know all about that little male habit, believe me," she said. "I get the same look from my husband—that vacant stare while I'm in the middle of saying something terribly important."

"Yeah, well, cut us some slack," Bruce said. "We can't multitask as well as you women can."

"Tell me about it." She laughed. "I bet you can't find things in the pantry or refrigerator, either—that's another masculine deficiency, you know."

She was right, of course. Bruce recalled the time he had cut his hand back during the summer and couldn't find a Band-Aid anywhere in Kimberly's house, the time he had gone over to Celia's to beg one. Later, when he had complained to Kimberly, she had opened the medicine cabinet in the bathroom and pointed right to them.

"Okay, okay, enough," he said to Elizabeth now. "Quit picking on us. What I was thinking about was this. How do you feel about separate schools for girls and boys?"

"What? Well, when? You mean middle school or what?"

"Everything—nursery school, elementary, middle, high school, college, grad school, the whole works."

Elizabeth laughed. "Well, it's an idea. Not a very good one, though. I wouldn't want to teach only girls." She got in her car and looked up at him. "What a boring educational experience. No men or boys around . . . to make fun of." She closed her door and waved good-bye.

33

This World of Toil and Snares

On the Tuesday evening before Thanksgiving, something occurred which, though it lasted only seconds, Bruce knew he would never forget. He knew he would replay it endlessly, probably expanding and embellishing it a little each time. On the one hand he wished he had a videotape of it so he could watch it over and over, could play it in slow motion to observe every detail of the way it actually unfolded, but on the other hand he knew his imagination would supplement his memory to produce a version far more entertaining in the long run.

The gist of it was this: One minute Matt, Kimberly's husband, was getting out of a car at the front curb, calling to Maddy, who had been sitting on the front steps waiting for half an hour, "Come here, sweetie," and beckoning to her from the open car door. And the next minute, before anybody could react, Celia was whirling out of nowhere, swiftly bearing down on Matt, her arms raised like Moses ready to strike the rock. All this Bruce and Kimberly were watching through the bay window inside.

The Incident—that's how he would always refer to it from this day forward—showed Bruce yet another side of Celia. He knew it was a story they would be telling for years to come. Thinking about it later, he supposed Celia could rightly be called the protagonist in the anecdote, while Matt would be the antagonist, and Maddy—well, she would have to be the source of conflict, the motivation for the action.

And what fine action it was. It would make a great movie scene. From Celia's angry righteous advance, with the terrible swift sword of her tennis racket raised above her head, to the initial shocked yelp emitted by Matt when he comprehended her intent and lifted his arm to ward off the first blow—what a nugget of high drama.

It was certainly understandable that Celia wouldn't have recognized Matt. Even though she knew by now that Bruce wasn't Maddy's father, she didn't know that Matt *was*. The rare times when he was at home, which hadn't been for a long time now, he didn't spend much time out in the yard, and because their two driveways weren't adjacent, she wouldn't have seen him getting in and out of the car.

Furthermore, since The Incident occurred after five o'clock, it was already sliding toward dusk and therefore getting hard to see. Besides all this, Matt had, for some reason, decided to grow a beard over the months he was in Germany, which made him look older and, combined with his olive complexion, a little sinister in Bruce's opinion, like one of Saddam Hussein's relatives.

"Think about it from her perspective," Bruce was telling Matt moments after it happened, after he and Kimberly had rushed out of the house to set things right. "Let's go through the whole scenario," Bruce said to Matt, who was still wincing and flexing his wrist. "This nice neighbor looks out her window and sees a strange man—" Celia interrupted him. "Oh, okay, this nice neighbor is getting things out of her car when she sees a strange man pull up at the curb next door. Then she sees the man open the car door—" Again Celia interrupted. "Oh yes, and it's not a car she recognizes, since the strange man rented it and drove it home from the Atlanta airport. And she then sees the strange man motion for someone to come, and she sees Maddy walking toward him—" Another interruption. "Yes, walking *slowly* toward him, a little shyly as though she's not exactly sure of herself."

"And then the man says something, and the—" Celia interrupted again. "Oh, so she actually hears him say, 'Come here, sweetie, I have something for you'—that makes it even more suspicious to her—and so the nice neighbor, having heard about such men in the news, grabs the nearest thing she can get her hands on, which happens to be her tennis racket, and rushes out to save the little girl, disregarding her own safety and any potential damage to her expensive piece of sporting equipment." Bruce didn't really know whether the racket was all that expensive, but it sounded better that way.

"This nice neighbor," he continued, "has no idea that the whole thing has been planned at the suggestion of the strange man himself, who happens to be the little girl's father returning home after a *long* absence and wanting to see if his daughter will know him, or that the little girl's mother is watching from inside." He doesn't add, "or that the little girl's uncle is also inside, though he has strongly objected to being part of this tender little homecoming scene and plans to make himself scarce as soon as he has given the strange man a quick perfunctory handshake and helped him carry in his bags." Bruce realized he should probably drop the word *strange* now, since it had somehow metamorphosed into meaning odd rather than simply unfamiliar.

So he couldn't blame Celia one bit, Bruce said. In fact, he said, they ought to thank her. "Oh yeah, sure, way to welcome me home," Matt said, "*thank* somebody for almost breaking my wrist." He was half smiling as he said it but was still massaging his wrist gingerly.

"I'm thanking her for coming to Maddy's aid," Bruce said, almost adding, "You know, Maddy, *your daughter,* who has quintupled her vocabulary since the last time you saw her." By now Kimberly was showering Matt with kisses and hugs, though the hugs were somewhat compromised by her rotundity and by Matt's concern over his wrist. Kimberly was laughing and crying at the same time and flapping her hands around, overcome with so many emotions she couldn't even put words together.

Somewhere in the middle of all this, Madison, totally bewildered, had leapt into the arms of the closest person and the one who must have seemed to be most in control of his senses, which was Bruce. Evidently she wasn't quite convinced yet that the bearded man really was the same daddy who had left her almost four months earlier, had sent her a stuffed bear from Germany, and talked to her on the telephone every week.

Meanwhile Patsy Stewart had materialized in her front yard during all this, wearing an apron over her knit pants and holding what looked like a wooden spoon in one hand. Whether she had merely rushed out of her kitchen without thinking or whether she had armed herself to help Celia, it wasn't clear. At any rate, she remained rooted in one spot like a pointer spotting a pheasant.

Bruce smiled at Celia, who looked humiliated now that she realized her mistake. He had to hand it to her—she sure wasn't afraid to get involved. He knew it was the kind of image destined to appear over and over in his dreams—Celia, quivering with courage and outrage as she raised her racket to strike again.

She was trying to stammer out an apology to Matt, who wouldn't even look at her, who was still rotating his wrist, then gently shaking it, apparently to see if his hand was going to fall off. Bruce wanted to give him a swift kick and tell him to stop acting like a baby, to be a gentleman and listen to this brave woman's apology, then accept it graciously.

At last Kimberly finally regained her powers of lucid speech and started nodding her head yes, yes, and blubbering that it was absolutely clear how Celia could have misunderstood. She even turned to Celia and gave her a sideways hug of gratitude, then went back to Matt's side and started smooching kisses all over his wrist. Matt, still acting like he had suffered some kind of mortal blow, reached back into the car and pulled out one of those cheap, glittery pinwheels he had obviously picked up for Madison at the airport gift shop. He held it out to her. Madison wriggled free from Bruce's arms and went forward to accept it.

Don't fall for tawdry enticements, Bruce wanted to say, but he reminded himself that Matt was, after all, her real father. His heart was filled with despair as he watched Matt take her into his arms.

To cover his defeat, he turned to Celia and asked to see her racket. He swung it a few times in what he hoped was considered good tennis form, then examined the logo and the writing along the side, as if he knew all about rackets. "Good old titanium," he said, wondering when they had started using *that* for tennis rackets. "Great stuff. Low density, noncorrosive, high temperature stability." He stepped back and pretended to serve a ball. "Atomic number twenty-two, which means that's how many protons are in the nucleus of a single titanium atom, and atomic weight somewhere around forty-eight, I think, which makes it heavier than, say, aluminum, but not as heavy as something like copper."

Oh, smooth, very smooth, he told himself. Rule number one, whenever you can't think of the right thing to say, just start spouting scientific data. That should warm the heart of any woman.

Celia nodded—he couldn't tell whether it was from pity or politeness—and took her racket back. She apologized to Matt again, who must have heard her this time, because he at least had the courtesy to say, "Oh, forget it."

At that point Kimberly let go of Matt long enough to issue an invitation for Celia to join them for Thanksgiving dinner, to which she replied with a hasty no, thank you, she was leaving for Georgia the next day around six to visit her aunt and uncle, which was a little over four hours away, which would get her there by ten-thirty or so if she didn't stop, which she didn't plan to. She had to be rattled, Bruce thought, to give out such a wealth of information.

Bruce walked back to her car with her, noting that Patsy Stewart hadn't moved. Put a beacon on that woman's forehead and she could be a lighthouse. Bruce gave her a friendly wave of dismissal and called out, "Everything's fine—just a minor misunderstanding. No need to call out the National Guard."

He thanked Celia again for what she had done, asking her if she needed any help checking her oil or anything before her trip, then backing off immediately when she said no, she'd had that done by her mechanic on Monday along with several other things.

He stood in the driveway as she zipped her racket back into her case, which was in the trunk of her car. It was getting darker now, and he thought he smelled rain. "You planning to play tennis with your aunt while you're in Georgia?" he asked, and she had answered without turning around.

"My aunt is eighty," she said. "She's actually my great-aunt."

"Will the rest of your family be there, too?" he asked even though something told him not to, that she might think he had already been enough of a busybody.

"No, there will be only the three of us." Still not looking at him, she shoved her tennis bag over to the side of her trunk, then rearranged a few other things and took out a bulging plastic bag, which seemed to be stuffed with other plastic bags, and looped it over one arm like a large purse. She closed the trunk and brushed her hands together.

He motioned back toward Kimberly's house. "Well, we'll only have you beat by one." He laughed. "I'm not sure what all Kimberly's cooking up, but she was talking last week about fixing Cornish game hens instead of turkey. And macaroons instead of pumpkin pie." Celia glanced up at him quickly, as if to see if he was teasing. "So is your aunt a good cook?" he asked, then added, "I used to have an aunt who made the best corn-bread dressing and giblet gravy every Thanksgiving. And my mother made this boiled custard she served in these white cups shaped like flower petals. Then my grandmother made sweet potato pie that was—"

He stopped. This was ridiculous. She couldn't possibly care about his grandmother's sweet potato pie. He sighed. Just once he wished he wouldn't act like an imbecile around this woman. "Sorry, I don't know what it is about you that makes me do this."

"Do what?"

"Talk like this, on and on. I'm usually very . . . well, polished and poised. Very suave, very cool. I've even been told that I'm sometimes witty."

The look on her face said, "Well, you sure didn't hear it from me."

"But for some reason every time I talk to you," he said, "I get all, well, sort of rambly and random and tongue-tied. So I'll shut up now and let you get on with whatever you need to do. Sorry for wasting your time. I won't bother you anymore, I promise." There, he had said it. Let her think whatever she wanted to.

"Oh, it's okay," she said, shrugging, "it wasn't a total waste of my time. At least I learned that the atomic weight of titanium is twenty-two."

"No, that's the atomic number," he said. "The atomic weight is forty-eight."

"Right," she said, nodding. "Just seeing if you would catch the error." She appeared to be on the verge of actually smiling. "Well, I've got to go." She took a step back. She seemed to be staring at his shirt. It was one of his favorite ones out of the few he owned—a maroon polo style, short-sleeved with a zipper instead of buttons at the neck. Immediately after spotting it on a revolving rack in Wal-Mart a year ago, he had found a size large and draped it over his arm as he headed to the checkout with his twelve-pack of root beer and box of Tide detergent. The shiny material reminded him of the nylon pajamas his father used to wear. What had been tacky in pajamas was probably even more so in a shirt, but for some strange reason it had struck his fancy, and he continued to pull it out of his closet and put it on time and again, even in cold weather.

"I'm not cold if that's what you're thinking," he said to Celia, who was dressed sensibly in a navy sweater and white turtleneck.

She shook her head. "No, that's not what I was thinking." But she didn't offer to divulge what she was thinking.

"Can you hear that train whistle?" he said. "It's the one that crosses Harper Bridge Road down by the old feed store. Same time every Tuesday. You hear it?"

"Oh yes, I have a very good ear for train whistles," she said. Again she took a half step back.

He hated to let go of the moment. "Everything okay at the art gallery?" he said. "Any exciting new paintings lately?"

She nodded. "Yes. We've got a very good show up right now." Again she moved to leave. "Oh, by the way, that's a great painting you've got over your sofa." She immediately looked as if she wished she could take the comment back. "I saw it that night I kept Madison. I had to go over to get a couple of diapers, and I meant to tell you . . . I mean, I wasn't trying to—"

"Oh, listen, hey, thanks. I don't know if I ever really told you how much I appreciated what you did that—"

"Yes, yes, you did. It wasn't anything. I just didn't . . ."

"Say, do you need any help with that big bag of . . . bags?" Bruce said, stepping toward her.

She answered quickly, firmly. "No, thanks. It's only plastic bags. They're light as feathers. I've had them in the trunk to take to the grocery store, but I keep forgetting, so I'm going to put them in the recycle bin here." And she twirled around and headed off as if such an important job couldn't wait another minute.

"I know what you mean," Bruce called after her. "My plastic bags are piling up like crazy right now, too. Why, my apartment is practically overrun with them!"

She stopped and turned around, her small chin lifted, her nose slightly wrinkled if she were standing downwind of a slaughterhouse. "Well, you better go take care of them," she said tersely, then turned on her heel and disappeared inside.

After a brief cordial conversation with his next-door neighbor, Bruce ruined it all with an ill-conceived attempt at humor. That's how this scene would close if it were in a book, he thought as he walked back up to the front yard. Well, this was one more confirmation of what he already knew—this woman was supremely touchy. One minute she almost smiled at you, and the next she treated you like you were a skunk trapper. Of course he didn't know her well enough to tease her like that. She obviously thought he was making fun of her and her plastic bags. Definitely not suave or cool.

Two days later, on Thanksgiving morning, Bruce heard Kimberly's voice in the backyard, the high-pitched, singsongy quality telling him she must be talking to Maddy. Though he had been awake for a few minutes, he was still in bed, having decided that the best way to start Thanksgiving Day would be to list all the things for which he was thankful. He started with his parents, who, in spite of their faults, had given him much. On the table beside his bed was a small framed picture of his parents on their wedding day.

He picked up the picture and looked at the youthful faces of his mother and father. His mother's hair was like Kimberly's, dark and thick but shorter and a lot curlier. She had some kind of little headpiece nestled in it, like a tiara, with beads and sequins and a wisp of white netting poofed up behind it. She was wearing a white two-piece suit instead of a traditional wedding dress, with a sparkly flower design appliquéd on the lapels and decorated with tiny pearls and more sequins. Up near her face she held a nosegay of white roses tied with a white ribbon, her hands clasping it in such a way as to display her diamond engagement ring and wide gold wedding band.

If he could somehow separate himself from the woman in this picture, forget the sound of her voice, her touch, how he last knew her, Bruce knew he would pronounce her beautiful. As it was, he could see her only as his mother, far beyond simple modifiers, someone he had known from his first breath and had observed through all her evolutions, his last view of her being three years earlier when she lay in her casket, gray and grim.

Slightly behind her in the picture and pressed protectively against her was his father, with his clean-sculpted features and a headful of wavy brown hair that he would lose thirty years later to chemo. When it had started growing back in, the wave was completely gone, which dismayed Bruce's mother to no end. In comparison to everything else, the wave was a small loss, but one she never got over. The last thing she had said before the lid on his father's casket was closed was "Oh, the wave in his hair—they took that away, too." She spoke the words with clenched fists and followed them with a curse. The funeral director had flinched slightly as though she were accusing him, though no one really knew who it was she was blaming.

The wedding photo was a closeup, taken from the waist up, so it was hard to tell whether they were sitting or standing. They had such open smiles, such youthful eyes, such anticipation of a long and happy marriage. "Thank you," Bruce said out loud right now. "Thank you both for what you gave me." Which in many ways was a fortune, for it was his mother who had taught him good manners and showed him how to pick himself up after a failure and move ahead with a smile, while his father had taught him patience and self-esteem. It was his father who had taken one look at him after the fire, after all the bandages were off, and had said, "Hey there, pal, what's a few little old scars? Why, nothing at all! You're still the best-looking kid around."

And the lessons had somehow stuck even though the teachers had abandoned their own advice, his father surrendering and wallowing in self-pity the last two years of his life and his mother throwing all her good manners and fortitude out the window at the same time.

Elizabeth Landis had lost her father to cancer also, she had told him not too long ago. Had it drastically changed her mother's personality? he had wanted to know. "Well, not really," she had answered after a pause. "Did *your* mother change?" And all he could do was shake his head and say, "There's no way to describe it."

Suzanne had once asked Bruce if he thought their parents had loved each other too much. "Too much?" he had said. What did she mean? How was that possible? "Like they were a private club," she said, "and no one else could join. Like they were singing a duet they had written, and nobody else knew the words and music. Like they were drinking tea for two all the time. Like they were—" "Okay, okay," he said. "I get the picture. But no, I don't think you can ever love too much," he said glibly.

"You mean you never felt like they overlooked you?" she asked. "Well, no, not really," he said, realizing that Suzanne was champing at the bit to get started on one of her favorite topics: the way their parents spent their money, in particular the injustice of their not taking her to an orthodontist to straighten her teeth, yet plunking down two thousand dollars to go on a cruise for their fifteenth anniversary. "I can't believe you," she said. "What about those twenty-four-carat gold cuff links she bought him for Father's Day the year you graduated from high school? The year she gave you a *shirt*, which you had to take back and exchange for the right size. Remember that, huh?"

"Hey, give her a break," he said. "That was right after he was diagnosed with cancer. She was trying to cope." "Yes, and weren't we all," Suzanne said, then added, "You're in denial about this whole thing, you always have been." To which Bruce replied with an air of superiority, calling after her as she flounced out of the room, "Love is not something you carefully measure out in controlled, equal amounts, Suzanne. And no, I still say *you can never love too much.*" As if he, with his vast experience, were the final authority on the subject of love.

That conversation was probably a good ten years ago, when he often said things off the top of his head with great passion to compensate for the fact that they didn't come from the bottom of his heart, things that sounded right, even exalted and idealistic, but wouldn't bear close scrutiny.

Now that he was the same age Suzanne was back then, he wondered what his answer would be if she asked him again.

An idea came to him now. Could it be that his parents' love for each other had in some way discouraged him from marriage? No, he argued with himself, a strong bond like theirs should inspire their children to copy them, to find their own soul mate and steal away together to their own little deserted island. Or might it scare a child to think of trying to progress at a normal pace through life attached so closely to one other person, like those frustrating three-legged races?

Those unity candles in certain wedding ceremonies had always made him uneasy. "Wait, do you really want to extinguish your flame?" he felt like calling out to the couple, who evidently *did* want to do precisely that or else weren't thinking about what they were doing, for when they had lit the middle candle and snuffed out their own, they didn't even seem to notice the two pathetic sorrowful little puffs of smoke wafting up from the blackened wicks. He didn't have a problem with using the two candles to light another candle, but why did they have to blow out the first two? Wouldn't it be making a positive symbolic statement to leave them burning, something about the whole being greater than the sum of its parts?

Somehow his parents' two little candles had come together to light a bonfire instead of another single measly candle. Maybe a child with parents like that might be a little nervous about the whole concept of marriage. Might he wonder, every time he met a girl, not if she could provide enough flint to get a fire going but enough fuel to keep it burning hot for years and years? Starting a fire wasn't any big deal—there was kindling aplenty. But the sustained, steady heat of a perpetual flame—was that possible? Was it even desirable? Might you not want a little relief from the heat from time to time? That was something to think about, something to make a wise person hesitate before leaping into marriage.

He set the picture back on his nightstand. There were some thickets too thorny for him to push through in this weary life, in "this world of toils and snares," as that hymn said—the one he had been so surprised to see in the old red hymnbook at church a few weeks back. He hadn't gone looking for it, as he had others, in fact hadn't once thought about it since watching the movie *Cool Hand Luke* years ago. One of the convicts sang it in that movie, slow and mournful—"Just a Closer Walk With Thee." And then there it was years later, jumping out at him from a hymnbook, right across the page from another song they were singing in church.

It was the second stanza that he hadn't been able to get out of his mind since reading it. "Through this world of toil and snares, if I falter, Lord, who cares? Who with me my burden shares?" Those were good questions, very similar to the ones Bruce had been asking himself of late. And the answer, though it was a comfort in one sense, was also sad: "None but Thee, dear Lord, none but Thee." Could it be true? Would he ever reach the point where God really was the only one who truly cared about him? If he could somehow distill all the love other people had for him right now, exactly how many milliliters would it measure in one of those graduated beakers? If he suddenly vanished off the face of the earth, how many people would mourn his loss?

Well, how depressing. This was certainly not the direction he wanted his thoughts to go on Thanksgiving Day. *Get back on track,* he told himself. *Count your many blessings, name them one by one, and all that.* So from his parents he moved on to his sisters, giving thanks for each of them in turn—for Suzanne, whose love for him he didn't doubt for a minute in spite of her disapproval of so much about him. And for Kimberly, whose optimism and even-tempered disposition was a miracle considering that she hadn't had a lot of nurturing for a good part of her childhood. She loved him, too—no question about that.

He still heard her voice outside in the backyard, talking with Maddy. He could pick out only a few words here and there: turkey, Daddy, birdie, Uncle Brucie, pie, Celia, Mommy, ambulance. Madison had never forgotten the thrill of the ambulance showing up in front of their house a few weeks earlier and still talked about it frequently. Bruce wanted to buy her a toy ambulance for Christmas if he could find one. He would love to get one she could actually sit inside and pedal around like one of those little kiddie cars. It would have to have a siren, too, which would probably drive them all crazy.

And, of course, Madison—he stopped to give special thanks for her. He was looking forward to the new baby, due in only two months now, but he didn't see how any baby could ever be as perfect as Maddy. He was hoping he wouldn't show his partiality too much. The ultrasound had revealed that this one was going to be a girl, too, and Bruce felt sorry for her already, having to live in the shadow of her clever and gorgeous big sister her whole life.

He heard his brother-in-law upstairs walking through the house calling for Kimberly. Over and over he called her name, then Madison's.

Sometimes, even though he could put a computer together blindfolded, Matt simply didn't seem bright enough to deserve Kimberly and Madison. If he himself ever had a wife and child, Bruce thought, he couldn't imagine not being aware that they had gone outside. Wouldn't most husbands and fathers develop a sort of radar about things like that?

Not that he would ever be a hoverer. Women needed their space the same as men did. He would never want a woman who depended on him exclusively for her happiness and well-being. His mother had been that way with his father, and look what had happened to her. And he would never expect any woman to account to him for every minute of her day, every penny she spent, every thought that crossed her mind. He would never want a woman whose mystery was solved, whose complexity was unraveled so that there was nothing left to wonder about.

Bruce got out of bed and opened his blinds. Kimberly was sitting at the patio table in front of something that looked like a kind of old-fashioned hole punch. It quickly came to him what it was, though, when he saw her pull a pecan out of a paper sack, insert it in the contraption, then pull a lever. Maddy was puttering around the patio in her footed pajamas swiping at acorns with a stick.

How typical of Kimberly, not only to let Maddy go outside in her pajamas in November but also to go to the trouble of cracking her own pecans when she could buy them already shelled at the grocery store. For that matter, he had been standing in the yard with her when Milton Stewart had given her a plastic bag full of shelled pecans last week. Why didn't she use those? Surely she had something better to do with her time on Thanksgiving morning. How were the *dinner plans* coming along, for instance?

He looked over at the Stewarts' driveway and Celia's empty parking pad. He wondered how many days she'd be staying with her aunt and uncle in Georgia. He didn't remember her mentioning when she'd be back. His mind went back to what had happened two days earlier in Kimberly's front yard, and he couldn't help smiling.

It was funny enough the way it had played out, but it might have been even funnier if Celia had indeed dealt a blow to Matt's head, as she had intended, instead of merely smacking him once across the wrist, if there could have been a big lump the size of an egg above his eyebrow, say, something as a visual reminder of The Incident for days to come. Maybe even a laceration and a few stitches. Bruce thought of Matt trying to look dignified as he carved the Thanksgiving turkey with a big pad of gauze on his forehead. Not that he wished Matt ill. He was okay for a brother-in-law.

No doubt Celia could have inflicted a serious wound if Bruce himself hadn't run out of the house shouting, "Hey, hey, stop. It's okay! That's her father!" And he wondered later how much damage she could have done, catching Matt unawares as she did and wielding a weapon which, though lightweight titanium, was nevertheless a sturdy, unbendable metal.

As Bruce watched Madison now, squatting down to pull the cap off a large acorn then fit it back on with a look of pure delight, his heart overflowed with gratitude that someone had been looking out for her safety and had sprung into action, misguided though it was. That was something else to give thanks for while he was at it.

Bruce tapped on his bedroom window, and Kimberly looked up from her pecan cracking and waved. Maddy saw him, too, and came running over, swinging a stick over her head. Bruce opened his window a little and knelt down in front of it. "Hey, there, Maddy. How's my girl?"

"I got acorns," she said, opening her fist to show him two.

"Nice," he said. "But don't eat them." He made a face. "Icky."

She squatted down again and dropped the acorns onto the patio, then set about trying to decap them.

"I'm going to make a pecan pie," Kimberly called to him. "This old relic was Mom's." She pointed to the pecan cracker. Bruce knew what this meant. She would get so involved with this one little part of Thanksgiving dinner that they would be lucky to eat by midnight. She would have to shell and clean all the pecans after cracking them, then hunt up the recipe, which could be anywhere, then find a store open to buy an ingredient she didn't have on hand, then make two or three piecrusts before she got one right, and so on. He and Matt would end up in the kitchen trying to help her finish things up, all of them bumping into each other and getting out of sorts. But at least pecan pie sounded better than her original plan of macaroons for Thanksgiving dinner.

"Why not use the pecans Milton gave you?" Bruce asked.

"Oh, I put those in the freezer," she said, as if this explained everything. "I got these fresh from that man that sells them over on Highway 11."

"Oh, I see," Bruce said. "So what time are we planning to eat?"

She looked up at the sky as if to see how high the sun was. "Oh, maybe . . . how does four o'clock sound?"

That meant six o'clock at the earliest. "Okay by me," he said. "You need any help with anything? I make a mean batch of mashed potatoes, you know."

" 'Tatoes," Maddy said, looking up happily. She threw one of her acorns toward the window.

"Nah, Matt said he'd help," Kimberly said. "He learned to make this German potato salad overseas and some kind of meatball dish he wants to try."

Potato salad and meatballs? For Thanksgiving dinner? Bruce felt another part of his day fall into line. He'd find someplace open for lunch and eat a triple-decker turkey sandwich. Or maybe he would drive to a cafeteria over in Greenville and eat a whole traditional Thanksgiving meal around three o'clock so he could just pick around at whatever ended up on Kimberly's table.

"I was going to j-o-g over to the p-a-r-k," he said. "Want me to take you-know-who in the s-t-r-o-l-l-e-r?" Which would modify his jog into a slow run or fast walk, but he didn't mind. The resistance of pushing the stroller could actually give him a better workout if he did it right. Or he could ride Kimberly's bicycle and fasten Maddy into the seat on back.

"Matt said he was going to take her somewhere when he got up," Kimberly said.

Oh, of course. Daddy was home now. What was he thinking? Uncle Brucie's services were no longer needed.

"He's still sleeping," Kimberly said. "I think he's still got a little jet lag."

"No, actually, he's been wandering around the house calling for you," Bruce said. "I think he's in the shower now. I hear water."

Two little boys suddenly appeared in the Stewarts' backyard, racing around a stone bench over by the clothesline, squealing and flailing their arms, followed presently by a younger taller version of Milton Stewart, ambling along, gazing up at the treetops as he smoked a cigarette. Evidently the Stewarts were having a family Thanksgiving. No doubt Celia was happy to be missing out on all the commotion.

That was the thing about a basement apartment. You were at the mercy of the herd overhead. Kimberly and Maddy padded around as softly as the cat, but since Tuesday night, Bruce had been constantly aware of the fact that Matt was home. What was he doing up there? Clogging? Bruce was glad his bedroom was beneath Maddy's, not Kimberly and Matt's. He surely didn't want to hear any thumps and bumps above him at bedtime to remind him that he was living in a house with a married couple.

He put on a pair of sweat pants and a hooded sweat shirt, and when he stepped outside ten minutes later, Kimberly and Maddy had left the patio. On the wrought-iron table sat a small bowl of pecan halves with broken shells strewn all about. He heard an excited shriek from inside—no doubt Maddy was being informed of her special outing with Daddy.

The Stewarts' grandsons were now on their knees scooping together a pile of leaves, stopping every few seconds to throw handfuls at each other. Bruce saw his neighbor on the other side splitting a stack of wood while his wife stood on the back step talking on a cell phone. She threw her head back and laughed, a high ringing laugh. Somewhere nearby he heard the deep woof of a dog and, farther off, the sound of a chain saw. It was ironic, he thought as he jogged slowly up the driveway, that on a day when the neighborhood was hopping with activity, he should feel more alone than ever.

34

Out of Distress to Jubilant Psalm

It was a Friday three weeks later, on the last day of school before Christmas vacation, when the ice storm hit, eventually bringing down entire trees and knocking out power throughout much of the area. Rain and low temperatures were a bad combination here in the foothills of South Carolina. By nightfall, Berea, Derby, and Filbert were plunged into darkness. According to the news reports, Greenville still had power except for a few outages on the northern side, for though they had the low temperatures, they had escaped the rain, at least so far.

It had started misting around nine o'clock but increased to drizzling steadily by ten, and parents had begun arriving at Berea Middle School soon afterward to pick up their kids before the roads got too bad to drive on. There were loud complaints about why they hadn't canceled school to start with, and the principal was kept busy trying to tell parents it hadn't been his call. It came from higher up. He kept reminding them, too, that the weather forecast hadn't helped any. They had predicted light freezing rain for tonight, but not this early and not this much.

A December storm was rare, especially one this bad. Real winter weather usually didn't come to South Carolina until January or February, if it came at all. By one o'clock the teachers were told to go home. Bruce stayed until the bus kids got on their way, then offered to follow Elizabeth Landis home because she was nervous about driving on ice. By the time they left together a little before two, the power had already gone out and the parking lot was like glass.

Most of the students were wishing the bad weather had arrived earlier in the week so they could have missed several days of school, but the teachers were glad for the timing. None of them wanted to give up part of spring break for makeup days, yet none of them minded one bit getting out of their afternoon classes on the last day of school, when the kids were pumped up with vacation fever and ripe for mischief.

Elizabeth made it home okay, and she waved her thanks as Bruce pulled into her driveway behind her to turn around. The garage door was up, and Bruce saw her husband step out the side door, as if he had been watching for her. He waved to Bruce, too, as Elizabeth pulled on into the garage. There was a curl of smoke coming from the chimney, and as Bruce drove away, he saw her husband opening the car door, holding out his hands to help her carry things in. How nice it would be, Bruce thought, to have someone waiting to welcome you home, even if it was a home without power for the time being, even if you couldn't use your stove to cook a meal together or your television to watch a movie together. You could still make sandwiches and sit by the fire together.

The news reports were already warning that power restoration could be delayed because the temperatures were expected to stay below freezing for the next two days and there was a fifty percent chance of heavier rain tonight. Maybe Elizabeth and her husband would drag out sleeping bags and bed down in front of the fireplace. Maybe they had a kerosene lamp to read by and lots of candles for atmosphere. Maybe they had an old transistor radio and could listen to classical music as Elizabeth read poems aloud. Her husband was a musician—Bruce had met him a couple of weeks ago at C. C.'s Barbecue. Maybe he would tell Elizabeth tonight about a new piece he was composing, get out the manuscript and play the melody for her on his trumpet. Later they could make milkshakes out of the ice cream that was starting to thaw in their freezer.

Driving home very slowly, Bruce wondered how many married couples would be able to transform the inconveniences of tonight into happy memories. He liked to think that it would be in his power to do that someday, to carry a woman through such a time with laughter and good cheer, to play off a disaster and shape it into a fine moment in a relationship. He used to be good at thinking up resourceful ways to rise above bad circumstances, but he wondered if he still had his touch.

Kimberly still liked to talk about the time she was seven and Bruce, who had recently gotten his driver's license, promised to take her to the community swimming pool one Saturday. But when they got ready to go, the battery in their parents' Chevy Impala was dead. Kimberly had burst into tears at the disappointment, but Bruce had whisked her out of the car and into the little red wagon they used to play with, then had handed her an umbrella to shield herself against the sun, and off they went. It was the ride of her life, she liked to say, from their house over to the pool some fifteen blocks away. They had even stopped at the Sunshine Grocery for cold bottles of Nehi grape soda on their way.

For most of his life, Bruce had always handled setbacks as challenges to be enjoyed. A forty-five minute wait at a restaurant? No problem. Whip out a deck of cards, play Twenty Questions, make up stories about the other people waiting—there were all kinds of possibilities. The lead actress in your play loses her voice the day before the big performance? Have her go through all the motions on stage and mouth all the words while you read all her lines over a microphone off stage. Luckily, the play had been a comedy, so his male falsetto had simply added to the effect. But there was always a way to make a bad situation better if you used a little creativity. Every time he watched that silly movie *The Out-of-Towners,* he imagined how he would have handled all those catastrophes differently from Jack Lemmon.

But in most situations there needed to be another person for motivation. For instance, he never would have pulled an empty red wagon across town by himself at the age of seventeen. So though it might be fun to tough out an ice storm someday, he had no desire to do so by himself this weekend. There was a fireplace upstairs in Kimberly's den, so Bruce knew he could keep warm, but without power what would he do tonight? He didn't have much to eat in his apartment, and he surely didn't trust Kimberly to have laid in a supply of food before she'd left town with Matt and Madison yesterday to visit Matt's parents in Tallahassee, Florida.

Maybe he should throw some things into a duffel bag and drive over to a motel in Greenville for the night. He could go to the old Sleepy Town Inn on Highway 25 with the trim little marquee out front that proudly advertised *VCRs and Movie Library,* only he would take his own movies along. He could imagine what kind of movie library a motel called the Sleepy Town Inn would have.

He had planned to go Christmas shopping this weekend, so he could do that tomorrow. He usually didn't buy many Christmas gifts, but he always tended to get extravagant with the ones he did buy. With only seven shopping days left, he should probably go ahead and get started.

Everyone he passed on the road looked worried. Not that he could see their faces, only the rigid slant of their bodies, their heads thrust forward, both hands clutching the steering wheel. It irritated him to hear northern aliens joke about drivers in the South when the roads were bad. So they were careful on ice—was there anything wrong with that? And all those other snide worn-out comments about everything shutting down and all the bread and milk disappearing from grocery shelves at the least suggestion of a possible snow flurry—it all got so tiresome. Those were the only things northerners seemed to be able to laugh about as they moved in and acted so superior. Take us or leave us, Bruce liked to say—preferably, leave us. Go back home to Yankee land, where everybody thinks it's a crisis when you have a whole week of ninety-degree weather in the summer, where the soles of your feet are so tender you couldn't begin to go barefoot on hot asphalt the way we used to do as kids.

He saw no lights on anywhere as he got closer to his own neighborhood. It was raining seriously now and freezing immediately. What a weight the tree branches had taken on in only a matter of hours. Already they were coated with ice and bending over like tired old field hands. Even though the storm would bring everything to a grinding halt, it would be a beautiful sight in the morning—a glittery crystal world like that scene in *Dr. Zhivago*.

A half mile from home a large tree branch lay right in the middle of the street, one end ripped jaggedly where it had broken off. Thankfully it had landed parallel to the curb so there was room to ease by. Maybe he should have headed south without coming home first. He could have bought toiletries somewhere and worn the same clothes tomorrow. But then he would have had to watch one of the motel's movies or whatever happened to be on television. He thought of some of the pathetic one- and two-star stuff he had sat through, with titles like *Cries from the Tomb* or *Tender Caress* or *Swamp Leech,* all of which had two things in common: pointless plots and very bad acting.

A night away from home might be a good way to start his Christmas vacation, Bruce decided. It would provide a clear dividing point from the concerns of school, and he was more than ready for a break from all that, even if it had to start out with an ice storm. This past week had seemed way too long. The prize rock collection of one of his eighth graders had disappeared from his classroom without a trace, and the girl's parents were irate. Two boys in his homeroom had gotten into a fistfight out in the hall, and his seventh graders had bombed another test—this one on vertebrates—the average grade being sixty-eight percent. These were setbacks he hadn't been able to counter very cheerfully. He had been every bit as exasperated as Jack Lemmon, had even shouted at the two boys, had actually pulled at his hair when he looked through the test papers.

He stubbornly refused to admit the test was too hard. If *one* student—someone like a Nate Bianchi, for example—could remember that frogs had two sets of teeth, the maxillary and the vomerine, then why couldn't all the other lazy sluggards? Maybe he was imagining things, but his students back in Alabama had seemed a little quicker than the ones at Berea Middle. He certainly wasn't willing to consider that his teaching skills might have diminished.

Then again he had taught mainly math classes in Alabama, so maybe that had something to do with it. Maybe he was better at teaching math than science. Although he really enjoyed science, especially life science, there was nothing like the solidity and exactness of math. He liked the fact that an equation always had a specific answer, not something you could argue about. It wasn't iffy like the weather—this fifty percent chance of more rain tonight, for example. Math was dependable.

A few months ago he had run across a copy of *Gruber's Complete Preparation for the SAT* in a used bookstore in Greenville and had bought it just to see if he could get all the math questions right. It probably should have alarmed him that he had spent one entire Friday evening zipping through pages and pages of practice algebra problems, writing down his answers, then checking them all. He especially loved the ratio problems for some reason: *If $m + 4n = 2n + 8m$, what is the ratio of n to m?* Easy as pie, he'd say. It's $7 : 2$. *If $P + Q = R$ and $P + R = 2Q$, what is the ratio of P to R?* In a flash he had the answer—$1 : 3$. Nothing but child's play.

Ratios were such an interesting way to look at life, to consider its problems as simple relationships. Maybe he should take his Gruber's SAT book along with him to the motel tonight. He could watch a movie, work a few math problems, eat a snack, watch another movie, and so forth. He shook his head. That wasn't one bit funny.

Since Kimberly and Matt's driveway was sloped, Bruce decided to play it safe and park on the street for now. He half skated down to the back of the house. The patio in front of his apartment door was glazed over in a solid sheet. No sign of Celia's Mustang next door, though the Stewarts' Buick was there. Evidently Patsy and Milton were holed up inside their house. They had a woodstove in their kitchen and kept a stack of oak logs beside the front door. He wondered what scintillating conversation would go on between them tonight in the dark.

He wondered how Celia would spend an evening without power when she got home. No doubt she was well stocked with candles and flashlights. She would probably do something sensible like eat a peanut butter sandwich, then straighten a few closet shelves and go to bed early. It would get awfully cold in her apartment, though. The Stewarts would probably invite her upstairs to sit by the fire.

Inside, he quickly got his things together, then stopped at his bookcase on the way back out. So which movies should he take along with him? He wasn't in the mood for anything really intense, nothing like *The Fugitive* or *Day of the Condor* or *Clear and Present Danger,* three of his favorites. He didn't want to watch anything tonight that would increase his heart rate. And nothing really long or fantastical—no *Star Wars* or *Lord of the Rings* tonight.

Driving Miss Daisy—now there was a possibility. He pulled it off the shelf and put it in his duffel bag, then added *The Trip to Bountiful.* Though he had watched it only a few weeks ago, he wouldn't mind seeing it again, a Hollywood movie with all those hymns in it. Okay, two movies about old women—well, he wasn't going to try to analyze that. They were both good stories, and he liked old women fine. *Singing in the Rain*—it was the only musical he owned. He pulled it out and put it in his bag with the other two. Okay, so now he had old women and dancing men. He quickly added *Citizen Kane.* There, that was a movie for the true cinema lover, somebody with an interest in the history of technique, camera angles, special effects, and all that.

Heading back up the driveway to the street, he was glad he wasn't staying in a cold, dark house by himself tonight. He stood for a moment beside his truck, looking up at the treetops, feeling the sting of rain on his face. All was quiet in the neighborhood except for the creaking of a tree limb somewhere nearby. Bruce wondered where it would land when it fell.

As he got into his truck, he saw a cat sitting in the window of the neighbor's house across the street, peacefully watching the world turn to ice outside. Thankfully, Kimberly had given her cat away a few days after

Matt had gotten home from Germany, so he didn't have to worry about checking on it while they were in Florida. Matt claimed to have developed an allergy to cat dander while in Europe, but Bruce had his doubts. He suspected that Matt didn't like the way Kimberly baby-talked and cooed to the cat, who never returned one iota of her affection. He further suspected that Matt wasn't crazy about the fact that the cat had been sleeping on his side of the bed during his absence.

Even in a species known for its hauteur, Kimberly's cat was in a class of its own, nothing like the sweet cat he had had as a boy, the one that had died in the fire. Tabitha would lie contentedly in his lap for hours at a time and let him knead behind her ears. Out of all the legs in the house, his had always been the ones she had chosen to rub herself against. Kimberly's cat, on the other hand, acted like humans were a step below squirrels and field mice.

Out on Highway 11 cars were creeping along. Even in good weather people had grown wary of this road, and they surely weren't going to take chances on a day like this. More people had been killed on this stretch than any other place in the county. *Be patient,* Bruce told himself, *keep your place in line, stay on the road, and within fifteen minutes you'll be on I-85.*

Maybe he would eat supper at the Cracker Barrel off the interstate outside Greenville. He liked their food. Then he'd have the whole evening before him. Maybe he'd do a little shopping tonight if the malls were open, then check into the motel and start his movie marathon. Or maybe he'd forget the malls and go straight to the movies.

He suddenly realized how tired he was from four months spent with middle schoolers. Right now he didn't even want to think about facing another five months after Christmas was over. How would he ever find the energy to tackle the chapter on human reproduction? "Cover the material in a straightforward manner," the teacher's manual said. "If you treat it maturely, your students will respond in kind." He would like to have a talk with those textbook writers someday and find out what planet they were from.

Forget school for now, he told himself. *Think about a whole evening in a comfortable motel room with a supply of snacks and some of your favorite movies to watch.* A question presented itself to him: What was the ratio between the number of different movies he had seen during his life and the number in his current collection? Well, what did it really matter, since so many of the ones he had seen were so bad? Here was a better one—what was the ratio between the number he now owned and the number he would have a year from now? Given the fact that his conscience had started protesting so much lately, he wouldn't be surprised if the first number in that ratio turned out to be larger than the second.

Things he had seen dozens of times before without even batting an eye were beginning to bother him. Only last weekend, for example, he had found himself stopping and ejecting a video when the scene suddenly shifted from a man and dog trekking up a snowy mountainside to that same man in bed with a woman. And it wasn't so much that the bedroom scene, to which he had never objected before, now seemed largely irrelevant to the main plot. The real offense, and the one that he actually shouted at the television screen, was the fact that the couple barely knew each other. "You just met her yesterday!" were his exact words, directed at the man—an actor Bruce had always admired for having won three Oscars.

And the worst thing, the part that let him know he shouldn't hang on to such a video, was the way it burst open the floodgates of his past. No sooner had the words left his mouth than he replied to himself, "Well, aren't we pious?" And as the faces of many girls suddenly rose up before him like clouds of little bubbles someone was blowing through a plastic wand, he added, "What about all these, Mr. Sanctimonious? How long did *you* wait after you met them?"

He was glad his pickup had four-wheel drive, but even so he wasn't going to push it. In his younger days, he had hotdogged all over the place, whether the roads were slippery or dry, but that was only another of the many ways he had changed.

What would the ratio be between the number of dollars of damage he had done to cars due to his careless driving, he wondered, and the list price of the Ford pickup he now drove? That might be interesting to know—or discouraging. He wondered how parents of boys could ever let them get behind the wheel of a car. He couldn't imagine the responsibility of rearing a son. He was too aware of male weaknesses—he would make the poor boy's life miserable. Of course, it didn't look as if he would ever have to face such a responsibility. Somebody like Strom Thurmond might have married at sixty-six and sired four children after that, but it made Bruce tired to think of having teenagers when you were in your eighties. He could barely keep up with the ones at school. Some days he couldn't wait to send them all home—and he was only forty.

The rain was getting considerably lighter now. Even a fine mist was treacherous, though, when the temperature was below freezing. He passed a car that had slid off the road. No one was in it or he might have stopped. That could have been nice, to have someone in the car with him—some distraught person who needed his help.

All of a sudden it hit him that an evening watching movies alone left a lot to be desired. And what if the storm migrated this way and knocked out all the power in his motel room, say right in the middle of Gene Kelly's great dance scene in the pouring rain? Then he would be in a cold, dark, *strange* place all alone. So what if the news said the storm wasn't likely to reach Greenville? *Likely* was a mighty precarious word.

Maybe he should drive farther south—on toward Anderson or Commerce, Georgia. That should be even safer. He had heard all the teachers at school talk about the good shopping in Commerce, all the women teachers that is. None of the men cared much about outlet stores. Or maybe he should forget Commerce and drive all the way to Atlanta. He could no doubt find a really spectacular gift for Maddy in Atlanta, maybe even that ambulance he was still hoping for.

But wherever he went tonight, he needed to be back home by Sunday to help with the children's Christmas program at church that night. Of course, if the power wasn't back on by then, they might not be having a Christmas program—and then what would they do? All the props for the manger scene and the shepherds' bathrobes and staffs had been collected and were stored in the choir room. If they put it off a week, it would be after Christmas.

Goodness, he was letting himself get entirely too keyed up over this little ice storm. He was acting like an old person. Where was his flexibility, the attitude of let-come-what-may that he was feeling so proud of only moments earlier? Calm down, get a grip, everything's going to be okay, he told himself. If Greenville gets hit, then you can get in your trusty truck and move on down the road. If the Christmas program gets canceled, life will still go on. School's out. You're a free man for two whole weeks.

He was nearing the little strip mall now where the Trio Gallery was, only a couple of miles away from the 85 exit. Though the sky was still the color of slate, it appeared that the rain had now stopped altogether. Maybe the weatherman would actually be right about something for a change.

It was almost three-thirty, but Bruce was already feeling really hungry.

Lunch had been totally confusing with all the announcements over the intercom, kids leaving, the cafeteria helpers trying to hurry things up. Bruce had eaten a single piece of pizza while helping patrol the front hall and office area. Other teachers had been scurrying to take down their Christmas decorations and pack up to go home early.

A good hot meal would definitely be first on the agenda. He would be at the Cracker Barrel before four o'clock, so he could get right in. Slowing down slightly as he passed the strip mall, he glanced toward the Trio Gallery. There were lights on in most of the shops but only a couple of cars in the parking lot. He wondered if any of the shop owners would close down early today. Surely Celia would have been listening to the weather on a day like today. Surely she knew about the broken electrical lines in Berea and Derby and wouldn't want to wait until almost dark to drive home and see if her apartment had power. He thought again of how cold her apartment would get without electricity and hoped the Stewarts would look out for her. Maybe she would stay the night at the gallery. Maybe there was a cot in a back room somewhere.

Suddenly he had an idea, a very silly one, but one that he could almost imagine himself acting on. He was already past the gallery by now, fortunately, but the idea kept growing in his mind. It was totally ridiculous. He would never do it. He wouldn't dare. He wasn't in the mood for another snub. But it could be different this time. He wouldn't get all flustered and talk too much.

He saw himself open the front door of the gallery and saunter in. He saw Celia lift her head from . . . whatever it was she did all day. Besides bookkeeping, that is. Milton had said not long ago that Celia had "taken over the books" at the gallery, which meant she was working longer hours during the week than she used to and wasn't working on Saturdays anymore.

Driving on, Bruce pictured himself in the gallery, standing by the door, looking around with a detached air, trying to decide if this was really worth his time. Very cool, very nonchalant. No nervous stumbling around for words this time. He did not even so much as glance in Celia's direction, though he could tell that she was looking at him, her fingers poised over the computer keyboard.

Humming a tune, something she would recognize—maybe "Precious Lord, Take My Hand"—he would proceed around the gallery perusing the works of art, maybe making notes on a pad of paper, as if he was seriously considering a purchase or was going to write up a critique on the show for the newspaper. She would resume her work at the computer, but hesitantly, the irregular clicks of the keyboard giving it away that she was eaten up with curiosity about why he was here at the gallery.

He skipped over ten or fifteen minutes, still walking around humming, before returning to the door, stopping to make one last notation on his pad. She had risen from the desk by now and was kneeling by a large painting on the floor, measuring its length and width. He could tell that she was only pretending to be busy, though, that if he asked her the dimensions of the painting, she would have to measure it all over again. He opened the door, which triggered an electronic bell sound, and watched her head spin around to see if he was leaving. He saw the stricken look on her face as she saw him step across the threshold.

At which point he pretended to take notice of her for the first time and step back in, at which point her face flooded with barely disguised joy, at which point he spoke to her: "It's pretty nasty outside today." She stood and came to the window, a worried look in her sad eyes.

"How will I ever get home?" she said, wringing her hands. "The tires on my car have almost no tread left on them."

"There's no power at your house," Bruce said gently. "I just came from there. The whole neighborhood is out."

Her hand went to her throat. "It will be so cold," she said. "And I hate the dark."

A car honked, and Bruce edged back into his lane. Good thing he had snapped back to reality—he barely had time to veer onto the 85 exit. Way to go, Walter Mitty, he told himself. He remembered the movie, with Danny Kaye playing the role of the addlebrained daydreamer. But at least he wasn't going to extremes like Walter Mitty—no World War II ace pilot heroics, no life-or-death surgical procedures or courtroom dramas. But then maybe he was going to extremes. In fact, he most definitely was. What was more extreme than dreaming about somebody like Celia melting at the sight of him, hinting for him to take care of her?

You ought to be ashamed, he told himself. And before the other side of him, the defensive whiny side, could say, "What for?" he provided the answer: "The only reason you keep thinking about her is that she doesn't give you the time of day." And he recognized it as the absolute truth. If she fell for him the way other women always had, he could mark her off and forget about her.

How many times had he watched women submit to him after he had plotted just the right word spoken at just the right time with just the right amount of innuendo and a suggestive smile, a long knowing look, a flippant nod—whatever it took for that particular woman, which was always something he seemed to know instinctively.

And though he had never ever forced himself on a girl, would have considered that the height of bad manners not to mention an empty victory, he knew in his heart that he had done exactly that by his smooth talking and subtle gestures. What did it matter, really, whether you used charm or brawn to get your way? Soft manipulation or manhandling—both resulted in the same thing. He had known exactly what he was doing. How could he ever forgive himself? How could God stand the sight of somebody like him in heaven with all the white-robed saints who deserved to be there?

And then, right there on I-85 heading toward Greenville, he again heard a chiding voice: *But grace, don't ever forget grace!* Part of him wanted to say, *But my sins are so many,* while the other part scolded, *You have got to be the slowest learner in all of Christendom.* God's grace, he told himself firmly, is big enough to cover the blackest sins. It's strong enough to lift the heaviest load of guilt, to blow the dirt of shame from the darkest corner and scatter it to the four winds. It's good and bright enough to shine into a man's heart and clean out all the filth of the past forever and ever.

Heading toward a hot nourishing meal on an icy day, Bruce allowed the truth of God's grace to envelop him like a warm bath. That's how he would write it someday, to help someone else who was having trouble remembering that when God forgives, he does it once and for all. He doesn't keep dragging out reminders the way people do.

Bruce was past thinking that grown men didn't cry. If they didn't, they probably should once in a while. He wasn't afraid to admit that he did sometimes cry, for that matter had cried less than a week ago during the closing invitation hymn at church: "Out of my bondage, sorrow, and night," it started, and the whole song was a back-and-forth list of things a person was being taken out of and being led into instead.

The *out of*'s all fit him perfectly—"shameful failure," "unrest," "life's storms," "earth's sorrows"—and all of the *into*'s were things he craved— "freedom," "joy and light," a "sheltering fold." And then there was his favorite line of the whole hymn: "Out of distress to jubilant psalm." How could anyone resist a trade like that? "Jesus, I come to Thee"—those were the last five words, words he hoped he never forgot. He needed to sing to them every day to remind himself once again of where he could go for reassurance every time he loosened his hold on the concept of grace.

35

And Grace Will Lead Me Home

Bruce was happy to see that the Cracker Barrel parking lot hadn't begun to fill up. Maybe he could get in and out within an hour. He had learned a long time ago that you could eat fast when you were by yourself. He never took a paperback book or newspaper to read the way he saw other singles do in restaurants.

He didn't need a menu, he told the waiter, a twenty-something with a pageboy and a friendly smile who introduced himself as Peter and told Bruce he would be "taking care of him." The boy had some kind of accent, too—German, Belgian, Danish, something like that. Or maybe he was Dutch, with his little Hans Brinker haircut. Greenville was attracting so many foreigners now with all its international industries that you could walk through one of the sidewalk cafés downtown and not understand a word. It was pretty amazing, though, the way they could shift into fluent English when they wanted to.

Bruce ordered a pork chop dinner with carrots, green beans, and mashed potatoes. Both corn bread and biscuits, he told Peter, with blackberry jelly for the biscuits. Sweet tea to drink, with extra lemon. After Peter left, Bruce pulled the little jump-a-peg game over to give it a try but stopped and shoved it away as soon as he saw he was headed for the "ignoramus" category. He used to have the pattern memorized, but it had been too long ago.

Though there were still plenty of tables available, he was a little surprised to find so many people eating full-fledged meals at four o'clock.

He looked up at the walls at all the old signs. He supposed they had been real products at one time, but he surely hadn't heard of most of them: Norka Ginger Ale, O-So Grape Soda, Morrell Snow Cap Pure Lard, Tops Snuff, Pollard's Tablets for Stomach Disorders, Beau Monde Corsets, Arpeako Sausage.

The hostess escorted a couple to the table right across from him. The man said something, and the woman emitted a shrill, tittering laugh. Bruce thought of a girl he had known with just such a laugh. He had taken her out once—and only once, after listening to her laugh for three solid hours. There were worse things than eating alone, he thought as the woman laughed again, then slipped off her shoe to rub the man's pant leg. She had a little blond corkscrew of a ponytail sprouting from the top of her head, and it bounced up and down every time she laughed. Bruce hoped his food would come soon.

He looked over at the window. Everything outside had the defeated look of early winter. No sign of rain here, though, which was a relief. How strange to think that a mere thirty miles away tree branches were falling onto power lines because of ice. He heard someone at a table behind him say, "Yep, Teddy says his crew's gonna be working all night."

The couple across from him ordered and then began scuffling over the peg game. "Hey, give it back, Gracie, I wanna go first," the man said. How old were these two anyway? Bruce wondered. The woman released another ear-piercing giggle and let go so suddenly that pegs went flying. One landed by Bruce's foot. "Oh, Grace, for crying out loud," the man said, getting up to retrieve them.

Of all the names in the world, her name had to be Grace. Bruce wished it wasn't. That was too pretty a name for somebody like her. He reached down to pick up the peg by his foot and handed it to the man, who said, "Thanks—sorry, she's a real live wire" and cut his eyes back toward the woman, though the self-satisfied grin on his face said, "But I'm the kind of man who can handle live-wire women."

While the man continued gathering up all the pegs, the woman stood up and made a big production of taking off her coat, which looked like a long limp sweater, then undulated her way over to the coatrack by the big stone fireplace, making it clear, with all the extraneous movement of her hips, that she wanted everybody in the place to notice her. When she turned around, Bruce saw that she had on a fleecy red sweater with a V-neck—a capital V—and a little black clingy skirt that hit her about

midthigh. Her long legs were bare all the way down to her highly imprac-
tical shoes, which were skimpy red backless heels that made a flip-flap
sound with each step she took.

Bruce quickly looked up at the wall again, fixing his gaze on a metal
sign that said Aunt Tidy's Foot Powder. There was no safe place you could
look at a woman like that. Someday he'd like to address all the women of
the world and tell them a few things about the clothes they wore. If he ever
had a daughter, he would never . . . But no use getting off on that.

She sat back down and the man said, "Okay, Grace, here we go. Whoever does best gets to . . ." Thankfully, he dropped his voice and leaned
across the table to inform her of the prize for winning the peg game, at
which Grace slapped his hand and said in a little-girl voice, "Oh, you bad,
bad boy, you."

Bruce felt like groaning out loud. There should be a law against
couples who acted this way in public. He took up his own peg game again
and decided to try figuring it out by going backward. At least he would have
something to look at while he was waiting. He emptied it of all the pegs,
then started inserting them one at a time, thinking back to the previous
jumps that would result in each configuration. It was hard to concentrate,
though. At one point he heard the man at the next table say, "Hey, you're
cheating. You can't jump two." Grace laughed giddily and told him to
shush, *she* was making up a *new* game with *new* rules.

Bruce was so grateful when Peter appeared with his food that he
decided right then and there to give the boy an especially generous tip.

He stared down at his plate of good food, then closed his eyes briefly.
This wouldn't take long. He would eat fast. He would block out everything and think about . . . what? "Cut it out, Grace!" he heard from the
next table.

That was it—he'd think about *grace* as he ate his supper. It was one
of his favorite topics, one big enough to dwell on for days on end. He
started eating his carrots. It was something he and Elizabeth Landis had
talked about several times after school—the marvel and mystery of God's
grace.

"Amazing grace, how sweet the sound"—it was a favorite hymn at
Community Baptist. Pastor Monroe, a gem of a man though not exactly a
gifted preacher, had told the story in one of his sermons of John Newton, a
converted slave trader who wrote the words and music to "Amazing Grace."
Bruce liked the way the hymn encompassed the past, present, and future

of a believer—that was exactly what grace did. In the back of the hymnal he had found a listing called Topical Index, in which he had discovered five hymns with the word *grace* in their titles. They had sung only three of them, however, during the time Bruce had been attending.

Sometime he would like to have a word with the song leader, who often had them sing little catchy choruses that weren't in the hymnbook. Though Bruce didn't know much about music, he recognized these songs as sort of a bridge between popular tunes and traditional-style hymns. If anybody had asked him his preference, Bruce would have voted to stick to the hymnbook, but because no one had, he didn't say much. As Virgil Dunlop had explained it, the new songs were for people like Bruce, who were new converts. "We're trying to provide something more familiar and contemporary," Virgil had said.

Although in Bruce's opinion it seemed a little like serving Spaghet-tiOs to an Italian, he had already begun to learn that the kingdom of God included a wide variety of tastes. He could quietly prefer the old hymns—there was nothing wrong with that. It was probably one more piece of evidence illustrating a recurring theme: "Bruce Healey is over the hill." But that was okay, too. After cresting a hill, the view could be breathtaking.

He finished his carrots and started on the green beans, proceeding in his usual one-food-at-a-time method of eating. Next would come the mashed potatoes and then the pork chop. He always saved his meat and bread till last.

But back to grace. Maybe someday he would learn not to keep beating himself up over sins that God had eternally forgiven. When you find yourself alone in a dark valley, he told himself, you've got to keep coming back to the mountaintop of grace. It was grace that found you, opened your eyes, saved you, and kept you safe. "And grace will lead me home," as the hymn said—what beautiful words.

But an old niggling question kept intruding. What if the day did come when he could finally consistently remember that the mercies of God were from everlasting to everlasting—that would be fine, but what about the mercies of people? How could he ever expect a good woman anywhere on the face of the earth to want a man with such a history as his? For it wasn't just any woman he wanted to make a life with—it had to be a good woman, someone who knew about the grace of God. And what right under heaven did he have to hope for the love of a good woman?

How ironic that he could finally see a permanent, binding relationship with one woman as a desirable and holy thing—a God-sanctioned
gift, one of the highest goals a man could set for himself—yet at the same
time he now realized how ineligible he had rendered himself to a godly
woman. He could have had marriage any number of times in the past,
but he had never wanted it. And now that he was beginning to want it, it
wasn't available.

Loretta Vickery hadn't been the only woman who had tried to talk
him into marriage, but she had come the closest to getting him. Though
she had used deceit, it had almost worked. *Don't think about Loretta,* he
said to himself, but almost immediately a reply came: *Yes, do think about
her. Review the lessons you learned from her.*

Okay, he would do that, and he wasn't really getting off the subject.
Being rescued from Loretta Vickery was certainly under the category of
grace. He slowly pulled apart his biscuit and spread it with butter. *Lesson
number one: Physical beauty isn't the most important thing.* Loretta had had
plenty of that. Even the early warning lights that had flashed in his mind
over some of the things she did and said didn't have enough wattage to
overcome the sight of her. He kept thinking, foolishly, that he could help
her change.

He cut into his corn-bread muffin and also spread it with butter. *Lesson
number two: Sins of the flesh lead to destruction.* Oh yes, it had been fun at first,
until he started learning about all the lies. Loretta, one of the trainers at a
fitness club he belonged to in Montgomery, had lied to him both by what
she said and what she didn't say. She *hadn't* told him she was still married,
for example, which was a fact, and then after they had kept company for
a couple of months, she *had* told him she had tested positive with one of
those home kits from the drugstore, which wasn't true. What had started
out as an exciting little fling ended up as a nightmare.

By the time it was all sorted out, thanks to an anonymous phone call
from one of Loretta's co-workers, Bruce had rued the day he first laid eyes
on her, that day he had seen so much that he couldn't think straight. If he
hadn't already known by then how unstable she was, another phone call
a couple of days later would have clinched it, this one from a neighbor of
Loretta's who had discovered her in the process of slitting her wrists in a
final effort to convince Bruce that she couldn't live without him.

And then when the husband finally got involved, showing up at school
one day waving a gun at Bruce in the parking lot, Bruce saw why the man

and Loretta had married each other in the first place—they were both a couple of wackos, crazy out of their minds. The police came and there were questions and paperwork, then rumors and tearful phone calls from Loretta, even a visit to his classroom right in the middle of a math lesson one day. No one had told Bruce to leave town—it was a demand he placed on himself. He couldn't wait till the last day of school, when he could load up his pickup and get out of Montgomery, Alabama, for good.

Lesson number three: Prevention is the best remedy for trouble. He shuddered to think what his life would be like today if he and Loretta had gotten married somewhere by a justice of the peace, as she had almost talked him into doing "for the baby's sake." It was enough to scare any sane man away from women for the rest of his life. He thought of the verse in Colossians: "Touch not; taste not; handle not." That would sure head off a lot of problems.

Unfortunately though, even as horrible as the situation with Loretta had been, as much as it had scared him, it wasn't enough to keep him from now imagining the joy of finding a good woman who could love him in spite of the things he had done. Also, and this was worth remembering, that verse in Colossians wasn't condoning total abstinence from everything enjoyable. So Lesson number three could bear reexamination, at least in its specific application.

He lifted his buttered biscuit again and spread it thick with blackberry jelly, then took a big bite and chewed slowly. He had to think this through. Virgil Dunlop had read that very passage from Colossians in Sunday school recently. The verse wasn't really warning against touching, tasting, and handling as such, but against all the rules people hold up as visible proof of their better-than-thou sanctification. Not that rules were bad, Virgil had stressed, not at all. Just because you had liberty in Christ, you didn't scrap the law. The law was like your rudder on the sea of life.

He took another bite. Who needed dessert, he wondered, when you could eat a warm buttered biscuit with blackberry jelly? So because a person could pig out on biscuits and commit the sin of gluttony, did that mean you couldn't enjoy *one*? Maybe he was forcing parallels now. He wished he could reduce it to a simple ratio.

But back to grace. He still had much to learn, but on this one point he was sure: If God's grace was full and powerful enough to cancel out bad things, wasn't it also generous enough to replace those bad things with good things? And the answer to that was easy: Yes. So maybe—it was coming to him now—maybe he ought to try something very basic to Christianity, something else he kept forgetting about. Maybe he should ask, seek, and knock, as that verse in the Sermon on the Mount instructed. That was it. He would pray. If God cared about supplying the food you ate and the roof over your head, surely he cared about something as important as a wife.

He looked up to see Grace and her boyfriend staring at him. What had he done? Maybe he had chuckled out loud or hummed a bar of "Amazing Grace." Well, who cared? He wasn't ever going to see these people again—at least he earnestly hoped not. He lifted his corn-bread muffin to them, as if toasting, and said, "Sorry, just had a nice thought."

Grace laughed, her ponytail bobbing. "Oh, that's cute."

"Well, good," Bruce said. "That's my goal in life, to be cute."

Another burst of giggles. "Oh, I *like* him," Grace said to her boyfriend. "I like him a lot." She reached over and cupped the man's face in her hands. "But not as much as you, Willy-boy."

Good grief, Bruce thought, he had to finish up fast and get out of here. Thankfully, he was nearly done. He took a huge bite of his corn bread, then a long drink of tea.

The Cracker Barrel was filling up. There were now only three empty tables that he could see. He nabbed Peter on the way by and asked for his check, and as he left a five-dollar bill on the table a minute later the thought came to him—and he hoped it wasn't a sacrilegious one—that Jesus had not only paid it all, but he also gave big tips and bonuses, as well. He stood there for a moment with his hand still touching the money, and when he looked up, Grace and Willy-boy were staring at him again.

Bruce smiled at them and with perfect composure said, "And grace will lead me home." As he left, he heard Grace erupt into a fit of spasmodic laughter behind him, then stop suddenly and say, "Hey, what did he mean by *that?* I'm not going home with *him!*"

He was standing in line to pay at the cash register, studying the glass jars of candy behind the cashier—red-hot jawbreakers, strings of licorice, malted milk balls, lemon drops—when it occurred to him that he could pray anywhere. He didn't have to wait till he was alone. A verse came to him, one Pastor Monroe had preached on not too long ago: "Pray without ceasing." And so he did. He fixed his eyes on the canister of caramel chews right then and there and prayed a very simple prayer.

Standing in line at Cracker Barrel, behind a woman wearing fuzzy brown earmuffs, Bruce Healey prayed that God would give him a good woman. That's how he would write it in a story someday. As the cashier gave him his change, he wondered how loudly she would laugh if she knew not only that he had just prayed for a good woman but also that he actually felt something he could describe only as absolute confidence that God had heard his prayer and was already making plans to answer it.

He wondered if this was a new-Christian phenomenon. Maybe after time Christians got used to praying anywhere and being filled with anticipation over seeing those prayers answered. Maybe it was like anything else—maybe it got old with time. Like the way most married couples seemed to look right past each other without seeing the miracle of being husband and wife. Like the woman with the fuzzy earmuffs, who had stopped to look wistfully at a set of Christmas glasses with holly berries hand-painted on them, her husband pushing at her elbow impatiently, a toothpick sticking out of each side of his mouth. Bruce felt like saying it to him, "Buy her those glasses, you fool! Can't you see the look in her eyes?"

Whenever he saw a woman with that defeated look on her face, wishing yet knowing it was useless to wish, Bruce felt sad. A man should understand how much pretty things meant to a woman. He should devote his life to getting them for her, even if she had let her figure go, as the earmuff woman had, and even if her face was as plain as a round of corn bread in a cast-iron skillet. Maybe she would have a little more motivation to keep herself looking nice if her husband made her happiness a priority.

Oh, the things he could tell husbands if he could gather them all in one place. But as he walked out the door behind the earmuff woman and her husband, he thought of how he would be laughed offstage if he ever were to stand before all the husbands of the world to give a speech. "Come back and give us your advice after you've been married a few years!" they'd shout. Yes, he had it all figured out on this side of matrimony, just as he could see, from his childless vantage, all the things parents did wrong. He should plan a double seminar while he was at it: How to Be the Perfect Husband and Father.

And then it happened. He lifted his eyes and saw her pulling into the parking lot at Cracker Barrel. At the first instant Bruce was so shocked that he didn't connect her with the prayer he had prayed only a couple of minutes earlier. His first thought was to wonder why God was playing a joke on him. For one thing, he had prayed specifically for a good woman—not necessarily one with a spotless past, but certainly one who had heeded the call of God to come and receive his grace. And though he had never spoken with her about it, he felt sure that Celia, with her sad eyes, was a stranger to God's grace. Besides that, he thought God understood that he wanted a woman who would enjoy his company, not one who went out of her way to avoid him.

But the second thought was that maybe he himself was supposed to be the messenger sent to acquaint Celia with God's grace. But then the very next moment, he remembered the lessons he had learned from Loretta Vickery and wondered if maybe Celia was placed in his path to test his sincerity. You didn't try to change a woman, he knew that. Had he really learned anything, or was he as ready as ever to fall for a pretty face?

There he was, standing by one of the rocking chairs under the covered sidewalk in front of the Cracker Barrel along I-85 a few miles outside Greenville, watching his next-door neighbor open the door of her Mustang. He knew it was Celia before her left foot touched the pavement. He knew her car—not only the make, model, year, and color, but also the tires, the hubcaps, the Triple-A bumper sticker, the license plate.

And, strangely, before he had time to argue with himself that no way, this couldn't be happening to him, that the split-second timing was too unreal, that God didn't pull rabbits out of hats, he suddenly remembered something out of the blue from a book Elizabeth Landis had brought him six or seven weeks ago.

It was from a book a friend of Elizabeth's had written. He had even met this friend, who was at C. C.'s Barbecue with her husband the night he had eaten there with Elizabeth and her husband. And the words that came to him now were from the epilogue of the book Elizabeth had lent him, in which her friend Margaret had set down the moral of her story: "Given sun and rain, a flower *will* bloom. To the human heart, love is irresistible. Though I have not solved the mystery of suffering, I have felt the healing work of love."

So what did it mean? He understood the words clearly enough, but what did it mean for him right now, and did it relate in any way to Celia? Could it be connected somehow to his prayer? If God was going to answer a person's prayer, he wouldn't try to confuse him and trip him up, would he?

"To the human heart, love is irresistible." Were these words sent as a message to Bruce? Did God mean for him to keep knocking at Celia's door time and time again? But wasn't it a dangerous thing, a campaign like that between a man and a woman? Was he capable of simply being a friend to a beautiful woman like Celia? God wouldn't hear a Christian's prayer, then deliberately send a temptation instead, would he?

Well, at least he could be cordial to her right now. After all, he did owe her a lot. Once again he thought of her swooping down on Matt, tennis racket raised like a club, with the fury of a mother defending her young. And wasn't there a verse in the Bible that was relevant here—"inasmuch as ye have done it unto one of the least of these"? She hadn't really saved Madison's life, of course, but she would have if she had needed to. So in God's sight, maybe it was credited to her account anyway. If somebody could commit adultery in his heart, surely somebody could do something good in his heart like save a life.

And then she saw him. Bruce would have time later to wonder what innovative techniques a good movie director would use to illuminate and enlarge the moment, but right now as it was happening, the only thing that came to his mind was one short sentence, something you might read in a book, though totally devoid of the sweeping diction and syntax such a moment warranted: *They looked at each other across the parking lot.*

She didn't exactly stop, though she did hesitate almost impercepti-bly in the middle of a step. But she kept coming, and as she did Bruce couldn't help thinking of all those dreams he sometimes had of being the main character in a play yet not knowing his lines, but the moment was there and it was his turn, so somebody pushed him out onstage under the bright lights, and there was nothing to do but take a deep breath, open his mouth, and start ad-libbing.

They both spoke at the same time, and when they talked about it later, neither had really heard what the other said. Bruce knew exactly what he had said, of course. It was the first thing that came to mind—a line from *A Midsummer Night's Dream,* spoken by Puck to one of the fairies in act 2: "How now, spirit! Whither wander you?"

Somehow in the awkwardness of the moment, it was agreed upon—or maybe Bruce simply announced the plan—that, though he had already eaten, he would sit back down with her inside and maybe have another biscuit and some tea, maybe even some apple cobbler. He was relieved when they were shown to a small table close to the fireplace, a consider-able distance from Grace and Willy-boy, who were still there. *Take it slow and careful,* Bruce told himself as Celia studied the menu. *Weigh your words before you open your mouth. And if you can't think of what to say, just be quiet.*

He thought of how a man could so easily mess up because of the smallest details. One of the math teachers at school had told everybody in the teachers' lounge about her husband's bright idea of paying all their bills online, for example, which wouldn't have been so bad if he hadn't forgotten to enter the decimal in his sixty dollar payment to the phone company, which was transacted as six thousand dollars, which in turn led to "checks bouncing all over the place," as she put it—a significant inconvenience here at Christmastime. What a difference a little dot could make.

Celia ordered a grilled chicken sandwich plate with a Coke but requested some corn bread on the side. "I really like the corn bread here," she told Bruce, and he nodded. He asked the waitress for more tea and told her he would have some corn bread, too, and dessert later. After the waitress left, Celia opened her purse and appeared to be looking for something. She pulled out a postcard and handed it to him. "You asked not long ago about the gallery," she said. "Here's the mail-out for the show that's up now. It's coming down right after Christmas."

On one side of the card was a reproduction of a painting: an old woman sitting on a porch shelling peas. The sordid details were astonishing— the frayed holes of her dingy tennis shoes through which her bunions protruded, the clumsy patch over the rip in the sagging screen door, the peeling paint on the uneven floorboards, a huge beetle on its back, the rusted chair legs, the chipped bowl, the woman's swollen knuckles, a blackened fingernail, her smudged apron over her rounded belly, three flies feeding on the pile of discarded hulls, a messy stack of newspapers beside the door, the headline on the top one reading *Fire Guts Old Mill.*

And yet, the focal point of the picture—the old woman's very wrinkled face—completely reversed the bleakness of the setting, for her jaw was clinched with determination, her eyes steady with the satisfaction of useful work. The expression wasn't anywhere close to smiling, but it clearly said, "I am a contented woman." There was a light in her face that was both surprising yet altogether convincing. Her hair was pinned up loosely, a couple of straggly gray strands hanging down over one ear. The whole picture, in fact, seemed to be executed in shades of gray, one of the few touches of color being the blue bowl.

On the back of the card was the title: *The Last Time I Saw Her.* Beneath it was the artist's name: Macon Mahoney. It was identified as oil on canvas, thirty by twenty-four inches.

"Let me guess—his grandmother?" Bruce asked.

"Yes."

Bruce turned it back over and studied it again. "It's . . . honest, isn't it?"

"Yes, that's a good word for it."

"This artist, this Macon Mahoney, he must be good," Bruce said.

"Oh, he is."

He handed the card back to Celia. "Wouldn't you hate to think of a world without grandmothers?"

But before Celia could respond, Bruce heard another voice. "Hey, isn't that that *funny* man who was sitting by us a while ago?" He looked up to see Grace standing by the coatrack, pointing straight at him, the other arm thrust through the sleeve of her coat, into which Willy-boy was trying to assist her.

Bruce smiled up at her and shrugged. "Just can't get filled up," he said. He was ready for the giggles, which spewed forth like a sudden leak, and for some parting banality, which came in the form of "That guy is an absolute *scream!*" Looking back at Celia, it struck him that he should thank Grace. If it hadn't been for her, he might have taken more time to eat, and Celia might have been shown to a table on the opposite side of the trellis-like partition, where he never would have even seen her. And though he knew there was no limit to the number of ways God could have arranged for their meeting, he liked the way it had worked out.

"So . . . where were we?" Bruce said. "Oh yes, grandmothers. I had a great one. Very Old South, but not so much that she couldn't see the humor in that whole way of life. She could do a very funny parody of a tea party." To demonstrate, he pitched his voice higher. " 'Mildred, where *ever* did you find this darling chintz for your tablecloth? Oh, at Bennington's? Well, I'm going to send Marie around tomorrow to pick up a bolt so Irma can whip me up some little curtains for the sunroom.' "

Celia smiled as she tucked the postcard back into her purse.

Bruce almost didn't ask the next question, but something gave him the go-ahead. "Do you have a grandmother still living?"

She shook her head, but not in a way that warned him to stop.

"Did you ever know either one of your grandmothers?"

"Yes, I knew them both," she said.

The waitress brought their drinks, along with a plate of corn bread and butter pats.

"And . . . do you remember much about them?"

"Oh yes. Yes, I remember quite a bit." She paused, then added, "Especially my grandmother in Georgia."

This might have been a good place to call it off, but again Bruce had a strong sense that it was all right to proceed, that it was something he ought to do in fact.

"What was she like?" he said. "Was she a good woman?"

36

Deeper Than the Mighty Rolling Sea

The first thing Bruce heard when he woke up on Valentine's Day, which fell on a Saturday this year, was the sound of a stump grinder. He looked out his bedroom window to see Milton Stewart standing in the middle of the backyard next door observing another man who was operating the machine on the stump of the large oak they had lost during the ice storm back in December.

Not the most romantic way for Celia to start such a special day, with a sound like that outside her front door, but at least he knew now that she would be awake in plenty of time for his first move. He had been plotting this day for several weeks.

All he had told her was that she needed to stay home today, that she couldn't be dashing in and out all day. Though she had pretended to object, claiming to have dozens of errands to run, she had finally given in. "You'd better have an awfully good reason," she had said. He hoped he would remember to ask her later if she thought his reason was good enough.

Nor was he going anywhere himself. He needed to stay home to make sure everything went according to schedule. He looked at the clock—not quite two hours before things got started—plenty of time to wash and wax her car and his truck, then vacuum them both out. He needed to check with Kimberly about a couple of details for this afternoon, too. He didn't want any last-minute glitches after all the time he had put into this. He ran through the day in his mind, hour by hour. He didn't care if the whole world thought his plan was corny to the hilt. He was forty years old and could be as corny as he wanted to.

When ten o'clock finally rolled around, he was watching from his bedroom window as Celia received the first delivery at her front door. Celia knew a lot about him by now, but he had never told her about the good view he had of her front door from his side window, about how often he had stood here over the past months and watched her through the blinds, which he could adjust so they appeared to be closed yet still allowed him to see out.

The first delivery was flowers, and from his vantage they looked exactly like what he had specified—red roses, the deep crimson red of blood, not an orangey red, and a dozen of them, naturally. No baby's breath— that stuff cheapened an arrangement in his opinion—but a few fronds of fern instead.

Bruce watched Celia take the vase of roses from the delivery man. He saw her smile and put her face close to them. So here it was—this was the beginning. He left the window, sat down at his desk, uncapped a pen, and began writing on the first page of a small black notebook he had bought especially for today. *On February 14 at 10:00 A.M. Celia opened her front door,* he wrote, *and received her first delivery, a dozen red roses.*

This was part of his plan for the day also, to record in writing every detail of the planning and execution of each delivery, which was the main reason he had to stay home today. Later he would give the notebook to Celia. He wrote now about how he had gone to the florist's shop in person to place his order for the roses.

This was going to be fun. He would try to recreate it all for Celia. In the years to come they could read back over it together. After the woman handed him a small gift card and a fine-tipped black pen, Bruce carefully printed these words: *"But the greatest of these is love,"* then added only his first initial, *B,* below. Then he offered to pay whatever extra fee it would take to have the roses delivered as close as possible to ten in the morning on Valentine's Day. The woman studied him for a moment before saying she would see what they could do. Then she wrote 10:00 A.M. DELIVERY!!! at the bottom of the order and underlined it three times.

Bruce was glad he had thought to add a PS on the back of the gift card, which said, *I'll see you tonight. Don't try to call today. I'll be in and out.* And it was true in a sense. He was going to be in and out, mentally, as he wrote all this down, traveling between now and the past several weeks. It was going to take a lot of concentration, and he wanted to relieve her of feeling like she had to call and thank him every time her doorbell rang throughout the day. He wanted to wait until the whole campaign was over before getting her response.

Bruce decided early on that this writing business was harder than he had expected. He stopped often to think about the best way to say something. He wanted the pages to be as neat as possible, not full of crossed-out words and details stuck in as afterthoughts. He barely finished with the story of the roses before eleven o'clock rolled around.

Watching again from his bedroom window, he saw Ollie pull his van into the Stewarts' driveway and park right behind Celia's Mustang. He watched him remove a large painting-sized present, which had been artfully wrapped in swaths of silver foil paper and white ribbon by Ollie's wife, Connie, who worked at the same florist where Bruce had ordered the roses. It was Macon Mahoney's painting of *The Last Time I Saw Her,* the one that reminded Celia of her own grandmother, the painting she had specifically chosen for the postcard mailing because she liked it so much. Though she had pronounced it the best piece in the whole show, it hadn't sold right away.

Celia came to the door after Ollie rang the bell. She looked bewildered, glancing up and down between Ollie's face and the painting resting against his leg. Finally she came to her senses and invited him inside. Bruce wished he could see her eyes as she unwrapped the painting, but for now he had work to do. He sat down at his desk again and uncapped his pen. There was so much he could write about this gift.

At 11:00 Celia found her friend Ollie standing at her door with the second delivery of the day. From there he went on to record how the idea had first come to him after going to the gallery back in late December and standing beside Celia in front of the painting.

"It's too bad so many people are in the market for something pretty," Celia had told him that day. "So look what gets ignored," she continued. "Something truly beautiful." And he understood exactly what she meant. People probably looked at *The Last Time I Saw Her* and saw the dead bug on the floor, the dirty apron, and the rusty chair legs, while completely missing the old woman's face.

That was okay, though. It had kept everybody else from buying it. That, and the hefty price tag. But it was worth every cent he paid for it. Bruce knew that his own grandmother would have approved of such an expenditure, and because he was using her money, it gave him all the more pleasure.

Celia told Bruce she was thinking about buying the painting herself, Bruce wrote, *but Ollie showed up at the gallery one day and put a red dot by it, saying he had an anonymous buyer. Bruce pretended to be disappointed for her when she told him, never letting on about the talk he'd had with Ollie.*

But she was also glad in a way, she had gone on to tell Bruce, that somebody else, some lucky intelligent sensitive person, had recognized the value of the painting and was going to get to enjoy it for the rest of his life. Anonymous buyers, she told him, were quite common in the art world, and they always fascinated her. Maybe the buyer of this painting was afraid everybody would laugh at him for buying what amounted to the ugly duckling of the show.

The noon delivery was modest—a heart-shaped pizza from Pop's Pizza Palace over in Derby, where they were running a Valentine special for only ten bucks. Bruce was watching for the delivery car and met the kid in the driveway to give him a tip and to stick a note to the top of the pizza box that said, *Save room for dinner tonight. See you at six.*

At one o'clock Bruce saw Elizabeth Landis knocking at Celia's door with a long, flat, triangular-shaped gift, wrapped in white paper with little red hearts all over it and a tag, which read, *Looking forward to many more love matches.* No doubt Celia would know at first glance what this gift was, and furthermore, she might even suspect the ulterior motive behind it. If he gave her a new racket, Bruce figured, he could use her old one, the one with which she had whacked Matt's wrist, instead of borrowing Milton Stewart's ancient wooden racket again.

From his bedroom window, Bruce saw Celia smile when she opened the door to let Elizabeth in. She laughed when she read the message on the gift tag, and they both disappeared inside.

Milton Stewart's wooden racket had provided Bruce with a good excuse for not winning a single game out of the twelve he and Celia played during their first match several weeks ago, which in turn had provided Celia with the opportunity to explain to him that the term for that particular score in tennis lingo was "double bagel."

"Well, just wait till I get a better racket, one with a decent sweet spot," he had said, waving the wooden one around. "Then you'll have to eat a few of those double bagels yourself." Whereupon she had insisted on trading rackets with him for another set, then proceeded to find the sweet spot on Milton's wooden racket time and time again while winning another six easy games in a row.

Bruce's main problem right now, he wrote in the black notebook, *is keeping the ball inside the lines, but as soon as he learns to control his massive power, Celia will have trouble on her hands.*

He wrote about driving to Greenville to talk in person with the pro at the Greenville Country Club, who recommended the Dunlop 900–G racket, advertised as "heat refined" in a "hot-melt carbon process," producing a racket with "explosive power and strength." For strings he had chosen natural gut, which was the best according to the pro, and for tension he selected something midrange between high, which he was told resulted in greater control, and low, which was for power.

"Let me tell you, she will love this racket," the pro said, "and with a little luck, some of that might transfer to you." And how did he know she didn't already love him? Bruce asked. The savvy pro replied that Bruce's very personal interest in every aspect of this gift didn't strike him as coming from a man who already had the cat in the bag, so to speak. Bruce took issue with the pro, telling him that he would always be as particular about the gifts he bought this woman as he was being right now. And though the wise pro only smiled as he took Bruce's money, Bruce could tell he was thinking, Oh yeah, right, I hear you. (Bruce is therefore putting this in writing so that Celia will someday be reminded to pay that pro a visit and inform him that not every man becomes careless and forgetful over time.)

Promptly at two o'clock Bruce watched Patsy Stewart plod down the driveway holding a present wrapped in shiny red paper topped with a silver bow. He had asked her to please deliver it to Celia's front door instead of going down through the basement.

One night a couple of weeks ago Bruce had looked in Celia's bedroom after she had paused *The African Queen* and gone to the kitchen to pop another bag of popcorn, right after the scene where Katharine Hepburn had pulled all the leeches off Humphrey Bogart's back. He was looking to see if Celia had a jewelry box, and as far as he could see, she didn't unless she kept it hidden in a drawer somewhere.

He had gone shopping the next day and found one at a gift shop in Greenville—not one of the tacky imitation leather kind stacked up with multiple little drawers, nor one of the more expensive tall wooden ones, some of them very pretty but still with all the drawers and doors, like miniature armoires. This one was a small elegant silver case. A scroll design was worked into the metal, and in the center of the lid was a plain oval silver nameplate for monogramming.

He had given a great deal of thought about what to have inscribed on the plate and had finally chosen a verse reference—Proverbs 1:9. It was a verse he and Celia had discussed almost two months earlier on the day of the ice storm, when they had met by God's design, as Bruce always described it, outside Cracker Barrel, the day Bruce discovered that Celia had, as she put it, "been sought, found, and brought back" during her recent trip to Georgia over Thanksgiving. What a day of surprises that Cracker Barrel day had been.

"For they shall be an ornament of grace unto thy head," the verse in Proverbs said, "and chains about thy neck," the "they" referring to the wise instruction of parents, grounded in the fear of God. Celia had told him about her grandmother that night, haltingly at first but gradually with greater freedom, after which she had gone on to speak of her parents.

"And you know what I've finally realized?" she had said. "Even though my grandmother's way of loving was totally different from my parents', it was still love, through and through. And even though I thought her way of looking at life was hard and cold and stern, she was right about a lot of things. Behind all her rules was a heart that wanted to please God more than anything in the world." She had realized, she said, that Christians weren't perfect, that some of their methods weren't the best, but that you couldn't throw out God's truth because of man's faults. Besides, she'd had plenty of faults herself during the three years with her grandmother.

From the pages of her grandmother's diaries, she told him, she had gotten a glimpse of what their three years together had cost her grandmother, not only in the careful scrimping to put away every penny she could in order to provide for Celia's welfare after high school, but also in the countless hours spent in prayer on her behalf, and finally in the deep sorrow she carried to her grave over failing to "keep my precious Celie safe." She had written about the dread of facing her daughter in heaven someday with the news of that failure.

Over Thanksgiving, three weeks before their meeting at Cracker Barrel, Celia had visited her grandmother's church again and talked at great length with the pastor's wife, with whom she had been corresponding by letter since August, a woman who, according to Celia, "had a lot more to her than you'd ever guess from just looking at her." Denise Davidson had met Celia's every question head on. "Never once did she look shocked at anything I said," Celia told him.

One thing Celia had wrestled with in particular was how sad her parents would be if they knew the things she had done. "I couldn't figure out," she told Bruce, "how I could have turned my back on everything they taught me if I had ever really been converted in the first place. So I kept struggling over whether I needed to start at the beginning and ask God for salvation, or if maybe I was just what everybody used to call 'backslidden' and needed to repent. I wasn't really sure I had ever understood that salvation was more than keeping a long list of rules. I don't think I had ever really caught onto the concept of God's grace."

And the answer to her quandary was so simple, she said, that she was a little embarrassed that Denise Davidson had to spell it out for somebody who had always considered herself well educated, somebody with a healthy IQ and a master's degree, not to mention years and years of churchgoing in her background. And would she please spell it out for him, too, Bruce requested. What exactly had Denise Davidson told her?

"She said why don't we leave it up to God to decide, that if I bowed my head and confessed my sins and repented and asked for his grace to be poured out on me, I didn't need to worry about which category I fit into. He would take care of it." Celia shrugged and smiled. "So I did exactly that."

Before she left Dunmore after Thanksgiving, Celia told Bruce she had visited her grandmother's grave, had stood there for a long time, praying for God to let her grandmother know right now that she would be joining her in heaven someday, and that she loved her and thanked her for all she had sacrificed and was sorry for all the grief she had caused her.

So the two o'clock gift, the jewelry box with its inscribed verse reference, is meant to be a symbol, Bruce wrote, *of the ornaments of grace in a Christian's life, and of Celia's circling back to the instruction of her parents and grandmother. The interior of the case is lined with soft velvet the color of atoning blood. Every time Celia opens the lid, she will see the red velvet and be reminded of how much God loves her.*

At first Bruce had resisted the idea of resorting to someone like Patsy for the two o'clock delivery, someone with such a total lack of dramatic flair. But the more he thought about it, the more fitting it seemed, since he and Celia had been talking about taking Milton and Patsy out for dinner some night soon and sharing with them the story of how God had brought them to himself, first of all, then brought them to each other.

Bruce had already told Milton about Celia's mistaking him for Kimberly's husband, which Milton thought was very funny.

At three o'clock Milton Stewart walked down the driveway to Celia's front door, Bruce wrote after the next delivery, *carrying a gold gift bag with musical notes stamped all over it and tissue tucked inside.* There were six CDs in the bottom of the bag, all of the ones they had at the Barnes and Noble over in Greenville recorded by a clarinet virtuoso named Richard Stoltzman, whom Elizabeth Landis's husband, Ken, had recommended. Richard Stoltzman had a vast repertoire, everything from classical to jazz. One of the CDs even had "Amazing Grace" on it.

Bruce had already told Elizabeth that he and Celia were planning to visit her church tomorrow, on the day after Valentine's Day, and he had even been so bold as to ask Elizabeth if she could make a couple of requests of their song leader, which she had promised to do. He knew Celia liked the song "Wonderful Grace of Jesus" as much as he did. Of all the hymns about grace he had heard so far, that one had the happiest melody, in his opinion. He particularly liked the chorus, which described grace not just in moderate terms, as a flowing river, but flamboyantly, as "the mighty rolling sea." He liked the men's line "Broader than the scope of my transgressions, sing it!"

At four o'clock Bruce carefully guided Maddy down the Stewarts' driveway on her little ambulance car, the one Celia had helped him locate the week before Christmas from an upscale toy shop she found on the Internet.

Bruce placed the gift in Maddy's hands. She held it gingerly, as if it were a fresh loaf of bread she didn't want to squeeze. He helped her ring the doorbell, then stepped around the corner of the house to wait for her. Celia opened the door and stepped out on the concrete stoop. She asked Maddy to help her open the present. He heard them laugh as they tore off the paper and ribbon.

"Oh, look," Celia said, "it's a video."

"Cartoons?" Maddy said.

"No, it's a story," Celia said. "A very nice story." Then she told Maddy to wait right there while she went inside to get a Valentine treat for her, which turned out to be a big lollipop wrapped in red cellophane. When she came back, she called out, "When you see your uncle Bruce, tell him I like the present very much."

At his desk a few minutes later, Bruce wrote, *At four o'clock Maddy brought Celia a video of* Emma, *the one with Gwyneth Paltrow, which Celia had told Bruce was one of her top five favorite movies, along with* Pride and Prejudice.

She had told Bruce she liked *Emma* even a little better than P & P, as they had come to call the other one, because she could identify so much now with Emma Woodhouse, who thought of herself as very alert and observant, although she had completely overlooked all the virtues of the man right under her nose, her neighbor Mr. Knightley.

She was very fond of Austen, "now that I have grown up," she had said. On a bookshelf next to her sofa was a dark blue volume titled *The Complete Works of Jane Austen,* and she had taken to reading Bruce excerpts from it in the past several weeks. She was still ashamed to think how she had once considered Austen's works nothing more than Victorian twaddle. Now she was full of admiration for them.

"Her humor is so understated," she had told Bruce one day. To illustrate, she read several passages, among them the famous opening line of P & P, with which Bruce was familiar, since it was also in the movie: " 'It is a truth universally acknowledged, that a single man in possession of a good fortune must be in want of a wife.' "

Bruce pretended not to catch it. "I don't see anything so funny about that," he said.

And she pretended to explain the meaning patiently. "She's using irony. She's really saying that it's everybody else who thinks the man needs a wife to help him spend all his money. She's just making an observation about all the mothers in the neighborhood who can't wait to get their eligible daughters married off to somebody rich."

"Well, then, that's good for him, I guess. He's got his pick of the whole lot."

"Oh, like women are apples or something? Like a man can stroll through the orchard looking them over, then whenever he feels good and ready just reach up and pluck one?"

"Well, yeah, or like watermelons. He can thump them all on the head till he finds a good one."

"And I guess he ought to check their teeth, too, like when you buy a horse."

"Not a bad idea. Here, open up."

They had talked at length by now about how each of them had been more than a little guilty of both pride and prejudice toward the other.

Bruce didn't believe it when Celia first told him that the original title of Austen's book had been *First Impressions.* She had to prove it by showing him the exact sentence in the introduction to her *Complete Works.*

"That's funny," Bruce said. "I had a little discussion once with Elizabeth Landis about first impressions. You were mentioned in the conversation, as I recall."

"You and Elizabeth talked about me? I would have expected it out of you, but I thought she was my friend."

"Oh, she was on your side, believe me."

"Well, she was on your side, too," Celia said. "Seemed like she was always finding a way to work you into a conversation—'He's so good with kids,' 'You should see him in play rehearsals,' 'He's got a great sense of humor,' 'He's a true gentleman,' blah blah blah."

"Blah blah blah? Are you suggesting none of it was true?"

"Hey, I wasn't born yesterday."

"I'm not touching that one. No way am I going to comment on a woman's age."

The five o'clock delivery was made by Kimberly, along with her new baby girl, Reagan, wrapped up in a white blanket. Bruce was a little nervous about this one, realizing the method of delivery was a gamble. He had told Kimberly to give him a signal when she left Celia's apartment, and twenty minutes later, after saying good-bye to Celia, she looked straight toward his window, raised one thumb, and nodded.

The last gift had to be a book, Bruce wrote. *Specifically, Bruce wanted poetry. So he asked their mutual friend Elizabeth for suggestions, and she told him without hesitation that he could do no better for Valentine's Day than a collection of Elizabeth Barrett Browning, who, she said, not only had a lovely first name and an underappreciated literary gift but also, interestingly enough, had found the love of her life at the age of forty.*

He had decided on a slim, gorgeously bound volume of Browning's *Sonnets From the Portuguese,* which he had ordered over the Internet from a bookshop in London that specialized in rare editions. *None of your ordinary mass-produced books would do for this gift,* he wrote.

First he had gone to the library and done some reading of Browning's poems on his own, thinking he might like to get a complete collection. But many of them had such melancholy subjects—deserted gardens, the tears of an angel, a dead person's hands, lost bowers, exiles from home, and that horrible one about the children weeping. Never would he give

Celia a book with such lines to stumble across: "But the young, young children, O my brothers, / They are weeping bitterly! / They are weeping in the playtime of the others."

So he had settled on the *Sonnets From the Portuguese* for the five o'clock gift, the final one before he came to her door at six. When the book arrived from England, he was tempted to underline certain passages: "How do I love thee? Let me count the ways." But it was Celia's book. He would let her do any underlining.

When Bruce had gone to the hospital right after Reagan was born three weeks ago and had looked at her through the window of the nursery on the maternity ward, he had received a small glimmer of understanding about how it worked with parents and their children. All the love he had felt for Maddy these two and a half years was miraculously reproduced and heaped upon this new baby he had never even held yet, without an ounce of it being subtracted from Maddy. It had to be one of the most astounding properties of love, that ability to multiply itself. Bingo, just like that, he had loved her. All those other babies who looked pretty much like her behind the window—well, they were okay, but nothing to compare to her.

When Matt had appeared at his side there at the window, Bruce had shaken his hand and asked what the baby's name was. When Matt told him it was Reagan, Bruce had said, "Oh, I get it," and when Matt had looked confused, Bruce said, "Last names of U.S. presidents—that's how you're naming your kids." Matt, who was in perfect control of himself, had laughed, then told Bruce he was starving and asked him if he wanted to go down to the cafeteria with him and get a cheeseburger.

After writing about the book of sonnets, Bruce paused and looked at the clock. Five-thirty—time to get dressed for dinner. He wanted to add one more sentence, but first he had to check on something. He left his bedroom and bounded upstairs. Kimberly was in the kitchen, peeking into the oven, where a large heart-shaped pizza was warming. Evidently Matt had heard about the Pop's Pizza Palace special, too, and had splurged for Valentine's Day.

"I don't want all the details," Bruce said to her. "Just tell me one thing—did she hold the baby?" Kimberly nodded. Celia had come forward and taken Reagan from her arms, she said, before she had even offered. Bruce went back downstairs. *After opening the book of poetry,* he wrote at his desk, *Celia held Reagan for the first time.* He closed the notebook and went to take a shower.

When Bruce appeared at Celia's door at six o'clock with a box of Godiva chocolates, she was wearing a red dress he had never seen. He wished there were truly special-occasion words he could pull out at such a time to describe how she looked. All the standard adjectives fell far short. Finally he said, "Wow."

He stepped inside, handing her the box of candy, which she set on the couch, where she had the other gifts laid out. She spread her hands to take them all in and said, "Wow, yourself."

The restaurant was one Virgil Dunlop had suggested to Bruce: Capriccio over in Greenville—a small classy place with real art hanging on the walls. "For a genuine once-in-a-blue-moon type of celebration" was what Virgil had said. And the restaurant lived up to the recommendation. It was clear that the owner of Capriccio knew a thing or two about the fine art of dining out. Everything—music, decor, cuisine, service—was perfect.

Over dessert, which was something called Bavarian Cloud that the two of them shared, Celia smiled and said, "You know that time Kimberly sprained her ankle and you came to my apartment to get Madison?"

Bruce almost said, "You mean the time you practically shoved me out the door?" but decided against it. He knew by now, of course, why his mention of the movie *The Cider House Rules,* about an abortion doctor, had affected Celia so strongly. Instead he said, "You mean the time you fed me sugar cookies?"

"Right, and the time you tried to show off by throwing your napkin into the trash can."

"Yeah, but at the last minute I decided you needed to see I wasn't totally perfect in every way, so I missed on purpose."

"Right, that time. Well, anyway, you were saying something that night about how things that happen to you in real life can seem like something in a fairy tale."

"Are you sure I said that?"

"Oh, absolutely," Celia said. "I always pay very close attention."

"You mean like that night a year ago when Kimberly and I came to your apartment and Patsy introduced me as Kimberly's *brother?*"

"She never said that."

Bruce shook his head. Out of the corner of his eye, he saw the waiter standing a discreet distance from the table, as if wanting to ask something. Bruce motioned him over. "What would you do with a beautiful but difficult woman?" he said.

The waiter gave a little bow. "I'd bring her to Capriccio at least once a week, sir."

In a way it seemed totally wrong—like a desecration of sorts, most certainly an anticlimax—to take Celia to the mall after such a dinner. What a contrast in atmosphere. But Bruce had planned this whole day as seriously as if it were a military maneuver, and the mall was part of it. In the end it would prove right, he knew that. And if Celia complained about the bright lights of the mall seeming a little on the unromantic side for Valentine's Day, he would remind her that she had started the day by hearing a stump grinder in the backyard.

37

The Song of Harvest-Home

And now for the finishing touch on his day-long Valentine extravaganza. As they walked past the fountain in the middle of the mall toward Hanneman's Fine Jewelers on the Mall, Bruce imagined years from now telling his children all about today, maybe when his son found the woman he wanted to marry and was planning the details of his own proposal. Perhaps the boy would roll his eyes and laugh about it—"Oh, Dad, how embarrassing! Mom, how could you marry such a dork?"—but then again, maybe Bruce would be able to teach his son that sometimes it was okay to embarrass yourself for a woman.

He hoped the man he had talked to at Hanneman's would be ready and would remember everything they had discussed. He had assured Bruce that he would be working tonight, that he would inform whoever else was working with him as to the specifics of the ruse, that they were "always happy here at Hanneman's to accommodate the customer." It didn't hurt, Bruce knew, that the store would be making a nice profit on the ring.

There were four small display windows at Hanneman's, draped with black velvet and white satin, all dressed up for Valentine's Day with organdy bows and red and white hearts and little fat cupids suspended from silver threads above the jewelry. Bruce guided Celia from window to window, and they admired it all together. He knew she had to suspect something. Before they could move to the last window, they had to wait for two fiftyish couples who were crowded together, gawking at the centerpiece.

As often happened, a story took form in Bruce's mind, and as they waited, he told Celia that the two women in front of the window were sisters, one of whom had donated a kidney to the other one. One of the husbands was a bus driver, while the other was supervisor of the stock boys at Thrifty Mart. At Christmastime both of the men dressed up in Santa Claus suits and visited the children's ward at the hosptial. The two couples shared a duplex with fake deer in the front yard. They had gone out to eat at KFC earlier and were now walking through the mall to get ice cream sundaes at the Frosty Cup, a dessert all four had obviously indulged in too many times already, judging from the amount of space they filled up, hip to hip, in front of the window.

"You gonna buy me a ring just like that one, ain't you, Jake?" one of the women said, and the other woman said, "Yeah, I'll take one, too." The men laughed. "Sure," one of them said, "all's we gotta do is sell our houses and trucks, and we might could make us a down payment on that baby," to which the other one replied that he was thinking hard about doing just that, but didn't they see the little tag that said it was already sold, and ain't that just the way it goes when you got your heart set on something?

As the two couples moved away, one of the women wondered aloud what kind of lucky woman would be getting that ring, and the other one remarked that it didn't look like whoever it was would be getting it for Valentine's, since obviously her sweetheart had done forgot to come pick it up. As the two couples walked off holding hands, something in Bruce admired Jake and the other man. You could think what you wanted about men like that—overweight and underrefined—but their wives looked happy, and that said a lot.

Without being too obvious about it, Bruce kept an eye on Celia's face as they stepped up to the window. In the center of the display a small raised platform rotated, and the ring in the black velvet box on the platform was another one of those things, like Celia in her red dress, that none of the ordinary words for beautiful could approach.

You could start out with the plain facts, of course: "The one-carat diamond was encircled by rubies, and the twenty-four carat gold band was an eighth of an inch wide." But there was no way to capture how truly fine it was. The little tag neatly positioned in front of the black velvet box was gold, embossed with the word SOLD in miniature block letters, not something you usually saw in a jewelry case. Bruce was impressed that they had come up with it.

"Hmmm, pretty ring, isn't it?" Bruce said, very casually.

Celia laughed softly without taking her eyes off the ring. "Oh yes, you could say that."

"A diamond can be so generic," he said, "but the rubies make this one unique. I've always been partial to rubies, you know."

"No, I didn't know that."

"It's one of the two corundum gems, you know—along with sapphires. An extremely hard mineral, mostly aluminum oxide."

"No, I didn't know that, either."

"Of course, diamonds are nice, too," he said.

"Oh yes, very."

"Highly refractive, diamonds are."

"Right."

"Which isn't the same as reflective. You know that, don't you?"

"Oh sure."

"A crystalline allotrope of carbon—that's all a diamond is."

"Uh-huh." She leaned closer to the window, her eyes still fixed on the ring. Bruce wondered if she was trying to hide a smile.

"Interesting, isn't it," he said, "that an impure diamond or ruby ends up being used in abrasives, but in their purest form . . . well, there you have it right in front of you."

"Yes, there you have it."

"Too bad it's already sold."

"Hmm." A small sigh.

Bruce couldn't read the look on her face. Maybe she was only pretending to be wistful, not wanting to spoil it for him. Or maybe she was trying to act only mildly interested, afraid to hope too much. Or maybe she truly wasn't expecting anything. Maybe she thought the surprises of the day were over.

She had already teased him at the restaurant, asking him how much of today had been Kimberly's idea, how many of the gifts she had helped Bruce plan and execute. He had objected, as if insulted, and she had apologized but explained that any woman would find it hard to believe that a man could think it all up, much less have the patience to synchronize all the details. Maybe she was wondering if it wasn't a little unnatural for a man to do all those things.

"But, hey," he said now, "why don't you try it on for fun anyway? Doesn't matter if it's sold or not."

"Oh no, I wouldn't—"

"Wouldn't what? Come on."

He urged her inside, although maybe she was only acting resistant, and he asked the man behind the counter if they could see the ring in the display window. The man, being the very one with whom Bruce had conspired, replied stiffly, "You may see it, sir, but you know, of course, that it is already sold."

"Yes, we know. We read the tag," Bruce said, very chipper. "But we'd still like to see it, and if you don't mind my saying so, if it's already sold, then maybe you shouldn't leave it on display for other people to covet. Maybe you should pick up the phone and tell whoever bought it to come get it." Celia shot him a look.

"In fact," Bruce continued, unperturbed, "I've never heard of anybody buying something at a jewelry store and not taking it home right then, unless they needed to have the ring sized or something, but . . . are you sure this person can be trusted?"

The man looked at Bruce stonily. "I assure you that our client will be coming for his purchase very soon, sir."

Though Celia was looking mortified by this time, she allowed Bruce to slip the ring onto her finger, at which point Bruce smote his chest in a theatrical way, put a hand over his eyes, and said, "Wait, it's too beautiful. I can't look at it." He was secretly pleased at how close he had guessed on the size.

Another sales associate appeared at the end of the counter, this one a woman with spiky frosted hair, bright coral lipstick, and dangly crystal earrings that looked like little clusters of ice chips. "Say, Quinten, I need that ring from the window," she said to the man, who was standing beside Bruce holding the empty black velvet box. "I told the man I'd gift wrap it for him." She glanced at the clock on the wall. "I sure hope he gets here before we close at nine."

"Well now, if he doesn't," Bruce said, "maybe we can work out a little deal."

"The other man has already paid for the ring, sir," the dour Quinten said. Bruce had to wonder whether Quinten had had some acting experience or was just naturally this kind of person. "Tight-lipped and testy" was how he had requested the part be played, and the guy was doing a bang-up job.

"Aw, but it looks so good on her finger," Bruce said. "How about if I offer to pay just a little more than the other fellow? Then when he comes, *if* he comes that is, which he probably won't, you can say mistakes were made and you'll have to order another one and . . . well, you can think of something. I'm sure things like this happen all the time in the jewelry business." Celia was staring at him now, shaking her head as she pulled the ring off and handed it to Quinten, who was glaring at Bruce with the look of a butler who has discovered a house servant tampering with the silver in the pantry.

"I am appalled that you would stoop to suggest such a thing," he said frostily to Bruce. What a very nice line—*I am appalled that you would stoop to suggest such a thing*. Bruce made a mental note to compliment him on it later.

Quinten put the ring back into the box and sidestepped it down to the woman, as if afraid to turn his back on Bruce. "Here is the ring, Ms. Ayers," he said. "Please wrap it quickly." Bruce wondered if Quinten had ever seen Anthony Hopkins in *Remains of the Day*. He had the voice and manner down pat. He even looked a little like Hopkins, only with more hair.

And the upshot of it all was great fun. Bruce insisted that Quinten tell him the name of the other man so he could call and offer him a little margin of profit if he would sell this ring to Bruce and wait for another to be ordered, to which Quinten replied that they did not release the names of their clients and, besides, this ring had been specially designed. There weren't clones of it sitting around in some factory warehouse somewhere.

And then Ms. Ayers got in on it, taking Bruce's side when she returned with the ring box, now ensconced inside a slightly larger gold gift box secured with a gold stretchy cord and affixed with a red Hanneman's Fine Jewelers on the Mall seal on top. Quinten and Ms. Ayers even staged a little altercation, during which Ms. Ayers went to the display window and got the SOLD tag, telling Bruce that the buyer's name was on the back of it, at which point Quinten claimed to be "astounded at such a breach of professionalism" and tried to snatch it from her as she tried to hand it to Bruce.

Celia was standing apart, observing them all with an amused look, as if they were misbehaving monkeys at the zoo. Though Bruce knew they weren't fooling her, he was still enjoying himself.

When the truth was made known, Celia laughed and cried at the such a vow, or did she want to give the ring back and call the whole thing off same time. "Can you tell he teaches middle school?" she asked Quinten and Ms. Ayers. "And coaches drama?"

And then right there in Hanneman's Fine Jewelers on the Mall, Bruce put the ring on Celia's finger again, for real, and asked the question he had been waiting to ask and heard the answer he had hoped for.

Maybe someday their children would ask Bruce why he had proposed to Celia in such a public venue, surrounded by people he didn't even know. Why not do it in private, out by a lake under the moonlight?

And Bruce, though he certainly didn't dismiss such triteness whole-sale, knowing that he himself had resorted to more than his own share of triteness that day and also knowing that any old idea could be freshened up in the hands of a skilled romantic, would wave a hand scornfully and say something like "Why do something so special in such a common way?" or maybe "Well, I was so proud of your mother that I wanted to show her off." And he would be ever grateful to the mall crowd that night, normally a fairly self-absorbed group, for their smiles and good wishes as he stopped them all along the way to present his future wife and show them her ring.

Another part of the reason for the mall proposal had to do with Bruce's vow, the one he told her about when he pulled into her driveway thirty minutes later. Besides being memorable because he had never heard of anybody else doing it that way, he said, proposing to her in Hanneman's Fine Jewelers on the Mall made it easier to keep that vow.

There in her driveway, sitting in his truck in the waning hours of Valentine's Day, Bruce told Celia that his vow was a personal decision, something he didn't want to share with anyone else. He wasn't saying it was the way everybody should do it, but he was sure it was right for him—and he was hoping she would understand, wouldn't laugh at such an old-fashioned idea.

He took a deep breath, then came out with it. Though he wanted to take her into his arms, he said, he couldn't. Not yet. He wanted to wait until they were married for . . . for things like that.

"You mean for . . . anything?" she said.

He paused, then said, yes, for everything. Not that depriving himself of all physical contact now was some form of penance, he went on, some kind of feeble effort to make up for all the thoughtless and godless liber-ties he had taken in the past, but he had sought God in the matter and felt very sure of his blessing on this decision. Could she go along with such a vow now that she saw how weird he was? She could keep all the other presents, of course.

No, she said slowly, she could go along with it. In fact, she liked the idea. She liked it a lot.

But with this vow in mind, Bruce said, he wasn't all that interested in an extended engagement, which was why he was wondering what she thought about . . . well, what she thought about a wedding on the first day of spring, which would be just a little less than five weeks away. Could she . . . could they pull it all together by then?

Celia laughed. "There used to be a time when I thought a decent wedding would take at least a year to plan."

"And what about now?" Bruce asked. "Do you still think that?"

Well, actually, no, she said, she didn't think that anymore.

"So it's settled," Bruce said. " I guess this is the place in the script where it says, *couple kisses passionately.*"

"I guess so," Celia said, "if it's one of those formulaic plots."

Bruce got out of his truck and went around to open Celia's door. It was a cold crisp night. He knew it was a Thanksgiving hymn, and Thanksgiving was long past, but he heard the words anyway: "Come, ye thankful people, come, raise the song of harvest-home." He had no idea why this particular hymn should come to him now. Maybe it was because he suddenly felt overwhelmed with thankfulness, with the sense that he had labored well and now the harvest was in and he was coming home.

"Have I ever told you how the words of hymns race around in my head all hours of the day and night?" he said as he helped Celia out.

She stopped and looked up at him. "Really?" she said. "How strange."

They walked to her porch stoop. "Are you happy?" Bruce asked.

"Happy?" she asked. She looked into the treetops. "That's sort of like asking if the sky is big." She took her key out and unlocked the door, then looked up at him. "Yes, I'm very happy."

And after loving God with his whole heart, Bruce thought, what higher aim could a man have than to make a good woman happy?

PART THREE:

THOU HAST LOVED US, LOVE US STILL

Through the Storm, Through the Night

At the Church of the Open Door the next morning, the usher escorted Bruce and Celia to seats on the aisle just as the choir was filing in. Celia saw Elizabeth and her husband in the choir and Margaret Tuttle at the organ. The pianist looked familiar, too—oh yes, it was the woman named Jewel she had met at Elizabeth's house the night of the poetry club meeting. The daughter of Eldeen. Celia glanced around for Eldeen but didn't see her. She felt a sudden thrill of hope at the thought of meeting the old woman again.

Early in the service, Celia decided one thing: Though she had heard a lot of preachers in her life, there was something about this one that called out to her soul. Pastor Monroe over at Community Baptist, where she had attended with Bruce a couple of times, was a good man, and even though his style of preaching was like bland cooking—it did provide nourishment, but without much seasoning—he seemed solid in his theology and solicitous in his care for his people.

It was clear, however, during the preliminary announcements that the preacher here at the Church of the Open Door had a gift for public speaking, which, all other things being equal, could only serve to enhance the effectiveness of a pastor in Celia's opinion. To be able to listen to God's truth imparted with such fluency and clarity of style, well, it would be like sitting down to a banquet every Sunday. It would be like the difference between the meal last night at Capriccio and the sandwiches she often threw together for supper when she didn't feel like cooking.

The song leader also seemed to stir the people to worship in a way she hadn't seen before. All the music seemed purposeful, not just perfunctory. She could imagine attending this church every Sunday. As the choir sang an arrangement of "I Love to Tell the Story," she wondered if Bruce would ever be interested in joining the choir here at this church. For herself, she would love to. He would probably hold back, claiming that he knew nothing about music. But he could learn. After all, she would point out to him, there was supposed to be a high correlation between mathematical and musical skills. Some famous musician, she couldn't remember who it was right now, had also been a respected scientist.

Celia closed her eyes during "Wonderful Grace of Jesus" when they came to the words "Taking away my burden, setting my spirit free," and again in the chorus when she sang with the women, "Wonderful grace, all-sufficient for me, for even me." How perfect that they would sing this particular song on this particular day. She and Bruce had had long talks about God's grace. They had laid their sins open, had looked full into each other's eyes, knowing the hard truth about themselves. And God's grace had covered it all.

After the offering was taken, a quartet of boys appeared at the pulpit and began a tightly harmonized rendition of "At Calvary." They were all tall, good-looking kids, two of them obviously twins. How odd, Celia thought, that four teenagers in the twenty-first century would be singing such an old gospel song. She knew the words by heart, from the opening of the first stanza, "Years I spent in vanity and pride," to the closing of the last, "Oh, the mighty gulf that God did span at Calvary." And those glorious words of the chorus: "Mercy there was great, and grace was free; pardon there was multiplied to me; there my burdened soul found liberty, at Calvary."

The boys' voices blended well. Something like this had to take a lot of time. Celia wondered when they rehearsed and how long. What had they had to give up in order to prepare this song? She could hardly take her eyes off the boy on the end who was dressed in a madras plaid sport coat, seventies style, a red polyester shirt, and a wide navy necktie. She remembered a certain photo of her father holding her when she was a little girl. He had been wearing a sport coat just like that one.

When Ken Landis came out from the choir before the sermon, lifted his trumpet, and began playing "Precious Lord, Take My Hand," Celia kept her eyes straight ahead. She didn't know how he had managed it, but she suspected that Bruce had something to do with this. Probably with the "Wonderful Grace" song, too.

As Ken played, the words of the song spoke themselves to her, taking her back to her grandmother's house, "through the storm, through the night" of their years together. But, what a happy ending to the song— being led by the hand to the light of home.

After Ken Landis's trumpet solo ended, the pastor prayed a prayer rich in allusions to all the songs and Scripture passages of the service thus far. His closing sentence was "And now, take us by the hand, precious Lord, and lead us to the light of the truth within your Word," after which he began to read one of Celia's favorite chapters in the whole Bible: "Though I speak with the tongues of men and of angels . . ." What better passage of Scripture for a sermon on the day after Valentine's Day than First Corinthians thirteen? What better passage to remind Celia of the source of all love, of God's wiping away the sin of her past and reclaiming her as his own, making her heart ready to give and to receive love?

At the end of the service, the song leader encouraged everyone to greet the visitors after the closing prayer. By the time they had made it back to the vestibule, Celia's hand felt numb from all the squeezing and shaking, and just as she was wondering if there was anyone in attendance that morning who *hadn't* greeted them, she heard a voice above the crowd and saw a large form looming over a dozen or more heads, waving what looked like a man's handkerchief. "Wait just a minute there, hold on, don't let 'em leave yet. I been hittin' snags right and left tryin' to work my way back here!"

And as the people fell back like waves against the shore, she came chugging into full view, a great steamboat of a woman, rounding the bend with continuous tooty blasts. Bruce leaned down to Celia, who looked up at him, and, as they had done more than once before, the two of them spoke simultaneously, the general message practically the same: "Just wait till you meet this woman. You won't believe it."

Eldeen greeted them warmly and at great length, telling Celia, "I remember you! You came to our poetry meeting and gave us a little talk about a picture. And you're still pretty as a picture yourself!" After they finally left Eldeen, Elizabeth Landis invited Bruce and Celia to meet her husband and her at Juno's for Sunday dinner. "It's not fancy," she said.

"It's a buffet, just good country cooking." She laughed. "Sort of like a southern family reunion."

"Oh, I know all about southern family reunions," Celia said. "I'll feel right at home."

On their way to Juno's, Bruce looked over at her and said, "Have I ever told you how beautiful you are? If I was writing our story, here's how I'd start this scene we're in right now. 'He looked across the seat at her and knew he'd never get tired of looking at this woman.' "

"That's not very flowery," said Celia. "No one would want to read a romance novel like that."

Bruce laughed and told Celia about the sappy novels he used to snitch from Suzanne's room when he was a kid. He would read them aloud through the closed door as she soaked in the bathtub and yelled at him to stop: " 'Thaddeus clutched Miranda's limp, white-clad form to his broad, heaving chest, lifted his contorted face to the driving rain, and bellowed his impassioned grief into the leaden skies.' "

She smiled and shook her head. "And the pictures on the covers of those books . . . oh my."She looked down at her left hand and touched a finger to the ring. "Our story could never make a good book, you know that, don't you?"

"And why not? We wouldn't write it like that dimestore trash. Ours would be simple and beautiful."

Again she shook her head. "Nope, too many problems."

"Like what?"

"Like every literary cliché under the sun."

"Well, we wouldn't have to put in all the sentimental Valentine stuff," Bruce said, then added with a wounded expression, "although I sort of thought you *liked* it all."

"Oh, I loved every minute of it. But it's more than just Valentine's Day—the whole story is riddled with clichés."

"Like what?"

"Think about it," she said, and when he continued to look puzzled, "Okay, listen, let me help you out here." If they gave even a little background for themselves, she told him, her part would be loaded with clichés, starting with her being an orphan and having an unhappy adolescence. "You know, right along the lines of *David Copperfield, Jane Eyre,* and all the rest." Then there was her grandmother's death, she said, and the obligatory funeral scene, where the worldly wise heroine returns home to her roots to bury the family matriarch—or patriarch, take your pick—and has some kind of Revelation with a capital *R.*

He interrupted her. "But you didn't have any Revelation with a capital *R* until months after your grandmother's funeral."

"Yes, yes, but it all started with that trip to the funeral and then bringing her Bible home and then her hymnbook and all her diaries and her quilts and dishes and . . ."

"Well, I don't think any of that qualifies as a cliché."

She made a scoffing sound. "And then the whole mistaken identity thing with you. That's the oldest gimmick in the book. The heroine hates the hero at first, until she has yet another Revelation with a capital *R* in which she realizes his *true identity* and suddenly appreciates all his *sterling qualities.*"

"Wait a minute. You still hated me even *after* you realized my *true identity,* remember?"

She ignored this. "And there's the boy-next-door element, too. How many times has *that* been used? The heroine all of a sudden discovers she loves the boy who's always been like a brother."

"And when did you ever think of me as a brother?"

She frowned at him and hurried on. "And then, *your* background is full of them, too. The tall, dark stranger shows up with secrets in his past. The good old Odysseus figure."

"You forgot handsome—tall, dark, and *handsome* stranger."

"Well, okay, yes, that's another one. The hero always has to be incredibly good-looking and strong and brave."

"And extremely intelligent."

"Yes, usually that, too," she said. "And the hero and heroine always seem like total opposites at the beginning, but—"

"No, no, that's not true. *You* were incredibly good-looking and extremely intelligent at the beginning, too, just like me—and still are, in fact you're even more intelligent now since you've gained an appreciation of the sterling qualities of the boy-next-door, that strong, brave Odysseus figure."

" . . . but then they always, *always* eventually find out by the end of the book that they have much in common." She paused and spoke melodramatically, as if reading from a bad story: " 'And suddenly the scales fell from their eyes as they both realized they were looking into the very mirror of their souls.' "

"Well, that's a funny mirror if you ask me. I mean, good grief, think about it. He's dark and she's blond, and he's tall and she's short, and he's got scars and she doesn't, and he's a musical moron and she's not, and his apartment looks like an army barracks and hers"—he lurched to a sudden stop at a red light—"hers looks like the Golden Age of Greece, and I could go on and on, not to overlook the most obvious fact that he's a man and she's a woman—the ultimate contrast."

She nodded. "Yes, and she can play tennis, and he . . . well, he tries."

"Oh, of course, the hero might have known the heroine would bring that up." He pointed his finger at her. "You just wait, sweetheart. You are going down." The tires of his truck squealed a little as he took off from the red light.

"And we can't forget the Day-It-All-Turned-Around," she said. "The Chance Meeting when their eyes locked in that Grand Moment of Illumination—there's another cliché to stick in."

But how could she call it a *chance* meeting, he asked indignantly, when she knew good and well that there was a lot more of the supernatural than of chance in that meeting in the Cracker Barrel parking lot? Why, she had said herself that after hearing about all the power outages in Derby and Berea that day, she had been fully intending to drive all the way into Greenville to shop a little and then eat supper at a place called Aunt Cassie's Kitchen, but that upon seeing the billboard advertisement for Cracker Barrel on I-85, she had suddenly felt strongly and inexplicably compelled to stop there, even though it was earlier than she really wanted to eat. It was almost as if "somebody else turned my steering wheel"—isn't that exactly what she had said?

And she looked chastened and said yes, yes, he was right, it wasn't a chance meeting at all but an appointed one. And forgetting about all the clichés, she said, which didn't matter anyway because they certainly wouldn't ever write their story for publication, in her opinion the two of them had more than enough differences to provide interest and variety.

They had already talked at some length about the ways they were alike—their mutual dislike of storms, for instance, the fact that they both drove Fords, their disapproval of sweet corn bread. They both loved the South, had moved to other fields of work outside their original college majors, and dreamed in color. And they had found out less than fifteen minutes ago that they were both fascinated by Eldeen Rafferty.

"By the way, did I ever tell you I had a grandfather who was a science teacher?" Celia asked Bruce. No, he said, and had he ever told her that his grandmother had been a portrait artist as a young woman and had a small gallery in Mississippi where she displayed her work?

But all the coincidences would never fly in a book, Celia pointed out. "I mean, two messed-up single people over thirty-five living in basement apartments right next door to each other and falling in love? Why, readers wouldn't stand for such tripe in a plot."

Tripe? he said. How could she call reality tripe? And who was she calling messed up? Even if there was a little bit of truth in it, well, the world was full of messed-up people. The chances of two of them living next door to each other were enormous. He ought to know. He had taken math courses in probability.

"Well, besides all that," Celia said, "another big reason we could never write our real-life story would be because of all the parts we'd want to leave out. A lot of readers want to see everything right out in the open, you know, and a lot of writers feel compelled to give it to them in living color." She groaned. "You wouldn't believe some of the stuff I've edited. No sense of subtlety—it all just slaps you in the face."

Bruce nodded. "Yeah, same goes for plays and movies. The worst ones show it all."

Readers would complain, Celia said, if the story wasn't finished. "They'd want to be seated in the front pew to observe every detail of the wedding. They'd want to stand by the car to throw rice and peek out from behind the curtains in the honeymoon suite. They'd want to know if we bought a house, how many kids we had, and on and on."

"Well, hey, I can sympathize," Bruce said. "I want to know those things, too."

Celia laughed and related something she had read once about Kafka's story *Metamorphosis,* in which the main character turns into a gigantic insect. When the publisher was considering ideas for the cover art, someone suggested a picture of the insect, to which Kafka replied, "No, please, not *that.*" His point being that you had to leave certain critical parts to the reader's imagination.

"And *you* would never be a convincing male character in a book anyway," Celia continued. "Nobody would ever believe a man like you could exist. It would all sound made up. And it would cause strife in homes everywhere. Women would be reading it out loud to their husbands, saying,

'Why can't *you* be like that?' and you'd get calls from all kinds of men threatening your life."

"But think of what a difference our story could make in marriages all across America," Bruce said. "After our book hits the New York Times Best Seller list, then we'll start the talk-show circuit and . . ."

"Books about Christians don't hit the New York Times Best Seller list," Celia said.

"Yeah, you got a point there," Bruce said. They were pulling into the parking lot of Juno's now. He parked his truck, turned off the engine, then looked up into the sun. "Too bad it's not later in the day."

"Why's that?"

"Because when we leave here, we'll be driving west."

"And . . . ?"

"Well, that would make a great thing to stick in the ending some-where—you know, driving off into the sunset and all."

Celia shook her head. "Enough already."

"No, one more thing. I have the perfect closing sentence for our book."

She sighed. "What?"

" 'And they lived happily ever after.' "

She moaned.

Bruce smacked his palm with his fist. "No, think about it! Christians everywhere should rise up and reclaim that ending for their stories. We're the ones who really will live happily ever after. That's what eternal life is all about, right?"

One thing she knew for sure. Life was never going to be boring living with Bruce.

Bruce snapped his fingers. He also had an idea for a good title for their book, he said.

"You mean the one we're not going to write?"

Yes, that one, he said. To go along with the fairy tale ending, they could use something like *The Prince's Good Fortune.*

"The prince being you, I assume?"

Yes, he said, and the "good fortune" part could mean so many things—for starters, wasn't it in the opening sentence of *Pride and Prejudice,* some-thing about a single man with a good fortune?

Celia nodded and held up her left hand. "Although, of course, you made a considerable dent in your good fortune when you bought this."

But the word fortune went far beyond mere money, Bruce pointed out. *The Prince's Good Fortune* would be a wonderful, multidimensional title, including a spiritual reference to the fact that the title character was a son of the King, with a capital *K*. Furthermore, he hurried on, it would indicate a love story, since a prince would necessitate a princess.

"So I'm the good fortune in the title?" Celia asked, and when he nodded, said, "Okay, I don't mind being somebody's good fortune."

And then there was the whole future implication of the word, too, he said, your fortune being your destiny, your ultimate success, and all that. "So there you go, we're back to living happily ever after. See, it's a great title."

She smiled. "And it adds one more cliché to the pot—the title with tricky multiple meanings. That's something amateur writers really go in for."

Bruce scowled. "You're a very critical woman, you know that? Very hard to please."

Celia laughed. "Okay, you've got the title and ending. Now I'll do the beginning: 'Once upon a time a tall, dark, handsome prince knocked on Celia's door and asked for a toilet plunger.' "

He suddenly grew serious. Was she sure, he wanted to know, that she could live with a man like him?

Celia appeared to be considering this. Well, to tell the truth, she said at length, she didn't see how she could live without him.

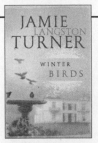

Looking for More Good Books to Read?

You can find out what is new and exciting with previews, descriptions, and reviews by signing up for Bethany House newsletters at

www.bethanynewsletters.com

We will send you updates for as many authors or categories as you desire so you get only the information you really want.

Sign up today!